IDA ELISABETH

SIGRID UNDSET

IDA ELISABETH

Translated by Arthur G. Chater

IGNATIUS PRESS   SAN FRANCISCO

Original Norwegian edition:
Ida Elisabeth
© 1932 by H. Aschehoug and Co., Oslo

English version © 1933 by Alfred A. Knopf, Inc., New York

Published by arrangement with Alfred A. Knopf, an imprint of
The Knopf Doubleday Publishing Group,
a division of Random House, Inc., New York

Cover art: *The Seamstress*, Thomas Wade, Bridgeman Art Library

Cover design by Riz Boncan Marsella

Published by Ignatius Press, San Francisco, 2011
ISBN 978-1-58617-424-8
Library of Congress catalogue number 2009935082
Printed in the United States of America ∞

CONTENTS

BOOK ONE

Chapter One

AS IDA ELISABETH WALKED the few steps from the door of the clinic to the taxi, she had a feeling that the night, which hung high over the town, was impenetrably dark and dense. The yellow light which fell upon the swept-up heaps of snow along the street seemed to leak out from under a heavy lid of darkness. On the opposite side of the street there were shop windows lighted up, but above them the house-fronts rose with only a feeble glimmer here and there behind drawn blinds. Down the middle of the street ran glittering tram-lines, and above them hung a row of pearly white electric lamps, shedding a bluish gleam on the darkness around them. The town lay as it were at the bottom of a cauldron; the white mountains surrounding it were just visible through the darkness, with little specks of light in the houses on their slopes. But then came black night, abysmal and frost-bound. The stars must be shining, she guessed, but one could not see them down here in the lighted street.

One of the nurses who followed her out handed her the boy in his bundle of wraps, while the other disposed her baggage in front by the driver. And then she drove off with Kalleman in her lap. Fleeting lights from one side or the other glanced across her in the dark taxi, and the impression she had got on coming out remained with her—that all this artificial light was as it were at the bottom of a well, and overhead brooded the night, vast and heavy.

The weather was clear, calm, and bitingly cold. The clatter on the quay rang so terribly sharp over the frozen paving stones. Chains shrieked loud and crudely, wheels grated so harshly as lorries drove on or pulled up. Voices on the quayside and the shouts of the crew on board sounded as if everyone had a cold in the head. Along the edge of the quay stood all the people who were seeing friends off, talking loudly and shouting up to the deck. No one had come to say good-bye to her—but then Aslaug had let her know beforehand; she hoped to get a job this evening, to take the place of a friend who played in a café. And now she knew nobody in this town but Aslaug—nobody she cared about, anyhow.

It gave her a grateful feeling to come below deck; the light was so tranquil, and then there was that steamer smell, stagnant and snug, as though it was never aired except a little at a time and no more than was necessary. Oh, all the old smells that hung about these cabins—fat, oily smells and suggestions of tobacco smoke and the fumes of beer and the odour of dust in plush sofas, and a faint, indefinite smell which made her think of voyages in boisterous weather, with sea-sick passengers and the sound of heavy seas around the boat, and lamps jingling and crockery getting smashed. Ida Elisabeth was always cheered by this strange atmosphere—it must have been a relic of the days when she was a little girl; then of course she had always been half-crazy with joy when she went on board one of these boats that was to take her to Vallerviken for her holidays, though it was long enough in all conscience since she had had anything to make her cheerful when she took this voyage. Dead against all common sense, however, the old happy excitement reasserted itself the moment she boarded one of the local boats.

The stewardess greeted her familiarly and inquired how the operation had turned out—it warmed Ida Elisabeth and made her feel happy. And now a lovely fresh smell of frying beefsteaks was wafted down the alley-way; she discovered how fearfully hungry she was. There was always such a delightful supper on board this boat; now she would have a really good feed. All the time she was in town she had been as economical as possible, not knowing how much the doctor's bill and the stay at the clinic would come to. But the doctor had been extremely reasonable—and so kind and attentive to Kalleman; the boy had been looked after as if he had been a prince.

The dazzling light in the little white cabin hurt her eyes, but she liked it all the same; it was so motionless, calm, and steady. Ugh! both the other berths were taken; they were full of baggage.

"Just like a prince", she murmured, and kissed the boy's cheek; it was so white and so soft and still cool from the fresh air. "But now little Kalleman is going home with his mamma, yes, he is, now Kalleman and mamma are going to be together again all the time—" The boy showed no particular sign of gladness, or indeed of any interest at all. Poor child, no doubt he was tired, and still pretty weak.

She sat down on the edge of his bunk and unwrapped him from his rugs and shawls. Better to put him to bed before there was any motion of the boat. The nurse had dressed him for the night and changed his bandage before they left the clinic.

"Kalleman! Kalleman—have you quite forgotten mamma—?" She cautiously hugged the boy to her. "Aren't we just a *tiny* bit glad to be back with mummie again?" At that he showed the faintest of smiles. Oh, how small and yellow his face had grown inside all the white gauze bandages! "And now Kalleman shall have some milk— lovely num-num milk!"—she got out the bottle and the cup and the bag of bananas.

"Beg pardon!" Ida Elisabeth looked up. Two quite young girls in fur coats had come in; they filled up all the little space between the berths. "Why yes, it's Fru Braatö!"

After a moment it dawned on Ida Elisabeth that they were the eldest daughter of Herr Meisling of the iodine works at Rostesund and her cousin, who lived with them. "Oh, isn't he good?" they said both at once, and "tit tit" they said as they hung up their coats and were told that Kalleman had had an operation on his ear; yes, it had been serious enough, and no, he wasn't the eldest; she had a little girl who was older, and now they were living at Berfjord. Ida Elisabeth did not ask them any questions, and Cecilie Meisling powdered her face in front of the glass, saying something about meeting presently in the saloon. With that the girls dashed out again.

Ida Elisabeth stayed behind. She was sitting very uncomfortably, bent forward under the upper berth. Now the water was roaring round the propeller, little vibrations ran through the boat, and then the sea began swashing and gurgling along the ship's side. She heard people going into the saloon; there was a clatter of plates and cups. But she would have to sit with Kalleman until he fell asleep.

For that matter, she had no desire to meet people she knew. And these Meislings too—they were so superior; everybody said that about them. Not that they gave you that impression when you met them. But they kept to themselves and scarcely mixed with other people on the fjord. Fru Meisling was English too, a sister of Oxley, who had founded the iodine works. And then the Oxleys were Catholics. She remembered how sarcastic their schoolmaster, Myking, had been because Ciss Meisling and Cecilie Oxley were not to take religion with the other children, the year they were living at the doctor's in Vallerviken to attend the grammar school, "The Two Sicilies", as he called them.

She had not seen that this was meant for a joke. As far as that went, a good many of her schoolfellows had not seen it either. But it was always at her and Frithjof that Myking's caustic remarks were aimed. "Any jocular allusion of a historical or geographical nature is lost upon Elisabeth Andst and Frithjof Braatö, for excellent reasons."

She could not bear to sit any longer doubled up on the hard edge of the bunk. Standing in front of the little mirror, she put her hair straight and pulled her travelling hat over it again. Her face no longer seemed to be anything at all—except ordinary: narrow, colourlessly fair, with fading eyes. There was no longer any lustre in her hair, it was a greyish cinder-colour, and even her curls were strangely dead and inert when she tried to coax them out under her hat. Ida Elisabeth looked at her reflection seriously, without a sigh—merely noted the fact that so it was. And it was not many years since she had been very pretty—at least as pretty as Ciss Meisling. Ciss *had* turned out pretty—much more so than she promised as a child. The other had always been charming.

They must be eighteen or nineteen now. For she herself was four-and-twenty. She and Frithjof were in the top class the year they entered the school.

She and Frithjof. As far back as their school-days the talk had always been of Ida Elisabeth and Frithjof though she hardly thought she had liked him even then. On the contrary, it had felt doubly humiliating; she had felt her exclusion even more for being excluded in Frithjof's company. He looked as if he never washed properly, and he couldn't see that he was only laughed at by his schoolfellows for his bragging. No, Myking could safely make fools of her and Frithjof—the school-fees were not often paid for either of them. Then as now the Braatös were badly off, but that did not worry Frithjof's father the least; he only cared for his violin. And everybody knew all about her father—

She and Frithjof must have been predestined to share their ill fortunes.

AFTER having supper Ida Elisabeth climbed up to the promenade deck.

It was lovely to feel the current of air which tugged and sang in the rigging as the boat steadily made for the open sea in the calm night. Not so frightfully cold either. Thank goodness they had such fine weather; she had been rather anxious about travelling with Kalleman so soon after his operation; it might not have done him any good if they had come in for bad weather.

They were already far out. As her eyes accustomed themselves to the darkness, she began to distinguish things. The sea was as smooth as glass; the waves made by the ship glittered feebly in the gleams of light from the ports as they foamed and rippled past the side; up in the rigging hung the little lanterns shining calmly. The masts pointed up into the black star-strewn sky; the thick smoke that poured out of the funnel drifted almost straight aft. And the old absurd happy feeling of her childhood bubbled up in her again in spite of all, that she was walking here on deck and looking at the night through which the ship bore her lights, and looking out across the black sea: it was a living, *bright* darkness, full of presentiment, but over there, where the land lay, the gloom was dense and as it were piled up—and the sky—

There were northern lights in the north-west too—not very strong, but an arch of whitish glimmer, just enough to make the mountain ridge stand out clearly against the pale stretch of sky. Ida Elisabeth plunged her chin into her fur collar, buried her hands deep in her coat pockets, and began to walk up and down the deck.

Someone was talking on the other side of the saloon skylight. And the answer came:

"Yes, but I *shan't* be able to sleep, I'm sure of that. And then that nasty smell, of iodoform or whatever it is they use on those dressings—just like being in a hospital—"

Ida Elisabeth turned scarlet in the darkness. Defiantly she tossed her head: surely one was allowed to travel by boat with a sick child even if a couple of spoilt brats—but it hadn't occurred to her that it could upset anyone—

She tramped harder on the deck, swung round, and marched back on the starboard side. Against the skylight she caught sight of two red gleams in the darkness—so they were smoking cigarettes, the young ladies. There were no chairs on the top deck at this time of year, so they must have had them brought up expressly. Oh yes, they knew how to make themselves comfortable.

It was more sheltered here, all the same, still as the night was. Ida Elisabeth halted by the rail. They were nearly at the mouth of the fjord now; the islands were quite low. The northern lights appeared like a calm, broad arch, faintly reflected in the water. And above the arch at its western end was a great star shining brightly.

"Fru Braatö—won't you sit here?" It was Cecilie Oxley who came up to her. Ciss Meisling had said that about Kalleman.

"Thanks, but I'm going below in a moment."

The other girl now came up:

"Isn't it fine? Oh, I think it's lovely to be back at home—for there's no place so beautiful as Norway after all! I wonder what star that is—is it Venus, do you think, Cecilie?"

"Venus, no—that can't be up yet—it can't be Venus we see there. Do you know what star it is, Fru Braatö?" asked Cecilie Oxley.

"No idea. I know nothing at all about stars."

"One might really imagine it was *the* star", said Ciss Meisling wistfully. "The one that guided the wise men of the East, I mean. That must be frightfully romantic, don't you think? For they must have been a terribly long time on the journey. A whole year perhaps, they may easily have been as long as that on the way, so I've read—even if we keep Epiphany only a fortnight after Christmas Eve. I've always thought Twelfth Night was such a lovely festival—for one seems to be so full of *longing* when one thinks of that about the star—"

Twelfth Night—it had not occurred to Ida Elisabeth till now, but of course, it was Twelfth Night tonight. To travel and travel after a star which showed one the way somewhere. Ah, if one only could! With a sick, failing sensation in her tired heart she felt for a moment that she too was filled with longing, as little Ciss Meisling put it.

"Oh, you!" Cecilie Oxley laughed indulgently. "But I expect we ought to go below and turn in now, Ciss, it's late—"

"Oh, those American verses that Sunniva Aarstad translated, I think they were so pretty. Positively charming!" The girl began to declaim them under her breath, with a good deal of sentiment:

> Melchior brings Him heavy gold.
> (All I have for you
> Is the gold mist-ring the moon
> Thrusts her fingers through.)
>
> Frankincense from Balthazar.
> (Can I make you know
> How the blue smoke curls above
> Flames upon the snow?)
>
> Out from Gaspar's scarlet sleeve
> Comes the box of myrrh.
> (O precious is the bitterness
> Of memories astir!)[1]

The three women stood for a moment looking out into the night towards the northern lights and the bright star over the mouth of the fjord.

"No, I'll have to go below and see to my little boy", said Ida Elisabeth.

KALLEMAN was sound asleep. Ida Elisabeth got out the detective novel that Aslaug had given her to read on the voyage. She seated herself in the saloon with it—there was not a

[1] By Mary H. Dwyer. Reprinted from *America*, December 20, 1930, by courtesy of the publishers.

soul there. So she drew up her feet under her on the sofa, prepared really to enjoy it all—the warmth and the soft plush sofa, the faint jingling of the lamps, the steamboat elegance, which roused distant memories of holidays and freedom and comfort from the days when she was a child.

But scarcely had she gone a dozen pages into *The Murder in the Swimming-Bath* when the girls appeared. In fur coats and with their arms full of plaids—who couldn't sit on deck and get romantic about stars?

"Would you like to go to bed first, Fru Braatö, or shall we? For there's only room for one of us to undress at a time."

Ida Elisabeth would rather wait till the last. Whereupon the girls went to the cabin and got rid of their wraps, but then they came back. Ciss Meisling offered her candy from an enormous box—and so they stayed sitting and chatting.

Ida Elisabeth remained reticent, suspicious. They've set themselves to be nice, she thought. *She* had never asked anyone to be nice to her—or to pity her.

Without being asked, Ciss Meisling informed her that they had been in England, first a year in a convent school and then a year with their grandmother Oxley. She chattered on and on and irritated Ida Elisabeth unspeakably with her enthusiasm. She had stupid sky-blue child's eyes and was altogether dollishly pretty with a milk-white, finely freckled skin, cherry lips, and reddish golden curls—an angel off a Christmas tree, if any angels are shingled, that is.

Ida Elisabeth broke into the middle of her flood of words, turning to the cousin: "How is your mother, Fröken Oxley?" She felt somehow prompted to show her teeth, for she guessed that this was a sore point with Cecilie Oxley. People had said all kinds of things, she had heard, about Fru Oxley and that engineer, Næser, whom she had married such a very short time after Oxley's death, and she had let her daughter stay behind with her uncle and aunt at Rostesund when she moved to Oslo with her new husband.

And sure enough, Ciss Oxley blushed. It suited her charmingly, for that matter, making her look enviably pretty with her light grey eyes and her face which was usually quite dark—she had long black eyelashes, a brownish skin, and raven-black hair.

But she answered with calm civility: quite well, thank you. They had just come from Oslo, had been staying with her mother for Christmas. Yes, she and Næser had two children, fine little boys.

Ciss Meisling went on and on with her prattle—how topping it was in London, and how kind Grandma Oxley was, and what a splendid time they had had with the Ursulines. Mother this and Mother that and Mother so-and-so—she couldn't say which of them was the sweetest.

"But in heaven's name!" said Ida Elisabeth contemptuously; "how many mothers were there at that institution of yours?"

"Well, among the Ursulines all the nuns who take charge of children are called mothers", explained Ciss Meisling.

"What ridiculous nonsense! But that's how it is when people try to set themselves up against nature. Of course they have exactly the same passions as all the rest of us, and so the whole crowd of these old maids get themselves called mother by other folks' children. Foh!"

"It's not like that", said Cecilie Oxley, blushing again. "Some of them have a call for it. And that's not so strange either, if you think for a moment. When one sees how egotistical many people become through family ties and all that—one can understand that merely as a set-off God chooses certain ones to be all to all, in such a way that they feel that they cannot bind themselves more closely to anyone than they are bound to all those who need them—" Her face was now perfectly crimson and she stopped dead.

"Oh, that takes some believing! We're all made alike, aren't we?—with the same natural passions—I don't think it's much use any of us trying to go beyond that."

"If I believed it was so!" Ciss Meisling's blue eyes sparkled with anger. "Then I don't know what I should do! Go straight up and jump into the sea, at the very least!"

"Ciss, dear!" said her cousin aghast.

"Oh, bosh. Just wait till you fall in love, my child", said Ida Elisabeth.

"Thank you! If I may be allowed to wait till I fall in love, then . . . If I can wait as long as *that*, I may just as well renounce it for good and all, if there is One I love, whom perhaps you don't believe in—I don't know anything about that. But He had neither house nor home. Fancy if I never fell in love with any man—there are masses of women who never meet anyone they *can* fall in love with; but simply because it's supposed to be so humiliating, they try to imagine they *are* in love with somebody—"

Ida Elisabeth laughed scornfully:

"It's much more likely to be nature asserting itself and playing them a trick, my dear Fröken Meisling. And there we are, caught in the trap."

"Yes, if one has such beliefs as *that*!" The girl's voice was icy with contempt. "Then of course one has to put up with anything nature may do, even if it plays one a trick with a rank loafer or a regular cad."

"Ciss!" whispered Cecilie Oxley in terror.

There was a silence which was positively appalling. Both the girls were scarlet in the face. Ida Elisabeth felt as though paralysed. Ciss Meisling stole a glance at her, shy and ashamed, her eyes glistening with tears—and for a horrible instant Ida Elisabeth thought she was going to beg her pardon—and then she would certainly have flown at her and given her a sound box on the ears.

But Ciss simply sat there looking miserable. Then Cecilie Oxley murmured that it must be getting late—there was a clock over the sideboard right in front of all their eyes, surely the child could see it. "Good-night", whispered both the girls, and slipped out, as though they had pains in their stomachs or in their consciences.

And her fury boiled up in Ida Elisabeth—she felt bursting with it. If only she could have taken the two loathsome young hussies by the neck and shaken them like a pair of kittens—banged the two sanctimonious little fools one against the other. Oh, they were cruel, cruel, as cruel as only children could be.

IDA ELISABETH lay in the narrow lower berth with the boy asleep in the crook of her arm. The darkness was so stiflingly warm down here in the cabin, the child's body made her hot, and the smell of the bandages round his head sickened her after a while. She was wondering if she dared crawl up and get into the upper berth for an hour or two—later on; just at present she could not let Kalleman lie by himself, as the boat was pitching a good deal in the long swell: they were outside the skerries now.

Cautiously and with mournful tenderness she hugged the child closer. O God, yes—when she brought him to town, so long as his life was at stake, she had felt, oh, if she were to lose one of her children she would surely go mad with grief. But now as she lay here holding him in her arm, she could not help thinking of a play she had once seen when she was a little girl—about a Greek lady named Medea, who took the lives of both her children on realizing what kind of man their father was. Now she could understand that.

Though Kalleman—oh, she was not so sure that Kalleman was the least like Frithjof. He had always been so sweet, so quiet and good, and so fond of her—ever since he was no more than a few months old he had seemed able to show her that he knew he was her own little boy. Sölvi was far more egoistic—but then, she was so small. But she *was* like her father, with just the same apish liveliness that Frithjof had shown as a child. And in those days people had taken it to be a sign that he had talent.

No doubt she had thought the same herself, sometimes at any rate, or at least she had persuaded herself to think so. If she and Frithjof were to be made a sort of scapegoat, it was a kind of consolation to believe that this was because he in any case was too gifted to feel at ease in that stupid school.

It seemed to her now that it must have been something of the sort that had made her accept the situation, when Frithjof first tried to chum with her, the spring they were to be confirmed. He wanted them to be sweethearts. That was the time when he was so keen on playing the violin—in the beginning it was so that she might hear him play that he insisted on going off with her and hiding in outhouses or away in the fields. He had learnt with astonishing rapidity to play a few pieces quite decently. And when he stood like that, young and weedy, almost with a grown-up look, holding the fiddle against his cheek with a white handkerchief stuck in between, just like a proper violinist, when he swayed his body and kept flinging his long fair hair off his forehead, while his fingers played so nimbly and delicately on the strings—why, then no doubt she believed, because she wished to believe, all his fantasies about becoming a great artist and bringing all Europe to his feet, as he used to say.

She thought him handsome when he was playing—and she had made the discovery that she herself had grown pretty, much, much prettier than any of the other girls she knew. Perhaps she was going to be a beauty. She could positively fall in love with her own image as she stood in front of the glass combing her fair hair, throwing it forward over her breast and shoulders and holding a string of beads across her forehead or draping her figure with silk handkerchiefs and scarfs. *That* was of course what the others had seen the whole time, long before she herself had guessed it—that she would be better-looking than they. That was why they had set their faces against her.

She began to romance about her future, weaving it into Frithjof's romances about himself. And at any rate she offered no resistance when he got spoony. Though she often thought him horrid—there was apt to be something about him that reminded you of a dog torn between the desire to snatch a bite and fear of the whip. But at other times she herself went altogether crazy—she romped with Frithjof and egged him on, cuddled him and pushed him away, just as she might have played with their dogs at home. Precisely because she knew it was wrong, on the very border-line of what she knew to be the worst thing that can happen to a young girl. That was what made it exciting, that was the real spice in this game—that it was frightfully improper, and if any-one found it out, God help them! It was just as if she were getting her own back after all the miseries at home—her father's drinking and rioting: at times he would sit drivelling and lamenting over all the misfortunes that had overwhelmed him quite undeservedly; at other times he was perfectly wild and furious, abusing her and her mother, and what language her mother used in return—! And when he wasn't in, her mother said the beastliest things about him, calling him an alcoholic and bewailing their poverty, and then she turned on her daughter for being bad at school and for flying out of doors early and late. Ida Elisabeth had guessed long ago that her mother was not above nipping at her father's bottles on the sly—rather too often.

For a confirmation present Frithjof gave her a ring with a little red stone in it. That made her feel she had bound herself to him in a sort of way. Though she had no present to give him in return. But directly after there happened what she knew to be the worst. Though she had no rec-ollection of having thought it so awful. Pooh, was that all? she had thought, in disappointment and regret. But then it became different after a while. All the same, the essential thing about it—the thing that made her perfectly wild at times, and still wilder when she found she could frighten Frithjof—was her feeling of defiance, of taking her revenge. Let them just see, all those who had been unkind to her and Frithjof, how daring *they* were ... She imagined all the answers she would give them, if they discovered it. And when she thought of what the results might be, her excitement was almost greater than her terror. For she could never have really imagined either that they would be found out or that anything would result. In effect her only thought was probably that they were playing a frightfully dangerous and forbidden game, and all she could suppose was that it would go on indefinitely in the future.

Then came that night—a dazzlingly bright, warm night just after midsummer. They had rowed up to Ervik intending to fish. By the farthest of the Ervik farms they landed and went up to an outlying barn, and there they went to sleep. They were roused by a man coming in with an electric torch. It was the doctor; he had taken shelter in the barn from a summer shower.

Frithjof had to row home by himself and she had to go in the doctor's motor-boat. He talked seriously to her; not that he really said anything she didn't know before—but it was as though she realized for the first time that this really concerned herself in earnest. It was so terrible that she thought she must surely die.

He said her parents must not be told of it. But he went to the Braatös, for he wanted them to send Frithjof away. And Fru Braatö was in such despair that she could not help confiding in a woman friend, and so it was spread abroad.

The day she was called to account at home—that was a day she wished she could forget. No abusive name was too coarse for her father to apply to her, he yelled and shook his fists in her face, threatened to kill her. And then it was supposed to be the climax of her depravity that she had

17

carried on with Frithjof while being prepared for confirmation. Her father, who had never done anything but laugh at religion and churches and parsons—had *he* thought she ought to pay any attention to what Pastor Söndeled said? He was so kind, poor man, but it had never occurred to her to take Pastor Söndeled seriously.

And then—then Frithjof was sent for. Oh! How could she ever have had anything more to do with him after that—no, that was beyond her! Nothing more miserable—a lad scared out of his wits, who blinked his eyes and put up his arms as though to ward off a blow every time her father moved, and when her father did strike, he screamed at the top of his voice: "Mamma!" And—yes—he blamed it on her.

And her mother—she almost thought that was the worst of all. At first she was quite beside herself. Oh, that voyage to town with her parents—how was it she didn't jump overboard? But when it was clear that at any rate there was nothing wrong with her—then it was that her mother seemed to calm down and soften towards her. Thank goodness, then what had happened was not such a terrible misfortune after all—

She preferred her father a thousand times; he roared like a beast and swore the most awful oaths—it didn't matter at all; whether she had a baby or two babies or none made damned little difference compared with the fact that the child was disgraced, disgraced and defiled, "the last remnant of beauty and refinement and purity I had in the world", and then he wept and suddenly threw his arms around her: "Oh, Ida Elisabeth, would to God you had died rather! If one's dog is maimed, one shoots him, any man who has a heart—but nobody's man enough to do that to his child—"

AND yet—four years later, when Frithjof came up to her that day in Oslo, saying he had got her address and thought he would call on her, she did not show him the door.

Those years had not been very amusing ones for her. She had been sent to a friend of her mother's, and all this "aunt" appeared to expect was that she would break out again. She failed at the Commercial College, and the examination she afterwards passed was not a very brilliant one. Office work was the last thing she would choose. But as for dressmaking or millinery, which she wanted to learn and knew she had a turn for—no, she must not think of taking that up for a living; it was not ladylike enough, in the eyes of her parents. After her father's death she tried it nevertheless—she got a place in a draper's shop and attended a dressmaking school in the evenings. The two years she spent in Fröken Myhre's shop were the pleasantest part of her stay in Oslo. But then the old building was to be pulled down and Fröken Myhre, who had carried on business there for forty years, thought she might as well retire. So she was left. Quite by chance she met a friend of her father's, and he found a place for her in his office. It was barely enough to live on. When Frithjof turned up she knew she was likely to be given notice before long; too many of these entirely superfluous berths had been found in that office for daughters of the partners' friends, and all the others were more capable than she.

She had been so careful during these years. She had been so scared and ashamed at the outcome of that business with Frithjof that she shrank up like a frightened animal as soon as a man attempted anything like an advance. They were not very tempting either, the kind of adventures that lay within her reach. She had indeed met a few fellows who were ready to take her out and give her a little amusement. But she knew the price. And she did not want to sink any deeper. She had to keep herself in hand now. Once more— and she'd be going straight to the bow-wows.

Frithjof came, and she thought he had improved in looks. Even then he reminded one rather too much of a fat cherry, yellow and red. But he was properly grown up, and properly dressed, with clean nails—it was that more than anything that gave her the idea he was no longer a boy. He had a job in the office of a cousin of his mother's—music, no, he had shelved that; there were more than enough budding musicians in the world without him, he told her with a superior air. No doubt he was repeating what he had heard somebody say. What he did not tell her was that it had turned out like everything else he had put his hand to: it was always fairly easy for him to start at a thing, but all at once he found himself stuck fast, and he never got any further. Now he had a great deal to say about his prospects with his uncle—he was altogether indispensable there. Of course he could easily have found something better—at the moment, that is—but his uncle advised him not to; his uncle was only waiting for him to be old enough to be taken into partnership. Frithjof had friends from whom he could borrow a car, and Frithjof asked her out—and when he wanted to have her as in old days and she refused to have any more of that sort of thing, he proposed: why shouldn't they get married? Now, at once. He was just of age. And her mother approved—enthusiastically.

But she thought the same now: it *did* look as if she were doing a sensible thing in marrying Frithjof, but that was only an excuse she made to herself for yielding to her ardent longing for rehabilitation. She desired rehabilitation for herself, and she desired it for Frithjof—she wished to convince herself and all the world that it had been *love* that played the mischief with them that time. All the distressing and humiliating side of it was merely due to their being so much too young.

It seemed like a rehabilitation for both of them that Frithjof now had a chance of showing that what had involved him in the mess of his boyish sin with all its resultant misery was after all a feeling to which he remained faithful now that he was a man. Now that he could provide for her, he came back and married her. The unbearable scene in her father's office—all that was only because he was a young lad at the time, and in his fright he became a child again, poor fellow. She had done her best to forget that she had always known Frithjof to be a coward.

In reality she had always known too that one could never rely on anything Frithjof said. But she pretended not to know it. For the first months of their married life they probably agreed in believing they were happy. He was much in love—and then he was so delighted at having a home which was his. They were living in a nice little top flat out at Oppegaard. He thought a lot of himself as a married man and was almost ridiculously proud when she told him she was going to have a baby—touchingly proud she called it at the time, though it pained her that he ran round telling everybody about it. Even then there was something that roused a secret repugnance in her, by the very manner in which he loved her: he seemed to think a lot of himself for being such a devil of a fellow, frightfully passionate and all that—and at the same time he gave her the idea of being always afraid someone might come and pull him up for it.

Well, and then it came. They had only been married some five months when Frithjof came home one day, fearfully dejected, but trying all the time to persuade both her and himself that, pooh, it was nothing to worry about. His uncle had promised to help them till he found something else, but after all he was not quite the right man for his uncle's business.

Their furniture was bought on the instalment plan. So when they had taken a room in Pilestræde they had nothing to put into it but the few things that had come from her home. Frithjof's uncle gave them a monthly allowance which just covered their rent and a little food. Through Fröken Myhre she got some dressmaking, so that she was able to earn a few crowns weekly. And then it was that she began to see in sober reality what sort of a man Frithjof was.

Not that she saw through him altogether—for he was kind, fond of her too, and as proud as ever of the fact that he had a wife and was going to have a child. And he drew a rosy picture of the life before the three of them—charming home, white lacquered perambulator—he was keenly interested in all the little clothes she was making, and entirely satisfied with the world and with himself. He never stirred a step to get anything to do again. Perhaps it wouldn't have been so easy either—it dawned on her after a while that she might be just as glad she had been kept in ignorance of the real reason for his dismissal by his uncle. But when he promised her a mine of wealth in a dim and distant future, he was just as pleased with himself as if he had really given it her, and he expected her to be just as enthusiastically grateful as if she had received it.

At that time she was still capable of being scandalized at him. And it revolted her that he must needs be always telling lies—even about the most indifferent trifles, where it was impossible to discover why he could not just as well have spoken the truth—he lied all the same. She had not yet found out that Frithjof was given to lying just as another person might be given to laughing.

They lived in that room for six months, until she went to the maternity clinic. From there she went with Sölvi to Sandefjord, to her aunt Mathilde and her mother; the two sisters had been living together since her mother became a widow. Frithjof followed her there. And from there it was that she wrote to the only person in whom she could trust to help her when he heard how desperate was her need. She dared not let her aunt and her mother suspect that she was going to have a second child before the first was a year old. And then she thought, if they could only get home, back to their own surroundings, there must surely be some way out. So she wrote to the doctor at Vallerviken and asked if he could not get Frithjof some work in that neighbourhood.

He did so. He actually got Frithjof into the canning factory, and he helped them to find quarters in Esbjörnsen's
house, where there was a little shop, and he helped her to
start the little draper's business that she had thought of opening, now that there had been so much building at Berfjord.

Kalleman was born, and then Doctor Sommervold had a
talk with her. He tried to get her to separate from Frithjof.

"But can't you see, Ida Elisabeth, that he's nothing else
but an infantile individual? Big and strong physically and
man enough to get you as many children as you please—and
with that his mental development is that of a child of ten or
twelve. And a damned unattractive child, in my opinion."

By that time Frithjof had already been done with the
canning factory. She earned just enough to keep them going
from day to day. And Frithjof was quite pleased with the
way they were going on. He pottered about in their little
strip of garden, rowed out and was proud if he brought
home some fish for dinner, looked after Sölvi—and all the
time she had this big, lazy, jabbering young man hanging
around her. And she realized that it was always going to be
like this, if she did not follow the doctor's advice.

"Only think of the two children who are your own",
said the doctor. "You may have enough to do providing for
them in the years to come, without being obliged at the
same time to keep this big child of other people."

Perhaps it was this that made it impossible for her to
follow his advice. She felt she could not turn a person like
Frithjof out of his home and say to him: sink or swim. And
she had not the heart to throw him on to the old Braatös.
She could not help thinking—what if somebody should do
the same one day with Sölvi or Baby. And she shrank from
imagining Frithjof's face, if one day she came and told him
she wanted a divorce and now he must leave the house.
She remembered very well what it had been like when she
herself was a child—the day she was told that they must
leave their home at Holstensborg.

23

For the desperate part of it was that now she realized Frithjof *was* really fond of her and fond of the little ones— that in any case was not lies and play-acting. He was fond of her, because he relied on her implicitly—she would see that he never suffered want. He was fond of his children, because he was proud of being a father, and then he always had something to play with. He was what Sommervold had said, a child; his egoism was like that of a child, he clung to anything that formed a wall about his existence and protected him, and like a child he romanced about all he was going to give them and do for them—some day, in a future which would never arrive—but to him it was as though he had discharged his obligations when he boasted of all he intended to perform one day. Then he felt like a good boy and wanted to be kissed and praised for it. His own feeling was that he was happily married, and therefore he was sure she felt the same, in her heart.

Now and again Ida Elisabeth dozed off, lulled by the gentle rolling of the ship in the swell of the North Sea and by the wash of the waves against the ship's side, by creaking and jingling and grating sounds on board. But every time she was on the point of dropping off into a real sleep she was roused by a pain in some part of her body, which was lying so uncomfortably. And each time she was thus snatched back into full consciousness she felt that her heart was a lump of physical pain; it ached, it ached. Myrrh—a heart like a casket of bitter myrrh—oh, yes. They ought just to know what they were talking about, those two silly little things.

Ciss Meisling, by the way, seemed to have been lying awake too, and she had been snivelling, as Ida Elisabeth could hear by the way she blew her nose. Now she seemed to be asleep. But when Kalleman began whimpering, at first faintly and sleepily, then louder and more insistently: "Cup, cup. Cup, mamma", till she had to get up and switch on the light—Ciss Meisling sat up in her berth:

"Fru Braatö, is there anything I can do to help you?"

Her red curls were all in disorder and dark wisps of hair were sticking to her hot and tear-stained face. She had on the most enchanting pajamas, of flowered white silk—which made her still more irritating to Ida Elisabeth.

"No, thank you", she said curtly, getting out the cup and the bottle of milk.

While Kalleman drank, Ciss sat upright in her berth and watched him with a mournful little look.

"Are you angry with me, Fru Braatö?" she asked in her thick and tearful young voice. "I know I was rude to you this evening and answered you impertinently—"

Ida Elisabeth jeered:

"Dear me, Ciss—you can surely guess that grown-up people don't take it very seriously when a flapper gives them a cheeky answer. Just you lie down and go to sleep, my child."

Ciss sighed good-night and got under the bedclothes, and Ida Elisabeth put out the light and crept in to Kalleman. The boat was now steady and the water streamed along the ship's side with a quiet and gentle rippling—they were inside the skerries again and due in five hours.

Oh, how tired she was and how sick of everything! In a way she almost thought she could not stand Frithjof any longer, and yet she *could* not turn him adrift. He was quite unsuspecting, to such a degree that he completely disarmed her. She could nag at him, ask him to be quiet, refuse to answer when he spoke to her—he hung his head for a moment, looked unhappy—and directly afterwards he was just the same as if there were nothing at all the matter.

So it had gone on these last two years, since Kalleman was born. Frithjof had had some small jobs now and then—and her business was beginning to go quite well. The only annoying thing about it was that Frithjof had no idea of money. He thought now that she was earning "such stacks" they ought to put it into something or other, which *he* would be able to run so splendidly, silver foxes, of course, or poultry farming, or growing rhubarb and fruit wines. Just lately there was an old tin can of a Ford which had ended its career on their fjord. Frithjof had wild plans of buying it and opening a road service to Langeland and Vallerviken and Ut-Helle—all the boats that called at Berfjord put in at those places too. Or even to Mokhus, where at present the commercial lorry dealt with all the traffic there was.

Her position was not so bad as to be unbearable—if only she could keep away from the thought that it would be like this for ever. And if she could only cease to think of what had been and to grieve over her own folly. And heavens above, there were thousands of wives who had to feed a waster of a husband, provide for themselves and their children, while the creature they kept alive claimed to be treated as a man and the master of the house. At any rate Frithjof was not a bad man and did not expect her to give way to him if she was to escape a beating.

If only, if only—no, she would not think of that. And the two children she had—oh, *she* thought they were lovely—yes, for their sake she would gladly have travelled on and on, as far as the star would go before her, if only in the end she might find her way to a place where she could make her offering, as it said in those verses. The smoke that whirled in the breeze above their home and the heart with all her bitter memories, like myrrh.

It was just before sunrise when Ida Elisabeth came on deck. The vault of sky was light and clear, pale yellow above the mountain-crests, where the dawn breathed blue shadows over the snowfields, but higher up the air became greenish, passing into the unfathomable depth of blue which veiled the stars.

The ice-floes scraped and scraped against the ship's sides. They were already so far in that the Berfjord was white with ice from shore to shore. The boat stopped, backed, and charged forward again through the new ice in the channel. The dark water came whirling up with a shower of greenish foam and flooded the new flakes which shivered and chinked against the old ice-edge.

In the usual way it was not so often nowadays that Ida Elisabeth was equal to feeling the beauty of the Berfjord. But now it took her by force as she tramped up and down to keep herself warm—up and down the deserted deck. The houses looked so touchingly small and patient, as they lay along the shore under the mighty mountains: they were off the Ruskenes farms with the ice-green waterfall hanging irresistibly down the cliff from the break at the top, right up against the sky, down to the narrow strip of beach, snow-covered and in shadow, at the foot of the mountain. All her night thoughts were focused into a single longing—for a tolerant endurance that should resemble that of the little farms, with the morning smoke twirling over the snow-covered roof, for a spirit of daring so dogged that it would last out a long journey over mountain beyond mountain and would be so familiar with the stars as to dash after them, even when they were hidden by the daylight.

THE steamer swung in, rounding the Gaupholms, and the inmost creek lay before her like a round white plain. At the far end of the open channel stood a little group of people on the ice with hand-sleighs and cases, a sledge with a little dun horse, and—God help her—Ida Elisabeth discovered the Ford. In front sat a little mite bundled up in something bright red—Sölvi in her own old golf jacket.

In her anxiety something seemed to break within her, and despair surged up like the cold black water round the ship's bow as it broke through the ice. Frithjof had gone and done it after all, while she was away.

There he came, running towards the boat as she lay to—young and tall and already inclined to fat; the lock of

27

fair hair under his fur cap was white with rime, his fleshy face had a healthy colour from the cold. He waved to her and shouted "Welcome!" in a ringing voice.

Ida Elisabeth replied with one feeble wave; then she turned and ran. She had to go below and fetch Kalleman.

As she dashed down the companion her mind and senses gathered it all into one image—the black water with the drifting, clinking ice-flakes, the white surface of the frozen fjord, and her husband's unsuspecting face, radiant with health, and the houses along the shore under the huge mass of mountain—and high up above it all the first golden rays of the morning sun shining upon the snowfields against the sky. She had an irresistible feeling, instinct rather than thought, that in some way or other *she* must keep something buoyant in her soul, as a fountain drives its jets of water unceasingly into the air, up towards the prospect of white, sun-gilt mountain-tops and the great bell of heaven—though she were held down never so fast among the shadows of the shore.

Chapter Two

THAT WINTER AND THE FOLLOWING SPRING Ida Elisabeth felt at times—no, she couldn't stick it any longer. Then she gripped herself by the scruff of the neck: of course she could stick it. For she *had* to.

She was expecting again, there was no doubt about that. The certainty of it roused in her the same turbulent feeling she had experienced the other times: she would fight for what belonged to her. She had only herself to rely on—she must do something.

But there was so little she could do. Send out bills to customers who owed her money—the amounts were not large, but it would have made a difference if she could only have gotten in half of what was due to her. But there was not much money about. For days together not a soul entered the shop, unless it was a little girl who wanted a reel of cotton or a woman buying buttons and tape. And all through February the weather was so frightful, storm and rain, leaving the whole surface of the country slippery with ice, and then came blizzards and rain and more storms. The children could scarcely ever go out of doors, and Kalleman especially was fretful and fidgety; it was a slow business getting him properly well again. He had quite lost his appetite; she gave him eggs morning and evening—her hens had begun to lay fairly well—but it was often difficult to get him to take as much as that.

She felt consumed by this fiery fighting spirit—if she could but get the better of some of the things that made her life so uncertain. There was nothing she could do but mind the shop, look after her house, her children, her chickens. Now that business was so quiet she employed her time in making a spring coat for Sölvi out of Aslaug's old coat and skirt, and some new blue shirts for Frithjof. Meanwhile she tried to resign herself—this was all she could do. And to console herself with the thought that there were many whose difficulties were far greater. Deep down in her mind anxiety gnawed like a kind of toothache: she too might easily find herself in far greater difficulties; she was thinking of all the debts of which she must pay an instalment at any rate, before she could get in any new spring goods. There were many who were worse off and appeared to be resigned, or else they became embittered and rebellious and demanded that somebody should help them or that the world should be rearranged, for then they believed they would be better off—but she had a vague suspicion that such people had not her defiant temper or her invincible desire to win through alone, without saying anything to anyone—or else their spirit had been broken; but if she let hers be broken they would all be better dead.

Therefore it had brought her, in spite of all, a kind of relief and satisfaction to clear up that affair of Frithjof's purchase of the car. She went up to Eriksen, who owned the Ford, and told him in so many words that *she* could not pay for it—not a farthing. So he took it back.

Frithjof came home. He tried to appear very cock-a-hoop, seemed to be throwing out his chest and flapping his wings. His voice was apt to break into a loud, thin shriek; what always made this sound so queerly was that he had a big and burly frame—might be taken for a regular manly fellow, if he kept his mouth shut and one did not notice his expression.

"But, Ida Elisabeth! You surely understand it was never my idea that you should *pay* anything—if you'll just sign your name, you see, I can get the money from the bank, and then I'll manage the rest—"

Ida Elisabeth let her sewing-machine whirr on to the end of the long seam before she replied calmly and unconcernedly:

"You understand, don't you, that *I* can't go surety for anyone?"

"Oh yes, the bank's willing to take you. And then you know, I shall get Sommervold too, he won't refuse to sign if you do."

"Don't talk such nonsense, please", she said indulgently, adjusting her material again in the machine.

"No, pardon me, Ida Elisabeth, I really think it's you who are talking nonsense. I don't understand how you can be so unreasonable. Of course you'll reap the benefit too, I really think you might see that, if I start something of my own which will bring me in a heap of money—"

"Five or six crowns a week, if you're lucky enough to get any orders." She jumped up—something was boiling over in the kitchen. She stroked his hair in passing, with teasing benevolence: "How much do you think repairs would come to, to say nothing of the tax and all—"

He followed her, but she was clattering with the rings of the stove.

"Ugh, Ida Elisabeth, why are you so absurdly anxious? Bless you—we've got on all right so far—we've never yet actually had to go without—"

She made no reply. Frithjof went on, encouraged by her silence:

"Do you remember before Christmas—when you were in such an awful state—hadn't an idea where you'd get the money for Kalleman's illness and all that? And didn't they come and ask me to take Arne's place at the Co-operative Society, so that I was able to give you the money for the journey and all—have you forgotten that?"

It was true too. Frithjof had brought her sixteen crowns which he himself had earned, and he had been able to buy for himself the rubber boots that they had been talking about for so long. He had been so proud and happy—and she had thought she must encourage him and make a show of being impressed. Presumably it was of that she now had to take the consequences.

"Well? Do you know what, Ida Elisabeth? I really think you might have a little confidence in your husband. You really might show me a little confidence—"

"Certainly, Frithjof. And I really think I have shown you confidence. But there's moderation in all things, you know." She laughed quietly. He came up and tried to put his arm round her. She gently pushed him away:

"Go back now, Frithjof. You're so in the way here in the kitchen."

"I can tell you it'll be a disappointment for Sölvi. So delighted she was with papa's car, as she calls it. And I'd been looking forward so to all the trips I was going to take with you this summer. Home to the old people—and up to Breistöl—do you know, they say one can drive right up to Breistöl now? Fancy that, Ida Elisabeth! You haven't been there for ages. Aren't you frightfully keen on going up to Breistöl once again?"

Ida Elisabeth shook her head. High up and far inland among the moors, a few little sæters on both sides of a clear and rapid little stream—from there it was half an hour's walk up to their hut on the saddle of the Svartdalsfjeld. From the hut you had a glimpse of the fjord infinitely far below, and in clear weather you could look out to sea, but inland in the other direction there was nothing but grey mountains with blue mountains beyond and the gleam of the glacier in the far distance. She did not even know if she cared to go up there any more. Or whether she preferred to leave it as it was—a part of her memories of a time that lay infinitely far behind her, almost unreal it seemed to her now, in a haze of bygones and untroubled joy.

It took some time before Frithjof gave in. She could not help feeling a little sorry for him—if there had been any possibility of affording it she would almost have welcomed his having this toy for which he begged so insistently, poor fellow.

He made a suggestion—couldn't he borrow what there was in the children's savings bank books? It would be a financial operation, of course, and he would replace the money with interest and compound interest. Sölvi had been given a book with a hundred crowns as a christening present from Aunt Mathilde; Ida Elisabeth herself had managed by hook and by crook to add a few crowns to it, and to open a book for Kalleman. Besides this Doctor Sommervold had put something in for Carl on his first birthday, but she did not know how much, as the doctor kept the book himself.

"That's not to be thought of. The children's money is not to be touched."

But she felt sorry for Frithjof all the same. And in March, when Frithjof got a temporary job driving for the packing-case factory, he came and told her about a second-hand bicycle that he could buy for thirty crowns.

That same morning she had sold four golf jackets at one swoop—to a party of people from far up Svartdal; there had been a big funeral in the place and a lot of people had come to it from a distance. And the schoolmaster's married daughter had sent her forty-seven crowns for purchases made when she was home last summer. So Ida Elisabeth said yes, it might be a sensible thing to buy that bicycle.

"Then you think I ought to do so?" he asked anxiously. Ida Elisabeth gave a little laugh. When he saw that she was not going to oppose one of his ideas, Frithjof always insisted on discussing the affair endlessly, simply revelling in her approval.

"And then you know," he said, "it'll be awfully handy when I have to fetch parcels for you from the boat and so on, I can put them on the carrier—"

Ida Elisabeth could not help smiling. It was five minutes' walk down to the quay. "Yes, of course", she said seriously. She was filled with the same quiet surprise every time she found that in spite of all she was really fond of Frithjof—or at any rate felt a queer, deep-seated tenderness for him.

Poor fellow, he made such a frightful exhibition of himself with his desperate efforts to be amusing, when he was in company—never had a suspicion that he was saying anything ludicrous.

SOME weeks of radiant spring weather followed. Frithjof trundled about all day long on his old bone-shaker, always with Sölvi sitting in front of him. They brought home bunches of primulas and branches covered with catkins which shed a yellow dust all over the house and put out little silvery felted leaves, which made Ida Elisabeth shrink from throwing them away.

Her best time was the early morning hours. She got up as soon as Kalleman was awake, dressed the boy and took him out. Tired she was, but it passed off as soon as she came into the open air—it was still cold and laden with the smells of the beach and of the raw, bare mould of the garden; coming into it was almost like plunging into cold water—and with a stab of regret she thought of summer days long ago, the sun sparkling on the fjord and the thickets of bushes around the bay, where she had undressed with the breeze and the warm sun caressing her skin. Oh, to be able to wade out, with the reflection of the ripples over the sandy bottom flickering all up her body—till the water was deep enough for her to strike out and feel it streaming about her, deliciously soft, and her limbs had such a funny look, foreshortened and tinged with the green of the sea. To think that she would not be able to bathe this summer either. But there was no place in the cove here where she could be certain that nobody would see her. Ugh, she remembered a trip they made to Ervik the summer before Kalleman was born. Her mother-in-law's bright girlish twittering: Oh, but Lisken dear, you don't mean to tell me you're shy about *that*? Why, it's really *such* a natural thing for a married woman ... Else and Merete were there too; they were just at the most disgusting age—

Cautiously Ida Elisabeth hoed in the manure around the perennials, which were shooting so that it was a joy to see them. She picked off the withered leaves of the auriculas. That was the kind of thing she could not entrust to Frithjof, but he might dig up the beds in the kitchen garden one of these days, so that she could get them ready and sow them.

She wiped her hands on her rough apron and blew Kalleman's nose, then stood for a moment straightening her back, as she watched the child running off to his place by the fence. There were some sheep feeding on the slope above. He was so fond of her chickens too. When he was a little bigger perhaps it would amuse him to keep rabbits. It had been good to have them to fall back upon in other years, but if she always had to go herself and see whether Frithjof hadn't forgotten to attend to them ... No, this year at any rate she could not keep rabbits.

He was not a pretty child, Kalleman—Ida Elisabeth could see that herself. His head looked very big, his neck being so thin and white; altogether he was small and thin for his age. And his forehead was so big and bulging, "a regular parson's noddle", said Fru Esbjörnsen; she thought too that Kalleman had such intelligent eyes. They were large and dark, blue really—handsome, she thought. But his mouth was perfectly charming, small and a very pale pink—otherwise his face was not at all pretty, puny and compressed under the heavy forehead, with hardly anything of a nose.

Oh, her own little boy! In the shadow of an apprehension which she would not allow herself to express in clear thought, she stood watching the child. Now the sun was shining on the highest of the moors. The Yridal peak, still covered with snow, stood sharp and golden against the sky. Down here the shadows lay blue and chilly upon the little houses around the quay and the pale waters of the creek beyond. In the morning stillness the murmur of the river could be heard so plainly, and the chuck-chuck of a motor-boat far out.

But above the mountains the whole sky was already full of sunlight, and the little drifting clouds which were golden a while ago were now white, and the blue of the sky deepened from one minute to the next. Now she could hear that Sölvi was awake; she was choking with laughter and Frithjof was humming some sort of tune—he must be playing with the child. Better to go in and get them up, and then get their breakfast ready.

Another thing was that Kalleman had been very backward in learning to walk. And as far as she remembered she had heard before now of children who could not talk much until they were about three. In other ways he seemed quite intelligent. Sometimes she cut out the coloured figures from old fashion papers, as she herself had gotten such fun out of playing with paper dolls when she was a child. But Sölvi did not care a bit for them—if she took any notice of them it was only to tear them up; and then Kalleman brought them to his mother and showed her the disaster: ow-ow, he said, in great distress. Kalleman could spend hours propping up his paper ladies and paper children against the back of the sofa, sprawling on it and chattering. "There, that's a boy, that's a girl, look, mamma—Oo, flop!" he said, when they tumbled down. He was *not at all* unintelligent, she believed. For instance, when there were pictures in the paper of things he knew, he always noticed them. And when they had put up a new Singer poster at the store he pointed to the woman at the sewing-machine the first time she took him there. "That's mamma!" he cried, delighted—

It gave him a much better appetite for his morning porridge too, if she had taken him out into the garden first.

IDA ELISABETH decided to go over to Vallerviken one Monday—then there was least chance of meeting anyone she knew in the churchyard; they would all have decorated their graves for the Sunday. It was about five miles, if she walked by the old road over Standal, so she could not take the children with her. Fru Esbjörnsen promised to look after them and the shop while she was away.

Frithjof went down to the quay as soon as dinner was over, and Ida Elisabeth made haste to get the washing-up done so that she could slip out without his noticing it. Otherwise of course he would have gone with her, and then she could not escape calling on his parents.

The road lay before her, bright and dry; among the withered grass at its edge fresh green blades were shooting up and little red bunches of new leaves were appearing on every side. The points of her shoes were grey with dust almost as soon as she started—the sight filled her with heartfelt joy: it was so summer-like. The road turned into the alderwood and dropped towards the bridge; now she could no longer be seen from the houses. Ida Elisabeth breathed freely—she had a whole long afternoon to herself, right up to supper time.

She saw and felt everything around her as she walked—as one renews acquaintance with everything the first day, on returning to a place which one has often visited in previous holidays. It is all as one remembers it, only much more beautiful. In the noonday sun the stems of the alders glittered like silver, and behind the open trellis of their leaves there was a white shimmer of water. The alders had almost shed their blossoms; the brown veil of catkins on all the twigs had darkened and shrunk; the pollen had floated down covering all the puddles in the wood with a dirty yellow film. Around the stumps the celandine showed with succulent green leaves and yellow star-like flowers shining like butter. A cow broke through the undergrowth and hung its head over the fence. Ida Elisabeth had to go up and pat it: "poor thing"—it was shaggy and dirty, sharp as a knife along the back, and its haunch-bones stood out like boards. A couple of birds darted across the road with passionate and frolicsome cries and vanished among the trees. Ah, thank God it was spring.

On the other side of the river the slope was thinly covered with firs. Here the heather was dark, with no life in it as yet, but on the level ground above there was water everywhere between the tussocks, and the moss was swelling green and fresh in the pools. Unconsciously she quickened her pace, for there were long stretches of shadow here. But when she had passed the summit and left the wood behind she walked more slowly. With half-closed eyes and face turned to the sun she went on foot by foot and allowed herself to be baked through.

The long, narrow Standal water lay before her, reflecting the blue sky, with some calm strips of dazzling white farther out. The shore here was quite a pale green around the rocks and tree-stumps. Scattered about were rowan-trees whose tops were perfectly round—all the trees and bushes here showed signs of having been stripped of leaves, no doubt people had done that for hundreds of years. The buds were big already. Ida Elisabeth broke off a twig of rowan; the leaf which was on the point of bursting looked like little grey claws trying to show themselves. The path on which she walked was running with water.

The Standal farms lay on the other side of the lake. The dwelling-house at Upper Standal was fairly large, ochre yellow with verandas to two stories. She had never been up there since that house was built. But the other farm, Johan's and Kristine's, down in the corner between the sheer mountain-side and the sea, was exactly as it had been in old days, when her father had taken her there. Little grey houses roofed with turf, stone fences topped with cut furze-bushes, which were withered and rusty, giving the whole an untidy appearance. The place was reported to be in a very decayed condition of late. Frithjof said that Johan Standal was now quite blind, something had shot up into his eye the winter before last, when he was chopping wood. Ugh, so now it was over a year ago, and all the time she had been thinking she would go up and see them—but then she thought she could not come empty-handed. Johan and Kristine had always been so kind to her.

She sat down on reaching the lake, and looked across. A fat bumble-bee was buzzing close to her feet—trying to fasten itself on a tiny grey pansy. Then it let go and floated humming into the air. Ida Elisabeth watched it. Behind where she sat was a scree, and among the stones grew some hazel-bushes. Long yellow catkins drooped from their branches.

She suddenly came to think of some branches of hazel that were passed round the class—it was while she was in the lower school. The mistress explained about male and female flowers, the little round buds with three fine purple filaments at the top—how the stigmas received pollen from the catkins, and how the same process was repeated throughout nature, up to man. A fierce red flame spread over Ida Elisabeth's face—what bosh! Styles and stigmas, bumble-bees and nectaries, birds that help each other in building nests and feeding their young, cows and calves and charming little foals—what in the world had this to do with men and women? She felt this with painful sharpness. The brightness of the spring day, the scent of mould and of all the growth that was forced on by this weather, the trickling of water in the screes behind her—there was a separating gulf between her and all this that was growing and living, unfeeling and lovely. It would change from one beauty to another, the light catkins would become dark and luxuriant foliage, the grass would grow high and full of flowers and be mown and become scented hay. In the little grey beds between the stone-heaps turnips and potatoes would shoot up and spread their rank leaves till the mould was hidden from view. Has this much to do with human beings letting themselves drift from obstinacy, and because they are unhappy and desire to be petted and believe they can force themselves in upon another person—and are afterwards ashamed of having been so naïve—? One sees that one was mistaken in the other person, but it was one's own doing, and so ... The other one is also human, poor fellow, it won't do to be shabby about it, and one knows that *he* has no idea of what it is like to be *me*, so that one cannot raise a hand in self-defence.

Animals—they do not know what it means to be in a constant state of anxiety about one's children. They are alarmed when the danger threatens, close at hand. But they do not know the feeling of dread that comes of being forced to think of the future and having children to think of.

What sentimental old maids' talk, that children ought to be told frankly and honestly and not to be allowed to form ugly ideas about there being anything mysterious or degrading in it! Styles and stigmas, pollination by insects and by the wind, sheep and little white lambs, mamma and papa standing hand in hand and watching baby asleep. "Is there anything on earth so lovely as a little child?" said Frithjof's mother, as she took the hand of Frithjof's father. It was exactly as if they were *playing* at father and mother, she had always thought. Frithjof's mother was one of those who were so frightfully given to all this talk about what was natural and pure and beautiful. And there was nothing mysterious about it, except in the way of sacred mysteries. Ugh, people like Fru Söndeled or Mathilde Baur—but thank God they belonged to an age which happily was past and gone, when women looked upon natural cohabitation as something impure and were so frightfully full of affectation and prudishness.

Perhaps it was merely that Aunt Mathilde and Fru Söndeled were rather less prudish. They knew a good deal more than Borghild Braatö, and in any case they were not prudish enough to pretend ignorance of what they knew.

The afternoon shadows were already long and the sunshine was golden, warm and as it were flickering, when she entered the churchyard. A light breeze stirred the fjord into flashing ripples. Their family grave was almost at the far end, where the wall came down to the beach; the soil here was yellow and sandy and soft to walk on.

The stones that had formed a kerb about the grave had become detached from each other and the headstone was crooked, leaning over the new grave. But they had told her it was no use doing anything until her mother's grave had sunk a little. When her name had been cut on the stone it would have to be moved to the middle of the space. Then Ida Elisabeth would plant another rose-bush, of the same kind as that on her father's grave.

She laid on her mother's grave the bunch of spring flowers which she had gathered as she walked and put a flat stone over the stalks so that they should not blow away.

"Carl Fredermand Andst. Late Master Mariner"—her father had himself chosen the inscription. Not "shipowner" nor any of the other things.

She had been fond of him—that was just what had always been the worst part of it, that she was really fond of him, though she struggled furiously not to be. For he grew to be so horrid—oh, how disgusting he had been when the drink got on his nerves and he felt so sorry for himself and accused everyone of playing him false and said all the nastiest things about people who had been his friends. It made her heartily ashamed to see him like this—it was almost a relief when he took a real crazy fit and roared and fumed and flew at her and her mother. And what things he could say to her, if she came home late some evening when he was drunk—and he was nearly always that. Was it strange that she had ended in doing what she did?

And yet she knew it was true, every word he had shouted at her—at that time—that she was the only one in the world in whom he still believed, the last remnant of purity and beauty that he still looked up to and loved. It was true that he had done so, though it was not enough to keep him from soaking till there was nothing left of him but a loathsome sloppy mess. He had been incapable of doing anything to protect her; he had done everything in his power to drive her to ruin—that was his way of being fond of one. But she knew that he had been fond of her—terribly fond. She knew in her heart that her mother was not exaggerating—not much at any rate—in asserting that her father had died of it. He had begun to die from the evening he saw her off in the train to Oslo.

And the strange thing was, it was precisely for his sake that she must not fail, so it seemed to her. Because he had failed her, although he was fond of her, she must not fail anyone—not even those she was not fond of, did not like. It was just like an inheritance that had come to her—an obstacle he had not been able to take, and so she must try whether she could clear it.

When she thought of her mother she was always reminded of a verse she had learnt in the singing-lesson at school:

> Little wavelet, gently breaking
> With the sunlight shining through,
> Colourless thyself, but taking
> Colour from the sky's deep blue—
> Heaven, no; but heaven's image ...

She did not remember any more. But "heaven, no, but heaven's image"—those words always made her think of their home, as it had been in old days, before the war, when her father commanded the *Frostdalsegg*—and when he was at home a light seemed to shine from him. He looked exactly as she imagined Olav Tryggvason—and her mother mirrored his joy in life, as it were, and her passion for him was like a reflection of his; she had realized this later. No doubt he meant it seriously enough in his heart, in spite of the jesting air he gave it, but he used to complain of having to be so madly and unhappily in love with his own wife. "Yes, you *are* fond of me, I know that—a little, so long as I'm with you. But supposing I were lost at sea, I should be to you as if I had never existed, when once you had got accustomed to the idea that I should never come back. At most you would remember our married life as a dream—quite a pleasant dream, I dare say." "Oh, but, Carl," her mother would protest, and a shadow of dismay would come over her bright face, "how can you say that! I do really love you—" "Oh, love!—you haven't the least idea what it is, you little—"

Afterwards, during the war, when her father was mixed up in all the racket of shipping and water-power and mines and forests, she knew that there had been something going on between him and other women. At least a couple of times there had been a talk of divorce. In some way or other she had gotten the impression that her father's love affairs were always unhappy—it was the kind of thing that suited him, when his ladies raised tearing scenes and broke with him, and he could love them in real anguish of heart. In the old days, when all at home was sunshine and happiness, he had been wild about sentimental songs and books which made the tears run down his cheeks as he read them. He had been a happy man at that time, she felt that; enormously strong, with a health that could stand anything, an unusually capable seaman too he was said to have been—and it must have been a disappointment to him that her mother was what she was, colourless as water, a woman on whom nothing made any lasting impression. So he transmuted his disappointment, got sentimental over it and even enjoyed it. So long as nothing could deprive him of the feeling that he was fortune's favourite for all that. When things went to smash and every attempt he made to recover himself only led to fresh disasters, he broke up altogether, just as a really ripe and juicy fruit goes rotten after a blow.

Her mother's maiden name was Siveking, and Ida Elisabeth had always thought that name had a strange, enchanting sound. Her mother's father was a watchmaker, but his father again had been a painter, and in 1914 he was discovered. The pictures he had given away to relations and friends or sold for a trifle were routed out and exhibited, and a book was written about him. The two great views of the Sognefjord, which Ida Elisabeth had loved to sit and dream over when she visited grandmother Siveking at the institution and which had afterwards hung in her and Connie's attic, were cleaned and given new frames instead of the old greeny-bronze ones with fir-cones nailed on them. The one with the stormy sky went to the National Gallery; the other was given the place of honour in the music room at Holstenborg, and after the bankruptcy it was bought by a Swedish collector. But long before great-grandfather Siveking was discovered her father had been in the habit of saying that by gad he thought the old man's pictures were much nicer than many of the paintings folks paid a heap of money for at the exhibitions. And when he saw Ida Elisabeth's drawings he laughed and said maybe she'd be able to do something in that line—she seemed to have inherited old Siveking's talent. Of course when Siveking became famous he was fearfully proud of having seen all the time that this was good stuff, and now there could be no question about it, Ida Elisabeth must have a chance of perfecting her talent. She herself was then more inclined to do something else—she did not quite know what, to learn weaving or working in metal or designing furniture. Or perhaps to be a jeweller; they had been to a jeweller's in Copenhagen, and this was a lady who had herself made the loveliest things. Her father was all for it—Norway's first woman jeweller, that wasn't bad!

Even in his sea-going days her father had been a great one for buying pretty things to bring home. Such objects as had come down to her she had been forced to sell while living in Oslo—a casket of carved sandal-wood and mother-of-pearl, some great ornaments from North Africa with lovely blue and green enamel, set with big blood-red corals. The only thing she had left was a little ebony elephant with real ivory tusks—it must have come from Ceylon. Sölvi and Kalleman were just as fond of it as she had been, when she took it down from the shelf and allowed them to pat it.

Anyhow her mother was always delighted to receive presents. She loved arranging her things and dusting them and laying her table tastefully when she had friends to take coffee with her. In other ways she was not a very domestic person. It was a shame to think such things, but Ida Elisabeth had the impression that in a way she got over Herman's death more lightly than the loss of her home and all the things she had been accustomed to have about her. She seemed to drift away from her children, or they drifted away from her as they grew bigger—no, it *was* their mother who had withdrawn herself from them, almost as if she had grown shy of them or as if the big children made her feel insecure. It was the inanimate objects that gave her a feeling of safety when she handled them.

In the years of abundance she had been a frightful spendthrift—but her father had positively encouraged her in it. She gave one the idea of a woman of the world who had stepped straight out of a film or an English magazine. But Ida Elisabeth had had the feeling that her mother was not nearly so happy as she had been when they lived in that little villa of theirs by the churchyard. At the same time, no doubt, she was hurt at her husband's infidelities—once more it was as though she were frightened by something she did not understand. For that matter she herself had probably had something on at that time—it was impossible to say whether there was any truth in what her husband cast in her teeth when he was drunk, but she was certainly not one to offer any great resistance when she had to mix with people whose ways were of that sort.

The last few years, after they had landed here at Vallerviken, she too grew pretty bad. Especially after she had begun to tipple, and when she tried to pay her husband in his own coin. It sounded utterly against the order of nature, when her mother used coarse abusive language and accused her father and his friends of committing all sorts of debaucheries.

And then, when Ida Elisabeth saw her again at Aunt Mathilde's in Sandefjord—one would not have believed there was any truth in what she remembered of the last years at home. She was as it were nothing but the sister of Fru Baur, the dean's widow—much younger, much prettier, for she had really grown charming again, bright in the face under her fair hair, with eyes a pure porcelain blue, and always dressed as suited a widow. They both gave you the idea of being widows to such a superlative degree. Entirely of one mind about the difficulties of marriage, which was nothing but a trial, and nevertheless they mourned their husbands so deeply. Aunt Mathilde, by the way, hinted that Wenche might easily marry again, if she had a mind to. And her mother spoke sorrowfully of "Carl, your father"—how much he had felt Herman's death, and what a blow it had been to him when they lost Connie, but as to Ida Elisabeth's misconduct, that had simply been the death of him. But her affection for Sölvi had been touching.

And now they were lying here, both her father and mother. Ida Elisabeth had not been able to go to Sandefjord when her mother fell ill the summer before. If only they had thought of sending her money for the journey—but she had always pretended they were getting on quite well in writing to her mother. And when the coffin came she had not cared to allow it to be opened. She had been dead a whole week, and it was in August. She preferred to retain as her last memory of her mother that blustering grey February morning when they said good-bye to one another on board the boat at Sandefjord. Her mother had worn a little black hat, and the black fur collar of her coat was turned up; it was not light enough for Ida Elisabeth to see her face clearly, but her mother's cheek was cold and soft as that of a young girl, when she bent down and kissed her daughter, and her voice was faint and despondent: "Now do take good care of yourself, my dearest child, and of the little one—"

As she came out of the sexton's she ran straight into the doctor.

46

"What—are you here, little Ida—?"

"Yes, but don't tell anybody. I couldn't get out to Vette-haugen, and now I must see about going home."

"Are you going to walk all the way back to Berfjord?"

"Why yes, in this lovely weather—" She smiled. "You're a worshipper of summer too, doctor!" He had on a grey alpaca jacket and an old panama hat.

"M'yes. You're very well, I hope?" He looked her over with a smile. And then—all at once his great fleshy face contracted. It was tanned by the weather, with black eyes beneath straight, pepper-and-salt brows, but his mouth was the special attraction, with delicate, narrow lips and a mass of fine little wrinkles running perpendicularly to his upper lip. He was always so freshly shaven too, and the skin of his cheeks and chin was dotted with tiny holes, almost like the end of a thimble. But she thought it looked nice, because it was Doctor Sommervold.

Ida Elisabeth was annoyed with herself for turning so red.

"Lord!" he said under his breath. "Have you gotten yourself into a mess again!"

She shrugged her shoulders, trying to put a brave face on it:

"The fortune of war, you know. Speaking seriously—it's no use being downhearted over a thing like that."

"If you don't deserve a whipping! What are you thinking of—?" He held her hand in his great soft palm, patted it once or twice with his other hand. "A thrashing you want! But anyhow you can come in with me now, and I'll drive you home. Are you hungry?"

"I've just had coffee—" She nodded in the direction of the sexton's.

"But no proper food since you left home? Come along then!"

IT was lovely all the same, thought Ida Elisabeth, as she let herself sink into the deep chesterfield. The blinds with

47

pictures on them of German baronial castles were half-drawn to keep out the sun; they waved gently in the draught, and below them on the window-sill stood the doctor's cactuses full of pink and scarlet flowers through which the sunshine glowed. "You must take a proper look at them presently, Ida Elisabeth", he said with pride.

She took a gulp of the ice-cold drink. Vermouth and seltzer was good. And good to sit in a big room again for once—it rested the eyes to dwell on such a wide surface of dark carpet. There was plenty of room between the groups of large furniture. The old baroque chairs were upholstered in cross-stitch embroidery, parrots and tulips, and the table with the black marble top inlaid with flowers in many-coloured stones had been brought home from Italy by Fru Sommervold's parents years ago. There was a grand piano, and there were handsome things on the walls, and here by the window was the place where they always sat, in the deep leather arm-chairs. It was so gratefully quiet—the doctor lived here alone. In summer, to be sure, he always had the house full of visitors.

"So *that's* why Else is to come and stay with you this summer?" asked Doctor Sommervold.

"Else? Not at all—there's been no question of Else coming to us."

"Then I may tell you that that's what your mother-in-law is saying. 'Else is to stay with Frithjof and Lisken this summer', she told me; 'Lisken can no longer manage everything by herself.' "

Ida Elisabeth turned red and knitted her brows. The doctor went on, quickly and earnestly:

"Now you're to be sensible, Ida Elisabeth, you mustn't agree to this. Poor Else, I suppose she's quite a nice little girl, but she'll only be a bother to you and no use at all. Of course, one can understand that the Braatös are anxious to find some place for her—they seem to be in worse difficulties than ever. But Else will never do anything for her living, unless she finds herself among perfect strangers—"

"Perhaps that won't be so easy. For Else to get a place among strangers. You know, it's always been the family's affair to see about that sort of thing. And they can't go on finding places for them for ever."

"No. No, of course it'll get more and more difficult. But you mustn't let yourself be talked over, Ida, my dear; you have your hands full with Frithjof and your own affairs—"

"Besides, I haven't heard a word about it", said Ida Elisabeth with annoyance.

"You will then. But you're not to agree to it!"

Ida Elisabeth thought for a moment: "Well, you know—I simply *can't*. But it's going to be horrid—if mother-in-law comes and proposes it—to say no. Because I *must* have *some* help, for a little while at any rate, in the autumn. And then mother-in-law won't be able to understand why I couldn't just as well take Else. She'll be frightfully hurt, naturally."

"Let her be hurt. You can't take any more burdens on yourself, Ida Elisabeth, just because the Braatös have no idea that other people find it a bore to be saddled with their charming children."

"That's just it, she has no idea." Ida Elisabeth was silent for a moment. "I know mother-in-law's an excellent woman in many ways. Kind at any rate. And she really means it when she's like that—affectionate and solicitous and sweet— with her Lisken dear this and Lisken dear that. But I must tell you, I know very well that all the time she's saying: 'Poor Frithjof, he did get let in for this far too young. And when he got such a big family to support all at once it's no wonder the poor boy has lost heart. If he'd been allowed to have only himself to think of, till he was really grown-up— and he had such a splendid future before him with my cousin. But then he must needs go and marry this Lisken Andst—'"

"I see, you know that. Yes—"

Ida Elisabeth said nothing for a while. Then she furtively got out her handkerchief—struggled to keep back the tears.

"Excuse me! Ugh, I hate to cry—it's only because I'm not quite normal at present. You know I'm not usually one to howl—"

"No, goodness knows you're not. But come in now and have something to eat."

How inconceivably better fish tasted when one had proper fish-knives to eat it with. And then it was so perfectly fried, and the piquant green sauce looked as charming as it tasted. The table showed as it were every possible modulation between what was good to eat and what was beautiful to look at—from the glass dishes of radishes and salad to the great bowl full of bluebells and those little crimson and sulphur-yellow auriculas which are the first to come out. Hers had not yet begun to bloom. But here at Teie everything was earlier than elsewhere.

When she was at school they used to run up in their playtime and pick snowdrops and bluebells in the copse outside the fence of Teie—well, they climbed over the fence too and helped themselves from the lawn, where it was blue with flowers under the big lime-trees. High up in front of the outhouses the forcing frames shone white in the sunshine and there was a sparkle of rays in all the colours of the rainbow from broken glass on the ground.

"We'll go and have a look at my hot-beds afterwards. Then you can take home anything you like. Borghild was here at the end of last week and I gave her some plants. That was how it was she told me that about Else."

"You see, it's true enough in a way, what she says", the doctor went on after a pause. "If only Frithjof had been let off having to think of others besides himself until he was grown up. Only he never will be grown up. And when you come to think of it neither Jens nor Borghild has ever grown up. They were just two delightful children—and they passed for being something like infant prodigies in their time. She with her brilliant matriculation at seventeen—and she was

lucky enough to have the chance of using her studious little brain just at the age when it is easiest for children to
assimilate such knowledge as is stuffed into their heads. *There*
she stopped—as the model schoolgirl. Jens was looked upon
with a little more scepticism—because he really *is* a good
deal of an artist. And because he was full of everything that
was in the air at that time, all fire and flame whenever he
came across anything that passed for a cause or an idea. So
folks who were inclined to be rather matter-of-fact discovered at once that he could never have thought out anything
properly, since he was always so enthusiastic. Besides, he
played so well that nobody expected him to be fit for anything practical. I suppose that's why he's always found friends
at need—up to now at any rate. We humans are always
rather more kindly disposed towards a person who does us
the favour of turning out as we have prophesied."

"Yes, but there *is* something about them which—well,
something touching. Sometimes I almost think I've never
met anyone who has managed to get so much out of life.
Fancy being able to say, after nearly thirty years of married
life, that there is no evil in the world that Jens and I cannot
forget in one another's arms. And such enthusiasm and optimism where their own children are concerned. And so
happy-go-lucky as soon as a scrap of prosperity comes their
way—"

The doctor nodded:

"Oh yes. They're artists in life in their way—if the art of
living consists in getting as much as possible out of one's
moments and one's own sensations and avoiding reflection.
They have practised vitalism."

"And that sometimes makes me think that Frithjof ...
For he did have a happy home. When he left it he cut a
fairly woebegone figure—though I'm not sure that he's ever
been aware of the fact that he was looked down upon. You
see, he's always had pretty lofty ideas of his own excellence,
instilled into him at home, where all the children were so

tremendously admired. He has no suspicion of his own lack of enterprise, for he doesn't know what it is. He seems to imagine that if no one comes and fetches him and sets him to do something, he can't be expected to find anything to turn his hand to of his own accord. And when he has been given work ... Why, he treats it exactly as he used to do at home, when he was asked to chop wood or weed the turnip-field—when he got sick of it or happened to think of something else he wanted to do, he just went off and forgot to come back. Father-in-law got furiously angry at times, and mother-in-law made a bit of a fuss, or else she lectured him in her kindly, improving way—and then Frithjof hung his head till it had blown over and they were in a good temper again. So it's really no wonder that he has no inclination to grow up—resists growing up, without being aware of it. For one can't suppose that he couldn't—? Do you know what, doctor! In many ways he's not at all stupid. There are many men who have less *intelligence* than Frithjof and who nevertheless manage to do their work and to be master in their house and really look after their children as a father."

"Have you never thought over what I said to you here a couple of years ago? That you ought to try to get out of all this—"

"I'm afraid it can't be done. As things are I get along, at any rate; I manage to provide for my children. And you can understand—living here divorced from Frithjof and having him running in at all hours to see the children, and then the Braatös—to know that they were discussing me with everybody ... No, it wouldn't do—not in a little community like ours."

"But what if you came here? To Teie."

"Here? To you?"

"Yes. You could come and keep house for me, couldn't you?"

She burst out laughing:

"I fancy I can see Sina's face! And what about me—divorced too! With three children! Are you quite crazy?"

"Sooner or later I shall have to pension off Sina."

Ida Elisabeth looked round at the immaculate tidiness of the room:

"There doesn't seem to be any sign of your having to do that for a long time yet."

"There might be another possibility—when we had seen how things were going, and if we agreed it would be a happy arrangement—you might marry me."

Ida Elisabeth laughed aloud:

"Well, you know, that *would* be a solution!"

"Yes, you laugh at it. But I'm serious." He pursed his lips for a moment, accentuating the vertical wrinkles around his mouth. "In many cases there is some justification for the prevailing prejudice against old men marrying young women. But by no means in all. And I don't believe that in this case the factors would be present which make this prejudice more than just a prejudice. Even though I am more than thirty years older than you—thirty-six to be accurate. People have such queer ideas of what it means to grow old—well, for that matter they damned well can't help it, it's one of the things one has to experience for oneself—and the process may assume so many different forms. But I'll tell you one thing, my girl: if a man can put up with remaining the same as he has always been and yet undergoing a ceaseless transformation—continuing to be the same in another way—then I can assure you it's exciting to grow old. Assuming of course that the organism continued in good condition. You don't know how exciting it is. One gets round things, is able to see them from one new side after another. That's what is the critical moment in a person's life, Ida Elisabeth—when he gets frightened because his outlook is changing, frightened because what he took to be a mountain in his young days turns out to be a multiplicity of peaks and crags with valleys and moors and lakes dividing them, and one can no longer see the trees for the forest. If a man tries to pull up at that point and to be himself in the old way—! Well, that corresponds exactly to the situation that may occur to one the first few times one is climbing a mountain—when one feels tempted to give up. If one does so, one's done for. The day a man no longer dares to see that a thing has more sides than he has already discovered—he's done for. Then senility sets in. Therefore an old man ought not as a rule to marry a young girl—he mustn't do it if he has come to a stop, and still less if he's still in motion. But now in the first place you're not a young girl—and even as a young woman you've had a fairly thorough experience that life is more manifold than one is apt to believe, so long as one feels oneself to be the most important thing in life. It would hardly astonish you very much, I think, if you were shown in a microscope the structure of what you had hitherto regarded as smooth, soft skin. Therefore I'm not sure that you and I wouldn't be able to get a good deal out of it, if we decided to join forces—

"Well, it couldn't occur to me to say that I've long been languishing here in a profound and secret attachment for you, Ida Elisabeth. To tell you the truth, I've never thought of it before. But it struck me a little while ago that you match this house so well. I believe it would be quite a success—hanged if I don't think it's an inspiration. You know I've been fond of you since you were a little girl. And certainly not with any kind of paternal feeling." He gave a little laugh. "Companionate affection, call it that—"

Ida Elisabeth shook her head slowly.

"Oh no, doctor. It sounds too fantastic. Ugh, I almost wish you hadn't said this."

"Well, we won't say any more about it. But at any rate you can think about it. That is to say, of course you can't help doing that. But I mean—think over what I have said. And then one more thing. If I can help you in any other way—well, I know, you've told me before, you won't accept anything which would disturb our comradeship; but situations *may* arise where one comrade can accept another's help without being ashamed? In that case you mustn't let this stand in the way. You understand, even if after mature consideration you come to the conclusion that you don't want to embark upon any such thing as I have proposed—you won't imagine that you've inflicted a wound on my heart, as they used to say in old days. At my time of life one no longer feels that sort of thing with the heart in particular—one never does that, I may tell you, it's only a figure of speech. One feels with the brain and the whole organism. But one is no longer to be compared with a locomotive which rushes forward along a laid track; one is more like an instrument of precision ...

"And there's yet another thing. If you agree, I don't think you need be afraid of anything in the way of—old man's love-making. For I myself haven't the slightest feeling of having been thrown out of the front-door and sneaking in by the back-stairs—so as to bribe my way in like one who properly speaking no longer has any right to be there."

Ida Elisabeth kept her eyes on the floor. Then she gave herself a little shake, as though waking up:

"Ugh, no—all this is nothing but—you must know yourself that it's impossible. Think of my children—!"

"You may be sure that at any rate they would have a good home here."

"And what about Ragna? What do you think she would say? And your grandchildren?"

"I'll see about that. You may safely leave me to arrange that side of the matter.

"But we can leave it at that, for the present. Now we'll go out and look at the garden."

IN a way she certainly did have a feeling of inward support, as she sat beside him in the car and was driven along the shore in the late spring evening. The farther she travelled in time from that conversation in his drawing-room, the more unqualified was the cheerfulness of her impression. It was as though she had been given by way of a bonus something she had missed as a girl. It was not after all a final sentence, beyond appeal, that her life was and must be bound up with that of Frithjof and no one else—it was a false idea that she had had hitherto, that she could not be worth anything in herself, because she bore as it were an invisible brand: has belonged to Frithjof Braatö.

But all the same . . . Without directly looking at him she saw the whole time Doctor Sommervold's weather-beaten face: his black and silver-grey hair and the dark grey cowls of his eyebrows, the coarse skin pitted with hair-roots on the cheeks and chin. She had always been conscious in a way that the distance resulting from their disparity in age was precisely what made it possible for them to be on such intimate terms as in a sense they really were. It is like two people talking together over a fence—there is such a glorious ease about it, one feels almost on a confidential footing. As to climbing over and joining him—ugh, no, the very idea roused repugnance in her, and fear—it would put a stop to their being friends in the good old way.

To be married to him would be downright unnatural. And she felt, no matter how she might revolt against nature being thus and thus, no matter what exasperation and despair she might feel at its being as it were closed against her, although she was caught in the midst of it, as in a man-trap—there was something in nature which was not in her, and something in her which it lacked or escaped. Nevertheless her place was in it, and when she had raged against it till she was tired, she felt its living warmth, felt that it was full of impulses and exhalations, not good, not evil, but lovely for their own sake.

Its opposite, anything that was against nature—something within her offered resistance to the bare thought of it. It was stronger and more obscure than dread; it had some connection with that feeling which makes people say: while there is life there is hope. There were things about which Doctor Sommervold had talked to her—well, in his mouth they sounded clean enough, like sterilized glasses and instruments in his hands. But they gave her the same feeling of invincible repugnance as the proposal that she should conform to custom and have her mother's coffin opened.

Chapter Three

IT ENDED IN HER TAKING ELSE after all. She did not do it with a clear conscience, for this was not cutting one's coat according to one's cloth. A confounded nuisance too that it should be so difficult to say no to those folks—

Just as she had a good deal of work for the confirmation there came a comparatively large order for various things for the new nursing home. Of course she had Doctor Sommervold to thank for that. But now she must have help. She got Olise Langeland to come in by the day.

They were sewing one afternoon in the sitting-room. The drenching rain streamed down the windows as if it had been flung against them by the bucketful, and the whole house shook as the howling gusts of wind struck it. Olise was engaged in binding some new wax-cloth—it was about the most unpleasant smell Ida Elisabeth knew of.

Someone entered the shop, letting in the blast so that the doors of the sitting-room and kitchen flew open. Ida Elisabeth dropped the white frock she was making, then got up—it was her father-in-law who came into the room, with the water pouring off his oil-skins: "God bless the work!"

"Heavens, have you come out in this weather!" Sölvi came dashing in from the bedroom; she had recognized her grandfather's voice. Ida Elisabeth took charge of his wet outdoor things, and Jens Braatö seized the little girl and swung her up towards the ceiling: "Are you my little girl today too? And there we have the master himself, that's the boy who hasn't forgotten grandpapa—how well he looks now, Lisken—no, no, don't put yourself out for me; I'd just as soon take a glass of milk if you have it"—he followed her out to the kitchen. "Oh, very well then, but at any rate you must let me light up for you ... What have you done with Frithjof—? Hey, look at her now—I believe she thinks Bebbe's got something for *her* in his bag."

The children were each given their sweets, while Ida Elisabeth tried to get the stove to burn and told him that Frithjof had been invited to the hotel—Clausen from Aarseth & Co. was here today.

The smoke continued to pour out of the door of the stove and leak through all the rings.

"You'd better go into the sitting-room and shut the door, there's good children. Sölvi, tell Olise to clear the sofa so that grandfather may sit down—"

"Don't trouble about that; I'd just as soon sit on the wood-box. But look here—this is from mamma; she was churning yesterday. And then I was to give you this letter—"

Ida Elisabeth thanked him kindly for the box of butter and put the letter down on the bench. "But do go in now—it's smoking so here—"

The envelope was damp and the ink had spread. Her mother-in-law's hand was large and round, with thick downstrokes and many flourishes round the letters—Ida Elisabeth never saw it on the outside of a letter without a little dark foreboding that here was something coming that she would just as soon be without.

She went and tentatively opened the outer door a little way. The wind came from the opposite quarter, but still the rain poured into the little porch as she stood holding the door and trying to dry her eyes with the corner of her apron—till a violent gust came down from the mountain on that side and slammed the door in her face. Fortunately at that moment the fire burst into flame under the coffee-pot.

She wiped her smarting eyes again and again, and then tore open the damp envelope:

"*My dearest Lisken!*"

Three sheets. The first two about how much mother-in-law would have liked to come across with Jens, and why she had not been able to, and how they all were at Vettehaugen. Then it came:

"And you, my dear child, how is it with you? My thoughts are so often with you at this time! Poor dear, I am sure it must be getting difficult for you to grapple with all the things you have to do. But now you shall hear of a plan papa and I have thought out, which seems to us perfectly splendid for all parties. You know we are anxious that our dear little Else should gain some experience of housekeeping elsewhere than in her own home...." Then came a page about Else's cleverness and good nature.

Not to be thought of. Ida Elisabeth thrust the letter into the pocket of her apron. She rehearsed her part, while getting ready the tray for her father-in-law—discovered one reason after another for saying no, till Jens Braatö came out to the kitchen again.

"Oh, my dear, you shouldn't have done that—making such elaborate preparations. But now I'd just as soon sit here; it'll be less trouble for you. The fact is I'd like to have a word with you in private."

"As you please." Ida Elisabeth rearranged the tray, taking off what was intended for the children and Olise and carrying it into the sitting-room.

"I say, Lisken; do you think it's *good* for Frithjof to hang about that hotel so much? These commercial travellers— well, many of them of course are excellent people, straight fellows—but you know what Frithjof is like, rather uncritical, so ready to be impressed when older men whom he takes to be experienced and who cut a bit of a dash treat him as one of themselves—"

This was as much as to say that his father was afraid Frithjof might acquire a taste for strong drink. "It can't do him any harm to meet Clausen, you know", she said curtly. Of course there was something in what Jens Braatö said— though most of the travellers she had done business with were steady men. And then she always had a hope that these acquaintances might be the means of getting Frithjof something to do in the end. Besides, it was so terrible to have him idling about at home when she was busy.

"In a way it's both a good thing and a bad thing," said Jens Braatö, "for children to grow up in a home where they are protected from evil, where the breath of impurity is not allowed to penetrate. Or rather, speaking generally it's naturally a good thing—and thank God, Borghild and I have succeeded in it, I think I may say that. But you see, one result of it is to make them in a way very confiding—ready to put their trust in everyone they meet. Well, that's what I wanted to talk to you about, what Borghild says in her letter about sending Else here for a while in the summer."

Ida Elisabeth sat on the opposite side of the kitchen table, watching her father-in-law as he talked. He was an unusually handsome man. As he sat there, broad-shouldered and powerful in his grey homespun, with wavy golden hair combed straight back from the broad, clear forehead, a warm, weather-beaten skin and great light-brown eyes, so fine and bright—why, he looked like someone out of a saga, Nordic and romantic, exactly what he wished to be.

He had been the only son on Braatöy. And of course it was true that they had had one of the biggest trading stations in that part of the country—though if, as he said, the people used to call his father king of Braatöy, they probably meant it as a joke. And he always referred to his mother as the daughter of the squire of Vetteland, and to the Vetteland folks as the celebrated family of musicians. In a way all his family stories were true enough, no doubt, but in Jens Braatö's mouth they became so dreadfully romantic—the big wedding at Vetteland when his parents were married, and the tragedy, when old Braatö went smash and hanged himself, and his own wedding, when Borghild von Post-Moe climbed out of a window one summer night and went off with him to town and they got married by special licence.

Though the Lord only knew who might have been interested in stopping the match. She was governess at Sheriff Ramstad's at the time and he was in the office there; when Jens Braatö had to leave the university after his father's death the sheriff had found a place for him and taken him into his house, because he and old Braatö had been good friends and he and his wife were also fond of music. But when Ramstad died, no successor was appointed; the work was rearranged and there was no place for Jens Braatö in the new office. Since that time he had tried a lot of different things—a soda-water factory, exporting eggs and fruit to England, a saw-mill—but somehow he could not make a success of anything. For many years now they had been living on their little farm, a piece of Vetteland which he had bought, and then he had some agencies for insurance companies and the like.

It was in connection with some insurances that he was now on his way to Mokhus: "But I think I'll wait till tomorrow, the weather may take up a little. But please don't put yourself out on my account—I'll sleep on the sofa in the sitting-room, you needn't make a bed for me. As long as I have a cushion under my head and a rug over me I shall do ... grandly!"

But then there was this about Else. She had made some girlfriends that they didn't like. And then there was this new manager at the co-operative store—he made a great deal of fuss over little Else; they were afraid he might turn her head. The fellow was a regular lady-killer, and the poor child seemed to be a good deal taken up with him. But it appeared he was married, and his wife was not coming to Vallerviken till after the summer holidays; she was a school teacher somewhere in the Aalesund district, where they came from.

Next day the weather was fine, but Jens Braatö decided to put off his trip to Mokhus one day longer. He tidied up the garden, which looked awful after the rain; he fixed some roof-tiles for Fru Esbjörnsen and sawed off a broken branch of one of the great willows. He sawed and chopped all the wood in the shed for Frithjof, and he repaired Kalleman's sports car, which had been smashed the year before. He cleaned Ida Elisabeth's cooking stove and tried the experiment of putting blocks under its feet—to see if it would draw better with a slight tilt.

He *was* obliging and helpful, frankly and honestly he was. But now her eyes were opened once for all and she could not help thinking of the kind of obligingness and helpfulness that possesses children just before Christmas and other festive occasions. Well, that too is frankly and honestly meant.

He was in earnest too in saying he did not want to give any trouble. He took off the sheets and pillow-case with which she had made his bed on the sofa and folded them neatly—no need for that, my dear. She had given him a jug and basin on a chair—no need for that: "I can wash myself under the tap in the kitchen." Ida Elisabeth couldn't stand anyone making his morning toilet in the kitchen; she couldn't stand having anyone there at all when she had work to do in the kitchen, except of course the children—it was the only place in the house which she could have to herself now and then. And she disliked having anyone sleeping in the sitting-room—she was obliged to use it as a workroom, so it was hopeless to think of keeping it at all tidy, but at any rate she would prefer not to have it used as a bedroom as well. And having a visitor at all, when she was so busy, and being always in dread, whenever she had to try on one of these confirmation frocks, that one or other of the two men would come bursting in without stopping to knock—

But her mother-in-law was just as happy and cheerful if she had people sleeping in every one of her rooms—visitors were always welcome in her house, "if only they would take things as they came—"

And all the time Ida Elisabeth felt how her resolution not to receive Else was being undermined. As her father-in-law chatted away she caught one glimpse after another of the difficulties they were in just now. He did not complain exactly, just talked as usual, in the quiet, resigned way that was peculiar to him and was rooted nevertheless in an everlasting vague optimism: something would turn up. But he told her a great deal without realizing how bad it was.

This fellow he was talking about was in the habit of taking girls into the back room after closing time and treating them to sweets from the shop. He had a motor-boat, and the use of the motor-van. It was a disgusting state of things, and more risky than the Braatös had any idea. That poor Else was keen on anything in the form of amusement or variety was not to be wondered at. And of course she was just as ready to get married as to live—and she had no small ideas of her own charms. She was really quite pretty, and her parents, the father especially, had never concealed their view that she was lovely—Golden Else they called her. She was certainly prepared to believe every word this manager fellow might take it into his head to say to her; he was a married man, but probably she would only think it thrilling and grand if a man got a divorce for her sake—and would never doubt his intention of doing so, if he hinted at anything of the kind.

All the Braatös' children had been brought up in an idyll of frankness and candour and taught to believe that all that about the two sexes was just like sun-bathing and nothing else. No doubt that was why their curiosity and desire to find out something for themselves had taken such nasty forms. And Ida Elisabeth had the impression that this was so, to a greater or less extent, with all those who were somewhat poorly endowed—who literally could not entertain themselves, but were dependent on others to feed them with news or with old, long-hung stories from which they could cut chunks and chew them. People of that kind always had a predilection for gossiping about anything that had a taste of horror or sensation in it, accidents and murders and fires and the like. Frithjof devoured everything he could find of this sort in the papers, and it was quite incredible how he remembered the smallest details of murders and shipwrecks and great disasters, even though they had happened many years ago. But he was attracted in a peculiarly intimate way by anything which lay, so to speak, outside the sun-bath. A case of rape in Bergen, a story from one of the coast towns farther south about a band of boys and two girls under age, sinister rumours about lay preachers and in fact any scandal about the doings of pious folks—he showed a consuming interest for all this. Trifles which did not necessarily point to anything wrong, but from which a certain class of observers drew fantastic and defamatory conclusions, imagining their suspicions to be a sign of subtlety—these things he retailed at home, just as innocently, with no suspicion of good or evil, as when he repeated for her benefit the detective stories which he picked up all over the place and read with avidity. He smiled slyly when she pooh-poohed his suggestions—"rubbish, nobody can possibly know anything about that"—and then he explained in detail how the scandal-mongers had arrived at their unsavoury results. And if she still continued to treat the gossip scornfully, he was as hurt as a child whose fondest illusions have been shattered by grown-ups.

Of course they might very well be lies, all the things people said about Margit Hamre's doings in town. And the girl who was to stay at the parsonage this summer need not actually have been planted there because she had done something that rendered her liable to deportation. But Ida Elisabeth knew Else well enough to be sure it would not make the girl any less eager to associate with them if she imagined them to be possessed of strange experiences.

However, she saved herself from giving her father-in-law any promise to take home with him. She said, as was the truth, that she had invited Aslaug Meyer for the holidays, and that it was more practical for her to have Olise Langeland's help this summer; Olise had her own hand sewing-machine which she could bring, and she could sleep at home, and she could not only work at dressmaking, but at anything else that was required. No, the more she considered it, the less she thought that Else would suit.

THEN there came a formal invitation for them all to come and spend a whole Sunday at Vettehaugen. Her mother-in-law had arranged for a motor-boat to bring them.

They had glorious weather up the fjord in the morning stillness; the jigging and coughing of the motor resounded far over the smoothly heaving water, and the mountains were bright with fresh green foliage against grey screes above and foaming white watercourses below. Vettehaugen lay within its little creek like a sanctuary, far removed from all the world in its own sweet summer life. Down the cliff under which the houses lay came the waterfall, magnificent after the rain; it filled the air with its roar, and then the stream ran on in a curve along the garden fence, dividing the little farm into two parts, and fell into the fjord beyond the old pier and boat-houses. It was true enough, as her parents-in-law were always saying: here was peace.

As they walked up from the pier the girls came running towards them in light summer frocks, tearing down the green, flowery meadow. Behind them came the mother-in-law; she embraced her grandchildren, her daughter-in-law, and her son: "Lovely to have you all here together!" Indoors the coffee-table was laid with flowers and a big cake, as for a birthday. Borghild Braatö drew her daughter-in-law down on to the old, soft, well-worn sofa, and stacked up cushions round her: "Now you're to make yourself really comfortable. No, children, Aunt Else and Aunt Jeja will look after you, today your poor little mammie must really be left in peace for once in a while. There, Lisken! You shall have some good coffee at any rate; I know you like it strong—though I dare say you *ought* not to drink such strong coffee just now, but for once in a while—"

"For once in a while", that was her mother-in-law's motto, Ida Elisabeth remembered. She could not bear this motherly fussing about what was good and what wasn't good for her in her present state. Though she knew it was well meant; one ought always to do what good one can to everybody, even though it may not be much in the eyes of the world; that was her mother-in-law's principle and she lived according to it. Poor Lisken, she doesn't always have a very easy time, no, but today at any rate she shall have a real peaceful, comfortable rest—that was how her mother-in-law thought. Ugh, they were so kind, so kind—and had no suspicion of how little adapted she was for such stuffy family intimacy.

In the course of the afternoon she had to submit to sitting alone with her mother-in-law. Jens Braatö took the boys and the children out for a walk, and Else and Jarngerd had to get ready the dinner. "Now you'll see how clever they are! They can cook very well, let me tell you, when they get a chance." Borghild Braatö was knitting a big white shawl: "They're so lovely and light, you know, and warm to wrap round them, when you have to pick them up and change them." And she cross-examined Ida Elisabeth as to whether she was thus and thus and felt this or that, and gave her good advice. Then she let her work drop into her lap and looked across at her daughter-in-law.

"But now, Lisa dear, with regard to what you wrote about Else, I've gone into the question whether it can't be arranged after all. For you understand, it would be immensely to your advantage too—you don't suppose we should expect you to pay Else any wages. Something to wear, whatever you see that the child needs most, but of course you get everything of that sort wholesale—a trifle for pocket-money now and then, if you don't mind, but it need only be so *little*, our Else has not been spoilt in that way, you know! At any rate it must be much, much cheaper for you than having to pay Olise by the day——"

Else would be able to borrow the old hand sewing-machine from the parsonage. And then Borghild Braatö had rung up the teacher's wife at Berfjord: Else could quite well sleep there while Fröken Meyer was to stay with Lisken. And if she had any difficulty in getting a nurse, when the time came, she would arrange to come out herself and nurse Lisken and the baby in any case the first fortnight.

Ida Elisabeth was on the point of revolting, when Borghild Braatö looked at her and her eyes suddenly filled with tears:

"You understand, Lisken, it is so terribly important for us . . . to get Else moved into other surroundings for a time——"

There was still a good deal of charm about Borghild Braatö. Her face was shaped almost like a heart, and although it was full of wrinkles, one was struck by its youth on looking at it more closely; her colour was such a faint rose and her skin was dotted with tiny freckles and as soft as silk. When as now her eyes were full of tears they reminded one of the bright eyes of a bird—they were not large and their colour was an ordinary grey, but they were frank and well shaped. Her features were small and straight, but her hair was pretty—she had worn it in the same way as long as Ida Elisabeth had known her: parted in the middle and combed down on both sides in gentle curls and waves like a picture of the Madonna. It suited her almost better now that her hair was as much grey as brown.

She was short and was now inclined to stoutness, but this was not unbecoming, as she was so light in her movements, like a little round bird, a wagtail. Or in her brown summer dress with light spots she really reminded one of a mother grouse.

"It makes me so anxious—for I'm afraid he's not a good man; I don't *like* him at all, and one hears one thing and another, you know. And Else is so childlike in that way, so simple-minded and confiding. I'm sure you understand me, Lisa dear—it would be such a sad blow to me if Else, who is so young and as soft as wax, should be the victim of a terrible disappointment. And you know what *cruel* gossips people are and how easily a young girl may get a bad name—"

Well, well, thought Ida Elisabeth, even if I can't stand her, it doesn't prevent my being really fond of her too, in another way. It's only that I can't stand her company, but she *is* an excellent woman, and she really does mean to be as kind as she can to everybody. *She* has no idea that anyone is so constituted as not to care for the way in which she shows her kindness. No, it won't do even to think of the terror and despair this poor mother grouse would be thrown into if one more of her brood went so far astray that even she couldn't help seeing how bad things were. If Ida Elisabeth could avert it, this time in any case, she would have to do so. And so she promised: "We can try at any rate. If it doesn't answer, then there's an end of it."

Chapter Four

I T DID NOT ANSWER very well. This was only what Ida Elisabeth had been prepared for. But she could not bring herself to send Else home.

To be sure, there was no harm in Else. Nothing really good in her either, as far as Ida Elisabeth could see. As for getting her to make herself useful, Ida Elisabeth had not time for that. Else was always willing, when her sister-in-law tried to set her to some piece of work, but Ida Elisabeth had constantly to explain everything to her and show her how to do it, the same thing over and over again. So it was much easier to do it herself. And when Ida Elisabeth was not by her side to correct her mistakes, Else simply sat dreaming.

Ida Elisabeth had been afraid they had not seen the end of that affair with the manager of the co-operative. And now, in summer-time, communication between Vallerviken and Berfjord was particularly active. And things had evidently gone pretty far with him and Else. The first week Else was obviously very anxious to talk. She made mysterious references to someone she knew whose marriage had been a mistake: "And so it must be better that they should separate. It's surely better that two should be happy than that three people should remain unhappy as long as they live. Well, don't you agree with me? But, dear me, why not?"

"Amongst other things because it sounds to me rather unlikely—either that two should be made happy, and one presumably unhappy, or that three should go about being unhappy for the rest of their lives, simply because this fellow is not to be allowed to enter into fresh engagements until he has gotten hold of one to suit him. If he changed wives now, there's every chance that in a couple of years' time the same situation would arise, with two of the three demanding permission to try a new arrangement. Who is going to provide for the children, and who is going to sleep with them and help them when they wake up at night and have had bad dreams or are thirsty or have to get up, while the parents are running around playing odd man out—?"

"No, of course," said Else eagerly, "people mustn't have children until they know whether they suit each other. But all we young people know how to manage that nowadays, you may be sure."

"Honestly, I think there are many other things that it's more important you should know about", said Ida Elisabeth, in spite of herself.

"Oh? I assure you, *that's* frightfully important. Tell me something you think more important?"

"Oh"—but after all he was her husband and the brother of this child. So she merely said: "For instance—you young people ought to know how deep is the mark one person leaves on another, when once they have been too closely connected."

Slowly Else's face turned red as fire. She was a good deal like Frithjof in appearance, had the same kind of coarse, luxuriant, straw-coloured hair, and she too was so full in the face that her eyes seemed more or less closed up. Her mouth again was like her brother's, fleshy, but the lips were red only on the inside, so that they passed imperceptibly into the tense skin of the face. But taken altogether she was nevertheless quite pretty.

"Ugh", said Else hesitatingly. "I really think you talk so—well, almost indecently sometimes. Downright coarsely almost, if I may say so!"

Ida Elisabeth felt so sorry for her all at once.

BUT by the following week Else had ceased to talk about her friend. For she knew many other people out here and they took up her attention. So perhaps that unfortunate business with the manager would blow over. Ida Elisabeth made her a present of a really sweet pale blue voile frock, which delighted Else—it suited her well too.

Then the summer holidays began, and visitors arrived both here and at Vallerviken.

It worried Ida Elisabeth a good deal that all these people should see she was expecting again. Many of the summer visitors came year after year, and the elder women especially were so friendly and sympathetic and full of questions, when they looked in at the shop to buy sewing things and bathing caps and so on. She was often invited out too, but consistently declined.

She let Else serve in the shop as much as she could, but she had to come in constantly to find things that the girl could not lay her hands on. Another thing was that she had told Else she might take an hour off in the forenoon to go and bathe, when there was nothing particular to do. The first few days Else asked: "May I go now?" But after that she took herself off the moment her friends appeared at the door and stayed away the whole forenoon, came home breathless to dinner: "Gee, I didn't know I was so frightfully late! Oo, I'm so sorry—it didn't matter, did it, Lisken, that I stayed a bit long?" In the evenings she was always out. Frithjof too was constantly on the go. There was a blessed peace about the house, thought Ida Elisabeth, when she had it to herself in the evening.

The bedroom was not so very small, with a window on the garden side as well as two big windows looking on to the road; but outside these were the great willows, obscuring the light of the room and casting a restless tinge of green over it like a reflection of the sea. When the wind stirred the pliant branches they whispered with a charming little murmur. Ida Elisabeth found such peace in here when she came to put the little ones to bed—a little undernourished gaiety welled up in her.

Sölvi's clothes were clammy, with an acrid smell of earth and perspiration, and the child's cheeks were hot and red as fire. It was almost impossible to pull her things off her; she could not stand still. She had the same kind of eyes as Frithjof and Else; her glance darted restlessly hither and thither from within their narrow cracks, and the eye itself was dark and strangely dense like some kind of metal, without any sharply defined pupil. It suddenly occurred to Ida Elisabeth that clear eyes are those in which the coloured surrounding ring shows up light against the black of the pupil. Her own mother's eyes had been clear, like shallow, bluish green water— when her mother's face was turned to the light there was only a tiny black speck in the middle of them, but when she was just awake they were large and black as coal, with a narrow blue ring around the dark hole. What handsome eyes her mother's had been really. Jens Braatö had handsome eyes too, clear and light brown with a living pupil which enlarged and contracted. It was from her mother-in-law that the children had these impenetrable eyes.

"No, Sölvi, stand still now! I don't at all want to wipe up another pailful of water off the floor." The little stool on which the basin stood was rather rickety. Ida Elisabeth soaped the child's hot and scrubby hands and held them down in the water, then noticed how they positively quivered with the desire to splash. "Ugh, child, one would think you had quicksilver in your body."

"I have too", said Sölvi eagerly. "I can feel it flying up and down everywhere inside me—"

"Oh, you—no, sit down so that I can wash your feet." Clammy little feet, grimy with road-dust—her mother knelt down and washed Sölvi's feet slowly and caressingly: they were still so lovely and small, and it was fun to see the white skin appear and the toes turn rosy pink.

"Mamma, what *was* the name of the little fishes that you said were inside me?"

"Oh, you! They're not fishes", laughed her mother.

"What are they then?"

"They're . . . they're like tiny little beads of a kind of silver."

"Then why don't they come out when you do like that?" Ida Elisabeth was pressing out a little matter that had formed in the raw place on her knee—Sölvi grazed her elbows and knees almost every day; the child was so boisterous. "Why don't some of those beads come out when I hurt myself?"

"Because they're so far inside you."

"Should I be dead if I hurt myself so frightfully that they fell out?"

"I dare say you would." Ida Elisabeth pressed Sölvi's face against hers an instant—the child's cheeks were so lovely and fresh after washing. "Now we've got to do your hair, Sölvi dear—"

That was always the worst. The thick yellow mop that served her for hair was most horribly tousled.

"Ugh, you pull so, mamma. Auntie Aslaug's much cleverer at doing my hair. Auntie Aslaug does it so nicely I don't even feel it—"

"Little noodle, you can't remember Auntie Aslaug; why, you were a little tot that I carried in my arms last time she saw you—"

"Oh yes, I can. Why, I saw Auntie Aslaug when she came and gave Kalleman and me our new shoes—"

"Oh, what stories you can make up! She's going to bring you those new shoes when she comes here." It had impressed Sölvi immensely when she and Kalleman had had to put their feet on a sheet of white paper while their mother drew a pencil round them—because Auntie Aslaug had written that she would give them some fine new shoes.

"Oh yes! Auntie Aslaug came back one day; she was on the pier, and then she gave us such *pretty* shoes. Mine are brown, and then they've got those *thick* white soles that look like pork and laces and gold eyelets—"

Ida Elisabeth shook her head with a laugh:

"I must say you have some imagination! There, up into bed with you. Now, Kalleman, it's your turn—"

He looked much better, and he could talk more—was quite chatty at times when he was alone with her. This was the secret spring of joy that welled up in her and caused her not to feel the weight of all the rest any more than she did. She kept it to herself as she had kept her anxiety to herself. But when she had finished for the day and the others were out, and she was here alone putting the children to bed, the sense of relief, known only to herself, was allowed to gush forth and fill her with joy.

Poor little Kalleman—he had been sitting as quiet as a mouse over by the window going through the box of old picture post-cards. He jumped down and darted across to her at once. He was sleepy and quiet—sat staring seriously at his sister, who stood up in her bed steering a motor-boat.

"Mamma, mayn't Kalleman come into my bed for a little, then he can be passenger, you see—"

"No, you're both to lie down and go to sleep."

Sölvi fretted and whined a little before she gave in.

"Mamma, don't go, will you?"

"No, if you'll lie down like a good girl I'll stay here till you've gone to sleep."

Ida Elisabeth sat down by the farthest window looking on to the road. From time to time the faint whisper stole through the willows and all their narrow leaves rustled. On stormy nights it was like a countless host of whips shrieking against the window, and in a particular kind of wind they grated against the glass with a strange sound like low wailing—but still she always thought she was fond of the two old willows here by the corner of the house.

It was grey outside—the grey light of a summer evening; she could feel there was rain coming tonight. And indeed the fine weather had lasted a long time. Between the trees and little houses she had glimpses of the sea with the reflected light on the water beyond the pier. The air was laden with

75

the smell of the beach and of the hay which hung drying on the slopes. There was the chuck-chuck of a motor out in the creek and some people were talking and laughing down in the road—and then a lamp was lighted behind a blind above the bank; the square of warm, subdued orange light seemed listening silently to all the faint and varied sounds that gave life to the evening.

Ugh—she ought to go and make up Else's bed on the sofa. If the child were left to do it herself when she came in, she would wake the whole house. But she did not feel equal to it—to getting up and setting about another duty just at the moment. And she felt she could not quite face the other room just yet—it smelt so, of shirting and cotton materials with dressing in them, and it smelt of Else, Else's lilac soap and Else's powder and Else's frocks and the dirty stockings she had changed before going out and thrown down on the sofa. Behind the curtain which Ida Elisabeth had put up in the corner by the kitchen door hung Else's clothes and there were her shoes. Piles of dressmaking materials lay by the sewing-machine and on the table; along one wall were stacked up boxes of hosiery and parcels of yarn—things she could not find room for on the shelves in the shop.

As she sank back in her chair Ida Elisabeth felt that this must be a kind of slackness that wrapped her round and plunged her into a deep animal lethargy. But her thoughts were in motion in this mild obscurity of weariness, like a forest in the night breeze or seaweed swaying in the current—thoughts of the children in the first place, but also of the other people who had a place in her life, those of whom she was fond and those she cared for less. In rapid gleams she recalled things which made her smile; rays of joy and shades of sadness chased each other through her mind. But this was life, much more than what she lived through in the harsh, exacting light of day, when she always had to be ready for action and was made sharper in her nature by the necessity of being continually on guard, of looking out for anything that might go wrong or that had gone wrong, since all such things involved threats to the welfare of those for whom she had to answer. But it was delightful to be able to sit for a while and feel the sweet drowsiness shrouding all this in its twilight, while all the joys which were not allowed to distract her during the labours of the day shone from out the dusk.

She got up. As quietly as she could she stole up to the two little beds.

Sölvi was in a profound sleep. But on bending over the boy she saw that he was lying with eyes wide open.

"But Carl ... are you still awake, my darling?"

"Mamma," he whispered anxiously; "may the brownie sleep in my bed?"

She gave a little laugh. The box of picture post-cards was in the other window. Ida Elisabeth searched through it by the pale light of the evening sky and found the dirty, crumpled card with the brownie and the Christmas pig that Kalleman loved so dearly.

"There! But now you must be a good boy; lie down and go to sleep."

The boy gave a blissful sigh and drew the card under the bedclothes. His mother stood there a moment, then passed her hand lingeringly over the round childish forehead, the slender softness of cheek and throat: "But now you must go to sleep, my little one—"

Then she went back and sat down by the window as before. There were the raspberries too. They couldn't be left till tomorrow, she would have to boil them this evening—but she would wait a little, it was so good to sit here.

OF course she was not glad she was to have another baby. Although at times she thought, all the same ... For instance, her mother-in-law had been here one day pouring forth her chatter: "Well, after all there's nothing so wonderful on earth as little children, when they're quite small! When they get to about six months old—and they can lie quite still for a long spell, looking at their fingers—*aren't* they charming!" Suddenly she saw it quite clearly in her mind's eye— the expression of unfathomable seriousness that may come into a baby's face when it lies watching the movements of its own hands. A thrill of joy went through her at the thought—and then it smiles, a bright and rapid smile, when its mother comes to pick it up—

But with it came her anger and bitterness against all that made it impossible for her to enjoy anything to the full. Like a tethered animal mother she had to stand behind the counter and look interested and listen to strangers who talked and talked and could never make up their minds, while she had to leave her children to look after themselves. She could not give her children properly cooked food at the right time nor change their clothes when they got wet, she could not listen to what they had to say about things they had discovered, she was not on the spot to smack them when they did something that was dangerous or wrong, because before all else she had to provide—well, all that a father ought to have provided for them. It made things no better that she had to admit she was herself partly to blame; she had known Frithjof almost all her life—so she ought to have known what she was doing when she threw in her lot with his. Nor was it any consolation to know that many mothers were far worse off. At any rate she did not have to leave her home, even if it fell upon her to provide for husband and children—and Frithjof was not a bad man; he was hopeless, but in any case he gave her no cause for fear.

Her own feeling was that she did not make unreasonable demands of life. She would be heartily content if they never had more to live on than they had at present—if only it were the husband who earned the money. The sense of shame was the worst—the shame of being married to a shirker. If only she could have been mistress of her own time, so that the children might have had the attention she was ready to give them, and the house might have been made into a home. But now her business encroached on everything. The shop overflowed into the sitting-room; figures and calculations overflowed every other thought in her brain—what items have I got to cover, how shall I find the money for it, how much can I have over for the house and the children and Frithjof? Ugh, and how ugly they were, all the things she bought and sold—but the people here would have them like that; they had little to spend and little sense of what was pretty; solid, dirty grey or snuff brown or leaden blue stuffs they wanted, or straw hats in poisonous colours and ugly, traced needlework. Just now there was a great demand for a dreadful kind of rubber aprons—it gave her such an unpleasant feeling in the tips of her fingers when she handled them.

If only she had been able to work with living things and have her thoughts on things that had life—her kitchen garden that she loved to work in, and her fowls; washing clothes was fun too, when one got as far as going out and hanging them up, and washing up and scrubbing floors were tiresome, but it was lovely to have gotten them done. And then she would have liked more plants in pots—it made her green with envy to go past windows which had swelling tea-roses and bright bunches of red and white pelargoniums pressing against the panes. Marit, for instance—she had a huge green window-box full of Jacobæa lilies; in summer it was like a regular thicket of long, narrow dark green leaves arching and crossing one another, and then in autumn came the flowers, as many as twenty at the same time. When they came out Marit always asked her in to coffee. They're quite a common flower, said Marit. But Ida Elisabeth felt wild with longing; she did not quite know for what, as she sat and looked at all these tall, stiff stalks with bunches of great staring red calyxes—the colour was so strange, so bright and clear, and the shape of each separate flower seemed so perfectly clean-cut and strong. Marit had given her some bulbs, and last year there had been a flower on the biggest of her plants—this year there would probably be one or two more. And then she wished so much they could have kept pigeons. Herman kept pigeons at home when she was a child, and she remembered how amusing they were— bad-tempered though, to any extent, and they made a fearful mess. But they were so charming with those pink feet of theirs and the red ring round their eyes. Some light brown ones were specially handsome, and so were the grey-blue ones with a glint of mother-of-pearl in their throats. Their cooing was so delightful, and the flapping of their wings when they flew up, and the sight of the flock of them when they turned high up in the sky on a sunny day and the light caught their wings at that moment—maybe Carl would like to keep pigeons when he grew bigger. If she could only have her wish to see and hear pigeons outside her windows once again.

Good heavens, it wasn't as if she asked for any luxury or a chance of being lazy, only a home in which she could see things living and growing and flowering—and where she could shut her doors against people she didn't care to have at close quarters and gossip she hated having to listen to. But even that was probably asking a great deal too much in our day—how many people nowadays are in a position to plant seeds in a garden and decline to see strangers? Frithjof's parents had managed to provide themselves with a home of this sort—but only by continually relying on relations and friends being ready and willing to help and keep the idyll going; they depended on others with the cheerful assurance of children.

ASLAUG MEYER had written offering to put off her holiday till the beginning of September, when Ida Elisabeth expected to be confined. Her presence would then enable them to avert the mother-in-law's threatened arrival to act as nurse, and they would get Else out of the house as long as Ida Elisabeth was laid up. It was a great deal to accept, as in this way the visit would be no holiday for Aslaug. But the prospect of having another grown-up person with her was too tempting—and Aslaug was one of the few people she knew whose nature was such that she could accept their help. And she would escape having to be nursemaid to great and small alike during the poor ten or twelve days she could afford to lie in bed.

But one day towards the end of August she received a thick letter from Aslaug.

"*Dear Ida!*

"*When you have read this letter I expect you'll be fairly shocked with me and think I'm a pretty despicable individual ... But what is one to do, when everything looks as black as you know it always has done for Gunnar and me, and then there's something else I've never told you; I know that Gunnar is pretty well tired of me—he has been so a long time, though he is far too honourable to have said anything about it, but one notices that sort of thing, you may be sure. And his prospects of getting anything that will enable us to marry seem slighter than ever. N.B.! if he still wanted to marry me, after the five years our affair has lasted. To marry somebody else—I'm sure he's keen enough. Mutual interests, you understand, and the girl is young, pretty, and—presumably—capable. And has* influential connections—*might at least be a chance for my poor old boy. You understand? Yes, life's a nice thing, isn't it? Now you mustn't think Gunnar's said anything about this to me; oh no, he's far too delicate for that, not a word about being tired or pro tem, otherwise engaged, as they say. But you know how many kind people there are in this world who haven't the heart to allow a poor wretch to remain in ignorance—!*"

Ida Elisabeth put down the letter—with a sickening sensation at her heart she sat still, feeling she could read no more—till she chanced to see that the next sheet began: "*So by the time you read these lines your devoted Aslaug will have put an end quietly and decently to her romance with Gunnar Vathne!"*

Good God! She hasn't gone and done something desperate——! Ida Elisabeth read on with a throbbing heart:

"It will probably astonish you to hear that when you read this I shall have gone to Oslo to be married to a man whose acquaintance I made at the teachers' congress this summer. You know I was engaged to play the accompaniments for some lectures on musical history——"

The man's name was Tömmeraas, and he was headmaster of a biggish country school in South-Eastern Norway—Furuberg post office; Ida Elisabeth didn't know where that was—a widower with an only son who was a missionary in Madagascar. Lord save us, could that be any match for Aslaug!

It was almost worse than suicide, in spite of all Aslaug wrote about Tömmeraas being a generous, high-minded person and that they had many ideas in common. *"I don't think I am likely to be unhappy with him. And it is to be hoped that Gunnar will be happy, now that I no longer stand in his light. At all events we have known the great happiness together, and how many people can say that? Ich grolle nicht!!!"*

Naturally Ida Elisabeth had guessed, when she was in town last Christmas, that it was wearing rather thin between those two. But she had never imagined anything like this. It was true Gunnar was a few years younger than Aslaug—well, something like six years it was. And the last few years had told badly on Aslaug, though to be sure they had told even more on him; Aslaug at any rate had had something to do all the time—he had been altogether idle for most of it. But this was so sad she didn't know what to say to it! Oh, Aslaug, how pretty she had been and what great expectations she had had! Of course it was a terrible disappointment to herself too, that Aslaug was not coming. She had never had any other woman friend.

When they first became acquainted in Oslo they agreed to share the little room in Thor Olsen's Gate—well, if she had been certain of anything it was that Aslaug would make her way in the world. They were as poor as church mice, both of them, but it seemed to give her fresh courage simply to share Aslaug's belief in the other's future. So it would fall to her lot to see *one* who made a success, who moved over to the sunny side of life, as Aslaug herself put it. Aslaug had come up to attend the conservatoire; she was from the north, but what she had to say about her home was rather vague and varied from one time to another—the only invariable point referred to an inheritance which she had already gone through when Ida Elisabeth met her. Altogether she had had an uncommonly lively imagination at that time. But she believed so firmly in herself: a debut concert with the orchestra of the National Theatre, a travelling scholarship, appearances abroad, fame—"You'll see, my girl!" It had reminded her by the way of Frithjof's dreams of the future before he was grown up. Perhaps it was her association with Aslaug more than anything else that had made her receive Frithjof so sanguinely when he turned up again— she suddenly saw that now.

But it was so desperately sad that with Aslaug too it had only led to trumpery results. She had had a chance of playing in public a few times—her own debut concert had never come off—but she *had* appeared, and there had been a few lines about her in the papers, just that. Then she met Gunnar Vathne, and the result was a love of which the world had not seen the like in all the years it had been spinning round the sun. Brünnhilde and Isolde—oh, they were only flat soda water compared with this! Vathne was an attractive lad for that matter, quiet and well-bred. He had come up to town to study law, but then there was such over-production of lawyers. When he got that appointment as correspondence clerk in the Cyclops works, Aslaug left Oslo in hot haste so as to be near him; she was so certain of getting as many pupils as she could take; it would all go swimmingly. She had never done more than just scrape along. Things grew worse still after she had been given notice at her first lodgings because she let Gunnar live with her, when the Cyclops closed down. And this craze for gramophones and radio made it difficult for a pianist to get pupils or any other work.

No, of course what Aslaug wrote was true, their prospects had really been hopeless for a long time. All the same it was terribly sad to think of—now she was called Fru Tömmervold, or Tömmeraas, was it?—and her husband was a schoolmaster and a widower and old enough to have a grown-up son, who was a missionary in Madagascar into the bargain!

AT the beginning of September Ida Elisabeth gave birth to a still-born boy.

A few nights before she had dreamt that the child lay in her lap and she was changing its clothes. It was a little boy, and he was so pretty—neither of her other children had been particularly pretty as babies, but this one was so charming. As she turned it over on its back she saw that it had light brown eyes—a curiously beautiful, reddish-brown colour, but they were quite clear and bright. On waking and recalling her dream she was filled with gentle, expectant joy. Although she had heard it said that no child is actually born with brown eyes.

The little dead child was not the least like her dreamboy. In spite of this she felt a despairing impulse to place a finger on one of the closed eyelids and peep underneath to see if the eyes were brown. But she dared not do it, it would be like profaning the little corpse.

The child had been born in the morning, and the same afternoon her mother-in-law came out. Borghild Braatö burst into tears as she bent over the bed and kissed Ida Elisabeth: "Oh, my poor, poor, poor Lisken! We were so distressed, papa and I, when we heard the sad news—"

The tears trickled clear as pearls down her soft freckled cheeks. But after a while Borghild Braatö began to chat.

Sitting on a chair by the bed, with Ida Elisabeth's hand in hers, she said one could never know—God has a purpose in all He does. Maybe it was for the best after all—

Ida Elisabeth knew in her heart—and it filled her with a bitterness not to be borne, and with a rebellious indignation with her fate—it was uncannily true that it was for the best after all ...

Chapter Five

THIS BITTER FEELING continued to prey on her. All sorts of people who had no concern with it offered her the consolation: perhaps it was for the best after all.

Sölvi complained loudly that she had not been given the little brother she was promised. Aunt Aslaug had sent the shoes by post, but Sölvi wanted to have a baby as well—

Frithjof had been tearing about all through the summer holidays—many of the regular visitors who had known him from a child invited him to make trips with them and were altogether very kind to him. In the summer holidays he could simply plant himself where he chose. He had scarcely had time to see anything of the children.

He was still away from home a great deal after Ida Elisabeth was about again. She assumed he noticed how depressed she was and went where he found more cheerful company. But then first one and then another came—in obscure hints to begin with and afterwards in plain words they gave her to understand that when Frithjof said he had been in such or such a place, he had really spent his time in the hotel at Vallerviken, making himself utterly ridiculous by flirting with the new girl they had there.

It was her customers who brought this information—they didn't think it right that she should be kept in ignorance of the state of things. Ida Elisabeth could not tell them to clear out; she had to pretend she knew about it and didn't think it need be taken seriously.

Nor was there any need to take it so, of course. He had tried that game before—all nonsense of course; there could hardly be any woman so stupid as to do anything but laugh at Frithjof's courting. But she was mad with him for having once more made a fool of himself. And then he hadn't the least idea that he was making a laughing-stock of himself. He believed he was cutting a dash when he fluttered about playing the gay dog.

One evening when Frithjof stayed at home on account of dirty weather Ida Elisabeth made up her mind to say a word or two about it.

Else was out, and when Ida Elisabeth had finished her washing-up she seated herself in the parlour with her basket of darning. Opposite to her Frithjof was sprawling over the table with his elbows stuck out and his chest leaning against its edge, exactly like a schoolboy over his lesson books; he was entirely absorbed in a copy of one of the popular weeklies, and he licked his finger every time he had to turn over. He looked so innocent sitting there with his bent head under the lamp and his coarse yellow hair bristling in all directions—it was time he went and had it cut again.

He looked like a picture of peace and innocence—and Ida Elisabeth knew to a nicety how he would look when he gave a start, if she asked him whether he thought it amusing to have folks talking about him and that Berta at Jensen's hotel. After all, why should she say anything? Let people gossip. Soon it would be winter, then there was never a soul at the hotel, except a chance commercial traveller—and Frithjof couldn't very well go off to Vallerviken in cold blood and sit down in the arctic solitude of Jensen's dining-room, with a cup of chicory or a small herb-beer, simply to have a talk with the lady—

The rain-drops pattered and pattered against the window. The wind had dropped, but it was still pouring. Ida Elisabeth let Kalleman's guernsey sink into her lap. Frithjof raised his head slightly:

"What makes you look at me like that?"

If he had not been so unshaven that the light stubble blurred the lines of his chin, he would have looked like a boy, as he lay with chest and arms resting on the table, sucking at one of his knuckles. The faded cherry-coloured pull-over suited him—there seemed to be just something or other wanting to make him a handsome man.

"It's so thick outside this evening. Oughtn't you to go and fetch Else—so she won't be by herself along the beach?"

Frithjof leaned back, tilting his chair. He dug out a packet of cigarettes and lighted one:

"There's sure to be someone to see her home."

"I say—now that Jarngerd's going to Aunt Gitta's, don't you think your mother would like to have Else home again?"

"No, mamma says she's to stay here for the winter. She'd rather get a girl to help her and let Else stay with you."

"No, I won't have that." Involuntarily she glanced at the bedclothes on the sofa, the washing-stand, the curtain in the corner with clothes hung behind it. Her mother-in-law would think it was only contrariness on her part to dislike having the whole house invaded by bedroom stuffiness—but now she had had enough of it.

"I must tell you"—Frithjof smiled slyly—"Else seems to be deeper than we thought, and that's what mamma's discovered. When we thought she was out with her girl-friends, she was more likely to be meeting somebody quite different. Several times. Went out to Helle in his motor-boat too. So it'll be safer if you keep her for the present."

"Why should I—when she's meeting him on the sly all the same?"

"Oh yes—otherwise it'll happen much oftener, you understand."

Ida Elisabeth shrugged her shoulders and went on with her darning.

"After all I suppose the whole business is nothing very serious? Only fooling—? Heavens, Frithjof, you don't believe what Else says, that he's over head and ears in love with her? And who's that Berta Helle that was at Vallerviken this summer? *She's* been boasting everywhere that *you're* her great conquest."

"Good heavens, Lisken!" He blinked his eyes in dismay and turned red as fire. "I've no *idea* what you're referring to! Berta—I certainly don't know anybody of that name—as far as I can remember. At least—unless I'm mistaken her name *was* Berta, that new lady Jensen engaged this summer—I'm not sure, but I almost think her Christian name was Berta—"

"Yes, she's at Jensen's hotel."

"Well, I never heard such nonsense! I was in the hotel a few times last summer; you know, Steffensen had his cutter here and I used to sail with him, I've told you that. And then I've sat there a few evenings since. You know it's just opposite the co-operative—I thought I'd better keep an eye on that fellow, she *is* my sister—"

"Well, have you known about this long—that Else was meeting him all the time?"

"Known? Well, you know what gossips people are. So I thought there'd be no harm in doing a little investigation."

Ida Elisabeth was silent for a few moments.

"It would have been better if you'd told me this before, I think. Why in the world haven't you said a word about it before?"

"I didn't dare." He gave her a rapid, unsteady glance out of his slits of eyes and turned red again. "Do you know what, Lisken, it isn't always so easy to talk to you. One never knows where one has you."

As she made no reply, but gave him a questioning look, Frithjof burst into a rapid flow of words:

"It *really* isn't easy—mamma says the same. You're not at *all* frank—there's something so ... secretive ... about you, we all find that. Poor Else complains so bitterly of it at times. Just when you're as mild as milk and we think there's no danger, you come jabbing at us with a reference to something we did so long ago that we thought either you hadn't noticed it or you didn't consider it worth talking about. Poor Else, she was really quite unhappy about it—last time we were at home she told mamma that one day you'd made her a present of some fine underclothes, but when she wanted to *embrace* you, she was so delighted; you switched over and gave her a lot of abuse about some soiled underclothes that she'd stuffed into the sofa and forgotten and some of your own that she'd happened to burn a hole in when she was ironing. Yes, that's what's so devastating; we never know where we have you—just when you're as nice and pleasant as you can be and we think you're in the best of humours and can't do enough for us—you come out with something or other which shows that you're not like that at all. You're so wanting in *frankness*, Lisken! Honestly, you're a pretty difficult person to live with, let me tell you, my dear."

Ida Elisabeth looked at him thoughtfully: "Perhaps so—"

No doubt they were right. That was how it looked, seen from their side. As a matter of fact she had spoken her mind to Else, that evening in the summer when she came home and found the kitchen full of stifling smoke. Else had gone out and forgotten to take off the electric iron, so that it had burnt through the clothes into the ironing board. It might have set fire to the house, she had said. Not much more than that, for what was the use? But when after that she gave Else the set of violet silk underclothes that the child had set her eyes on so long, she had tried to say something to her about her monstrous untidiness. The fact was, Else was a regular pig—but at any rate she hadn't used that word. The Braatös' children were accustomed to their parents losing patience now and then; at such times Jens would storm at the youngsters like mad, and there might be some slaps . . . Or their mother would abandon herself entirely to wailing and lamenting, till she found vent in a deluge of tears. But when they had worked off their rage they were as mild as ever and everything went on again in the old groove. Nobody had ever been disagreeable to those children except for the purpose of letting off steam—nobody expected anything else to result from it. In general they were accustomed to regard all they heard said as a mere outburst of feeling.

It was really a pretty hopeless state of things. She had accustomed herself to saying a great deal less than she meant, but at any rate not to say anything unless she meant it. If she did her best for them, since fate had made them her dependents—and they then discovered that she was not so passionately devoted to them after all—they must naturally regard her as false and secretive, the opposite of what they understood by frank and natural. So they filled her up with lies—it was the only natural course for them. Poor things, they were undoubtedly sincere when they answered in an injured tone: why didn't you tell me what I was to do; why didn't you ask me to do so-and-so—? Why didn't you say I was to stay at home? asked Else when she came home in the small hours, the night that Ida Elisabeth had had to go herself and telephone for the midwife. Before that she had been obliged to finish the boiling of some jam—but dear me, you might have asked me to do that, said Else. They meant it. But it never occurred to them to do a single thing unless they had been expressly told about it. And if it was a case of asking someone to do a thing for her, she preferred to do it herself, if it were in any way possible—

So it was, and there was no getting over it. But it was a pity, for the sake of the others as well.

"At all events I didn't mean any harm by it", she said with a little sigh.

"Dear me, no; you may be sure I understood *that*." With a wink in his eyes and his lips pinched in a significant smile he rocked his chair and nodded at her.

"So you *can* be a bit jealous of your husband, still?" he said with a teasing laugh.

Ida Elisabeth folded the guernsey she had been darning and took another garment out of the basket. Of course he believed it was *that*—

"At any rate I don't know why you need give all the old women something to cackle about."

"Oh, you're a good one!" he laughed with growing cheerfulness.

However, after this there was an end of his trips to Vallerviken. Else too stayed more in the house. She and Frithjof had doubtless discussed matters. Now and again Else would come of her own accord and ask if there was anything for her to do, and Ida Elisabeth began to think it might be her own fault that she had not succeeded in training Else at all. Perhaps with a little more patience ... Only it appeared that a little patience was not enough. Else had to have everything given her by the teaspoonful. Ida Elisabeth herself had not properly recovered from her last confinement—there was nothing definitely the matter with her, only she felt powerless and uneasy, excitable in a queer and horrid way. And this morbid feeling of disinclination was all the more tiresome when Frithjof and Else were really trying to show themselves kind and obliging—at this time they often let it be seen that they knew they were being well treated and appreciated it. But these were just the occasions when she had to make a serious effort to be calm and not cross.

Frithjof was running round on his bicycle again and took Sölvi with him—Kalleman was afraid to sit on the machine. "Do be careful", said Ida Elisabeth, when Frithjof proposed to Sölvi that they should go for a ride—the roads were pretty bad after the long spell of autumn rains. "You know very well I'm not rash", he laughed. Nor was he, she thought; it had never occurred to her to be seriously anxious.

And not a glimmer of presentiment had prepared her for what was coming. She was standing on the step-ladder in the shop, arranging on the shelf the new waterproofs she had gotten in; Else stood below and handed her the parcels one by one. From where she stood Ida Elisabeth could look out through the shop window; she saw the doctor's grey Essex come rushing in from the Mokhus road at a terrific speed and turn past here—someone being sent to hospital, she thought; the boat was lying at the pier. The car stopped just outside. "What are you doing, Else?" she cried in irritation; "come here and hand me up—", but Else was already at the door. "Ugh, what is it now", said Ida Elisabeth impatiently; then there came a loud scream from Else: "Oh! Frithjof—something must have happened to him—!"

Ida Elisabeth jumped down from the steps and followed the girl out. A lot of people were already standing round the car. The sun was shining, mild and autumnal; the water of the creek glittered and glittered behind bare trees and the grey gleam of slate roofs, and from below came the sound of a bell and the steamer putting out from the pier. Ida Elisabeth sensed it all, sensed the blue of the mountains rising up on the other side of the fjord through the light-drenched haze; on their summits the new snow was already lying white. She remembered afterwards something light lying on the dark, muddy ground—the fallen leaves of the willows on the road in front of the house, and within the garden fence the leaves of raspberry-bushes lying with their silvery under-side up. But beside the car stood Frithjof, and the blood was running down over his face, and it was smeared brown with mud; his clothes looked as if he had been rolled over and over in the road; he had lost his cap and his hair was caked with blood and dirt—and when he moved his hand that too was bloody ...

"But, good God, what have you done to yourself—where's Sölvi?" she asked, and the moment she asked after the child it was as though time and place faded from her and she was left hovering in sheer expectation.

But she did not even listen to Frithjof's answer; in breathless tension she bent down and looked into the car, where a red-haired young man, the locum tenens, sat holding the child wrapped up in something—

"Careful—can you take hold . . . so"; he passed the bundle out through the door of the car into Ida Elisabeth's arms, and trembling with horror she felt for an instant that the child's body was lifeless in its heaviness; she had a glimpse of the face, battered and bruised—and when the strange man stepped out his light grey clothes were bloody and stained with mud. He took the child from her again, went in front, and carried her in. She heard Else whimpering by her side and realized that the girl was hopping and tripping as little children do when they have burnt themselves, and she was gnawing at her knuckles.

They were in the bedroom, and there was one more with them, a young woman in a leather motoring cap, a light blouse, and breeches. She said something that Ida Elisabeth did not understand, and then she began taking the blankets and pillows from Ida Elisabeth's bed and putting them on Frithjof's. She smoothed out the under-sheet, and there the two strangers laid Sölvi, Sölvi with closed eyes and smeared with blood, a red stream oozing from her mouth, her clothes all torn and grey with mud—the heavy wrap that had been wound about her fell with a crash on the floor by the bed, and the lady said to Ida Elisabeth: "Oh, would you mind picking it up, to give us room—" Ida Elisabeth stood holding a heavy leather motor coat in her hands and heard the strangers asking for water, warm water, clean towels or sheets, then saw the lady cross the room and pull down the blinds, as some faces appeared at the windows trying to look in—

"That comes from the teeth; they've been loosened", said the doctor, as he opened Sölvi's blood-stained lips with a finger. "She fell right on her back, but she must have had a blow on the mouth from the handle-bar or something. No, I hope it isn't—but she's certainly got a concussion . . . My wife will see to you directly", he said to Frithjof, who loomed huge and dismal at the foot of the bed; "only we must attend to the little girl here first." Frithjof was talking in a loud falsetto: "I kept right out at the edge of the road as soon as I heard the lorry coming, but it was Ola driving, and he doesn't care how he drives, at least eighty kilometres he was going, and then the lorry skidded at the bend, you understand, doctor—it was loaded with boards—"

"Oh, Fru Braatö, would you be kind enough to get the others out of the room, so that I can examine the child in peace—" The doctor was cutting the clothes off Sölvi. Ida Elisabeth turned, as though awakening, from the sight of the motionless child on the bed. The others—Kalleman had somehow come in and stood by her knee uttering little screams; Else was in the room whining shrill and excited questions; Frithjof repeated over and over again: "It wasn't my fault; indeed I couldn't help it; I kept right out at the side of the road—" and Fru Esbjörnsen came in with a steaming kettle, which the doctor's wife took from her.

Then Ida Elisabeth got the boy and Frithjof and Else out to the kitchen, put on more kettles, fetched a pile of clean linen from the cupboard, brought the doctor what he asked for, got what she wanted for the doctor's wife, who had taken Frithjof into the sitting-room; he was still talking: "I hope to goodness he'll lose his licence for this, the road-hog—"

"We must hope for the best", said the doctor to Ida Elisabeth; "broken bones heal pretty quickly at her age; it isn't properly broken, you understand—it's like trying to break an osier twig. But there's her back, and perhaps internal injuries—it's impossible to ascertain that at present. The concussion—no, that *need* not be so terribly serious—"

Sölvi was now lying stretched out in her own little bed. Her mouth was swollen out of all shape. And on the bedside table lay two little white teeth streaked with blood at the roots—the doctor had had to take them out.

The shop bell tinkled again. Else was out there—and Frithjof; he was repeating his story to some fresh arrivals and telling them what Doctor Grönvold had said about himself and Sölvi. "Wouldn't it be better if you shut the shop for today, Fru Braatö? So as to keep the house quite quiet. My wife will come back and stay with you tonight at any rate— she's a trained nurse."

When Ida Elisabeth went to the door with the doctor and his wife it was almost dark and the fog had drifted in from the sea; the moisture gleamed on the fence and dripped from the bare branches of the willows in the light of the lamp above the door. The doctor's wife, slight and boyish in her leather cap and coat, put her husband's bag on the back seat; Else stood by the car, in travelling clothes and with suit-case in hand, and followed the others' movements, lost in admiration. Then Fru Grönvold got into the driver's seat, the doctor beside her, and little Else crawled into the car.

"Now don't frighten the life out of your mother, whatever you do—it might have been a great deal worse, remember to say that. She mustn't think of coming out here, tell her, for some days at any rate—" She simply could not have any of those people fussing and chattering about the place when she had two patients to look after.

Then the Grönvolds drove off with Else.

IDA ELISABETH closed the shop and switched off the light, then went through the sitting-room—it had a queer, unfamiliar look with Frithjof's bed where the sofa usually stood and him sitting on it with his arm in a sling. "I'll come and help you directly"—she went on into the dimly lighted bedroom; that too looked unfamiliar with its furniture displaced. Ida Elisabeth bent over Sölvi's bed, felt the child's face, put her hand under the coverlet, where it was warm from the hot water bottles, and came upon the great bundle of gauze, which was Sölvi's left leg. There was no change.

Again she was overcome by that sense of unreality—as though all everyday, familiar things were out of reach and she were suspended in mid-air, until she could know how it would turn out, that Sölvi was out of danger. The hospital odour left by the doctor's work gave her a numb feeling, light-headed and empty-headed at once.

Frithjof was sitting on his bed, in a blue shirt, one ripped sleeve of which dangled loosely, woollen pants and long felt socks. Ida Elisabeth knelt down and unfastened the buckles of his slippers, then drew them off: "I thought I heard you in the shop just now—you surely didn't appear . . . in *this* costume?" she said disapprovingly.

"You can guess I threw my coat over me"; he stood up so that she might pull down his pants. "They were only people I knew very well—" He sat down again, and she lifted the pants carefully over his bandages; he had received some abrasions on the legs. "You may be sure they were anxious to hear how it happened. And *I* certainly have nothing to conceal, I wasn't the least *bit* to blame for his running into us—"

With one hand modestly held in his lap he observed with interest the suffused patches on his broad, white thighs. "Have you seen my bicycle? Well, but you must go out and look at it—absolutely smashed to pieces—"

Still kneeling Ida Elisabeth drew the blue-striped pajama trousers up his legs—he stood up to let her tie them round his waist, telling her the while how the lorry from the saw-mills had come at a speed of at least eighty kilometres and had swung out at the bend, and as Ola was trying to get it back into the middle of the road it had grazed the bicycle, and as they were flung on to the side of the road they had been caught by the ends of some planks. "Yes, it's a marvel we got off as we did, say I—but that Ola Langhus is going to lose his licence over this, I'll see to that. It was a bit of luck anyway that that doctor turned up just at the very moment; it's all over with Anna Mokhus now, that's where

97

they'd been ... She's pretty smart, isn't she, that wife of his—charming lady, I must say—"

They had cut Frithjof's hair short on one side, and the tufts of yellow hair straggled over the edge of the bandage—he looked so comic. Ida Elisabeth got the pajama jacket on him, then fetched a reel of tape and tied it up over the bandaged arm. "There. You can brush your teeth yourself, can't you? What will you have—tea? Milk? And you'd better take one or two more aspirins. Poor you—tomorrow you'll be feeling pretty stiff; I expect you'll have to stay in bed three or four days at least."

"A couple of poached eggs—if you have any—I'd like", he called after her as she went out to the kitchen.

In a way it had irritated her, having to dress this great white, fleshy male person as if he had been a child. But at the same time there was something reassuring in it—it seemed that it *could* not be so serious, when Frithjof was so comic. Her anxiety for Sölvi receded to a distance when she could not help being vexed and at the same time amused over Frithjof.

The tea and bread-and-butter he could dispatch by himself, but she had to feed him with the poached eggs. And all the time he was explaining and explaining, and overhead at the Esbjörnsens' she heard Kalleman running about the room. There *could* not be any danger for Sölvi.

She tucked Frithjof well in his blankets and put out the light before going in to sit by Sölvi. He was sleeping like a stone when there was a tap at the window and Ida Elisabeth went to let in the doctor's wife.

NOT till the evening of the fifth day did Ida Elisabeth realize that danger threatened.

She had grown used to the new state of things in the house; it seemed to have lasted an age already. Sölvi moaned a good deal, the fever went up and down, and it was impossible to know if her head was clear when she was awake.

Now and again she said something, but it was not easy to understand her, as she had lost two front teeth and her mouth was so swollen. "You'd better not try to talk to her", said the doctor's wife one evening; but she seemed to think everything was going normally. She had forbidden Frithjof to have visitors, so he had to content himself with chatting to her and Olise Langeland in loud whispers, when they had time to pause by his bed.

Olise served in the shop and helped Ida Elisabeth with the housework; without being asked she washed all the muddy and blood-stained clothes after the catastrophe. She was a little middle-aged person of intermediate social position; Ida Elisabeth had always thought it such a comfort to have her about. She was scarcely aware that this was due to Olise's taciturnity even more than to her capability. If anyone wanted a chat with Olise Langeland they had to do most of the talking themselves—this was a grand thing just now, when everyone who came into the shop had questions to ask.

Ida Elisabeth learnt to change the child's sheets almost without disturbing her position, and to arrange towels under Sölvi's chin, to prevent her getting wet with what was spilt when her mother gave her medicine and soup by the teaspoonful. As she washed the soiled linen in the scullery and hung it to dry in the yard she chatted with Kalleman; when preparing Frithjof's tray she cut a few slices of bread and jam for the boy, and he sat on the kitchen door-step and talked and ate—he evidently enjoyed staying with the Esbjörnsens. One day she took him on her arm and carried him in; he was to be allowed to say good-morning to Sölvi. But he appeared to be terrified at his sister's red face and swollen mouth, and Sölvi did not show a spark of interest in her brother. Afterwards, it is true, Kalleman had a great deal to say about Sölvi being ill.

Frithjof was driven to and from the inquiry in the doctor's car, but had to go to bed again as soon as he reached home; he had a headache and was still pretty stiff. But he was greatly excited by the trip, reported everything that had been said and what he had said himself, and he cut out some paragraphs about the collision that had appeared in the local press and preserved them in his pocket book. "But that old Essex, you know—I really think Sommervold might stand himself a new car; goodness knows he can afford it—"

It always irritated Ida Elisabeth to hear people say, oh, Doctor Sommervold, of course he can afford anything he likes. He had his daughter and her family; Ragna Sommervold had married a German naval officer—that was in the good old days before the War, when German warships visited the fjord every summer. During the War Hans von Dettingen had been disabled, and they had lost all their money, and there were two sons to be educated. He also had to help his son's widow—in fact, it was always the doctor who had to put his hand in his pocket when anyone or anything was to be kept above water. Frithjof's parents, for instance, had certainly received not a little assistance in the course of years.

And the same thing annoyed her the day her mother-in-law was here. Fru Braatö had come out by the steamer; she was to drive home with the doctor, she explained, when he called in the evening. And then she began to complain about Doctor Sommervold's being in Germany as usual; not but what she was quite ready to believe Doctor Grönvold was *quite* clever, and his wife was *certainly* an excellent person, even if there was rather a modern air about her; but indeed it *was* annoying that Doctor Sommervold should always happen to be abroad when it *would* have been more reassuring to have *him*—

Ida Elisabeth had to serve her mother-in-law with coffee in the kitchen; they sat with the door open to the bedroom, where Sölvi lay with drawn blinds, breathing audibly and moaning feebly in her feverish doze.

"But don't you think the same, it'll be better if we send Else out to you tomorrow?" asked Borghild Braatö. "This is just the time when you might need her—"

"Need her!" Ida Elisabeth replied hastily. "Good heavens, mother—you can't seriously imagine there's any help in Else. And as long as I have two children lying ill I'd rather be excused having to keep an eye on that young woman as well."

But she regretted it at once, on seeing her mother-in-law's expression, like a child flinching at a box on the ears—only this was something that struck deeper than a blow. Dear, dear—did she really know all the time how other people regarded those children of hers whom she loved and worshipped and bragged of and always had a thousand excuses for—?

On the morning of the fifth day Ida Elisabeth was sitting with Sölvi. The drawn blinds were aglow with sunshine and shadows flickered across them of branches swaying in the wind; the roar of the fjord was so loud today—it was glorious weather outside. Sölvi moved her head the least bit; her stiff eyes seemed at the same time dull and bright, and there was a strange, anxious look in them—perhaps it's the restless light she's afraid of, thought her mother.

"It's mamma, Sölvi—mamma's sitting with you." She tried to show a real smile. "You're not afraid, are you, when mamma's here?"

"Mamma—" lisped Sölvi.

Thrilled with joy Ida Elisabeth took the clammy little hand in hers: "It doesn't hurt you so much now, does it, Sölvi?" She had given her medicine a little while before; it was an anodyne.

"Yes!" It sounded so pitiful, a feeble wail, as though the child's patience had been strained too long.

"But where does it hurt you most, my darling? Can't you tell mamma *where* it hurts most now?" Sölvi made no answer. "Is it in your leg? Your head perhaps? Shall Mamma put another lovely cold cloth on your forehead?" Again she received no answer, but she went out to the kitchen and got the compress ready. While doing so she had an idea; she darted into the sitting-room.

Frithjof lay peacefully reading; he had a whole pile of magazines and weekly papers on the floor by his bed. Ida Elisabeth went to the shelf and took the little ebony elephant that her father had brought her from Ceylon, once upon a time.

She laid the compress on Sölvi's forehead and passed her hand cautiously over the child's hot cheek. Then she produced the elephant:

"Do you see who's come to pay you a visit?" Sölvi showed no sign of interest. "The illiphant, Sölvi! It's for *you*, my dear—do you hear, Sölvi, mamma's *given* it to you, it's your *own* now. When you get well again it'll be *yours* and you can play with it whenever you like—"

But still Sölvi showed no reaction. Ida Elisabeth placed the elephant on the bedside table among all the bottles and the rest of the sick-room gear—it had quite an encouraging look there, she thought, with its smooth and shiny black body, its white tusks and little glittering mother-of-pearl eyes.

"Has she shown any interest in toys and that sort of thing today?" asked the doctor when he made his evening call.

"Not yet. She was very restless this afternoon—and I haven't been able to get her to take anything; it gets into her nose, and then it seems as if she was going to vomit. Poor child, I'm sure it hurt her frightfully—"

He took a very long time examining Sölvi and asked to see the sheet which Ida Elisabeth had taken from under her that day. He and his wife exchanged some words she did not understand; Ida Elisabeth looked at their faces, and then it was that it sank into her, sharp as a knife—the possibility that until now she had never for a moment believed in. Her eyes fell on the little elephant, and all at once it had assumed a horribly threatening aspect; the little mother-of-pearl eyes in the black figure had an evil stare.

"You had better stay here for the present, Gerda", said the doctor to his wife.

Ida Elisabeth kept back her questions till he was gone—as though the answer would be more hopeful if it came from the young wife. There was something calm, a certain chilliness, about her manner, but in the way she went about her work there was a kind of energetic human sympathy.

"Well, you know, we must hope for the best. But it is impossible at present to ascertain the extent of the . . .internal injuries she has suffered." She spoke as if there was a good deal she would rather not say.

But at last she persuaded Ida Elisabeth to lie down for a while, and the mother was so starved for sleep that she went off almost at once.

She was roused by a sound—after a few moments she realized that it was the little iron bedstead shaking. Sölvi was wailing with a strangely jarring sound. Ida Elisabeth started up—Fru Grönvold was bending over the child, but when her mother came to her side, Sölvi seemed to collapse altogether; she was terribly changed in some way or other.

Fru Grönvold thought for a moment—then she tore off her white apron: "I must run to the telephone exchange—I daren't give her anything without asking my husband—" She dashed out.

Ida Elisabeth heard the back door quietly close. Then there was not a sound in the house except that fly buzzing inside the shade of the bedside lamp and hitting against the bulb with a ring. But outside the fjord was booming, the wind roared and the branches grated against the window. It was a little after three when she looked at the clock.

She sat bending over Sölvi, staring and listening to the child's breathing.

Again the little frame was shaken by spasms, the eyes rolled and rolled under their lids, which had grown so thin—there was a pause, but soon the spasms returned, more feebly, and the collapse was more marked than before. And after another while—she did not know how she knew it, she *saw* it, but it was not a thing she could see with her eyes. It was as though she had been through this before, in giving birth—the moment the child was born a wave from an invisible and infinite ocean had swept over her, had torn something asunder, but when the wave withdrew again the little twitching, puling creature lay beside her, as though the two had been washed up on a beach. The same wave from an invisible eternity now went over her again—and it was as though the fierce, tearing pain she had then felt in her body was but a crude image of that which now tore her in two. The wave drew back, but now it had taken Sölvi with it—what was left in the bed was not Sölvi.

Lying prone upon the bed Ida Elisabeth pressed her bosom hard against its edge, as though the pain of it might deaden the other. Then the door opened—Fru Grönvold came into the light, with rain pouring from her oil-skins. She tore them off on her way to the bed. There she stood; Ida Elisabeth looked up at her; they looked at each other. As the doctor's wife bent over the child, the mother rose and sat upright, pushed the hair back from her face—and when the other looked up and their eyes met, Ida Elisabeth's face gave way. She began to weep, first a low and agonizing wail, but then the tears came and she sobbed outright—but quietly, as though there were someone she did not wish to disturb.

Once the other came up to her: "Fru Braatö ..." She took one of Ida Elisabeth's hands, stood holding it: "Fru Braatö ..."

All at once the door of the sitting-room opened and there stood Frithjof in striped pajamas, with his tufted, half-cropped head, his eyes nearly closed with sleep. When he saw the two he dashed forward and then burst into a loud, harrowing fit of weeping: "Sölvi—oh, Sölvi—oh—"

He fell on his knees by the bed, beside his wife: "Oh—oh—oh—" Ida Elisabeth held out her other hand to him, behind her. "Hush, Frithjof, you must not cry so loud", she begged him, as though there were someone in the room who must not be waked.

Chapter Six

FRITHJOF WAS ENTIRELY FREE from blame for the accident—she knew that. But in the period that succeeded Sölvi's death Ida Elisabeth thought at times: it will end in my hating him—

He talked and talked about it to anyone who would listen to him. It was true that he had really been very fond of Sölvi. If he had scarcely asked after her during the days when he was himself in bed, it must have been because it had not occurred to him that there could be any danger. But at any rate he was utterly distracted at her death. But it almost seemed as if he had been compensated for the loss of the child by having such a lot to tell people—about the accident and about how sweet and funny she had been, papa's little playmate, and about her death-bed and what the doctor had said and about the inquiry and the funeral and what there had been in the papers. He was constantly meeting someone who had not heard it before—on board the boats, on the pier, down at the trading association. When he came home he repeated to Ida Elisabeth what he had said and what so-and-so had said. The story changed with every time he told it. At first he had said he remembered absolutely nothing from the moment the lorry struck the bicycle till he was helped into the doctor's car. But by degrees he came to remember more and more. "Sölvi", he had thought; he had been afraid they would get the load of planks on top of them, and he had thrown himself forward to protect the child with his own body. Ida Elisabeth knew well enough that he believed himself all he said. It was the first real sorrow Frithjof had had, and it excited him tremendously.

Only she was not like that herself. She would have preferred never to hear another word about it. After the first few days she had scarcely shed a tear. She felt as though she were full to the brim of inward weeping, and quite instinctively she compressed her lips and stifled the tears, as though afraid her sorrow would run over. But she thought and thought of the dead child, fell asleep thinking of her, and on waking felt as if the same thought had gone on weaving itself within her while she slept. She recalled what Sölvi had said last summer about the little beads that flew up and down inside her. When the little body had grown stiff in death she had thought it was as though a volatile, fluid substance had congealed into heavy metal within it and transmitted its icy chill to skin and flesh. And then she could not help thinking of the two milk-teeth that she had thrown into the stove: "Mouse, mouse, here's a gold tooth for you; give Sölvi a bone tooth!" The child had been conscious then, and Ida Elisabeth had hoped she might get Sölvi to smile.

But at times the same feeling came over her as she had had in church. She did not hear what Pastor Söndeled said, and probably she was the only one who was not in tears; but she was fighting against a terrible impulse to scream aloud, to tear her clothes in pieces, tear the hair from her head and scratch her face till the blood ran ... Thus her father had seen people behave at funerals somewhere in the tropics—she felt inclined to curse because it would not do to act in the same way here and deaden her fearful despair with physical pain.

Kalleman had scarcely spoken of his sister since her death. Ida Elisabeth had the impression that he did not even listen when Frithjof was talking about her. But indeed he had a way of avoiding his father—it looked as if he did not care for Frithjof's noisy manner. He himself was quiet, and besides herself he seemed to get on best with Olise and the Esbjörnsens—the Esbjörnsens were also of the quiet sort.

But one morning she and the boy were alone in the shop. Outside the snow was driving in great sticky tatters, and Kalleman stood at the door trying to look out between the bibs and advertising placards that hung behind the glass. Ida Elisabeth was busy counting the stitches on a big piece of embroidery which she had promised to begin for a customer by the next day. The colours struck her as so pretty— subconsciously she felt it did her good to work at it.

"Mamma," said Kalleman from the door, "isn't it a bore that Sölvi's dead? Now we have nobody to play with any more."

"We must try to play together as well as we can, you and I."

"Yes, but we can't play, mamma. Only Sölvi could play."

"Oh, I don't know." She tried to smile. "Are you so bored, poor boy! Look here—" She found a piece of paper that had lined a cardboard box. "And a pencil—now you can draw pictures. You may sit here by me, nobody will come in this weather."

The boy took the paper and pencil; he seemed quite pleased and crawled up on to the chair she placed for him. "But we can't *play*, you know!"

"Oh yes, we can. It's fun drawing pictures, Carl—"

"Oh yes. But that's not playing—"

A week or so before Christmas Doctor Sommervold looked in on her one morning. Ida Elisabeth had not even heard he had come home; she knew they had tried a new operation on his son-in-law and that the doctor intended to stay there till they saw whether it had any result. So she made haste to inquire how things were at Ragna's, before he had time to ask after her.

"Oh well, at all events it looks as if Hans would be able to use his limbs a little more. And how are you?" he asked in a low voice, as she showed him into the sitting-room.

"Quite well, thanks. Have you time to stay a little while?"

"That's what I thought of doing—if I'm not taking up your time. Ciss Oxley was to pick me up here—she's driving for me today, we've been to the almshouse. She was to take Sjur up to Mokhus, he's been given leave to visit his daughter for a few days."

"Oh, is she home again?" Ida Elisabeth was not very pleased at the prospect of having a visitor.

"She's going to stay with me for the present—till Sister Laurentse's well again. She's very capable. You know she's been trained as a nurse."

"Oh—" said Ida Elisabeth without interest.

"There's a great deal of sickness about this winter." The doctor paused. "I don't know if you have heard," he said hesitatingly, "about little Merete—?"

"No—that is, they mentioned that she'd had a very bad cold in the autumn. She wasn't at the funeral either, as far as I remember."

"Well, it's t.b. I wanted to tell you, because I hear you're going to Vettehaugen for Christmas. So you must be rather careful with the children—with Kalleman", he corrected himself and hastened to continue: "You know, when it's taken in hand so soon there ought to be a good hope— there'll be room for her at the sanatorium in February—"

"I'm so sorry for the old people—I suppose they're quite beside themselves over this?"

"Oh, you know, Jens and Borghild are optimists by nature. Yes, they knew it before the funeral. Grönvold examined her. So if they haven't mentioned it to you—I thought it just as well that you should know it. You needn't show any sign, of course."

Ida Elisabeth's lips showed something like a smile.

"Well, well, I must tell you, Ida, I was there to supper yesterday. It's not merely that they're trying, as a purely spontaneous reaction, to conceal the fact that there's infection in the house. They're a little afraid about you too. You have scared them by the way you've taken this. It seems to them quite uncanny—that you're so unapproachable."

"I see." Ida Elisabeth was silent for a moment. "I suppose that's why mother-in-law has left me in peace ever since ... For that's what she has done."

Doctor Sommervold nodded: "To them, you see, it's quite incomprehensible—utterly abnormal—that you don't manifest any need of seeking consolation and so on. Well, you know all about that just as well as I do", he said rather impatiently. "And all the same, little Ida, they're so fond of you. It's true, my dear, they are! Unconsciously, or consciously, I can't tell which—they know that you're a support for them all." He smiled a little crooked smile. "You're one of the fixed points in their existence. That's why they love you—and are so anxious about you now!"

Ida Elisabeth sat looking at the floor and made no answer.

"Well, well, well. No, it's deuced awkward, I know, when humans have to act providence for other humans. Life must have looked considerably less hopeless to folks in old days, who believed providence sat high up, above the whole mess—that it could survey the interconnection of all human destinies and had an insight into everything that we humans can never have insight into."

"You mean, the Lord knew his own—mother-in-law asserts that he does so, and God knows we don't!" She gave a little laugh. "For that matter they believe in providence too in that house. And if they know that I've been some use to them, they probably think there's a providence in that too—I'm only an instrument in the hand of providence."

"But you don't believe it."

"No, God knows I don't!" Ida Elisabeth smiled bitterly. "I don't know why I should think so badly of providence. For in that case it would have been pretty beastly to me."

"Precisely." The doctor nodded. "If you had had the same belief as Ciss Oxley, for instance, you would perhaps have accepted patiently enough the role that had been assigned to you—as deputy providence for certain people who are pretty helpless. Because you would take it for granted that all human beings possess a mystical value in addition to the value they have or have not as members of society. Nowadays we avoid taking the consequences of no longer believing this by saying, there is *some* good in all men. And no doubt there is—but when the good is so small in proportion to all the rest of their make-up, the stupidity and egoism and laziness! Is there any sense in it, from a purely realistic point of view, that a person as capable as you should wear yourself out for the incapable—for a downright moron, for instance? Ought one not to look at the good in people as one looks at an outcrop of ore for instance—ask if it is rich enough to pay for the working? If one has thrown overboard these religious notions about a human soul being an infinite value—be it never so small and weazened and frugal a soul in a big and greedy carcass?"

"Ugh, no." Ida Elisabeth shrugged her shoulders, wearily. "You know it doesn't do to ask such questions."

"Not for you and me, no. We cannot liberate ourselves from the old estimate of human life, even if we don't believe in the dogmas it is based on. But in a generation or two from now—do you believe those people who are fully efficient will then be willing to keep alive all those who cannot furnish a fraction of the money's worth it costs to keep a human body going? We needn't speak of good and evil, for there again their opinions will be different from ours."

"That's their business." Ida Elisabeth gave a toss of the head. "We at any rate can't watch people drowning because they can't swim, and not care."

"No. But there have always been people who could do that ... That must be my car ... And talking of cars: there seem to be quite a lot of people now who can run over another person and drive on without stopping to see what's happened!"

Ciss Oxley came in, her round cheeks red from the winter air. She greeted Fru Braatö with slight embarrassment and said thank you, a cup of coffee would be very grateful.

If Fru Braatö would excuse her—she put out one foot in a high ski-boot which was fearfully muddy. But it hadn't been possible to take the car beyond the first of the Mokhus farms. Oh yes, she had delivered Sjur all right; poor fellow, he was as light as a feather now. So it went finely, they had tramped up arm in arm—the daughter had been so glad to get him home again—

"There you see, Ida, what we were talking about, when humans have to act providence for other humans. I'm no out-and-out advocate of almshouses—if old people prefer to suffer hardship and keep their freedom it's devilish to shut them up against their will, except when it's quite unjustifiable to let them have their own way and do without nursing. And Sister Klara means well, poor creature, but I can't listen to her for five minutes without wanting to chloroform her—the way she cackles! But this Sjur, with senile eczema and rheumatism—and the daughter who grudged him every bite of food and didn't even attempt to conceal her longing for the day when he would peg out, verminous and under-nourished he was—"

"She was very glad to get him home now", said Ciss.

"Yes, for a few days."

"She's anxious to have him at home over the New Year; I was to give you that message and say you must please arrange it."

"Hm, well, people are queer."

"But is it so queer after all? That Sjur should feel miserable living in a brick house surrounded by whitewashed walls where none of those he associates with has known him in the days when he was an able-bodied man. Brite may push him aside as much as she likes and let him feel that he's only a broken-down old wreck—but still she knows what he has been, and he knows that she knows it, and every stone and every tuft of grass and every chip in the walls up there is familiar to him from the time when he was in full work. And even if she's not very kind to him, there's the family tie—and he's fond of Brite and her children. No, I think it must be horrible, when one's too old to form new habits and new acquaintances, to be shoved like that into a house full of nothing but old gaffers and gammers. Why can't the commune help them so that they can stay in their own homes instead—?"

"Economy, Ciss!"

"Pooh! It must have cost so much to build that almshouse that they could have let the old people stay in their homes and be better off than they'd ever been in their lives, many of them—for what the almshouse cost. And I don't suppose it's run for nothing either—"

"It was built in the boom, Ciss, and the people who brought it forward talked about the almshouse cause. And those who get control of things in this country are very seldom the sort of people to understand that there really are folks who are willing to do without a great deal—even the chance of gossiping and poking their noses into other folks' private life, simply in order to retain the right to shut their own door against those they don't want to have on top of them. Those who nowadays pass for leading personalities are often the kind who are not happy unless they feel the mass around them on every side. And who themselves possess mass mentality in a superlative degree, which keeps them from making themselves impossible as leaders. But they always bear in mind that, if it is difficult to get the masses to believe in unpleasant truths, it is downright impossible to take away their belief in flattery and pleasant lies."

"It's fairly difficult to make them give up that, even if you take them one by one", said Ciss Oxley. "None of us likes unpleasant truths, and we're all open to flattery—the only difference is that some can take their flattery neat and others have to have it stirred up in a little truth, like cod-liver oil in beer froth, before they can swallow it."

"Nevertheless there is just one thing to be said in favour of an aristocracy of birth. It makes it possible for a man to attain power without having to echo the views of those whose welfare he's responsible for."

"And the worst thing about it is," said Ciss hotly, "that in an aristocracy a man is given power over others' welfare whether he feels responsible for them or not."

The doctor gave a little laugh:

"That applies to all systems—aristocracy and democracy and capitalism and State capitalism; the qualities which put a man in power and those which make him feel responsibility are not necessarily associated, nor do they necessarily exclude each other. He may have both qualities or he may have one of them. For that matter it was just the same in the hierarchies, eh, Ciss? But the worst thing about all democracies is that they give us these leaders who don't know what's what—they don't even try to make it clear to themselves when they're thinking about the people's welfare and when about the people's goodwill. We had an institution here in Norway in the saga times which was called debt-servitude. When a man had incurred more debts than he was able to pay, he could hand over his children to his creditors, and they had to work as thralls until they had earned enough to cover their father's indebtedness. I don't believe children are told anything about this debt-servitude in the schools nowadays. But they're destined to experience it."

Ida Elisabeth nodded: "They won't have a good time, those who come after us."

"No. And that brings up the question we were talking about a little while ago. Will those who come after us be content to bear all the burdens which *we* still feel it our duty to shoulder? To help all that neither can nor will help themselves? Submit to all old people living on till they die a natural death and even do what they can to prolong their existence? Especially when the young are aware that the old have taken upon themselves to determine, *that* they should come into the world, and *when* they should come, and how many should be put into the world to take over the burdens when they themselves are no longer able to bear them."

Ida Elisabeth turned red: "Does that mean that you've entirely changed your opinions, Doctor Sommervold?"

"No, I haven't done that. I am still unable to agree with Ciss here, who thinks people ought either to get married and accept all the youngsters the Almighty chooses to send them, or go into a convent. But I admit that those of us who are of a different opinion might do well to adopt the lofty morality which the gipsies of old are said to have practised—disappear of our own free will, when we begin to be troublesome to our successors. Otherwise we may run the risk of finding ourselves in too painful a situation. When the offspring fully realize that their parents have emancipated themselves from the old religious subordination in their family life—I'm not speaking merely of the Christian religion, but of fertility religions, and ancestor religions and belief in fate and all the rest. Of course it is something entirely new that people are to grow up with the knowledge that they owe life a decision made for them by their parents, unfettered by considerations for a higher power to which the parents had to submit. So I expect we'll have to take it gracefully if the family suicide rock comes into fashion again in some form or other."

"Ugh, how you talk!" said Ida Elisabeth.

Ciss Oxley said seriously:

"But I've heard other people talk like that—young people who say, why couldn't our parents have bought a dog or a car or a camera when they thought they must have something that would make their life interesting? Are we to smart for it for sixty or seventy years because they got an idea that it must be so delightful to have a little baby, and perhaps into the bargain they suffered from the delusion that they were fitted to bring it up and that they themselves were estimable people—and may easily have been so according to the standards of their time. They were fond of us, naturally; we were provided in order that they might indulge in the pleasure of having children—and when their pleasure in us is a thing of the past we have to adjust ourselves to the world as they have organized it—see what we can make of the data they have provided, no matter how impossible and disgusting we may find them. Voluntary fatherhood and voluntary motherhood have thus been practicable—but what is to be done to preclude involuntary childhood? Well, I've heard many argue like that, and at any rate it's consistent. And I suppose that's just what the sin consists in—starting people on a line of rails that must end in the suicide rock, if they follow it the whole way."

"Just so, Ciss", said the doctor. "That is, if one looks upon the suicide rock as such a terrible thing."

"*I* do, you may be sure. But if I belonged to *your* confession," she said defiantly, "I expect I should consider it mere sentimentality to have any prejudice against it. Merely one more instance of people rejecting the demands a religion makes on them, long before they renounce the consolations it offers them."

"You strike me as pretty cynical, my girl—at any rate for one brought up in an English convent."

"I don't know about that. At all events Mother Anselma taught us that all religions are views of life—the more perfect they are, the more consistently they determine one's notions about all phenomena that crop up. Your faith is not my faith—but that doesn't prevent my understanding your co-religionists when they draw conclusions according to the doctrines they learnt as children?"

"And what about you, Ida Elisabeth?" asked the doctor.

"Me?" She scoffed. "I confine myself to doing what I have to do and feeling what I can't help feeling. Perhaps that's why Fröken Oxley's god punishes me. 'The children', you said just now, Doctor Sommervold. Isn't it strange, I too find it so hard to get used to—that I can no longer

speak of my children in the plural. Last summer I kept thinking to myself, three children, no, God knows how I'm going
to provide for three. And then the question was settled for
me. Do you believe it was done to help me, Ciss, or to
punish me?"

Ciss turned very red:

"If *we* believed that all misfortunes were punishment, we
could not keep festivals to commemorate an apostle being
beheaded or some young wives having their children taken
from them and thrown to wild beasts—or missionaries being
crucified or roasted alive and all the work of their lives wiped
out by fire and murder."

"Here comes Frithjof." Ida Elisabeth jumped up. "Now
you'll hear the whole story of the accident, Doctor Sommervold. But I must go and relieve Olise—she was to do
some mangling for me this morning—"

DOCTOR SOMMERVOLD examined Frithjof thoroughly before
leaving. There was nothing in the world that he could find
wrong, either in his knee or in his arm. "It's a bad job that
that big strong fellow should hang about here and not find
anything to do", said the doctor as he was saying good-bye.

"There's not much chance of his getting anything round
here", said Ida Elisabeth resignedly.

"No. But if one could get a situation for him somewhere else—do you think he would accept it?"

"I'm sure I don't know."

ON Christmas Eve the day was stormy and thick with snow.
According to the time-table the steamer ought to have called
at Berfjord at nine in the morning. As she had not yet
appeared by midday Ida Elisabeth suggested that perhaps
they would have to stay at home.

"No, I say! When they're expecting us—and Christmas
Eve's such an occasion at home—mamma always makes such
a lot of preparations. Here we have nothing—"

"I've made some cakes, you know." She looked about the room, which she had cleared up, covering some of the piles of shop-goods with an old rug and a new plush carpet from her stock. But it had no very festive appearance, and their suitcases stood ready packed on the table. "And I have some pickled pork and trotters too—I dare say they're still rather fresh, but—"

"No, that won't do—we'll celebrate Christmas Eve properly as I've always been accustomed to. With roast pork and sausages and a Christmas tree—poor Kalleman, last year he was in hospital, and isn't he to have a proper Christmas Eve this year either?"

About two o'clock the boat came in to Berfjord. She took nearly four hours to reach Vallerviken, and Kalleman was miserably seasick, fretting and whimpering and screaming aloud with impatience when the boat fairly stood on her head. There were two others in the ladies' cabin, and they were also seasick—a half-grown girl who had been at an eye clinic in town and her sister who had been to fetch her. They came from an upland farm fourteen miles above Vetteland.

The shreds of snow whirled about the lamps on the quay, streaking the light, as Ida Elisabeth came on deck with the boy in her arms. Everywhere in the darkness there were white gleams of surf and spray which filled the air with a roar and a hiss, there was a howling and clattering and creaking—the gangway heaved up and down and skidded this way and that on the edge of the quay—and there came father-in-law; the water was pouring from his oilskins, his face shone red and wet:

"Christmas weather, what! I couldn't get a horse, worse luck—but it isn't so far, you'll manage it all right!"

In fine weather one could reach Vettehaugen comfortably in twenty minutes, but in this storm and darkness! Heavens, if only it doesn't make Kalleman ill, thought Ida Elisabeth.

The two little girls stood just inside the cabin door talking to the mate—nobody had come to meet them, there must be a misunderstanding. They were terribly exhausted by the long voyage; the one who had had the operation was crying. Jens Braatö rushed up to hear what was the matter. The girls knew some people here, but it was a long way to walk, along the shore.

"I think you'd better come home with me", Jens Braatö decided. "Oh yes, mamma will manage to put you up, you're very welcome. We'll have to put your luggage in the shed till tomorrow—just for one night you'll have to make shift with a rather casual toilet."

Of course there was no stopping it. Ida Elisabeth had her Christmas present for Kalleman in her suit-case, a couple of flowered plates with a mug to match and Sölvi's christening spoon and fork. In this way she had counted on having an excuse for washing up the child's things herself.

In the darkness around there were glimpses of lights which seemed to be blinking, as the storm-tossed trees and the driving snow swept past the lighted windows of houses along the road. Jens Braatö stamped along in front, carrying the boy, the two strange girls kept just behind him, and then came Ida Elisabeth; she had to take Frithjof's arm so as not to be blown over, for there was ice under the snow and it was driving so fast that she could scarcely keep her eyes open. She got simply buried in snow, and then it began to melt and trickle down her neck—and her coat was very thin. Frithjof's big, solid body against which she leaned made her feel like a dishevelled crow at the mercy of the weather, and she was so nervous about the boy.

It was even harder to scramble along when they came into the open fields, but at last they reached the forest, where the road ran across the little promontory and there was some shelter. Ida Elisabeth slipped again and again and Frithjof held her up, but once they both came down, and through the darkness she had a glimpse of the two girls sprawling on the ground in front of them—the roar of the forest made it impossible to hear anything.

At last the road began to go downhill, but that made it even worse to keep one's feet on the slippery surface. Inland here the wind was far less felt; the roar of the fjord had a different sound, wave followed wave thundering on the long sandy beach of the bay, and through the darkness and the howling of the wind they heard the drone of the waterfall, and now they could make out the lights of Vettehaugen.

It was surely good to get under a roof and be met by warmth and light and to hear the front door shut out the roar of the stormy night, which had boomed right through her head for so long. A rich smell of cooking and the sound of frizzling meat accompanied her mother-in-law as she dashed out from the kitchen, flushed by the fire and full of welcomes and attentions—Else and Jarngerd were sent to look for dry stockings, slippers, and shoes; "You're not so very wet, are you?"—she felt Ida Elisabeth's arms and back; "it'll dry so quickly, all these candles give such warmth—mustn't take cold, Lisken dear"—and then she flew on to the two strange girls. They were very welcome—all were welcome here, at all times.

And here it was delightful. The low-ceilinged dining-room was full of mellow golden light and soft shadows from little living flames; slender tallow candles stood in brass candlesticks and iron clips on wooden feet all down the long table: "Without them it wouldn't feel like Christmas to me", said Fru Borghild. "Jens insists on tallow candles for the Christmas table, for that's what they always had at his grandparents' at Vetteland. And green in every nook and corner, that's what *I* insist on." There were sprigs of heather and fir round all the picture-frames and behind the mirror. Kalleman kept looking about him with bright eyes that reflected the lights; he was too overwhelmed to utter a sound.

It was festive too in a way to see so many faces round the table; they looked so well in this light. Merete was quite charming with her glossy reddish plaits hanging forward over her bosom. On the whole she was the best-looking of them all, not so fleshy as her brothers and sisters; her eyes were more open and her hair was darker and softer. She must have been about eighteen now, little Merete—

And it was lovely to get something to eat. They ate the roast pork with solemn enjoyment and said very little while so engaged. And afterwards it was good to feel satisfied. Ida Elisabeth got rather sleepy; her cheeks were burning so from the weather. When Else came in with the coffee-tray Ida Elisabeth found that she must actually have taken a little nap.

Then the girls cleared the table, and the little boys, Vikarr and Geirmund, grew restless with impatience before the closed door of the drawing-room. But at last the signal came—a long-drawn violin note from within. The boys flung themselves at the door, burst it wide open, and there stood the Christmas tree beaming and glittering and Jens Braatö in the gleam of the candles with the fiddle under his chin: "In heaven, in heaven—" It was an old folk-tune he was playing, and meanwhile all the others stole away and sat quietly round the room—till Jens Braatö laid aside his violin and bow, took the huge old Bible and opened the brass clasps.

Ida Elisabeth remembered, two years ago, how impossible it had been to keep Sölvi quiet while Bebbe was reading the Christmas Gospel. Kalleman lay with his head against her breast—on looking down at him she discovered that he was asleep.

So she did not move when Jens Braatö took up his fiddle again and her mother-in-law sat down at the piano. The others formed a ring about the Christmas tree. Borghild Braatö struck a chord; the violin led off, clear and full, and they all joined in, singing: "Ring out, ye bells, ring out before the dawn—"

But after the first verse Borghild Braatö broke off, jumped up, and came to her: "You must come too, Lisken dear— and Kalleman—come along"—she gave Ida Elisabeth a rapid, affectionate kiss on the cheek. "It's Christmas, you know!" Ida Elisabeth mumbled in confusion, the slippers—they were too big for her—and her mother-in-law burst out laughing, in happy relief: "Nonsense! We take things as they come here!"

She broke the chain between Frithjof and Helga, the elder of the strange girls, put Kalleman's hand into his father's, hooked his mother in on the other side: "There! Now Kalleman can dance round the Christmas tree between his mamma and his papa—" With a happy smile all over her face she turned back to the piano, and the music began again.

IT was late before they got through the whole program, for at Vettehaugen every Christmas Eve had to be celebrated in the same fashion and nothing could be left out. The parents played and the children sang all the Christmas hymns, and then came Cutting the Oats and The Juniper Bush and the other games, and then the dancing ballads. After that came the distribution of presents, and Christmas sweets, and finally the Christmas supper with pickled pork and salt meat and home-brewed temperance beer—but then Borghild Braatö, outside the usual order, had to arrange sleeping accommodation for her two unexpected guests.

It was decided that they should sleep together in one bed up in the little girls' room. And Borghild Braatö brought a pile of bedclothes and sheets down into the drawing-room and made up a bed on the sofa—Merete was to sleep there tonight.

The room was nearly dark now, only the piano candles were alight and there was a cosy smell of snuffed wicks and spruce. Ida Elisabeth was half asleep in the rocking-chair by the window. Outside the wind roared round the house, now and again the snow hissed against the panes, though the storm had subsided a good deal. Jens Braatö was saying that if it was fine tomorrow and no one came for Helga and Lovise, he would borrow the sledge from Teie and drive the girls home; it would be a grand drive, there was room for six anyhow, and Kalleman.

She had had great trouble in getting him to bed—the boy was fearfully overtired and howled at having to sleep in his underclothes, he *would* have his combination. And she had helped Jarngerd with the washing up. Now she was tired. But it had certainly been a jolly Christmas Eve, and they *were* sweet, in their cheerful happy-go-lucky way, and it was wonderful how her father-in-law could go on playing like that all through the evening. And then she was glad they had not said a word about *that*—Frithjof had been so taken up with everything else that he hadn't even mentioned her.

Little Merete came in, undressed in the corner, and slipped into bed. The Christmas tree was moved to one side, so that its branches overhung the foot of the sofa.

"Are you comfortable, my treasure?" asked her mother, as she came in with a jingling tray of glasses and a bottle. This was Frithjof's present to his father, a bottle of port that had been given him by a commercial traveller a few days before.

"Oh yes, mamma, it's lovely and comfortable—"

"Don't sit over there, Lisken dear, I'm afraid you're in a draught"—her mother-in-law lighted the old blue moonlight lamp and arranged the glasses on the table; "come and take a glass of wine, it'll do you nothing but good."

The house was still—the tramping and clatter from the rooms above died away in a few last pattering footsteps and muffled thuds; the roar of the forest and of the sea outside grew so plain; a gust of wind struck the walls, making them creak, and went howling on. Only the parents, the son, and his wife were still up, seated round the table.

"Mamma, mayn't I have a little wine too?" asked Merete from the sofa.

"It can't do her any harm", said Frithjof. "Do give her a glass, mamma."

The Braatös had been abstainers for many years; Fru Borghild was still a member of the Lodge, but Jens Braatö had taken his name off on coming to the conclusion that the ideal was not total abstinence and prohibition, but ceremonious drinking. "Such as our people practised in former times. Then every farm had brandy in the house, but not that they touched the bottle—it was allowed to stand in the cupboard for months at a time. But if a guest came to the house, the bottle was brought out, and the dram glass and the sugar bowl! A dram, and a lump of sugar, and then another dram, for the other leg—in handsome and ceremonious fashion, let me tell you! And a drink for all hands when anything extra was called for, a tough job on sea or land, to put life into a tired and frozen body. Teetotal all the rest of the year— but at merry-makings and funerals, hey, hey; well, I'll go so far as to say this: hanged if I think it such a terrible thing if they did take a drop too much when it *was* to be a festive occasion—those fellows who *never* abused alcohol in the ordinary way. But now—Lord save us, what a state of things— illicit sale and smuggled liquor and pocket pistols that they swig at as soon as they're round the corner . . . But of course, if Borghild thinks differently I respect her opinion; I ask to be let alone with *my* convictions, but I respect *everybody's* convictions when they're sincere—"

He enjoyed his little glass of port in a way that was quite touching to see. Poor man, he was indeed as temperate as could be—but how he relished it when he had a chance of preaching like this, as he sucked up his wine in blissful little sips—

Oh, dear me, I am fond of them after all, thought Ida Elisabeth; they're somehow so innocent—middle-aged, without a penny, battered in the rough-and-tumble of life; grown-up they have never been. And I am without a penny, battered by life, because I never had a chance of being really a child. But this evening at any rate we've had a good time— and even that is no small thing.

Jens Braatö divided what was left in the bottle among her glass and Frithjof's and his own: "I'm sure mamma's tired—and I dare say you are too—so here's a happy Christmas, right up to Easter"—he kissed his wife: "that's for *you*—instead of the drink!"

It was nearly two o'clock—Ida Elisabeth was reeling with tiredness when she got up and tried to stand on her feet.

With their arms about one another's shoulders her parents-in-law had gone to the sofa, where little Merete was asleep under the Christmas tree. Borghild Braatö beckoned to the young couple.

"Isn't she *charming*?" she whispered with emotion. Merete lay with her cheek buried in the pillow and her thick plaits lying like chains over the delicate curve of her shoulders. "Our sweet, lovely child, papa!"

Ida Elisabeth and her husband stood waiting rather sheepishly while the older couple leaned in adoration over the young girl, who looked in her sleep like a Christmas angel. Then Borghild Braatö turned and embraced them both.

"Oh, my poor little Lisken!" She kissed her warmly on the cheek. "But you mustn't forget—yes, it makes me think of those lovely words of Grundtvig's:

"But two who love one another
Can heal the deepest wounds
Just by a glance that is mutual
And stroking each other's hair."

"That isn't Grundtvig, mamma, it's someone quite different—I believe it's—"

"Well, well, but it may be just as true for all that", Fru Borghild replied quickly, a little piqued; "oh, it is so true, so true! It *is so* true, Lisken dear!" She kissed first her and then her son. "And now I think we must go to rest. Happy Christmas once more, my dear children—"

THE day after Christmas they always went to a party at Teie.

There were only the family from Vettehaugen, but they were nine strong, and then the Meislings—the engineer and his wife and Ciss and Sunniva and the two eldest boys, who had now arrived at the dinner-jacket age. That was already a big party.

Ida Elisabeth felt hopelessly out of it. She had smartened up her old blue georgette, but not succeeded very well with it; it was *too* old now. And Fru Meisling and her daughters in reality were not so fearfully stylish, but they gave that impression. Fru Meisling was really almost ugly, with a little wrinkled face and prominent teeth, but she appeared elegant, always in black. The daughters looked as if they had stepped straight out of an English magazine, with fair bobbed hair framing their healthy faces, and pale green evening frocks cut far too low. For once Ida Elisabeth agreed with her mother-in-law, though she made no reply when the other remarked on the Meisling girls' naked backs.

But the food and the wine were excellent, of course. Jens Braatö gave his little lecture on "drinking culture" and seemed to be having the time of his life.

Ciss Oxley acted the part of hostess more or less and had on a perfectly lovely dress of steel-grey chiffon velvet. It occurred to Ida Elisabeth—surely that old buffer, Lars Sommervold, could never be casting his eyes on Cecilie Oxley now? If she had taken him at his word that time last summer, perhaps she might have been the mistress of this house. Not that she had any regrets; not for a moment had she thought of taking his proposal seriously. But that he had never so much as hinted at it since, that gave her after all a slight feeling of disappointment. Her father had told her that in Spain it was the custom, when a guest praised one's house or anything in it, to say: everything I have is yours. But one had to beware of taking them at their word. Perhaps there was something of the same sort in Doctor Sommervold.

They sat about in the big drawing-room with their sticky liqueur glasses in front of them and the last cold drops of coffee in their cups; Fru Meisling was at the grand piano in the middle of an endless sonata—when Doctor Sommervold came across to Frithjof.

"I should like to have a few words with you—if you'll kindly come into my room." Frithjof looked up in alarm, but rose and went with the doctor. Whenever anybody said he wanted to have a word with him he put on that air of exaggerated jauntiness, as though he expected to be called over the coals for something he had done wrong and was getting ready to act surprised.

But after a minute or two the doctor returned:

"If you can spare a moment, Ida—there's something we'd like to discuss with you."

Well, she too expected nothing but unpleasantness ... In the consulting-room Frithjof was seated in the patient's chair—his face was perfectly slack and stupid, but as she entered he straightened himself, took a pull at his cigar, and looked business-like.

"The thing is, Lisken, I've been offered a situation, through Doctor Sommervold—and so we'd like to hear what you think—"

It was a place as chauffeur at a big private clinic outside Bergen. The wages were a hundred and sixty crowns a month with free lodging, light, and heating, "but there's this in it: the doctor thinks I should have to be there alone for the present; you couldn't give up your business that you've taken so much trouble to work up—it would be dropping a safe thing for an uncertainty—"

"You needn't ask—I think you ought to be very glad!" She saw that he must have been hoping she would raise objections. "In times like these, to be offered such a good job! And a permanent situation too—!"

He *should* take it—she had made up her mind to that the moment she heard what it was. And the more she became aware that both Frithjof and his parents would rather he were let off, the more irrevocable was her determination that he should take it.

They discussed the matter at great length on returning to Vettehaugen the same evening. Jens Braatö had fastened upon a clause in the letter about a uniform allowance: "You know how cordially I have detested uniforms all my life! At bottom they're nothing but a sign that a man is pledged to obey the commands of another person—the sign of a free man's abasement. Thank God, poor I have been all my life, but a free man—my own master, and I must say I don't like the idea of my son being forced to accept orders."

Is it better to be forced to accept help? thought Ida Elisabeth defiantly. Too proud to take orders, but not too proud to be clothed by one's wife or to accept one's friends' signatures on bits of paper. But she said nothing.

"And then this again! It isn't even a uniform properly speaking; it's a livery, nothing less. One couldn't imagine a position that was less free!"

"Oh, but really, father, it's necessary in a hospital—they must have people who can carry out the orders of those in charge. It's the same on board a boat for that matter, or on a farm—or anywhere—"

"Of course, of course, there must be someone in charge; but it must all be based on voluntary, intelligent co-operation—"

"Frithjof must be intelligent enough to see that he ought to co-operate with me in providing for us all." She was herself dismayed at having spoken her mind to *this* extent.

But now her mother-in-law took her up:

"It's just *there*, dearest Lisa, that I think you're so mistaken. I *don't* believe there'd be anything gained if you're to have two establishments—even if Frithjof lets one of his rooms to the porter and arranges to board there. There are so many other things, you see, in a town. Money flies . . . Oh, my dear little Lisken, it's *not* so important whether one has a little more or a little less to live on; the great thing is affection, that the children may feel surrounded by the warm, secure, loving atmosphere of the home. *Think* of what difficulties Jens and I have been in many a time; well, you have no idea ... But I really ask you: *have* you ever seen a happier, more harmonious home than ours?"

"No ..." She admitted it. But *I* am different. And perhaps you have been happy because you are as you are, and because there are others who are different.

"Well, there you see!" said Borghild Braatö radiantly. "No—keep together, my dear children. Hitherto you have never been in *want*, I know. And it's very likely that Frithjof may get something to do here—in the herring season, for instance—"

NEXT morning—they were to go home by the boat that afternoon—her mother-in-law came and confided to her the truth about Merete. She wept a good deal as she told it. She had not mentioned it before for fear of spoiling their Christmas.

"But I'm wondering how many of us will meet together here next year, when the Christmas bells are ringing! Herjulf is gone already, over two years, and he's so little given to writing, you know. Else is to go to Oslo, and Jarngerd to Gitta's, and now we have to send little Merete away from us in this way. And if Frithjof is to leave home too ... Oh God, Lisken, can't you understand what it feels like to me who have been used to having all my flock of children around me—and now at a blow to be stripped of half my earthly treasures—"

"Well but, mother, nobody can expect to keep her grown-up children at home for ever, just for the pleasure they give her. Some day they too must be given a chance of taking responsibilities." You ought to know what it is to lose them while they are still so small that one has the right to give them all and to be all to them ...

"Oh yes, indeed." Borghild Braatö dried her eyes. "That's just the point, responsibility—it seems to me you'll be taking upon yourself a great responsibility if you let go of Frithjof in this way. Remember how young he is, and so good-looking—I'm sure he doesn't mean any harm, but you know yourself how attractive he's always been to the ladies, ever since he was a child. And in a way he's still so impulsive and boyish. And accustomed to a married life. You understand what I mean?" She saw that her daughter-in-law had turned deep red. "Oh but, my dearest Lisken, that is just what is natural and beautiful in life, that we were born to be so to each other. And that is just why we women must guard the sacred flame, lest our men be driven to form unseemly and immoral relations—*that* is all I wanted you to understand. You must not jeopardize the happiness of you both."

He *shall* go. If he can make up his mind to stick to his place and attend to his work, I shall be ready to join him—I can sell the business; I can take up dressmaking or something in Bergen. Even if we are more pinched than we are now, I shall be content. If only I can see Frithjof at work.

It was useless to let oneself be so upset by her mother-in-law's words. If she had thought she must try to make the best of a state of things in which she had gotten herself mixed up—it would never occur to these people that perhaps she did not feel comfortable in her position. By making the best of things she meant that she would have to provide as best she could for the people with whom she had become entangled, that she must restrain herself and avoid scenes, refrain from saying disagreeable things to them except on the few occasions when there seemed to be a hope that they might be of some use. A sort of kindly feeling she had for them too, though she did not like them. And her mother-in-law thought—sometimes, at any rate— that she was a good wife for Frithjof. But then of course she could only imagine that this was because she loved Frithjof. Her mother-in-law took it for granted that they loved one another. And Frithjof believed the same.

Loved ... It made her wild in her heart of hearts when she recalled that once, long ago, she must really have loved Frithjof. Incredible as it might seem now, ashamed as she was to think of it—once she had really been happy as she lay in his arms. She had been ardent and unrestrained when his behaviour showed her that he still felt they were on forbidden ground even after they were married—she wanted to make him feel safe, to strengthen his proper pride. My dear boy, you're a man now—

It was intolerable to remember this now—in between was the time when she had to learn little by little that all day long he would insist on remaining her irresponsible, immature, well-fed, chattering boy, always full of self-confidence, entirely lacking in pride.

And he never even discovered that there was any difference. Now and again no doubt he had a sort of vague feeling that she received his caresses—well, not exactly as in their newly married days. But he comforted himself with the reflection that after all they were not newly married, it was reasonable enough that she should be rather tired at times, she had so much to attend to. But it did not occur to him that it made any essential difference in their relations, whether he had her because she wished to bind herself to him, or because she had bound herself to him once for all, and, as her father had been in the habit of saying, what one has signed in one's cups one must abide by when sober.

Chapter Seven

IDA ELISABETH KEPT a stiff upper lip—parried all the objections raised by Frithjof and the old people, pictured to Frithjof all the joys and advantages of town life. When he had properly settled down to the life of the hospital and she had found someone to take over her business, she and the boy would join him—she discovered with a bright gleam of surprise that it was actually *true*: she did look forward quite hopefully to a change of this sort. In town there would surely be no one who would care to discuss their affairs—a chauffeur and his wife who did dressmaking. Perhaps it meant descending in the social scale, as her parents-in-law called it, and to begin with at any rate they would scarcely be better off financially. But it would put an end to what had disgraced them both so long—that he lived by living with a wife, and that she was the wife of such a man.

It was true that until this day Frithjof had never shown that he was in any way embarrassed by it. But even if his nature was such that he would never of his own accord have gone to look for anything to do, but on the contrary tried with all his might to avoid anything that looked troublesome, it was not impossible that he might learn to like it, when once he had been thrust into the ranks of men who *were* something. Perhaps he would come to feel a certain pride in himself—and he had always been more interested in cars and motoring talk than in anything else. True, he was also expected to do some work in the garden, when he had time—he liked that less, but they could surely arrange so that she helped him with it. Oh—it would be all right—it *must* be . . .

She got his clothes ready, and it seemed as if Frithjof gathered courage to face the wide world in proportion as he saw the piles of shirts and underclothes and stockings growing on the sitting-room table. He handled them and examined the little woven marks with an F. B. in red which she had sewed on every garment.

She would really have preferred to have made the journey with him, to see what sort of quarters he was to have. But she could not possibly afford it. All the same she was in a good humour on the calm winter afternoon when she stood on the pier and waved as the boat stood out towards the rust-red skerries in the frost fog—leaving behind her a thick, sluggish trail of smoke which was mirrored in black on the grey sea.

THE house was very quiet after he had gone.

Kalleman was not at all good at staying out of doors. Now and again of course there were spells of bad weather, when she was obliged to keep him in. But if there were only one or two degrees of frost he was back at the door almost as soon as she had put on his things and let him out: "Mamma, I'm so cold." He never cried, but he had such a fearfully troubled look. Even when she took him to join a crowd of other children, he slipped out of their games at once, just stood there—

At times it made her rebelliously impatient—that she could never have time to take him out for walks! Just once during the winter they had been for a walk together over the bridge and up along the river—the Sunday after Frithjof left. It was a cold day, but he had said nothing about feeling it; he had been too busy talking and asking questions—and he had had such a lovely colour in his cheeks when they came back.

But she could only be glad that the shop gave her so much to do. It was wanted badly enough. Merete had to have a quantity of new underclothes before she went to the sanatorium, and Else and Jarngerd required all sorts of things before leaving home. For all this she received nothing in cash; her mother-in-law promised her a ham and butter and fish. Sometimes Ida Elisabeth could scarcely see how she was going to meet her own outgoings.

As a Christmas present for Kalleman Jens Braatö had made a little table and chair, and he was allowed to have them in the shop, half hidden behind the counter, now that his mother had to keep him indoors so much. He sat as quiet as a mouse, if she just gave him pencil and paper.

His drawings looked like mere scribbles, but no doubt they meant something to him. He made some long thin sausages with a sort of fringe at the lower end, and they were supposed to be people: *that* was mammas and papas and children, he explained, and *that* was the men standing on the pier when the steamer came, and *that* was two who were angry with each other. One day he had drawn a round and filled it in with black shading. What was that meant for? asked Ida Elisabeth. Carl looked up, whispered in a strange, frightened tone, "That's when they're buried—" and quickly pushed the paper away.

FOR Easter she bought the boy a box of coloured pencils. On the Sunday it rained in torrents, so they sat in the kitchen after she had cleared away the breakfast things. That was the only room Ida Elisabeth had been able to make at all pretty. She liked the fresh yellow colour of the walls, and for Easter she had made herself new kitchen curtains from a remnant of cotton voile with little green flowers on it. Olise had polished the tinware for her, and she had arranged the plates and cups according to their colour, and had put red checked cloths on the table and dresser. She felt a certain comfort now in sitting here—the window-box of chives and parsley was so fresh and green. She felt inclined to sit awhile and simply enjoy her ease—not start on anything useful just yet. If only she had had an amusing book, she thought, and a piece of chocolate—

"Mamma—can't *you* draw?" the boy asked all at once.

"I used to be able to draw a little—when I was a little girl."

"Can't you draw now?"

"I don't know, Carl—it's so many years since I tried."

The boy came and put his drawing things into her lap: "Oh, do try, mamma—I expect you can!"

She had tacked together a sort of drawing-book for him of packing-paper in different colours. And she had a sudden impulse to draw with the white pencil on brown paper— the rough side. Birds she had been specially good at drawing when she was a child.

"What's that going to be?" asked the boy eagerly; he was leaning over the table opposite her.

"A pigeon—it's supposed to be—" The first one was not very good, but her fingers seemed to remember as she went on—how she had done it when she drew them facing her and from the side and from below as they fluttered and flew, and a dovecot, and the roof of a house with a dormer window and the face of a girl looking out and green trees behind—

When she had once started it was such fun that it was almost impossible to stop. "And now with *this* one!" Carl begged her, holding out the violet pencil. Ida Elisabeth turned over the pages and drew on the light blue paper, a mountain and water below it and a little steamboat under the cliff, and took up the white pencil again and put in some white streaks on the top of the mountain: "That's snow, Carl." The boy's warm breath came against her forehead; his eyes were nearly starting out of his head; he was so absorbed that he could only utter a breathless word now and then—as she drew baskets of flowers and two kids butting and children with a skipping-rope and three ladies sitting on a bench and putting their heads together, which made Kalleman burst into a little laugh of delight—

Afterwards she wondered to herself—why it had never occurred to her to draw for her children. But on thinking of Frithjof she felt a sudden repugnance: she could not have done it even now if he had been at home—why, she did not know, but so it was.

It led to her drawing for Kalleman fairly often after this—if he saw that his mother had a moment's leisure in the evening he came at once and asked her to draw. And it was funny to see how obviously it reappeared in his scribblings—he was trying to copy what his mother had drawn for him.

FRITHJOF had never been much of a correspondent, so his letters were infrequent and there was not a great deal in them. But he seemed to be in fairly good spirits. He told her about the new clothes he had bought himself—a blue suit, a spring overcoat, shoes with raw rubber soles. Well, he wanted them, poor fellow. But one day there arrived a vacuum cleaner and a letter from Frithjof—he had bought it for her on the instalment plan. She wished he had sent home a little money instead—she was so desperately hard up for cash. The food which her mother-in-law had sent came in very handy, but she was everlastingly short of ready money—for the wholesale people in the first place, and then there was lighting and taxes and Olise's wages on the days she came to help. Milk and bread and a little sugar she had to buy—a few other groceries too; she and the boy could not live entirely on ham and butter from Vettehaugen. She took her eggs to the store, but the price was so low that her fowls scarcely paid for their own food. She had put off buying shoes for herself again and again and it looked as if she would have to put it off for a long time yet; to provide Kalleman with new foot-gear she had been obliged to draw something from his savings-bank account.

The vacuum cleaner might have been a good enough thing to have, especially for cleaning the shop—if Frithjof kept up his payments on it, but she doubted whether he would meet the instalments regularly, and it was more than she could do.

It was hopeless to think of getting rid of the business now. There were indeed two women who would be very glad to take it over, but the cash payment they could offer was so insignificant; she dared not risk any of the proposals they made her.

But by this time she was used to money troubles—as one gets used to a chronic illness. And in spite of all she was happier and easier in her mind than she had been for a very long time—felt that after all she was a young and healthy woman. In the evenings when she was working in the garden or sitting at supper with the boy and listening to his chatter, it sometimes happened that all her anxieties sank below the horizon as it were for hours at a time. Carl, she usually called him now—in her heart she had always thought Kalleman a nasty sticky name for the child, but it was Frithjof who had put it on him; actually no doubt it was due to the grandparents; it was the Vettehaugen way to have all these pet names. She had never been able to bear their calling her Lisken either; nobody else had ever done so.

She did not see much of them that summer. When the weather was fine she went for a walk with Kalleman almost every evening after closing time—up the bank of the river, along the beach to Vestnæs, or by the roads inland. She was more inclined to stop and talk to people they met. "He's grown finely this spring", they said of Carl, and, "How well you're looking, Fru Braatö." She was more willing to chat with her customers and laugh at what they told her—subconsciously she assumed that there was no longer much to be said about her own life; it did not occur to her that the summer visitors discussed Frithjof's absence and what it might signify.

Sometimes she was invited upstairs to the Esbjörnsens' for coffee on Sunday afternoon, and occasionally she looked in on Marit to see her flowers. She was given some cuttings of her fuchsias and a little Louis Philippe which was already in flower.

Carl was not nearly so good at letting himself be put to bed without protest that summer—at times she had to be downright severe with him. And when at last she had got him into his combination he would try to escape—he hopped away with little unpractised skips and feeble, tentative screams of wildness. His mother caught him, took him up in her arms, and carried him to his bed:

"There, that's enough for today—now you'll lie down like a good boy and go to sleep! My boy, my boy, my little, little boy—" She hugged him to her and kissed him, with eyes tightly closed to keep back the tears. The thought of Sölvi was always close at hand; it followed her like a little shadow; now it seemed to be just behind her, now at her side. But when she was struggling to get the boy to bed in the evening it seemed as though Sölvi's laughter haunted every corner, and it was inconceivable that the child was not somewhere about the rooms, waiting for her mother to catch her in her turn.

FRITHJOF wrote once in a while, telling of great plans he had in his mind. He had bought a fine violin very cheap, and now he had taken up his music again; next winter he would stand himself some lessons; perhaps he might earn something in that way. Then he proposed to Ida Elisabeth that they should buy a second-hand car, he wanted to start for himself: "Hurry up and get your business sold and come along here; you'll see how finely we'll get on." Some time in the autumn he wrote that he was "brushing up his knowledge of book-keeping and accounts"—a lady whose acquaintance he had made at the hospital had offered to give him some lessons and teach him English too, if he felt inclined.

Ida Elisabeth wrote back and encouraged him to stick to the place he had been lucky enough to get. She laughed at herself as she wrote—the letter was so smugly prudent! She praised his virtuous intentions with regard to the violin and foreign languages—and laughed. Well, well, it had to be done. But now that she had him at a distance it did not hurt her so much that her husband had to be treated like a child, with praise and admonition.

When the firm from whom Frithjof had bought the vacuum cleaner dunned her for overdue instalments she did feel rather annoyed, but still she laughed. For once in a way she rang up Doctor Sommervold: "Don't you really think it's time you had a vacuum cleaner at Teie—?" She got him to take it over and rescued the fifty crowns that had been paid on it for her own shrunken coffers. That evening she bought four cream buns and treated Carl and herself. "Wasn't it lovely—what?"—she gave the boy a smacking kiss on the cheek; it felt round and firm; he had crumbs of cake right up to his eyes. "Your mamma has been extravagant—"

Heavens, yes, that was it, and her extravagance had come to no more than this! She laughed to herself recklessly— half-forgotten memories of her childhood floated through her mind: a palm court in Copenhagen where she had had tea with her father; Langelinje, and round the shops with her mother—she had been given a ball dress entirely of Irish lace and a nutria coat and tortoise-shell brushes with a coronet and monogram and coat of arms in gold, things that had been sold by war refugees, no doubt. And at the hotel where they stayed the bath belonging to her room had looked like marble ... Imagine that once she could have anything she liked to ask for ... Goodness knows how it would have turned out if this magnificence had lasted. She had almost forgotten what it was like—but of course she loved all kinds of luxury at that time. And probably if the truth were told she had a turn both for passion and extravagance—so uncontrollably indignant had she been at all the sickening unpleasantness at home, and so light-headed when she threw herself away on Frithjof. Well, life had managed to catch her and drive her in. Now she thought, almost with a kind of arrogance—it did not matter so very much. If she had been wild as a filly, she felt strong as a horse now; she would be equal to her load, it's fun to pull through ... Four cream buns, it's droll after all to make a dissipation out of as little as that! "Come, Kalleman, mamma's going to do gymnastics with you. Haven't we had fun this evening—?"

ONE day in the course of the autumn her mother-in-law came, bringing with her a big basket of pears: "They're so delicious, Lisken; I felt I *must* bring you some." Borghild Braatö was radiant. No sooner had they reached the kitchen and Ida Elisabeth had put on the kettle for coffee than it burst out of her:

"Oh, my dear Lisa, I'm so happy—I could fall on my knees this moment and thank God; well, I've done so too, you may be sure! Fancy, Merete's engaged! And such a splendid husband she'll have too!"

It was a patient at the tuberculosis sanatorium; Frede Nordbö was his name, and he came from a big farm up in Nordmöre with a store and a mill and everything. And he was such an exceptionally fine character, and handsome and every inch a gentleman, wrote Merete.

Borghild Braatö began to sob quietly:

"You see, little Merete *was* much more seriously attacked than we liked to tell you. Oh, I have been so alarmed about her, Lisken—she has always been so delicate, not nearly so robust as the rest of our children, and then, you know, there was that indescribable air about her, as though she did not really belong to this world. But now I feel so safe, you understand, now that love has touched her God cannot *choose* but let her recover, for God is the God of love, Lisa!"

Ida Elisabeth brought out the coffee-cups. She looked down at the other, who was smiling through her tears—and she refrained from asking whether Merete's sweetheart was also on the road to recovery. And Fru Braatö said nothing about it. She pictured in glowing colours all that Merete would now be able to do for her brothers and sisters: Vikarr would become a businessman, for no doubt he would be able to join his brother-in-law, and Merete could take either Jarngerd or Else into her house, as she was not strong and would need plenty of help: "Oh, you know, in a big place like that there's sure to be work for many people—"

"Help yourself, mother", Ida Elisabeth offered her the plate of ham sandwiches. Again she was overcome by that strange feeling, tenderness and antipathy at the same time. There was indeed something grand in this confident affection for one's own—and this blindness to everything outside one's nest.

"What delicious ham—no, you don't mean to tell me it's the one I sent you? I don't know, Lisken, but everything seems to *taste* so good in your house." Borghild Braatö chatted as she ate: "Well, really at times it's almost as if God meant to heap coals of fire on my head. When I think how unhappy I was last Christmas. And then just that was to mean happiness for Merete; fancy, perhaps we shall have them both home this Christmas! And my Fiffi boy whom I used to be so anxious about—that too has turned out for the best, yes, for you've made him such an excellent wife, Lisken; that's what I always write to him; poor fellow, I'm sure he's longing to get back to his home. But now, thank goodness, he'll be coming for Christmas—"

"Yes, he's hoping to get a week's holiday. But it's a long time till then, you know, and of course something may happen to prevent it." But then she thought it was detestable of her not to be able to refrain from throwing cold water on the other's glowing visions of the glories to come.

Chapter Eight

FRITHJOF DID COME HOME for Christmas. He looked splendid—too fat if anything, but that was a sign that the life agreed with him. It had been an experiment, and apparently it had turned out well. So Ida Elisabeth allowed herself to be infected by his delight at being home again—submitted with a sort of good-humoured sharing of his joy to Frithjof's tripping at her heels wherever she went. He was effusive in his descriptions of the terrible loneliness he had to struggle with in town: "But you've been longing just a little for your husband now and then, haven't you, Lisken? You can't deny that?" He caught her in another violent embrace. She felt how small and slight she was in his arms, had an idea that she must be hard and sharp—she would have to take care she did not grow into a regular catamaran, for there was something in this too-plump, unsuspecting fellow which always roused a protest in her. So she gave a little laugh, as she freed herself: "A little—as you may guess", and tamely accepted his kiss.

It was fine, calm weather that Christmas—a gleam of sun within the fog and a tinge of green over the bare fields, when they arrived at Vettehaugen on the morning of Christmas Eve. Merete and her fiancé could not come, but a big photograph of the couple stood on the Christmas table among candles and heather. The fiancé had a very ordinary, rather good-looking face with an enormous mass of curly hair brushed straight up—and he was so tremendously musical, Borghild Braatö declared. Else too was missing from the Christmas table this year; she had gotten a domestic situation in the neighbourhood of Oslo. But she was more or less forgotten, in all the fuss that was made about her sister.

They went through the whole of the usual Christmas program, but Ida Elisabeth could not succeed in working up any such feeling as she had had the year before. She remembered that then her heart had warmed in spite of all—because there had been something that touched her in these people's affection for one another and their delight and their singing and music with the storm howling about the corners of the house and the snow hissing against the windows—and there was sorrow and anxiety in the hearts of all, which they kept to themselves for the sake of Christmas. This year all the others were in such high spirits that she could not keep up with them: even the little Vikarr boy was already quite solemn, vaunting his dignity as a coming businessman. In reality they were rather to be pitied; if this were to turn out a disappointment . . . But in any case there must be *some* disappointment, and she knew that she would be the one who would have to listen to their complaints, to witness her mother-in-law's tears, which always affected her so terribly, and her father-in-law's innocent, mournful surprise at being disappointed once more. She could not help shuddering in anticipation at the sympathy which she knew would be required of her—in addition, of course, to all the other demands they would make on her.

For the present all she was asked to do was to make new dresses for her mother-in-law and Jarngerd; Borghild Braatö had the material, so it was only a question of the work and the trimmings. But it was always so difficult to find time, and just now her hands were a good deal tied by Frithjof's visit, and she had to make up her books for the year. But they must have the clothes in January, when it was possible that Frede and Merete might come on a visit.

Frithjof spread himself tremendously the days he spent at home with his parents; he boasted of his exploits and talked motoring till all was blue, played the violin to his father too. *That* was a thing of which Jens Braatö ought to have been a judge—but he seemed quite pleased with his son's performances on the fiddle; Frithjof had left it alone for so long, but allowing for that his father thought he had made great progress. Frithjof had also a good deal to say about that lady who had given him some commercial training; he hinted that she was rather gone on him, but of course he didn't care for her in *that* way; she was easy to get on with and very friendly with him, but fairly old and not a bit pretty. Even that did not appear to shock his parents—though it was shabby of him to speak thus of his friend Kamilla Arne. To Ida Elisabeth he had never mentioned her, and she had not cared to ask him about his studies, because, for one reason, she was not so sure that there was any truth in what he had written about them. For that matter, most of what he told his mother and father might easily have been invention.

The house at Teie was closed that Christmas; Doctor Sommervold had gone to his daughter-in-law who was ill—it was believed to be cancer, Borghild Braatö had heard. Nevertheless it almost seemed as if the Vettehaugen people were a little offended at being done out of the Christmas party at Teie this year.

All through the holidays Ida Elisabeth was longing for the return of working days. She had made a great wreath of pine twigs, and she intended to go down to the sexton's and buy some snowdrops or tulips; his wife generally forced some of these for decorating graves. Subconsciously Ida Elisabeth was looking forward to this walk to the churchyard, for there she could be alone, could weep undisturbed and enjoy a brief respite from being unnatural, gentle, and balanced. But Frithjof had seen her go off with the wreath on her arm, and so he came running after. She gave up calling at the sexton's for flowers, and after laying her wreath on the grave she simply stood waiting, while Frithjof looked down at the tangle of frosted grass with a stiff emotional stare: "Our lovely little darling! I feel as if I could scarcely grasp it even now, that she's lying there. Oh, you may be sure I've thought of Sölvi very often, as I sat alone in my room in the evening, in town—"

ON the second day of the new year Frithjof went back. Ida Elisabeth left her stocktaking to see him off. The last few days, since their return from Vettehaugen, she had scarcely had time to talk to him. And now the rush of new year's business was full upon her.

She was a good deal upset on becoming aware of certain sensations in her body which she knew of old. Of course, it might turn out that they did not mean anything—but she had no great hope of it. Well, in that case she would have to take it calmly. For Carl at any rate it might be just as well if he were no longer the only one. The boy's nature was such that he needed her most careful attention; but she often thought it could not be good for him to notice how unremittingly she watched over him. He was terribly fond of her, thank God, and surely it was not possible for a mother to be too fond of her children. It must all depend on the kind of fondness. She herself in her heart of hearts had been so fond of both her father and her mother that she was quite astonished to discover how little her affection for them had suffered from the furious revolt they had excited in her when she saw them destroying themselves. It reminded her of rust on solid iron objects: they may be perfectly red outside and one may be able to knock great flakes off the surface—but this is after all very little in comparison with the massive core which is firm and unaffected. But she would be very unwilling to see her children fond of anyone in that way. Though perhaps that was better than being fond of one's parents as Frithjof and his brothers and sisters were fond of Jens and Borghild; there was not even calculation in their feeling, so little did they think of their parents; they merely clung to them as young birds cling to the nest, so long as they cannot shift for themselves. And they were as fond of their children as anyone could possibly be—it was only the manner of their fondness which must be so utterly crazy. Never do a thing without bearing in mind what was best for the children, but never let them see that they were her constant occupation—something like that ought to be her rule—and then she ought not to make too much of a pet of Carl.

But at present she could not help a certain shrinking of the heart whenever she had a reminder of the new possibility. She needed all her health just now, so as not to have to think of her body; in fact, she needed to be so well that she could put off its claims with the minimum of food and sleep. And an affair of this kind must involve some additional expense, even on the cheapest scale.

At the end of January she had a letter from a lawyer in Sogn. He wrote that it had come to his knowledge that she was thinking of disposing of her business, and in that case he might open negotiations with her on behalf of two elderly ladies, daughters of the former clergyman at Rostesund. If she were willing to consider their offer he would come, if she wished it, to Berfjord for a personal conference.

Ida Elisabeth replied without a moment's delay that in any case she would be glad to hear further particulars; it would be best of course if they could meet and discuss the matter personally. As things stood it was better to realize her plan of joining Frithjof. She would have to put forth her utmost strength in the endeavour to help him, so that he might keep his place. If they both worked for their home they would surely get along, and she would be rid of that feeling of disgrace, which was the worst of all—the feeling that she could neither respect nor rely on the man who was the father of her children.

THE correspondence with the lawyer in Sogn developed on quite promising lines; he held out a prospect that he might visit her at the beginning of March. So she wrote to Frithjof that she now had good hopes of disposing of the business so that she and Carl could join him. She would not say anything at present about the new factor in the situation. It was no use frightening him yet awhile with the prospect of increased responsibility.

A week or so after dispatching this letter she was in the shop measuring long-cloth for a woman from Helle. She heard the back-door open, and a voice—but surely it was Frithjof's—and next moment Carl appeared, ran up to her, and whispered in a frightened voice:

"Mamma, papa's here again—he's sitting on the wood-box—"

"Excuse me", she said to the customer, and to Carl: "Oh, I want you to be quick—put on your things and run up to Olise, ask if she can come here at once." She went out into the kitchen.

There sat Frithjof, leaning forward with his head in his hands, and both his suit-cases stood before him on the floor.

"But good gracious, Frithjof—what is it—are you ill?"

He raised his head, looked up with a woefully tragic air. Then he stood up and came over to her:

"Well, here I am again, Ida Elisabeth!" With that he embraced her. "It's my nerves, you see—and so I couldn't do anything else, I *had* to come home! Oh, Lisken, how I've been longing for you!"

"Well, but take your things off, won't you—and go into the sitting-room, there's a fire there. Excuse me a moment, I'm serving a customer—"

The woman from Helle wanted three yards of stuff for a child's frock too, and Ida Elisabeth took down piece after piece of woollen material: "Something in muslin then, won't that do? Or tartan? The same that Ola Markussen had a piece of for a Christmas present for his twins—oh yes, I remember very well, but I see there's only a small remnant left of it, not quite two yards ... No, that won't be enough—" She felt her heart like a heavy lump in her breast—ugh, what new bother could this be? At last the other finished her shopping, and Ida Elisabeth went back to her husband.

"But to think of your being ill, Frithjof—and you didn't write me a word about it?"

"No, what would have been the good of that—when you couldn't do anything for me? But now I couldn't stand it any longer."

Had he lost his job? But she felt she couldn't ask about that straight away. He must have something to eat first anyhow. It was Wednesday, when they generally had minced meat and sausages at the butcher's. The thought of the red mince lying there in white enamelled bowls made her mouth water; unconsciously she grew more cheerful for having an excuse to buy it. That winter she had only cooked a dinner on the days Olise was there; it took time even to prepare a dish of fish. She gave Carl milk and bread and eggs—it was good food for a child, and he liked it. Poor boy, how glad he would be to get Sunday fare in the middle of the week.

It was impossible to make anything of Frithjof. He said he was ill—suffering from his nerves. No, he hadn't had any accident on the road, none that mattered anyhow, none that he was to blame for—but he felt in himself that his nerves would not stand this everlasting strain any longer. No, he hadn't been to a doctor, and he wouldn't go now either—at any rate not before Doctor Sommervold came back. There was once more only a locum tenens, a new one who knew nothing about him or his family history.

"I must tell you, Ida Elisabeth, I'm not *suited* for town life. I've always felt unsettled everywhere else except at home here on our fjord. I don't feel *happy* in town."

"I've never been asked if I felt happy in Berfjord."

"Well, but you do, don't you? One can't imagine a more beautiful spot, and we know everybody and have father and mother close by, and we've got on quite well up to now—"

The news of Frithjof's return had naturally been carried by the boat to Vallerviken; she might expect one of them to come tearing down at any moment.

"No, I haven't any confidence in a locum—remember how it was with Sölvi! After all it was madness to ask me to take a post as chauffeur just after such an experience. And I'll tell Sommervold so, as soon as I meet him."

"It's not certain that he'll be home before Easter."

Frithjof gave her a hesitating look but said nothing.

"Can't you tell me exactly how it is, Frithjof?" she asked. "Have you lost your place at the clinic?"

At that he flared up and swore solemnly that he had not; his place was kept open if he chose to go back; he had merely gotten leave. The only thing was that it was utterly impossible for them to live together at the hospital, for many reasons.

Perhaps it would be doing an unscrupulous thing, thought Ida Elisabeth, to force him to go back to a comparatively responsible position in the distracted state in which he appeared to be. That is, if he was not play-acting, for her and for himself.

"You didn't say a word about all this when you were home at Christmas", she said despairingly. "Then everything was as rosy as it could possibly be."

"At Christmas! Well, but then I hadn't a notion you were *thinking* of anything of this sort! Breaking up our home and plunging us all into uncertainty—"

"But we were agreed about that the whole time, Frithjof—"

"No! How could I imagine you would act on it in earnest?" His voice had changed to a kind of blubbering: "I don't understand how you can have the heart—destroying our little home where we have been so happy."

It must be that and nothing else, she saw now—consciously or unconsciously he must have counted on always being able to come back here, and he had lost his head altogether when it looked as though her plans of moving were to be taken seriously.

No, indeed it was not easy to know what she ought to do now. She had been in the habit of thinking that at any rate she had one great advantage: there was no one so near to her as to know her thoughts and feelings. Doctor Sommervold was the only one in whom she had confided a little now and then; but afterwards she had always felt rather clammy and washed out, as after an attack of fever. Even when it had resulted in his helping her she had thought the help dearly bought by talking about herself. But now she wished indeed he had been here to consult.

It was Jens Braatö who came out on the third day—mamma was in bed with inflammation of the ear after her cold, he explained. Thank God—well, of course it was horrid to think that, and inflammation of the ear is said to be very painful, but anyhow Ida Elisabeth preferred having her father-in-law to talk to. She was pretty desperate by this time: the only thing she had gotten clear about was that Frithjof had made up his mind he would not on any account go back to Bergen. She almost began to fear—there might be something behind it . . . Had he done something which made him afraid to face—? Well, in that case she would be sure to hear of it soon enough.

While Frithjof talked on and on, his father sat and looked at him with the expression which always disarmed Ida Elisabeth. His light brown eyes were so handsome, and he seemed to be just as much surprised and hurt each time anything went amiss with him. This time she found a kind of backing in her father-in-law—he expressed the opinion, very feebly, it is true, that Frithjof ought to go back to town and at any rate give it one more trial. "Do that, my boy—if you can't manage it we'll find something else, you'll see." But at the same time he thought Ida Elisabeth ought not to give up just yet—that was the expression he used. "I quite see that you may often have been in difficulties—but it *has* succeeded so far; it's not a *bad* business that you have here." "To tell the truth," he said when they were alone for a moment, "I don't believe you'll get Frithjof to go back unless you promise him that you'll keep up your home here for him."

"But what if I won't promise that—?" She dared not sell if it was a fact that Frithjof had already lost his place or guessed that it was only a question of time when he would be given notice. But if she were to stay on here and be burdened with this impossible lout of a man who wouldn't do a hand's turn … Oh, if only there had not been this new arrival in prospect! For the first time in her life she fervently desired—that she might be rid of it.

THE next day was a mail-day, and Frithjof went to fetch the post. As Ida Elisabeth took her letters from him she noticed casually that they had a disgusting smell of scent. There were some bills, a new price list from the firm which supplied her with overalls and the like, and a letter from the lawyer in Sogn. Frithjof stood watching her as she opened her mail.

"Is that the man you've been in correspondence with— about selling?"

She nodded.

"Are you still thinking of that?"

"Certainly I am."

"But father advised you not to—"

"I have a great esteem for your father, Frithjof, in many ways. But not exactly as an adviser in business matters."

Frithjof blinked his eyes a few times. Then he turned and left her.

Soon after, when she went into the kitchen to start the dinner, her eye was caught by a letter in an oblong violet envelope, lying in the middle of the floor. Ida Elisabeth picked it up. It was addressed to Frithjof, and it was responsible for the smell of scent. Ida Elisabeth put it on the dresser, but the stink of it was so penetrating that she moved it outside to the scullery.

Presently Frithjof came in. "You haven't seen a letter, have you?"—his face showed an expression of tense anxiety. "I believe I must have dropped it out of my pocket—"

"It's in the scullery—on the top of the cupboard."

He crossed the kitchen in three leaps and returned with the letter in his hand. "Have you read it—?"

Ida Elisabeth laughed: "Are you crazy—?"

"Oh, thank God", he exclaimed in a loud whisper.

When she came into the sitting-room, after washing up the supper things, she was sitting down to sew. The letter lay on the window ledge by her machine.

"Can't you take care of this letter of yours?" she asked with irritation. "Put it away or burn it, but don't leave it lying all over the place—!"

Frithjof got up hastily from the table, put down the paper—and now he came, took the letter and stood facing her, holding it in his hand. He looked so ridiculous—and suddenly the idea struck her that he had been dangling this envelope in front of her nose to excite her curiosity. Dear, dear, had he made a conquest in town, and did he insist on her hearing of it?

"Oh, I say, would you mind looking after the stove for me—I must finish this tonight."

Frithjof did not move and seemed to be revolving something in his mind.

"You don't ask to see it?" he whispered in a stifled voice.

"No, indeed I don't."

The letter was dropped on the sewing-machine in front of her: "Read." He went back and sank upon the table, burying his head in his arms. "It is best you should know all—!"

She looked at him disapprovingly. Then she picked some sheets of paper out of the envelope:

"*My darling boy!*

"*Now night has come again and I am sitting here alone in the corner of our sofa, so you may well imagine that my thoughts and longings go to you, and I am wondering how you are, my dearest darling."*

"What damned rubbish is all this?" asked Ida Elisabeth, and Frithjof groaned: "Read it, won't you——" So she went on reading:

"You know how eagerly I am waiting for a letter from you. Have you found an opportunity of having a straight talk with your wife, and how did she take your announcement of the resolution you have come to? Of course I understand so well that you shrink from having to say this to her, but then she is a sober and sensible woman of business, at any rate that is the impression I have gathered from all you have told me about her and from her letters, and fortunately the financial side of the question is of no importance to her, as she is entirely independent in that respect, so it must be possible to make her realize that it would be extremely ill-bred of her to refuse to set you free."

She had a strangely cold tingling sensation all over her face as she read. It was sickening, mawkish stuff to have to do with—Ida Elisabeth folded the sheets, looked at the signature: *"Your own Vera, who is longing for you."* But then some words caught her eye at the top of the last sheet:

"be able to understand how unreasonable and vulgar it would be of her to insist on your being bound for life by a marriage which was contracted as the result of a juvenile faux pas. Naturally I understand how painful it must be to you to cause her sorrow, especially after the misfortune of losing your little girl last year, but then she will be able to keep the boy, and as the sexual side is dead between you it would not be even moral if a new and deep and ardent feeling were to be sacrificed on the altar of a marriage which has lost its deepest meaning."

"I see." She put the letter back in its envelope. Her fingers had turned so cold that they trembled. "So you want a divorce. Well, there's nothing to prevent that, you may be sure."

"Yes, but that's just what I don't want!" He screamed aloud. "How can you imagine such a thing! Do you see *now* why it's impossible for you to come and join me? Her sister's in the office there! I *can't* go back there, surely you understand that at last!" He seemed quite hysterical.

"Indeed I do nothing of the sort. On the contrary, I think you have every possible reason for going back as quickly as ever you can—to this Vera!" Ida Elisabeth was about to fling the letter away, but then she checked herself and put it in the pocket of her apron. "I dare say I'd better retain this document."

Frithjof glanced up rapidly. "Are you going to answer her?"

"I?" She laughed. "But by the way, who is this person?"

"Why, it's she who was giving me lessons—Kamilla Arne's her name, but she liked me to call her Vera. But you understand, I never thought it would go so far, I assure you . . . She's much older than I am for one thing, and to begin with she was just sort of motherly, it really never occurred to me that she meant anything of this kind! But you see, I was absolutely alone there, and we sat together in that room of hers every blessed evening, so you can imagine . . . But I won't *have* any more of it, no, God knows I won't. That's why I came home, you understand, after I'd been at home here at Christmas and been with you again and the boy and all of them at home—but then she noticed a change in me . . . Well, then I ran away, Lisken. For I saw that I *must* get out of it, I *wanted* to be out of it, you understand!"

"Well, that must be your affair. But at any rate I too am going to get out of this now."

"God! Ida Elisabeth—what do you mean—I don't understand—"

"Don't you? One thing is that I didn't want—if one has taken the devil on one's back, one has to carry him over the stream, I thought. But if the devil himself does one the kindness to jump down, you don't suppose anyone is going to be so foolish as actually to squat down and beg him to be so good as to get up again? I propose that you take the boat back to town tomorrow and inform your friend Vera that you and she can be married as much as you like, I give you my blessing."

"Ida Elisabeth—you can't mean this—"

"Oh, you great fool—do you believe you've ever known anything of what was in my thoughts?"

He looked up at her, helplessly, from where he sat.

"But, Ida Elisabeth—it's *you* I'm fond of, don't you understand? That other business—why, it's only the sort of thing one's apt to say when one has gotten oneself into a certain kind of situation. You really ought to be able to see that, a sensible woman like you. But you're the only one I'm fond of—"

She looked away and made no answer.

"Ida Elisabeth—we've been so fond of each other always—ever since we were children! Just think of when I was home at Christmas—well, and now too—"

"Be careful!" she said quickly, under her breath.

On looking at him again she saw she had really given him a scare. And at the same moment she recalled fragments that she had read of that letter—details the meaning of which detached itself from the general foggy sense of disgust.

"So she's well posted about our affairs, your new flame ... She knows that you're married and have a child and that we've recently lost a little girl and that I have a business, etcetera. Taking it all round I think Vera has honestly deserved to *get* you—and so she shall, damn it, if I can bring it about. Fond of you!" she said on seeing him cringe. "M'yes, if she's as good as her word and really marries you, I'll wish you joy with all my heart, I shall be pleased if you're happy with her. But then you'll have to buck up and behave decently, or she may get a fright before it comes off and you'll be left!"

Frithjof lay with his face against the table, crying softly.

"Oh—oh—oh—I never thought—you'd take it like this! I felt so sure, so sure that when I'd told you all, you'd help me. I was so certain you were fond of me and would help me out of this mess—"

A sickening fear seized her—that she might allow herself to be borne down, from habit and from all the deposits that their life together had left within her, layer upon layer—if he should go on like this. Weeping and wailing and saying he had relied on her being fond of him and willing to help him—if he were allowed to carry on with this long enough, she did not feel sure of herself, did not know what she might end by doing. For he hadn't even a suspicion of the shabbiness of his conduct. All he thought was undoubtedly that he had been guilty of a trifling infidelity, but now that he had come back and begged her pardon all would be well again. With a sharp pang she saw in a flash—yes, so it might have been if she had had a properly grown-up man for a husband—if there had been that between them which neither could destroy entirely nor blab about to any third person. And in that case she could have felt real sorrow now, could have been made furious by her pain, but would have yielded in the end and tried to continue her life with him, since they belonged to each other after all.

"And then the children, Lisken!" he wailed. "Think of Sölvi—do you remember when we went together to look at her grave, only this Christmas! And Kalleman—you wouldn't separate me and Kalleman, would you?"

She gave a little sigh. No, there *was* nothing to bind them together. Never more would she have to drag him with her, if she wanted to go out to her grave. She would be free to fight for her child without the feeling that she had a heavy log chained to her foot. She would be rid of them now—him and all his crowd—would have her hands free to support what was her own flesh and blood—

"Well, I'm sorry, Frithjof," she said gently; "but there's nothing else for it. As this friend of yours writes, I must naturally be given custody of the boy. And it's sad that it is so, but you've never been up to much as a father. You are not fit to take care of what you have yourself put into the world. And so it's better for Carl too that I be excused having to take care of any others than him."

"How you talk!" He sobbed despairingly. "Didn't I take— may I *ask* you who it was that looked after Sölvi all the time—but I suppose I'm to be blamed for what happened to her. But I tell you, it *wasn't* my fault—" Now his loud falsetto scream had come back again.

"No, no, Frithjof, I know that. You'd better go to bed now", she begged him suddenly, in a low, tired voice. "Oh, do go, please—"

She seemed to see all at once that this was just the awful thing about it. A mother can be both father and mother to her children, and perhaps a man too can be both mother and father, if the worst comes to the worst and he is left alone with them. But when a mother has to take the place of a father while the father hangs about seeming to assume the part of the mother—why, that is simply iniquitous, utterly against the order of nature—there is something in it which seems to threaten all sorts of disasters; it made her think of dissolution and corpses full of breeding corruption.

"Oh, oh, oh", he moaned. "Oh, that doctor—yes, he did me a nice turn when he got me packed off to that clinic! I shan't forget to tell him so too. As far as that goes I know very well it was he who put it into your head that I don't do anything for my children—he's been at me before with that tale, that I don't help you enough to keep the family—"

Ida Elisabeth took her sewing out of the machine, folded it, and put on the lid. "Now you must go to bed", she said quietly.

ALL the same, the last thing he said had given her a shock. There was probably something in it. It made her hot to think of all she had told Doctor Sommervold about herself and Frithjof. People never *can* know enough of others to

157

judge them fairly in what they say and think—this was a conviction that had grown strong in her during all the years in which she grew out of her childhood and saw her parents going to the bad. She had tried as well as she could to conceal her own feelings about all this—it's no concern of others! Folk talk an endless lot of nonsense when they retail all their misunderstandings and scraps of information about other people, putting this and that together and drawing conclusions and feeling sure they know what they only imagine themselves to know. But even Sommervold could not know enough about the relations between her and Frithjof to pass judgment as he did. As a doctor he knew that she was a healthy person who must be responsible for what she did, and that Frithjof was not altogether accountable in this way—there was something in her that rebelled when Sommervold laid all the blame on Frithjof—and as a matter of fact he *had* tried to influence her to cast Frithjof adrift.

But now she was firmly resolved to do so after all. The disgust which now welled up in her washed away everything else—the half-understood suspicions that the lowest stratum of all in what she had felt for Frithjof until this very day was a sympathy with something she saw, though she could not clearly express even to herself what it was she understood. That born and brought up as he was, allowed as he had been to loaf on the outskirts of orderly human life, to accept a rather tolerant sympathy here and to close his eyes to obvious contempt there—that being so, he was condemned to be worsted perpetually, and it only made it more heartrending that he himself saw so little of what awaited him. But now it would have to do, she couldn't manage any more either—he was *too* sickening. The letter rustled and stank in her apron pocket as she went about finding things to do. There was evidently not a thing in the relations between him and her about which he had not talked to this dona of his in town. God, how she would rejoice the day she heard that Vera had married him!

And indeed it was not impossible that Frithjof might take a turn for the better if he had another wife. Her mother-in-law had been fond of saying that the trouble was, Frithjof had too many children by her. That there were so many for whom properly speaking he ought to have provided, that took the heart out of him. Well, he certainly wouldn't have any children by this new wife—she had captured him with motherly airs. And Ida Elisabeth knew this much, that women who put on motherly airs with grown-up men, younger than themselves into the bargain, don't go and have real live children, if they can anyhow avoid it. Women who feel that their purpose in life is to bear children and rear them as well as they can into full-grown men and women hate and abhor to have grown-up men coming and forcing them to be motherly with them too. When Frithjof had forced her to bestow on him some such feeling as would be normal in the case of a child, it had seemed to her that this must be what is meant by taking the children's bread and casting it to dogs.

Her heart began to beat violently—she knew what the latent thought had been that had murmured and fretted within her these last few days. Now she could simply drop it and forget that she had harboured it. If something had to go overboard, better a person proved to be impossible than a life which still had possibilities.

At last she could hold out no longer—she was *too* tired, and shivering with cold too, relaxed after her excitement, and besides, the fire in the stove had gone out long ago.

Ida Elisabeth paused outside the door of the bedroom. For the first time she felt that poverty can drive one to red-hot fury. Poverty had been a worry, and it had been a struggle, but even the degradation of her life had been bearable, since she had had others to fight for. Now it was a disgrace and an offence which lashed her into flaming indignation. That two people could find themselves in this position, after saying to each other such things as she and the man in there had said this evening, and be forced to remain together under one roof in a narrow little home—and now she had to go in and sleep in the same room with him.

She stole in on tiptoe. The beds stood end to end along one wall—they were two wooden beds that were not a pair, bought at an auction when they came to Berfjord. While Frithjof was away she had slept in his bed, because it was much longer and broader than her own, and Kalleman's bed still stood by the side of it. So she dared not steal up to see if the boy had kicked off his clothes.

As noiselessly as possible she undressed in the dark—listening now and again whether any sound came from Frithjof. But he seemed to be fast asleep. As she got into bed it creaked horribly. And a moment later she heard Frithjof moving.

She lay still and held her breath—had he gone to sleep again? But soon she heard him sit up in bed—then his bare feet stepped on the floor.

"Stay where you are! Don't come here—" Her voice seemed to stick in her throat. He was close to her, his big body loomed in the darkness just at the edge of her bed.

"Ida Elisabeth", he whispered miserably. "If you only knew how unhappy this has made me. It's you I'm fond of—I don't care a scrap for the other one—" His hand was searching on the coverlet over her breast.

"If you attempt to touch me," she said calmly and distinctly, "I shall pour paraffin over you as soon as you're asleep and set light to it."

"Did you ever hear the like—what a cruel thing to say!" he groaned in dismay. But he did pad back and get into bed again.

She lay wondering what could have put it into her head to say such a thing. One Midsummer Eve she had seen them burn a bed that was full of bugs—that must have been it—and then they had so many books at home about negroes and other savage folk, and all at once she thought of her sister, and Torvald, who had married Connie. She had not seen him once since Connie's death—but what if she went to him—? She had had the impression in those days that Torvald was kind and ready to help—their mother had been enthusiastic about the match. Father had been strongly opposed to it—though he and Torvald belonged to the same set, and Torvald was certainly very rich, at that time anyhow. She herself had not cared much about him, she remembered—but then she was only a little girl at the time. At any rate this was a lawyer whom she knew. Ida Elisabeth tried to work out a plan—what she ought to do now; as she did so memories cropped up of people and things in old days, and suddenly she fell asleep and forgot it all.

SHE woke at her usual time next morning, dressed as quietly as possible so as not to wake Frithjof, and then carried the boy out to the kitchen, put on his clothes there, and sent him upstairs to the Esbjörnsens'.

She got ready a breakfast tray for Frithjof, then went in and woke him:

"And when you have had this you must get up. You'd better take the boat to Vallerviken and stay a few days with your parents."

He lay blinking with sleepy eyes, rather confused, but obviously much relieved to find she was no longer angry. Ida Elisabeth had almost a guilty feeling, for she saw that he took her composure and the appetizing breakfast to be signs that this tiresome business was on the way to being forgiven and forgotten.

"Go home—well, no, I don't think that will be very convenient." He took a gulp of coffee and began to eat. "I must tell you, I rang them up yesterday and talked to father— this was after I'd gotten that letter, you understand. But father said they were expecting Merete and her fiancé today.

And when they're in the house, you know, I can't get a proper talk with the old people. And they wouldn't like Frede to know we had had any jar."

"No, no; then say nothing about it. But you'll have to go there."

"Well, but I'm not sure it will suit them to have me now. Papa promised that we should be invited there one of these days to meet Frede—"

Ida Elisabeth shrugged her shoulders: "You must be good enough to do as I say. I wish to be left alone here for a while."

He seized her hand. "I assure you, Lisken, it shall never occur again . . . It's a thing of the past now. You shall see, you can trust me for the future. I promise you I'll pull myself together—"

"Yes, that's all right, but get ready now."

She hurried him again and again, and actually got him out of the house.

That left her five hours before the boat called again on the outward trip.

She sat down and wrote to the lawyer in Sogn that she had entrusted the sale of her business to Herr Torvald Lander, barrister. Then she took another sheet and began: "Dear Torvald—" She supposed she must address him familiarly—ugh, it wasn't easy. His present wife she had never seen, but the second, the one he had married a year after Connie's death and who had left him, had been very pretty and frightfully smart. Ida Elisabeth tried to recall Torvald Lander: tall and thin, pale and sandy he had been, but good-looking in a way, or rather, he had the kind of figure which sets off well-cut clothes. Once more her impatience flared up—that the poverty with which she had been so long familiar should suddenly reveal new annoyances. She did not possess a pair of shoes in which she could be seen in town; her hat was nearly done; her coat looked comparatively decent, but it was the one she had bought to be married in, really a spring coat which she had lined with woollen material. She flinched at the idea of calling on Torvald at his office—it would have been easier if she had been well dressed. Better to do it early tomorrow and get it over. She tore up the letter she had begun to her former brother-in-law—it would now be superfluous to write.

There were two or three business letters that she had to answer, and then she emptied the shop till and entered the amount in the book. Twenty-three crowns in cash—she must remember to cut sandwiches and take milk for the boy; they could not afford more than a cup of coffee on board.

She got out her trader's licence, her testimonials, the children's savings-bank books, and put them in her hand-bag. The bank was not open today—she would have to ask Torvald to draw out what was in Sölvi's book. Hard pressed as she had often been this year, she had nevertheless been firmly resolved that Sölvi's money must not be touched, it was to go to Carl some day. Well, it was a piece of luck in the midst of misfortune that the money was there—

As she went through in her mind what she still had to do and in what order she should do it, the sense of defeat and disappointment dragged at her. So she had been forced to give up. Oh, and now she thought, in this house, from which she was about to steal away, as soon as it grew dark— here she had known more than anywhere else in the world how *good* it can be to live ... As she watched her children unfolding before her very eyes, growing and eating and play- ing and eating and falling asleep. She thought of the kitchen out there, when it had been put straight for the afternoon, the floor not yet quite dry after she had gone over it with a swab—there seemed always to be something about it which reminded one of the eve of a holiday, when Sölvi and Baby sat at the table watching her cut bread into dice and fill their two mugs with borders of roses and "good boy" and "good girl" on the outside—and then came the smell of boiling milk. When she had put them to bed in the evening and sat alone in her parlour with some sewing—every now and again she had to get up and listen at the bedroom door which stood ajar. The two little children were breathing quietly in the dark—it was like leaning over a deep pool of black water in which two little living springs welled up pulsing from the bottom. Time after time she had left her work to listen and refresh herself.

She had come to the end of it here. But she must surely be able to find some place in the world where she could be *safe* ... For just as she realized how much of happiness there had been in life after all—in the toil of it, in all the commonplace things that happened over and over again every day, a kind of happiness of which she had known nothing when she was a rich little girl and a poor little girl and thought that happiness was something quite different—just then an image seemed to form before her eyes: it was as though she had been threading a string of beads; the big beads in the middle were the children and all that had to do with them; and all the rest that she had accomplished and put in order and all the evil she had averted—all this was the smaller beads she was threading at both ends. But every time she had finished threading a piece of the string, he and those other people came and tore it out of her hands and the beads fell on the floor and rolled away into holes and corners, and every time those she found again were fewer and fewer—

She must rescue herself and the children while there was yet time. Suddenly it struck her as an impulse, though she fancied she could divine a mysterious significance in it: if she managed to bring this new child safely into the world and it was a boy, its name should be Tryggve.[1] Sölvi—and the little one who had not had so much as a name in this world—no, such things should not happen again, so long as she had strength to fight for a living soul—

[1] The Norwegian word *trygg* means "safe".—Tr.

Ida Elisabeth packed her trunks. She fetched from the shop four sets of good warm underclothes, stockings, and a guernsey for the boy, a dark-green jumper and three pairs of stockings for herself. In her fine, commercial-school hand she entered in the books what she had taken. Olise followed her movements with those strange brown eyes of hers which guarded a secret so closely.

"If you could sleep here at night too," said Ida Elisabeth, "perhaps that would be best. You're not afraid, are you? The Esbjörnsens will hear you if you knock on the ceiling. You can stay here, can't you, till you hear from me?"

"You know I can." She saw that Olise understood the whole situation.

Naturally—it had not occurred to her before, but it was quite likely that Frithjof's doings in town were all over the neighbourhood long ago.

It was no use being vexed about it. It was no use being vexed because Frithjof gossiped and discussed her with maternally sympathetic female friends, and with his mother and his father and his sisters and the fiancé from the sanatorium, if he was one of the same breed. They *were* like that—it was only natural that they should hold together, consult each other as to how to take her when there was anything they wanted to get out of her, and help each other when they had anything to conceal from her. It was quite reasonable from their point of view, and it was useless and irrational for her to be annoyed about it. But she was different, and now she would get away from it all—go to some place where she could shut the doors on her home and her nest, without having to give house-room to one who ran in and out leaving them wide open to all and sundry.

IDA ELISABETH pulled back the blind and looked out. It was already quite dark. Fine, calm weather—so the boat would be more or less punctual.

Overhead she heard Carl running about. Fru Esbjörnsen had offered to let him have dinner with them. That was a good thing—then she need not fetch him till it was time to put on his things; she would not have to answer questions and so on till the last moment.

There was a customer in the shop; Olise was serving. It seemed as though it did not concern her any more—as though she had already finished here.

Olise—no doubt she would miss her very often. She had an idea. She took out of her trunk the queer old-fashioned brooch that Doctor Sommervold had given her the year before when he came back from Germany. Ida Elisabeth made a parcel of it, wrote outside "In remembrance of your affectionate I. E." and put it in Olise's old and well-worn leather bag which lay on the window ledge in the kitchen. The brooch represented a kind of ship in enamel, with a disproportionately large pearl for a sail—perhaps Olise would think it more odd than pretty. But it was the only thing she had to give her.

It was just time to put on the kettle—she could take a cup of coffee and a little bread and butter and then it would not be too early to go down to the pier.

As she came back from the kitchen her eye chanced to fall on the little shelf above the side-table—there stood the black elephant. Ida Elisabeth took it down—and that made her think of Carl's coloured pencils and drawing-books— and her boxes of picture post-cards and paper dolls must certainly go with her. She collected them all and stuffed them here and there in her two trunks. Ida Elisabeth locked and strapped them, got her own and the boy's outdoor things and hung them near the stove. There could be nothing else that she had forgotten. All was ready now.

BOOK TWO

Chapter One

IDA ELISABETH MOVED all the flower-pots on to the table in the middle of the room; they would do fairly well there, even if they were only watered once a day while she was away.

It was almost a pity to go away and leave them. She bent over the white cactus—it had such a strange scent, intensely delicious, but with a hint of something loathsome at the same time. When it flowered last year she had been obliged to leave a crack of the window open all the time, in spite of the awful dust of the road.

Thank goodness the main road had been diverted last spring. Unconsciously Ida Elisabeth went to the east window and looked out. It was by no means so small, the piece that had been added to her garden when they straightened out the bend in front of the house. This year she had not been able to do much more than put up a fence and have it filled with mould. But next spring she would plant a hedge on the side of the new road—Siberian acacia or perhaps rugosa roses—at any rate something that grew quickly.

The dust nuisance had been awful here in past years. Cars dashed past the house all through the twenty-four hours, hay carts rumbled by and wagons loaded with rattling milk-cans—they raised a cloud of dust and the wind came and carried it along. It found its way into her house, through closed windows and doors; it even seemed to filter in between the logs of the wall—it lay thick and dirty grey on the window ledges, white on the furniture and curtains. She wiped and washed and brushed, but it was fairly hopeless work. But of course the dust had been even worse where she lived the first two years—it was a poorer house. When it rained the rooms were filled with that strange smell, as the dust was laid—she liked it though, in a way: there was something about it which made one think of mournful things, but at the same time there was a note of expectancy in it. As though it reminded one of renewal and reserves of force in nature or within oneself.

Under the windows, close to the wall of the house, grew a row of old perennials. In former years when all the traffic passed close to the house they had been perfectly white with dust all the summer. This year they were healthy and flourishing: the narrow, ribbon-like, pale green leaves of the day-lilies grew thick, and from among them the flower-stalks rose with bunches of pointed yellow buds—they would have come out by the time she was back. The columbines were in full bloom with airy pink and blue flowers waving among the white and purple blooms of the Dame's violets, but the monk's-hood still showed its dark lobed leaves with their queer tinny glitter, and was hardly in bud.

The disused piece of road in front of the row of perennials was already being overgrown with all kinds of hardy little plants that can live in a soil of road metal—slender sorrel blazed in the sunshine, little grasses formed tufts, and grass-leaved stitchwort spread with clouds of white flowers. It looked pretty, and besides, it would cost too much to break up the old piece of road which now ran through her garden; after all it might not be a bad thing to have a strip of main road of one's own—she could walk up and down it in the evening, if she had time. Ida Elisabeth smiled at herself. Now that she had a garden to attend to—

The new piece between the old road and the new was only bare greyish brown mould in furrows. Potatoes had been planted but at present only a dark-green tuft here and there was to be seen above ground—she could not even see them from the window, but she knew of them, for she went out to look every morning. Along the path from the door to the gate she had planted some lilac bushes, but they looked rather thin and scraggy; they had been put in very late—all the same they seemed to be getting on.

Tryggve was standing by one of the lilac bushes. The little donkey—he was digging with the point of his shoe in the puddle she had left after watering her flowers.

Ida Elisabeth went out into the hall. Even so early in the morning there was that warm and friendly smell of the well-sunned timbers of an old wooden house long inhabited. There was this huge roomy hall, with low, broad doors leading to rooms on every side and the broad steep stairs to the first floor, which had made such an impression on her when she came to view the house that she forgot to notice what bad repair it was in.

By the front door stood their trunks and the case with her hand sewing-machine; a roll of fashion papers was tied to the handle. Marte Bö always said she need not bring her machine with her—but she would be sorry to use Marte's old machine. Ida Elisabeth smiled at the thought; she was looking forward so much to these few days she was to spend at Marte's. From the moment they arrived, and Marte showed them up into the big room where they were to sleep—it smelt of sunshine and summer and clean white beds, and of pink almond soap when the boys began to wash—she was overflowing with holiday sensations. For the boys of course these days up at Marte's were a holiday, and to her the very work was pure fun. Marte had coffee and cream and waffles for them when they came down, and before they got up from the table Marte had to go through the fashion papers and they began to choose models. The blue room where she worked looked out over the steeply sloping fields and the valley which was full of blue haze—and she heard her boys running about, making the dry ground ring, and Tryggve's voice shrilled; they were right under her window one moment and away again the next; they had a fine time there from morning till night.

Ida Elisabeth went out on to the door-step—lovely weather they would have. On the slopes opposite, the spruce forest was light green with fresh shoots, sucking in sunshine, and above the highest summits floated white summer clouds.

The house she lived in was the old main building of Viker, but it stood some little distance from the other houses of the farm, and when the old road which used to run right through the yard at Viker was diverted this year, she was allowed to put her fence across the abandoned piece of road, so that the old house was now quite cut off from the posting station. When the railway came, the father of Kristian Viker, who now had the farm, had put up a new main building on the north of the yard, with open and closed verandas and gables in all directions, intending to make a hotel and summer boarding-house of it. But it had never done much good, so when Kristian married he moved into the new house and let the old one. He had calculated that four families could live there, but during the two years for which she had occupied the southern half of the ground floor and Hansen the schoolmaster the flat above, the northern half of the house had stood empty—it was rather far from the station, and Kristian was not inclined to spend much on keeping the old house in repair.

It still looked imposing, for it was built of heavy timber, which sunshine and weather had turned brown and grey, but the white paint around the small-paned windows and on the big front door had peeled off badly. And all the signs that had been put up on the front contributed to give the handsome, extremely well-built house an air of having seen better days. Hansen held some agencies for insurance companies and had therefore put up signs which were resplendent with red, yellow, and green enamel, and on the other side of the door she had a big tin plate, painted white with black letters: "Ida Braatö, Dressmaker. Boys' Outfits." But she liked living here—it made her positively happy; every time she went out or came home and looked at the fine old building and thought to herself, *this* is where we live—

North of her garden fence a wing of the Viker barn turned its long red back this way, and she could get a glimpse of the green farmyard with many outhouses, great and small, around it. It wafted a breath of summer stillness and warmth towards her, a smell of byre and stable, and of hay and straw and fresh planks; they had taken the cattle to the sæter a few days before, and now the outhouses gaped with open doors and were to be repaired after the winter. And this stillness and this smell now formed part of her sense of summer at Viker.

"What is it you're doing there, Tryggve? Didn't I tell you not to get into a mess?" But her voice was gay; she was not in a humour to scold the boy. "Come here and let mother have a look at you!"

He came running—oh, that little face of his was far too innocent; his smile was like an angel's, but his eyelashes blinked and blinked. When he saw that his mother was not really angry he threw himself upon her and embraced her hips.

"Your cap—do you know what you've done with it?" She dug her fingers into his curly flaxen hair, forced his head back, and looked down into the warm little face. Ugh, it wasn't easy to keep up one's severity when this little pig had to be scolded—he had such lovely red cheeks and his skin was golden from the sun; his lips had a sort of transparent look, like the pulp of a cherry or a raspberry.

"*What* a sight you are!" He must have been in a thicket full of wild chervil and dandelions, for he was covered with white fluff from the top of his head right down his new light blue coat. "Where *have* you been?"

"Carl told me to find his cat—mother, aren't we going to start soon?"

"As soon as Kindli comes back from the dairy ... Ugh, where can Carl have got to now? He ought to have been back long ago."

"Carl has come back, mother, but then he flew out again to find Puss, because I hadn't found him, you see—"

This love of animals that Carl showed was rather troublesome. She had assured him that the kitten would be all right; Fru Hansen had promised to leave out milk for it every day while they were away—but Carl stuck to it that these white cats with blue eyes were always hard of hearing; Puss could hear well enough when they called him, but he couldn't hear motor cars or dogs, and so he must needs get hold of him and carry him up to the Hansens' himself before they left. Poor boy, he was so kind, Carl—he had offered of his own accord to run over with those two blouses for Fröken Hagen—but she would like to know if he had gotten the money for them, if only he hadn't dropped it in his running about. He was always so eager to make himself useful, and then he was so forgetful, and so hopelessly clumsy, and he was never on time—.

Ida Elisabeth fetched the clothes-brush and the box of boot-brushes. Sitting on the door-step she brushed Tryggve's shoes. He could not stand still—he had managed to get soaked with perspiration already, and the warm, acrid smell of the child reached her every time he wriggled. Behind this restless boy she always seemed to glimpse the reflection of a love and a life—and cares and anxieties and joys belonging to a time long past, a world that had sunk into the ground and the darkness. She was not actually thinking of Sölvi while she was busy with Tryggve, but the memory of the child she had lost flickered like a glistening halo round the little floundering body and about her love for her youngest—

"Here he comes—now he's caught Puss!" It had gotten into Viker of course.

"Oh, mother, come and take him, won't you!" Ida Elisabeth went up and received the cat over the fence. It was a really sweet kitten, soft and white and warm it lay purring in her arms, as she watched Carl climb over the rails in his delightfully clumsy way. In one hand he grasped a bunch of yellow flowers:

"Look what I've found for you, mother!" He smiled so beamingly and there was such a sparkle behind his glasses that she had not the heart to remind him that they were going away and that there was no sense in pulling up flowers now. They were lady's slipper—the first she had seen this year: "Fancy, are they out already—that was very nice of you! Did you get the money from Fröken Hagen?"

"Oh yes, mother, and she gave me ten öre for myself, so I bought some cream caramels—" He dug in his pockets and shared them out, one caramel for his mother and one for his brother, and Fru Hansen was to have one, and there was one left for himself. He had the money too, quite correct.

"And now stay here, boys; Kindli may come any minute. Don't get in a mess again, Tryggve—Carl, you must run in and wash your hands—no, where are you off to now—?"

It was the cat of course. She had put it down to take the money, and then it had walked off. White and solemn, with its tail straight in the air, it was wandering about her grey potato patch—Carl after it, and every time he made a grab it hopped playfully aside, made a few long, soft bounds, and wandered on, as gravely as before. Ida Elisabeth stood for a while smiling as she watched them. Then she went in.

She moved the last of the flower-pots, then took another look at the white cactus. The outer golden-brown leaves stood out like rays around the wide-gaping creamy white flower, which turned to a greenish hue down at the centre, where a thick tuft of stamens protruded, silvery white with white buds. It was a pity to leave it here in its beauty, when no one could have any pleasure of it. Ida Elisabeth took a pair of scissors. She could at least make up a bouquet to take to Marte Bö—Marte shared her delight in flowers—

She paused for a moment with the cut cactus flower in her hand. Then she took up the scissors again. The delicate bittersweet perfume of the rose-leaves and the pungent, spicy scent of the pelargoniums was diffused under her fingers, as she cut with slow and tender strokes. She found some thread and began to bind the bouquet, choosing the cut blooms one by one—the two half-opened yellow roses projecting from a bunch of scarlet pelargonium, and a sprig of the purple English geranium against the burning red, the pink among the violet. She remembered that grandmother Siveking used to bring bouquets like these on her mother's birthday. But grandmother's bouquets had always contained some sprigs of Louis-Philippe. She thought she would like to have a Louis-Philippe again—at Berfjord she had had one of those with red bells. The thought drifted through her mind like the shadow of a cloud. She drew the thread tight and bound it. Really it was quite a nice bouquet—

She was roused by noises in the road—somebody screamed, a car was braked sharply, and then came some indefinite sounds; Ida Elisabeth put down her bouquet and went to the window. A tall lady flung her gate open wide; a tall man in grey carrying something big and blue in his arms came walking towards her between the newly planted lilac-bushes—then she guessed that it was Carl the stranger was carrying. With a low, shrill cry she darted out—

The boy lay lifeless in the stranger's arms with his bleeding face against the man's blood-stained blue shirt; the boy's legs in socks and yellow sandals dangled long and thin in front of the man's grey trouser-legs. White in the face, with open, distorted mouth, the mother met them—

"Perhaps it's not so bad as it looks." The stranger looked up. His eyes were clear and grey, his head bending over the child was smooth with brown, close-cut curls. There was something curiously feminine in the way he held the lifeless child—it reminded Ida Elisabeth of pictures of the Madonna.

"The doctor will be here directly—my cousin has gone to fetch him. He's been rather badly grazed—"

Ida Elisabeth felt as if she had expected something of this sort to happen. She had tried to escape from a monster—it had played with her, giving her time to recover breath and believe herself safe, then it leapt upon her again. O God, O God, O God—wailing softly she looked at the young stranger, as she backed towards the door in front of him and the boy. She thought of the angel of death or something like that—his forehead was broad and clear, the upper half snow-white, the lower brown, and the grey eyes, which looked straight ahead, were full of tender seriousness.

"It may not be so bad as it looks—he got under the car, but the wheels didn't go over him. I must say I didn't quite see how it happened—he flew out into the middle of the road right in front of the car, and when she tried to steer to the left he turned round and tried to run back and so we ran into him, but we hadn't much speed then—"

White and rigid Ida Elisabeth went in front to show the way. The empty window-ledges in her work-room, the curtains pinned up—it was as though the mortuary chamber had been prepared already. Through the cosy little room where she herself slept on the divan she led the man into the boys' room, took hold of Carl's bed, and pulled it out from the wall so that it stood free—all this she had been through once before.

With infinite caution the stranger laid his burden on the bed and withdrew his arms.

When she came with a basin of water and some towels he took them from her and placed everything on a chair which he had brought to the bedside—she did not know whether he had asked for water or whether she had remembered of her own accord that that was the next thing she had to do. She saw that the man had taken off Carl's socks and sandals; he raised the boy's legs carefully, bending and feeling them—the knees were fearfully grazed—then he took hold of Carl's wrists and moved his arms. The palms of the hands were covered with blood and sand, Carl's face was smeared with blood and earth, and the stains of blood were spread over the pillow and sheets.

As Ida Elisabeth touched the boy's face with the wet towel, he turned his head slightly and muttered something. The man was engaged in washing Carl's hands with another towel. "There are splinters of glass in them?"

"Perhaps that's from his spectacles", she heard herself say.

The man was cautiously attending to the cuts on the hands. "Then it's a God's mercy he didn't get glass in his face; the spectacles must have fallen off as he was struck—"

The boy whimpered loudly and impatiently, then opened his eyes a moment and tried to sit upright, but shrieked as he leaned on his hand. "No, no, lie down quietly", said the stranger. "It's nothing dangerous—just lie still till the doctor comes." Ida Elisabeth had unbuttoned the boy's clothes and they both felt the child's body all over. "I really believe it won't be so bad as it looked", said the man. "But poor boy, he's got some nasty abrasions—"

As Ida Elisabeth straightened her back the room went round with her. She felt her heart beating in a wild flurry— all within her was in confusion and she was plunged into a chaos of darkness and stifling sensations. Now she seemed to come to the surface again and regained her foothold in the everyday world. Carl had been run over by a motor car, but it looked as if he had come off fairly well; the black flood of torment, the memory of horrors she had gone through once before, ebbed back—

"You must sit down", said the stranger, taking the basin from the chair. "It's not so bad", he said quickly to the boy; "you've bled a little, but it looks such a lot when it's in the basin." He took it out; Ida Elisabeth heard him in the kitchen, emptying the water and letting the tap run.

"There—there—there—" she said softly, stroking Carl on the cheek that was least scratched; "you mustn't be afraid"—he made a wry face and was going to cry, but no doubt his wounds hurt him badly. "You mustn't cry—it's nothing dangerous—there, there", she bent down and gave him a light little kiss.

The stranger came back. "I've put some water on to boil, for the doctor when he comes. My name is Toksvold, lawyer Toksvold", he said, as though suddenly remembering to introduce himself.

He went over to the window, stood with his back to it, and looked at the bed. "Phew—it was awful! Never in my life have I felt so bad as when I saw the boy lying under the car—"

Ida Elisabeth suddenly laid her head against the end of the bed and burst into tears. She tried to check herself. "I can't help it—I'm like this—when it's over", she sobbed in excuse.

"Yes, I can understand", he said seriously. "Poor Kari, I expect she's quite beside herself—she was driving, you see, my cousin. She doesn't know yet how it's turned out—"

"Mother"—she heard the patter of little feet running through the work-room. Ida Elisabeth got up to stop Tryggve before he could burst in.

"Mother—Kindli's here—"

She had to go out and explain to Kindli what had happened; he must go and tell Marte Bö that they would not be coming today. As she was talking to Kindli she grew quite calm, the everyday world had hold of her again. Coming back through the work-room she caught sight of the bouquet lying on the table. She put it in a vase, carried it in, and put it on the boys' little chest of drawers. It would cheer Carl up by and by.

Lawyer Toksvold was still standing by the window. Behind him was the daylight and the shimmer of leaves and the sunshine reflected in the river; the bedrooms looked out on to the old garden of Viker, and below the garden the water lay far out over the fields; the floods had come early this year.

Ida Elisabeth took her seat again by the boy's bed, and the stranger remained standing and they said nothing—and it did not strike her as at all strange that this man, whom

179

she had never seen before, should stay here waiting with her—until he said:

"Well—perhaps you'd like me to go? I can just as well wait outside, you know—but I should like to hear what the doctor says. I only hope she found Eriksen at home— they ought to have been here by now, I think."

Ida Elisabeth made a motion of the head—it might be yes and it might be no. He went up to the boy's bed:

"Poor child—what a sight he is—"

Again her tears were very near. Carl had almost stopped bleeding, but the whole right side of his face was fearfully abraded; his eyes were nearly closed with swelling. She saw with distressing clearness that he was no pretty child, this poor little boy of hers with the pale, wizened face under a forehead which was so big and bulging; his hair was of no proper colour—rat-coloured they had called it at school; he had cried so when he told her that. And they made fun of him because he had to wear glasses. Now that he lay here all scratches and bruises he looked quite pitiable— with an involuntary gesture his mother bent forward as though to protect him.

"You have a telephone, haven't you? I think I'll ring up—find out if Eriksen was at home—" he slipped out. Instinctively she sat up and listened for his voice, when she heard him at the telephone in the work-room: "Fru Eriksen?—yes, this is Toksvold—oh no, we were unlucky enough to run over a little boy down at Viker—no, I hope not—well, then I'd better ring up Fjeldberg—" He rang off and called up the sanatorium: "Fröken Presttangen—ten minutes ago, do you say?—ah, thank goodness, then they'll be here any time now—"

So Doctor Eriksen had been out, Ida Elisabeth understood, and then Fröken Presttangen, that must be the cousin, had driven up to the sanatorium and fetched the doctor from there. So it was Kari Presttangen, the lady dentist down by the station, who had run over Carl . . . It struck Ida Elisabeth that she had always thought there was something unattractive about that person—though she had never spoken to her—and she was really good-looking in her way.

Toksvold seemed to have gotten into conversation with Tryggve—she heard the boy's chatter and the other's calm and even voice. All at once he ran out—it must be the car with the doctor. The tension returned and took the strength out of her knees as she got up at the sound of several people in the hall and Doctor Lund's voice.

"He's rather a nervous child, isn't he?" asked Doctor Lund, when he had made his examination.

"Oh yes, he is."

"As I say—you must keep him in bed till he's gotten over the shock—and in *case* he should have any internal injuries. But as I told you, I don't think he has. But I'll look in again tomorrow—and you can ring me up if there should be anything before then. I'll give you a prescription for a sedative—" Doctor Lund passed his hand again over Carl's bare chest and arms, the skin of which was rough, like sand: "Pretty nervous, yes, I can see that . . . Look here, Fru Braatö—you're not forcing him on, are you? Don't let him overstrain himself. He was Number One of his class this year, my little girl tells me—"

Ida Elisabeth shook her head:

"He's pretty quick, it seems." She tried not to betray her pride, but it gave her a warm feeling of joy to hear the doctor speak of it. Doctor Lund was really very kind—he was always so friendly with her five years ago, when she went to the sanatorium to see Aslaug, and once or twice he had asked her to come into his consulting-room to talk about Fru Tömmeraas. That she had avoided Doctor Lund since then was by no means due to her thinking he must be so busy; that was only an excuse she made to herself. In reality it was something he had said, which had come round to her. This told her that he too assumed she had naturally had an affair—when she turned up here, expecting a child, and had left her home and was about to be divorced from her husband. That she was a friend of Aslaug Tömmeraas had also had something to say to it, no doubt; for Aslaug had confided to the doctor every scrap of her own history and a bit more, that terrible summer before she died.

She had seen, of course, that it was perfectly natural people should take this view. She had realized it already, when she had to tell her brother-in-law why she wanted to leave the West and why she could not accept the post of manageress he had obtained for her. But at that time she had said to herself, it did not matter what folks believed—if only she got clear of Frithjof. And when she guessed that people here must think the same—that it was she who had been unfaithful to her husband—she had still thought: I don't care, if only I get something to do, so that I can live with my children; and who inquires about a dressmaker's virtue, if she is capable and keeps herself to herself? And as it was, she had had as much work as she could get through, almost all the time—she had made regularly for patients at Fjeldberg too during these years. It was now long since she had thought at all about these old stories, and she doubted whether anyone hereabout still interested herself in the least about Fru Braatö's past; what did interest them was that she was a very good dressmaker and hardly ever disappointed them.

Why it should suddenly have given her a sense of discomfort when she heard Toksvold speaking to Fjeldberg and guessed that it was the sanatorium doctor who was coming—she did not know. Unless it was that the whole of that past which she had deliberately banished from her thoughts for so long that it had almost faded from her memory—had now as it were risen like a sudden storm and swept over her, as she saw Toksvold appear with Carl in his arms. But now that was over—this time disaster had only grazed her, without striking. And so it seemed rather a bore to have Doctor Lund in the house. But that was foolish—for he was a pleasant man as well as a clever doctor, which was the main point.

As she showed the doctor out, the two strangers were sitting in the work-room waiting—he by the big table where all her flower-pots were assembled, she by the window. She was turning over some fashion papers which lay on the little basket-table. They both sprang up on seeing the doctor.

"Ah, thank God", said Toksvold, when the doctor had explained that the boy had probably gotten off very easily. But Fröken Presttangen broke into a discourse of how the accident could have happened, in that easy bend where there was a clear view of the road and no other cars in sight at the moment. The boy had jumped out into the road after a kitten. Well, she ought almost to have guessed, thought Ida Elisabeth—that it was the cat.

Ida Elisabeth regarded Fröken Presttangen thoughtfully, while the other was talking. In her outdoor clothes—a long, light dust-coat and a kind of grass-green béret which sat very oddly on her old-fashioned high coiffure—she did not look particularly attractive. There was no doubt something about her which gave her an air—not exactly repellent, but as though she meant to keep people three paces off—an attitude of challenge differing from that which other women adopted nowadays. She was not satisfied with refusing to cut off her hair—Ida Elisabeth herself had let her hair grow again; she could not afford to be constantly going to the hair-dresser's to have it trimmed, so she simply parted it on the forehead and fastened it in a kind of knot low down on the neck. But Fröken Presttangen had stacked up a huge crown of light golden plaits on the top of her head, reaching forward almost to the fringe on her forehead—Ida Elisabeth had seen this style of hair-dressing in old photograph albums, but never before in the life.

Perhaps that was what gave her the idea that there was altogether something about this lady dentist that recalled the jersey fashion—one had the impression that her clothes fitted her broad, round shoulders and high bosom more tightly than was now the vogue. And the very face of Fröken Presttangen was of a type that was more in place in old photographs—there was something bare and tightly drawn in the way her bones showed under the skin. This was handsome too in a way, presumably it was what people meant by a look of breeding—broad forehead, high cheek-bones, a slightly hooked nose, and long, rather thin cheeks. Her complexion was dazzlingly white and pink, but the skin was rather dry and scrubby—there was something about it which put one in mind of a consumptive tendency; the nostrils too showed a little of the pink membrane dividing them, and the lips were very light and dry.

Although she had been assured by Doctor Lund that in all likelihood Carl was not in any danger—she might at least have said a few words to the mother of the child she had run over—she could surely realize that it had given her a terrible fright. Instead of that she merely went on explaining to the doctor how entirely blameless she was for the accident. Beyond the few questions and answers they had exchanged when Ida Elisabeth and the doctor reappeared, the dentist actually did not say one word to her until just as they were going. The doctor saw the trunks standing in the hall, and in reply to his question Ida Elisabeth explained that they were to have gone on a visit to Marte Bö. Then Fröken Presttangen said:

"I didn't know you went out dressmaking in people's houses."

Ida Elisabeth gave a little laugh:

"I don't either—only to Fru Bö. She was so kind to me when I first came to this part. And now it's very difficult for her to come all this way; so I go up to *her*."

But she was a queer fish all the same, this young woman.

IDA ELISABETH followed them out to the car. The lawyer and Fröken Presttangen were just getting in.

"Will you drive, Kari—?"

"Oh no!" A long shudder seemed to run all over her. "Ugh, I don't believe I'll *ever* be able to drive a car again in my life!" She jumped in quickly and took her seat behind with the doctor—and now she looked ready to cry. "Well, good-bye, Fru Braatö—"

Yes, indeed she was an odd character, this dentist lady.

LATE in the evening Ida Elisabeth was walking home from the station; she had only been able to get the parcel from the druggist's by the eleven o'clock train.

On the wooded ridges west of the valley the spires of spruce stood out sharply, almost black, against the pale yellow sky; they were all that reminded one of darkness in the light summer night, and a reflection of the light in the sky lay upon the peaks of bare rock where they towered above the forest. The river rolled through the valley, mighty and swollen with flood-water, reflecting the evening glow brokenly in its silent, level whirlpools. Thick yellow logs came drifting past in endless procession; they appeared to be sailing along quite slowly, but if one stopped and fixed the eyes on a particular log, one saw what speed there was in these masses of water that travelled past, with their smooth surface ringed and ruffled almost imperceptibly wherever anything on the bottom opposed itself to the force of the current.

In that strange, strong light after sunset even the ugly houses around the railway station were tinged with a kind of beauty; their colours seemed to shine back at the sky. Ida Elisabeth walked past Björkheim hotel; the massive timber building with gables and projections and verandas in all directions was painted reddish brown with dirty yellow bargeboards and window-frames and twisted ornaments, but this evening its sun-baked walls seemed to exhale a breath of cosiness. In the boxes along the verandas it actually looked as if the red and white and pink clusters of flowers were sparkling, and the broad shingle-strewn space in front with the gasoline pump in the middle was so light that it reflected the brilliance of the sky. Magda Björkheim, herself a bright spot in her pink overall, came running down the steps—to attend to the dusty old Buick that stood honking by the pump. On catching sight of Ida Elisabeth she waved to her: "Wait a moment!" Ida Elisabeth stopped and felt the evening around her as a deep, indefinite sense of well-being. Although it was so still there was a faint rustling above her head in the pliant birches.

The car drove off, and Magda ran across to her; she wanted to hear how Carl was. At first they had said at the station that the boy had been so terribly injured that there was no chance of his recovery. "But folks are always so fond of exaggerating—ugh, that Fröken Presttangen, she's a queer one, frightfully nervous, I'm sure—she ought to lose her licence for this, for a time anyhow, that would teach her—"

"But look here, Magda. I might just as well take that dress of yours while I'm about it, as we're not going up to Bö after all. You know, I've given my dressmakers a holiday—but it shan't be any worse if I do the whole thing myself."

"That's fine! how lucky—" She ran off. Ida Elisabeth walked on, warmed with pleasure. They had made so many inquiries about Carl at the station too. "They say that boy's got such uncommonly good brains", said the stationmaster banteringly. Perhaps they would be kinder to Carl at the school after this.

As a matter of fact she would have been glad to take a few days off—but now she had promised to make Magda's dress at once. And it is always satisfactory to get things out of the way. A good deal of the work she could do while sitting with Carl. He would not be allowed to read for the first week at any rate, but a good thing about Carl was that the boy was never bored when left to himself. Goodness knows what his little head busied itself with all the time. Precocious, yes, poor boy. It's easy enough for the people who write in ladies' papers and the like that children must not be allowed to get precocious; they ought to be sent out to play games with other children. One would think they had never seen children in reality or known how their nature inclines them to treat one who is a little different from the crowd. A little boy who is frail of body and near-sighted and wanting in looks—and shy from having been told of it—what is one to hit upon to prevent his being precocious, when he is already intelligent and suffers from an inclination to cogitate about all sorts of subjects—?

Poor child—and then his own idea was that he would be a farmer! He spent a lot of his time at Viker; he was fond of animals—but how clumsy he was, and his legs were like pipe-stems! And where was he to get the money to buy a farm? But that was just the point—in one way or another she *must* try to get some financial backing, so that she could help her boys on in the world. With Frithjof and his brothers and sisters she had seen well enough what the result is when the parents lack both money and common sense and the children are imperfectly endowed in one way or another. And she had been too deeply involved with that family to yield to the temptation of refusing to see what was lacking in her own children. Carl was really a plucky little fellow—he *was* nervous and he was sensitive and shy, and at times he would break down and complain to her. But at the same time he had it in him not to give in and let outsiders see that he took things to heart, and for quite long spells he was her brave little boy. Tryggve of course was still very small—but all the same she had discovered that he was much more of a coward; he made no attempt like his brother to clench his teeth and show no sign; Tryggve had a disposition to take refuge in boasting. And he lied like anything. Perhaps he was still too young to distinguish between what really happened and what he imagined might happen and what he wished to happen. And no doubt it would be no easy job for her to teach that boy to keep fancies and desires and facts apart from each other. But it was tempting to adopt the same attitude towards her children as Frithjof's parents, for instance—deliberately to make oneself even less critical than one is by nature and to make up for it by criticizing other people a little more, in order to reassure oneself: one is not so idiotically simple after all. But she was aware of her own reluctance to notice Tryggve's little flaws—because the young rascal was so pretty—and then he reminded her so much of Sölvi.

Ida Elisabeth turned into the main road. In the big new office building on the corner—a three-storied pea-green brick house in a sort of "rational" style—Fröken Presttangen had her dental surgery. Behind a window on the ground floor with her name on the glass blind Ida Elisabeth caught a glimpse of a big reflector and the top of a drill. Herr Toksvold also had his offices in this building—of course she had seen his name-plate many a time, but never taken much notice of it before. Tryggve Toksvold was his name. Whereabouts did they live, she wondered. Somebody had told her that the new woman dentist lived at Solhaug pension. Perhaps he lived there too—

Probably he had the management of the Pea Soup, as people called the house. So they had not yet succeeded in letting the shop at the corner. Ida Elisabeth stopped for a moment and looked in through the big, empty window. The shop-fittings had some pretension—counters and shelves were coloured pearl-grey and brick-red; paper and boards lay about the floor, left behind by the painters. She had only laughed when Marte Bö suggested that she should take this shop. Marte had preached to her all these years: you ought to start a business again. And last spring, when she told Marte about those bank deposits left her by Doctor Sommervold, Marte had been insistent: You may be sure, if you leave the money lying in a bank it'll go smash some day—put it into a business, Ida, before somebody else comes and starts here, then they'll buy everything ready-made and you won't get any dressmaking to do either—

There was something in that of course. And a draper's shop here ought to be a paying thing—and she had a name for good dressmaking and excellent taste. If only times had not been so bad—and if a whole row of similar shops didn't crop up when it was seen that she was making a success of it.

She had never dreamt that Sommervold would leave her such a lot of money. A couple of hundred crowns for Carl was her idea—she knew the doctor's christening gift to the boy included a bank-book. But it turned out that there was over three thousand crowns for Carl, besides a bank-book which had originally been in Sölvi's name, but had been transferred to her. This deposit amounted to two thousand five hundred odd crowns. And that money in any case she could do what she liked with. It was a question too whether Carl's money was safer in a bank than it would be if invested in a business.

But that would mean being away from home nearly all day, and she would have to have someone in the house to look after the boys. Ida Elisabeth sighed. She had been comfortably off, she thought, since she moved to Viker. She had been able to supply the boys' needs—and for herself there was the stillness, when the day's work was done and her workwomen had left. Then she and the children had supper together out in the kitchen, and she helped Carl with his lessons, or sat with a piece of work and said nothing and listened with half an ear to what the two were about. One could ask for nothing better, if one could provide for one's children and at the same time be a mother to them. The children saw this too in a way; Carl had been quite upset the day he heard Marte Bö talking to her about the shop. Well but, my dear boy, as it is I'm busy all day long in the work-room, she had said. Yes, but we always know you're there, so we can go and tell you at once, if we have anything to say. That, no doubt, was just the point. The children often got on without her all day long, apart from the routine of meals. She did not have to herd them; so long as they knew they would not look in vain if they wanted to find her.

It was terribly dusty on the road—heavy and soft and noiseless to the feet. The grass and flowers along the edge of the ditch were buried deep in dust, spruce and alder were grey with it, where the trees reached to the edge of the road—a long stretch of heather and moss was stifled in dust, and the scent of the woods seemed blunted by the smell of the road. Ida Elisabeth passed the house where she had lived the first years she was here. It stood on a lower level than the road, squeezed between a steep overhanging rock and the curbstones which had met her eye every time she looked up from her work.

The two windows which had been hers were dark and blind—an old Norwegian-American lived there now, and he always hung something dark before the windows that looked out on the road. The house had been draughty and in bad repair even when she was a tenant, and certainly nothing had been done to it since. It was as ugly as a house can be, with a ground floor of unpainted, grey dovetailed timbers and above it an attic which was panelled and painted with one coat of a kind of thin yellow ochre. In her time the panels had always been working loose and rattling and banging whenever there was a high wind.

On the other side of the road was a flat stretch of heath with gaunt, unhealthy pine-trees. Their stems were yellow, a colour which had always put her in mind of rancid salt trout; their scanty tops were faded and turned to a pale olive green quite early in the summer. She had walked on this heath with the children on summer evenings, when she could spare the time. Marte Bö had lent her an old mail-cart for Tryggve—he enjoyed himself when it bumped and splashed over stones and rough ground on the old track which led to a gravel-pit. The soil was bare and grey with moss and dark clumps of scrubby heather and big stones which might have been left behind by a river in old days. Perhaps it had once been broad, the little Aasdal stream which ran through the heath—it was the stream that came out into the big river a little below Viker. Her usual walk was as far as the river; it ran with a cheerful roar peculiar to itself in its bed of pale rounded rocks, and Carl ran hither and thither throwing gravel and pebbles into the stream and searching for berries among the heather. The sound of the running water and the hot dry smell of firs from the heath were profoundly grateful to her. But how ugly she had thought this East Country when she first came. These low wooded hills that seemed to recede so leisurely could not take the place of mountains. And it was dry and sun-scorched here, no colour either in sky or earth—the sky was either bare blue or bare grey; the forest greenish black and the hills on which the farms stood were burnt yellow early in the summer. Down here at the bottom of the valley all was dust, so that everything was perpetually grey. That she knew nobody here made no difference to her, but that it was so dry and monotonous everywhere made her feel terribly lonely, driven out into the wilderness together with her children.

But round Viker it was pretty. And that made her feel as though a new phase of her life had begun with the first morning she woke there and looked out into the old farm-house garden with its bare gnarled apple-trees—and below the garden the yellow fields still streaked here and there with snow. The great loop which the river made just below Viker reflected the spring clouds in a steely blue, but below the surface there was a green shimmer of ice in many places, and on the other side of the river the wooded hill-side shone in the morning sun. She would never forget it— for it was years since she had waked in a room that did not look out on to a road. And no doubt it was for that reason that it could never grow commonplace to her, this view over the river and the northern slopes in the morning light—when the weather was fine and she sat by herself in the kitchen drinking coffee before settling down to the work of the day, she had imbibed as it were a restful sense of joy which remained latent in her mind and showed through from time to time as she dealt with all the tasks and events of the day.

Ida Elisabeth walked quickly home. Birds were singing in the wood, although the cars rushed by one after another, hooting and leaving behind a fresh cloud of dust streaked with bad smell. Here and there the trees receded a little from the road and formed a ring about a new little home with a newly planted garden around it; Ida Elisabeth peeped with interest over every fence and made comparisons with her own garden that was to be.

The warm, living smell of the farm greeted her as she passed the northernmost houses of Viker. Had Carl been asleep all the time she was away, she wondered—

The light of the summer night had faded into a light dusk; Ida Elisabeth saw that a man was standing by her gate. The cigarette that he threw away as he went to meet her lay glowing for a moment on the road.

"I only wanted to hear how the boy is going on—?"

"Oh, thanks; he's as well as he can be, in the circumstances."

Lawyer Toksvold shook his head:

"My goodness, when I think of how it might have been! The one who opened the door to me said you had gone down to the station for a parcel of medicines. So I thought I'd wait and inquire of yourself. It was stupid of me, by the way, not to think of that this morning—I might have offered to fetch it for you. But to tell the truth, I was myself a good deal—well, you understand, Fru Braatö. And then, to be frank, I was afraid there might be some bother with Kari—a nervous breakdown or something of that sort—"

Ida Elisabeth smiled rather sceptically. She had not exactly had the impression that Fröken Presttangen was on the verge of a nervous breakdown.

"She sent her kindest regards—she wouldn't venture to come herself, but she asked me to leave this—for the boy." He handed her a bag, evidently containing bananas and other fruit. "And then this—I didn't quite know what to get, but children are generally fond of sweets—"

Ida Elisabeth took from him the other parcel, a big box of candy, she could feel. When she had thanked him there was a pause, as though each were waiting for the other to say something.

Toksvold leaned forward over the fence:

"Kristian Viker told me it was you who paid for all this"—he nodded towards the grey potato patch. "Fancy your caring to spend so much money on laying out a garden for a house that isn't your own—!"

Ida Elisabeth shrugged her shoulders:

"I wanted so much to have a bit of a garden again. And if I were to wait till I had a house of my own, perhaps that would be never. And this piece of ground looked so ugly and was no use to anybody. You know, Kristian carted the mould gratis and let me have materials for the fence quite cheap—"

"Wouldn't wire fencing have been cheaper, don't you think?"

"Yes, certainly. But then one doesn't feel properly hedged in. I've been thinking of planting a hedge here on the side of the road. But of course it'll take some years to grow up."

"But what if you were to leave here just as your garden was beginning to grow?"

"M'yes." Ida Elisabeth gave a little laugh. "Then at any rate I should have left a garden behind me. But you know, it would make me sick if I heard that my successors weren't treating it nicely. There was such a lovely old garden at the place my parents owned in the West Country. It made me quite sad when the people who bought the place after my father's death cut down the old trees and let the terraces and the rosary and everything fall into neglect."

"Well—I mustn't take up your time. You must let me look in tomorrow to hear how the boy is. Good-night now, and I hope he'll soon be better—"

Ida Elisabeth opened the gate, then walked slowly up the path to the house. The leaves of the newly planted lilacs were drooping after the broiling hot day. But the green of the potatoes had grown tremendously—the tufts of dark leaves were now showing all over the place.

On the doorstep sat the cause of all the trouble: the white cat; with one leg sticking straight up in the air it sat polishing its hinder part assiduously. Ida Elisabeth bent down and took it on her arm. She buried her face in its soft warm fur—it seemed like an eternity since the morning, when she had taken the kitten from Carl, while he struggled over the fence. If he was awake now, she might let Puss pay him a short visit—that would be sure to please him.

Chapter Two

A MONTH HAD GONE BY; Carl was up and out again, fit as a fiddle, though still bearing some yellow stains on face and body from his bruises. One morning one of her workwomen came and told Ida Elisabeth that Fröken Prest-tangen was outside asking for her. Ida Elisabeth was in the middle of a trying-on. "You'll have to ask her to wait a minute—you can show her into the sitting-room."

They had not met since the day of the accident. Ida Elis-abeth had caught a glimpse of the other once or twice near the station—and had had the impression that Fröken Prest-tangen was no more anxious for a meeting than she was herself.

Kari Presttangen was sitting on the divan; as Ida Elisa-beth appeared at the door she rose quickly. She had on a bright sky-blue linen dress and was bareheaded—she held a white washing hat in her hand—and it struck Ida Elisabeth that she looked simply splendid in this get-up, but her move-ments were strangely abrupt and angular. She stood full in the sunshine, which poured in, broken by the light flutter-ing of the curtain in the summer breeze and by the flowers on the window ledge. The spots of light flitted across the visitor's high bosom in its blue dress and made her heavy crown of plaited hair gleam like gold—she was handsome in such an unusual way, and so big that it looked as if she could not possibly fit in anywhere.

"Well, I only wanted to ask how your boy is getting on", she said rapidly, when they had exchanged greetings and Ida Elisabeth stood as though waiting for her to speak. "That is, of course, Tryggve has given me the news when he has been here. But I thought I would like to call one day myself and ask after him—"

"Thank you. Yes, he's quite well again now. And a thousand thanks for all the things you sent him while he was in bed—"

"Oh ... That's nothing ... Is he at home now?"

"No, both my boys are up at the Viker sæter. They were invited to spend a few days there—"

Then they stood without saying anything. From the field below came the metallic clicking of a reaping-machine, and at the open window the summer air brought a warm breath laden with the scent of hay and a reflection of the sunlight gleaming on the river and on the leaves of the garden.

"It's pretty here at Viker", said Fröken Presttangen. "I think I should like to live here—" She looked about the room, as though in search of something.

"Yes, it's pretty here." Ida Elisabeth maintained an expectant attitude.

"Well, then there was one other thing." Kari Presttangen looked aside; she was playing with the white linen hat in her hands. "Of course I shall pay the expenses of the doctor and so on. All the expenses you've been put to by the accident—"

"No, why should you do that?" Ida Elisabeth put a note of friendly surprise into her voice. "It was not your fault. You explained that yourself the day it happened. And it was what I could have imagined", she added, on seeing the queer look on Fröken Presttangen's face; she positively made one think of a schoolgirl charged with something downright wrong. "I'm afraid it's Carl's nature to be easily flurried—"

Fröken Presttangen tugged and tore at her hat.

"Well, but I think that ... Can't you allow me, Fru Braatö—? Ugh, I've been so angry with myself ever since ... I really think you might accept it—?"

Ida Elisabeth shook her head:

"You would not accept it yourself, Fröken Presttangen."

The other looked up—she was standing with her head slightly inclined. The sunlight fell right on her pupils; she had large eyes, a slightly greenish grey. All at once Ida Elisabeth knew what this person reminded her of—a big light dun mare they had had at Vallerviken when she was a child. This mare had been so fearfully shy—because her former owners had treated her with senseless cruelty, her father said.

All the same she repeated what she had said:

"You would not accept it if you were in my place— would you now?"

Kari Presttangen stood there, blinking and glancing at her sideways. Then she said in a low voice: "I don't know. It's never easy to say what one would do in another's place."

"But of course I'm grateful to you for having thought of it." Ida Elisabeth made a little gesture—couldn't this young woman understand that there was nothing more to talk about, and that she at any rate had her work to go back to? "As I say, I am deeply grateful for your offer."

Kari Presttangen understood.

"Ugh no—I'm afraid I must be taking up your time—"

Ida Elisabeth looked at her wrist-watch. "The fact is, I'm expecting someone to try on, in a moment—"

"Well, I won't detain you any longer—"

She looked so mortally embarrassed that Ida Elisabeth felt bound to make some little show of friendliness: "You can go out this way, then you won't have to go through the workroom." She opened the door to the hall and showed her visitor out through the great empty room, where the warmth of the sun and the cosy air of long habitation filled the space between the unpainted walls. Ida Elisabeth accompanied the other as far as the gate.

"Ugh—I hope you're not angry with me", said Fröken Presttangen distressfully, as they separated.

"Dear me, no—it was such a kind thought of yours."

Ida Elisabeth paused for a moment at the gate, watching the tall stranger in blue as she walked away. She tried to put on her unfortunate hat, but it was reduced to a mere swab. So she let it swing, as she walked off rapidly with her long stride.

Poor girl, I expect I was rather too short with her, thought Ida Elisabeth. But it *was* a queer way to behave—first not make a sign for a whole month and then come blurting out that of course she would pay—

IT was rather strange being altogether alone in the big house at night. The Hansens upstairs had gone away to some gathering or other. Old Hansen usually sat down to play his harmonium at this time of the evening, and Ida Elisabeth caught herself listening for it—it was so quiet here without the drawling whine of folk-song or hymn dragged out of the teacher's wheezy old instrument upstairs.

After her two workwomen had gone she slipped quietly about clearing up the rooms. Before the long mirror in the little trying-on room she paused for a moment to examine her own image. She could not help smiling as she recalled the stories her grandmother Siveking had told her of people who had met themselves in a doorway or on a stair and had gotten such a fright that they died of it. If it should ever happen that she met her double, she would certainly take it calmly. Presumably she would greet it with a bow and think to herself as she passed on—now who was that? I'm sure I know that lady, but at the moment I can't think who she is—

Pretty, but ordinary face, ordinary height, ordinary slimness—and a figure as it were effaced by the long apron with big pockets and loose belt. Quite a neat apron all the same, grey with pink stripes and trimmed on the cross—it was part of her trade always to be neat and smart, but never so as to attract attention. She had buried herself in working clothes for so long now, ever since she was grown up almost, that she had nearly forgotten to think of her figure. Well, indeed there were so many women who were in the same case nowadays. But some of them, perhaps most, when they took off their apron in the evening, dressed up and made themselves pretty, so that those they were going to meet might think they were as they imagined themselves to be. That was a thing she had never been able to do. She had always been forced to hold out through the twenty-four hours and to be what other people assumed her to be—one who was ready and willing to attend to them in every possible and impossible way. Thank God, now at last this was true and natural—now that it was her boys who were certain that mother will look after us, and mother will keep all bad things away from us, and if there is anything bad from which she cannot protect us, it must be because it is a thing that no human being can keep away from others. Children have a right to demand this of their parents—that they give them the feeling that there is something they can rely on in this world. It is good that parents love their children, it is good that children love their parents, but her experience showed that this is jolly well not good *enough*. There must be something more—and God grant she might never let her children feel the want of it.

Ida Elisabeth took off her apron and hung it up—went back and looked at herself again in the glass. A sweet little dress it was—especially considering the price: a dark blue pleated skirt and a silk jumper of the same colour, with some modern-looking stripes in silver-grey on the front, dark blue stockings and shoes. With a smile that was something like a grimace she looked herself in the eyes: oh yes, you're dressed according to your station, no mistake about that—

And now it was delightful to be left absolutely alone for once.

She went back to the work-room. Strictly she ought to be sewing the smocking on the two voile frocks for Doctor

Eriksen's little girls. She found the box of sewing silks, then tried them against the material. The green that Fru Eriksen wanted to have the white sewed with would anyhow be difficult in the wash, and steel-blue against pink looked rather ghastly—but if Fru Eriksen had chosen it ... She would make a nice job of it—but all the same she did not feel up to starting on it now. She had all Sunday tomorrow to do it in.

Ida Elisabeth wandered into the boys' room. There was something almost uncanny about the unaccustomed tidiness here; the two children's beds showed up white in the evening light—how deserted they looked! It was the first time the children had been away by themselves. They must be having a grand time up at the sæter. She would have to write to them this evening—she had promised them each a letter.

Standing by the dresser she drank a glass of milk and ate up the dry rolls that had lain there since Mari Kleivmillom had been in at the beginning of the week. Really she might very well take the yarn Mari had spun tomorrow morning—it would give her a walk too. It was such a lovely path along the hillside to Nyplassen—and a good thing to arrange about the boys' winter stockings in time. And no doubt Anne would like to get to work as soon as possible. By autumn she might have other orders for knitting.

Heavens, what a glorious evening it was! There was that strange blue reflection again in the river below the woods on the other side. Perhaps it meant rain before long. Kristian Viker had predicted that the fine weather was going to last—he would not have to use frames for drying his hay this year, he thought. Ida Elisabeth leaned out of the window, looking at the swallows; one or two of them had not yet gone to rest. Clouds in the sky, but high up—a thick canopy of little balls of cloud packed closely together, reddish grey and some edged with gold—and now a great part of the reflection in the river was a light mother-of-pearl colour. No doubt they were the sort of clouds that are called strato cumulus. Her father had taught her the names of the different kinds of cloud when she was a child.

From the larder a little door led out into the old farm-house garden at the back. In winter she had to hang empty sacks and old bits of carpet over it, to keep out the driving snow; even then one almost froze to death whenever one had to fetch anything from the larder, and it was impossible to keep any food there which would not stand a hard frost.

The latch was almost rusted fast, and the hinges shrieked painfully as she opened the door. Outside the clouded sky seemed ribbed, and through the gaps in the clouds came the intense white light of the summer evening. This garden had been allowed to run wild; the gooseberry bushes were like little dark tufts almost buried in the tall rank grass. Even among the mouldering steps outside the door the grass sprouted—they were so rotten that it was probably danger-ous to tread on them. The idea struck her that this utterly meaningless little back-door was to her a secret sally-port from all the cares and worries of the day into a world of summer night, full of mystery and stillness, into the free open air.

Before Ida Elisabeth knew what she was doing she had jumped down and stood knee-deep in grass—felt that it was sopping wet with dew—and laughed quietly at herself. She began to wade through the garden, sticks and stalks giving before her with brittle cracks as she pushed her way through. She took refuge on the little path leading to Fru Viker's kitchen garden, then stopped to shake out her skirt: dripping, soaking wet, and my feet are all wet too—I must be crazy to go on like this. She laughed in quiet rapture.

A bat shot quick as lightning across the light patch of sky between the apple-trees. She had always enjoyed watch-ing bats; there is such grace in their darting flight, and then it is only on summer nights that one sees them. There it was again. The old trees were so dark against the pale sky, and among the branches the fruit showed as little round knobs—she had only to see them to feel in her teeth how sour they were.

There was such a lovely scent in the kitchen garden—damp earth and burdock and dill and celery. She went up to the fence, climbed over, and began to walk across the field, where the hay was raked into little cocks.

It was so light here after the darkness under the apple-trees, and so spacious all around her. In this twilight it seemed so far down to the river that she did not know if she could walk that distance. The sky was now clear at the zenith and there were a few small stars, and the reflection of the sky in the river seemed even brighter than before, but under the woods on the other side of the valley the water was so dark that it seemed one with the land.

Ida Elisabeth crossed her arms tightly with a shudder—she felt cold in her wet clothes. Standing in the middle of the field she abandoned herself to the voluptuous feeling of being swallowed up by the summer night—space was so infinite on every side, the clear twilight unfathomably deep above her. Darkness had its home in the black woods along the sides of the valley, among thickets and bushes and all growing things, but over the new-mown field the summer twilight seemed rarefied and filled with the raw scent of hay. As she stood thus, sensing within herself all her sur-roundings, she seemed to cease to be herself—

All at once she recalled a sort of vision she had once had: she thought she saw a little hollow in a meadow, which was full of water from a spring, and a little brook trickled out of the hollow, but in the pool itself the water was black and clear as glass and seemed perfectly stagnant, only quiver-ing slightly on the surface above the spot where the little pulse was beating—

SHE paused at the window in her own room, not knowing whether to shut it or not. If she left it open so many flies and moths would come in when she turned on the light.

But if she shut it, the room would be too close; these old timber walls held the heat so.

This evening she noticed the smell which accompanied her wherever she lived—from the material she was using, the dressing it contained, a suspicion of sewing-machine oil, the smell of fresh woollen stuffs. She was so used to it that as a rule she was not aware of it. Anyhow it was not so bad as the smell of some other trades. A delicatessen shop smells much worse—of cold meat and milk and cream in the ice-box. In the long run the smell of home baking is the most disgusting. Aslaug and she had had a room for six months with a lady who went in for that. And, heavens, how that smell had made their mouths water when they moved in one afternoon—in those days they never suffered from over-feeding—but the suction in their stomachs was unbearable when they entered that woman's parlour—what was her name now?—and were met by the warm smell of greasy vanilla-flavoured cakes. And how horrible they thought it when they had lived there a little while! Greasy and cold and nauseous, it hung about the furniture and in their clothes and hair; they lost their appetite altogether—and to that extent it was of some practical value to them. Not that it filled their stomachs by any means; they were just as hungry, but food was repulsive.

Ah, poor Aslaug. Every time she thought of her she could not help asking and wondering—what is the meaning of it all? *Is* there any meaning in it? And is Aslaug living on in some other place, and has she there found out why her life was so miserably fooled away—?

Ida Elisabeth stayed sitting by the open window without turning on the light. Aslaug—it was strange though that it should be Aslaug's death that had brought her to think of that sort of thing, whether there was anything after death, and if so, what. She did not even know whether she believed her father and mother to be still living, in some form or other. Sometimes no doubt she had felt as if she believed it, and sometimes not. Sölvi—to her the child was never far away, in her life Sölvi was eternally alive—but she did not know whether she believed that Sölvi too still had a kind of independent existence outside the days of her own life. At any rate she had never attempted to clear up her thoughts about her own dead—until Aslaug's life came to an end, the last fiasco which could not be repaired here on earth in any case. And if she had been allowed to live, it would only have been the beginning of the next fiasco. That made her ask—is there something which we ought to have known, but have never been told, and is that why we do such terribly stupid things with our lives—?

Aslaug however came from a religious home—she said so herself. The Bible was always in evidence in their parlour, on a little table of its own, with a white crochet cloth on it. Aslaug and her girlfriends had read all the nasty stories in it, when her parents were out. She had insisted on reading them to her too—and in that way Ida Elisabeth had acquired most of her knowledge of the Bible. For that matter she had never been able to persuade herself that they were so bad—they were told in such a queer old-fashioned way. Aslaug was quite disgusting and very silly, she thought, with her prurient laugh, as she read for instance of David after that affair with Bathsheba, when he tried one way after another of avoiding discovery—her own feeling was simply one of cruelty, just as if a hand took hold of her heart and squeezed it; and afterwards, when the prophet came and told that story of the poor man's only ewe lamb—it was really more calculated to make you cry. And then that expression that Aslaug was never tired of giggling at, about these old Jews, that they "knew" their wives—she took good care not to let Aslaug know it, but in her inmost heart she thought it must mean something lovely. No doubt this was due to her having had that miserable affair with Frithjof—but then she had never let Aslaug know either, that she was not such a piece of innocence as the other imagined. That business with Frithjof had ended so wretchedly that she could scarcely bring herself to recall it—and besides, she had heard both her father and her mother use such coarse and ugly expressions about that kind of thing that it was enough to make one sick. But "knew" ... She thought of people she had read of in the illustrated works her father had, of savage folk and Italians and Moors and Arabs, when she heard of these women who dwelt in tents. They must have had great brown tents woven of camel's hair and goat's hair and there was a smell as of a sæter around them—there they lived, with a fire outside the tent, at which they baked hard little loaves and roasted kids on spits, and they gathered grapes in great baskets which they carried home on their heads and emptied into great stone vessels. Half-naked, bare-footed servants and maids trod the heaps of grapes so that the juice spouted, sweet and sticky, and they were stained as with blood up to the knees and their clothes were splashed all over with the juice. And when the sun was about to set her husband came home driving his flocks and herds—grey woolly backs huddled together and grey cows with huge black horns straight out to each side jostled one another as they came down the mountain. And she imagined the man who drove the flocks to look like that Arab she had seen in Copenhagen, who went about selling carpets—he was so handsome with all that white round his thin, dark face. He came up and seated himself outside their tent, and she fetched milk and food and stood watching him eat. Then they went together into the tent, and in the farthest corner a bed was made on the ground of skins and coloured rugs, and the thin, dark man with the great dark eyes embraced her with a narrow, brown hand that smelt of byre and mountain and thyme, then stroked her breast and whispered in a deep voice, with strange guttural accents. The worst thing about Frithjof had been his fleshy hands, which had as it were no *intelligence*—and his voice, unctuous when he thought himself safe, but flying up into a falsetto when he began to make excuses. Ugh—if she had understood it at that time: she might marry this fellow and have children by him, that was *one* thing, another was that he could never in this world come to know her, or anyone else for that matter—

But if Pastor Söndeled—not to mention Fru Söndeled—had known what kind of Bible studies Aslaug and she carried on, he would certainly have thought they were one as bad as the other.

Perhaps it was *that* which was to signify the centre and meaning of it all—of life, that is. Love and that. And then one had children and existed for them, as the leaves on the trees breathe and absorb sunlight for the bud which is growing within the stalk and will burst out next spring. But that made it simply unbearable that in this very matter most people conduct themselves in such a way that life becomes a fiasco and a disaster. Well, Jens and Borghild Braatö had come through on love, and indeed her mother-in-law used to assert that "love between man and woman" was the meaning and object of life and a foretaste of heavenly bliss—but good heavens, was everybody else to be at their beck and call, as Borghild Braatö thought she had a right to expect, because they had been lucky enough to find happiness in love? And their children did not seem able to manage either to be happy themselves or to make anyone else happy who had to do with them.

Aslaug—that was the maddest case after all. She had felt quite sick every time she came away from her, that summer before Aslaug's death, and she made herself almost sick in anticipation, so much did she dread every visit she had to pay to her at the sanatorium. Of course there had been a certain amount of personal disappointment and bitterness in it: her own position was not exactly pleasant either, and when Aslaug wrote again and again insisting on her coming here, she had had some idea that the other intended to help her with advice if nothing else, until she could start something. But she soon found out that Aslaug had only wanted to bring her here because she needed someone to whom she could talk and talk and talk without end. But poor girl, when she spent her life in bed ... There hadn't been a word of truth in her story about Gunnar Vathne being tired of her and in love with someone else—so she said, anyhow. It was Aslaug herself who had turned desperate or hysterical or whatever one was to call it, because that affair with Gunnar seemed to offer no prospect, and so when Tömmeraas fell in love with her she had had the sudden idea that now she *would* get married and put her life straight and have some comfort in it like other people. It was not that Ida Elisabeth couldn't see that anybody might well be turned a little crazy at times by the sort of life Aslaug and Gunnar were leading—but to go and take Tömmeraas! It was not only that they did not suit each other, not even that Aslaug had filled him up with stories about her past and future as a pianist and that he hadn't heard very much about her relations with Vathne until after he was well and truly married to her. But everything Aslaug was and said and did was interpreted by her husband so falsely—as was to be expected—and everything appeared to him in such a light that Aslaug was never for a moment free from torment. So said Aslaug herself, and at any rate there must have been something in it. And then Aslaug lay there, afraid to die, and afraid to get well, for she could not face going back to her husband, nor could she face the idea of a divorce and of trying to make her own way again. One was inclined to think it a mercy that she was allowed to die. But she could not help asking herself at times— what if there was a hereafter? For to a certain extent Aslaug was herself to blame for the failure of her life. When she did not care to see how things really were, she invented an imaginary situation and believed in it. But if, for example, one were forced after death to confess how much one really knew and understood, but was unwilling to admit to oneself that one understood, during one's life on earth—well, that must be like a kind of purgatory. Hell perhaps—if one had deliberately chosen to live in one's imaginings, refusing absolutely to allow the truth to exist.

In an unthinking way all men did that—tried to overlook facts the admission of which might be painful, and persuaded themselves that one's own fancies might very well be realities also. Religion for instance was nothing else, at any rate for such people as her parents-in-law, and they were the only ones she had known who were properly speaking religious—her mother-in-law in particular had tried pretty hard to influence her in this direction. But all she had been able to get out of it was that Borghild Braatö's god dwelt in Borghild Braatö's heart and broadly speaking was of Borghild Braatö's opinion on all questions, spoke to her through her conscience and gave his approval whenever she made a decision. But of course, it might well be that God existed to that end ... Perhaps there was even something in the idea that he tried to get a hearing in men's hearts, and that men cut him short with some such words as—well, that's really just what I think myself—in the way people do when they contradict anyone.

Well, in all conscience, it was not that she herself hadn't done all this—tried to believe in things which in her heart she knew very well were only her imagination, otherwise she could never have married Frithjof. Only when she realized that her children had no one else who cared to make an effort for their sake had she begun to cure herself of that habit of sailing away from tiresome facts. She had then thought she must try to take any bull by the horns if it threatened to gore her young.

Now she had come so far that life no longer meant mere endurance, taking each day as it came and struggling through it till she could tumble into bed and lose herself in sleep for a few hours. Now she had courage and means to look forward, to next week, to next month, to the time when the boys would be bigger. She dared to settle what they would have for dinner next Sunday; she dared to decide that Carl would have to make do with his old rain-coat this summer, because she was comparatively certain of being able to get him a new, thick winter coat in the autumn; she dared to think that they would require more as they grew bigger. And she had dared to lay out a little garden and was now planning what she would do in it next year. And now it was that she caught herself asking at times—she would very much like to know what is the meaning of it all, of our being alive.

Of course she had met people who go about saying that if one has work to occupy one there is meaning enough in life, and that it is only when people are too well off and can afford to be idle that they think they must at all costs discover a higher meaning in life. And Doctor Sommervold's opinion had been that when people were too badly off, when life was an everlasting fight against want and suffering, so hard that they had continually to risk their wretched lives in trying to save them—that it was then that people took refuge in religion in order to find a meaning in everything that happens. And it was really the very devil; yes, she thought it looked as if there was something in both these views. Perhaps some natures are such that they ask the question during the struggle, in order to find consolation, while others who are more hot-headed forget to ask while they are in the midst of the battle, but as soon as they have breathing time they begin asking: why—?

As a matter of fact she herself had had enough to occupy her in her work during all the years when it was only permissible to take thought from one day to another, how she was to get the boat to carry her and all those who more or less by her consent were in the same boat with her—and who took care to make her life one of constant anxiety: at any moment one or other of them might give a sprawl and capsize the whole caboodle.

At times she had actually come near to feeling something like a prick of conscience for having run away that time and saved herself and her children, for instance, when she had had letters from Doctor Sommervold in which he told her how they were getting on at Vettehaugen—that little Merete was dead, and that Else was married and divorced and had been home and handed them over a child which the old people had to keep, and that Frithjof spent most of his time there and had nothing to do. In her heart she did not think she could have acted otherwise than she did—but she was not sure that she would have made a break of it, if Frithjof's last exploit had not come to light just when she had discovered that she was to have another child by him and that he was even more of a duffer than she had always known him to be.

But he and all the rest of them were what they were bound to be—with the nature that was in them, and with nobody to see the necessity of any discipline that might constrain their nature. And she had met a fair number of people like them—the sort that Sommervold called infantile types. But in times like these, when things are so difficult, it is only too tempting to divide people into those whom it is some use to help, because they are willing to help themselves and are trying to swim as well as they can—and the rest. Doctor Sommervold indeed often talked as if he thought one ought to leave off holding up those who have no buoyancy in themselves—but if he did think so, he did not act according to his opinions. He did all he could for all he could in any way reach and do anything for. But then he belonged to another age.

Nor was she doing badly now, with her work from day to day. The very fact that it was waiting to be done over again, as soon as she had finished a job of work, was no bad thing. What Aslaug complained about till she positively shrieked—that housework was so monotonous: no sooner had she prepared a meal than it was eaten up, and then it was soon time to think of another, and when one had washed up and put things away, one knew that in a couple of hours' time one would have to take them out again and let the others dirty them, and the rooms had to be done and the beds made every day simply in order that folks should get into them again at night. There was something in that, of course. Folks must have clothes, and then they get worn out and folks must have more clothes—luckily for her. But she herself thought one might also look at it in this way: that it was the good, happy moments when one had finished one's work that recurred—when she had finished the morning's work and put the rooms in order, when for instance she had gotten the stove to burn nicely, with the window still open so that she felt the fresh draught of air through the room—or when supper was laid in the kitchen on Saturday evening with something out of the ordinary and she could call the boys in. Getting a thing off her hands she had always liked— whether it was packing up a dress with tissue paper and pins ready to send, or simply putting away a pair of shoes that she had polished and washing her fingers afterwards.

But just now, when she was to some extent free from the daily strain: how shall I find the needful simply to get something to cook, something to burn in the stove, and something to buy shoe-cream with? Now she could not help thinking: this life which demands such constant work simply to be kept going—what is it in itself? For this daily work, no part of which can be neglected without bringing the whole to a standstill—it was like everlastingly plaiting a basket. But what was to be in the basket? Or like the potter's work she had begun to learn, when she wanted to take up arts and crafts. But what are these cups and jugs to be filled with?

It was Aslaug's death that had impressed her, in a way more deeply than any other death in her experience. For she had admired Aslaug so tremendously when they were girls; in her case she had indeed expected to witness an instance of human happiness, for Aslaug was one of those who thought life was sufficient in itself, life was rich, merely to live was a delight. God knows how she had managed to fool away her life so completely. It was almost as if Aslaug's fiasco had caused her to take a different, more sympathetic view of all the failures of the world—but perhaps this was just as much due to her having cut herself off from the birds of ill omen with whom she had been thrown and having succeeded in bringing her own children more or less into safety.

THE window might be left open. She pinned the curtains together and lit the lamp.

What a state her skirt was in—and it was almost new! But at the same time she was thrilled with joy at the thought of her walk in the summer night. She took off her wet things. In a kimono, with her bare feet in slippers, she put them straight—pulled and shook the skirt as well as she could, before putting it on the hanger, wrung out the silk stockings, and stuffed the shoes full of paper. But she was still full of joy over this sense of vitality that she felt within her, and of longing for something towards which it seemed to be feeling its way—while all the time she saw to her clothes with a careful and practised hand, like a sensible and economical housewife.

There were those letters to the boys. Ola would have to take them in the morning. Her writing materials were in the trying-on room—but on going there she stood looking out of the window. It was already growing light—a car which dashed past on the road had a curiously up-all-night air in the grey dawn.

She had a sudden inspiration, went back to the boys' room and took out Carl's drawing things from the top drawer of the chest. It was long since she had drawn anything for her children; she had so little time for that sort of thing now, and Carl had given up asking her; he could draw for himself now. But this evening she would *draw* a letter to each of the boys.

She found a drawing-book with a couple of clean sheets in it, made a few strokes of brown and filled them in with blue and green wavy lines. That was the pool, and then she had to have the stream running out of it and the grass around and some big stones. She saw that she could not get on without the box of colours, and fetched water in a saucer. Now there came some life in it—she changed back to the coloured pencils. There, the pool with the spring lay at the bottom of a slope; Carl would be able to see that. It was best not to do any more to it; she would only make it heavy and lifeless. But she would have to put in a little blue above the crest of the hill—that was fine; now it was a bright summer sky with fine white clouds blown across it—

Ida Elisabeth sat looking at the little picture she had made. Why, yes—it was something like what she had been thinking of a little while ago out in the field. Only that this looked like morning—she had imagined it as a vision in late evening light. But she was not clever enough to try to paint that.

She wrote a few words to Carl on the back of the picture. But she must do one for Tryggve too. He always wanted her to draw something that would make him laugh—otherwise he did not care about her pictures.

Ida Elisabeth took a fresh sheet and put a little bluish green spot in the middle of it. That was the béret that a tourist lady had left behind at Viker and that Ola, the farm lad, had appropriated to his own use—he looked so comical in it, as Tryggve and she agreed. Ola could be walking by the side of a load of hay; against the brownish hay and the green field his blue-green cap would look just as incongruous as it was in reality. The horse drawing the load must not be too dark, or she wouldn't be able to make it look like walking when she had to draw it coming towards her. There—that would do for the Dun, which Tryggve was so fond of talking about. True, the horse was away on the mountain now, but what did that matter? It was quite a funny drawing—if only Tryggve would think it amusing.

When she had finished she sat there with her hands in her lap. This room was so cosy—and the joy of having at last got a nice room filled her afresh every time she could spare a few moments to sit still in it. She had made a patchwork carpet to cover the whole floor, and she had hung the wall behind the divan on which she slept with the same and covered it in the daytime with the charming Lapp rug Marte Bö had given her. The big semi-circular corner cabinet and the chest of drawers were so handsome with their reddish brown colour, worn slightly yellow at the edges— she had bought them quite cheap at an auction together with the two darkened oleographs in dark gilt frames. The pictures were exactly the sort she had seen as a child in the old houses of old people—when she used to sit and think of the places abroad where there were windmills and houses with thatched roofs and castles on the tops of mountains and hunters with feathers in their hats under great oaks— the places she would go and see when she grew up. Ida Elisabeth laughed a little at the memory, as she looked up at her pictures: one of them represented a green huntsman with hounds and a stag he had shot, and the other had a lake with high alps around it and a white church with an onion-shaped spire. But they did not look so bad as they hung here after all—

Well, she would have to make her bed. Pussy was asleep in the corner of it, half-way up the sofa cushion. White and fine with a pink little nose. Talk about a sleeping child—a human youngster can't succeed in looking half so innocent and peaceful as a sleeping domestic cat. "Excuse me, Puss"— she caressed the lazy creature as she moved it into the rocking-chair. Then she began to make her bed—

That too would fill her with an overwhelming, almost savage joy—each time she realized in earnest what it meant. That she could stretch her limbs, absolutely alone and safe, between the cool white sheets, bury her cheek in the cool white pillow—without having to be afraid of anyone coming.

It was daylight outside when she put out the lamp and slipped in under the bedclothes. It had not escaped her when talking to Fröken Presttangen—the dentist was evidently surprised at the comfort of her living-rooms. Ida Elisabeth smiled slightly at the thought.

Chapter Three

CARL CAME DASHING into the work-room one day in September:

"Mother—look what I've got!"

His whole face was shining to match the convex glasses of his spectacles. He held up his arm and exhibited a wrist-watch.

"Fröken Presttangen gave it me, mother, because she ran over me—isn't she kind! She came to see me at school, and do you know what she says! If you give me leave she'll give me a dog—oh, you don't know how sweet they are! We went to Evensen's and looked at them—I can have whichever one I like. The one I want is perfectly black and it has white on its chest and then the white goes in a ring all round its neck and it's white on the tip of its tail."

"I must say it was kind of her. I hope you thanked her nicely." Ida Elisabeth looked at the boy—poor fellow, how radiant he was! It *was* very kind of Fröken Presttangen—

Carl scarcely had time to look at the food, as they sat at dinner in the kitchen a little later. He talked and talked. She had said that it wouldn't do for him to keep pigeons here, for it would only make him so sorry when the hawk took one of them, as *she* had been when she was a child—he had told her he wanted to have pigeons, but she said he would get far more pleasure out of a dog. And then there was no truth in it that the blue dragon-flies over the pond down at Bru flew in people's faces and tried to put out their eyes—"they're not at all dangerous, says Kari—yes, mother, she told me to tell you that; you can just say Kari said so, she said—"

"If I'd been run over I'd have gotten something", Tryggve consoled himself. He evidently felt quite put into the shade by his brother.

It was of course very nice of her—but Ida Elisabeth was rather surprised: it actually looked as if she had a way with children. Carl was not one to take to a stranger. But obviously it was not entirely on account of the presents that the boy was so full of the lady dentist. They must have had a lot to say to each other as they went.

In a way she was not at all inclined to accept this dog from Fröken Presttangen. It would be difficult to bring up a puppy in this house—and it was bound to do a great deal of mischief at first.

But she had not the heart to say no. Memories of all the dogs she had known and loved came back to her: from the first, the big Leonberg she lay and played with when she was so small that she seemed to remember the dog stood taller than herself. And a poodle that had lived on board one of her father's boats. Whole dynasties of pointers and setters that they had had at home, and harriers that were boarded out in the country, and her mother's ruby spaniel—nobody in the house had liked him, by the way, not even her mother. And then the dogs that had been hers—the lovely Airedale that died of distemper, and the last she had had, Sonny, the Llewellyn setter, he had turned out no use at all for shooting, gun-shy and all the rest, but his pedigree was frightfully grand, and so she was given him. Oh, Sonny was the sweetest of all the dogs she had known, so handsome and so good and so terribly fond of her. He could never bear to see Frithjof touch her, so she used to lock him in her room when she went out, that last summer—

Oh yes, it would be fine to have a dog in the house again. It would make Carl so happy. And those little black sheepdogs that Evensen bred, they *were* handsome.

IDA ELISABETH had a great deal to do that autumn and well into the winter; she had two workwomen to help her all the time. She scarcely saw anything of her children except at meal-times. Tryggve was out amusing himself in the snow all day long, but Carl too was not so bad at going into the open air as he had been in other winters, and he had the puppy. Burman was its name—after a dog Fröken Presttangen had had—but anyhow it was frightfully sweet. And it was comic to see it with the cat: the poor pup frisked round Puss, confiding as ever and full of play, whenever the cat came into the room—and the little white creature was just as unapproachable in its dignity and made a dab with its paw if Burman became too impertinent. And Carl was so consequential and solicitous about these two domestic animals that were his. Poor Tryggve would really have to have something next summer—rabbits perhaps—he was quite left out in the cold. It would end in a regular menagerie—

It still remained with Ida Elisabeth like a feeling for which she could not account: that day last summer when Carl had escaped unhurt from the accident seemed to have marked a point of departure in her life. She had found courage to be cheerful in a new, calm, bright, and easy way. The old feeling she had had, that life was essentially something good which was perpetually being pursued and attacked and struck by something evil, had suddenly been transformed. Happiness was not *merely* like a pursued outlaw who took refuge with one by stealth and had to be well hidden the short time he dared to stay in one's house and get his breath, before his pursuers came on his trail again and hunted him.

Formerly she had felt as though she must enjoy each little happy moment with eyes and ears closed to yesterday and a moment ago and tomorrow. Hectic in its warmth and sweetness, almost so that it hurt, she had felt the joy within her, when she could steal out in an early morning hour and be alone, or alone with her child; or at such brief moments when she seemed to be snatched out of her thoughts of the whole daily effort by the boys laughing and making a noise or being so absorbed in their play that they grew perfectly still—and her mind became so clear as she wondered: how happy the children are, and that happiness must be something they have within themselves.

Now she took her boys much more calmly. For they were well, they had a lot to amuse them, they found amusement all round them—in outward experience and within themselves. And seeing this she was no longer afraid lest something might be lying in wait, threatening to extinguish the children's unsuspecting joy.

A DRAPER's shop had been started at the corner of the Pea Soup building, but it was not doing much good. It was kept by an old maid, daughter of one of the big farms in the next parish, and though she had once served in a shop in her younger days, she had spent the last fifteen years at home, keeping house for her brother, until he married. But it seemed she had neither capital nor experience enough in starting this business—people said she already regretted it and would be glad to be rid of it again.

Ida Elisabeth was playing with the idea—she discovered that she had a positive fancy to go into business again. When she passed the shop she could not help thinking, for instance, how she would have dressed the window. Fröken Torstad's windows would certainly not tempt anyone to go in and buy, unless they had gone out for that very purpose. And if one went into the shop she scarcely ever had what one wanted, and should she propose anything in place of it, the suggestion was not likely to be very helpful. There should undoubtedly be room for a properly run drapery business here by the station. For one who had some knowledge of how to carry it on, understood buying and had taste. People in these parts were more inclined to spend money; they came to her, for instance, and wanted to have a piece of material made up that they had bought on a visit to town, simply because they had seen the stuff in a window and fallen in love with it, though they didn't actually need it. And if she combined the shop and the dressmaking business—

At Easter she was invited to Marte Bö's with the boys, and then she and Marte discussed this project of the shop. Not that she really imagined it would be realized. But it was fun to sit and explain her ideas about it all, and it was always fun to discuss plans with Marte, whatever they might be. She fell in with everything, and she was always certain that it would turn out all right—

She had chiefly Marte Bö to thank that she did not lose heart altogether the first autumn she came to the valley here. She had left in a tremendous hurry, when things became too involved for her in Bergen. Torvald had certainly been extraordinarily kind—had even invited her to stay in his house: thus she discovered that his second wife, that is, the third, counting Connie, had also left him, no doubt for good. Torvald was going to get her a situation, and he was going to introduce her to people. But she could not get on with his acquaintance. Perhaps it was she who was stiff and prudish, or she took everything too seriously—or it may have been merely that she could never bear people who were inclined to encroach. She had been like that as a schoolgirl, when any of the mistresses tried to get their fingers under her outward manner, as it were, and touch the bare skin of her nature—gain the child's confidence, they called it—or when her mother-in-law was in one of her cordial and intimate moods. Torvald and his friends were on such unpleasantly free-and-easy terms—most people's object in life is to have comfort and amusement, but their amusement consisted to a great extent in a promiscuous propinquity. She was not a likely person to be squeamish; she must surely have been cured of that before she was grown up. It would never have occurred to her that people had to wear clothes because there was something shameful in their being made thus and thus; her idea was that one puts on clothes as one has a home—in order in the first place to be able to say "not at home" to all those one doesn't want to have at close quarters. But at times she had really had the impression that in the clique to which Torvald belonged they unbuttoned both their clothes and their minds, stuck together and chattered incessantly, because they were afraid of being left alone—just as some children get bored or imagine all sorts of uncanny things, when they are left alone in a room for a little while.

At first she had not told Torvald that she was to have a child again. But that only made her feel more out of place in that set. Once he had asked whether it was on religious grounds that she was scandalized at his goings on, for he could see she was, he said, chaffing her. To that she could only answer that she was probably just as much of a heathen as one could be. Far from it, he laughed; you're as moral as you can be. That had made her think of all she had read about negroes and savages and so on—it would do my worthy Torvald good to be dumped in the middle of a tribe of real savage heathens and be forced to observe their morality or suffer the savage and heathen punishments customary among savage heathens when anyone tries to take a liberal view of their system of morals.

But in the end she had to tell Torvald why she would not stay in the West. Amongst other things she was afraid that it would drag on her divorce interminably if Frithjof or his parents got wind of the new baby that was coming. Then of course Torvald wanted to make her confess: it was she herself who had someone else in view; to be sure, he wouldn't blame her for that, but as he was her lawyer she must tell him how things were. His intention was good enough, but it was a horrid thing to say.

So then she left Bergen, at Aslaug's instance. All that came of it was that she had to sit by the bedside of this dying person who was never tired of turning herself inside out.

The money she had received for her business and with which she had thought of starting something else melted away with fearful rapidity. Nor could she bring herself to say no when Aslaug lay there perfectly wild with terror lest her husband might find out about these bills which were being sent her. He was keeping her at this expensive sanatorium, and altogether it could not be said that he had been close-fisted with her, but he was very strict about regularity in money matters.

In the middle of all this she found herself obliged to see a doctor or a midwife. She chose the latter, as being cheaper—and as it were not so serious. For if there should really be something the matter with her—she dared not even think of it, what would become of Kalleman then—? But she thought she had never in her life been so miserable and downhearted as on that broiling hot day in August when she dragged herself uphill all the way to Bö Farm. But at last she arrived at the summit and saw the whole valley lying beneath her, north and south, with the shining river at the bottom and the haze quivering over dark blue wooded slopes with green patches where the farms lay on the hillside. Beyond were bare moors with hazy hollows and then more bare and rocky country, with snow mountains in the far distance. It was the first time she saw that this was beautiful country—not merely pretty as down by the sanatorium with its birch-woods, or at Berg where she was then lodging. Up here the view was grand in the way which induces an inward calm, since one's own cares and troubles slip away and lose their reality for a while.

The last piece of the road ran between rail-fences surrounding cornfields and a paddock, and when she arrived at the yard gate Fru Bö received her on the steps. She still remembered that Marte had been wearing a light blue washing dress in a large check; she was already immensely stout, but there was something so intensely charitable and yielding in all the curves of her figure. Ida Elisabeth felt she had been given fresh courage the moment she greeted the old midwife. Her big face was so healthy and kind under her neatly parted hair, black with streaks of grey, and her shrewd light-brown eyes were full of light; her lips looked quite young and pink in the fleshy old face. Coolness and comfort surrounded her soothingly in the little parlour with its pearl-grey walls—it had that old-fashioned panelling of broad flat boards cut long ago in some local saw-mill; great fuchsias stood in the window, hung with a wealth of flowers, subduing the light. There was such a solid and reserved look about all the old people in the enlarged photographs on the walls—old men with a white fringe of beard under their chins and men with keen clean-shaven faces, women with silk shawls over their smooth parted hair and women with their hair done in a huge crown on the top of their heads and a lace frill with a big gold brooch at their throats. Even the sofa covered in American cloth did not look a bit forbidding among this unpretentious birch-wood furniture upholstered in green check linsey-woolsey.

Actually Ida Elisabeth had always thought the worst of the whole business was that one had to hand oneself over so helplessly and humiliatingly to other people to be felt and squeezed and manipulated. It had been horrid at the maternity clinic in Oslo, and she had not been able to bear the widwife at Berfjord. For the first time in her life she felt that a strange person's hands may do one good—it was as though the mere touch of Marte gave her comfort and consolation. And when Fru Bö finally declared, oh yes, there was nothing wrong here, it would go quite satisfactorily—Ida Elisabeth believed her without hesitation. It would all turn out well.

All the same she could hardly understand how she came to tell Marte Bö so much about herself as she did the very first time she saw her. But she had said a lot—that she had left her husband and had to keep herself and her children without any assistance, and that she must look for work the sooner the better, and there was really nothing she could turn her hand to except dressmaking and tailoring.

Marte said afterwards that she too had taken a fancy to her at once—"a straightforward person without any nonsense about her". Marte made the suggestion that she should take up her quarters near the station and helped her to get the lease of two rooms and a kitchen in that ugly uncomfortable house which lay half-buried under the road; but when Marte came to see her there one day and assured her: you'll see, you'll come to like this place—Ida Elisabeth came near to believing herself that she might find it quite comfortable. Marte helped her to buy some second-hand furniture quite cheap and to get a sign painted. Marte sent her her first customer. Heavens, yes—she had never made a coat and skirt before, except at the school of dressmaking, that is, never since. But she got it right—as a matter of fact, she had perhaps never succeeded in getting quite such a smart cut again. It bucked her up tremendously to have turned it out so well. And Marte Bö positively advertised her.

Only three weeks after Tryggve's birth it happened that Marte Bö was crippled by an accident as she was driving to a case in the Aas neighbourhood. She was over four months in the hospital, and Ida Elisabeth sent her flowers at Christmas, and flowers when she went home—she wanted to show some slight sign of her gratitude. But she was greatly surprised to see how highly the old midwife had appreciated it.

Since then there had been a kind of friendship between them, genuine and unaffected, in spite of their being so different. Besides, Marte Bö had a sort of predilection for Tryggve, as being the last child she had brought into the world, and because he was so nice-looking and big and strong. It was like a holiday to Ida Elisabeth when she went up to Bö to make for Marte. In her company she could sit and weave fancies about her own and the boys' future. Not that she believed exactly that her wishes would be fulfilled, but it was so amusing. The mere fact that she now ventured to talk so much about the future was a great thing—and never did she dare to talk about such things so freely and cheerfully as under Marte Bö's bright and kind brown eyes.

"You can go and talk to this man Toksvold, can't you?" Marte was saying. "He can't charge you anything for *that*." And one day, just after her return from Bö, she actually did so. She had been to the station to fetch a parcel of sewing materials—odds and ends that she could not get at Fröken Torstad's but had to telephone to town for. On her way home she went up to the lawyer's office. But she came near to regretting it, when his lady clerk said he was engaged, would she kindly take a seat. She was left sitting a fairly long time, heard the hushed buzz of voices from the next room and once Toksvold's voice—he was speaking on the telephone, very clearly and distinctly. No doubt everyone did that, spoke more distinctly when they used the telephone; only she had never noticed it before. Ugh no—she had better get up and go; what had she to say to him after all?

At that moment he appeared, showing out the dairy manager and another man. He looked a good deal surprised as he caught sight of her—and that made her regret still more having come. But now she had to accompany him into the inner office.

"No, I haven't heard anything about that", he answered in surprise, when she asked if it was true that Fröken Torstad would like to sell her business. Where had she heard it? And then he gave a little laugh: Fru Bö, ah yes, she always knew so much—

Well, well, then there was nothing more to be said about it. Ida Elisabeth got up and asked him to excuse her.

"Oh, dear me, that's nothing ... No, as I say, I haven't heard of her having any such idea. But if she should say something about it, would you like me to let you know? Or you might yourself broach the subject with Fröken Torstad?"

Ida Elisabeth buttoned her gloves:

"No—no, times are so bad now, perhaps it's rash to start anything. But if she herself should hint that she would like to get rid of her business or anything of that sort, I would certainly be grateful if you would let me know."

"But tell me, Fru Braatö—do you think you would have a better chance than Fröken Torstad of making anything of the business here?"

"I have had a shop of my own before, where I was living while I was married. For about five years. And I made it go. Though there were not nearly such chances of custom as here. And I had a husband who was out of work most of the time. And then, you know, I could combine it with dressmaking—Fröken Torstad only makes a few child's frocks and aprons and so on. You know I have to think of my boys; they will have to be educated when the time comes—"

He fixed his clear, serious eyes on her:

"And you have to manage all this alone—?"

"Yes, that's so."

He shook his head:

"That seems to me wrong. That there are so many children nowadays who have only one parent. And it falls more and more on the mothers to see to it all themselves."

"Yes, you may well say that. But what is one to do? If one must, one must."

He put his hands in his pockets, then stood for a moment balancing on his heels. Then he asked rather shyly:

"Excuse my asking, it doesn't really concern me—but is it a fact that you have a husband alive?"

"Yes. He's at home with his parents."

"Ah, I see. Well, then he can't contribute very much for the children."

Ida Elisabeth could not help laughing:

"No! That comes under the head of downright impossibilities."

"Well, I'm sure I don't see how it's going to end", said Toksvold. "I had a case not long ago—a woman who was trying to get some contribution towards her children out of their father. And he's a man who has never been able to keep himself even, but now he had gotten married again to a woman who has money and a good position. Separate estate, of course. Well, one can't expect *her* to help and provide for the children he had by another woman, that's plain. But there's something about it that's utterly wrong. Talk about a midwife's husband living on his wife— there was always something ridiculous in that, even with a man like Haakon Bö, though goodness knows he was master both in his own house and on the district council and all the other boards he sat on. But now it seems no longer to be a disgrace for a man not to be able to provide for his family unless his wife too has to go out and work— and there are many who are not even ashamed to be kept by their wives. Shocking! They used to cry out that it was such a disgrace if a woman married in order to be supported—but if she keeps her home in order and brings up children to be decent men and women she has certainly made a good return for the support she has received. But as for a kept man—God knows what use he is. Unless he can console himself like the street-walker that there are other ways of making a living that are a good deal less respectable than hers."

"Oh well—" Ida Elisabeth turned red. It occurred to her that she had been disappointed to hear that it was all off between Frithjof and that lady of his. But that was of course because she had regarded it as a sort of safeguard for herself if the other took over Frithjof—and she would just love her to get him. And in reality she had never had enough respect for Frithjof for it to suffer any diminution ... It was merely a thing she had tried to work up in her own imagination.

"If we women are stupid enough, why then—"

It looked as if he was going to say something, but he did not, and Ida Elisabeth took her leave, with excuses for troubling him.

Chapter Four

IDA ELISABETH WAS WATERING her garden one evening of the week before Whitsuntide, when Herr Toksvold stopped outside the fence: "May I come in, Fru Braatö?"

She had imagined it was something about the business, so she was extremely surprised when he asked if she would care to accompany him and Fröken Presttangen on a trip to Valdres at Whitsun. They would spend the night there with an aunt of his who kept an hotel.

"Thanks, but you see, I can't leave the children."

"No, of course they must come too."

The sun had sunk below the mountain in the west and the evening light was dull and cool down here in the valley. But on the top of the ridge opposite, the firs were still blazing in orange sunshine, and the woods were so full of the song of birds this evening. It was frightfully tempting to think of—getting away for a real long trip—

"Thanks, but . . . I don't see how I can—your aunt doesn't know us even—"

"Aunt will be very glad indeed. She's always so glad to have visitors." He had already telephoned to her about it.

Ida Elisabeth dried her hands on her wet canvas apron, and stood looking at him reflectively. It was so curious—she scarcely knew these people.

He smiled, a trifle bashfully, it seemed. And that became him very well, she noticed.

"I must tell you, Fru Braatö—to be quite frank, you would be doing us a favour. Kari is to meet someone up there, and so perhaps it wouldn't look so well if we arrived alone, just she and I."

"Well, but wouldn't it be better if you got someone else whom you both know better?"

"Kari knows nobody here. She finds it rather difficult to make friends. And she has such an immense respect for you—"

"For me? But I've scarcely spoken to Fröken Presttangen."

"Haven't you? I really thought—well, after all it doesn't matter." Again he looked as if he would like to say something but didn't quite know how he was to do it. "Yes, she has a huge respect for you. For having made your own way— not giving in when you had to drop your art and so on, but courageously turning to something else. That is just what she has most at heart, I must tell you; she insists on being independent at all costs. I'm afraid she'll fritter away her life altogether with these independent notions of hers. That's what made me think, if you and she could see more of each other—perhaps you would be able to put some sense into her. From our talk the other day when you came to see me I thought . . . She and I were brought up together, you see, and I'm very fond of Kari. So I should be only too glad, I really should, if you could get some influence over her."

"I'm afraid I can't imagine that." Ida Elisabeth could not help smiling at the man. Why, she had really had the impression that her feeling for the dentist, not exactly one of sympathy, was fairly mutual.

"Oh yes, surely. She has such a tremendous respect for all women who *are* something. And the fact that you were a painter too—"

"I?" Ida Elisabeth laughed aloud. "But in heaven's name, where did Fröken Presttangen get that idea from?"

He looked rather surprised:

"It was your boy who told her—Carl. He had shown her some sketches you had done—and then Carl said you were a well-known painter before you were married. Had a big picture in the gallery—"

"Oh, that boy!" Ida Elisabeth laughed aloud. "It's all stories and imagination—there are some pictures by my grandfather in some of the galleries. That must have put the idea into the child's head. Jacob Siveking, you know, the landscape painter."

Toksvold nodded, in a way that showed Ida Elisabeth he had never heard Jacob Siveking's name before.

"But isn't it true that you paint yourself—?"

"I do a few little daubs for the boys sometimes. We can all draw a little in our family. My brother wanted to be a painter. Well, so did I for that matter—but then my father lost all his money, so I had to give up the art school."

He nodded and looked very sympathetic. But now what about this trip?

Ida Elisabeth asked if she might think it over till tomorrow. They could talk about it on the telephone.

Oh, that Carl, she thought when Toksvold had gone and she went back to her watering. To think that he too was so given to boasting and making up stories—? Then it struck her that after all she had done the same thing herself this evening—something like it at any rate, when she talked about having had to break off her studies at the art school because her father had lost his money. Actually she had stopped long before, because she was sick of it ... And she had promoted her great-grandfather Siveking to grandfather and spoken as though she assumed that everybody knew about him ... She laughed a little at herself. Perhaps everybody is tarred more or less with the same brush—

If *he* rang up about that trip, she believed she would accept. But *she* would certainly not ring *him* up, without hearing from him again.

It was strange though that they should want her in particular to be chaperon. And not easy to understand what he meant by her influencing Fröken Presttangen. People said that the fillings she put in fell out again at once.

SHE had had a thousand belated scruples for having accepted this invitation. They vanished like smoke on the morning of Whitsunday when they were waiting for the car: she saw how Carl was looking forward to it!

He stood before the mirror in the trying-on room:

"I say, mother! I expect they'll all think it's *motor* goggles I'm wearing!"

Ida Elisabeth seized the youngster and hugged him to her so hard that he gave her quite an embarrassed look.

"You've got a different car to the one you ran over Carl with", remarked Tryggve with the air of an expert, as they were ready to get in. "Then you only had an old Dodge."

"Yes, that's correct." Herr Toksvold gave a little laugh, but it sounded as if he was a trifle annoyed. "But get in now."

"Let Fru Braatö sit in front with you", said Kari Prest-tangen. Ida Elisabeth was just thinking how strange it was that pretty girl hadn't a better idea of how to dress herself. With her style of hairdressing it must be hard to get any form of head-gear to sit properly, but anything more unfortunate than that boy's cloth cap she could not possibly have found; her hair filled out the crown so that it looked like a stuffed cushion. And the ulster in a brown mixture was outrageously unbecoming. She looked incredibly untidy and this exaggerated the awkwardness of her manner. And then her coat stank of naphthaline—

"Then you'll see more, I mean", she added clumsily, as though abashed at her former tone of command.

"Thanks, but I'll have to sit with my boys."

"There's less draught in front too", said the other eagerly. "And you won't notice the dust so much either. I'll take good care of the boys—"

Have they had a row? Ida Elisabeth wondered, as she seated herself beside Toksvold. The whole thing looks rather odd. But it's all the same to me. I'm simply going to enjoy a lovely drive. What weather!

The car purred and flew along towards the mountains, which stood out a pale purple in the morning light—they seemed to draw together blocking the valley and the winding river. Then the road curved back upon itself and one guessed there was some place where it could slip through at the foot of the huge mountain masses. It was so fine and so interesting to watch them change their shape continually as they drove towards them. Ida Elisabeth sat still enjoying the view and resting in the happy sense of speed and the present moment.

Now and again Toksvold mentioned the name of a big farm as they dashed past, and Ida Elisabeth answered, "Oh yes", and, "I see." They all stood some way up the hillside and were all alike, with great brown timber houses and a dull gleam of slate roofs and huge red barns, and some had dwelling-houses painted in bright colours. "Don't you think it's fine here?" he asked once, and she nodded. She had a feeling that he saw the beauty of it from the point of view of the farms, they were the essential thing in the valley in his eyes. And instinctively the scenery they were passing through began to take for her the form of pictures, in which the brown or many-coloured groups of houses became centres around which all the rest arranged itself. The broad green meadows and brown ploughed fields spread out from them, white spouting streams running down the hillside formed dividing lines between a strip of wood and the paddock of a farm. Clumps of bird-cherry which were already quite green and sprouting birches and aspen thickets with tiny bright reddish leaves grew around heaps of stones that had been cleared from the fields in old days.

She had often wished herself over on the other side of the river, for she had imagined it must be so much finer there on the northern slopes. The dark fir forest grew from the water's edge right up to the mountain brow, where the bare ground showed through, and the little green patches in the forest, where was a lonely cottage or a farm with a few small houses, were so far apart. She had never really seen before today how beautiful it was here on the sunny side.

They entered a forest, and the road ahead was dark and wet. Remains of snow-drifts reached to the edge of the road, frozen on top and dark with fallen pine-needles. "It's no more than three weeks ago that I got stuck here", said Toksvold. There was something so intensely spring-like in the tall, slender spruces with their coat of lichen wet and black and their needles bright and green as though freshly washed after the snow. High up the sky was a clear blue above the tree-tops. The cold smell of wet crumbling rock and the carpet of pine-needles was lovely—

"What a lot of blue anemones there are here! We don't have them at home in my part of the country. Perhaps that's why I can never get accustomed to them—they're so pretty that I can scarcely believe they're real."

"If you like we can take some up with the roots as we drive back tomorrow. They do quite well to plant in your garden. We had a whole ring of them at home round the flagstaff."

Behind her in the car Ida Elisabeth caught Tryggve's voice calling out; evidently he had questions and remarks to make about everything they passed. "Ugh, that boy—I'm afraid he's worrying Fröken Presttangen shockingly, he's such a fidget."

"Oh, you needn't be afraid. Kari likes children."

He was a good driver and a safe one, Ida Elisabeth could see. They left the forest behind. Here the river broadened into a lake and in the morning stillness the reflection of the hillside with forest and farms sank indistinctly into the water, as a mere brightness of colour, blue and green. At the end of the lake a rounded hill rose; it was not so very high but its shape was curiously beautiful. "Do you know the name of that hill over there?"

"Torstad Brae I believe they call it. Those farms you can see below it are Torstad. You don't know these parts very well?"

Ida Elisabeth shook her head:

"I have only once been here in the train. When I came here first. And then it was raining, I remember."

"Well, then it was high time you came for this trip. And lucky we had such fine weather. You'll just see when we get up on Tonsaas how grand it is. And going down to Aurdal—"

Their quiet chatting about nothing in particular, with long pauses when they sat silent and there was nothing but the hum of the motor—this made her feel even more secure in her delight in everything. He had such a calm, warm voice—every time he mentioned the name of a farm or a dairy or a church they passed there was a note of solicitude in it, that she might enjoy the drive. Now and then her conscience troubled her a little when she heard how noisy the boys were behind her—scattered over a green slope by the side of the road was a whole herd of goats, and on some of the farms they had let the cows out into the paddock, and she guessed that the boys bombarded Fröken Presttangen with questions every time they passed anything of this sort. Ugh, they must be worrying her to death. But at the same time it was good to have a little peace for oneself.

THEY had been driving for several hours, had driven a long way by the shore of Lake Mjösa—this was the brightest country she had seen, the whole vault of heaven free and blue above the broad smooth surface of the lake and the low border of hills around. It was already quite summer-like down by the water, a quantity of different flowers were blooming by the roadside, dusty already. The first white bunches of cherry blossom were out where the trees got the full warmth of the sun, and the meadows were so advanced that the grass waved like flames when a gust of wind came. She had never really imagined so open a landscape could be so beautiful. "I wonder what sight will meet my eyes, over the mountains yonder—" The lines came into her head, but that made her think of Vettehaugen, where this had been a regular national anthem—and it was one of the tunes Frithjof could play—

At that moment Toksvold had turned to her to say something: "You're not feeling cold, are you?" he asked. "Would you like a plaid over your knees?" "Oh no—" She smiled and made haste to chase away the expression that her memories had brought into her face. "You're not feeling ill, are you? Some people get seasick when they're motoring—"

HE had put on speed—they had a long stretch of straight clear road before them through a wood. Then there was a terrific noise at the back of the car and Kari Presttangen stood up and tapped Toksvold on the shoulder: "Stop—you must stop—"

When the car stopped she could hear Tryggve bellowing with all the strength of his lungs—and in an instant they were all out, standing around the boy, who was howling worse and worse.

"You haven't swallowed anything—?" Kari Presttangen took her fingers out of his mouth. She opened a handbag, took out a cup, and ran down to a brook which shot under the road close by. Carl made haste to explain—Tryggve had stuck his hand into Kari's ulster pocket and found some white balls which he thought were sweets, and when she tried to take them from him he hurriedly stuffed them into his mouth, but they were something to keep away moths—

"Fancy my forgetting to take them out before I came away", Kari Presttangen was full of sympathy. "Poor little chap—here, be quick and rinse your mouth out!"

"It's just what you deserved", said Ida Elisabeth hard-heartedly. "For putting your hands in other people's pockets. Now stop that horrid shrieking!"

"We might just as well take a rest here", suggested Toksvold. "And make coffee." He drove the car into a little green clearing in the wood; Kari Presttangen and the children galloped up the bank of the stream. "Here, here!" they shouted; they had found such a grand place.

They were collecting wood for a fire when Toksvold and Ida Elisabeth came up with plaids and a suit-case.

"No, look here, Kari, that'll take too long—we must boil it with the spirit stove—"

"Is there any fun in that! No, we're certainly going to make a proper fire!"

They stood facing each other and it looked like coming to a quarrel between them—as to how far they had still to drive and how late they might arrive, when the aunt expected them to dinner, and how long they could rest here. She at any rate grew excited—turned very red about her high cheekbones. The boys too tried to join in the discussion, they voted for a bonfire—

"Come here, Carl and Tryggve", their mother called. "You'll be good enough to keep quiet; it's not for you to interfere in grown-up people's business." Her voice sounded very cheerful and decided. What the two had fallen out about was no concern of hers. The boys were so sulky that they said nothing.

Ida Elisabeth's head was in a whirl after the long drive. It was delightful to sit and listen to the soft sighing of the breeze in the tree-tops, which bore with it the sound of a church bell far away—sometimes it died away completely, but then she heard its notes again. And close to where she was sitting the little brook purled over stones and roots.

"There's nothing I can help with—?"

He had won the victory; on a flat rock stood the spirit stove with the coffee-pot over it. Kari Presttangen looked crushingly offended as she knelt and laid a cloth on the grass with cups and plates of cake. Of course it was rather depressing to be on a trip with a pair of lovers who had quarrelled, but she would just have to take no notice of it.

"Won't you sit here on the plaid, Fru Braatö?" asked Fröken Presttangen with marked complaisance. "Or shall I bring you your cup? All the same, you're more comfortable over there, I think I'll join you—"

She did so, sat down beside Ida Elisabeth and looked as if she had been badly sold. Now and again she got up, fetching this or that and handing it to the other. Toksvold sat by the cloth, cutting cake for the boys.

Fröken Presttangen would not hear of changing places with Ida Elisabeth when they went on again.

ABOUT three o'clock they arrived at a big place lying between the main road and the river. "Hotel" was painted on the nearest of the great white houses, one with verandas all over its front. The whole place looked frightfully comfortable—a great grass-grown courtyard with several white dwelling-houses and some huge red and grey outhouses around it. The lady who came out to receive them reminded one a good deal of Marte Bö; she too was stout and brown-eyed and kind. It was the aunt; her name was Fru Björnstad.

They were sitting at the dinner-table when a maid came and said Fröken Presttangen was wanted on the telephone: "from Galby". She jumped up and ran out, more awkward and abrupt in her movements than ever. Toksvold watched her go and forgot his food for a while. It was some time before she came back.

"Sigurd's in bed. He's hurt his leg—they had been to the sæter and he had a fall on the way home early this morning. So he can't come here." She went over to the window and stood looking out over the pots of flowers. "He wants me to come up—"

"Well, that's quite natural. Shall I drive you up?"

"I can just as well drive myself—if I may borrow the car?"

"All right, as you please. Is it anything serious?" asked Toksvold, as she slowly made her way to the table again.

"Don't know. They didn't think so. It was Marit I was talking to. The doctor has been. He's not to go to the hospital anyhow." She gave a very heavy sigh as she sat down again.

IDA ELISABETH sat in the big glass veranda that looked on to the garden and saw Fröken Presttangen drive off on the road to the south. In a moment Toksvold came and stood watching the cloud of dust—and then came Fru Björnstad, who poured out the coffee.

"Well, I must say it's a strange thing—that this should happen to Sigurd today of all days!" said the aunt meditatively.

"There may be a purpose in it." His voice sounded so hopeful.

Toksvold and Fru Björnstad conversed about people in the neighbourhood; Ida Elisabeth listened with half an ear, keeping an eye on the boys, who were busy by a pond in the garden. Then, in order to draw her into the conversation, as she guessed, he began to tell her of a case of manslaughter a few years before, when he was acting sheriff here. But she could see that all the time the others were thinking of this visit of Fröken Presttangen's and that for some reason or other it had put them in a good humour.

Then Fru Björnstad was called away—a car had arrived with some visitors. "Shall we go down and look at the garden?" he proposed. "It's very pretty. Perhaps there's not much to see in it now, but . . . But you're interested in gardening, aren't you?"

Poor man, he was quite at a loss to find something to entertain her . . . Saturday's paper lay there, she hadn't seen it yet. But she went with him all the same—along a garden path with old apple-trees on each side. The buds were just about to burst, showing bunches of little yellowish beads between tender compressed leaves. Along the edge of the path there were beds of sun-warmed grey mould in which the green shoots of perennials were coming up.

"Don't get yourselves in *too* much of a mess", she said as they passed the duck-pond where the boys were sailing bits of bark on the muddy water.

The path ended at a stone wall towards the river. On the slope down to the water was a thicket of slender half-wild cherry-trees whose shiny brown branches were covered with buds ready to burst. On the other side of the river the cliff rose perpendicularly at first, grey with clefts in which ferns and little trees had taken root, and above was the steep hillside covered with dark firs.

"Isn't this pretty—?" He waved his hand towards the view. "This terrace was my uncle's pride. I'm really very glad you could come. Will you smoke—?" He held out his cigarette-case.

Ida Elisabeth had begun to smoke again. It was like a little happy assurance that she could afford the time and money to indulge herself again, every time she bought a box of cigarettes. At Berfjord she had had to cure herself of all superfluities. As she accepted the match he handed her she felt the cool caress of the heavy ivory silk blouse against her skin—a Vienna model that she had bought to copy. She had changed into it when she came out—good to feel fresh and chic.

"You can guess," he said, "it's Kari's fiancé, Sigurd Mælum. He took over Galby four years ago after an uncle of his. A very good fellow, straight and sympathetic. Well, it isn't public yet, though goodness knows it's no secret either. And as far as I can see it would be far better for her to marry him than to go on with that dentist business of hers. She's not even very good at it—hard of hand, I've heard it said. To be sure, it's no great fun to be a farmer either in these days. But to have to root about the jaws of anybody who comes in—no, that's the last job I should choose—"

"I expect there are lots of people who think it's interesting work—"

He scoffed:

"It's only that Kari absolutely insists on being something—professional. It's the result of her having had a stepmother—one who had been our governess. We were a few families who had clubbed together for a governess who was to coach us for the grammar-school. So when Kari's mother—she was a sister of my mother—when she died, Tor Presttangen married this Ella. But she and Kari didn't get on. It was then that she came to live with us. Not that I believe Ella meant any harm really. But she gave Kari no peace, trying to cure her of being as she was in every way. She was pretty genuine in those days, a regular country girl, handy and straight—and extremely sensitive with it all. Well, then she turned obstinate and did exactly the opposite of all her step-mother told her—but imitated her all the time, or tried to, so long as Ella wasn't within hearing. In a way too I believe she admired Ella—who was really a handsome person to look at, but rather affected. At any rate she was out of place as mistress of a big farm—

"But another thing was that Kari saw well enough that her stepmother could do what she liked with her husband—Tor's head was quite turned by this woman. At first, that is. For no doubt he grew thoroughly sick of her after a few years; she lost her looks pretty soon. But then Kari was no longer at home. Her father was absolutely against her con-tinuing her studies—he had probably had quite enough of that sort of thing, and he wanted her at home. Then it was that she and Sigurd began to see a good deal of each other, and at that time they were *very* much in love. But then Kari came into some money of her own, a legacy—

"You know, Kari's real mother had not been treated as Ella was, and Kari did not forget that. Gunhild, you see, my aunt, was a regular countrywoman of the old type. She never spared herself, and I don't think she expected anyone to think of sparing her. No, she had no pretensions. Or rather, she made no demands on her own account, other-wise she was far from what we should call unassuming; what she considered fair dealing and behaving 'like folk' was no small thing, I can assure you—and she insisted on this both from herself and others. Ella never made any demands except that people should have due regard for her. And when all's said and done that is a great deal less than what Gunhild demanded. So it's not to be wondered at if Ella had things more to her liking. But this was the state of things that Kari turned over in her mind all the time she was growing up. Well, it was the same in our home too—though both my father and we children did appreciate mother in a way. But not as we ought to have done, of course, and it would have done no harm if we had shown it more.

"The result of this was that Kari grew up as she did, you see. For really she is the kindest of persons—but she takes everything to heart in such an unreasonable way, especially if she's fond of a person—so she's positively afraid of anything of that kind. I'm certain that if you hadn't been with us today, she would have insisted on my turning back when we'd come half-way."

Ida Elisabeth was sitting on the wall a little way from him, looking down at the budding cherry-trees and the river running past in the shadow of the steep grey cliff.

"Well, but if your cousin is like that—" She searched for a word; "she must surely be allowed to decide for herself how to arrange her life? If she's afraid of marrying this fiancé of hers? The engagement must have lasted a good many years—perhaps they have both changed . . . Aren't you taking a pretty big responsibility—for if I haven't misunderstood the situation, both Fru Björnstad and you—well, at all events it wasn't to *break it off* that you brought her here?"

"She must anyhow have a real *talk* with him, in my opinion." Toksvold had turned red. "Sigurd must have a right to be told where he stands—

"And do you know what? A person can't let her whole life slip away simply because she's afraid it may hurt her to live."

Ida Elisabeth sat plucking the dry sun-warmed moss from the stone wall—it crackled so pleasantly between her fingers. It was an odd question, the one he had just put. She had never thought of it before—if indeed she had ever been so placed or so constituted that she could stop and consider: shall I?—shall I not? before throwing herself into any of the experiences she had been through—it would have been hard to say what she would have done. But she had come through it all in a way—and had come out of it quite well, she was beginning to think latterly. She had her boys, and they were healthy and brim-full of vitality and pluck to discover the world into which she had put them. When she put her arms round them and felt the warmth of their young carcasses, she thought—after all there are lots of people who manage things so that they can enjoy being alive—

As though he had heard something of her thoughts, he said:

"So you would rather be in your present position and have your children than have made a name as a painter, for instance, and be an old maid?"

"Supposing I had become a painter, it's not certain that I should be an old maid." The idea made her laugh.

He frowned:

"No, of course not. I didn't really mean that either. But it would have made things rather different, wouldn't it?"

"Different from having a dressmaking establishment? Yes, I presume so."

"Well, now you're laughing at me! But don't you see what I mean? That such a life as has nothing—grand, or striking, about it in people's eyes is worth more than if a woman makes a name for herself in art, or takes up a practice or any other work that comes first with her, and is only a mother in the second place as it were, or in her spare time—"

Ida Elisabeth nodded:

"But you admit that all Fröken Presttangen's mother and your mother gained by it—I mean, by thinking of themselves last of all—was that all those they lived for did the same. They too thought first of themselves and last of the one whose only thought was of them."

"That is true enough. It's a thing that was brought home to me when I'd seen a little more of the world. One can understand to a certain extent why so many girls have got that idea of wanting to be independent and to develop themselves before all. The only thing is that the world grows even worse than it was when those who formerly were willing to devote themselves to goodness will do so no longer. For you mustn't imagine that men are made any better by women becoming egoistic. On the contrary. For, you see, there will never be more than a small percentage of either men or women who can create for themselves a field of work which they could not exchange for another without feeling it as a sacrifice. But because a few women have succeeded in making themselves a position which it would be a sacrifice for them to give up if they married, perhaps nine times as many are to be forced to go out and do a full day's work as breadwinners, and to do the work of a mother and housekeeper the rest of the twenty-four hours, or as many of them as they can stand on their feet without dying for want of sleep. Because a few females of the middle class have discovered that it is a disgrace to be kept by a man. In reality, I suppose, there were always devilish few who did nothing in return for their keep. The great majority at any rate had more to say than all the men in the country put together, as to how the generation that was growing up should turn out. But this talk about women not allowing themselves to be kept, you see—the ordinary average man who is no better than the majority of sinful folk takes this to mean that he needn't provide for his wife; she can look after herself, and if she wants to have children she can do her share in providing for them, since as a rule she is keener on having them than a man. And if you come down to the real scallywag type, they reckon on being kept for life if they've been fortunate enough to have a child by a decent and moderately good-hearted girl. You may be sure I've seen more than one example of the type in my practice."

Ida Elisabeth laughed nervously:

"You give your own sex a nice testimonial, I must say!"

"Well, but the majority of people are a pretty rotten lot, you know. And always have been. And God knows if there's anything that can make them keep within bounds and behave decently except just this—that the women, the best of them anyhow, are willing to take upon themselves what my mother and Aunt Gunhild and their sort went through. Even if they never got the thanks we owed them from their own family. They were after all the ones who carried the whole concern, even if they were hidden beneath what they carried, just as the soil of the cornfield is hidden under the corn. And it's no small thing to be that—"

Ida Elisabeth gave him a serious look, but said nothing.

"But of course, having seen that, one knows one ought to cherish and respect such persons. At any rate I imagine I should do so *now*, if I met anyone of that sort."

She laughed, rather bitterly:

"I too was promised that, once—to be cherished."

He looked at her, almost sadly:

"And you were not—no, I can guess that."

"You see, Herr Toksvold—it's natural for children to be egoists. All their needs must be satisfied by other people. And there's little they can do to help either others or themselves. Imagine if all the grown-ups fell sick at the same time and could do no work, and the children had to keep the world going for a single week—that would be a nice state of things. And such people as never grow up—you know what one reads in the paper: the accused's mental development was that of a twelve-year-old child. You must have had to do with a number of such cases. But there are still more who are on the twelve-year-old level, or the eight-year, or five—who get along without bringing themselves into court; they marry and have children and vote at elections and help to make up public opinion. Well, there was a friend of mine who was a doctor; he used to say that all

these ideas about democracy and so on came from a time
when nobody had yet dreamt of anything like psychiatry.
But one ought to excuse such people if they show the egoism that belongs to their age. But it's true, I do think really
grown-up people ought to be kinder to each other than
they often are."

Toksvold nodded:

"That day last year when we had the misfortune to run
over your boy—it was quite odd how you reminded me of
Kari's mother, when you received us and attended to him.
Kari noticed it too. Well, she was in such despair at what
had happened, as you can guess. But it was that likeness
that made such an impression on her that, for instance, I
could never get her to come with me to inquire after the
boy—she got quite hysterical when I asked her. There was
a boy too, I must tell you, Elling—he was younger than
Kari. He was a cripple from infantile paralysis, and his mother
looked after him for five years, besides all the other things
she had to do—and was just as kind and ready and calm all
the time. But when he died she seemed to be fit for nothing more—she went out the year after. No, it's not in outward appearance exactly—though Gunhild was also fair and
thin, but she was a farmer's wife, and it's easy to see that
you're not a countrywoman. But there's something of the
same, for all that—" He looked at her for a moment and
looked away, as though embarrassed.

Ida Elisabeth could not help smiling faintly:

"Was that why you were so keen on getting me to join
this—expedition?"

With increasing embarrassment he replied:

"You know it was a great pleasure for me too—I greatly
appreciated your coming with us."

Ida Elisabeth sat in silence. But she was thinking of the
day when he came in carrying Carl—there was something
in his expression at this moment which reminded her of
that. And she realized as a thing the significance of which

she could not ignore—his handsome, serious face with its clear grey eyes, as it looked at her over the boy's head, was a part of that day which to her was like the entrance to a new, brighter, and more confident time.

The sun had now left the place where they were sitting, and down the garden path came Carl and Tryggve running at full speed:

"We're to tell you from Fru Björnstad that you're to come in to supper—"

As they turned in to the grass-grown courtyard they discovered that his dark-green Chevrolet was standing there among the three or four other cars. Fru Björnstad met them in the passage:

"Kari came in to fetch her suit-case. She was going to stay up there a few days, she said. So I expect you'll have to drive home without her. She said she'd ring you up in the morning, by the way—"

As they went into the dining-room she told them at great length about Mælum's accident. "Poor Kari, she was fearfully upset about it", Ida Elisabeth heard her whisper to Toksvold.

Of course she can't break it off while he's lying with his leg in plaster of Paris, thought Ida Elisabeth, and she felt rather sorry for Kari Presttangen. But she dismissed the feeling—the others were so cock-sure that it would be best for her to become Fru Mælum of Galby. And they knew both parties.

IT was no easy matter to get the boys to bed; they were perfectly wild about all they had seen during the day and chattered incessantly. Ida Elisabeth's body felt strangely light, almost as if she were floating, as she went about the dusk-filled room, unpacking the boys' night things and clean stockings for the morning. It was a very large room, low-ceilinged and irregular, with nooks and corners where the dusk seemed to collect.

It was on the ground floor and looked out on the yard. Outside she heard Toksvold talking to one of the motorists who had arrived the night before. The other was inquiring about the state of the road over Tonsaas. And she remembered a lake they had passed up there—it was still covered with ice, dark and rotten and full of leaden cracks. There was still a good deal of snow in the forest there and great blue-grey clouds collected from all quarters, till the sunshine was extinguished altogether. They ran into a scud of driving snow which passed over the forest. But he said he didn't think it would come to anything—and a moment later they were out in the sunshine again.

She inspected the boys' necks and ears—what a mess they had gotten into. With the clothes-brush and Tryggve's breeches in her hands she went up to the window.

Toksvold, in shirt-sleeves and overalls, was engaged in washing the car. On seeing her at the window he came across:

"Perhaps you would like to have an evening drive? There are some waterfalls here, about seven miles to the north; they're generally splendid at this time of year. Or we might drive down to the westward past Galby, then you'd have a view of the farm—"

"No, many thanks. I've had plenty of driving for today." She laughed.

"Are you awfully tired? You'll come into the drawing-room presently, won't you? Aunt wants us to come in and have coffee."

Properly speaking she had had enough coffee too for one day, she thought, still smiling. But she would have to join them all the same. This place was uncommonly homelike.

THERE were no lights anywhere as she went through the house. In the dining-room the doors stood open to a veranda, and the strong pale light of the spring evening was reflected with a bluish tinge from the long table with its white cloth. When she opened the door of the drawing-room it seemed quite dark. The light rectangles of the windows were entirely filled with an outlined pattern of leaves from the big pot-plants. There was a scent of Virginia cigarette, and now she saw the little red glow.

"Come over here, Fru Braatö; here's a good chair. Would you like me to turn on the light?"

"Oh no, that seems almost a pity." She settled herself well in the deep, square arm-chair; its plush was bristly and felt like moss against her cheek. Ida Elisabeth slipped off her shoes and drew one leg up underneath her. She was rather proud of her high insteps, but it was inconvenient when she wanted to be neatly shod, pumps and straps were always too tight for her.

"We've been uncommonly lucky with the weather. And it looks as if it would hold for tomorrow."

So tomorrow I shall have to sit in the back of the car, she was thinking. The boys can't sit alone—

"It was awfully kind of you to bring us. It's been quite an experience for the boys. Fru Björnstad has been so extraordinarily kind to them. She brought them in milk and cakes when they had gone to bed. And I'm sure they've been allowed to run all over the place and poke their noses in everywhere—"

"Oh!" he gave a little laugh. "Poor aunt—she doesn't like this new-fangled motor traffic. Parties who come and demand meals at all hours of the day and never two of them together. And far fewer people who stay. Only two parties staying the night here and they're going on again early tomorrow."

"Yes, it's strangely quiet this evening. But people can't sleep in tents so early in the year—with the nights still so cold and the ground so raw?"

"Oh, that's half the fun. Comparatively cheap to get about too in that way."

Then they sat in silence—as though each were waiting for the other to start talking again.

He went over to a corner and lighted a little lamp. The globe was shaped like a rose, giving an orange and deep pink light. The bronze figure of a dancer held it with raised arms. Her hair was puffed out over the ears and she wore a kind of Empire gown which spread out to form the stand. Ida Elisabeth remembered having seen lamps like that when she was a child.

He was manipulating a radio receiver over there—in the red light of the lamp he studied the programme in a paper. The apparatus roared and grated, then came a talking voice, and Toksvold turned the button again till he got the music of a dance band.

"From London", he explained. "Shall we dance? Are you fond of dancing?"

Ida Elisabeth fished up her shoes and got on her feet. At the far end of the room was a free space of floor without furniture or carpet, with windows on two sides and dark shadows playing on the glass. A tall pier-glass was full of dark coppery reflections from the windows—like the waters of a tarn on a summer night.

A soft thrill of voluptuousness passed through her as she felt his arm on hers and his hand against hers, the scent of his skin and his clothes so near her. It was long since she had danced, but at the first step she took with him a memory awoke in her whole body—the languishing rhythm of the tango flowed into it, as light as nothing her body felt as he guided it. Her eyelids drooped; she felt herself turn pale with pleasure. The room was now so dim that she could see nothing but obscurity and pale light floating around their movements and two distant red lights like beacons turned with them—the one by the radio and another far within the mirror each time they reached a certain spot in the room.

"Oh, but it's lovely dancing with you—" he whispered, and she could hear the delighted surprise in his voice. "You're madly fond of dancing, aren't you?" She only smiled and abandoned herself more intensely to the joy of motion.

When the music stopped they stood still; he did not take his arm away, and she felt the rough cloth of his jacket under the tips of her fingers.

"We'll go on dancing, won't we?" She only nodded, and they stood quite still waiting for the music to come again. There—and he gave her a happy little squeeze, as they glided on again over the little bit of floor; and they danced and danced till a door opened and they stopped abruptly.

"Well, I must say you're two sensible people", said Fru Björnstad's voice. She set down a jingling tray and turned a switch. The light leapt out so dazzlingly white and hard in the middle of the ceiling that Ida Elisabeth stood blinking—it was like being waked out of sleep, or as in the theatre, when an act comes to an end and one is suddenly hurled back into a glaring auditorium—

"That's what I like! That man from Askim and his wife went off to bed as soon as they had had supper."

"He said he had to drive all the way back tomorrow", Toksvold explained. "And had driven pretty far today. A drive I'd like to take too—" His voice was lost in mumbling, as he took a map out of his breast pocket and unfolded it: "Nesby—here you see it—"

Fru Björnstad shook her head—Ida Elisabeth need not help to arrange the cups. So the younger woman crept into the big chair again.

"You'll take cognac, I suppose, Tryggve?" Fru Björnstad handed Ida Elisabeth a liqueur glass. The liquid in it was thick and black with flashing gleams of dark amethyst.

Toksvold picked up the cognac bottle and regarded it critically:

"Thanks—but I believe I'd rather have some of your brew, aunt. Well—did you say 'skaal'?"

The thick sweet liquor that burnt like fire as she swallowed it and smelt and tasted of bitter almonds was wild-cherry ratafia; she remembered having been given some as a child on a visit to her grandmother Andst, but never since. It was frightfully good.

Fru Björnstad complained that the spirit one got from the wine monopoly was too weak; she had had to alter all her receipts for liqueurs. From that the other two went on to talk of all the prizes she had taken at exhibitions, for syrups and jams and bottled fruits and liqueurs, and then of the prizes won by people they knew at exhibitions of home industries and cattle-shows and so on, and finally of horses.

Ida Elisabeth took in the whole picture of the room, with the utmost intensity, as though its appearance was of overwhelming importance. The walls were pearl-grey, panelled with broad flat boards, and the ceiling was panelled with narrow boards arranged in a kind of star pattern and divided here and there with mouldings and knobs painted brown. There were masses of flowers and green plants in the windows and on old-fashioned stands made of birch-stems, and the bulky and angular furniture was covered in bluish green plush. Along the walls stood heavy carved farmhouse cupboards, but they had been painted a bluish green with much gilding and silvering of the carving. On the walls hung enlarged photographs and old rugs and mangling rollers and embroideries representing boys and girls dancing in national costume against a pea-green woollen background—and there was a black piano with a white Cupid and Psyche on it. But all the same the whole effect was wonderfully pretty—

It was long past midnight when she entered her room. The window stood open, rattling a little on its fastening; the room was filled with cool night air, and the bed looked cool and white and tempting. She had drunk a little too much of that cherry liqueur—but it was such fun watching the heavy pale purple drops creeping down from the edge of the glass like a scalloped border after she had drained it, and she remembered that of old—

Ida Elisabeth went across to look at the boys, who were asleep in the broad double bed. As she bent down and kissed first one and then the other of the two warm faces she noticed that her lips were sticky and sweet—

It would be lovely to get to bed—but it was lovely to feel tired like this—after a whole long day that had been a glorious time from beginning to end—

Chapter Five

CARL AND TRYGGVE were never tired of talking about their Whitsun trip. Almost every day at dinner or supper in the kitchen they recalled some point or other of which they had to tell their mother.

Ida Elisabeth was busy from morning to night cutting out, trying on, putting her workwomen right, and finishing what was difficult. Everything seemed to go so easily—the two young sempstresses were infected by Fru Braatö's cheerful mood, they worked gaily and with a will, and when they had finished in the evening they dawdled over their clearing up and confided to her all sorts of things about their private joys and sorrows, till Ida Elisabeth went with them to the gate and all three stood there chatting a good while before they parted.

It was the same with the children. Carl and Tryggve scarcely noticed that their mother perhaps did not pay very much attention to *what* they said; but they had discovered how easy it was to make her laugh. She was so disinclined to be peremptory and vigilant, and they took advantage of it. The evening hours were filled with long and merry skirmishes, which ended at last in Ida Elisabeth getting them driven into the boys' room: now they *were* to go to bed; she would soon be angry in earnest, she told them; just look how late it was. And Carl looked at his wrist-watch to find out how much he and his brother had won from their mother—it was actually so late that all little boys with sensible mammas ought to have been in bed long ago.

Then at last she had finished all she had to do, in house and garden; she too could go to bed. But she didn't feel inclined—

One of the many things she liked about this house was that here she need not have blinds in her bedroom. She had always liked so much to be able to look out if she woke up at night, and see what time it was. Whether the window was black and a few solitary stars twinkled brokenly where the pane was slightly warped, or she saw that it was already growing light and there were clouds in the sky which were flushed with the sunrise, or the two light squares of window were frosted over in patterns of rays and tendrils, or the rain was pattering against the panes—she always thought it so delightful to have these glimpses of the time and the weather between one sleep and another. But she had not had that since she was a little girl. All the time in Oslo, and the time she was living at Berfjord, and the first years here in the house near the station, she had slept in rooms which looked out on to a street or a road, so that she had to hang something over her window.

The nights were now light, so she had left off lighting the lamp when she went to bed. She dawdled over making her bed on the sofa, dawdled over her undressing—went over to the window and looked out. The river and the wooded slope on the other side of the valley and the old garden just outside came out more and more clearly as the dawn approached, but still the whole world lay in a sunless, chilly light. Her flowers in the window-box were no longer a play of shadows against the glass—they spread luxuriantly with grey-green leaves and red and white blooms. It was almost a sin to sleep away so much time, the little while the light nights last.

And it was another lovely feeling to be the only one awake in all this big house.

She herself thought it rather comic that this Whitsun trip continued to haunt her thoughts so incessantly. Of course her existence had not been spoilt exactly with diversions. She could not forget having danced. But she *had* really been madly fond of dancing when she was young—and she had not even thought of it for years; everything of that sort had seemed so utterly past and done with in all the years she had been married to Frithjof. In reality she was still a young woman—but there had been a long time during which she had had as it were no age, she had merely been one who had to get through a certain amount of work every day.

But it was strange how the mere fact of having danced once again called up in her body all kinds of memories of a physical nature. Images kept cropping up—they appeared in strong lights and were accompanied by memories of music and the hum of voices, but far away, almost like old dreams that one happens to recall—a place in Copenhagen, to which she and Connie had driven in a car with their father and mother. And she envied Connie for having gotten a partner with whom she could flirt, a tall, handsome, dark young man, while she herself had fallen into the clutches of one with horn spectacles and thin wisps of fair hair through which his shiny red scalp could be seen. That must have been when her father was down there placing a contract for a steamer with a Danish shipyard and had brought the whole family with him. That time, though, was so strangely unconnected with all her other memories, before and since, that it appeared quite unreal; she could not even work up any particular feeling of loss when thinking of all the glories of those days, though she remembered many of them with extraordinary vividness, for instance, a cormorant's skin coat she had had with a big bunch of artificial violets on the revers.

But behind all that again was a time that she often thought of now, with a sharp stab of longing. She fell to recalling the children's dances of those days—one in particular: her mother had curled her hair all over and had tied a big bow on one side of it, of broad green silk ribbon with silver thread. She had had on a frock of a kind of shot silk, very light and shifting from blue to green—something her father had bought for her in England. And she had enjoyed herself so frantically that she was in a kind of daze—every time she came upon her own reflection in a big mirror that stood in the room, it gave her the impression of seeing a strange girl. But then came the terrible disaster—somebody upset a plate of yellow cream and red syrup over her. A lady had taken her up to a bedroom and tried to wash it off, but the frock was spoilt for good and all, and she had cried with despair, and her mother had been so angry when she got home—though it was not her fault. And then she remembered a Christmas dance at Teie; there were two boys there from Trondhjem, nephews probably of Doctor Sommervold. She had wished so tremendously that one of them might stay in the neighbourhood, for then she was sure she would have fallen in love with him. That was the winter she was to be confirmed. Her parents had been there too—she remembered how afraid she had been that they might drink so much that the Trondhjem boys would notice it. Frithjof was there too. Yes, to think how little was needed to make everything turn out differently.

The last time she danced—she remembered that too. It was in Oslo, on the first floor of the Park Café, the evening after Frithjof and she had been married before the mayor. They had supper there with their witnesses, Aslaug and one of the friends of whom Frithjof had so many at that time, and they danced. Yes—they had been happy. She must have been fond of Frithjof at that time—or of the idea that she was in love with a man and was married to the one she loved and was to have her own little home with her boy and they would live happily ever after. And so she had assigned Frithjof the part of the husband in her romances about happiness. She was then nothing but a child, a great big girl—though to be sure she was not what one would call innocent; but that had only been a kind of accident. She had been a child in spite of it, a little goose she might well say. And Frithjof too had been a child then. And he had never grown up, but she had. That was the whole story—really poor Frithjof was not to blame for it all, nor for being such an unprepossessing lad either.

She was not unaware of the drop of bitterness that lurked in every one of these memories of dancing. And in spite of that she thought it so lovely to sit and recall them. Even the memory of her wedding evening—that was indeed infinitely sad, but all the same—she had come *through* all that that had led to, and that was no small thing. It was true, as Tryggve Toksvold had said, that one cannot refuse to live simply because one is afraid it may hurt. Certainly it does, perhaps life hurts more often than not, but "more often than not" is not the same as "mostly". The good things come first.

A little while ago all the colours in the valley were already awakening, as though with a dawning light that came from deep within. But now all was grey again; the sky had clouded over. And all at once there was a rustling in the leaves outside—every tree in the garden flinched under the first heavy drops of rain. That was good—rain was wanted now.

By degrees she had gotten so far as to be standing in her nightdress—enjoying the coolness of the morning against her body through the thin stuff. She would take a look at the boys first.

They had kicked off the bedclothes. Their mother handled their limbs gingerly, as she covered them up and laid their hands on top of the turned-down sheet: "Heavens, how fond I am of them! Of Tryggve because he's such a little rascal and so entrancingly pretty, of Carl because he's my own good little boy who's not at all pretty, but queer and difficult." Even while it felt like a pain to love them so boundlessly, when she was besieged by uncertainty and knew there was no one but herself who cared to do anything for them—even then her love for them had been a happiness which nothing could *entirely* suppress. And to be able to love them as now, without too much care and anxiety for the future—O God, how good that was!

Half-past two—and at seven she must be up again. But she really had no feeling that she required more sleep now in summer-time. The first flute-like morning notes of the birds intruded, sweet and cool, upon her jumble of thoughts, weaving themselves into the mists of sleep the moment she had stretched herself between the sheets.

THE local paper announced the engagement of Fröken Kari Presttangen, dentist, to Sigurd Mælum, farmer, of Nordre Galby. Poor girl, thought Ida Elisabeth. But perhaps she has arrived at the conclusion that this is her best choice.

A week or so later Ida Elisabeth met Fröken Presttangen in the village; she went up and congratulated her. Kari Presttangen received it with a curious expression, as though trying to ward off something of which she was afraid. She asked abruptly after Burman, Carl's dog. She had with her another fluffy little black thing; this was an own sister to Burman, she explained, and entered into a long dissertation about these shepherd's dogs. Ida Elisabeth was now able to tell her more than enough about their dog, its talents and its misdeeds, so they had an animated chat and walked together as far as they were going the same way.

Poor girl, she thought, when the other had gone—if she had gone up there to break it off with her fiancé and had then been captured, on finding him on a sick bed. But perhaps it was the best thing for her—she seemed in a fair way to become an oddity, if she had been left there as an old maid. And it's no use being afraid of life because it may hurt—

SHE had met Toksvold once or twice by chance and he had given her a lift one day when she had to go to the bank and he happened to be driving in that direction. Next day he called on her in the evening: he was on a committee which had been formed to build some baths on the plot between the dairy and the savings bank. Ida Elisabeth laughingly promised a subscription of ten crowns, and he sat and chatted for nearly an hour, and as he was going he stopped outside the front door and talked to her about her garden. He had an idea that that strip of the old road in front of her door would just suit for a croquet lawn. Ida Elisabeth thought it was too narrow. He admitted that of course it was narrow, but all the same ... He had an old croquet set lying in his attic: "I'll bring it one evening, if you like, and then we can see." He evidently enjoyed having a chat with her.

The boys had seized the opportunity to make off—it was past eleven before they chose to come in, and past twelve before she had them in bed. She sighed and shook her head with a laugh, when at last they had stopped their noise. It was summer anyhow—one mustn't be too strict—

She lighted the lamp in the work-room: she was anxious to finish the tussore silk dress she was making for herself by Sunday—when all at once Carl's little form in light pajamas appeared at the door:

"I say, mother—what did he really want—that Toksvold?"

"He wanted to rent a piece of ground from me for a croquet lawn", Ida Elisabeth replied seriously.

"Oh, bosh—don't try and humbug us!"

"Well, you'll see. They're going to start a croquet club, he and some others, and they'll come and play here in the garden."

The boy had come right up to her, stood looking at her with an expression she could not quite make out. But she threw aside her sewing, then took Carl in her arms and pressed him to her with a laugh: "You little silly! Go off to bed—"

She went in with him, shook up his pillow and turned it, smoothed out the top sheet. Carl threw his arms round her neck and drew her roughly to him: "Mother—I'm so fond of you!"

"Are you, my darling?"—she kissed him. "That's nice of you—but now lie down and go to sleep—"

THE following evening, as she was working in her garden, he came to the gate with a young lady and a man whom he introduced as Herr Berge, the engineer from the slate-quarry. Ida Elisabeth knew the lady slightly; she was Fröken

Sörli, the schoolmistress. They wanted her to come over to Björkheim with them and dance.

"Ever so many thanks, but I don't think I can. I can't go off and leave the children alone in the house."

"Those big boys—why, what difference can that make—?"

"No, I really can't."

"There are the Hansens upstairs—if anything should happen. And then there's the telephone—"

They kept on for a while, trying to get her to come. It was Herr Berge's birthday and she should have champagne: "Now don't be so slow!"

But Ida Elisabeth stuck to it and assured them it was impossible. She gave the hero of the day a rose for his buttonhole and found a rosebud for Fröken Sörli and another for the lawyer, then waved to them from the gate and hoped they would enjoy themselves—

She hadn't even wanted to join them, she discovered with some surprise.

NEXT evening she was standing at the window of the trying-on room arranging some fashion papers, when she heard the click of the garden gate. She had now gotten to know Toksvold's way of swinging it to.

He caught sight of her at the window and stopped outside. The old perennials growing against the wall of the house were like a spreading hedge between them, with the white and pink flowers of the columbines floating above, intensely bright in the evening shadows.

Over the hedge of flowers he handed her a huge parcel in brown paper:

"It's those blue anemones I promised you once. I'm told by an expert that it doesn't do to plant them while they're in flower, so I didn't bring them before—"

"But really that's far too kind of you—"

Ida Elisabeth undid the parcel. Inside were several layers of newspaper, and the last wet and crumpled sheet was full of mould that had sifted off the roots—raw, loose brown mould with pine-needles and moss among it; it brought before her the forest they had driven through. The old leaves were brown as leather, but each root bore a tuft of this year's leaves, soft as silk and brilliantly green with fine silver hairs at their edges, lying limply in the paper. With a little pang of sorrow she thought, ugh, I'm afraid they won't thrive; I'm sure he ought not to have taken them up before the new leaves were more developed.

"I may as well put them in for you, while I'm here—"

"Thanks, but you really shan't do that ... There's no need—"

"Well, but suppose I do it all the same? If you have any tools here—"

When she came out he had hung his coat on the doorhandle.

"Where would you like to have them? At home we had them round the flagstaff, but as you haven't any flagstaff—"

You told me that once before—she felt inclined to say that and laugh, and blushed, with a delicious little thrill. It would have established a kind of intimacy between them, and she wished she had dared—and she had imagined that flagstaff with a ring of blue anemones round it as vividly as if she had seen it—a part of his home—

Instead she proposed that perhaps they ought to put them under the hedge of roses she had planted on the far side of the old piece of road: there they would get the sun at the time they were in flower and would be in shadow afterwards, when the leaves of the rose-bushes had grown. And there she would be able to see them from the windows of the work-room.

She brought a spade, a trowel, and a watering-can, and he set to work putting in the plants according to her instructions. Ida Elisabeth carried water and sprinkled each one as he finished.

"Did you have a pleasant time at the hotel, yesterday evening?"

"Oh, not enough to hurt. You didn't miss much—"

"That was a pity. Poor Herr Berge—not to have a more cheerful birthday party—"

"All the same I think you might as well have come. As you're such a good dancer. It was rather mean of you, Fru Braatö—"

She only laughed: "It's not so easy. It isn't as if one was a free and independent person—"

"No, I see that, but—"

It was a terrific quantity of anemones he had dug up. The sun had gone below the gap in the hills to the north; not a cloud was to be seen in the sky, which was pale and clear, shading to light yellow over the northern ridge. Some swallows were still darting in giddy curves high above the house and under the eaves to their twittering nests, but more and more of them had slipped in to rest. Toksvold planted away as hard as he could, and still there was a whole heap of roots in the paper.

"Have you thought of doing anything on Midsummer Eve?" he asked.

She shook her head: "As far as that goes I don't know what folks *do* here on Midsummer Eve—beyond putting up leafy boughs. And Hansen does that here. Don't you light midsummer bonfires in these parts?" She was reminded of the great bonfire on the mountain above Vettehaugen, and the waterfall and her father-in-law's fiddle, to which the young people danced.

"Some of those who've been to continuation schools and the like have had a try—but strictly speaking we haven't that custom here. But one can find something else to do. Go up to a hut and dance. It's sure to be open up on Kallbakslia now. They have a big new house at the Svensrud sæter, where ten or twelve of us could sleep. We should have to take a gramophone, and cream—we'd have to take

Kari with us to make cream porridge, or perhaps you can? *Can* you make cream porridge? If it would amuse you—I'll see about getting up a trip for Midsummer!"

Something dark squeezed itself under the fence on the Viker side—Burman, the puppy. Noiselessly it dashed at Ida Elisabeth, jumping up and squealing and wagging its tail and making little snaps at her hands—then it went off to bark at Toksvold. First Tryggve, then Carl climbed over the fence and plumped down into their mother's garden.

"What in the world—what are you thinking of, coming home so late! Carl, you'll be able to find things—the milk and butter are in the cellar, you know. And you'd better finish up the rissoles that were left from yesterday. But then you must be quick and get to bed. You see, I've got to get this finished tonight—"

Carl inspected the plants that his mother and Toksvold had put in.

"There! Now you must go in and have your supper and hurry off to bed—"

"Will you come in and say good-night to us?" asked Carl, hesitating.

"Yes, of course I will—no, Burman! Carl—oh, do take this wretched beast in with you! Ugh, puppies and gardens", she laughed despairingly. "Like dogs? You may be sure, we're as fond as we can be of the little rascal—but oh, what a lot of mischief he does", and she began telling him of it.

At last he had finished his planting, and then he had to go into the kitchen to wash. Ida Elisabeth went to get him a clean towel.

"Come a little way along the road with me, Fru Braatö! It's such a fine night. A little exercise will do you good—"

"Very well. I'll have to go in and say good-night to the boys first."

At first they walked without saying anything. It must be late—getting on for midnight, as one heard no sound from the village and there were no lights anywhere. The road stretched before them pale and dusty in the twilight, which was clear enough to distinguish every object one passed, only the colours were absorbed by the dusk.

"It would be fine if we had rain now—"

"Yes, it's extraordinary how dry it's been—for so early in the summer—"

From behind they heard the hum of a car approaching—the glare of its lamps flooded the road in front of them and lighted the dusty alder thickets on each side. He took her hand and drew her out of the road—on to a little dry slope where they stood with eyes closed for the cloud of dust that whirled after the car.

Then he twined his fingers round hers, squeezed them, and did not release her hand. On the little hill where they were standing were some little old timber houses—they belonged to the farm on the other side of the road; from them came a warm smell of byre in the summer night. The meadows below the farm were light with the reflection from the river, but under the hill on this side water and forest were merged in one dense shadow.

Ida Elisabeth held her breath in a kind of terror, for there was something new trying to force its way up within her—then he drew her with him back on to the road and walked on, but he still held her fingers entwined in his and did not let go. And as they walked his hand gave hers one short squeeze after another. It filled her with a languishing sense of happiness which made her incredulous—here was this man *wanting* her, and she felt that he wished her nothing but well.

Suddenly he said, speaking rather low in the stillness:

"But how is it you don't get a hose to water the garden? You could have one to screw on to the tap in the kitchen and bring it out through the passage—"

But his voice had none of its usual sound, and she understood that he was only talking to persuade himself she would not notice his agitation.

"Then it would have to be a very long one—" She heard her own voice, there was no ring in it—it made her think of a glass bowl that has been filled; then it only gives a faint dead sound when you strike it.

They gave up the attempt at chatting as if nothing had happened—abandoned themselves to silence.

The lights at the station showed far ahead—but what's going to happen now, she thought; I'll have to go back—? They were just outside the house where she used to live; there was a dim light behind the dark green blinds of the Norwegian-American.

They were walking on the opposite side of the road, along the fir copse. The scent of pine-needles still floated out from the darkness of the wood and she caught the distant murmur of the little stream rolling the bright pebbles in its bed farther away. Is that where we're going? she thought confusedly—

There was laughter on the road by the station—a group of people came towards them, talking loudly and laughing. "I must go—" She drew her hand out of his.

"Oh no?" He put his arm round her—for an instant she felt herself held against him, between his arms, with his face above hers, and then he kissed her—first on the edge of her cheek, but then he found her lips in the darkness and kissed her properly.

She seemed to lose consciousness—short or long, she could not tell. "Let go now—" she said in a low voice, and on feeling that she was free, she turned and began to walk, at a furious pace, back towards home.

Is he following me—? She did not know whether she wished it or was afraid he might—both, perhaps. But when she stopped to get her breath, outside the little farm where they had stood before, she could hear nothing. She started to walk again—more slowly. In reality it was only five or six minutes' walk from here to Viker—

With a feeling as of trying to get oneself awake—now I *must* get up—she tried to rouse herself out of this vague, unreal feeling in which she was borne along. Dear me, yes, he kissed me—that's not so very terrible. You've been kissed before now, Ida Elisabeth—

But inwardly she knew it was not true. She had never been kissed before. Even if she was dimly aware that she had allowed someone before to do this or that—which she now scarcely remembered—to her, and she had more or less taken part in it; nobody had kissed *her*—

God knows what he thinks of me—? But in reality that did not affect her a scrap. He thought neither one thing nor the other about her—it was something quite different, she knew that very well.

Happiness, and all that has never come my way before—

FROM habit she looked in on the boys, when she had made her own bed on the sofa. She arranged the children's blankets, bent down, and kissed them lightly on the cheek. But it was as though she stood outside herself in a way, while she did it; and when she looked into the kitchen to see if the boys had cleared up after them and remembered to put the milk and butter back in the cellar—all of which she did from habit—she herself seemed to take no part in it.

In reality—in reality there was only herself, filled with dizzy rapture and freakishness, and all else that she sensed outside her, that she knew she would be forced to think of again, did not concern her *now*—

THE moment she opened her eyes next morning and remembered, she made up her mind to take the whole business lightly: it was by no means certain that he had meant anything much by it all. She went through her morning work gaily and calmly—got Carl off to school, Tryggve out to play ... All the time she was possessed by the most intense conviction—he meant, O God, what a lot he meant!

Precisely at nine o'clock the telephone rang:

"Good-morning! This is Toksvold. Is that Fru Braatö?—may I call this evening?—there's something I'd like to talk about—"

He had avoided either familiarity or formality in his way of addressing her, she noticed. That made her smile so that she infected her sempstresses with her inward gaiety, and the girl from the sanatorium who tried on two summer frocks of artificial silk went off home in the best of spirits and perfectly certain that she would be quite irresistible in her new clothes.

Ida Elisabeth went over to look at the anemones as she took out Tryggve's lunch. Their leaves looked pretty limp, but they might very well pick up for all that—

The thought struck her—what was she to do with the boys when he came this evening? About half-past eight, he had said—she couldn't drive them off to bed at such an unchristian hour on a bright summer evening. Ida Elisabeth thought furiously—having something on from which the children must be excluded was a situation that had not occurred before.

They spent a good deal of time at Viker in the evenings, and they had playmates at a cottage a little farther south along the road. But they were in the habit of dashing back home at any moment—she had them running in and out all day long.

Then she remembered it was a cinema evening at the young people's hall. But they had never yet been to the pictures without her; they were too small to go alone. The Hansens' adopted daughter, that was an idea—Snefrid, who sometimes did messages for her; she had invited her once or twice when she took her boys to the cinema. But the girl was about thirteen; if she gave them the money Carl and Tryggve could very well go with her. It lasted from a quarter past eight to a quarter past ten, and the children would certainly be about half an hour on the road—

IDA ELISABETH did her hair again and changed into the tussore frock. Then she went and put her own room straight—moved some vases of wild flowers and grasses.

Burman was tied up in the passage—poor chap, he couldn't be taken to the cinema. And at last he began to bark at the approach of someone.

Ida Elisabeth stood in the middle of the room laughing, as Tryggve Toksvold appeared at the door.

Then he flung away the straw hat he held in his hand—it spun like a wheel through the air and landed on the divan, and the two were in each other's arms, laughing for all they were worth.

"Well, you know, I'd actually gone and got a speech ready—'I don't know, Fru Braatö, what construction you may have put on my conduct yesterday evening'—or maybe I'd thought of asking if I'd offended you, for that was not my intention—"

They laughed so that they had to sit down on the sofa, and he took her hand and laid it on his knee:

"Well but, Ida, what did you think of me for being so bold—?"

"Think of you? Do you imagine I was stupid enough to do any such thing?"

He looked at her, as though uncertain and at the same time rather offended:

"Well, to tell the truth I did think you had been thinking about me—"

"Yes, thinking about you! I've done nothing else."

"You mean," he said thoughtfully, "thinking *about* a person—is not the same thing as thinking something *of* him? No, naturally." He drew her to him and kissed her. "Natur-al-ly it's not the same thing!

"But you are a queer person, Ida!"

"Not a bit. I'm as ordinary as I can be."

"You? Oh no, that's too much to hope for, I'm afraid—that people like you should be ordinary. It would be a much better world if it was so."

She laughed quietly: "If that's meant for a compliment I must say it's an uncommonly delicate one—"

"It isn't a compliment. You should just know how I look up to you. And what lovely hair you have—there's something so soft about it—"

"Now don't be angry if I ask you to go." She had dreaded having to say this for the last twenty minutes at least. But now she was obliged to say it. "The children will be here directly—and you understand, they might ask questions. I'm not in the mood for that—this evening at any rate."

His face grew serious:

"No, perhaps not. But walk a bit of the way with me anyhow—"

She fetched the box with the little golden yellow straw hat that belonged to her dress, then put it on with care in front of the glass.

"That yellow suits you so well, Ida—you look like a young girl in it."

She smiled fleetingly at herself in the glass. As a matter of fact she must have known all the time why she had such a fancy for getting something really charming and becoming to wear this summer—something altogether different from the neutral, business-like clothes she usually wore.

"We'll go along the south road, won't we?" he said when they came to the gate.

She nodded. And when they turned into the first side-road, a farm track leading into the forest, she was all expectation. A cart was jolting and lumbering over the stones farther up the slope, but when it had passed them he took her hand and they walked shoulder against shoulder, happy to be so close to one another.

Chapter Six

B ut, Ida, you must see about getting your divorce put in order."

She was in his office one afternoon in July, sitting in his revolving chair, with all her parcels piled on his desk. It gave her a real childish joy to see them lying there—as a token of their intimacy and solidarity.

Tryggve Toksvold sat on the window ledge looking down at her.

"Do you hear, Ida? I can't make out why you haven't done anything about it before. Don't you know that you may be liable—in certain circumstances—to contribute to his support, so long as you're not divorced?"

"His family are not *that* sort, though. And with him it's out of sight, out of mind—to such an extent that I wonder if he really believes any longer in our existence, mine and the children's. As it's so long since he saw us."

"Oh, rubbish. The man can't be quite abnormal. If he discovers one fine day that he still has a claim on you, you may take your oath you'll hear from him."

Ida Elisabeth shook her head:

"I think you're awfully quick to assume the worst of people, Tryggve. I suppose you must have come across a great many cases in your practice to show that when people lie, as a rule they believe themselves what they say, more or less. People who lie and are fully aware that they do so are much rarer. But it's very much the same with those who seek their own advantage at other people's cost—they generally manage to persuade themselves that what they propose is merely what would be to the advantage of both parties. But that would be impossible here, you know, and therefore I'm certain they would never do what you think they might take into their heads."

He smiled sarcastically:

"You underestimate folks' rascality, my friend. At any rate—it may be that I'm too much of a countryman to draw such fine distinctions among all the shades of deception plus self-deception and deception minus self-deception. We're in the habit of saying there are two sorts, honest folks and the others, and there's an end!"

That was the line he took, and it was rather absurd of her to be so discouraged every time she noticed it. But it made her feel sorry—not for anyone in particular, simply for everyone in general who was not exactly one thing or the other.

"I just can't understand why you haven't been more anxious to get your position cleared up."

"You know, as I've told you, it was my brother-in-law who arranged the separation. And when he died I didn't feel in the mood to find another lawyer and give him the old story from beginning to end."

Toksvold frowned slightly. It had surprised her to discover that apparently he knew quite a lot about Torvald Lander. Of course she too had had a suspicion that Torvald's affairs were pretty shady, and that no doubt he had put an end to himself. Did lawyers all over the country usually know all this kind of thing about one another? she wondered. He had positively disliked her having had this man for a brother-in-law—though that was such ages ago; she had told him that Constance died before she herself was grown up.

"You see, I didn't think the question would ever become urgent for me. I looked upon it as Frithjof's affair, as it was he who had formed another connection. As concerned myself I had but one idea, to be left in peace in some place where I could provide for my boys and myself. For a time I even thought of changing my name. Not to Andst, for we are the only people of that name, and I didn't want anyone who had known me in former days to discover what had become of me. But I thought of calling myself Fru Carlsen. Or Fru Aanstad, after the farm my father's family came from."

"Yes, poor dear. You've had a rotten time. And have been wonderfully plucky. But that's just what makes it seem strange that you've let it slide like this."

"I've had so much to do all the time, you know. At first to make both ends meet—to provide the needful from day to day. And afterwards, when I began to do pretty well, it was difficult to find time enough."

"I know that." He jumped down from the window ledge, took off her hat, and kissed her on the top of the head. "But now, thank God, there's going to be an end of that. But you know I'm proud of you. You see, perhaps it will hardly do for me to arrange this for you. But I can find someone. It can all be settled pretty quickly. I confess I don't quite like it, so long as you're not free—legally, I mean."

He crossed the room and put on his overcoat.

"*Won't* you, all the same, when you've thought it over? You might for instance come only as far as Fosli hotel— then we'd have supper together and I'd get you a car to take you back. You could be home again before twelve tonight, one at the latest."

"You can guess, I'd like to very much, Tryggve. But I can't."

THE sun broke through as she was walking home, lighting up the rain-drops, which hung like sparks of purple fire in the spruce-trees. Along the edge of the road the shooting corn was dulled and bent by the moisture, but farther off it glistened wherever the sun reached it. It would have been lovely to drive with him up the valley—he said he thought this case of the common lands would take at least five or six days; that would be a long time without seeing him. And it

273

was so fresh after the rain, the road dark and free from dust, with big patches of blue sky reflected in the puddles, and the shadows were lengthening in the warm yellow evening sunlight.

Naturally people were busy about them already, she could tell that. And that she should be severely criticized was only what she had to expect; there were not so many bachelors here, and Tryggve was very eligible, a good deal more so than she had any idea when she became engaged to him. However, those of his acquaintance whom she had met had been pleasant to her—the midsummer trip to the Svensrud sæter had been a success as far as that went. Although they were unlucky in the weather, which was bitter and windy, so that they had to sit in all the evening, and next morning the snow was lying in the sæter paddock, so they had some snowballing before breaking up in the afternoon. But they had sat around the fire, and they had danced, and the bank manager's wife and Fröken Svensrud had made cream porridge and waffles. Kari Presttangen was not there.

Tryggve and she had not had much of each other's company. But as in the ordinary way they were together every single day—

This must have been noticed even before that, for when she rang up Marte Bö to ask if she might send the boys up there on Midsummer Eve, as she was invited to join in a trip, Marte had laughed: "You're going with Toksvold, aren't you?" "Oh, you know that?"

They were playing croquet in the yard at Viker, she heard when she reached home.

He had actually arrived post-haste with a brand-new croquet set one afternoon shortly after he had spoken about it. "You said you had an old set stowed away in the attic?" "Oh, did I say that?" He had laughed. "No, I had to buy this new one. You see, I had to have an excuse for coming to see you again so soon. And I couldn't tell that things were going to develop so rapidly."

The old road however turned out to be much too narrow for a croquet lawn, and the boys were too small to understand the game properly. Tryggve had undertaken to teach them one afternoon, when he called while she was still at work. It was not a success, she could hear through the open window. Her Tryggve, little Tryggve that is, only wanted to fool about; he kicked the balls and flew after them and tore up the hoops. And Carl of course went about it clumsily, and the dog joined in the game—and big, grown-up Tryggve lost his patience and got angry because the children wouldn't learn properly but only romped about. Carl had now taken the set over to Viker, where it was mostly used by Kristian's little girls.

When she entered the trying-on room Carl sat there drawing.

"But why aren't you out in this fine weather, my boy?" She laid her hand on his shoulder and looked at what he was drawing. It was men as usual: one was standing at a reading desk on which his fists rested. Another was shown in a back view; he had narrow shoulders and a huge posterior; with a long pointer he was indicating places on a wall map. Then there was one running and four others pursuing him with threatening gestures. Carl's drawings were not like any other children's that Ida Elisabeth had seen: it was with evident intention that he always made the faces ugly, like caricatures; but there was expression in them, and he had discovered a good deal about the foreshortening of running legs and gesticulating arms. There was something strangely alive, but malicious, in many of them—extraordinary, for Carl was the kindest little boy imaginable, and essentially so soft.

It had suddenly dawned on her lately—what if Carl really had talent? One evening she had yielded to Toksvold's request and shown him all the pictures she had drawn for Carl, which the boy had kept with his own drawing-books. She had done so however with a rather guilty conscience, as these drawings were really a secret between her and the child. Tryggve Toksvold had been loud in his praises of her pictures, but she saw that he did not know much about it: if they represented such subjects as he liked, sunsets and flowers and children dancing and sæters and snow mountains, that was enough to make him think them altogether first-rate. But on that occasion she realized for the first time how good Carl's drawings really were, in a curiously unamiable way—and it struck her that perhaps he possessed a talent which she ought to take seriously.

She had earnestly begged Tryggve not to let it out to Carl that she had shown him the contents of the drawer where they kept these things. Ugh, she almost wished she had not shown them. Although, on recollecting Tryggve's admiration, she did not wish that either—

Ida Elisabeth sighed rather impatiently, as she unpacked the boy's new white gymnastic shoes:

"Here! Put them on so that I can see if they fit. But then you must remember that you promised, you're to whiten them yourself—here's the bottle you're to use for them."

"Thanks." He came back, after putting on the shoes. "You are kind, mother!" Rather shyly he took her hand and caressed it.

"Well, well, my boy—now you've got what you asked for. Do you know where Buster is, by the way? He ought to come in now—"

"I expect he's with Leif—shall I go and fetch him in?"

"I may as well go with you." Hand in hand with Carl she went out along the road to the south. Coming home she took Tryggve's hand; Carl walked on the other side of her.

"If you like I'll make you 'kompises' this evening—"

Bread and milk with butter and sugar in it had been called "comrades" by her mother when they were children. But one day when Tryggve was small he had said the right name for it was "kompises", not "comrades". After that it was always known as "kompises" in the family jargon.

She made the boys undress while she boiled the milk. They always thought it was such a treat to be allowed to come into the kitchen in pajamas and have their supper; it meant that they could stay up while she took an extra cup of tea and smoked a cigarette.

This evening again Tryggve crawled up in her lap and pestered for one thing or another—he wanted so much to be given a pull at her cigarette, just one pull. "No, stop it—"

Through the evening stillness they heard the north-bound express thunder through the cutting under the ridge on the opposite side of the valley.

"*Kastens-kunstens, kastens-kunstens*, that's what the train says", Tryggve interpreted, clinging closely to his mother in his enthusiasm. "And then when it goes over the bridge it says *rakkedelakkede rakkedelakkedera*. And just before it comes to the station it says *patty paw pusscat-patty paw pusscat-patty paw-pusscat*. But the big freight-train, that says *grorgram, grorgram, grorgram*", he imitated its heavy lumbering noise. "Isn't that right, mother?"

"Silly little thing!" She kissed him. "You're mother's little Buster, aren't you?"

"Why do you always call Tryggve that?" asked Carl with some disapproval. "That was only when he was a baby—"

"No, but you must go to bed now! In with you—then I'll come and read to you a little."

It was always Elisabeth Welhaven's old Bergen stories they wanted to hear. She had come across the book again one day when she was rummaging in the drawers and had tried reading it to her children, because her father had read it aloud to her when she was a little girl. How much the boys understood she did not know, but it amused them immensely to hear her imitating the dialect, which to them was a foreign language.

Carl was in fits of laughter with his face in the pillow, and infected his little brother so that he spun round and round in bed like a puppy chasing his tail.

"But *now* you must be quiet for tonight!"

IDA ELISABETH did the small amount of washing up, pausing now and again to look out of the window into the summer night. The river shone faintly beyond the meadow.

Perhaps it was not so very unnatural if the children were rather mystified at her having begun all at once to go out fairly often in the evening. They were not used to such things.

It had never been her habit to fuss over them early and late; she had simply never had time to follow them about and herd them and pet them and take note of all they said and did and reflect about their characters to any great extent. Her mother-in-law had thought her good, but oh, how dry and matter-of-fact, and compared with Borghild Braatö, for instance, she did no doubt show a great lack of motherly sentiment. But the boys had always been accustomed to know where they could find her. In the work-room all day—if anything turned up, they had to be as brief about it as possible, but she *was* there. And they had her evenings entirely at their disposal; they played, Carl did his lessons, they had supper and went to bed; but all the time they were running to and fro, and at any moment they would come to her for help or to ask some question or to hand over a button that had come off their clothes or to show her a bruise or a scratch that they suddenly remembered having got.

But now there was a strange man who came nearly every day during their evening hours—to take her out or to stay here. It was not so strange that this bewildered them a little and dashed their spirits, and their manner was not very exuberant or gracious when Tryggve was present.

No, she was none of the Braatö breed, and she had never imagined that everybody must think her children so delightful. The main thing was that Tryggve thought and felt as she did in this particular: if a person has once gone in for breeding children, that person must stick to the task till the children are finished and turned out as successfully as one is able to make them. He knew what he was doing in wishing to marry a divorced wife who was providing for and bringing up two little boys unaided. He had talked about it in a way that was almost too business-like to her feeling—though her whole nature apart from sentiment could but approve of his way of approaching the matter. If she gave up her independent livelihood to become his wife, it was a natural consequence that he would provide for her boys so that they did not lose by it, materially in any case. Tryggve was not rich, but the position he offered her was well-to-do in comparison with what she had been used to. Certainly she had no sense of giving up hard work for idleness—as he said, she was about to take up a more responsible position—she knew very well that she was capable of accomplishing her share of the work and responsibility. Whatever the times might have in store—so long as there was a chance for active and efficient people to get on, he and she would do so. And if for instance that forest he owned began to yield a profit again, he could at any rate promise his stepsons a good education. Carl, who was never at his ease among strangers and was slow at learning any subject for which he had not a special aptitude—it was impossible to say how much it might mean to that boy if a good and honourable and capable man like Tryggve Toksvold were willing to take the place of the father her children had never had.

It was true that it had jarred her slightly to hear him talk in such a matter-of-fact way about the financial side of the affair. But probably this was because she herself had always been obliged to think of money and say nothing about it: none of the people with whom hitherto she had been closely associated had been so constituted as to give her a chance of discussing money matters with them, without running the risk of hearing so many unpractical wise sayings and so much babyish good advice that she was in danger of losing patience and forgetting herself altogether. And the men had been worse than the women. So it was new for her to hear a man talk like this—he it was who had the initiative and it was her part to listen and give her assent. It was rather comical that to begin with she had felt this to be something strange—

And assuredly she was not so stupid nor so inexperienced as to think it improper to discuss money matters because they were wildly fond of each other. He did not overrate money if he was willing to marry her, whose only contribution to their joint estate was two children by another man. It is only idiots who suppose that any of the things that make life worth living can be bought for money, he said. It is equivalent to thinking that the whole pleasure of travelling consists in wearing out the seat of one's trousers on the place for which one has bought a ticket. But it is a fact that one cannot travel without any money at all—even if one often gets most fun out of a journey when one is obliged to travel economically. But however fond two people may be of one another, it is madness to suppose it will turn out well if one marries and lives the life of two bachelors each with an independent livelihood, merely living together and sleeping together, but unable to afford to keep a home and have children—or if one provides oneself with a child or two who have to be content with a "part-time" mother.

At heart she entirely agreed with him. She had really thought at times, for instance, when Doctor Sommervold died, that perhaps she would have acted more rightly towards her children if she had snatched at his proposal of marriage. To be sure, she was in doubt to this day whether it was any more than a sudden impulse on his part. But if she had taken him at his word, she knew Lars Sommervold well enough to be sure that, even if he had been rather puzzled at the moment, he personally would have gotten something satisfactory out of their relations. Nevertheless she had never had any regrets. Teie would always be to her the most delightful spot in the world and Lars Sommervold the only friend who had been able to help her in spite of knowing all there was to be known about her. But she could never have faced being married to him. If one has put oneself in the position of having to live with a man whom one objects to as a husband, it is certainly better to be on such terms as she was on with Frithjof—to have the right to be angry with the man, to have enough to contend with outside, and to be compelled to be continually on the look-out for dangers ahead. When it is one's most sensitive nerves that are attacked—when one has an earache or toothache, for instance—the pain feels worse if one is lying in a warm and comfortable bed; it is already more bearable if one can get up and set about something. Marrying for the sake of an easy life, with a man whom one does not care for in *that* way, is no doubt the stupidest thing a woman can do—in any case it would have been the summit of stupidity for *her*. She had seen long ago that, if she had been able to put up with Frithjof as long as she did, it was simply because he had only been one thing among all the others she had to put up with.

But even a really passionate love like that of Aslaug and Gunnar Vathnes—even that might turn out a misfortune, almost as stifling in the long run as a loveless marriage. And that simply because they could not get anything to marry on. They wore each other out, through never being able to enjoy each other in a perfectly natural way so that they were satisfied and could go calmly on side by side till of its own accord the warm wind blew on them once more. So they lived everlastingly at half-cock; the one could never leave the other in peace, neither having the courage to admit that this insatiable excitation was only an unsatisfied remnant from last time, and it got worse and worse as they became worn out and felt like broken springs with no resilience left. Of course they were not married—but a wedding ceremony surely makes no difference, so long as a couple cannot accept it as an initiation to something more than this sterile and futureless relationship between two only—

It was perfectly true that she believed herself to have realized, even before she met Tryggve Toksvold, that what she had been through was nothing to shriek about. It had appeared to her as something like what one experiences when walking in a storm. So long as one is out in the open country, where the wind has full force and one has to crawl forward against the driving snow, the feeling only lies smouldering deep within, but no sooner does one reach shelter than it leaps out into the mind: it is simply joy of living, just as the vital warmth is repressed and exists only as the hidden motive power deep down in the body, so long as one is struggling along the hardest bit of the road, but breaks into heat in face and limbs as soon as one is in shelter. Some perish on the way, of course. She had come through—she had nothing to whine about.

But now she had made the acquaintance of an entirely different kind of joy in life. Precisely, *made its acquaintance*, for it was something quite new that she had met with, intensely different from the old joy which used to well up as it were from the depths within herself, draw nourishment from her own forces and from what she herself had to win for it. Oh, my beloved!

This was so unlike the old feeling—as the sun-drenched summer air when it bakes the sides of the valley, warming earth and stones and penetrating to every leaf and blade of grass, is unlike the lonely little fire within a man's body which he himself must feed as long as he lives and which goes out when he dies. Probably she had never seriously believed that there is such a thing as a happiness that merely flows from one person to another—they need do nothing; it is enough that they are together. No doubt she had seen that people can help each other and do each other a great deal of good—but then they must be active all the time, must do their share without ceasing. Happiness in love— Ida Elisabeth laughed quietly at the thought—no doubt she had imagined it as a kind of picnic to which each of the parties brought his own provisions and then they exchanged. There was something in *that* too, of course—they had to contribute something of their own, if they were to be happy together. But all the same it began by their having made each other happy without making any effort to that end. Tryggve said the same.

"Well, no, I don't believe I thought I was in love with you, when I first got to know you last year", he said quite seriously. "It was *more*, in a way, at the very beginning. I came to like the whole world better. It didn't shock me or revolt me so much to see that people were stupid and mean. Since I knew there were also many good and courageous and sensible people in existence. Many absolutely white people, in spite of all. You see, I had always known that there were such people. But you mustn't imagine that on making your acquaintance I merely thought: here is another of those who make life decent. When you came they were an overwhelming majority. When I bowed to you going through the village it was as though I had taken my hat off to humanity. Well, I suppose that's what it really means to *love*. It's a silly word to apply to decent people in general, but for once in a way it's no exaggeration. So we may say that I loved you already all last winter—and that was why I took so much trouble to get to know you better. Got you to come for that trip at Whitsun, and so on. You see, I had to find an opportunity to fall in love with you—"

But then she thought, this was exactly how it had happened with her. She too had acquired a new kind of confidence in life from the day she met him, and she had fallen in love with him when she already loved him.

But if their love were *that*, confidence, then it must indeed be invincible. In her idea, the little everyday troubles might worry and disturb them, when they were together—but in reality they could not affect their love, since it consisted above all in their having provided each other with a new and better climate, simply through having met. Naturally

they must get rid as well as they could of all such disturbing factors—and no doubt these would turn up from time
to time as long as they lived—but all that was merely
transitory—

Of course she guessed that the boys might get on his
nerves at times. She would never forget his expression as he
carried Carl in that day. So full of tenderness and sympathy
and desire to help that it made her think of pictures of
guardian angels and Madonnas and everything of that sort.
That was how a man like Tryggve Toksvold would show
himself in the presence of a little child who had met with
an accident. It was quite another thing to have to show
patience with a pair of active and not invariably attractive
youngsters, whose presence was not always desirable at the
moment. They were *not* particularly well-behaved; unfortunately she saw that better than anyone, when a stranger
was present. They were allowed as a matter of course to
romp rather unceremoniously in the company of people
whom they saw every day—but practically speaking they
had never seen any others; it was new to them for a stranger
to call, so that they must please control themselves a little.
And they didn't like it. Carl actually demonstrated against
it—for instance, by appearing more ungainly than usual at
table if Tryggve Toksvold was dining with them, by making impertinent remarks and rudely emptying half the sugar-
bowl, by licking his fingers instead of using his napkin. "But
we never *get* napkins unless he's here", he grumbled one
day, when she made a remark about it. That made her angry
in her turn: "Well, if you'd rather wear your bib as usual,
you can." She ought not to have said it; she could see that
the boy was frightfully hurt. Carl *was* jealous of this man
who claimed so much of their mother's attention—there
was no getting away from that.

Little Tryggve, little Buster she had started calling him
again—it was such a bother with two Tryggves. Though
from the very beginning it had been one of the things about

Toksvold which had strengthened her feeling that he opened the door for her to a new and happier phase of her life—that his name was Tryggve. She had attached superstitious notions to that name when she decided that her last child should be called Tryggve, if she succeeded in saving herself and her children. Perhaps she had actually taken it as a good omen when she heard that the man who carried home Carl after an accident like that which had killed his little sister, bore this very name. As to her little Tryggve, he didn't care a hang whether she called him Tryggve or Buster or Sausagemeat. But she noticed that Carl didn't like it.

And Buster, poor little chap, was fearfully given to fibbing and bragging. She made fun of him when he tried that sort of thing with her, but she had never taken it very seriously. All little children tell lies. The only thing to do was to call him to order, till he saw for himself that it was a habit he must get out of as he had gotten out of wetting his breeches. When he had occasionally brought her a trustworthy message, she gave him to understand that now he was getting a big boy.

But Tryggve regarded it as a serious moral blemish in the child. It made things no better when one day she let him look through an old photograph album which she had been given as a confirmation present. Among the rest it contained a portrait of Frithjof as a boy of ten; he was taken together with Herjulf and Else. She had done this with intention: now that she and Toksvold were constantly seen together and people were no doubt discussing whether they were to be married, she assumed that all the gossip there had been about her when she first came to the village would be revived. Probably Tryggve was aware of the hints then dropped that her husband was not the father of her youngest child. And sure enough, when Toksvold saw the portrait he made the remark she was expecting:

"It's extraordinary what a likeness there is between that youngest boy of yours and his father!"

"Oh, do you think so? Well, you know, in a way it's the family type. But really the little lad's much more like the young Braatös—an aunt of his named Merete—she's dead now—" and then she told him something of little Merete's history.

But afterwards she noticed that Tryggve seemed to suspect little Buster of being somewhat untrustworthy by nature. That he had a tendency that way was so far true enough. But surely something must depend on the home in which such a boy grew up, whether with a couple of visionaries who left everything to chance, or with sober-minded people who kept things in order and were not in the habit of throwing dust in their own eyes.

It was an unfortunate thing that Tryggve constantly gave the boys money, telling them they could go to the shop and buy goodies—to get them out of the way for a while, and the boys guessed that to be the reason. They went reluctantly—but still they went; they were so little used to having money, and sweets they hardly ever got. She always made something good for Sunday's dinner—mamma's English apple pie or Aunt Mathilde's gingerbread—telling the boys she could not afford to give them both, and how they would miss the good smell of cake on Sunday morning—it wouldn't be Sunday at home at all without it. But now they were always crunching chocolate or sucking sugar-sticks—the most disgusting sight she knew—with an injured air, and in Carl's case often with a look in his eyes, of uncertainty or whatever she was to call it, but it hurt her whenever she saw it.

She would have to tell Tryggve one day—that he mustn't do this.

Of course he only meant well by it. And they *must* be together. And she had no other leisure than the short evening hours. But she felt a little ache in her heart as they sat together in her room and she was sure that Carl was lying awake and in low spirits. He was not asleep, only pretending, she could see when she looked into the boys' room before walking part of the way back with Tryggve.

"Do you think it's good for that big boy", asked Toks-vold as they walked, "to run in and out of his room after he's gone to bed—watching him as if he was a little child—?"

"No", she said tamely. "I dare say I do too much of it—" But it had never been so before—she had never had a feeling that she was fussing over her children, if she did look in on them now and again in the course of her evening work. And indeed she had not done that even—for she had to pass through the boys' room in going to and from the kitchen.

In a way they were freer where he lived. He had a couple of rooms at Björkheim Hotel—that was where he had lodged all the time. But only in a way—for there they were always under observation. Magda Björkheim, for instance, was a charming girl but a terrible one to talk. And of course she had herself had a fancy for Tryggve—though that was not much to worry about; Magda was always in love with such a lot of men, and just at the moment she seemed to be engaged to one at the telegraph office.

But when they were married all this would be different. To a great extent it was only a question of time and space. In the villa which Tryggve owned by the station they would have plenty of room to turn round—he had given notice to his tenants on the floors above and below. When she had the whole day at her disposal she must surely be able to manage both Tryggve and the boys. It was a good thing the children were so small—otherwise it might have been difficult for them and their step-father to get used to each other.

Chapter Seven

E VER SINCE THE FIRST DAYS of their engagement Toksvold had talked about their driving over one Sunday
to visit his sister, Ingvild Brekke.

He was very fond of her, Ida Elisabeth could see, and it
was probably her fate more than anything else that had turned
him so much against irresponsible men. It was this sister
and her husband who had taken over the farm of Toksvold
when the eldest brother died unmarried a few years after
their father. But Torstein Brekke launched out far too
freely—it was while the boom was on—and then he plunged
into dissipation to an inordinate extent; in the course of
five or six years he had run through all they possessed, and
then they had to give up the farm. Then came a few years
during which he tried one thing after another in the Opland
towns, but he was drinking harder and harder, and finally
he bolted with the wife of a veterinary surgeon. Ingvild
was left with four children and not a red cent. The family
arranged the separation and helped her to start a boarding-
house. It was quite a success—she was brave and capable
and worked as hard as she could, but then she was happy in
her children, who were talented and good. The eldest boy
was at college, and then there was a "big" girl who was
going to a training school for the hotel industry when she
had passed out of the grammar school. But then this husband turned up again, absolutely down and out. And the
end of it was that Ingvild took him back in favour. He
stayed with her about a year, looking after the stoves and
doing odd jobs about the place—and practically ruined his
wife's business. She still had boarders and customers for meals,

but they were not the sort she had had before; decent people who had stayed with her for years gave notice; the scandal was more than they could bear; schoolchildren were sent to her no more, and there were constant difficulties with her cookery pupils—Ingvild had always taken five or six girls who were learning housekeeping. "If he's to stay here mother will have to shut up shop, unless she wants to keep a regular brothel", Elling, the eldest boy, had said, when Toksvold was there last year. And Marit, his sister, said she wouldn't stand it any longer—she would leave the grammar school and go to Oslo, take a place there, anything she could get.

There had then been a sort of clear up; the man no longer lived with Ingvild, but he was about the place and was given food and money and worried her and the children. Toksvold had little faith in her ever being able to get rid of this beast of hers; she could not face letting him go under. She had been desperately fond of him once and had married him in the face of her parents' strong opposition to the match.

IDA ELISABETH was not looking forward very keenly to the trip. For one thing she did not expect Fru Brekke to be wild with delight at her brother's approaching marriage, to a divorced woman into the bargain—that would be unreasonable, even if it were not the fact that Tryggve paid for the schooling of the two eldest children and had helped her in other ways, to a considerable extent, of late years.

It was Toksvold who proposed that the boys should come with them—then they would get the long drive, and Ingvild Brekke's youngest boy was about the same age as Carl.

The sky was restlessly bright, full of sunshine and cloud, on the August morning when they were to go. There had been some showers during the night, but Toksvold thought they would have fine weather. And when he said to Carl that they would have to take Burman, it was a shame to leave the poor puppy alone in the house all day and he would be sure to raise a fearful noise and make messes too—the boys were in radiant humour as they drove off.

Ida Elisabeth sat in front with Toksvold, but she was rather nervous about having the boys alone in the back of the car. The dog was a fairly restless companion; he kept jumping up and standing with his fore-paws against the top of the door—supposing it were to open and one of them fall out. But Toksvold laughed rather impatiently at her anxiety: "They've got to learn to look after themselves some day—use their brains a little."

That was true of course. She was reminded of something that happened during the summer; she was out driving with him, and all at once he had asked: "Don't you want to drive? I think you ought to learn." She had replied no, so curtly—rudely, it had probably sounded—that he had looked at her in astonishment. Then she said: "I lost a little girl—our eldest—she was run over and died." After a moment he had said, and his voice was infinitely tender and gentle: "My poor Ida. Then it must have been far worse for you than I had any suspicion, when we brought in Carl." She could only nod at the moment. But presently she managed to say: "I thought it would be the death of me. But when it turned out that the boy was not in any danger after all, it seemed to me that you had brought me a pardon, when I had been condemned to death."

Afterwards he had asked her whether perhaps she disliked motoring altogether. "When you're driving I don't think about it. But I should never dare to drive myself—I should be terrified the whole time of running over somebody—"

But the next day he had suddenly returned to it. "Fancy your never having said anything about it to me. About your having had a little girl." But there were a great many things she had never told him.

He had told her all sorts of things about himself. The idiotic affair of his engagement, as he called it. That was in his student days in Oslo—a girl he met at the boarding-house where he lived. It was just after the summer holidays, he was the only male in the place who was not ancient, and he was ignorant enough to believe she cared for *him* in particular, because she appeared to be taken up with him, gave him such frightfully earnest glances when they were chatting together and altogether laid herself out to be agreeable. So they got engaged—she made no difficulty about that. But by degrees, as she got to know more people in town and a few more men came to live in the boarding-house—well, then he was so damned slow to realize that she cared neither more nor less about him than about any other tolerably passable male person. She wanted to flirt with them all; with him too she only meant to have a little flirtation—it was he who had misunderstood the situation and would not admit that he had done so, but insisted on keeping up the engagement at all costs. Oh yes, she was an excellent person; she married a few years later, and by all accounts she had behaved splendidly to her husband in exceedingly difficult circumstances. No doubt it was her nature to go through a weathercock period at the age when he made her acquaintance, and the foolishness was entirely on his side. But it had hurt abominably—he was in love with the girl, and of course in love with himself too, at that age—

Naturally there might have been other things which Tryggve had not told her, but she knew that this was because they were things which meant nothing to him in comparison with her—things which had not penetrated beneath his skin. But all that she could not tell Tryggve was of such a nature as had contributed to the formation of her character and to determining how her life was to shape itself.

FRU BREKKE's boarding-house was a long, low, red-brick building of two stories. Viewed from outside, the place was not very attractive—the street in which it was situated was as ugly as any street in a small town could be, with neglected wooden houses and mean brick buildings and unpainted wooden fences and sagging gates all higgledy-piggledy on the slope of a hill, where the road was full of holes and puddles with humps of the road metal sticking up. But then they entered a big courtyard, with borders of bright summer flowers everywhere along the walls, and flowering creepers trained over some ruinous outhouses.

Tryggve's sister came out to meet them on the steps; she greeted Ida Elisabeth in a very friendly way, but with some reserve. She resembled her brother—she had the same low, broad, smooth forehead with the soft, handsome curve over the arches of the brow, and her eyes behind the substantial steel spectacles were clear and grey-blue like his. Her short hair was curly and much streaked with grey, quite white at the temples, but one could see that it had been light brown. Her face was thin, so that the cheek-bones stood out and the cheeks were fallen in; the chin was narrow, as though she had lost a good many teeth; it gave the delicate, thin-lipped mouth a peculiarly melancholy, but resolute look. But her figure was corpulent, as is often the case with women whose work consists in standing over a kitchen range, and she was tall—noticeably taller than her brother, and he was no small man. Ida Elisabeth thought her appearance very sympathetic—not that she expected the other to feel any immediate sympathy for her.

Fru Brekke had the coffee-table ready for them in her private sitting-room—it was quite a cosy little room casually furnished with faded and worn things, old crocheted antimacassars on the backs of the chairs and new embroidered sofa cushions with tulips and jazz patterns in glaring colours—they looked like presents and gave the room a homely look, in spite of their frightful ugliness. The window stood open, but, for all that, Ida Elisabeth could tell by the atmosphere of the room that someone slept here at night. Perhaps Fru Brekke herself remarked it, for she said something about its being a good thing they had had rain—the dust had been so bad that they could scarcely open a window.

Ida Elisabeth was given a seat on an old birch-wood sofa covered in faded yellow flowered plush—she could not help thinking how charming that sofa could be made if it were suitably upholstered again, in horsehair or linsey-woolsey; she and Tryggve had talked a good deal about the furniture they would buy. But hardly had she seated herself when she had to get up again to greet the four children who came in.

They were uncommonly pretty, the little girls, Marit and Signe—quite strikingly so. And the youngest boy, Borger, the one who was a few months younger than Carl—Ida Elisabeth felt a pang at her heart on seeing that he was a good head taller than her boy, slight and well built, with a skin as brown and rosy as crab apples. For an instant a shadow of mingled sweetness and pain passed over her mind—would she too one day have strong and handsome children like these, hers and Tryggve's, around her, and would the two whom she had loved and worked for so long be thrown quite into the shade—?

It continued to lurk within her as a profound discouragement—now that she saw Tryggve with his own people she felt so clearly that they were a different kind of person. It was hard to say in what this consisted: this Ingvild and Tryggve had also been torn out of the surroundings in which they had grown up, just as much as she had. Tryggve too had had to shift for himself since he was quite young: what he ought to have inherited from his parents had to be left in the farm, and when Brekke went smash, that went too. Ingvild's life had not been very unlike her own; she too had kept a home for her children as one holds a trench, forced back upon a little room behind those in which she worked and received strangers; she too had been obliged to lead her private life and her life with the children as it were in the margin of the life she had to

293

carry on in order to provide for them; Ingvild Brekke too had had to take the place of the man, since she had made a wrong choice and had bound herself to one who was no good ... But good Lord, how different she felt them to be—!

She felt this disparity as though it were something purely physical, right in to her bare bones—all her bones were thin and long, her skull narrow with thin and hollowed temples and a slight lower jaw with a long, almost rectangular chin. These Toksvolds had foreheads to press on with, shoulders that could bear a good load, but there was something angular about their handsome heads with the strong crisping hair which had such a bright gleam of gold in its brown. Their grey-blue eyes were not hard, far from it, but even when they looked their mildest they could avoid seeing what they did not *wish* to see, and there was a dash of bigotry in their narrow, finely drawn lips. There was something obstinate in their nature—she herself had had obstinacy enough in hers, but it had not sufficed to set her free from seeing more than she wished to see, when she would have preferred to judge blindly and without understanding.

But at the same time she felt quite painfully the longing to belong to him entirely. That he might take her and be one with her—until then she was not safe from all the shadows she felt to be floating in the space between them. A terribly coarse expression of her father's suddenly occurred to her memory, but the grossness had gone out of it, as it were; all it meant now was a union so close and firm that no dividing breath could penetrate between two human beings who *must* not separate again.

"Well, I suppose you know Kari's here?" asked Fru Brekke. There was a strange caution in the way she said it.

"No—?"

"Yes, she came yesterday midday. Just after you had telephoned. I believe she's going on by the six o'clock train today. To Oslo. She's taken a place there. As assistant."

"You don't say so!" Tryggve put down his pipe and sat looking at his sister. "Perhaps she's to be locum tenens?" he asked cautiously.

"It sounds as if she meant to stay there for the winter", replied Ingvild Brekke non-committally.

"That's the strangest thing I've heard—"

Kari Presttangen's wedding was to have been in October; she had gone home directly after midsummer to arrange about her trousseau and so on and to hand over her practice to another dentist, a male one this time.

Toksvold seemed to be pondering both deep and long.

"Well, she can't have broken it off with Sigurd, can she?" he asked in a low voice.

Ingvild Brekke threw a rapid glance over her spectacles at the stranger. "That's what it looks like", she said curtly, below her breath.

"Well, I never heard anything like it—"

"I dare say she found she didn't care enough for him", said Ingvild as before. "And in that case perhaps it's best—"

"It's the worst I've heard", repeated her brother.

"Well, you're going to meet her at dinner."

He didn't look as if the idea roused his enthusiasm.

The children came stumbling up the steps and burst into the room—they had disappeared while coffee was being drunk without anyone taking much notice of it. Breathlessly they all shouted at once that Burman had run away! They were down at the wood-shed looking at a canoe that Borger was building himself, and they had tied the dog up outside the wall of the shed and then another dog had come and Burman had broken loose and run off with the other dog, and Carl hadn't managed to catch him again—

After a lot of cross-questions, and after scolding Carl and Borger and Signe very thoroughly, Tryggve Toksvold declared that they must go out and see that they found the dog—he might get caught in something and strangle himself, running like that with the lead after him: "You'd better come too, Ida—he's more likely to come if you call him."

Outside the gate the children ran off in different directions—Carl was crying as he trotted after Borger, but the two Brekkes were evidently in high spirits and tremendously busy.

Toksvold and Ida Elisabeth wandered up one street after another. Never had she seen a town that looked so unattractive. They crossed great desert-like squares surrounded by ugly low houses—there was a curiously crippled look about the buildings here—and they went through broad, ill-kept streets with houses high and low and wooden fences and brick walls all huddled together so that the line of buildings looked like a rotten set of teeth, and all at once at the end of a street they came on a view of Lake Mjösa, grey and green in sunshine and shadow under the restless open autumn sky.

And of course it was not very amusing to wander about here searching for a runaway dog. Tryggve could not resist making a few remarks—and it was true enough that Burman was sadly wanting in good manners and that was a pity, for he was an uncommonly good specimen of his breed, and Ida Elisabeth herself had regretted it many a time; she knew very well how the dog ought to have been brought up, but as she hadn't had time to look after him and he was always in the hands of a pair of little boys ... And they didn't see a sign of the brute—

But she knew very well it was not *that*. That was responsible for their ill humour and having nothing to say to each other—beyond animadversions on the dog and suggestions as to what could have become of him.

And Carl would be in despair, and Tryggve annoyed, if they had to drive back this evening without having found Burman—

And then they met him coming round a corner, pulling at the strap of which Signe Brekke held the other end. Her face was flushed and her curls were falling into her eyes—eager and radiant she told them all about it, as she joined the two. Till she handed the lead to Ida Elisabeth, swept her hair back, and took a deep breath: she would have to run and find the boys—

Ida Elisabeth watched her go—she was about twelve, long-legged, and shapely, and there was something altogether charming and powerful about her youthful figure bounding along. And there was nothing to make one feel so disheartened—

"Well, you'll have to give him a thrashing for this when we get home", said Toksvold referring to the dog.

"Yes." Poor little beast, he doesn't get a chance of running loose all the summer. But Burman chased sheep—

They had come in sight of the red brick walls of the boarding-house when Kari Presttangen came striding towards them. Ida Elisabeth knew her at once by her walk, but at the same time noticed a change in her: she appeared to much better advantage—

She was slighter and not so loose-jointed—in a black tailor-made; there was now an elegance about the tall girl, which was her own and unlike that of anyone else. She had on a little black straw hat with the brim bent up high in front; for a change it *sat* on her hair—something like a coal black tiara above her fair, boldly cut face. Her manner was very quiet and calm as she greeted them—and then they had the dog to talk about.

Ingvild Brekke showed Ida Elisabeth into an empty guestroom, if she would like to tidy herself before dinner.

She took down her hair, ran the comb through it, and looked at herself in the glass as she did so. She had grown much prettier again this last year, it was as though her face had awakened. Her hair too—it was thicker and seemed to have more vitality; it had recovered its bright silvery lustre, and its long waves no longer hung so limply; Ida Elisabeth shook her hair so that it fell in ringlets on each side of her face.

At that moment Kari Presttangen appeared at the door, stopped and mumbled an excuse—she had not knocked. Then she drew nearer, so that Ida Elisabeth saw her eyes behind her own face in the glass.

"Do you know, Fru Braatö—I believe it would suit you awfully well to wear your hair half-long in the way that's fashionable now ... With your long, fine neck and all—if you let it hang loose on the shoulders—"

It was just what she herself had been thinking. As she began to twine her hair into the knot at the back she smiled at the girl behind her:

"I can't wear it that way, you see—it would be so in the way, when I have to bend down all day long cutting out and trying on—"

"No. But—when you give up dressmaking! Then you'll be able to pay more attention to your own taste and so on!"

There was the strangest expression in the eyes behind her in the glass—a kind of staring crystal-clear wonder. Again Ida Elisabeth was reminded of the shy mare they had had at Vallerviken.

"I'm not going to lead an idle life though, you may be sure. That style of hairdressing doesn't do for people who have a good deal to see to."

"No. I dare say you're right." The other turned away and disappeared from the glass. Ida Elisabeth heard her pouring water to wash her hands.

She finished doing her hair, but involuntarily closed her eyes once or twice as she did so. In reality she had known it all the time. It was Tryggve Kari wanted—she must have wanted him for ever so long. And Kari had probably seen how things were going, almost before they knew it themselves. That was why she had accepted the other man, as a trial—but found it wouldn't do after all. What she had been through this summer had changed her. And whatever the result might be, Ida Elisabeth was aware of something which touched her: Kari wished no one ill, even if she saw that she herself had lost. She was no doubt one of those people who perhaps are not much good at fighting, they are too nervous or passionate for that, but who can take a beating, because they never allow themselves to complain.

"I've been thinking about it too", said Kari Presttangen from the wash-stand. "I think I'll have my hair cut off when I get to Oslo. It's such a weight—"

And Ida Elisabeth had a notion that this strange girl had had some secret intention in wearing the golden crown of plaits which she now wished to be rid of.

"Oh no, don't do that, Fröken Presttangen. It would be a pity—" No sooner had she said it than she had an uncomfortable feeling—as though the words were ominous of she knew not what.

THE atmosphere at the dinner-table was rather depressed than otherwise, and it was not much livelier when they moved back to the private room. They had coffee—and all at once Ida Elisabeth felt a kind of spiritual heartburn—whenever something had upset her she had always had to take coffee with somebody. Tryggve disappeared into the drawing-room—there were some people there he knew. And he stayed away till it was time to drive Kari Presttangen to the train. Ingvild too wanted to see her cousin off at the station. Ida Elisabeth was left alone with some worn and crumpled copies of illustrated weeklies. She looked through them with repugnance; they reminded her of doctors' and dentists' waiting-rooms.

Relief came when Carl and Borger tumbled in; the Tryggve child toddled after, a fairly played-out little creature. Strange enough, but it seemed the two boys of the same age got on grandly together. Borger hinted that he would have liked very much to be going with them—he had never been so far on the road—

"If your mother gives you leave," proposed Ida Elisabeth, "we can give you a bed. I'm sure your uncle will think it fun to have you. And a big boy like you can go home alone by train—"

BORGER's spirits had an enlivening effect on the whole party, when the others returned from the station. It would soon be time for the rest of them to start for home, and the interval of waiting was mainly occupied in getting Borger ready for the journey—for Ida Elisabeth suggested that he might as well stay for the week that remained of his holidays. Both Tryggve and his sister were evidently pleased at her inviting Borger.

The weather looked doubtful as they were leaving—it was quite thick to the northward—so Toksvold thought it as well to put up the hood at once, in spite of the boys' protests. Burman was fetched from the wood-shed, Ingvild Brekke gave her son some final admonitions, and Ida Elisabeth thanked her once more for her hospitality. Then they drove off. So *that* was over!

The two sat side by side hardly exchanging a word—nor had they gone more than seven or eight miles before they ran into showers; the rain poured down the wind-screen and drove in on them. "Did you ever see such filthy weather! I hope you won't catch cold, Ida—" "No, but I wonder how they're getting on behind. Keep yourselves well covered up, boys!"

"It was nice of you to think of that—asking Borger to stay. Ingvild was very pleased about it."

"But dear me—you can guess, it'll be a pleasure to have him."

The rain stopped as they came farther up the valley. The sky was now gorgeous with the setting sun; shining and burning in every shade of gold under the tattered dark-blue and cinder-brown clouds. When the sun had gone down behind the mountains they turned to copper and purple, and little shreds of cloud floated across the clearing sky, gleaming in rose-pink till they melted away in the blue-green vault, where the stars were beginning to leap out. Ida Elisabeth sat watching the river as it reflected the red glories of heaven—but it had turned frightfully cold.

The three boys had slipped half off the seat and lay asleep in a lump like a litter of puppies, when they reached Viker. It was fairly dark already—in her little front garden the big clusters of phlox were bright and fragrant in the cold, rain-soaked air. The sky was clear now, only a few belated rags of dark cloud floated low in the pale green air above the ridge, as Ida Elisabeth piloted the sleepy and shivering boys into the house.

She had a good deal to attend to; there was the children's supper, and she had to get out clean sheets and remake Tryggve's bed for the visitor. The little boy would have to sleep with her on the divan these nights—fortunately it was good and wide.

SHE had gotten all hands to bed and was just beginning to undress when the dog sat up and barked. There was a knock at her window—it was Tryggve outside in the garden. "Come out for a bit", he asked her, as she opened a crack. "But put on plenty of things—it's horrid cold."

Ida Elisabeth wound about her a big white woollen shawl and stole through the boys' room and the kitchen and out through the little back-door into the garden.

Her friend stood to receive her as she jumped to avoid treading on the rotten steps. And he continued to hold her fast in a lovely long embrace.

It was quite dark now and bright with stars—only in the north a pale white border lingered on the horizon. It was cold and wet under the old apple-trees.

"Tired?" He kissed her on the mouth a lot of times. But when he let go, it was as though he would have forgotten something, but saw it was no use—

"Certainly it was no great success", he said in a low voice. "Our trip, I mean."

"O-oh." She stopped to free the fringe of her shawl which had got caught in a bush. "One or two things did turn up, outside the programme—"

"O Ida!" He caught her in his arms again, then pressed her to him. "God, how I wish I could sleep with you tonight!" he whispered in her ear. "Don't you wish that too—that I could have stayed with you tonight?"

With her hands flat against his shoulder-blades as though she were feeling under his clothes she pressed against him, nodding her head against his breast, so that he must feel it in the dark. Had I been a young girl I might have said yes. Then I might have told you how I was longing—how often I have longed for you—

One of his hands came groping under her shawl, slipped into the opening of her dress till it lay upon one of her breasts—cold and firm.

"O my Ida!"

She clung more closely to him, so that his hand pressed hard and bony against the soft flesh. Ugh, you shan't feel that my breast isn't firm and young. Oh, would I had been young when I met you—

"I love you", she murmured with her head leaning on him; "you should just know how I love you, Tryggve—"

One doesn't have four children without being marked by it. Do you think I haven't grieved over it, shuddered at it—? I wanted so much to be beautiful for your sake—young and buoyant and unworn. One doesn't escape from all I've been through without being marked by it. Oh, I wish I could forget such a lot of things I know. There's such a lot of things I would have liked to believe—about life and all that—but I cannot, it's only a pretence. There's so much that one would be happier for not understanding—

"Tell me if you feel cold", he whispered. "Do you want to go in—?"

"No, no. I'd like you to stay a little longer—"

Oh, why didn't I meet you before? Fifteen years ago. Though it would have been too late even then. Both too late and too soon. For then I had already let Frithjof spoil me, and I had not yet done anything to make me feel I had redeemed myself. For one doesn't get over an affair like that until one feels one has worked one's own redemption. For now, you see, now I know well enough that you can use me. But it's wearing, a journey like that, deep down into the ashes and up again. I'm a worn woman, now that you get me at last—and you are the only one who should have had me always—

"All the rest doesn't matter, does it, Ida? It's nothing compared with our being fond of each other?"

"No. No. No."

But she felt a kind of rage—why should it happen to *me*? when so many others are allowed to spend their girlhood in peace? They must have the same restlessness within them; they must be rebellious and impatient to tear to pieces all that is stirring and smouldering within oneself; they must long to find out what there is in the visions that loom before one. But they are looked after and kept from committing follies, and somebody sees that they don't yield to the temptation to throw themselves away. Till they are grown up and the tempest subsides—then they are a new thing, as a beach gleams fresh and new on the first fine morning after the storm has passed. There was no one to look after me; there was no one who could prevent Frithjof or keep him away from me—

Naked Lady, that was the name of a flower, she chanced to remember. It was Torvald Lander who had shown it to her, telling her what it was called—she had never forgotten it, though she was only a little girl at the time, but Torvald had said it with such a nasty smile. It was like a crocus, a very light blue, and it raised its calyx upon a bare white stem straight up out of the black earth—no doubt that was why it was so called, for it had no leaves round it. It was a pretty name—and it was beastly to laugh at it.

Slowly they wandered down among the apple-trees, leaning closely on one another.

"You mustn't think I don't understand", he said quietly. He still kept his hand on her breast, but it lay quiet now, only the finger-tips moved in tiny caresses. "That you can't ... I don't want them to have any food for gossip at the hotel, for instance. I've never asked you to stay late up in my room, have I, Ida?

"Not but what it was a good old country custom in many places"—he gave a little laugh—"for engaged couples to be together in that way. But that was in the days when it was more of a disgrace to break off than it is nowadays to treat one's home and one's children as naughty boys treat a magpie's nest. So that in those days an engagement was like a honeymoon. Petting month, as the Swedes call it. There was no wedding trip or anything of that sort for country folks, you see. When the wedding was over it meant bearing the yoke together as long as they lived. It's not the way now, even in the country, for folks who call themselves folks to stick it ... Though even I can remember the first case of anyone getting a divorce at home in my parish. And he was one of those the old fogeys of last century called liberal-minded. But damn me if I'm old enough to be that—"

They had reached the fence at the bottom of the garden. Before them the faintly lighted field merged into the black night which swallowed up everything. Away on the other side of the valley gleamed a solitary speck of light, making the darkness yet deeper, but above them the whole sky flickered with great stars in a swarm of star-dust.

"That about Kari", he muttered, with some heat. "I don't like it."

Instinctively she took his hand away from her breast. Her heart began to throb—though there was no definite thought in her mind.

"At any rate she needn't have made a fool of him like that. First accepting, and then refusing him a few months later. I don't understand her preferring to flutter about in this unsettled state instead of getting married and helping Sigurd to keep Galby in the family—"

Ida Elisabeth did not know what she could say. She did not even know whether he had guessed how it was with Kari. And she had a queer feeling as if Kari had confided something to her which made it treachery to discuss her with this man.

"When it was decided that I was to study law," he said, "both my brothers were alive—nobody could have any idea of what would happen to Elling or that Lauris would take it into his head to go to Australia. But you know, if I had guessed that Torstein Brekke was going to make such a mess of things, I'd have tried at all events to hit upon some arrangement to prevent the farm going out of the family. For it's a bad thing that one after another of the farms that have been in the same family for ever so many generations should be constantly changing hands."

Ida Elisabeth said hesitatingly:

"But if she doesn't care enough for this man ... There must at least be a kind of fellow-feeling, Tryggve, if she's to think it worth while. For Galby anyhow is not her ancestral farm."

"Of course I don't expect you to understand it." There was a little cock-sure ring in his voice, which made her smile in the dark. "I don't suppose it's the same in your part of the world." What do you know about it? she thought, recalling the one occasion when she had been with her father to Aanstad. It was in a terribly dirty state, and the old people who had it, cousins of her grandfather, had an odd submissive air, and one of every generation had had to seek his fortune away from the farm. But for as far back as they had any record there had always been one of the family who toiled for a living on that bit of land between a sheer precipice and the grey sea.

"It's not that I imagine farmers to be *better* than other people. But at any rate it ought to be easier for them to remember that all the things on which life depends must take their time to sprout and grow and ripen. Children and trees and corn and beasts. It's not much use trying to increase the pace *there*. You can do that with factory products. And they *can* be dispensed with, nearly all of them. I'm not saying anything about folks being *unwilling* to do without a lot of them, I shouldn't want them to do that either. But if we were *forced* to do without them. That which takes its time to come to maturity, that is the indispensable. Pace and records and that kind of thing, all I say is that it's amusing. But if all the wheels that hum and buzz and race about the earth came to a standstill—we could still carry on. But if the seasons stopped their usual course, that would be the end!"

They had turned and were strolling slowly back towards the house. From her two kitchen windows a golden light fell on the nearest apple-trees and was drowned in the darkness of their foliage.

"And folks who have lived on an old farm from the day they were born to the day of their death and been put to work there by others who have lived their whole life on the farm before them . . . For it isn't only that when a farm has once come into the market and changed hands over and over again, it's nearly always misused and reduced in value. But in a firmly rooted family every member of it knows, whether he thinks about it or not, that there have been days before these days, and times have often been hard, and flourishing times have always come round; but good times never last long, and bad times come to an end some day—"

"You mean, you wish you had taken over Toksvold after your brother?"

"It's no use wishing that now. You know, the way I'd been brought up—they'd spent so much on my education

306

that they wanted some return for their money, I knew that was how my father argued. And I was placed with old Björnstad, the brother of my aunt's husband. And Ingvild had that boy of hers, Elling. When it was too late. But all the same I will say this: Kari is a woman, and I think it's *foolish* of her, just for the sake of her education, to refuse to marry into Galby when she might—if you had seen the farm you would understand that *there* is a task entailing both honour and responsibility. For a woman who *wants* to accomplish something in this world I for one can't imagine anything greater."

"Perhaps all she thinks is that *she* is not the one to occupy that place", said Ida Elisabeth quietly. "If she's not fond enough of the man—"

"Fond of, fond of—" He held her more closely to him with the arm that was round her waist. "It doesn't depend on that alone—not even with you and me, Ida. If it were not that we know our *wishes* are the same, in everything that matters. That we love one another, that is good for *us*, that is happiness—but it is a rare thing, the kind of happiness that one receives as a gift. Indeed, a red-hot love may just as well mean something quite different. Ingvild loved that fellow of hers beyond all bounds. He was in love with her too for that matter, for a time in any case. No, if one can't get both things, I believe it's better for most people to marry one they can rely on and whose aims they can share."

"That's asking a good deal of one who is still young like Kari. And good-looking too. Asking her to resign herself now—rather than wait to see if the future may bring—well, all sorts of things." The moment she had said it she had a vague sense of fear—why should I say that, what did I mean—? "Oh no, I'm cold—I think I must go in now, Tryggve—"

"Yes, poor dear. It's late too." He paused for a moment. "But what's to become of the world?" he asked, and his voice sounded to her so strangely confiding. "If nobody cares for the happiness that one has to *work out* as it were, by a kind of mining? Well, you and I ought not to be talking like this now. But you have said yourself, Ida—you were often happy, though in a different way, all the years when you had as much as you could do to make both ends meet—"

She drew his head down to hers, forehead against forehead.

"Oh yes. Oh yes. But you ought to know how difficult it was many a time! And the happiness that one receives as a gift—oh no, Tryggve, I could never say to another *now*, that she must please stop waiting for *that*, but be content with the happiness one can quarry out like a miner!"

"Heavens, how you're trembling! I'm afraid it was selfish of me to ask you to come out, it's so cold tonight—"

"No, no. I was glad you did, but—"

"I'll go now . . ." He kissed her again and again.

She laid her hands on his shoulders:

"You're not to say it either, Tryggve. That others can be content to work for their happiness. When you and I—?"

He laughed doubtfully between the kisses:

"No. I don't suppose I ought. My Ida!"

HE helped her in by the little back-door—she had to step on some stones that had slipped half out of the foundation wall. It hasn't been a good day, she thought with a shrinking at the heart, as she stood alone in her kitchen, stiff with cold in her damp shawl.

Carl and the visitor were asleep as she passed through the boys' room. It gave her a disproportionate sense of relief to see Borger lying there, as though the boy were a sort of pledge that his world and hers might harmonize after all. What a pretty boy he was, Borger! Very like Tryggve—

In the sitting-room lay *her* little Tryggve—right across the sofa, breathing quietly and healthily. He was hot and red in the cheeks after the drive; his golden hair was matted and touzled in the gleam of the night-lamp. One might search far to find a prettier child. But he *was* of a different kind—more luxuriant, but without natural firmness. The visitor in the next room looked, even when asleep, as though he would always go straight ahead through life, he had that in him. Her boy here would have to be *taught*, she did not quite know what—to hold himself erect, not to crawl and sneak by crooked ways, even if he were compelled to work to windward—

The moment she lay down beside him he wriggled against her in his sleep, and then he curled up, warm and soft and puffing like a young animal cuddling up to its dam.

Chapter Eight

TRYGGVE TOKSVOLD WANTED to take Ida Elisabeth on a trip to Oslo. She had not been there since she passed through the town the year she came from the west country.

"You don't mean to say you haven't been in a theatre for six years?"

"No." Ida Elisabeth laughed. "There are many people, Tryggve, who have to put up with that."

"But all the same—nowadays when the distance is nothing to speak of—"

"I had another use for my money, man—and I couldn't leave my children either, unnecessarily like that."

"That was almost too much of a good thing. One must be allowed to think a *little* of oneself too." So he decided it—they would make a trip there in the autumn and have a good time. Make some purchases too. "It's about time you made a little pleasure trip too."

HE planned this visit to town so that Ida Elisabeth had a lump in her throat when she was alone and recalled the expression of his face as he talked of it. She could scarcely believe it—that here was one who looked forward like a child, in sheer delight without the slightest reservation, to treating her to a really first-class time.

It *was* difficult for her, placed as she was between her lover and her boys. Tryggve was fond of children; he said so, and he spoke the truth, she had seen that during the week they had Borger with them. He went to the cinema with the boys; he had taken them all for a trip in the mountains—they drove off on Saturday after office hours and stayed till Sunday evening, and they had made a bon-fire and gathered cloudberries and fished. Borger had brought fishing-tackle with him, and so Tryggve presented Carl with a really fine fishing-rod and was going to teach the boy—he had taken the two little fellows with him some evenings along Vaadöla. Ugh, but that sort of thing was not at all in Carl's line. It went fairly well as long as Borger was here; Carl was excited at the new experience of having a friend of his own age on a visit, and he was inclined to worship Borger. But he was by no means willing to let himself be trained by a grown-up, who was his mother's friend over the heads of the children. Ida Elisabeth looked forward with some dread to the winter, when Tryggve Toksvold would realize his intention of making open-air beings of her boys.

As it was, they were full of a spirit of opposition to this man who was to be their step-father—they must have under-stood that, if they had not heard people talk about it. And as she saw how much Tryggve failed to understand, Ida Elisabeth gradually became aware how far her own treat-ment of the children had been guided by unconscious under-standing. Carl was by nature a stay-at-home. True, he was ready to help her in the garden or to run errands for her or take the dog for a turn or hang about the outhouses at Viker. But as for going out purely for fun or for taking exercise—no power on earth could make Carl do that, least of all Tryggve Toksvold. If Carl had nothing definite to take him out, he only wanted to sit over his drawing and reading, and he was as cross as a bear if he was not allowed to do so.

And it was impossible to do anything with little Buster, if one took him too seriously. It was no earthly use being grave and strict when he came out with his fables—that only frightened him, and then he grew assertive and invented a whole string of fresh yarns and lies to back up his first stories. But when she laughed and affected not to see that he meant her to believe a word of all he had dished up—when, on the contrary, they agreed that he was only rattling off a rigmarole that he had invented for fun—why, then the boy spoke the truth and gave her the story as straight as he could, if it was important that she should take what he said seriously. And it was the same with everything else—whether he was to join in a game of cards or pick berries and peas for her or kick about a football with the boys at Viker—if he only wanted to play monkey tricks the thing to do was to ignore him, say that now we big folks are going to do this or that, so we can't be bothered with a little baby boy who only wants to play. But Tryggve lectured him seriously—a boy who wants to be anything of a man doesn't play tricks, doesn't brag, mustn't be such a scatterbrain.

"You know, Ida," he said seriously, "that my wishes about the boys are no different from your own. I want them to grow into decent men. So you and I are agreed as to the things we wish them to respect. And I assume that you trust me, when I have given you my word to treat your children in every way as if they were my own sons."

That was true enough. But it makes all the difference in the world whether children learn a thing of a mother of whom they know, consciously or not, that everything she does and is and lives has their welfare and happiness for its ultimate object. Or whether they learn the same thing of a stranger who has definite opinions as to how they ought to be brought up—even if the children understand in a way that he means well by them and thinks of their good, amongst all the other things he thinks of.

And it could be no use his trying to treat them as his own sons. He behaved to Borger in a way that was natural to him with any boy he was fond of, and Borger's whole being responded as it were to that of the man. Tryggve was fond of children, but only as he was fond of people in general—in the case of folks whom he liked or understood or respected he was the best of friends, staunch and considerate, cautious and delicate in helping, happy in making sacrifices. Sacrifices, by the way, was a word he detested, and he certainly had no feeling that he was sacrificing himself, even when he made what people call great sacrifices in order to serve one with whom he was in sympathy. And he did not do it for others.

Perhaps in reality there were not so many people who are fond of children whatever they may be like. Ida Elisabeth had always thought it sounded rather schoolmistressy— sort of Borghild Braatö-ish, when anyone claimed to be that. Children differ among themselves just as much as grown-up people, and those who see children as they are cannot possibly like all children, any more than they can like the whole of mankind. Decent people make certain allowances for all children, because they are children—can't get on by themselves, can't defend themselves, and often don't understand. But unless one believes oneself bound to love all mankind for some mystic or religious reason, one certainly has no cause to love all children either—that is, if one really knows something of children.

Tryggve Toksvold was held up time after time, so that it was October before he and Ida Elisabeth could leave for their visit to Oslo. But it was brilliant autumn weather the day they drove off—bright and clear under a blue sky streaked with white, the trees were still thick with red and yellow leaves, but their tops looked thin, and under them the ground was pale with fallen leaves; little golden yellow birch-leaves lay strewed about the green paddock, where the cows were grazing.

HIS youngest sister lived in Oslo, married to a journalist named Mosgaard. He had been connected with a local paper in their parts when Anne Toksvold made his acquaintance. Now he was editor of a trade journal and on the staff of a daily, and his wife had something to do with the children's page of a Saturday edition—they had no children.

"I was always much fonder of Ingvild than of Anne. Anne always understood so well how to get what she wanted. And father spoilt her all he could. It meant a thrashing on the spot if Lauris or I did but point at Anne."

They were asked to dinner there one of the first days they were in town. The Mosgaards lived a deuce of a way out along Drammens-vei, beyond Stabekk. Their villa lay in a side road—a little salmon-coloured house in the modern style at the top of a little garden which sloped steeply to the road and was laid out entirely in stone steps and big stones with cushions of frosty grey rock plants among them. There was not a bush high enough for a self-respecting cat to hide behind.

However, Anne and Frits Mosgaard received them very pleasantly. She bore a likeness to her brother and sister, but with her close-cropped, glossy, and well-kept hair, her plucked eyebrows and reddened lips, she had adopted another style. She had a charmingly slim figure and was chic from head to foot. In a way it was reassuring to Ida Elisabeth to meet one of the family who had been able to change her skin—so it appeared. But she *liked* Ingvild Brekke with her untidy grey-streaked hair and her steel spectacles and her cook's figure—and her politely expectant attitude towards an unknown quantity whom her brother presumably thought of marrying—better than this charming and animated young woman who received her so cordially and proposed to be on sisterly terms as soon as her husband had filled the glasses and welcomed them to the table.

They had a comfortable home too in a way. One corner of the drawing-room was all window, and there were no windows in the other walls. There were chairs so low that one almost had to lie in them, little tables that broke up into a whole system of shelves, huge globular flower-vases holding but a single flower, and two delightful Scotch terriers, Pen and Ink were their names.

The Mosgaards were going out in the evening, so the visit was not too protracted. And they were engaged the whole of the following week, so nothing could be done about fixing an evening for going out with Toksvold and Ida Elisabeth. But they must be sure and come here again on Anne's birthday, in a week's time, when they were expecting some people to dance.

"It's been a pleasure to meet you, Ida, and make your acquaintance." Anne Mosgaard shook her hand vigorously.

"Well, you'll be seeing Kari, won't you?" she said to her brother. "Then you might ask her from me—you're going to invite Matthisen after all, aren't you, Frits?—you might ask her to come here on my birthday. I haven't had time to have her out here yet. Though, as she's really so much older than I am I don't really see that I need ... All the same, perhaps it'll be better if I ring her up and ask her myself—otherwise she might take it into her head to be offended ... Do you know where she lives? yes, of course you do—"

"It'll be nice for Ingvild, won't it, when you have a home of your own, then you can invite each other's children to stay in the holidays", mimicked Toksvold; he had taken Ida Elisabeth back to her hotel after they left the Mosgaards'. "Not damned likely *she'd* ever invite the children. Anne's never thought of anyone but herself. Pleasant? Oh yes, she's *that*. I imagine it would be worse for herself if she wasn't!"

He came across and kissed her:

"I suppose I must go? You're going to change ... Put on that red dress of yours this evening—it suits you so well."

It was charming and becoming, thought Ida Elisabeth, as she got out the dress Tryggve called red—it was plum-coloured, but rather on the red side, in a kind of artificial silk. But if they should go out to the Mosgaards' for Anne's birthday, she would treat herself to a really elegant gown. She was not at all inclined to look the country cousin in *that* house.

IDA ELISABETH persuaded herself after the event that she had had the first premonition of her past lying in ambush, ready to spring out on her, the moment she saw those chairs again.

Toksvold and she were to meet outside the Theatre Café and have a rather late dinner—they had each had engagements all the morning. He was walking up and down when she arrived:

"If you're not feeling too ravenous, I've seen some furniture in an old curiosity shop close by that I'm sure you will like. Six baroque chairs and two arm-chairs, uncommonly handsome. Shall we slip round and take a look at them before we go up and dine?"

It was not many steps to the shop. Two of the chairs were on view in the window. She was certain it was those, the moment she saw the covers—canvas embroidery, green and red dominating, with touches of yellow and violet—parrots and tulips.

Quite correct, the shopman was able to tell them that they came from a country house in the West, sold by order of the executors. He asked a whacking price for them, but it was scarcely unreasonable.

Afterwards, as they sat at dinner, she told Tryggve something about Teie and Doctor Sommervold.

"But then wouldn't you like to have those chairs?" he asked. "If you're keen on them I'll buy them."

"I don't quite know—" she said, hesitating.

"It's a hell of a price, but no doubt one could beat him down a bit. And one only gets married once—"

She did not think she really wanted them. She had a feeling that it might be a bad omen.

THE day they were to go to Anne Mosgaard's evening party Ida Elisabeth had spent an enjoyable forenoon.

She went early in the day to one of the big stores and introduced herself—she had been a customer there all these years. The head of a department and a manageress took charge of her cordially and conducted her to the department for orders and models. Three mannequins of different types were set going and paraded one ravishing gown after another for her benefit, and she examined them closely, went into the question of material and cut and niceties of taste and smartness, and talked shop—hour after hour.

Then she betook herself to one of the fitting-rooms with Fru Wilde, the manageress, and attendant spirits hovered to and fro, fetching and carrying, while she tried on. A corselet— the price to *her* was forty crowns—positively transformed her figure; fine and firm, with a girl's purity of outline, she stood letting Fru Wilde slip on one evening frock after another, each more lovely than the last. Till they burst into raptures—it was a gown of lemon-green crêpe Ranée—she had thought it would be too tight for her, but it was not, it fitted so exactly that not a stitch required to be altered; she had not imagined it could suit her—on the tall dark mannequin it had looked marvellous—but it did not make her appear wan, it really did suit her—quite brilliantly. It was sleeveless, with a simple belt of gold scales; the skirt was trimmed with a lot of narrow flounces, so that it fell about her in a kind of light profusion—and an enchanting little bridge coat went with it; it was a positive vision, as she turned and twisted among the many mirrors in the fitting-room. It seemed to be no time since her mother and she and Connie had ransacked the most fashionable shops and kept the assistants busy filling up the fitting-rooms, while they spent hours choosing and rejecting among the finest and most original models, without troubling about the price—

But Fru Wilde came and gave her the closest price for the lemon-green—it was simply a gift. She found stockings to go with it—shoes, well, they would have to be pale gilt; it would be impossible to match the colour—

Ida Elisabeth looked at herself again and again in the glass—it seemed incredible that this was herself. Or *was* this the charming Ida Elisabeth Andst? And it was—but then it was like looking back on a bewitched existence when she recalled Fru Braatö of Berfjord, in golf jacket and long dark apron, yellow and drawn in the face, thin as a rake except just when she was shapeless and expecting her confinement—or Fru Braatö the dressmaker, neat but unassuming. She too had sloughed her skin; she was young again, and charming, really charming—so that's how I actually look!

Tryggve Toksvold was dining with some business friends, so she went and got something to eat at a small restaurant in the centre of the town; meanwhile her thoughts dwelt with delight on the purchases she had made. The necklace Tryggve had given her, of polished amber beads mounted in old-fashioned gold filigree, would go splendidly with her dress. Ida Elisabeth felt perfectly happy for the moment.

From the restaurant she went to the hairdresser's. She had seen there was one close to the shop where the chairs from Teie were on view.

She had had her hair washed and was sitting well wrapped in white towels before the big mirror, while a woman dried her hair with the electric hot-air apparatus. Then it was that it dawned on her there was something familiar about the girl in the white apron who was engaged in waving the hair of the lady in the next chair. It was—yes, indeed it was Jarngerd Braatö, her former sister-in-law. Ida Elisabeth had not seen her since she was quite grown up. She was greatly changed, with a huge mop of golden yellow permanent-waved hair round her big, rather coarse face, and her features were improved with thin, dark eyebrow streaks and sealing-wax red lips, etcetera. But there could scarcely be a doubt it was Jeja. Next moment the other had recognized her; they nodded to each other.

It turned out that Jeja was to do her hair.

"That was a surprise, I must say!" she snapped the curling-tongs and jingled them down on the little heater. "Fancy your being in town! But perhaps you're here pretty often?

You're getting on so splendidly where you are now, I've been told—"

"And so you've come to Oslo? How are you—and how are they all getting on at your home?"

"Oh, not very grandly, as you may imagine. Well, you know Herjulf's come home—?"

"No, has he? No, you see, since Doctor Sommervold died I never hear any news from there. Olise Langeland and Fru Esbjörnsen are the only ones I hear from now—generally at Christmas. But they only tell me how things are going at Berfjord. I never hear from Vallerviken."

"Why, fancy, Lisken, your shop's changed hands three times already—nobody's made anything of it since your time—"

"Times have gotten worse too since then", remarked Ida Elisabeth.

"Yes, you may well say that! Why, fancy, now papa and mamma have got Herjulf and Frithjof both living at home—for it's just as bad in America as here, and so Herjulf came home last year. Well, Vikarr's at home too, but he's got a job, on the quay—Vikarr's turned out a worker, he has, let me tell you!"

Vikarr, Geirmund, and Jarngerd—the three youngest; it was true, she had always had the impression that they were rather different from the elder ones, with more go in them somehow. "And Geirmund?" she asked.

Jarngerd Braatö looked about her before answering. Ida Elisabeth was now the only customer in the saloon, and the three other young ladies in white aprons had withdrawn into the next room—the chiropody saloon, apparently—and were busy chatting there.

"Ugh, yes, Geirmund. He'd gotten a situation in Aalesund, you see, and then he got into some mess. Isn't it awful? You may be sure mamma and papa were in a state about it. Now they'll get him home by Christmas, and what they're to do with him then I'm sure I don't know. There's no place to send him either, it's just as bad everywhere, and there's not many of the relations left, at least not those that can help us. It won't be pleasant to have him hanging about at home—and after such a business as that too!"

But her voice ran on in the same practised tone, bright and lively, which more than anything else gave Ida Elisabeth the idea that Jarngerd must have cast herself adrift from Vettehaugen for good.

"I'm sure you did quite right to let your hair grow. Do you know, Lisken, I never thought it suited you to wear your hair short—every separate hair's so soft and thin that you never got any fall in it, it looked limp and straggly"— she gave a shake to her own imposing frisure. "So?" she tried, holding Ida Elisabeth's hair against her face. "Or perhaps a little higher up?" She seized the tongs again: "A little more here, I think. . .

"And so you're divorced from Frithjof now—mamma wrote that you'd done it. Well, you know, *I'm* with you there, you may be sure; poor Fiffen's been a flabby sort of fish all his days, and now that he seems to have got consumption too—"

"Has Frithjof—is there anything wrong with his chest?"

"Well, you know, they don't call it that—they've said it was bronchitis and phlegm on the lungs and all that sort of thing, but it's easy to guess what *that* means. Of course he got the infection from Merete; she was laid up at home almost to the time of her death. So then I got it fixed that Else anyhow came up here with her youngster, so now *we're* living together, but, you see, it's so hard for Else to get anything to do—she never gets a red cent from her husband and she's pretty well tied, with Bojan. But I can tell you, that *is* a sweet child—gee, I wish you could have seen her. Her name's Borghild, papa insisted on that, but we call her Bojan. The old people hated parting with her—only grandchild and all that, you know, but I thought it wouldn't *do*—Frithjof's not very careful, as you can imagine; it gave me the horrors to see him petting the child—"

But here was at any rate one of them who was willing to *do* something for the others. The rest of the Braatö children had kept together just as much and just as little as a litter of kittens: they stuck to their parents and their home as kittens to their mother's basket, and if one of them were offered anything outside, the whole lot made off after it. But as for keeping together in order to help and support one another like a family of grown-up people, she had never seen a sign of their having any such idea—until now in the case of Jarngerd.

Jarngerd showed her out by a long, badly lighted corridor: "Well, it was a real treat to see you again, Lisken, and have a talk with you. Are you staying long in town? Fancy if you could come and see us—well, we've nothing much to—not but what it's quite a nice place where we live; it's up at Bryn in a villa, an attic with an alcove, but it isn't easy to keep it tidy with two of us living there and a little child, and you know, Else's no great hand at that. But I'd like you to see Bojan. And it would be fun to hear a little more about what you're doing—"

"If we could meet in town tomorrow", said Ida Elisabeth rather undecidedly. "Then you could dine with me. What time do you have dinner?"

"Gee, that would be fine. Would you like me to tell Else, so that she can come too and bring Bojan? Oh, I can tell you she's sweet—"

Ida Elisabeth had some misgivings as she walked home to the hotel. But pooh! it couldn't matter much if she had invited Jeja and Else to lunch tomorrow. And if there was a chance of helping Jeja a little in one way or another, she would be glad to do it—it need not mean getting too deeply involved with the Braatös again. And as she had now heard *so* much about them, after all these years, she would like to hear a little more—how things really were with her father-in-law, for instance. Poor man—well, poor mother-in-law too, of course—

Anyhow Jeja was really fond of Else's child.—By the way, she hadn't so much as asked after her nephews, it occurred to Ida Elisabeth. Well, but in any case Jeja was capable of some feeling outside herself—

Her depression passed off as she dressed for the party. Only now did the frock show to full advantage, when she had shoes and stockings to match—and had had her hair done properly.

It was a slight disappointment that Tryggve was not more thrilled, when he came to fetch her:

"Yes, you look first-rate of course"—he kissed her bare shoulders, stroked them with his hands. "You're beautiful.— It's only the colour—it seems to me so odd? Oh no—I dare say it's pretty. But I've seen you in lots of things that looked prettier on you, in my opinion. That red you've been wearing here, for instance—"

He saw that she was not quite pleased, and then he laughed:

"But I suppose this is the last word in smartness? And you can trust Anne to appreciate it anyhow—and that's really the idea, isn't it?"

It was a late affair at the Mosgaards'—nearly six o'clock before she got to bed. So Ida Elisabeth was rather short of sleep and felt that she had smoked and drunk a good deal more than she was used to, when she had to go out to meet Jeja and Else. She bitterly repented having invited them.

When Ida Elisabeth entered the restaurant Jarngerd was already seated in one of the compartments. She was alone.

"Well, now you see, I didn't say anything to Else after all. Except that I'd met you and you sent your love. You know what Else's like—a bit slow in the uptake, and she's not improved with years, poor girl. We can chat much more freely without her sitting by. And Bojan's so lively that sometimes she won't give you a chance to get a word in—"

They gave their orders, and Jarngerd chatted as she ate:

"This is awfully cosy, Lisken!

"Teie? Why, fancy, it's standing empty. They're trying to sell it. You can guess there's nobody can afford to take it over, neither the people in Germany nor Thomas' children. Sommervold *didn't* leave such a fearful lot after all. And we all thought he was so tremendously rich. But he was never very good at holding on to his money. They had only to go to Sommervold and make out they were in a real bad way, and they got something—for interest and instalments and boats and cows and I don't know what all. He poured it out all over the place—that's what papa and mamma always said."

It was assuredly no small amount *they* had received in the course of years. But so like them to criticize. Ida Elisabeth frowned slightly—she was reminded of her fundamental antipathy to the Vettehaugen race.

"*You* were left quite a lot, weren't you?" asked Jarngerd inquisitively. "They said so at home anyhow."

"Carl was left a bank book with a few thousands in it", said Ida Elisabeth curtly. "The doctor was his godfather, you know."

"Carl, yes—by the way, how is Kalleman? He must be a big boy now? And you have one besides—that came after you'd left Berfjord?"

Ida Elisabeth gave her information about the boys as briefly as possible. She had run away with them, it was true. But not the slightest attempt had ever been made on the part of the father or his family to dispute her sole right to the children, a thing which struck her all at once as sufficiently monstrous.

"Well, you know it didn't come to anything with Frithjof and that dame of his? Thank God! She was awful, I can tell you—an old frump! Frithjof must have been *crazy* to have anything to do with her—"

"I assumed as much", replied Ida Elisabeth evasively. "Since he took no steps to be divorced when the separation period was up."

"And anything so ungrateful—after all we'd done for her. She came to Vettehaugen, you understand, as she required a rest in the country, and then mamma invited her, and then she stayed with us nearly three months and let herself be nursed and waited on. Then she went back to her situation and wrote and broke it off! What do you think of that?"

Very sensible. And rather what you might expect. But Ida Elisabeth said nothing.

"And that just as we had got Merete home. Poor mamma—but, you know, she's as confiding as ever. It was decided, you see, that she was to go to Frede's parents and stay there when she left the sanatorium—naturally they took it for granted that at a big place like that, a regular mansion it was, she'd be able to nurse herself and get cured, for she was to take care of herself and live really well for a time. I fancy I see it! Instead of that she had to serve in the shop, and it was *frightful* in winter-time, she froze nearly to death, she said, a horrible climate it was and her future mother-in-law was wicked and miserly. Frede they sent to the East country, some place near Lillehammer; he died too, by the way. But poor Merete they just packed off home again, when she couldn't slave for them any longer—and by then it was certain death. Poor Merete, she was in such despair, she wanted so much to live—"

Ida Elisabeth bit her lip. This was the Book of Job all over. And she felt her old compassionate tenderness for these people; it was just as fundamental as her antipathy to them, and it rose again in her like a returning tide—

"It must have been very hard on the old people, all this?" she asked quietly.

"You may be sure. Though in a way they're not much changed. It seems as if they don't rightly understand even now how difficult it is. To get anything for us young ones to do and that. They sit and wait for someone to come and offer us something. Ugh, yes, Lisken—Else's like that too, you know. Often I don't know *what* I'm to do—you can imagine what it's like when we actually have nothing to live on all three except what I earn. But I don't feel that I *can* send her home either, when there's such a lot of them already and poor Vikarr's the only support they have—he's got enough weighing on him as it is, at his age. And Bojan in a house full of consumption as it is now. I didn't dare stay there a day longer—

"And then Else can't do a blessed thing, you know. We've advertised and answered advertisements by the score for domestic situations—that's the only thing she can do. If only she could get something where there were no children, or to keep house for a gentleman where she could have the child with her ... But you know, situations like that don't grow on trees.

"*You* don't know of anything for her, do you, Lisken, up in your parts?"

Ida Elisabeth shook her head:

"I really know so few people up there. My work keeps me busy from morning to night, and then there's the house and the children—"

"Listen now, Lisken. My holiday starts next Saturday; I haven't had a summer holiday yet. *Couldn't* you ask Else and Bojan to stay with you a week or so, then she could look about for something to do in the neighbourhood—?"

"I'm sorry, Jarngerd, I can't do that. I have neither time nor room to have anyone staying with me."

Jarngerd slowly turned red under her powder, and her eyes filled with tears:

"To tell you the honest truth, Lisken—I'm often quite in despair about her. I don't know *what* I'm to do—I *must* look a bit decent, with my work in town. And Bojan at any rate mustn't starve if we can help it. Ugh, you don't know how hard it is sometimes. I owe two months' rent now. Ugh.

"You know, Else can quite well sleep on a sofa or a shake-down and have Bojan with her—there's no trouble about that. Ugh, Lisken—I really thought when you turned up so unexpectedly that you'd been sent from heaven—"

"I think it would be a better arrangement if *you* came", said Ida Elisabeth with hesitation. "For your holiday. You would have to put up with what I could offer, of course."

"I *can't* do that, you understand, don't you?—go away and leave her there with the child, without any money or anything, and the people of the house so ill-tempered and wanting to get rid of us. Oh no, I'll have to stay.—And to tell you the honest truth, Lisken—you can guess, I have friends and acquaintances. But whenever I'm going out to have a little fun it makes Else so sour—and it won't do to take her; nobody thinks she's a sport. You've no idea what a favour you'd be doing me if you took her just for a fort-night, so that I could be free and have a good time for once in a way."

Ida Elisabeth looked seriously at the other:

"Yes, yes, Jarngerd. I understand. But—"

Jarngard gave a toss of the head, at once defiant and despondent:

"You see, Lisken—you can easily understand that if we all three had to live just on what *I* earn at 'Irene's' we should soon starve to death. If I hadn't—well, an acquaintance, you know, who helps me a bit. But you can guess, he's quite likely to get sick of my being always so tied. It's only reasonable that he should want us to meet in a free and easy way and have a little fun together. If he gets tired of me and takes himself off, I really don't know what I'm to do. I'm quite fond of him too, let me tell you!"

Ida Elisabeth did not quite know what answer to make to this revelation.

Jarngerd looked up with her defiant toss of the head:

"Well, I suppose you're virtuously scandalized. But that's how things *are*, Lisken. It may be all right for people like you—you're a frightfully clever person, and strong. Or for girls who've had a heap of education or have influence or a family that are somebody, or talents or a turn for something. But there are very few like that, you must remember. The rest of us, we have to be glad if the men are moderately decent and kind. And he is like that, the one who—well, my friend, you know. You don't know what some girls have to put up with for a living. Oh, there are lots of fellows who give a lady a place simply to have somebody to work on the cheap from morning to night and to be used for you know what when he feels inclined, and if she grumbles all she hears is that he can get ten women to take her place.

"Not that that's happened to me, you know", she said provocatively. "But I know lots of others. But now I suppose you think I'm frightfully depraved?"

Ida Elisabeth shook her head: "But I think it's sad, Jeja. All you've been telling me. And I wish"—she blushed as she said it—"that I could help you in one way or another. So that you shouldn't get into—still greater difficulties. But could—but could—well, anyhow so that you wouldn't have to—simply in order to live. For you see, Jeja, this sort of thing leads very often from bad to worse—"

"You needn't be afraid of *that*. I'm not such a fool as you seem to think. I'm not so ignorant of human nature, you see, as Else and Merete for instance. I know the people I have to deal with. And as for a blunder like Else made—it won't be this little girl that'll be as clumsy as that. Bojan's enough for us. Oh no, you needn't worry about *me*, thank you!"

A sickening chill seemed to close Ida Elisabeth's lips. She thought of Vettehaugen, Midsummer Eve, and Christmas candles ... Then she said in a low voice: "I'll try anyhow—if I can find something—for Else—

"God knows what your father would say, Jeja—and your mother—if they knew this—"

"Oh, they! They live in another age, poor things! You may be sure I'll take good care they don't hear anything. It was only Else that was foolish enough for *that*. Even little Merete had sense enough to keep quiet about what it wasn't good for them to know. They haven't the least *idea* what folks are like nowadays—"

She burst out laughing, laughed like a great child:

"Can you imagine, Lisken—they still trot along in the Seventeenth of May procession every blessed year, both of them, in their old freshmen's caps!"

As they were leaving the restaurant they ran straight into a couple of men coming in. They and Jarngerd greeted one another beamingly. Ida Elisabeth listened instinctively—it was at any rate a slight relief to hear that Jeja did not address either familiarly; so it could not be one of these—for they looked so utterly loathsome, vulgar faces, insolent pig's eyes. Jarngerd introduced them, most unnecessarily. Ida Elisabeth did not catch their names.

"My sister-in-law, Fru Braatö." It was no longer ago than last night that Anne, enchanting in a stylish dress of red taffeta and tulle, had introduced her as "my sister-in-law, Fru Braatö" to a crowd of pleasant and cheerful and charming young people. In any case she had thought then—that they all looked so healthy and clean and straight. Tryggve looked so well in evening dress. She had enjoyed herself hugely. Now it seemed so long ago.

Next day they drove north again.

The evening before, when they were in the theatre, he had asked as early as the first entr'acte: "Have you had anything to bother you today?" And she had answered: "I met some people I know whom I hadn't seen for many years. And they're in a pretty bad way now—" Said he:

"Ah—there are a good many people who feel the pinch nowadays—"

He wanted to drive home by another road—along Harestuvand over Hadeland and High Cross down to Gjövik. They had come as far as the Gjeller ridge: "Are you cold, Ida?" he asked anxiously. "Oh no."

There was a black frost and the weather was grand for driving. In the thin, white mist the villages looked so bright, all colours were gentle and subdued under the wide pale-blue sky. The lakes they passed shone with a dull silver gleam and faded out on the far side where the belt of mist and the pine forest merged in a grey-blue mass. They drove through belts where the fog grew suddenly dense with a smell of smoke, till it was nothing but sour, raw smoke that stung the throat and eyes, past crackling red bonfires in a clearing. Now there was only here and there a solitary tree which kept its red and yellow leaves, bitten and faded by the frost; but copses and thickets rose in the air with an open tracery of bare branches and twigs, and in the forests they drove through the ground was grey with frozen heather and rime-covered bog. They passed fields where turnips had been dug and stacked in rows, and Tryggve sniffed in the fresh, rank smell: "Don't you like it? Talk about the scent of spring; I say it's nothing to the scents of autumn after all." A lad who was driving a cart could not get his horse past the car. At last Tryggve had to get out and help him to lead it. "Fine beast. It's queer, some horses never get really used to cars—

"There *is* something the matter, Ida?" he said inquiringly.

"For *one* thing, you know I'm not used to going out and amusing myself night after night. And it makes one fearfully tired to tramp along stone pavements when one's used to country roads—"

He laughed a little at this. "Is that all? You're not cold, are you? Shall I get out my rain-coat? It'll help to keep you warm if you put it on outside—"

She stamped some warmth into her feet on the frozen road, while he rummaged among the baggage in the back of the car. Just here where they had stopped there was a very fine view; on one side of the road the forest rose steeply, but on the other the ground fell away in folds, pale with stubble and green with aftergrass, towards a valley with a little river at the bottom. The fog had so far dispersed that there was a blue gleam on the little tarn from which the stream issued and the last of the yellow foliage on the hillsides shone out.

Tryggve helped her to put on the coat and poured something out of a thermos flask. It was strong, hot soup flavoured with madeira: "I'd almost forgotten it. It's good, what?"

"Ugh, Tryggve—my conscience is downright guilty—when I think how well off I am now. And then those people I spoke about yesterday, whom I used to know very well indeed—they're so terribly hard up."

"No, stop it! You toil and drudge as not many do nowadays—it would be too bad if you didn't get a little compensation sometimes."

"But, Tryggve, you yourself criticize Anne for never thinking of doing anything for Ingvild and her children."

"That's another matter. Her own sister. And such a hard-working woman as Ingvild, with such clever, promising children. Well, as far as that goes I don't know what these friends of yours are like. But I thought perhaps—if they were the same sort as Fru Tömmeraas, for instance. It's no use worrying oneself about that type of person. Nobody can do anything for them, Ida—for the very moment they're left to themselves, all the trouble you've taken to help them is wasted, as if you'd never done a thing—all they want is to get stuck in the bog. If anyone cares to give them a hand and try to pull them out, that's all right, then they feel they're interesting. But rather than make any effort of their own they'll just sink in."

"It's not that they won't—they *can't*—"

"Rubbish!" He took her in his arms. "Give me a kiss then. Hasn't that soup warmed you, Ida dear?—your face is so cold! Everybody *can* do *something*, but there are so many who *won't*."

His kisses sent warmth and a melting sense of happiness through her whole body. And Frithjof's at home with the old people and has consumption, she thought. And here I am driving with my sweetheart who loves me, whom I love—

It was already fairly dark as they approached Gjövik. The glare of their lamps flew before them over the road, lighting up fences and forest on both sides. When she looked up it was a moment or two before her dazzled eyes could distinguish the black tree-tops sweeping along the dark grey sky. Toksvold wanted to stop and have supper at Gjövik. "You can telephone home from the hotel and say that you'll arrive a little later."

After supper, as they sat at their coffee, she told him:

"I've done a thing which I know you'll think foolish. Invited a lady to stay with me for a week—a Fru Nilsen. One whom I knew pretty well in former days. In fact, she's a sister of my former husband."

Toksvold looked up from the pipe he was filling; he said nothing.

Then she gave him the story—all she had heard from Jarngerd, except that about Jarngerd's most private arrangement.

He sat watching her as she talked. And when she had finished there was a pause before he said anything.

"Well, we have an old saying in my part of the world," he said slowly, "to this effect: When misfortune's abroad it's wise to keep indoors."

With a little thrill of pain it struck Ida Elisabeth that this was just the way of thinking she could not accept.

They sat side by side and said nothing, as he drove on in the dark autumn evening. Once he said:

"Couldn't you write to that lady and say it's not convenient after all for you to receive her now? Send her some money instead, so that she can go somewhere else?"

It gave her such a strange sinking of the heart to find that he too had thought of this. Money ... She had given Jeja something for her rent, but that would not go very far. If she could get Else something to do, so that at any rate Jeja would not have to do that for the sake of the *money*. But perhaps that would make little difference—if Jeja had gotten used to that sort of life it was not easy to see what one was to do to get her on to another track. If she had got into a set where that was the prevailing tone, she was no doubt as ready as the rest of the Braatös to adopt the morality of those around her.

"For the sake of the boys, if nothing else, I think you ought to hesitate", said Tryggve Toksvold. "Are you anxious for them to resume relations with their father's family?"

No, he was right there. And she had done a stupid thing in asking Else. But on the other hand—not to stir a finger, after hearing all their story—she could not do that either.

WHEN they entered the dark passage at Viker the kitchen door opened and Carl's little form appeared in the light.

"But—are you still up, my dear!"

"I couldn't get him to go to bed", said Ragnhild, one of her sempstresses who had been staying here while she was away. "He would stay up to see if you were coming."

But the mother had seen the suspense and uncertainty of the boy's manner. Whether he should throw himself into her arms or should confine himself to a polite kiss and a "good-evening, mother" depended on whether Toksvold came in with her or not. He said good-night and left, almost as soon as he had carried in her baggage. And she and Carl drank the tea which Ragnhild had ready for her.

When he had gone to bed and she went in to say good-night to him, he threw his arms about her neck and held on to her like grim death. At last she had to free herself gently:

"There, Carl. Now I'm back home with you. Now you must lie down and go to sleep."

BUT she herself could not fall asleep. When she closed her eyes and tried, she saw nothing but the road rushing towards her and slipping under the car, and the changing landscape dashing past.

Then she lay tossing again, oppressed by vague fears—like presentiments of all manner of coming evil. Tryggve was *right*, she felt that now; she ought not to have let herself be fooled into taking up with those people again. Especially as she knew much better than he did, how quick they were to take an ell [45 inches] when you offered them an inch. But now that she had heard what a bad state they were in—and with her knowledge of them: incapable not merely of looking after themselves, but actually of forming a judgment. It quite took her breath away to think of it—such a mess as they were in; it might require a whole troop to get them more or less out of it. So no doubt she might just as well have spared herself. But she simply *couldn't.*

And then, when she thought of Tryggve, a feeling like impatience or anger, almost despair, came over her. Though she knew how *horrid* it was of her—for he loved her, he longed to possess her; she was not the kind of vain little goose who would take it into her head to doubt him or to imagine he could not be so violently in love after all, since he had never forgotten himself with her or tried to get her to forget herself. There were plenty of shallow-brains who argued like that, and it might be quite pathetic, if they were young and naïve enough. She could see and appreciate his view of the matter—she had two sons. No doubt he felt that the children were jealous of this new factor that had entered their mother's life, but they would have to put up with it; no child has the right to demand that a mother who has been left alone shall pass the rest of her life in celibacy. What they have the right to demand is that the new man who steps in shall deal fairly by them. Look after their true interests in the best way. Not behave so as to give them a *right* to hate him. But sons have a *right* to hate a man who makes their mother his mistress. If they do not, there is something wanting in them. If sons can discover extenuating or exculpating circumstances in their mother's irregular love affairs, they must be spiritually castrated. Children ought to have instincts and to assert them.

Tryggve had dragged her about in Oslo so untiringly that she almost thought it had been too much of a good thing. All the time he was not taken up with business had been filled with a programme of theatres, concerts, excursions, restaurants where they danced. And she knew full well what most men would have asked in return. So she too had to conceal with what painful violence she had desired, every single evening, that they could have ended the day by going home somewhere together and staying the night. She *saw* his point, when he said it was best not to stay at the same hotel: all their neighbours knew of course that they had gone to Oslo together. But one needn't give a damn what people think or say, so long as one doesn't prove them right.

But perhaps the most hidden secret of all was that she was afraid. Not of him. Not of herself either, in the sense of fearing that this love which now filled her might pass off. But afraid that something might happen—something might come in the way and force this current of passion into another channel, where it could not find the outlet for which it yearned, in Tryggve's arms. That some power or other which she suddenly seemed to feel outside her might forcibly possess itself of her new fullness of spirit and use it for purposes unknown to her, which were not *her* purpose. *That* she was afraid of. And that was why she was in despair— for now, as she lay here in the dark, it suddenly took the form of *despair*—at his not having flung all considerations to the winds, since she thought it impossible to feel safe in her happiness until the night had come and gone when she and Tryggve lay clasped in each other's arms. After that nothing could come between and part them. Though she knew very well this was only a fancy—she realized well enough that many things may come between a man and a woman afterwards as well as before.

But she was longing, longing, longing. She who knew what it is to have a man, but had never had a man whom she loved. She who knew that love is far from being always invulnerable and indestructible, it may be ruined by external agencies or one may ruin it oneself—but precisely for that reason she would fight to defend and preserve their love, and precisely for that reason she longed to throw herself into it heart and soul, longed as consumedly as a woman without her bitter experience could never have done.

Ida Elisabeth opened her arms in the dark: "Tryggve", she whispered. "Tryggve—" she called a little louder. "Tryggve—"

There was a movement in the boys' room.

"Did you call me, mother?" the little voice asked cautiously, as though afraid of the night.

Ida Elisabeth paused for a moment before answering:

"I only wanted to hear if you were awake. I thought you sounded so restless."

"My toes are itching so fearfully, mother", he said whimpering.

"Oh, nonsense!" she replied after a moment. "It's only something you've made up, Tryggve—"

"No, mother! It hurts so fearfully—" Now there were almost tears in his voice, and she could hear him scratching or rubbing so that his bed shook. "Can't you put something on it, mother—?"

Ida Elisabeth slipped out of her bed on the divan and into the boys' room: "Be quiet and don't wake Carl—" She turned on the light. The youngster started up like a spring; his face was shining with interest as he put out one little foot for examination.

It was really true—his toes were swollen, with glistening spots, red as berries. He had gotten them pretty badly frozen last winter—ugh, were they to have the same trouble over again this year—?

"Hush, hush", she whispered, searching in the medicine cupboard. She found the lump of tallow, gauze bandage, and talc. "You must come into my room, little one—" and she put out the light.

While she was warming the tallow in a silver spoon over the lighted candle on the leaf of the bureau Tryggve sat in the rocking-chair wriggling and writhing—with delight at all the trouble that was being taken about him, and partly because he was cold. His eyes sparkled in the light of the candle.

"But what have you been wearing on your feet lately?"

"Sandals of course. And they're so ragged, mother. And so Ragnhild said I must put on my ski-boots, but they've got too tight for me, so I couldn't get them on—"

With a pang of conscience she thought of her child running about and getting his feet frost-bitten in ragged sandals, while she was spending forty crowns on a corset and buying an evening dress and gilt dance shoes ... Though that was all nonsense, as she knew very well—only it ought to have occurred to her before going away to see whether the boy could wear his last year's boots—

The toes had been well smeared, bound up with gauze and a pair of clean stockings put on outside it all: "There! now off with you to bed again!" She gave him a kiss to conclude the ceremony.

"Mother—mayn't I sleep with you tonight, because I'm so bad?"

"All right. Come along then—"

She blew out the candle, picked up the boy, and carried him to the sofa. The moment she had lain down beside him the child curled up; with the top of his head jammed in her armpit and his knees in her stomach he gave a little sniff of satisfaction and fell asleep at once.

Ida Elisabeth sighed. Now perhaps she would be able to sleep too. There floated before her mind an idea that a mother has already left her children when she is in love with a man, even if she sleeps with them held in her arms.

Chapter Nine

ELSE'S VISIT WAS AN UNMIXED TRIAL. And Bojan was the most intolerable specimen Ida Elisabeth had come across in the way of children. Poor little thing, perhaps she couldn't help it—but oh, how gruesome children are who haven't an idea that they ought to listen when anything is said to them, and are still fretting from morning to night.

Ida Elisabeth had been given permission to fit up one of the empty rooms on the other side of the passage, and Fru Viker lent her a bed from the hotel. It was quite comfortable when she had gotten it aired properly, and hung up curtains and made a fire in the stove.

She would not have recognized Else if she had met her by chance in the street. Though she was not so very much changed if one looked at her feature by feature. Her face was coarser and more fleshy—but what struck one particularly was that the youthful prettiness Else had had in old days had gone off as the pattern goes off cheap crockery in the washing-up. Her hair was now lustreless and thin, her skin a dingy red—and her mouth had always been pale, but now the lips were not even smooth and young. She collapsed on sitting down and had no poise in walking—her figure reminded one of worn-out elastic.

It was an effort to think of anything one could talk to her about. Ida Elisabeth was busy in her work-room at this time and it got rather on her nerves to know that meanwhile the other simply sat moping on her sofa. Ida Elisabeth had provided her with yarn and knitting-needles; she was making a jersey for Bojan, but it grew with incredible slowness; the grey-blue wool only got greyer and greyer.

Else could not be persuaded to go for a walk; she read nothing but the paper—she just sat turning over old fashion papers or looking out of the window.

When they had gotten the children to bed, Ida Elisabeth took up some needlework and tried to entertain Else, till she thought she could decently suggest that we go to bed early in the country. Else did show a little interest in her customers—she wanted to know who this or that lady was and whether they were well off or not. She also expressed a desire to see the well-known sanatorium for tuberculosis—so they walked up there the first Sunday of Else's visit. Otherwise there was only one subject that could put a spark of life into Else: Jeja. Ida Elisabeth was not a little scandalized at the way in which Else spoke of her sister. She was bitter and jealous at Jeja's earning money and having friends, male and female, and "often" going out to amuse herself, but doing nothing to get Else included in the party. "Sitting at home and moping, of course she thinks that's good enough for me."

"Well, but, Else, what would you *do* if you hadn't Jarngerd?"

"Ph! I could take a situation, couldn't I? If I wasn't obliged to have Bojan with me all the time. Mamma and papa would be glad to take Bojan again. It's Jeja who absolutely insists on Bojan staying with us. *She* takes good care not to get a child of her own. But she's the only one who's to have any say about Bojan, just as if no one else understood what was good for her—"

But there was here a hope that perhaps Ida Elisabeth might find a solution, since it was not Else herself who made it an absolute condition that she must have the child with her if she took a situation. Ida Elisabeth rang up Marte Bö—and made an appointment with her at Björkheim hotel.

The old midwife promised at once to do what she could to get Fru Nilsen placed—Marte was always burning with avidity when she was given a chance of straightening out other folks' difficulties. She had two or three places in view.

She would speak to Tveito, the schoolmaster, tomorrow—
his housekeeper was to be married next month. Tveito was a
widower with six children; it was such a good Christian home.
They kept two cows, pigs, and fowls, but Else must be
supposed to be used to country ways from her life at Vettehaugen, and Tveito's eldest children were so ready to help.

Whether Else would be overjoyed at being planted out
like this with a schoolmaster's family right out in the wilds
was by no means certain. But she would hardly oppose the
scheme. True, she had not said very much about her past
life, and Ida Elisabeth did not like to ask. She had only a
very vague idea of who and what Hartvig Nilsen was, but
from things dropped by Else in passing Ida Elisabeth had
gathered that it was Aunt Gitta, old Fru von Post, who had
taken the initiative in getting her married to him—on the
understanding that they should be separated again as soon
as the child was born. Probably Else had never lived with
her husband—he was at home with his parents at that time,
and now he was "gone away"; Else did not know what had
become of him. Aunt Gitta had sent her and the child to
Vettehaugen as soon as she came out of the maternity home,
"to keep her from committing any more follies", and at
Vettehaugen she had stayed, till Jeja moved her away. It was
possible one could make it clear to her that if she took a
situation she would have to pull herself together—Marte
Bö promised to look her up now and again—and Ida Elisabeth would have to provide some outfit for her and the
child. Then Jeja at any rate would be let off having to keep
others besides herself for a while. Else, by the way, was already
looking rather less dull and slack—regular meals were no
doubt among the things she needed—and Bojan was not
quite so pale and thin and abnormally restless.

Tryggve Toksvold came in to take his coffee with them,
as they sat deliberating. They had agreed that he should
not come to see Ida Elisabeth as long as her visitor was
there. So that in ten days she had only met him for a moment

at odd times, when she was doing her shopping and looked in at his office or paid him a surreptitious visit at the hotel.

He sat on the arm of her chair, his fingers stealing a caress at the back of her neck, while he made fun of the ladies' fussiness and of Ida Elisabeth's anxieties: "I must say you've taken on a big job, Ida!"

"It's very kind of Ida to do so", replied Marte Bö. "Ida's too kind, that's the only thing—"

"Exactly! Ida's *too* kind. All the same—when I come to think of it, you're a pair of rather unscrupulous women. You don't think of poor Tveito. For she seems to be an out-and-out good-for-nothing, this Fru Nilsen. What if he should have the misfortune to get hooked by her!"

"Oh no, *he* won't do anything like that!" Marte was offended. "He's such a good, steady man—an earnest believer—"

Toksvold only laughed maliciously.

THERE was something in that, Ida Elisabeth thought as she walked home. For once she was inclined to subscribe to the old adage about taking care of number one. Ugh, if only Else didn't notice that she'd been drinking liqueur— she was surprised and sour because Ida Elisabeth "knew nobody". They had been invited to coffee at Viker and at the Hansens', and Ida Elisabeth had had Fru Viker and Fru and Fröken Hansen in one evening; that was all.

THEN there came a Saturday morning; Ida Elisabeth was in the kitchen cleaning a capercailzie that Tryggve had sent her. All three children were clinging round her to look on. Then Fru Viker came in, evidently in a great state. She hinted that she had something to say that the children were not to hear.

Ida Elisabeth happened to look at Carl—his face was red as fire, with the strangest expression—of shame and indignation combined, as he withdrew.

Poor Fru Viker was embarrassed and unhappy. It was a thing that was so awkward to talk about, Ida must excuse her, but she thought it was so bad for her children to hear such things, and so she would only say it to Ida: it was that little girl from Oslo that had told something to Anders and Jöda, and Jöda was so small that she knew no better than to go to her mother with it. Well, the thing was that Bojan had told them something about a man who had given her fifty öre to go with him into a wood-shed and then he had behaved in a nasty way—well, she had described exactly what he had done, in a way that made Fru Viker's hair stand on end when Jöda told her.

Ida Elisabeth listened to the other with an icy chill all through her. In her blind fury with the unknown who had misused the child she clenched her hands till the nails ran into the flesh. But through the desperate throbbing of her heart which sent the blood thundering in her ears she gathered what Fru Viker meant: she did not wish Bojan to come and play with her children any more.

Ida Elisabeth sat down on the kitchen chair and wept, when she was alone. And the likeness between Bojan and Sölvi which she could not avoid seeing—that had increased her antipathy to Bojan, for it was so like a caricature. Bojan was without charm; her monkeyish liveliness was exaggerated into something quite abnormal; she was always cross and shrieked in a downright morbid way if her whims were not humoured at once—Ida Elisabeth was now so shocked by the likeness that it seemed as though Sölvi was the one who had been abused. This unhealthy, unattractive little child was her own little girl transformed by the ruin and ravages of wickedness. Oh, you poor, poor little thing, what are we to do with you—!

She heard the children outside—glanced out of the window, as she dried her eyes again and again with her apron, not thinking that there was blood on it. They were running across the field with the bob-sleigh; there was no snow, only hoarfrost and ice, but they managed to coast down it. She guessed it was Carl who had gotten the others to come out, as he wished to keep out of her sight just now—Bojan must have told the same story to the boys, and that explained their bashful manner towards their little cousin. She remembered from her own childhood that it was the unwritten law never to say anything to the grown-ups about such things—that one had been scared by horrid men, spoken to on the way to school, asked to go with them; and that her schoolfellows enlightened each other in whispers as to what happened to those who did not get away from the man in time. No doubt poor Bojan was too small to feel that she must not talk about this—or she had been too demoralized.

But together with the bitter repugnance she felt at the thought that her boys had heard such things, it occurred to her that it was practically arranged for Else to go to Tveito—but now she could not take the responsibility of sending Bojan to mix with Tveito's flock of children. Two or three of them had been here, when she was making a confirmation cloak for the eldest—naturally they knew as much as most country children, but they looked as innocent as health itself.

She was still crying when Else came into the kitchen:

"But dear me, Lisken—what is it—?"

Ida Elisabeth tried to overcome her trembling and her tears. But she was forced to speak to Else about it. Perhaps, if Bojan could be sent to some place where she would have no opportunity of talking about it, she might forget. But where—?

"It was Fru Viker who was here just now. She told me of something that Bojan had been telling them about. Oh, Else, Else, it's too dreadful—"

"But gee!" said Else in alarm. "Is there anything wrong with Bojan?"

"No, no. It's—you know what—she's been telling—"

But Else did not know. Ida Elisabeth was forced to explain herself more clearly. Else looked at her in surprise—then she gave her foolish little laugh:

"Oh, that! But that isn't true, you know. It all comes of something like that happening near where we live, some time last autumn. Ugh yes, isn't it awful—? But you can understand, all the children round there were frightfully excited about it, so I expect lots of them have told the story to make themselves interesting. And Bojan, poor child, has such a lively imagination—you know, she doesn't understand that it's bad manners to go and tell about such things—"

It was bad enough that way, though not so bad as the worst. But now she saw for herself that Tryggve had been right: it was downright unscrupulous of her to try and smuggle Else and her child into Tveito's home.

She rang up Toksvold: "Have you time this afternoon? Can you spare me a couple of hours? I have to go up to Bö to talk to Marte. You're kind! Well, if you'll meet me at the crossroads with the car—"

Toksvold was so delighted at their having an hour or two together that it made her immensely happy to see it. He went into fits of laughter when she confided her anxieties to him; but on her entering more fully into the matter he became serious:

"There you see. You can't do anything there. Give her some money, won't you? And send her back to town. And make it clear to them that you can't go on regarding your divorced husband's family as your near relations."

It ended in Ida Elisabeth admitting *why* she thought it so wrong to send Else and Bojan back to Jarngerd. That made him angry:

"What beastliness! No—one must draw the line somewhere. You must think of your boys. I won't consent to their having any communication *whatever* with aunts of that sort—or uncles either for that matter, if they're to grow up in my house and I am to take my share of responsibility for them."

ON the way back they scarcely exchanged a word. It was a pretty bad road too, narrow and steep and covered with ice that glistened in the light of the car lamps, and full of turns. "You're nervous, aren't you?" Toksvold asked once, with a little mocking laugh.

Ida Elisabeth smiled apologetically.

"Well, poor girl, I won't say anything about that." What did he mean by that—?

"Come home with me for a moment—won't you?" he asked as they turned into the main road.

"I'd like to."

HE got out a bottle and some glasses, while she stood at the window. It looked out on the broad street-like approach to the station where arc-lamps on high masts made a few ragged patches of light in the frost-fog—it was now drifting up from the river and making the darkness spongy and unclean. She was cold after the drive and uncheerful—in the worst way, when one does not really know or dare to arrive at what is the matter.

A maid entered with a jingling tray and went out again. Toksvold called:

"Have a drink, Ida—I'm sure you want a stiffener. *Skaal!*"

Two deep leather chairs and a smoking-table with a copper top represented his attempts at making the hotel room a trifle less uncomfortable. "Here, sit down and take a little rest before you have to go home—

"In a way you *have* achieved something this afternoon. As far as that goes you have reason to be pleased. Marte won't give in, she'll get this fixed up—"

"I *am* pleased, you know." She gave a little sigh.

"Yes, you look jubilant." He sniggered. "All right as long as it lasts, you're thinking? Well, I know nothing against

345

these fellows at the Smithy—as far as that goes. I've had
something to do with Hans, the one who really owns the
forge, in the way of business—he made a very favourable
impression. But a young housekeeper and two middle-aged
bachelors—of course it depends a great deal on what sort
of person *she* is." The mocking smile flitted across his face
again. "I don't know whether you've thought about it, Ida—
you may have a good deal of trouble yet with this quondam
sister-in-law of yours!"

"I know it!" she said quickly, in a worried tone. "But at
any rate it's a solution—for the time being. I can't do
more—"

"No, if you'll only stick to it, all right. The thing is that
I *see* how you let this weigh on you!" He jumped up from
his chair, then came and stood before her. "*That's* the reason, Ida! My dear, you know, don't you—I don't shirk helping another any more than you do, if I can—and if it's *worth
while* helping him. But in times like those we're in now—
one ought to give all the help one can to such people as
may reasonably be supposed to be capable of keeping on
their feet, when pulled out of a tight place, and perhaps of
holding out a hand to others in their turn. So you can
understand, it is actually worse in the long run for the many
who are so constituted that they can never help themselves,
if a number of those who *can* do a little more than hold
their own end up were to go to smash."

He was right of course, in a way. They *did* form a race
apart, the ones who never cease to need help. The infantile, as Sommervold called them.

Tryggve Toksvold laughed with nervous annoyance:

"Ida, Ida, you sit there looking at me as if . . . One would
think you were one of those who believe all lawyers are a
lot of devils who haven't a scrap of heart in their bodies—"

She smiled palely and shook her head.

"Why, bless your soul—some people are born like that,
like trailer cars with no motor in them, and some like motor

cars. But if all the motor cars went to pieces, the others might stand there till they fell to bits."

Ida Elisabeth shivered a little, as though chilled:

"When all's said and done, Tryggve, I think you're exaggerating. My dear boy—it's *not* such a terrible business, my asking Else Nilsen to stay with me a fortnight—"

"—which has already grown into three weeks and more—"

"Just so. I was prepared for that when I undertook to try and find work for her. But now that's settled for the present. So don't let's talk about it any more."

He thought for a moment. "All right!" He took her in his arms and kissed her warmly.

"It's for your own sake, Ida. Can't you see that to an outsider this looks like merry madness? They've left you to shift for yourself—with both your children, year in, year out. Presumably never inquired how you were getting on? No; there you see. Then you meet one of them by chance—they discover that you're evidently getting on quite well—and so you have them on top of you—

"Remember that you have to act as the motor car for your boys—we don't know yet for how long. However much you may have me by your side—you will of course be the one who has most control over them, if any control is possible here—"

"What do you mean—?"

He looked away, without answering.

"Tryggve, what did you mean?"

"At present in any case that little one of yours seems to take a good deal after his father's family", said Toksvold in a low voice, as though reluctantly.

As he took her hand and bent down to kiss her, she resisted very slightly at first, but then let him do it.

"I wish your children nothing but well, Ida. I've told you that times without number."

She nodded. But why must you say it times without number—?

"Tryggve!"—she spoke quite low and slowly. "Do you think—have you the impression that they are specially *difficult* children, Carl and the little one?"

"Well, I don't know", he said quickly. "I haven't much experience of children. I thought that perhaps you—

"We live in difficult times, Ida. You mustn't think I don't see—not only that folk who are born with some defect or other can't get along by themselves, but that many people who prefer to spare themselves exertion, or who do not easily endure uncertainty—simulate defects in order to be let off. It isn't always easy to decide which is which—"

"What do you mean?" she asked as before.

"Oh, don't look so tragic, darling! All I meant was"—he tried to find the words. "Your children are children; they have the right to be given their chance. You are their mother, they have the right to expect you to do all you can to help them to get on in life. But that may give you quite enough to do, my dear—without burdening yourself with others whom you *know* to be scrap metal.

"Oh, don't look so despairing, my sweet!" With sudden passion he lifted her from her chair into his arms. "Well, but don't you see that it makes me perfectly furious at times? Aren't you the same? I *love* you, and so do you—love me, I mean—and we never have any peace! We never have a chance of being just you and me—but we ought to be allowed that too—oughtn't we now?—to feel just once—only for a short time—what all the others feel when they're young and in love, that now we two are one and all the rest of the world is something else."

She stood still with her forehead against his shoulder and let him fondle her.

"I know that perhaps it isn't possible—for you", he whispered. "And I shall do my best to accept it with Christian patience. But anyhow we'll go away—when we're married? You wish that too, don't you—?"

She nodded against his shoulder.

348

"Yes, I suppose you must", he said resignedly, when she suggested that now she would have to go home. He picked up his coat. "I'll drive you. Damn it all, it can't be necessary for you to tramp the whole way in black darkness just because that Fru Nilsen mustn't be offended at your going out motoring without her—"

Ida Elisabeth squeezed his hand. He was trying to think of something to please her ... But, but ...

In a way he was right, she thought, and the quality in him which had sometimes affected her as priggishness was not that after all. He stood by his people, and it was not merely his own family he meant by that, but the type they represented: sober-minded folk, who didn't care for big words and lots of butter, though it seemed to her they could swallow a good deal of that kind of thing on festive occasions, at meetings and the like. They were industrious too, and as Tryggve said, they knew how slow is the growth of all those things which life cannot dispense with, and how those who have to do with such things must be content to serve a long apprenticeship and to plod on steadily. They knew just as well as others what canting phrases can be made of such things as faithfulness and tradition and rectitude and self-respect and diligence and frugality—but God help us all if there were none who could thrust in their hand and feel the hard reality behind the phrases, for then we should all go to ruin. Tryggve was brought up in all that, and if he clung to it as he did, it was not merely because he believed in it, but because he had learnt this belief and these ideas from someone of whom he was immensely fond. He had something to defend, and that does not make one indulgent towards the attackers. The kind of people he called scrap metal—well, he only saw the mischief they brought about; he had never looked into them. Nor had any of these light-eyed people with the broad white foreheads—both he and Ingvild had such handsome, clear foreheads, but all the same there was something about them which reminded one of the forehead of a bull, all the more as their light-brown hair curled so rebelliously in a forelock. Ingvild had loved her piece of scrap metal of a husband, passionately and stubbornly—but if one knows how such a person looks on the inside, one does not *love* him; normal human beings do not fall in love with what is infected and deformed.

But one does not leave them to their fate either, when one has seen them on the inside—without once *trying* if one can help. Or some do so. And others *cannot*. And she herself—well, perhaps she was like one who has grown up in a hospital; her father and mother might certainly be classed as scrap metal—except that the fault in them did not appear until they were subjected to a certain strain, and then they broke. However, this was only metaphorical—human beings are not castings, and chance had taught her how they suffer, those who cannot meet force with force, who derive no benefit from adversity, never learn to understand why they are badly off, but wait like children for someone to come and help them—and then they either do not suffer anything to speak of, because they are convinced all the time that somebody will come and pick them up, or else they are beside themselves with despair like children lying alone in an empty house—

She had come by degrees to the conclusion that after all there was something in what Cecilie Oxley had insisted on in old days—it was perhaps necessary that there should be some who had a sort of call to be mothers and sisters to all and sundry. To be young and in love and to wish one could feel and act as though we two are one thing and all the rest of the world something else—that was *happiness*, no doubt most people felt that in their hearts. But if this instinct of happiness were really such that no one could resist it—if no one could hold out against this thirst within him—well, then there would be an end of mercy in this world. Then finally there could be no question of leniency for the disabled and those who can never help themselves—

But there was no need for her to apply this to herself—it was not a discovery that she need feel anxious or sad about. It was certainly a good thing that there were women who were willing to become nuns—she could now concede that much to Ciss & Ciss. But at any rate it was not a problem that was actual for *her* . . . Only it was madness to imagine Tryggve and the boys should be incompatible quantities.

But the moment she had thought this out clearly, it was as though a hand took hold of her heart and squeezed it. Oh, but it was all unreasonableness. The boys were unreasonable in their jealous dislike of him. And he was unreasonable in his distrust of her children—

Chapter Ten

THE DAY SHE COULD AT LAST PACK Else and Bojan and their baggage, which she had had to supplement and overhaul, into a car and see them drive off to the Smithy, Ida Elisabeth was so relieved and happy that she could not contain herself; she rang up Tryggve as soon as her workwomen had gone in the evening.

"Congratulations!" His voice was gay. "But look here— I've got to go to town tomorrow, to a conference. And then there are those Hungarians giving a concert. I'd like very much to hear them—wouldn't you? Can't you take a day off and come up with me? Honestly—don't you think we both deserve an evening off?"

He made short work of her little objections: hadn't she any shopping to do in town? They could dine late, just before going to the concert, and then if they drove off as soon as it was over she could be home in good time—and the next day was Sunday—and he didn't mind cutting out supper, "unless you'll stand me a cup of tea when we get home—"

Ida Elisabeth was very keen on going and accepted.

Carl was lying on the sofa in her room, buried in a book. He looked up as she passed through the room: "Are you going to be away tomorrow—?"

"Yes, I have some things to do in town. And Tryggve's just offered to take me in his car. So I may just as well go tomorrow."

She had planned a regular festivity with the boys for this evening. They were no more in love than she was with this aunt who stayed on and on—the longer her visit lasted, the more difficult it had been to restrain Carl in particular from manifesting his impatience too plainly. One day he had said, entirely without provocation: "I remember you stayed with us when we were living at Berfjord, Aunt Else—once when you were giving me my bath the water was absolutely boiling hot." "Fancy, I don't remember that", Else had replied with her silly smile. "No, it wasn't you that got scalded." "But Carl!" his mother admonished him, and the boy went on with suppressed rage: "Don't you remember either, mother? You had to powder me all over with potato flour."

—While she thought of it: "You'll have to have your baths this evening, boys, as I shall be away tomorrow evening. You shall have pine needles in your bath water for a treat—"

Carl said sulkily: "Must we put on our *dirty* things again after our bath?" "No, you'll have to change this evening." "Shan't I have a clean shirt on for Sunday then?" "Oh yes. I'll mend one of the check ones so that you can wear it tomorrow, and then you'll have the new green one for Sunday."

She took his old check shirts out of the drawer, turned them over to see which was least washed-out—better to mend it at once, of course there were some buttons missing.

"Am I to go to school with *that* on?" There was an abysmal sense of injury in the boy's voice.

"Yes—it's clean and there are no holes in it. I don't suppose your schoolfellows are so elegant that they've never seen a faded shirt before."

His face twitched and twitched—his eyes filled with tears behind the spectacles—the tears began to trickle down his cheeks. When his mother took off his spectacles, dried them, "there, there, Carl," and kissed him lightly on the hair, "you're too big to cry for a thing like that"—he was shaking with suppressed, convulsive sobbing.

Ida Elisabeth drew him to her: "Hush, darling. You must stop now, my dear—I'm going to get supper ready, I thought you'd have come out and helped me a little—"

His distress subsided a little when she set him to work; he cut the loaf and warmed the plates in boiling water. His mother prepared the meal—poached eggs on slices of white bread fried in butter, two for each; that was the established delicacy for *great* occasions—and Marte Bö's mutton sausage, which only appeared on Sundays in the usual way.

When they had had supper Ida Elisabeth brought out the old album of picture postcards from London and told them for the thousandth time about her going there with her father and mother. Actually she did not remember very much—she was only four or five at the time—a house full of cockatoos that screamed worse than anything she had heard, and there were birds of all the colours to be found in the paint-box—and a dromedary that wanted to eat Herman's straw hat. Little Buster yelled with delight as usual, but Carl only smiled in a doubtful way. And then there was a man who stood in the street selling tarantulas—that's a kind of spider, and these were made of coloured tin and had wire legs covered with chenille. The man wound them up and they flew about the pavement, and although there was such a crowd of people in the street, all English of course except grandfather and grandmother and us children, they got out of the way and took care not to interfere with the man's tarantulas, but none of them looked annoyed at having to walk round. She had been afraid of her own tarantula—for grandfather bought one for each of the children, but they looked so horrid, and besides, grandmother told them how dangerous the real live tarantulas were—and she was never really sure whether this one of hers *was* alive or might come to life. Grandmother didn't like them either: "I really don't think that was a thing to buy, Carl—"

After that the boys had a pine needle bath and marched off to bed in clean pajamas. And when she said good-night to them Carl's face was again wet with tears and his lips were hot and trembling.

The boys were at school when they left next day, and Ida Elisabeth's morning was entirely taken up with shopping and a visit to the dentist. Tryggve had invited a friend and his wife to dine with them at the Victoria, but when the others wanted them to come up to their villa after the concert—the young wife was very anxious to get up a supper party and to bring in two or three more of Tryggve's friends—Toksvold said straight out: "We'll have to leave that for another time, Agga—you see, Fru Braatö has two boys at home and must go back to them." Fru Agga then asked Ida Elisabeth all sorts of questions about her children, how old they were and so on—and plunged into endless descriptions of her own two little ones, a boy and a girl. And the concert was delightful. Tryggve was very fond of music: "When once we're married we'll come up as often as we can, when anybody comes who *is* somebody." And that would unquestionably be interesting—after all the years in which she had actually heard no music but that of Hansen's harmonium.

The night had turned quite mild when they drove out of town, with a few flakes of snow floating in the light of the lamps. They had not gone very far when the road in front was white with the first thin coat of snow. The firs were lightly powdered with it as they drove into the forest— thicker and thicker the snow-flakes danced in the light. The night air tasted quite sweet in its purity. "I expect this will be our last drive this year—"

Their clothes were fairly white when they entered the passage at Viker, and their voices were rather loud and cheerful, as is the way when people shake off the first snow of the year. Ragnhild had laid a tea-table for two in Ida Elisabeth's room.

As Ida Elisabeth went through the boys' room to make the tea in the kitchen, she noticed by his breathing that Carl was awake. She crossed over and said good-evening to him.

Then she heard Toksvold calling from the other room:

"You'd better come in and have a cup with us, if your mother will let you—as you're awake. May he, Ida?"

When she came in with the tea-tray the two were surrounded by a mass of packing-paper which was spread all over the floor round a big plant in a pot—a giant chrysanthemum only half unpacked. Carl had a finger in his mouth, the tears were running down his face, and Tryggve Toksvold stood looking down at him; he appeared annoyed.

"Well, this is for you—so I asked Carl to help me unpack it—you say he's so fond of flowers. And then he scratched himself on a pin—"

Ida Elisabeth stroked the boy's hair: "You mustn't cry like that, Carl. Go and sit down, both of you, and let me—" She removed the last of the tissue paper that was wrapped about each of the five huge pale green blooms. "How lovely they are!"

The most natural thing would have been to throw herself on the man and thank him for the flowers in a volley of kisses—if the boy had not been standing there. And it would have been equally natural to take her little son who loved flowers by the hand and let him share her admiration of their loveliness—if they had not been a present from Tryggve. As it was she looked at them with a vague melancholy— she had never seen these giant chrysanthemums without a plate-glass window between her and the flowers, since she was a little girl and smelt at them and touched them with the tip of her tongue, on early mornings at home at Holstenborg, before her parents were up. She had never had such flowers in her own house. She would tell Tryggve this, but could not do so now—

She poured out the tea. Carl still looked tearful—and it struck her again how thin and poorly he was looking this autumn, less attractive even than usual. She fetched the parcel of cream buns—they were really meant for tomorrow's breakfast, but he would have to have one now.

"I don't want it", said Carl in a low voice.

"Oh yes, you do—you like nothing better, your mother says. Take one, when she's bought them for you."

Carl gave a sidelong glance at the buns. His mother saw he *did* want them—it was a kind of impotent, childish attempt to demonstrate pride or self-assertion, when he refused to touch them. But the cream buns were too tempting—with a sour little grimace he took one. And this wasn't nice—since it was yielding to a temptation, however ridiculous.

Trifles, she tried to think, trifles. But she could not help it; these trifles reminded her of the instruments she had seen on board boats in old days, with little narrow pointers that quivered and swung. Little thin blue-black pointers, but their vibration denoted the whole course of the great steamship and the working of her engines.

"You're not sulking, a big boy like you, because your mother has been out for an evening?" No, no, don't say anything, thought Ida Elisabeth uncomfortably—but if she asked him to stop it would only make things worse. Carl gave the man a harassed and hostile look.

"Will you have any more tea—Tryggve?—Carl?"

"Thanks." Toksvold held out his cup. "She's been sitting at home every evening for a whole month to entertain your aunt—a lady who has nothing in common with your mother except that she's aunt to you boys."

Ugh, no ... "Well, no, Tryggve, I am really fond of Else in a way—you must remember that. She was quite sweet when she was a girl"—ugh, that didn't seem to make it any better.

Fear and shyness and defiance were struggling in the boy's face as Carl looked up:

"I suppose she won't be so much at home—now that aunt's gone—" he said in a low voice.

"Well, what then?" Toksvold replied sharply. "She's been sitting at home with you every blessed evening for several years. Do you think there are many mothers like that now-adays, Carl? You must learn to put up with it if she moves a few steps from home now that you're getting such big boys."

Ida Elisabeth got up and put her arm round the boy's neck:

"I never thought it a bore to sit at home with you, my children—because I'm fond of you. I've never cared for any company except that of those I'm fond of. It's because I'm fond of Tryggve too that I sometimes go out with him. My dear!" She kissed Carl on the forehead. What I should like best would be his company and yours at all times—she dared not say this aloud.

"Don't you think you ought to give that boy cod-liver oil?" asked Toksvold as she came out on the steps with him. "I don't know much about such things, but I've read that cod-liver oil is supposed to be good for nervous children—"

She was still clearing up and unpacking her purchases when the telephone rang in the work-room. Trembling with nervousness she went to answer it—it had never happened before that she had been rung up in the middle of the night; she knew it was a terrible business waking up the exchange.

"Ida!" It was Toksvold. "Brekke—Ingvild's husband, you know—died this afternoon. There was a message for me when I came in. So I'm leaving at once by the night train. Fracture of the skull, as far as I can understand—he had had a fall in the street the night before. Poor Torstein—it was a sad ending. I just wanted to let you know. I'll try and telephone on Monday. Take care of yourself till we meet again. Good-night, Ida dear, sleep well—"

Poor thing, she thought—and meant no one in particular— the dead man, and Ingvild and her children—and many more. Tryggve had sounded genuinely grieved ... No doubt he was so in a way—and presumably it was an intense relief in

358

another way, but he would not admit this until a sufficient time had elapsed to enable him to say with decency: after all it was the best thing for all concerned.

SEVERAL weeks followed in which Toksvold was constantly on the move—at home to attend to his own business and away to look after his sister's affairs. Ingvild Brekke had collapsed altogether. "It's quite incomprehensible", said Tryggve, with a thoughtful look. "She must have been fond of the swine right up to the last! Well, poor man—de mortuis etcetera, he was a stout fellow once upon a time, to look at anyway, and I must say he had no mean opinion of himself. But that she should never have done with him—" It was unpleasant to see the children unable to conceal the fact that their father's death relieved them of a terrible strain, but of course it pained their mother when she noticed it. Outwardly Ingvild was fairly self-controlled, but she had taken it into her head that she would sell her boarding-house and leave the town, feeling she could not stay in a place where everyone had known Torstein only as he was at the last.

The body had been taken home to Land—Brekke came from there originally—and a number of his family and hers had attended the funeral. Tryggve would have liked Ida Elisabeth to come, but she declined. At this gathering there had been a talk of Ingvild Brekke taking over Björnstad's hotel—the aunt wished to retire.

"The place isn't what it was. And times are bad for hotel-keepers like the rest. Though Ingvild ought to be able to work it up—for summer visitors." So that had entailed some travelling about—he had to find out how his sister's affairs could best be arranged.

This meant that he had to be away for the whole of Christmas. He was sorry for this, but Ida Elisabeth thought that after all it was just as well: this would be the last Christmas Eve she could spend alone with her boys—if all went as they intended.

LETTERS arrived the morning after Christmas Day. Carl fetched them in and laid them on the little table by the divan which served her as a bedside table. Ida Elisabeth was just clearing away the breakfast; she moved her cup and the coffee-pot over—would take another drop while she looked at her Christmas letters and the paper in peace and comfort.

"Be careful now—" The boys were going out with their new little sledges. Whether their dislike of Tryggve Toksvold were great or not, it did not extend to these Christmas presents of his. That was one of the things that weighed on Ida Elisabeth's mind. The boys' attitude towards her fiancé continued to be reserved, for all she knew downright hostile, but they had accustomed themselves to expect presents from him. Money too—

There were cards from Anne Mosgaard—from her sempstresses—and a thick letter, addressed in a handwriting that she knew was familiar and that called up a vague idea of unpleasantness even before she recognized it. Then she looked at the postmark—it was from her former mother-in-law.

She held it in her hand without opening it—laid it aside and looked through the rest of her mail. A little letter from Olise Langeland, a card from Fru Holter of Myhre & Co., one or two engraved cards from business connections—

But she couldn't *do* anything to her now. Just as well to get it over. She tore open the envelope and fished out the wad of crumpled sheets:

My dear good trusty Lisken!

To begin with you must have a real good Christmas hug in gratitude for all you have done for my little girls—oh, was that all? Ida Elisabeth ran through the first few pages.

Ah, Lisken, if I could only tell you how you have rejoiced and cheered papa and me by giving us this proof of your faithful, warmhearted nature. I can assure you, in these years when misfortunes have been positively showered upon us we have learnt to appreciate such faithful friendliness. Very often in the course of these years our thoughts have gone to you, who nevertheless for so many years were as dear to us as one of our own. You must not think I do not understand the action you took on getting wind of Frithjof's infatuation; I understand that you could not help feeling offended and wounded in your most sacred feelings—hell, and wasn't it fated too that I should run into Jeja that day—?

I assume that Else has told you the sad story of Geirmund. Yes, Lisa dear, we have made our preparations for Christmas as usual, and by the holy evening I shall have my poor boy home. Need I tell you that here he will be met with open arms, without a word of reproach. I don't think—

But, as no doubt you have also heard, Frithjof has now been attacked by the same insidious disease which tore our darling little Merete from us. And I cannot *bear the thought of exposing Geirmund and Vikarr to the same infection (Herjulf, who as you probably know has returned from America is at present employed at Rostesund, thanks to Director Meislings interest). So now for my children's sake I have gone on my last and saddest round of begging, writing to relations and friends to provide funds for sending Frithjof to a sanatorium. Papa and I have then had the idea that possibly the pure dry air of the East Country might offer him a last chance of salvation. (The opinion was expressed when Merete lay dying that perhaps a stay at an inland sanatorium might have saved her.) Our thoughts were then directed very naturally to the many well-known sanatoria which are situated in the immediate neighbourhood of your present place of residence.*

No, that'll do now! Ida Elisabeth let the letter drop into her lap. No, we won't have any of that!

So Frithjof is leaving here on the afternoon of Christmas Day— God the Father, he's already on the way! She glanced through the last pages. To Fjeldberg—the most expensive sanatorium of all, eh—? *Now he will have his sister near him, for you know what a bond there has always been between Else and Frithjof—* no, indeed I don't—*and will be able to see his children again, of whom he has so often spoken with ardent longing in the course of these years.*

Ah—that too! There was no avoiding it. Bitterness suddenly sent the tears to her eyes. After never having asked after his children for all these years he chose to turn up just at the moment when she herself had found out how insecure the relations between her and the boys had grown— between her and Carl in any case; Tryggve was so small that he was still like pulp, but an echo of Carl in many ways. And then their father bursts in just now ... Longing, he! To see them again—why, he had never even seen the little one.

She flung the letter down on the divan and sat thinking.

Telegraph to Tryggve, that was her first impulse. Ask him to come home at once. He must be able to find some way out. Stop Frithjof in Oslo, get him taken in somewhere— there must be several sanatoria in the neighbourhood of town. But that wouldn't do, on account of the boys—

Wasn't it the fact, by the way, that as a rule patients had to wait a fairly long time for admission to a tuberculosis sanatorium—?

She went into the next room and rang up Doctor Lund at Fjeldberg. Yes, they were expecting a patient, a Herr Braatö; they had been notified of him a month ago. "Is he a relation of yours, madam?" Ida Elisabeth explained that he was her divorced husband. "Is that so? Well, if there's anything you'd like to discuss with me about the matter, you know I'm glad to be of any service." Thanks, thanks—

I know I shall not appeal in vain to your generosity in asking you to meet Frithjof at the station and look after him, the letter said. And—*times are so different now from what they were when papa and I were young—it is an everyday occurrence for divorced people to meet and associate on a friendly footing, and no doubt we may regard this as an advance in the direction of broadmindedness.* Yes, wouldn't you like it, mother?

THEN she had a feeling that perhaps she was exaggerating. She had no objection to meeting him at the train and driving with him up to Fjeldberg—but she would have to do it in such a way that she would have no more to do with his affairs; she simply hadn't time to run all that way and visit him. And at the big sanatorium, where there were patients from every part of the country almost, there was nothing very remarkable—it was unpleasant of course, but not such a sensational affair as it seemed to her—in the fact that the man to whom she had once been married had also landed there.

God, how angry Tryggve would be when he heard it! And then he'd be sure to say she ought to have known she could expect something of the sort. But indeed she had been very far from that—!

She picked up all the sheets of Borghild Braatö's letter, laid them together, and was annoyed at the difficulty of stuffing the whole wad back into the envelope. So she was the one who had imagined she knew what these people were like inwardly, but not a bit of it—such a cunning, impudently calculating old hag was beyond her comprehension: the moment she hears that her girls have discovered my whereabouts and I've been fool enough to hold out a little finger to them, she comes dashing in—

Rubbish . . . The very worst part of it was that she knew very well the other *was* in good faith in her own way. She meant all those flowery phrases, and she believed all she *wished* to believe. She sang all these false notes just as much for her own edification as for the benefit of those from whom she wished to gain something for herself and those belonging to her.

Ida Elisabeth sat staring, without seeing it, at the little Christmas tree that stood in the corner glittering with glass balls and tinsel in the pale winter sunshine. Ugh, it was agonizing—and lucky if it were no worse than *that*.

If only Tryggve had been at home—

During the next couple of days she did her best not to let the boys notice how sorry for herself she was. Then came the telegram. Tomorrow, train due at half-past two. It was inconceivable that this was real ... All the time she had been expecting in a sort of way that it would turn out an empty threat, it would surely pass over.

When she sent the little one to bed she gave Carl leave to stay up a little longer. He curled up in the rocking-chair with a book the Hansens had lent him. Ida Elisabeth was knitting. Would she ever be able to see this blue jersey on her boy without recalling all the evil thoughts she had knit-ted into it—?

"What's that book you're so deep in, Carl?"

"'The King of Österdal'", said the boy with his nose in the book.

"Can't you put it down for a moment? I've got some-thing to tell you."

Carl did so—reluctantly; he looked up at his mother in a doubtful way, as though he did not expect any good news exactly.

"I've had a letter, Carl. To say that your father's coming here on a trip."

"Father—?" His face grew tense: "Do you mean—my *proper* father?"

Ida Elisabeth nodded.

"It's papa then?" He was beaming.

"Yes. Tell me, Carl, can you remember your father?"

Now it was the boy who nodded—rather uncertainly:

"Oh yes. I remember papa very well. I remember the time Sölvi died", he said in a low voice. "Papa bled so—he must have hurt himself too? And then I remember when he was at home for the last time—just before we came here, I remember—"

Mother and son sat looking at one another.

She had scarcely mentioned their father in all these years. She did not know what was in the boys' heads—if they thought about the matter at all. Did they know that she was divorced? Had Else talked to them about their father?

Had her friendship with the other during the last half-year made them think of their real father? She knew nothing.

But she had a suspicion that this sudden joy that flared up in the boy on hearing that his father was coming was due to an instinctive deduction that here was their ally against the stranger.

"When is he coming, mother?"

"Mid-day tomorrow."

"Then I'll go with you to meet him!"

"Yes, of course I'll let you do that." There was a sharper ring in her voice than she had intended—it made her anxious; if only the boy had not been hurt by it—

"Now you must eat your orange, my boy, and go to bed."

Carl finished eating his orange in thoughtful silence, and got up: "Good-night, mother—

"Have you told Tryggve that papa's coming?" he asked at the door.

Which Tryggve do you mean—? But she merely said:

"I have told no one but you. As yet."

She sat with her knitting in her hands and did not move till she heard Carl getting into bed. Then she went in, put out the lamp, and kissed him good-night. Are you glad your father's coming—? She was not equal to putting the question—and she felt deep within her that he was.

"Mother", Carl asked, as she was leaving the room: "Does papa know that I wear spectacles?"

"No, I'm sure he doesn't."

Oh—! It's come to that—it *cheers* me to see a little shadow come over the boy's delight at his father's arrival—

Chapter Eleven

W HAT THE BOYS might have said to each other in the morning she did not know.

"Is papa going to sleep in Aunt Else's room?" asked Carl in the course of the forenoon.

"No, he's going up to Fjeldberg."

"Fjeldberg—but that's—is papa *ill*?"

"Yes, he's not quite well. That's why he's coming here. Your grandmother thinks a stay in the air here will do him good."

Poor little fellow—now he had something more to puzzle over.

She made the car come to Viker to fetch them. Instinctively she had already begun to dread her future here: Tryggve's office at the corner, the hotel where she had gone in and out with him. People had talked about them; that had worried her very little—but now that the news of her former husband being here would soon be all over the place ... Ugh, how right Tryggve had been: it doesn't matter a damn what folks say so long as you don't prove them right in any of it.

Carl sat on the flap seat facing her. His serious little face looked as if a whole new world of thoughts were springing up in the boy's mind. Thoughts of which she knew nothing— she could only guess. Perhaps she would never get to know anything. She knew from her own childhood how much there is about which children cannot talk to grown-ups. If the grown-ups try to question them—that is the worst thing they can do. Or again, there are some children who like it, put up with it—she had always had a feeling that such children are like fruit the peel of which has been pecked through by birds; they cannot keep healthy. But it was a thing which had never before concerned *her* personally. Now she saw in a flash how happy and comfortable had been the relations between her and her children: right up to last summer there had never been anything in their life which made trust and confidence two separate things.

In black bitterness of heart she was thinking: and there is no way out. At any rate none that she could take. Not at this time of day. Now that the boy facing her had become an unknown quantity. And it was not her fault. The only miserable alleviation was to yield to spiteful thoughts, when her mind turned to Frithjof's mother. God, how she hated her! All of them for that matter.

The little one sat by her side, beaming with delight at being given a drive in the finest car in the place. It was upholstered in light grey cloth with a lot of fine straps and tassels, and there were cut-glass vases in it with bouquets of terribly faded artificial flowers. The car had been used for weddings in Oslo, the children said.

THE moment she saw Frithjof appearing on the platform of the railway car her agitation vanished. The irritation of the last few days became a bad dream from which she had awakened. Poor man, *he* was only an element in a past so distant that she had quite done with it. He had scarcely changed—though he had grown a good deal thinner, and the flesh of his face had become rather flabby. He wanted a shave badly—blond, young, washed out. He was quite well dressed, in an ulster and brand-new brown shoes.

"Ida Elisabeth!" He came forward with his arms stretched out in a way that reminded her of flippers, and she met his flutterings with her hearty greeting and the powerful handshake that stopped him *there*. She felt the boys' big eyes watching them—noting too that their father called her by what they knew to be her full name, but had never heard anyone use; here she was always Ida.

"Well, here you have me back again, Lisken!—And *there* we have the children—*no*, how big and bonny you've grown since papa saw you last! Kalleman!" Frithjof threw his arms round the boy and kissed him with emphasis. "And so that's Tryggve—"; he looked slightly confused for a moment, but then recovered heart and spread out his arms: "Will Tryggve give papa a kiss too—?"

I shall have to tell him that as soon as we're alone—that he mustn't kiss the children—

"But *how* like Sölvi he is, Ida Elisabeth!"

"Have you any registered baggage? Look here, Moe will get it for you. Carl, can you take your father's hand-bag?" At the head of the procession she hurried away to the car. Of course they had been observed with interest by all the six or eight people who were at the station.

TRYGGVE TOKSVOLD would be away till after Twelfth Day. And Ida Elisabeth could not bring herself to write anything about this new dispensation of providence—she had tried once or twice but tore up the letters again. For that matter Tryggve seemed to be always moving about—she had a card from him from Oslo and a letter written from an hotel at Röykenvik.

At last he rang her up one morning. He had arrived by the night train. "Can't you come and dine with me at the hotel? You can guess I'm longing pretty badly to have a talk with you again."

"If you're not altogether too busy this morning—I'd like awfully to come over at once—may I come up to the office?"

It had not been much more than a week, but it felt like years. Burman jumped up on seeing her fetch hat and coat. The dog lay down flat in front of her feet, wagging his tail and barking as she stood holding her coat to the stove, jumped up again squirming and whisking to the door and back—just as he went on every afternoon when Carl put on his things to go to the sanatorium. And that was another reason why she did not like it, knowing Frithjof's ways with dogs—and Burman's thick coat was just made for carrying bacilli. It was true they were out in the park all the time, when Frithjof had the children with him—Doctor Lund had seen to that—but all the same—

The mist along the river was bitingly raw when she came out. The rising ground on the other side of the road lost itself in fog, all grey with snow-covered forest which was coated all over with hoar frost. In her little garden only a few tops of the lilac-bushes stood out white as corals from the frozen, rime-covered snow. The dog darted away in front of her, black and round with his tail jauntily curled over his back, turned to her again, swimming with enjoyment through the snow-drifts by the side of the road. "Good dog", she patted him as he jumped up at her. "It's not good to be a human, Burman; it's better to be a dog on a big farm—" It was Kari Presttangen who used to say that.

Her heart was burning with anxiety and sympathy with Carl.

As early as the third day, when Carl gave his brother the order: "Put on your things now; we're going up to papa", the little one answered: "I don't want to."

"Yes, hurry up. I'll work the sledge—I'll pull you up all the hills if you like."

"No, I won't. It's such a bore talking to papa."

"Nonsense, Tryggve; you mustn't say such things", she had interposed. "Why, you hardly know your father yet."

"Oo—I think he's just like Aunt Else. I don't like him", said the boy with embarrassment. "I say, mother, why does he call you *Lisken*? I think that's so ugly. But Ida Elisabeth, *that's* a nice name, mother."

"I'm glad you think so. But now you can put on your things and go with Carl today as it's such fine weather.

Remember you're so small that you won't be able to go all that way when it isn't nice weather."

But poor little Carl—she guessed that his father represented a terrible disappointment for him—or worse, a defrauding. He kept a tight hold on himself. No doubt it was better too, if he could fight his way through this without speaking to anyone about it. But it was a bitter injustice that the boy should not have been spared this.

One thing was that Frithjof treated the boys as though they were still little children; she realized this when she went with them to see him on Sunday—as though his fatherliness had been put away in a drawer since the time they were at Berfjord, and he had now taken it out again. And then both boys were fairly bashful—were used to being left in peace as much as possible by their little selves. Any obtrusiveness made them bristle up instinctively.

Of course she was also terribly afraid of infection. Unless Frithjof had completely changed he would naturally be pulling the children about in season and out of season—the thoughtless petting which was the order of the day in his family. For he himself would not admit that there was anything much the matter with him; he declared in mysterious terms that the presence of tubercle had never been ascertained, but he had broken something inside him, which was the cause of the hæmorrhages, but some natural healer at home had said it might heal up with rest and good nursing, and that was why he had not opposed mamma's wish that he should enter the sanatorium.

TOKSVOLD jumped up and came towards her the moment she opened the door of his office. He grasped her hand:

"Bless my soul, you look quite—it must have taken it out of you properly—" he pushed forward the chair she usually sat in.

"Oh, then you've heard?" She had almost expected it. They heard everything at the hotel.

"Oh yes. Now we're in the soup!"

Ida Elisabeth took off her gloves, unbuttoned her coat, and took a cigarette from the box he pushed across to her.

"Well—what did I say, Ida?"

"You understand, it's mother-in-law"—she wished at once that she had used another word—"who arranged this."

"Just so, yes. The daughters write home to mamma that Ida is the same old—softy is what they have in their minds. And then you have the old woman on you—!"

It's not like that either, Tryggve. She called to mind that she had never told him of what there had been between her and Frithjof as adolescents—simply because she thought at the time that it had nothing to do with her present self. She might well have done so then—and Tryggve would have seen that she had been nothing but a little girl who was whirled round by everything and everybody till she was giddy. Now she could not possibly tell him—now it would make an entirely different impression on him.

"Well, excuse my asking. But is it you that are paying for him at Fjeldberg?"

Ida Elisabeth turned red.

"No. At least—his mother has got together enough to pay something like a couple of months for him. If he will move down to The Hill it will last a little longer. But you know—

"I had a long talk with Doctor Lund, after he had examined him. And it appears that the illness is far advanced; it's not easy to say how it may go. But he has not had a temperature since the first day or two after the journey, and he eats well. So I was thinking, he ought to stay here in any case till the spring. I have about fourteen hundred crowns left of that bank account, you know, and the money was originally intended for the little girl who died. So I think in a way it would be fair to use it for her father, as he's ill—"

"Well, that of course is a matter that doesn't concern me." While she was speaking he had been folding the top sheet of the pad before him over and over and cutting off the folds with the paper-knife—now he collected all the strips in his hand and crumpled them together: "I'm not very enthusiastic about the whole affair, as you may imagine—

"In this state of things I can only say it's rather lucky that I shall probably be leaving here. You know I was in my uncle Björnstad's business for a few years; I began there as articled clerk. Ola, my cousin who's carrying on the firm, wants me to join it again. Well, nothing is settled yet. But there are many things in favour of it—

"Now if this comes off, I propose that we get married pretty soon. Have we any real reason for waiting? And honestly, my girl, I think the situation here must be getting rather complicated for you? I'm willing to admit I don't find it at all amusing—here we are, you and I, secretly engaged, as everyone knows—and at the same time you've brought your former consort and his family here to play the good Samaritan with them."

Ida Elisabeth looked up at him, but said nothing.

"As I was saying—what you do with your own money is a matter I certainly don't intend to interfere with. But it seems to me for many reasons that the very fact of your paying for the fellow at a sanatorium here makes it advisable that you should live somewhere else."

"Frithjof personally is nothing more to me than a ghost—from a time I have left so far behind that I don't even seem able to feel that it is my own past. Well, I am sorry for him, naturally—"

"Oh, don't imagine I'm jealous of *him*—in his present role. But as a ghost, to use your own word, that's another thing. If you've done with that past of yours, you simply ought not to let its ghosts follow and annoy you. That's the stupidest thing anyone can do, Ida. Let the dead bury their dead, as the Bible says."

"The thing is that they're *not* dead. It's only I who no longer have any feeling that they concern me. But I *know* very well that they're alive; there's just as much life in them as there ever was, for suffering and being anxious about one another, and being impecunious and incapable of understanding why *they* should always be in such trouble—"

"Very well. But if you want to help them, do so in God's name, but do it by cheque—or better still, by money order; that renders all correspondence superfluous. But you yourself ought to disappear from the scene."

"There are the boys too that I have to consider", she said in a very low voice. "Can't you see, it would look odd in their eyes—if I ran away because their father has come here—"

"But they know that you're no longer married to him."

"I suppose they do. I've never said anything about it to them. It somehow never occurred to us to talk about what happened before we came here. I don't believe they ever thought of it either. We simply lived from day to day. Right up to the time when you and I got to know each other."

He said quietly:

"Of course I can well imagine there is much which those boys don't understand now. But they must get to understand it some day. When they're grown up, if not before."

"I dare say they will. But what one may get to understand when grown up, Tryggve—is no remedy for the suffering one goes through as a child. One suffers just as much while it lasts. And the effect on one of suffering and being compelled to brood on one's difficulties while growing up—I suppose that remains much the same, even if one gets to understand a good deal of it later."

"Surely children must be taught to be just?" said Toksvold hotly.

"Yes, but they're not just. Except in the way of sticking up for what they think are their own rights and those of their schoolfellows. For that matter the majority of people seldom learn more than that. But one can't expect children to see the rights and wrongs and all sides of a question, especially when it's dead against their own feelings. It would

373

be a pity, I think. It would be like putting little children who ought to be learning their multiplication table to study the sort of mathematics they do at the nautical school, for instance."

"Ida, Ida—you mustn't be always thinking of such things. You won't make any of us any happier by it."

She felt her cheeks go cold with sudden pallor:

"No", she said very low. "None of us, except—perhaps—my children in certain contingencies."

"You can't mean what was in your head just then", he said as before.

She drooped slightly in her chair and looked down at her hands.

"Tell me, Ida—" He broke off, got up, and went to the window. Once or twice he seemed about to say something, but checked himself. She was in sheer dismay at the turn things had taken—she had not *wished* this, but now it seemed the most inevitable of all things—

"Tell me", he asked, turning towards her: "Don't you care for me as you did?"

She looked at him, and then it was as though she could not take her eyes off him again. Not care for him—O God, had she ever cared for him as much as now! His face, and his body, which her longing seemed to embrace, stealing in under the clothes, and the man, his life and mind and desire of her, soul they called it, which set his fine, healthy limbs in motion and directed his eyes and determined what he said and did—all this she loved past endurance. Oh, it was as though she scarcely cared at all for her children when she thought of being his—they were only like a drab, heavy weight that was chained to her feet. But they were there, she could not come to him without them, could not go by his side without having to drag them along with her—

"Well, you see—I've had that impression—fairly often—lately—"

"It's not that, Tryggve—"

"What is it then?"

She felt as though perhaps she might ward off the evil in answering as she did:

"Can't you understand—it would make a tremendous impression on the children if I went away and married you just when their father is lying on his deathbed in a sanatorium. Well, it's unlucky enough that he should have come here just now. I expect poor Carl is thinking all sorts of things even as it is—"

"I should rather think so. He's a queer fish. Nervous as he can be."

"You don't like him", whispered Ida Elisabeth.

"At any rate I do my best to, I think. And let me tell you, Ida, to begin with—last year when he was laid up and so on—I really thought him quite an attractive boy. But he doesn't like *me*, no need for you to tell me that. He's jealous—"

She nodded. "And that's the point, you see, Tryggve—I should always find myself on your side. I don't believe—I can't *imagine* that I could ever do anything else. But take your part—against the boys. Always."

"I see", he said slowly. "And don't you think my part would be the *right* one, as a rule? Carl is very unreasonable, and your youngest has a good deal of the rascal in him, poor little chap. And in reality you and I are quite agreed about what we want, aren't we? I mean about what is right and honest and what line we ought to take with them and so on—"

Ida Elisabeth gave a little twitch of the shoulders as though she felt cold.

"Well—don't you agree with me?" he repeated.

"Yes. In everything I'm sure I should always agree with you."

"Presumably you must also have seen long ago that your children have in them a good deal of that nature which—well, at any rate I don't recognize much of your nature in them."

"That's just it. Alone, I know that I can cope with that streak in them—get them pulled over, I mean, every time they come to a jump where they try to refuse. Well, I'm not so sure after all. But if anyone can, it must be me. Who can teach them not to yield to all kinds of disinclination and bury themselves away in whims and fancies and nonsense, whenever they're faced with a difficulty, instead of trying if they can to work their way out of it. But if they had you and me *together* against them—" She raised her hands and let them drop helplessly.

He stood looking down at her, she felt. For a single instant she ventured to look up and meet his eyes.

"God help you, Ida", he said under his breath. "You are going to make yourself so unhappy!"

She nodded without looking at him. And it was a few moments before she had courage to answer:

"Don't you remember—we talked so often about these things. You said the same—when once one has begun to have children, one cannot leave the work half-done. Giving birth is merely delivering the raw material, you said; children are not finished and out of their mother's hands until they are grown up, you said. And in such times as those we live in, you said once, when there are so many who don't even *own* anything outside themselves, don't know what it is to have anything to prove false to—shame on him who calls it a sacrifice, you said, if he is called upon to give all he can to keep faith, when there are others who don't even own anything to which they can be faithful." She swallowed the tears that forced themselves on her. "I don't know why it didn't give me the creeps, our talking so often about these things. The same as when people say, there's a goose walking over my grave."

"Oh yes. But when it comes to the point—it *is* different. Faithful, you say. But I never intended you to fail your children. But what about me, Ida?"

"Oh yes. But I didn't think"—the tears got the better of her—"I didn't think it was like this, you see. That I can't come to you without dragging with me something which is my own flesh and blood and can never be anything but strange to you."

She gave him a rapid glance, saw the perplexity in his eyes, and then she felt that her despair was complete.

"Oh, how you will regret this, Ida!"

"Yes, I know I shall do that, Tryggve. Times without number."

"Why do you do it then?"

Ah, why *have I done* it! For now it cannot be undone. Now he too will discover more and more that the difficulties are too formidable—

"Oh, Ida, Ida—I think you ought to reflect more."

Yes, you may be sure I shall do that! But you too will reflect more upon it after this. Oh, how could I do this thing!

"Besides, it may shape itself quite differently from what you think, you see. If we move to the other place. Then, for one thing, we should have a good many of my family in our neighbourhood, you know. And you've gotten on well with all those you've met hitherto. Both Anne and Ingvild think a great deal of you. We should be living only a dozen miles from Ingvild—could send the boys there in the holidays and so on."

"The thing is, Tryggve, that they have nobody but me, poor boys. And it's my own fault. For I've known the Braatös nearly all my life, so I ought to have known how it would turn out."

"I expect you were too young for that. You were married when you were about twenty. Honestly—aren't you rather morbidly conscientious?"

"I don't know, Tryggve. But it's all I have to go by—my conscience—when I have to try and straighten out questions of right and wrong. God knows I wish I had someone

377

I relied on, whom I could ask for advice and guidance, but as I haven't? Not that I think anybody's conscience is such a grand thing to rely on", she said bitterly. "For they've all said, everyone I've known, pretty nearly, that one ought to be guided by one's conscience. And I've never seen that it kept them very much from doing what they wanted. I believe my father was the only one who couldn't get his conscience to back him up—I presume he kept it in alcohol for that very reason! So it's not that I believe my conscience to be more apt than other people's at plain-speaking, you understand. But as it's all I have to guide me—"

"What about your love, Ida?" he asked softly.

"It tells me that there's nothing else in the world that's worth troubling about. There's only you and I. And that's not true, as we know."

The dog had gotten tired of lying by the radiator and came over to Ida Elisabeth, laid his head in her lap, and wagged his tail invitingly; but as she took no notice of him, he padded across and stuck his nose into Toksvold's hand. Tryggve turned his face slightly and looked down, as he stroked the dog's handsome black head—his expression distantly recalled the look with which he had once helped her to wash the blood from Carl, and Ida Elisabeth felt her sorrow running over as it were within her.

"But what is it you want then?" he asked as before. "For you don't mean to tell me", he went on hastily, "that you intend to throw in your lot with those people—again?"

Ida Elisabeth shuddered:

"Oh no. I shall have as little as possible to do with them, you understand."

"No, I must say I don't understand. What do you think of doing then?"

"Fighting alone for my children, as I have done before."

But now the tears came again—she rose abruptly to make her escape. And then he was beside her in a flash and had taken her in his arms.

"Oh no, Ida! Ida, my dear—but this is sheer madness from beginning to end!"

She stood sobbing and let him kiss her and kissed him back, with her arms round his neck, while the dog bustled uneasily about them—

"Ida—we won't say any more about this now! Tomorrow will be a new day, you know. Oh, my poor girl, how you're crying—Ida, if we're fond of one another—? We'll think no more about this, for the present?

"Now you'll come along with me and have dinner? And then we'll go up to my room and sit there, and then—then we shan't *be* like this any more. You're overstrained, that's what it is, poor girl. Shall I send a message to Fru Björkheim, I expect she has something that you could take, to calm you? And then we won't talk any more about this for the present—"

She hung upon him, exhausted, and little by little she got the better of her tears: "And in the middle of your office hours too—and you only just come home. I'll have to go. Ugh, that I should have made such a scene—and they must have heard it in the outer office—"

"Yes, you've now compromised yourself in so many ways, Ida, that you'll soon have to do something about it", he tried to be jocular.

She smiled as well as she could:

"But now I'm going. No, Tryggve—I won't stay; naturally you have a lot to get through—"

"I can work late. The night's my own, unfortunately—?"

Ida Elisabeth laughed rather feebly:

"Unfortunately I too have a lot to get done."

"Yes, damn it all, you always have", he answered with a grimace.

And then he embraced and kissed her again. Oh no, it was not all over between them after all. But she knew, even as they stood thus in each other's arms, that she had severed the living bond between them. It felt *now* as though it must be able to grow together again; so it would feel as long as the wound still bled, but little by little it would cease to bleed, and then it would shrink up, and they might go their different ways; he would realize this in time—

Chapter Twelve

I T WAS NOT ALL OVER so soon as that. At times Ida Elisabeth felt herself longing for the end to come. Then an
interval passed in which she did not hear from him; she
could not help counting the days: it had never been so long
between his letters. And she was beside herself with impatience and despair: it was *not* all over; something or other
might happen which would make all well again. Then there
came a little letter-card from him; he had to come back
here for a while next week: "Looking forward to seeing
you again."

She was to dine with him at Björkheim's the day after
his arrival. Ida Elisabeth dreaded it as she walked there. She
had a feeling that she would find they had already moved
some distance apart.

It was such a fresh and sparkling winter day—the glare
of the sunlight on the frozen snow actually hurt the eyes.
Against the deep blue sky the firs stood almost bare of snow
after the late storm; in some way they reminded one of
flames, there was such a blaze of gold on the green boughs.
And deep within her lay a dull sense of oppression—she
seemed to know that she was going to be lonely in a way
of which she had had no knowledge in her previous life—
the contrast between the radiant beauty of the day and her
own despondency made her see this yet more clearly.

On the road in front of her a flock of children approached,
coming from school. A whole crowd of little sledges in the
middle of the road, and on the deep snow-drifts at the sides
were children on skis. The shouts of childish voices and the
crunching of the snow under their feet and the soft patter

of skis and sticks blended into something which reminded her of the noise of a flock of migrating birds. Ida Elisabeth looked out for Carl. The children were red in the face with the cold; their noses were chapped from wiping with frozen gloves. By the bye, thought Ida Elisabeth, I must remember to call at "Manon's" for vaseline and frost ointment.

Carl was among the last. His mother stopped and spoke to him, told him that Tryggve was down at the ski-jump in Enger's field; Carl must get him home, as Ragnhild had promised to get dinner ready for them, but she hadn't much time. Carl said yes and did not ask where she was going.

Close to where they were standing was a group of aspens on the edge of a field. In thinking of this day in aftertimes she remembered the fine, genial look of the grey-green stems with the winter sunshine upon them. Masses of golden yellow lichen grew upon them in round patches, and behind the trees their blue shadows lay across the snow.

Tryggve Toksvold was waiting for her in the hall of the hotel, and when he had brought her in among the rows of pegs he kissed her, as he took her coat and hung it up: "Won't you take off your hat?" Then she was angry with herself—she did not know what impulse had made her want to keep her hat on during dinner, as though to signify that their intimacy was on the decline. She took it off, but then she regretted *that*: as she stood powdering herself before the glass she thought the last few weeks had made a difference in her looks, but the little black hat was so flattering.

He had on a new suit, she saw, bluish grey, but far too blue for her taste.

There was an unusual crowd of people in the diningroom, for the time of year. A meeting, Toksvold explained: the only room they could give him when he arrived last night was a little den at the hack: "Pretty cool, don't you think, when I've lived here for three years. But at any rate Magda promised we should have coffee in her private room."

Never had the dining-room at Björkheim seemed so comfortless, she thought—it had a transverse panelling of oiled pine and there were posts and beams everywhere; they were hacked out in angular fashion with gaping dragon's jaws so that one had a downright physical feeling of hitting one's eye against a sharp corner wherever one looked.

Toksvold had come from Oslo last: "Anne and Kari asked to be remembered to you. Yes, I happened to meet them two evenings running. They had a party, the Mosgaards I mean, and then we were asked by some people who were there, for the next day. It was a kind of fancy-dress ball"—he gave a little laugh.

"How amusing! Were you in fancy dress?"

"I? Are you crazy? No, I was a chance visitor, you see, so I got off having to dress up."

"Your sister must have been awfully smart, I'm sure?"

"Can't say that. Some kind of pajama things—with a pack or two of cards for trimming. She was meant to be something about bridge, I believe."

"And Kari, what was she?"

"Goodness only knows. But it was something she looked awfully well in. A long train, I remember, for I happened to tread on it. And tremendously décolleté up here."

"An Empire gown perhaps?"

"I dare say it was. It suited her anyway."

Ida Elisabeth sat in silence. No—it *had* begun already—their ways had parted. In her thoughts she was already settling down in her work-room—I am fated to stay here—

After a while Toksvold asked:

"And that Herr Braatö? Is he still here?"

"We have got him to move down to The Hill. He's had to take to his bed again—temperature."

As Toksvold said nothing, she went on:

"It's a nasty thing to say, but I can't deny I'm rather glad Doctor Lund has forbidden the boys to go there, now that he's in bed. For I'm never very easy in my mind when I know they're with that sick person."

"No, that's extremely natural."

Then there was no more to talk about.

THEY were sitting together on a sofa in a little room belonging to the private part of the house, when Tryggve laid a parcel in her lap. "Properly speaking I had intended to give you a ring. But then I thought perhaps that wasn't quite the right thing now?"

Ida Elisabeth tried to smile. She undid the parcel. Inside a box was a silver cup—chased. "Oh but, Tryggve—what made you think of such a thing—!"

"It's supposed to be old Trondhjem work. I know you're fond of pretty things. Do you like it?" He kissed her.

"For you must promise me—no sending back presents or anything of that sort—whatever happens. At all events we shall always be friends, shan't we?"

Friends—I hardly think so, Tryggve—for I shall often have such terrible regrets, I'm afraid. And I don't know that my feeling will be one of friendship exactly, when I think I've been too badly treated and that you would not give me a chance—

But he *had* revolted, time after time, had begged and threatened—every single time they were together, until he went away, six weeks ago. He had tried to force her to be his mistress. And now she bitterly regretted having resisted—in earnest. But it would have been already too late at that time. She had thought in secret, full of bitterness—you might have taken me before. Though she knew very well *that* was no infallible preventive of divorce— even if for decency's sake he would doubtless have raised more difficulties before letting her go. But perhaps more for decency's sake than because it made him unhappy to lose her and to see all their hopes and expectations of a life together brought to naught—

He *had* been unhappy—he let himself go one evening, raged and broke down in tears—called her an overstrained female who found a perverse enjoyment in tormenting herself, said it was a sin against life if she parted from him when they were so fond of each other—

That was now six weeks ago. For six weeks their daily intercourse had been suspended, and he had met a lot of other people—in conditions which bore no resemblance to those in which their love story had been passed. It was neither more nor less than the sober truth that he was terribly fond of her, fond enough to be sure that he would rather have lived with her than with any other woman he had met. He was willing to take her children into the bargain, to provide for them and start them in life as well as he could.

But since at the same time it was the sober truth that whatever he might do for these children the only result would be continual dissension in his home, try as he might to be a faithful friend to them—they would repay it by disturbing his married life with her, fretting at his and her happiness and confusing their mutual affection—that being so, he gave up. He was not a man to indulge in any fancies—that honest intention will overcome distrust and good will prevail in the end, and that in time they will understand ... She did not believe in anything of that sort, and he knew that she was right. Better to abandon the attempt, even if its abandonment hurt horribly, when they both knew there was scarcely a dog's chance of its turning out otherwise than disastrously.

THE moon, nearly full, hung low in the pale green sky above the ridge, as he walked home with her. Their shadows on the snow were pale and vague and long in the feeble moonlight. It was going to be fairly cold tonight—the snow grated so loudly under their feet.

He was going up the valley on business next day—could hardly be back before the night train. "But the day after tomorrow? For we want to see as much of each other as we can, don't we?"

"O Ida, I'm so fond of you", he said again, as he kissed her good-bye in the shadow of her porch. And she knew it was true. But he had realized that she was not free to begin a life which should be shared with him alone, and he was sufficiently sober-minded to acknowledge that neither of them could be content with less.

AT times she thought of things she had heard—before she was grown up, for instance. A friend of her mother's was thinking of marrying again, and her children by her first husband made a great to-do about it. She talked about her new happiness—"our painful, sensitive happiness. But oh, what triumphant joy it is too, when we *can* have an hour of peace together, just we two." There was something about the children being sent out for a walk and the maid given an afternoon off and the telephone receiver taken off. And it was courageous—not to renounce one's happiness, but to pay what it cost.

Oh yes, it seemed tempting—she saw that even now. But if one looks into the dry meaning of all such humid sentimental phrases one arrives at a very simple question: Am I to take what I desire and let my children pay for it? Well, God knows, it is less simple when one has to answer it. Then one discovers that, when all is in tumult within one, the voice of conscience is only like the feeble crow of the mistress in a school-yard full of roaring youngsters. But the fact remains—when they are old enough and strong enough, children can refuse to pay the debts of their progenitors; they can take refuge in bankruptcy from morality or society or whatever the creditor may be called who holds all the unredeemed claims on their parents. But so long as children are children they cannot prevent it, if their parents choose to live their own lives at the cost of the offspring.

Perhaps it is true that people nowadays cheat and exploit one another with more barefaced assurance than formerly. Perhaps human nature remains the same, and it is some outside factor which makes it appear as though there had been more honour and fidelity in the world at some periods than at others. But whatever pass we may come to, even if everyone fails everyone else, the last thing to happen should be a mother's failing her children.

IDA ELISABETH shrank from the attempt to make out what was going on in Carl's mind that winter. It is so easy to misunderstand children, especially when one's own interests which are involved differ from those of the child.

With little Tryggve it was easy. He could not bear going up to the sanatorium, and he thought his papa was a queer person, and it was a bore having to go in and say good-morning to him when he lay in bed in the middle of the day. But mother was always at home now, and it was only when she had some trying on that the children could not get hold of her at once, if they had anything to say to her. Little Tryggve was really happy that things were cosy again at home—and he was still delighted at going to school; there was so much that was new there, and the mistress was kind, and she praised his writing so much. Ida Elisabeth had to examine his copy-book every day and hear him in his ABC's. And he was great at ski-jumping; this was true, not bragging; his mother had seen it herself when they came down from The Hill on Sundays. He was so eager to deserve praise and put his mother in a good humour that his obedience and good behaviour passed all bounds that winter and spring. Ida Elisabeth did not allow her illusions to go too far; she might have difficulties enough with that boy in course of time. But just now he had entered a good period—he was glowing with health and almost unnaturally good and sweet; it was a delight to see how he was growing and blooming from day to day.

With Carl it was more difficult. His mother thought she could see how he was torn between a loyalty to his father to which he would not prove false, and the feelings which his father aroused in him. His illness, and also presumably the years he had spent in idleness at Vettehaugen, had as it were stripped Frithjof of any appearance of maturity he had ever had. It was gruesome to have to think such a thing of a man who was not much more than thirty, but it actually seemed as if he was passing into second childhood. And he had never been a very attractive child. Though it seemed to her that in a way he was less unattractive now than when he really was a boy—at any rate no one could expect a sick man to think of much beyond himself. But probably what struck Carl most was that there was something abnormal in this childishness— for it could not be denied that the boy was in reality a good deal more grown up than his father. Doctor Lund took care not to let him be too much with the patient. But on the occasions when he had been there Frithjof had no doubt talked a good deal about Berfjord and Vallerviken and Vette-haugen, and that started Carl trying to sift what he remem-bered more or less of his early childhood. Once or twice it had happened that he came to her and asked what had been the facts about this or that—when Ida Elisabeth told him he was apt to be very thoughtful for some time after.

Then there was a Sunday evening at the end of March. Ida Elisabeth was in her sitting-room and had not yet switched on the light, as the moon was shining in so brightly; it glittered on the frozen panes, and the white light stream-ing across the floor and over the furniture fluctuated, mild as milk. She opened the air-hole in the door of the stove and sat huddled together in a corner of the sofa with her feet drawn up under her—it was so good to be able to sit and rest one's eyes a while, and she would not have to go and get supper ready for another hour.

The boys lay on the floor in front of the stove chatting. The firelight flickered red upon them and showed up the stripes of the patchwork rug. She must have been nodding, she found, on hearing Carl speak to her.

He was standing at the window, thawing peep-holes on the pane with the tips of his fingers. "I say, mother—are we going to leave Viker?"

She vaguely saw Tryggve and the dog as a dark mass over by the stove—the boy was breathing heavily, fast asleep. There was only the faintest red gleam in the air-hole.

"Oh, Carl, put some logs in for me, there's a good boy. Tonight we shall have to take in the flowers from the windows again." The cold was making the old timber building crack loudly.

The boy came over to her, when he had done as she asked. "Sit down here", said his mother, and Carl flopped down on the sofa a foot or two from where she sat in the corner.

"You were asking whether we're to go on living here . . . That's what I'm not quite sure about. Fröken Rönningen, you know, the one who was here for a few days last summer, she's manageress to Myhre & Stovner, and she's going to be married at Whitsuntide, and I've been told privately that I could no doubt have her place. I don't quite know what I shall do, Carl. It would be a regular thing, you understand—a fixed income every month and more than I make here. But rent and many other things would be more expensive there—and I should have to be away from home all day. But there would be many advantages for you boys if we moved to a town—education and so on—"

The boy made a bound and buried his head in her lap: "Oh, mother—but it's so cosy here! I do think we're so jolly and cosy here", he repeated again and again.

Poor child—she felt how happy it had made him. His very attitude, with his head in her lap, told her that he had once more found security amid all the uncertainty that had tormented him so long.

Ida Elisabeth sat still, her fingers playing with his hair and fondling his cheek. "You know, I can't tell yet how it will turn out. For that matter something might happen to prevent Fröken Rönningen's marriage, for instance—"

Carl did not move. Presently he began to tell her things—about a record trip on skis which the dairy manager and Berge, the engineer, had accomplished a week before—from the Musli sæter across to Österdal, Hanestad station. Ida Elisabeth was still winding tufts of his hair round her fingers, and Carl continued his accounts of records. She had not heard that lively, cheerful voice of his for ever so long—

BORGHILD BRAATÖ's fat letters came tumbling in at shorter or longer intervals. Ida Elisabeth glanced through them, vaguely wondering—how does she find time for it all? Well, but it must always have been her chief recreation and amusement, to compose these long letters. Ida Elisabeth dropped them into the fire and never answered any of the points in them, when, once a fortnight or so, she sent the other a brief account of how Frithjof was getting on.

Tryggve Toksvold also wrote fairly regularly, and now it was his letters that she shrank from opening—and longed for, when a couple of weeks had passed without her hearing from him. He had spent Easter somewhere up on the Bergen line, with a friend who owned a hut there. On the way back he had stopped for a day in Oslo.

Do you remember you asked what Kari was meant to be at that fancy-dress ball last winter? I was told when I was in town— Madame Sans Gêne! Anne and Fritz tease her about it shamefully, and I must say, poor girl, she could hardly have hit upon anything that was less in her line. I consoled her by saying she looked splendid anyhow. They sent all sorts of messages to you.

IN the weeks following Easter they had wonderful weather. A slight impatience stirred in Ida Elisabeth as she sat at her sewing-machine, while the sunshine filled the work-room in a way that was altogether spring-like. Oh, it didn't take you long to get used to an easy life, my girl—now you sit here fretting because you can never get out. She ought rather to be glad that the busy time had come round again. But she had no one but Ragnhild Moen in the work-room; in winter she had never had more than one workwoman, and now the other girl she used to get in when she required more help had left the neighbourhood. So it was a case of sticking to it.

But outside her windows the sunlight quivered upon snow that was melting and glistening; down on the river grey-green water was oozing over the white surface, and the lanes of water reflecting the blue sky grew wider day by day. Carl dragged home catkins every day and went off looking for anemones—here on the sunny slope the bare ground showed through the snow in dark patches.

Now and again she had to find time to visit The Hill, and every Sunday morning she sat with Frithjof. He was in a very bad way now—there was a terrible change in him; his throat had grown so long and thin with great hollows under the chin and by the collar-bone. His face too was almost unrecognizable; it was so thin and narrow—more than ever he looked like a mere child.

He had been incautious, and then the illness had passed into a new and worse phase—it was what people called galloping consumption in old days, Doctor Lund said. His voice was nothing but a whisper—but he was as sure as ever that he would get well again; he didn't believe a word about having consumption. He had called to mind a case that had happened at Vallerviken some thirty years ago; the son at one of the farms there was looked upon as a consumptive patient and given up by the doctor, but one day after a terrible fit of coughing he spat up a lump of matter and shreds of lung with a fair-sized eyebolt among it, and after that he got well. And now, when his racking cough was at its worst and his expectorations were really shocking, Frithjof was full of excitement and hope that an eyebolt or something of the kind might make its appearance.

It was a great pity that he had to be so much alone. The Hill was not a big place; it was a farmhouse. Sister Tonetta, who owned it, had been head nurse at tuberculosis sanatoria, and when she inherited it from her father she let the farm to a half-brother and fitted up the larger of the two main buildings to receive patients. It was a good situation, and Doctor Lund of the big sanatorium was its physician, but it was very quiet, as Frithjof complained bitterly: far gone as he was, he was ill fitted to dispense with company.

Ida Elisabeth was beginning to wonder whether she ought to write for his mother: it would be hard on Borghild Braatö if she were not to see her son again before he died. There were Else and Bojan too—Ida Elisabeth had only once had them to her house since Else went to the Smithy; she had really not been able to manage more. They looked well, though. Else complained greatly of the hard work in her new place, but the air of prostration that had been characteristic of her had become less apparent, and Bojan was stouter and not so restless.

One day when she was with Frithjof he asked her himself: "Can't you write and ask if mother couldn't come here for a few days? I'm sure she would think a great deal of it if you invited her. And I have such a lot of things I want to talk to her about."

So that same evening she wrote to Borghild Braatö and sent her money for the journey, in case.

IT meant getting ready the room she had borrowed before, when Else was here. She had a high-strung letter of thanks from Borghild Braatö, and Frithjof was probably more worked up than was good for him at the thought of his mother's visit. For that matter it could hardly make much difference now; the end was sure enough, and so it was a good thing he was granted this pleasure.

The next thing was a letter from Borghild saying when she was leaving Vallerviken and what day Ida Elisabeth could expect her. And finally, the evening before she was expected, a telegram from Oslo: "Papa coming too. Leave here first train tomorrow. Looking forward seeing you all again, Mamma."

Well, after all it was quite natural. But Ida Elisabeth could not resist a little laugh—that she couldn't say so before. So now she must run across to Viker and see if she could borrow another bed.

Carl came home while she and the maid from Viker were putting up the second bed. His mother told him that his grandfather was coming too. Carl stuck his hands in his breeches pockets and stood with an air of profound cogitation.

"Well but, mother", he said slowly. "Grandfather—we really *liked* him quite well, didn't we?"

NEXT day both the boys were at school, so she went off alone to meet the old people.

It could not be denied that she dreaded it a little, as she walked up and down the platform waiting for the train. It was going to be pretty stiff having them in the house for an indefinite time—

The feeling vanished the moment she saw the two old people hurrying towards her over the yellow desert of the gravel-strewed platform. Again she took in without knowing it one of those pictures or visions that she would never forget: the sunshine poured down over the ugly station building and the dreary railway line, with pitiless harshness it showed up the faded and poverty-stricken hideousness of things near at hand—but the same spring sunlight quivered over the thawing valley, and the woods on the receding slopes faded into the clear blue sky where fine white clouds hung motionless high up, as though blown across the vault of heaven. There was a loud clatter by the brake-van, where some men were loading and unloading boxes; several pairs of skis rattled noisily on the ground, but the wide expanse of sunny air resounded with the roar of the river; the water gushed in a rapid, babbling stream round gravel bluffs and vanished under the bridging ice with deep notes like a peal of bells. On every side there was a sound of running water: white brooks foamed down the hill-sides; from under the edge of thawing snow little watercourses oozed purling; from the dirty heaps which lay shrinking against the walls of the station yellow streaks of muddy water flowed across the gravel of the platform.

As the two old people approached her it seemed to Ida Elisabeth as though all the world's adversity had battered them, and at the same time it was as though all that makes human effort so futile came bodily before her in their semblance—and then they smiled at her, pathetically and without misgiving. But then Borghild Braatö's face turned red and wrinkled up like a little child's; the big bright tears came trickling down, a whole shower of pearls, and next moment Frithjof's mother lay in her arms:

"Oh, Lisken! Oh, Lisken! Oh, thank God, my child—how good it is to see you again!"

So Ida Elisabeth offered no resistance to the other's kisses—did not feel much reluctance even—only tenderness for this poor wet face that was puckered and soft as silk, as the skin of old women often is. And when at last Borghild Braatö let her go to take to her handkerchief, and she saw Jens Braatö standing there with his old violin-case in his hand, she raised herself on tip-toe and with a good grace allowed herself to be kissed by her former father-in-law.

He had not shaved that morning and the stubble on his puckered cheeks glistened like silver. His fine, golden brown eyes were sunk in their sockets and the skin around them had become filmy and brown and covered with wrinkles; his viking mane of shining, wavy dark-blond hair was white at the temples and withered like last year's grass.

"How nice that you could come too, father-in-law! I can tell you, Frithjof will be pleased!"

SHE was fond of them, that was the truth, when she had gotten them and their belongings under her roof and they were pottering about between the spare room on the other side of the passage and her kitchen and the boys' room and her own sitting-room. And of course mother-in-law had to have a look at the work-room and the fitting-room and be introduced to Ragnhild: "Oh, how snug you are here, Lisken dear—I must say you've known how to make a charming home for yourself! And a lot of work you have, I see"; she went over and looked at the dresses Ida Elisabeth was making, which were hanging in a row on a long rod. "And flowers everywhere—oh, what a lot of buds on your roses, fancy their being so far advanced already!"

They petted Carl and Tryggve in word and deed to an extent which made the boys shoot surprised and questioning glances at their mother. They bustled into their room to continue their unpacking and came back to say something, leaving the doors open behind them, so that Ida Elisabeth had to sign continually to Carl to go and shut them.

And the dinner. "Roast veal! Oh but, Lisa dear, you *shouldn't* have gone to such expense on *our* account! You know papa and I really *prefer* a simple meal. But it's *delicious*, no mistake about that!"

The dress she had on, of dark blue velveteen, had been made by Ida Elisabeth herself one time. It was loose in the back with a belt very low down, so that the body had the look of a big pillow-case from behind, and it seemed comically short now that one was used to long skirts—ugh, what a horrid fashion that was really, of short skirts and the waist down on the hips!

She was positively touched at seeing them again and there was no other feeling in her mind—Ida Elisabeth was surprised to find herself so touched. While it lasts, she thought—till mother-in-law irritates me beyond bearing again—

After dinner the Braatös went into their room to lie down for an hour; the journey and their emotions had fatigued them. Fresh surprise for the boys—they had never known people to take a siesta before. Then they had coffee, and then the car arrived.

Her father-in-law came out with his violin-case in his hand. Borghild Braatö was a little displeased that the children were not to accompany them, but their mother gave a decided no: "I'm not going in to see Frithjof today either. The first time you're with him I'm sure you'll have such a lot to talk about which you won't care for a stranger to hear." "A stranger—but, my dear child—?" Borghild Braatö looked at her in dismay.—Ugh, poor thing, had she been looking forward to a great family gathering around the sickbed—? Besides, Ida Elisabeth was nervous about harrowing scenes, when his parents saw how changed Frithjof was.

IDA ELISABETH took the old people down the long passage and showed them the door of Frithjof's room. Then she turned and went down to the garden. The paths were already free of snow; the mould lay black and raw, smelling of spring-time, on the sunny side in front of the old veranda which had been turned into an open-air shelter for the patients, but there was still some snow lying on the lawns, and over it the apple-trees cast long shadows in the late yellow sunshine. Thank goodness for the long light days—and the puddles froze in the shade, so that they crackled under one's feet.

Sister Tonetta came out—fresh and starched in her blue and white dress; her cap sat like a glazed, white diadem above her long, square-cut face, which was a light brick-red with elderly sunken cheeks that fell into folds about the mouth and chin. She greeted Fru Braatö in that voice of hers which was rather creaky and dry, but so gentle nevertheless—whenever Ida Elisabeth saw Sister Tonetta she thought of the word "genial", which seemed to express exactly what this woman was, from her stout black shoes to the white celluloid brooch with her badge. Ida Elisabeth and the nurse walked backwards and forwards in front of the veranda chatting.

From one of the first-floor windows which was partly open came the sounds of a violin being tuned. "Why, what's that?" said Sister Tonetta in surprise. Then the notes came pouring out into the evening air, bright and pure with dreams of longing and joy tinged with sadness. "The Blessed Day" he was playing. Sister Tonetta instinctively clasped her hands. And now they were singing upstairs—there was Jens Braatö's mellow barytone and Borghild's thin little voice, which still kept some of its old bell-like sweetness:

> The blessed day which now we see
> In gentle radiance growing,
> Brighter and brighter shine its beams,
> Heaven's grace and joy bestowing!
> As children of the light we feel
> That now the night is going!

"Oh, but that *was* beautiful!" whispered Sister Tonetta enraptured.

> That blessed hour of silent night,
> When deigned our Saviour to be born—

The notes of the violin swelled, growing in power and sweetness, drowning the voices in their flood. Moved, but at the same time with a vague feeling of repugnance or embarrassment, Ida Elisabeth stood listening. But good heavens, how he *can* play, when he's in the mood—and how queer they are—!

Some patients who had been out walking drew nearer. Over and over again Jens Braatö's fiddle flung the lovely old hymn tune out into the fading golden sunshine—and the little group of sick people stood stock-still, listening blankly. Then there came a humming, as one or two of them took it up. In the room above they sang the hymn verse by verse.

> Golden the early hour when day
> Brings back the hue of rising morn—

Sister Tonetta joined in and sang in a clear, pleasant voice, with great emotion:

> But golden too the lovely kiss
> Of sunset comforts the forlorn,
> Giving new lustre to the eyes
> And brightening features pale and worn.

> Then haste we to our native land,
> Whose gleams our strength restore;
> There stands a castle fair and grand
> Upon a golden shore,
> Where joyfully we may consort
> With friends for evermore.

A thin, elderly lady on the outskirts of the group was crying, with quick catches of the breath and suppressed sniffs. Moved, and thrilled by a vague alarm, mingled with a sense of nausea, Ida Elisabeth dared not look round at all these sick persons standing there. But Sister Tonetta dried her eyes with a happy smile: "Well, I must say! Think of our having a service like this right here this evening!"

Again the notes of the violin rose as if they would carry all hearts with them, away into the sunset sky:

> The great white army we behold
> Like snowy peaks a thousandfold,
> With them a sea
> Of waving palms

Before the throne. But who are these?
They are the band of heroes who
Have fought and won the fight below—

Instinctively Ida Elisabeth clasped her hands inside the sleeves of her coat. To her the music was painful. For it tore at her heart—lifting it up towards faith and hope and eternity, and yet there was in the very beauty of the music a denial of all that she knew to be also an aspect of life. Is there *nothing* solid in it then—is it only poetry and song and feeling and nectar for the spirit, and not a scrap of dry bread for hungry thoughts and tired wills—?

Chapter Thirteen

J ENS AND BORGHILD BRAATÖ quickly made themselves at home in her house. She was allowed to attend to her work without much disturbance—she had been afraid she would have her mother-in-law running in and out of the work-room all day long. But when the old people were not up at the sanatorium Borghild Braatö spent most of her time in the sitting-room, reading the papers or knitting or just dozing—poor creature, how tired she was! Carl's and Tryggve's manners were quite exemplary, but the boys evidently could not get over their astonishment at the remarkable ways of their grandparents. Their grandmother chirruped affectionately when she talked to them, and tried to win their confidence—the boys seemed to think she behaved as though she took them for little babies. But in fact she treated them much as she had treated her own children, even after they were grown up.

They were obviously not nearly so bored in their grandfather's company. Jens Braatö would go into the garden to see if there was anything he could do for her. There was not—the frost had not even begun to go off the ground; the little that thawed in the daytime froze again at night. But Carl followed him about and acted expert, and told him what had been planted everywhere and what they had had in the different beds last summer. Then they were in the shed; Jens Braatö wanted to look over her garden tools and put them in repair. That did not take long; she hadn't very much.

And then they had snow again. Day in, day out the loose May snow continued to float down in great flakes, till everything was buried deep in drifts. It would be gone again in a jiffy, as soon as there was a change of wind, but so long as the snow was lying the country had a look of midwinter.

ON the Sunday after the snow had come Ida Elisabeth had ordered a sledge for the old people; they were to drive over to the Smithy to see Else and Bojan. The boys went with them—if they had no particular longing to meet their aunt and cousin, they would not let slip a chance of driving in a sledge with straw and foot-muffs and fur rugs and bells on the horse.

They went off. Ida Elisabeth was washing up after breakfast, while the soup was boiling. The stillness of the house felt so grateful—even the sound of Fru Hansen's footsteps overhead, which made the beams creak slightly. Poor things, after all the old people worried her far less than she had ever ventured to expect. It was as though these last years had put a distance between them across which they could scarcely call to one another. They no longer fussed her about anything: they simply relied on Lisken, trusting like children in her ability to deal with all practical matters in a satisfactory way. But what is to become of them—she could not help wondering. They were not even so frightfully old in reality—probably neither of them had yet reached sixty; they might well live another twenty years or more. But they could never acquire more sense for looking after themselves, or more sense of reality—on the contrary, she had noticed in the fortnight they had been here that, the more rents had been torn by the fortunes of life in the airy illusions and sky-blue optimism in which when young they had dressed themselves out like a midsummer bridal couple, the more passively did they shrink into inactivity, wrapping the last remnants of their dreamworld about them and letting things take their chance. Such initiative as they had shown in their time—her father-in-law's numerous attempts and experiments, her mother-in-law's naïve and aggressive cunning when she sought to obtain advantages for her own family and at the same time imagined herself to be the least calculating, the frankest and most truthful soul on earth; their persistent and desultory diligence and their dawdling, that frugality of theirs of which they were so touchingly proud, since they were not merely frugal in their requirements of this world's goods, they also required very little in order to be pleased with themselves and asked nothing of their children in order to be pleased with them—even such activity as this on the part of these people had been conditional on their being surrounded by people who were fond of them, all things considered, on account of the kindly, endearing, ever-young side of Jens and Borghild Braatö's nature. They had to have someone who could encourage them with approval and good will when they were making an effort, and befriend them with advice and assistance whenever they were at a deadlock.

Now the ranks had been thinned of relations and old friends who had shown them affection and indulgence; those who were left of the family had grown tired or had all they could do to look after themselves, as times were now. As times are now—there is no outlook even for the young who are growing up healthy and normal; even those who are born strong, with the power of vigorous growth, are held down by depression, enfeebled by uncertainty, so that their growth is checked and their skin galled and hardened, and they come to a halt in an egoism like that of children and animals and neurasthenics. But what in God's name is to become of the old whose powers are ebbing and ebbing, and of those who are born so that they never cease to require help, and all those in whom the healthy see nothing but scrap metal—?

Ida Elisabeth brought in her outdoor things and laid them on a chair by the stove in the sitting-room. Why, Puss, are you at home today? The cat lay as he always did when indoors, on the best sofa cushion, sleeping in unruffled comfort. His coat shone white as driven snow—and no doubt it was the fresh snow that had made it so clean and fine; his nose was rose-pink and charming. "Yes, you're a pretty Puss—you catch mice and you catch birds and you go about fighting with the other tomcats and you decorate the neighbourhood with pretty white kittens and then you come home and get petted and given milk in your saucer. And yet I wouldn't wish to be an animal, Puss. But you'd be a great fool if you wished you were a human—"

A gleam of sunshine, pale golden and mild, shot in over the roses on the window-ledge and lighted up the snow-white grace of the cat on the blue-green cushion. The weather looked like clearing up.

As Ida Elisabeth opened the window she heard the faint rustling sound of spring snow falling from roofs and trees against wet snow on the ground. The garden's fairyland of white, airy, dome-like tree-tops was fast crumbling away. The blue of the sky showed through a mist as light as white steam, and behind the waves of cloud which curled along the slopes, the white hills on the far side of the valley changed colour; the forest burst out, slaty blue, as little by little the mass of firs dropped their burden of snow. But up above stood the wavy line of bare mountain, its eternal snows gilded by the sun, and the clouds descended; dark blue and white they rolled like smoke over the wilds; the vault of heaven came out, clear and blue as summer, and the sun shone with full power so that one could positively see the snow shrinking under the flood of light—the dull, lingering drip at long intervals from the roof became a rain of violet sparks in the sunshine.

The cat awoke, got up, and arched his back—with a light, noiseless spring he was up on the window-ledge, insinuating his head into Ida Elisabeth's hand and rubbing himself against it, narrow-eyed and purring with enjoyment. She took him up in her arm: "Oh, so you thought you might come here—and pull down my flower-pots for me when I'd gone. No, no, Puss—"

She carried him out into the kitchen and filled his saucer with milk, before turning to skim the soup for the last time. There—now it would surely do to put it in the hay-box, so that she could get out at last.

Long, bright drops fell glittering through the air and the snow was loosening and slipping down with a faint sighing sound from twigs and branches as she walked up the avenue of birches to The Hill.

"Such weather!" Sister Tonetta greeted her, smiling at the sun; she had come into the yard to meet Ida Elisabeth, blue and white and newly ironed. "No, I'm afraid not", she shook her head. "He's not getting on very well, no." Ida Elisabeth must please wait a little while; Sister Eydis was doing his room now, but it wouldn't take long.

Frithjof had been moved down to a room on the ground floor, as Ida Elisabeth knew—it was next door to the patients' parlour. Old Braatö was *so* kind, said Sister Tonetta; it made him so happy to be able to cheer everyone in the house with his music. Ah, and what a gift it was! To be able to play his son right into heaven like that!

Ida Elisabeth nodded. It was her mother-in-law's expression—Borghild Braatö had used it here the other day, when she had asked her if she wished them to see about getting the clergyman. Not that Ida Elisabeth had ever seen any sign of Frithjof's being in the least preoccupied with religion, in all the years she had known him. But now that he was ill, and his parents were here, with the old hymns which must have awakened all sorts of memories of childhood, children's prayers and so on—well, then it had occurred to her that perhaps Frithjof might like a visit from the clergyman. But Borghild Braatö dismissed her proposal with a little smile: "We don't know anything about the clergyman here—have no idea whether he would suit Frithjof. No, you see, Lisken—it is with our hearts we must turn to God, and I don't think anything could be

404

found which speaks to the heart like papa's music. Then I read to my boy a little—the most beautiful and comforting passages of the Gospels—but papa plays him straight into heaven."

Sister Tonetta went on talking about Jens Braatö's music. Nothing of the kind had ever been known before at The Hill. Up at Fjeldberg entertainments for the patients were fairly frequent, and those from here who were well enough attended them. But many of the more serious cases had not heard a note for ever so long—to them it was a real godsend to have Braatö's father here. And how kind he was about playing—not only hymns, but folk tunes and songs and all kinds of things. "And he plays quite like an artist, almost—"

"Yes, there's no doubt about that. Braatö *is* an artist."

Sister Eydis appeared in the creepered porch of the veranda, from which the melting snow poured down in glittering streams: "Now Fru Braatö may come in—"

SHE had not seen Frithjof since he was moved into the new room. Whether it was the effect of the light in here she did not know—nor whether he looked worse, but he seemed changed.

The room had windows on two sides; it was full of sunshine and there was a restless reflection from the walls, which were of rough logs, painted a glossy bluish green. The light was refracted in a multitude of lustrous points, and the reflection from a mirror flickered and quivered on the uneven surface of the back wall. The unsteady bluish light reminded one of the sea's sparkle.

His sheets had just been changed, she saw; the folds were still sharply defined. And the dead white of the bedclothes lent a peculiar hue to Frithjof's emaciated face—he was not pale, on the contrary, rather red about the cheek-bones, and elsewhere his skin had a brownish tinge; only it was a brown that had nothing to do with healthfulness but was a sign of withering, as though it had spread from the dark colour under his eyes. The pouches of fat that had puffed out his eye-sockets were quite gone, and the great wide-open eyes more than anything else gave him a strange look.

"You're looking pretty fit today", Ida Elisabeth said with an attempt at a smile, as she sat down by the bedside. "And what a lovely big room they've given you—"

"I'm not at all too bad either", he whispered eagerly. "I wasn't so well last night, but that'll pass off. If only I could get my digestion right again—"

Ida Elisabeth told him how the others were occupied today, and then cudgelled her brains to find some other news. He was not supposed to talk much, probably his voice was not equal to it. But it wasn't easy. He was not particularly interested when she tried giving him an account of the boys—their school and how they spent the rest of their time—evidently he had quite ceased to concern himself about his children. And she actually knew of *nothing* to tell him which would give him any pleasure—for years they had not even had surroundings and acquaintances in common; she could not even bring him such pieces of news as that so-and-so had gone away or arrived or had invested in this or that, or had had a letter from America or met someone or other. For that matter Frithjof had always been the one who purveyed that kind of news—and she had been accustomed merely to put in a word here and there, just enough to keep him interested.

O God, O God—was it wrong of me, while I was married to him, never to attempt to talk to him as to another grown-up person—? But what in the Lord's name *was* I to talk to him about? And now he was to die ... They could not talk about *that*—and she could think of nothing but the great darkness which Frithjof was about to enter, and the riddles to which perhaps he would find the answer. And on the other hand it was hopeless to try to talk about the life they had lived together—that she had ever loved him was merely a delusion of her own, and what he had called loving her was something quite different; besides which, he had probably all but forgotten it now—it was so long since the days when he had been used to come to her with his various requirements.

She took his hand and stroked it. It was heartrending that he should die—he had gotten so little out of his life, as far as she could see. But at the same time she knew that in all probability this had never occurred to himself, if he thought over such things as he lay here—in his very nature he had always had a sort of compensation for what he lacked—"sufficient to the day is the evil thereof" had been his constant motto; he had never taken thought for the future on his own account and never worried a scrap about what might happen to anyone else.

"Is there anything I can do for you? Anything you'd like to have—?"

"If you would draw down the blind—not all the way—like that—"

The room then lay in a brown-tinted shadow and the light was steadier. The reflection on the wall only showed faintly, and the blind clattered slightly against the cross-bar of the window in the draught of spring air.

"I don't think it'll be very long before I get out now", whispered Frithjof. "It'll be fun to come down to your house and see what it's like. You were always so clever at making a comfortable home. Mamma says you're so cosy there—"

"It's nice to hear she thinks so—"

"Yes, she's quite proud of this new home of yours. You may be sure, I've regretted many a time that I made such a fool of myself—I mean that affair, you know, when you got so angry that you left me. But I can tell you, the more I got to know the other, the more I thought of you—"

"Hush, Frithjof—there's no more to be said about that now."

"Well but, Lisken—we *have* made it up again now, haven't we? And once I get well again—you agree that we shall come together as in old days—?"

She felt her face turn stiff with paleness. She risked nothing in saying yes—in a way that was the most terrible part of it. If there had been any possibility of her having to fulfil such a promise—never in this world could she have given it. But now she stroked his hand and tried to smile as though it were nothing:

"First of all you must see about getting well, you know. That's all you have to think about now; you know what the doctor says—"

"Let's have a kiss anyhow, Lisken—"

She let him have it, bending down to him. As she felt the sick man's lips trying to fasten on hers, the unhealthy smell of him, the back of his pajama jacket drenched with sweat, an icy thrill of horror crept through her. At last he let go. She smuggled out her handkerchief—could do nothing else—and wiped her lips.

Frithjof smiled—a ghost of his sly smile of old days, when he imagined himself to be knowing:

"Oh, you needn't be afraid of infection, Lisken dear! It isn't what the doctors think, you see—nobody has really understood my case yet. I must tell you, I burst something inside me about three years ago, and as this heals and the matter from the internal wound drains out of its own accord—" Something of his old animation reappeared in his low whispers, as he began again, telling her about the grand piano that the parson's new wife had—

"Hush, Frithjof—don't talk so much, you know you oughtn't to strain your throat—"

But it was difficult to stop him, this was just the kind of anecdote he had always loved to enlarge upon—

From the parlour came some long-drawn whines—someone was trying to play an American organ. At first there came nothing but discords. But then it began to take shape. With helpless pauses and many wrong notes the player struggled on with the tune of "The great white army we behold". Involuntarily Ida Elisabeth followed, anxious to hear how it would turn out—

They are the band of heroes who
Have fought and won the fight below—

It sounded so deplorably different from the song of the violin in Jens Braatö's hands, when one's heart seemed to be ravished into high heaven, so long as he was playing—whether one believed or not in the glad tidings proclaimed by his fiddle—

But as she sat here, by this lad who was about to die, and listened to the organ's miserable droning—the hymn tune dragged on its wretched halting and disjointed course, verse after verse to the bitter end—she felt more vividly than ever before, precisely owing to the doleful contrast with the singing violin—there *may* be a reality behind all this of which they speak as though it were nothing but sentiment and emotions of the heart. Behind the mists of feeling there may be something solid, truth—and if I knew this truth, perhaps it would first freeze me and then quench my thirst, as when one drinks the living water of a spring in the mountains. Behind the consoling words there is perhaps a real consolation, a kind of spiritual law and order, and he who knew it would perhaps be constrained to love it—in the same way as I thought I must get to love the stars, those nights on the deck of the *Frostdalsegg*, when father tried to explain to me the courses of the stars and teach me their names and the constellations they formed—

He *is* only a lad, and he is going to die—and I have been married to him and had children by him; I have often been fond of him in a way—and I have never been able to like him, and never for a single instant have I been unaware of how strange he was to me and I to him. And yet it has always seemed as if there were something, from somewhere out in space, or from one who walked invisible by my side, or from something within myself—which warned me against judging anything but what I could see and perceive in clear, everyday light, phenomena as one would say; but the same voice also tried to make me understand how much else there always is in all men. Is it God—with hands in which repose all the irreconcilable contradictions; a kind of first cause in which we are united with something more in us than all that prevents our ever agreeing; a kind of magnetic pole of the souls which sets up a trembling of sorrow and shame within me for speaking untruths to this lad here— and which draws me away from the path on which my thirst for happiness would urge me, because it is now too late for me to follow it—which tells me that what I have signed in my cups I shall have to pay when sober, as father used to put it? But if it is God, then he must surely be able to help me, who am to live, in trying to bear the burden I have taken upon myself; and if he knows the meaning of Frithjof's life, which appears to have been so meaningless, then he knows what I have only been able to guess, why Frithjof remained a child always—and when the black wave that came and took Sölvi from me takes Frithjof too, it is into his hands that the child falls. And perhaps he is what Borghild asserts—an all-loving father. And it was only my lack of understanding that caused my unbelief to harden every time she said it—since I always thought of such fathers as I have known, each with his human frailty.

"It was papa who started them on that", said Frithjof with a proud smile. "Now there's always somebody trying to play. They never did that before in this house." His laugh cut her to the heart. "I can tell you, he's let the air into this place!"

"I can well believe it!"

"Yes, and I was thinking too I'd take up my music again, as soon as I get a little better. Papa's promised to get me a fiddle. I sold the last I had, but papa's going to get hold of a fine one and send it to me——"

"Yes, it's no wonder you feel you want to play again."

"Now you might pull up the blind again", Frithjof suggested. "The sun's more slanting now——"

She did so. On a little table by the window lay some books—no doubt Borghild Braatö sat there when she read to her son. There were some novels by an author called Runa—she remembered the name, a favourite of her mother-in-law's—and a New Testament. With some hesitation Ida Elisabeth took it up:

"Perhaps you'd like me to read to you?" she asked shyly; in reality she found it odd and foolish, almost—but something like a little flame flickered within her: she had heard of folks who were in the habit of opening the Bible at haphazard and hitting upon some passage which they took as an answer. And we *have* been married, we have brought children into the world, however strange it may be to imagine it now——

"Yes, will you?" said Frithjof eagerly. "I think you'll find *Tidens Tegn* in the parlour, the Saturday edition. There's such an exciting serial running in it, mamma or Sister Eydis generally reads it to me——"

Relieved in spite of all, Ida Elisabeth went off and found the paper. And it struck her as one of the most absurd things about it all, and at the same time so sad and touching—that here he lay, perhaps only one among many other dying people, who were all so intent on following the exciting serial which might not be concluded till long after they were dead.

THE old people were extremely pleased with their trip and quite elated to find that Ida Elisabeth had a late dinner ready for them. They were rather numbed by the long sledge drive. The two men at the Smithy had made *such* a sympathetic impression, and they thought *such* a lot of Else; she had really improved most strikingly, and Bojan had been so charming and sweet—

IDA ELISABETH was making her bed on the divan. She took the cushions out of their day-time covers and was just slipping them into the pillow-cases when Borghild Braatö looked in at a crack of the door:

"May I come in a moment? You're not too tired, are you—? I wanted so much to have a little chat with you before going to bed, you see—but don't let me disturb you, my dear—just go on making your bed; I shan't stay long."

She sat in the rocking-chair, glancing at Ida Elisabeth; the little face was sad and anxious, though she tried to make it appear that she had just come in for a little evening chat. But at last it came:

"Lisken dear. There's one thing Else said which really made me a little bit uneasy almost. What a charming kimono that is of yours, Lisken—you don't mean to tell me you got that material up here?"

Ida Elisabeth looked down at herself. The kimono was only artificial silk, plum-coloured, almost the same shade as the dress Tryggve had been so fond of. When she had to make herself a new kimono at Christmas time she had thought she might as well buy a material which she knew he would like to see on her—

"It was about Jeja", said Borghild in a low voice. "Well, of course you met her too, in Oslo. Tell me—did *you* have any impression that Jeja—well, that she had been mixing with some not very desirable—that for instance the other young ladies at that hairdressing establishment are perhaps not so—well, I mean, that she should have any associates who are not quite eligible—?"

"No—what makes you think that?" She tried to answer unsuspectingly. That stupid jerk of an Else!—Jeja had met her parents at the station in Oslo, had spent the evening with them and seen them off next morning, and they had been delighted to find her so attentive and looking so splendid. If they had been praising her sister to Else—why, then Else was such a fool that one could imagine her saying or hinting something, purely out of jealousy—

"I mean—" It was lamentable to see the lurking dread in her eyes. "There are so many dangers, you know, for a lonely girl in a great city—"

"But Jeja is very sensible, I'm sure. I can't help thinking she understands quite well that she has to look after herself."

"Then you didn't have the impression that Jeja might have gotten into any—well, that she might take it into her head to do anything—rash—?"

Ida Elisabeth hesitated a moment before replying:

"No, mother-in-law", she said decisively. "I certainly did not have the impression that Jeja is thinking of doing anything rash."

"Ah, thank God for it", said Borghild Braatö.

IDA ELISABETH woke in black darkness and a nightmare terror which continued outside her in a thrill of sound, and she could not come round—where was she? Then her consciousness righted itself again: there was the pale rectangle of the window, covered with frost stars, and her right hand felt the log wall with the rug hung over it, and the ringing sound was the telephone in the work-room. She started up and ran to it.

She had guessed what it was before picking up the receiver. It was Sister Tonetta:

Young Braatö had suddenly become much worse, so she would advise his family to come up at once. He had had some frightful paroxysms of coughing last evening; there was blood in his expectorations too, but no very serious hæmorrhage, and he had quieted down after Doctor Lund had been there and given him something. Even at eleven o'clock she had thought his condition was not so bad, all things considered. But a little while ago a change had come over him. The recent acute stomach troubles had weakened him very much. Sister Tonetta would send her car, so that Fru Braatö would not have to see about getting one at this time of night.

Ida Elisabeth found herself shivering in her thin nightdress when she came back to her own room—and as soon as she had gotten a few clothes on she was obliged to go and wake the parents.

It was bitingly cold and raw crossing the great dark hall, and as she opened the door of the room where they slept she was met by a thick velvety darkness that was warm and laden with the smell of humanity. Until now this bedroom odour which all the Braatös exhaled far more powerfully than other people had always filled her with disgust—tonight for the first time it seemed not sickening but rather touching; it put her in mind of animal innocence; it made it all the more painful to have to break in upon their unsuspecting sleep.

She felt her way through the thick darkness, trying to find the table and matches. This empty side of the house had not been fitted with electric light, and as the window looked out on to the road she had hung a shawl over it at night; not a ray of light penetrated from outside. Something she knocked over fell on the floor with a sharp metallic ring, setting her heart throbbing—there was a creaking movement in one of the iron beds. But when she had found the matches and struck one, she saw that they were lying quite still in the two narrow beds along the wall.

The flame of the candle flared up, and its gentle light made the room seem even bigger and barer with its unpainted log walls and the minimum of furniture—and the trunks in the corner and clothes hanging and lying about gave it an air of transient habitation. But on the table in the middle of the room stood a bowl of marsh-marigold; they had been gathered before the snow came and had grown in the water with long scaly stalks; the flowers had faded to a brownish colour—

"Mother-in-law!" She was forced to give the sleeper a gentle shake. Borghild Braatö was lying with two thin plaits of grizzled hair framing her little heart-shaped face, in a pink flannel nightdress. "Mother-in-law—you must wake up, please—" She thought her own words sounded quite ridiculous, and the other only grunted and was turning over in bed, exactly as the boys did when she waked them to go to school on dark winter mornings—and when she got her eyes opened they stared with just the same confused and drowsy look.

Then Borghild Braatö recognized her daughter-in-law, then started up in bed, whimpering as at a blow:

"Hush, mother-in-law. There's been a telephone message from the sanatorium. The head sister had to report that Frithjof has taken a bad turn tonight. She thought it might be safest if we all came up—in case—"

Borghild Braatö stuck her legs out of bed and began to fish for her slippers; Ida Elisabeth made haste to find them and slip them on the ill-kept feet. The pink nightdress only reached a little way down the calf, and the white flesh of the legs was enmeshed as it were in a network of thick blue veins.

Borghild Braatö sat bending forward, and in the light of the candle the tears glittered like crystal as they trickled down her round cheeks, fresh-coloured and soft as silk, which looked young with all their freckles, in spite of the wrinkles on her face. She looked quite young and at the same time old; with her bright bird's eyes from which the tears were pouring and the little plaits on each side of the face with its fine pointed chin she was a charming little girl who was also a poor wrinkled old mother.

Ida Elisabeth laid her arm about the rounded pink flannel back, then kissed her mother-in-law: "Mamma, poor mamma", and got a flood of salt tears on her lips. "You must be kind enough to wake father-in-law, while I go and get things ready."

415

What she was to get ready she did not quite know. But then it occurred to her that at least she might see that they had a cup of tea before going out into the cold. And it was a relief to be able to do *something*, were it never so little.

The stars twinkled coldly in the sky, which already showed a faint glimmering towards dawn, and the snow shone bluish grey and crunched under their feet as they went out to the waiting car, black with extinguished lights, outside the garden gate. When they had taken their seats and Sister Tonetta's nephew had thrown the lights on to the white road, Borghild Braatö sank weeping in her daughter-in-law's arms: "O Lisken! Lisken, Lisken—" Jens Braatö sat on the folding-seat, huddled in his great overcoat—not a sound had Ida Elisabeth heard from him since she carried in the tea before they started—

THE hill looked strange with only a single lamp burning outside the entrance to the sanatorium building, while the other houses of the farm lay in darkness and roofs and trees showed black against the starry sky.

Sister Tonetta came out and met them in the yard, whispered that they must keep on their outdoor things, as the window of his room was open. In the parlour a little table-lamp with a red shade was burning in a corner, and from the next room, the door of which stood ajar, Ida Elisabeth heard an unearthly rasping sound which rose and fell ... She was afraid, as she entered.

In Frithjof's room a cone of crude yellow light fell upon the bedside table and all it contained, but the bed lay in darkness—the brownish parchment shade of the little lamp was tilted over. Ida Elisabeth stopped near the door, while the other two went across to their son.

"It's mamma, Fiffi—it's mamma. Do you know me, my dear boy—?"

Ida Elisabeth gave them one rapid shy glance. Borghild Braatö sat bending over her boy, with one arm crooked about the pillow. It was as though time and years and all the rest became unreal—a child was lying in a bed, and its mother was bending over it: here am I, what is it—?

Well, of course, she thought, this is a thing I have always known. In reality it is a thing which never changes. They grow up into men and women, and then it all appears to be so different. But there is always a possibility that all the rest will scale off and that they will need their mother's presence. Remote and unsubstantial the memory recurred to her that not long ago she had been thinking much more of other things than of her children; a man had been much dearer to her than the two little ones ... It was a good thing I came to my senses, she thought—what if the boys had had need of me and I had not been there—?

Jens Braatö came over to Ida Elisabeth: "I believe he knows us", he whispered. "Perhaps he would like to see you too, Lisa—"

She took her father-in-law's arm firmly and squeezed it. With a stifling oppression of the heart she allowed herself to be led up to the bed.

In the brown shadow she could not see him very clearly. One of Borghild Braatö's arms was round his pillow; her other hand held her son's, resting on the white blanket. She looked up for a moment, fixed her young, tear-bright eyes upon the other, and said with a kind of smile:

"And here is Lisken too, Frithjof—we are all here."

His mouth was slightly open, and it was awful to hear this breathing which seemed to be struggling with obstructions everywhere, in chest, throat, and nose. His head looked so dark against the pillow, and his forehead glistened with a pale sheen, which his mother wiped off with a cloth. The narrowness of his face, which she had seen increasing week by week, had now become an unnatural distorted sharpness.

"Lisken is here, my dear", said his mother again, gently and affectionately as though she were talking to a little child. "Do you know Lisken, Frithjof—?"

Frithjof opened his eyes a little, enough to remind her of his look as she had known it of old—there was a metallic, opaque glint in the narrow slits. But it was impossible to say if he knew them.

But she thought she could now see that it was Frithjof, her schoolfellow of old, who lay there. The boy of fifteen had emerged again, as one recovers the oldest picture at the bottom of a drawer of old sketches. There he lay, a big boy merely, he who had been her companion in the days when they were both so young that neither of them had sense for anything but their own unrest, and they had both been full of anxiety and impatience in the face of something which they expected to open its doors to them—life no doubt. And now it was death.

All the rest was bitterly real enough; every single day they had lived since that time was just as real and inescapable as everything else that the sun shines on every day of our lives. And what is once done cannot be helped; nothing can be undone of all that takes place here on earth. But outside this earth is infinite space, before which hangs the veil of day. And as she stood here she felt overwhelmingly certain that there was something, as real and as invisible as are the stars in broad daylight, and that it was the same for all four of them, the mother and son here who were parts of each other's substance, and the old couple who were so infinitely one, and she herself and this man to whom she had been married through an error—it was God alone who really was the same for them all, of that she was just as sure as that there was not a thing they looked upon with their individual eyes that was the same for any of them. There was something beyond time and the day, in which youth and childhood and old age are one, though here they cross each other like the pattern of a woven fabric—

Jens Braatö squeezed her arm against his side:

"He doesn't feel anything", he whispered, as he led Ida Elisabeth back to her chair by the door. "It looks so painful, but they themselves don't suffer at all—so Sommervold said when Merete died."

From time to time Sister Tonetta glided in on noiseless shoes, went up to the bed, over which the mother was bending, and attended to the dying man, taking a look at him as she did so. She wiped his forehead and moistened his lips with a dab of cotton-wool. The painful gasping sound was changing; it broke off at times and began again, differently.

It was getting lighter and lighter behind the blinds. Jens Braatö sat motionless by the window, sunk in his great overcoat, with the collar turned up. He no longer loomed as a mere black mass; a pale morning light touched his flat cheeks and the smooth bent ridge of his nose; his coat showed faintly grey.

Ida Elisabeth got up and stole across to him on tip-toe:

"Father-in-law, don't you think you ought to move? It must be fearfully cold for you sitting here—"

Jens Braatö gave a start. He must have been dozing. He shook himself once and passed his hand over his withered mane. Then he got up, stiffly.

He let his daughter-in-law lead him out into the parlour. It was quite light outside, they saw, on entering this uncurtained room. In the sky a few light clouds were flushed with the approaching sunrise.

The steatite stove still held a little warmth, she felt as she put a hand on it. She made Jens Braatö stand with his back to it.

"Well, well, little Ida", he said in a hushed voice. "You have been through it yourself, poor child. But all the same, two grown-up children, at their most promising age; I don't think you can realize what that means—"

"No." She put her hand in his, as he held it out, and then he laid his other hand upon it and stood patting it.

"You're a good girl, Lisa; you always have been. And you mustn't think we have any reproaches to make, my dear child. Poor unhappy Frithjof—we understand that you must have felt wounded to the very heart. But for all that the blow fell heaviest on himself, Ida Elisabeth, you may take my word for it."

Ida Elisabeth shook her head slightly—she did not know why. It was all poor and blank enough; here she was with his father and his mother at the bedside of Frithjof, who was dying, and they had nothing in common but bare naked life. They were alive, and they would all die—it was Frithjof's turn first, but it would be the turn of all of them one day. All those things by which people make something of their lives—love, work, responsibility; they were and always would be big enough things—only just tonight a light, or perhaps a darkness, seemed to lie upon all that, so that the forms and colours which make one human life different from another disappeared, and she felt that the bare stuff each was given to fashion his own life with was like clay one grasps in the dark. The life which one was given to have and to use—not such a terribly long time before one must give it up again and die.

There was a little sofa by the stove, and Jens Braatö seated himself on it and drew her down beside him. His eyes closed again almost at once, and Ida Elisabeth found her own thoughts getting tangled with tiredness, and then she woke up again and saw that they were a little nearer sunrise—and then she was on the point of falling asleep again, and started up on seeing her mother-in-law in the doorway, weeping. And she guessed that now Frithjof was dead.

THE sun was high in the sky and the roofs had already begun to drip when at last they were ready to leave the sanatorium. Jens Braatö crept first into the car; he looked utterly worn out.

"I think I'd rather *walk* home", said Ida Elisabeth, "and get some fresh air. I'm rather tired—and you know, there'll be a good deal to arrange."

"But then I'll walk too." Borghild Braatö put her arm through Ida Elisabeth's. "I believe Lisken is right—it will do one good to walk a little, on such a fine morning—"

Jens Braatö got on his feet, resigned—his face seemed begging to be left in peace.

"No, no, father-in-law—you're to drive. And try to get a little sleep as soon as you're home."

The car drove off. Arm in arm the two women started to walk down the birch avenue, where water was beginning to seep into the wheel-ruts, and the crust of ice cracked under the foot with a moist squishy sound.

"Poor Jens", said Borghild. "He's not so young as he was—well, you must have noticed that already. He no longer has his old elasticity for meeting the blows of fortune. Thank God, I am tougher—I can ward off the worst of them from him in the years to come."

Ida Elisabeth gave her arm a little squeeze.

The sky was still cool and pale blue, and there was a silvery morning gleam on white stems and budding twigs. The snow lay crisp and fresh with night frost in the shade, but in the sun there was a gentle trickling and dripping from the edge of the hollow drifts, and a subdued gurgling of running water deep under snow and ice. The roar of the river sounded far away and hushed. But in a few hours it would be as dazzling and warm as yesterday when they went up to see him, with tree-tops like flames against the dark blue sky, and the valley lull of steamy mist and the murmur of the river and sound of running water on every side, and from the forest and fields voluptuous little sighs of the sinking snow.

All the time she saw before her Frithjof's face, as it had appeared after he was laid out. Handsome, in an incredible way—and young, altogether young. Not that she deluded herself that it was Frithjof whom she had ever known, or that beneath his nature and manner she had divined this beauty which was like the remoteness of youth, unapproachable and pure. It was merely incomprehensible and mysterious, what she saw in Frithjof's dead face. But perhaps it was like a vision of something he was meant to be, or would become—perhaps one sees a glimpse of what a person is destined for in the brief while after he is dead, before corruption has begun to destroy the husk he has worn out. For she had seen it before, this radiant and startling beauty which some corpses exhibit for a little while. But Frithjof, Frithjof with the black hymn-book under his chin and his hands clasped on his breast, it was more incomprehensible than anything she had seen, that he was so beautiful.

"He looked so sweet and peaceful", said the mother. She was weeping all the time, but quietly and simply. "It is hard for us who are left. But good for him whose struggles are at an end."

Perhaps. Or perhaps it is just now that his struggles are beginning—now that he is freed from all that kept him from making any struggle in this life. All that talk about purgatory and so on—perhaps that is where he has gone now, to a place where he may learn to understand, to love and fight, and that is what makes him radiant, almost as though triumphant. Perhaps that is what happens to us when we are dead, that we get to understand, and though it may be painful, that is the way out of the mists into clarity—how do I know—? But understanding, that must be the best of all, for love itself fails simply because we understand too little.

"Oh, yes." Her mother-in-law sighed. "You may be sure, Lisken, papa and I wish so much we could have taken him home with us. So that he might rest by the side of little Merete and Jens' father and mother. Where we shall all be gathered together one day. Not far from Sölvi either—little Sölvi whom he loved so unspeakably!"

"But his boys are living here, you know . . ." She felt ashamed at saying it. But she *could* not offer to send Frithjof's coffin back with them to Vallerviken. It was now broad daylight; she was forced to think once more of how she was to find means for all that had to be done. All her reserves were spent; before she was through with the funeral expenses she would have to borrow something from Carl's bank account.

"Yes, of course", said Borghild Braatö resignedly. "There may be a good deal in favour of it. Frithjof was a grown-up man; it would be reasonable enough for him to lie where his own family are living. Well, I suppose you will go into mourning for him too, Lisken—now that you were reconciled at the last."

Ida Elisabeth nodded. Yes, she could quite well do that. She had to get herself a new everyday dress anyhow; she might just as well choose black and white, for instance.

Borghild Braatö went on talking—and all the time she was weeping quietly—about all the things they had to arrange, and Ida Elisabeth replied, suggesting how they might best do it. And meanwhile she was thinking all the time of how strangely death had changed Frithjof.

THE boys were in the sitting-room. She had telephoned from the sanatorium; they were not to go to school. The divan was still in disorder, as she had left it on springing out of bed last night. She saw it, and at the same time she saw the children's faces, as their grandmother enclosed them in a wide embrace, while her tears overcame her again:

"Poor dears—so small, and to be left fatherless so soon. Yes, it's hard—"

Little Tryggve instantly burst into tears, and Carl stiffened; his face was pale and he looked at his mother as though seeking her help. Ida Elisabeth crossed the room and freed her sons—she put her arms round them and gave each of them a rapid little kiss on the cheek.

"Where's grandfather, Carl?"

"He went in and lay down at once—"

Ida Elisabeth whispered in his ear: wouldn't he be a good boy and go into the kitchen and put on a kettle? She set to

423

work putting the room in order. Borghild Braatö sat in the rocking-chair with Tryggve in her lap. He put up with it for a while, but then he asked if he might get down—

"Mother—mayn't I go out now?"

"Wait till you've had breakfast."

"Ragnhild has given us something to eat", Carl explained.

"Oh, I see. Then you may go if you like. But go quietly, so as not to wake grandfather."

Borghild also thought she would go in and try to get a little rest, when they had breakfasted. Ida Elisabeth was summoned to the telephone—it was the milliner's in town, which was sending up some black hats on approval. On coming back to the sitting-room she guessed that his grandmother had been telling Carl how beautiful his father looked in death.

"And this afternoon I think we shall all go up to him again, with flowers. And you boys will come too, won't you? You mustn't think there is anything uncanny in it, Kalleman; he is so beautiful as he lies there." Ida Elisabeth saw how the child stiffened again.

DIRECTLY after, Borghild Braatö went into her own room. Without looking at the boy Ida Elisabeth said in an even tone:

"What your grandmother was saying just now—about going up to the sanatorium to see your father—you understand, you needn't unless you wish it."

She heard the boy stirring. Then suddenly he was beside her and threw himself into her arms, sobbing violently.

His mother stood with her arms around him. The thin boyish frame was shaking with sobs.

"There, there, Carl. You know you needn't go if you don't want to."

"Yes, but I do want to, mother", he muttered in a smothered voice.

"Not unless you like." She held him closer.

"I—don't like—" he sniffed once or twice. "But I *will* go all the same."

Ida Elisabeth felt how the boy drew himself taut as it were, and a flood of joy or relief came over her. What it was that was stirring in the child's mind she did not know—nor would she ever have dared to ask. But she felt, as a purely physical sensation through her hands embracing the boy, that he was in process of growing. *What* had been taking place in him all this last year she did not know, but in any case it had caused his character to expand and develop and put out new shoots. And although she recalled Frithjof's dead face as a sort of token that perhaps the incomprehensible would not always remain incomprehensible, it yet sent a warm wave of relief through her to see this boy here growing up; he would one day be a grown man, for good and evil. He would have his own difficulties to struggle with in life, but it is a fortunate thing in itself to be man enough to face them—

"If you like," she said as simply as before, "you and I can go up there together. I have some things to do in the village afterwards. If you like I can go up to The Hill with you first?"

Carl shook his head resolutely:

"I would rather go alone. I can start out with you, then we can go together as far as the turning."

"You must do as you please of course." She stroked his hair again and again. "What your grandmother says is true"—she stroked his cheek lightly. "Your father looks very handsome. He was never so handsome while he was alive. It is quite wonderful—"

Carl thought for a moment.

"Well, but I would rather go up to him alone, mother."

"Do as you please then." His mother kissed him on the forehead. "Of course you must do as you please about that. For you're a big boy now, Carl."

THE LEGENDARY
KID DONOVAN

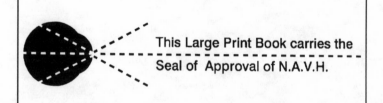

This Large Print Book carries the
Seal of Approval of N.A.V.H.

THE LEGENDARY
KID DONOVAN

E. K. RECKNOR

THORNDIKE PRESS

An imprint of Thomson Gale, a part of The Thomson Corporation

THOMSON

GALE

Detroit • New York • San Francisco • New Haven, Conn. • Waterville, Maine • London

THOMSON
GALE

™

LIBRARY OF CONGRESS CATALOGING-IN-PUBLICATION DATA

Recknor, E. K.
 The legendary Kid Donovan / by E.K. Recknor.
  p. cm.
 ISBN-13: 978-0-7862-9416-9 (alk. paper)
 ISBN-10: 0-7862-9416-7 (alk. paper)
  1. Frontier and pioneer life — Arizona — Fiction. 2. Arizona — Fiction.
 3. Large type books. I. Title.
 PS3618.E424L44 2007
 813'.6—dc22   2006039633

Published in 2007 by arrangement with NAL Signet,
a member of Penguin Group (USA) Inc.

Printed in the United States of America on permanent paper
10 9 8 7 6 5 4 3 2 1

THE LEGENDARY
KID DONOVAN

December 14, 1938
Phoenix, Arizona

Mr. Horace Smith III
Smith, Smith, Riley & Proctor
New York City, New York

My dear Trey,

I wrote these pages years ago, right after your father was killed in the Great War. I felt guilty for never having told him the truth. Still do. So I penned this confession, intending to leave it to you when I passed. However, your imminent inauguration as senator from my home, the great state of New York — and all the yellow journalism that will inevitably follow — forces my hand, and I herewith mail it to you.

Of course, you've heard of Kid Donovan. When your father and uncle were youngsters, they used to play at him, taking turns being the Kid or Cole Jeffries at that last shootout in Diablo. Years later, you played the same game with your friends — and accidentally set the garage afire, as I remember. I imagine half the children in the country played in the same way.

Your grandmother and I used to tell you the same thing we'd told your father — that there had never been a Kid Donovan, that he was nothing but a dusty old legend.

That wasn't exactly true.

Kid Donovan existed, all right, but only for a scant five months. It was just enough time to bring down a ring of scrofulous stock swindlers and avoid certain disaster on Wall Street; just enough time to kill countless men and burn down a town, and to turn part of the Arizona Territory — and half of New York City, I daresay — on their collective ears.

I should know, because I was Kid Donovan. I admit to the name — though not half the charges — and I also admit to a little whoremongering. After all, what else can a sixteen-year-old boy do when his only living relative — make that his last relative on this earth to die — bequeaths him the finest whorehouse in Pinal County, Arizona?

Shocked, are you? I know what you're thinking, but I assure you, your old grandfather is still in his right mind.

I have written the whole of it, from Mother and Father to Cole and Belle, to Jingles and Lop Ear, and to that larcenous backstabber Aloysius Dean, who hired none other than the infamous shootist John Henry Strider to come after me. That bloody incident marked the birth of Kid Donovan, and set me off on a course from which I barely escaped alive.

But I'm getting ahead of myself. Have no fear, Trey. Here in these pages I have laid it all bare with nothing held back for the sake of either modesty or shame.

Do with it what you will, my boy. Use as needed, as the doctors say.

Fondly,
Grandfather

1

I was sixteen years old on the very day I stepped off the train in Flagstaff, Arizona — fresh from the cosseted upper-middle class of New York City — but I hadn't much cause for celebration.

Quite the opposite, in fact. Just six weeks earlier, both my parents had been the victims of a freakish accident. They'd been on holiday in the south of France, taking in the sights from the comfort of a hired four-in-hand, when their coach went off a cliff. Their coachman leapt clear and the horses escaped injury, the shaft having given way, but Mother and Father were there one minute and sloshing against Mediterranean rocks the next.

I comforted myself that Mother had always loved the sea, and that she had finally gotten Father to take a dip, albeit permanently.

I don't mean to sound callous. I suppose I

hadn't seen much of them, having been away at school most of the years since I was quite small, and so it wasn't as if I had been constantly seeking — or receiving — their comfort and nurture. I admit that I was closer to my chemistry instructor and my riding master — and I daresay most of the groundsmen — than I was to my father. And I held Mrs. Slaughter, the housekeeper at Billings Hall, dearer than I did my own mother.

I knew her so much better, you see.

Home was a place I visited every two or three years, when my parents weren't in Europe. Or when my mother wasn't plagued by one of her frequent — and long-lingering — headaches. Sometimes they would last, very conveniently, for the entire summer vacation and recur again at Christmas break. At these times I was shunted off to the homes of school friends or, worse, sent off on "educational trips" with paid companions. So far as I was concerned, home was little more than the place the money came from.

It's probably a sin to say such things, but it's the truth.

At any rate, it was a very disheartened youth who stepped down to the Flagstaff platform that tenth day of May in the year

1882. There I stood, in my best charcoal suit of clothes — from which my knobby wrists and bony ankles were swiftly emerging — and there was no Uncle Hector in sight, not a blessed soul to meet me.

Sullen, I sat on a bench, my trunks carelessly stacked at my side, and sulked. I had quickly lost any fascination I'd once held for trains after the third day out. A fair-sized cinder in the eye will do that for a person. But I waited obediently on the platform with the trains coming and going, disgorging the flotsam and jetsam of America, it seemed to me, while reeking of hot metal and burned oil and sending out huge jets of steam. These jets turned the blowing dust from the streets into a slick slime and silt that settled into every pore, and shortly turned my dark gray suit to the color of ashes.

And all the time that I sat there, I was thinking that I didn't deserve to be bundled off to a town called Tonto's Wickiup. I didn't deserve to have to live above a place called Hanratty's. I had no clue what Hanratty's might be, mind you, just that it was Uncle Hector's place of business, and that he lived upstairs.

I deserved to have my life back, I thought as I sat there with the steam jetting and the metal complaining, and disreputable fellows — ax murderers one and all, no doubt — clambering off and on the trains.

I deserved to finish prep school, and set out for the ivied halls of Harvard when the time came. I deserved to be sculling the streams of New England and playing tennis and riding to the hounds, and investigating the mysteries of Miss Olivia MacKember's Academy for Young Ladies of Good Breeding, across the Hudson.

I considered everything that had happened to me to be a slap in my face by God, Himself, who had apparently — and for no particular reason — taken a sudden and distinct dislike to me.

At any rate, after two hours of feeling good and sorry for myself — something I'd honed to an art those past two months — and of pacing and sitting and checking my watch and pacing some more, Uncle Hector still had not come.

This was the final insult to my many injuries. Uncle Hector was my mother's only brother and my only living relative, and it was to his home in Tonto's Wickiup that Misters Dean and Cummings, father's attorneys, had packed me off.

I can't say that I gave them a great deal of argument. I can't say that I really took in a quarter of what they said in those dark, stuffy legal offices, amid the smells of old leather and ink and lemon oil.

I was only a boy, after all. A very cloistered boy, although I didn't see it at the time.

At any rate, the part that did sink in was that Father had been deep in debt, and there was nothing for me, nothing. Good-bye to Tattinger Prep, the only true home I'd known, for there was no more tuition money now that I had completed the term. No more Manhattan brownstone to visit on those selected holidays when I was invited. No more servants, no more thundering rides after the hounds, no more riding boots ordered direct from London. Hardly more than the clothes on my back.

I had studied a map, of course, to pass the time on the train. I had worn it to tatters, actually. And the only conveyance between Tonto's Wickiup and Flagstaff — between Flagstaff and practically anything south, west, or north of it — appeared to be the Butterfield stage route. If Uncle Hector didn't come tonight — and I had already decided that he wasn't coming, the thoughtless wretch — I determined to set out and meet him on his way.

Of course, this entailed finding a hotel for the night, and I reluctantly checked my purse. Mr. Dean had taken pity on me before I left New York, and pressed fifty dollars into my hand. It was a sum that I would have once spent on clothes or trinkets without a second thought. It was the only money I possessed, and I now had only thirty-two dollars and twenty cents remaining.

I left my trunks under what I hoped was the watchful eye of the station master, jotted down the directions he gave me, and made my way toward the hotel.

The town, if you could call it that, was appalling. I supposed I should have paid more attention to Clive's battered dime novels. Clive Barrow was my roommate back at Tattinger's, and he probably had hundreds of the things, mostly centering on the West and concerning desperadoes and shootists and cattle rustlers and wild Indians and the like. I had always thought they were silly, childish. But now, as I nervously walked the streets of Flagstaff, certain there were gunmen or bandits in every shadowed alley, I wished I'd read them like primers.

Luckily, the hotel wasn't far, but I almost didn't go inside. No stately marble pillars here, no uniformed doorman, no glass and brass and burnished wood. Just a sign that said COBB'S — CLEAN BEDS and a tiny dingy lobby with one weak lantern to light it.

The front desk was little more than a plank set on two barrels, with a few mismatched keys hanging from nails on the wall in back of it. Once I had cleared my throat a few times and the man behind the desk put his newspaper aside, he eyed me curiously.

"From back east, ain't you?" he asked by way of a greeting, and turned the register toward me.

I didn't deem this worthy of an answer, and elaborately wrote my name, as was my affectation of the moment, with many curlicues, and underlined it with a flourish. I returned the pen to its inkwell, flipped the register back toward him, and asked, in my most officious voice, "Where would the Butterfield office be, my good man?"

He didn't answer right away. He was too busy squinting at what I had written. "Horace Tate Pemberton Smith," he said at last, twisting his head back and forth and making the most of every syllable. He looked up. "By jingo, squirt! You sure they's only one a' you?"

I ignored the question, although I may have arched a brow. I did a good deal of eyebrow arching back then. "The Butterfield office, sir?" I repeated.

He leaned a hand on the desk and regarded me with a smirk in his eyes, as if he were privy to some secret joke. He said, "Well now there, Horace, the Butterfield's closed up for the night. Be open at seven on the dot, unless Jess's wife's been drinkin' again and don't wake him up. Where 'bouts you headed?"

The clerk provided me a wobbly handcart, with which I collected my belongings and brought them back to the hotel. After a furtive fried egg dinner at a hole in the wall called Aunt Mary's Eats, I fairly raced upstairs to my room and locked the door behind me. I also barricaded it with the room's sole chair. Shaking, I hunched across the narrow room on the bed, my back pressed to the wall.

If Tonto's Wickiup was anything like Flagstaff, where I'd just seen one man shoot another in the kneecap over a side order of fried onions, it was a place in which I had no business.

Somehow, I managed to sleep — still sitting up and in all my clothes — and woke with the dawn. After I ferried my things to the still-closed Butterfield office, I made yet another trip to the train depot to inquire

18

about Uncle Hector. He still hadn't shown his face, and I resigned myself to making the rest of the journey alone.

This saddened me tremendously. I'd come all the way from New York by myself, of course, but I was counting on Uncle Hector's company — even if it should turn out to be bad company — for the remainder of the trip. When you are just one day past sixteen, you can only stand so much of being alone.

True, I had been alone for most of my life. Surrounded by the other boys at school, certainly, and there were always servants at hand. But, all in all, I'd been alone, even in the crowd at Tattinger's. I suppose that somewhere deep inside, I was wishing that Uncle Hector would turn out to be a true uncle, not only in blood, but in heart. A secret part of me, you see, still lived in hope.

At any rate, when the 9:30 stagecoach arrived at seventeen past ten — "Right on time," quipped Jess, the lanky station master, with a glance at his pocket watch — I loaded my trunks with the help of one Mr. Muskrat Hutchins, the driver, then clambered aboard.

"Christ a'mighty, kid!" Muskrat Hutchins snarled through the open coach door. His grizzled and untrimmed mustache completely hid his mouth. "What the H-E-double-L you got in them trunks, anyways?"

"Everything," I said.

It was the truth.

The trip was long, and I was alone for the better part of it. We couldn't make very fast time in the mountains, and spent the next three nights at ramshackle stage stops. The food at each was worse than the last.

There was still no sight of — or word from — Uncle Hector, although I inquired at each stop. The only thing working in my favor was that while we changed teams frequently, we changed coaches but once, and so I didn't have to help unload and reload my trunks over and over. Trust me, a trunk that weighs only forty or fifty pounds on the flat seems to weigh a hundred more when you are called on to hoist it overhead.

Once we left the mountains behind, it was comparatively easy going, if you could ignore the dire condition of the roads. I had company for small spurts of time. There was a fat, silent woman who said she lived near a town called Milcher and got off in the middle of nowhere, where her husband, I guessed, was waiting with a buckboard.

A drummer joined me on the leg of the trip from Peach Tree to Hanged Dog. At least he was talkative, but since he was fairly well oiled when he got on — and more so by the time he got off, due to frequent sips from a pocket flask — none of it made much sense.

And all the while, the view became more and more depressing. We were making fast progress over the vast plains, now. Sometimes they seemed to go on forever, flat to a horizon edged with distant, jagged mountains, with nothing between to break the monotony but cactus. Other times, a small chain of arid hills or a stand of rock — red or yellow or white or tan or all four, like a layer cake — would thrust from the plain. Some stood singly, like a dog's canine tooth, and some were clusters and spires and hummocks of rock the size of small villages.

Not a scrap of it, however, looked habitable.

As the landscape grew drier and hotter and more alien, I found myself yearning for the sweet-smelling pines of Flagstaff. Funny, but I hadn't considered them sweet, hadn't considered them at all, really, until just then.

I wouldn't have minded so much getting shot over fried onions, I thought. At least it was cooler up north, and the dust filtered down softly instead of blasting you in the face.

It's all a matter of degrees, isn't it? The

things a person can stand, I mean, and still be alive.

And then yet another tatty little town came into sight. It was built right on the open plain, with no hills, no towering rocks, and hardly a tree to shelter it. Its mud-brick-and-plank buildings looked as if they'd just been dropped there by the hand of God, and some had shattered on impact.

"Welcome to Shit Hole," muttered the man across from me, who had boarded the stage three stops back and had suffered through the drunken salesman with me. It was the first thing that he'd said, although it was more of a mumble, and he said it more out the window than to me, person-ally.

He was a rough-looking fellow — about thirty, I supposed — with sandy hair, a stub-bly, unshaven jaw, a wide mustache, and a gun strapped to each hip. His guns looked to be in fine repair, even if he didn't. At least, they were shiny enough, and had fancy pearl grips with eagles carved into them.

It was all I could do not to ask to see one of them. Judging by his manner, though, I think I was wise not to.

We had entered the town by then. A hand-ful of squealing hogs parted as we slowed, then stopped, in front of the Butterfield office.

My companion stepped down from the stage almost before it had stopped, and directly into the arms of a young woman. I mean that just the way it sounds. She squealed, "Cole!" and gripped him in an embrace the moment his spurs clanked on the boardwalk.

He did nothing to stop her, and I was transfixed, watching them, only jumping a little when Muskrat Hutchins tossed the man's saddle down after him. After all, my parents were not ones for public displays of affection, and the meetings and partings I'd observed on train platforms across the country were far less . . . carnal. I couldn't think of another word to describe this one.

Just then, Mr. Muskrat Hutchins broke into my thoughts. Actually, he nearly broke my neck, it snapped around so fast.

"Get out here and help me with these trunks a' yourn, Horace," he shouted, roughly a foot from my ear. He was hanging upside down from the top of the coach at the time.

We were on a first name basis by now — well, he was, anyway — and I had learned he was hard of hearing, the result of having a rifle discharged directly beside his ear during the Battle of Bull Run.

He had also imparted various desert survival tidbits to me, such as to never let your testicles dangle down the hole of an outhouse. This, he told me, was because of the black widows that liked to web there.

"One gets her fangs into you," he'd said with a scratch at his neck, "and your balls'll get swole up like musk melons. She'll put you in bed for a week if'n she don't kill you."

While this was certainly valuable information, I would rather that he hadn't shouted it in front of the Peach Tree station master's wife.

"You hear me, boy?" he shouted, still upside down. "This here's Tonto's Wickiup."

"Are you sure?" I yelled back, certain it was someplace with the unfortunate name of Shit Hole, but he only gave me an annoyed look.

As I struggled to get my land legs, Muskrat Hutchins pushed down trunk after trunk to me. The first one, I caught, and while I was still staggering under its weight, he tossed the other two to the ground. I heard something break. Muskrat Hutchins didn't, though. He just went on about his business.

Dejectedly, I shoved my luggage together and slumped on the nearest trunk, wondering whether it was the glass in a picture frame that had broken — and if so, which one — and watching for anyone who looked like he might be my uncle.

By the time they'd changed the team, Muskrat Hutchins had waved goodbye, and the coach had left me in its dust — a trick accomplished in less than ten minutes — I was alone on the boardwalk. But across the way and down a little, through the space newly vacated by the stagecoach, I spied a large sign. HANRATTY'S, it proclaimed in large, elaborate letters.

To be honest, I nearly wept from the abject relief of it.

However, I did the manly thing. I swallowed the lump in my throat, stood up, gave my suit coat a tug, and dusted myself off the best I could. I grabbed hold of the first of my trunks and proceeded to drag it up the dusty street, past more squabbling hogs, toward Hanratty's.

2

Hanratty's was, of all things, a saloon.

I stood there, just inside the batwing doors, with my mouth hanging open. My uncle — my own mother's brother, for God's sake — owned a saloon?

I had ignored the CLOSED sign on my way in and the room was void of customers, but it was enormous. Perhaps a dozen large tables and as many smaller ones, their tops ringed with upturned chairs, sat round the floor. Above, chandeliers constructed from wagon wheels depended on ropes from the high ceiling, and in between the chandeliers, there hung several large five-bladed fans.

Lining the wall on my right were banks of glowing windows, edged with stained glass dragonflies and pond lilies that streamed fingers of purple and red and green light across the plank floor. Also to my right was a long, narrow staircase that led up to a railed balcony, perhaps eleven or twelve feet above me. It wrapped the flanks and back of the second floor, and multiple doors opened off it.

A sleek bar of polished cherry, complete with a brass foot rail and findings, ran nearly thirty feet along the wall to my left. The back bar was elaborate, and punctuated every few feet by paintings of naked women. There were long shelves for liquor bottles and glasses in between, and a huge mirror, flanked by cut crystal lamps, at the center.

At the rear of the room was a stage, draped by a red velvet curtain. I began to see a glimmer of hope. Not only did Uncle Hector have a prosperous and well-kept establishment, but he was in show business!

My parents wouldn't approve, but then, they weren't here, were they? And Uncle Hector had marvelous taste in paintings. My eye kept traveling back to one of a buxom blonde, invitingly stretched out on an electric blue sofa.

Oh, she was grand, just grand! You could see her nipples — both of them — and so far nobody had smacked me on the back of the head for looking at her, as had Mr. Haskell when he found us passing around Bobby Trask's French postcards in European History.

"Can I help you, kid?" said a sour voice,

and my hand automatically flew to cover the back of my neck.

There was no danger, though — at least, none that was imminent. The man who had spoken stood behind me, wiping his large, chapped hands on a bar towel. He was tall, muscular, and clean-shaven, with a square, dour face. Dark hair fringed a wide bald spot.

"Y-yes," I stammered as I turned toward him, "you may indeed be of assistance."

"I asked what you wanted," he repeated.

"I should like to see Mr. Hector Pemberton, if you please," I said, and belatedly remembered to stand up straight and be a Smith, by God.

"Too late" was all the man said.

My heart sank. Uncle Hector had gone to meet the train after all, and was probably scouring Flagstaff for me at this minute. Probably cursing me, too.

It was not the most propitious start.

"When did he leave for Flagstaff?" I asked, rapidly calculating the time it would take him to get back in every possible instance. Mathematics was among my stronger suits. I hoped this man would see reason and allow me to stay at Hanratty's until Uncle Hector's return. I wanted to peruse that painting at my leisure.

The bartender tucked his chin and gave me quite a look. "Flagstaff? Why the hell would Mr. P. go up to Flag?"

Obviously, this man knew nothing. I needed to talk to his superior, and was about to tell him so when a flutey voice called out, "Willie? Hey, Willie, whatcha got down there?"

I looked up to see a woman leaning over the balcony rail. Wild red hair spun over her bare shoulders and framed a heart-shaped face. She had nothing on but a flimsy white chemise and short silk knickers of some sort, with a gauzy pink feather-trimmed robe tossed recklessly over them. The robe was open, and as she leaned casually on the railing, arms splayed, I could see deep into the shadows of her cleavage.

Now I had never seen a female in such an advanced state of undress — not a living, breathing one, at any rate — and it stopped me cold. Or hot, more likely. The sweat that had been seeping relentlessly from my pores since midmorning began to pour from me in rivers, gluing my clothing to my body, and all I could do was stare at her and gulp damply.

"That's what I'm tryin' to find out, Belle," the barkeep shouted back at her. Frowning, he turned back to me. "Your mama know you're in here?"

The thought of Mother — socially fastidious, always tastefully attired, and doubtless heartily disapproving of this situation, even though she was dead and therefore past doing anything about it — was the thing that at last allowed me to tear my gaze from the woman on the balcony.

The barkeep was snapping his fingers beside my ear by this time. "Hey! Over here!"

I took a deep breath. "My name is Horace Tate Pemberton Smith, sir, and Hector Pemberton is my uncle. I should like to wait for him here, if you don't mind," I said, and added, a tad pompously, "Even if you do."

Willie the bartender pulled back a little and tucked his chin. "Well, I'll be dogged," he said. "Believe you do look a little like him round the eyes. Your mama that gallivantin' sister of his? You Helen's kid?"

From up on the balcony, I heard the fair Belle shout, "Hey, Dixie! Hey, Pony Girl! It's Mr. P's nephew!" and looked up again in time to see door after door open, and tousled female heads pop out all down the row.

It was a veritable cornucopia of feminine pulchritude, and I marveled that Uncle Hector could fit so many actresses on Hanratty's small stage. Perhaps it was deeper than it looked. Perhaps they all danced in a close row with their arms linked, while they kicked their legs high and squealed.

I had heard of such dances coming newly from Paris, but needless to say, I hadn't seen them. Quite suddenly, I was looking forward to the prospect of sitting front row, center.

An anticipatory leer barely had time to take hold of my face when, over the hum of excited female conversation, Willie called, "Back inside, you hens, and paint your faces. Fifteen minutes till we open."

Like so many turtles pulling into their shells, the heads disappeared and the doors closed, although Belle remained where she stood. "He all right, Willie?" she called. "You all right, boy?"

It was nice of her to ask, but I didn't see why I shouldn't be absolutely champion. The worst of it — the wrench from Tattinger's, the disbursal of my parents' property, and my grisly trip west — was over. Now there was only Uncle Hector to wait for.

The thing had turned a distinct corner, I thought. Considering what I'd seen so far at Hanratty's, I'd fallen into the proverbial cream. Uncle Hector could teach me the business, and what a bold and exciting business it was! The West would not always be so wild, I reasoned, and the country was growing smaller every day, what with the railroads. Twenty or thirty years from now, I could see myself husbanding a vast chain of fine drinking establishments — no, hotels! — across the country.

I determined to write a letter to Clive Barrow the first chance I got. While he would be back at Tattinger's next fall, mooning over his Western dime novels, I would be living smack in the middle of his favorite setting, surrounded by high-kicking actresses, and well on my way to becoming a captain of industry.

Of sorts.

Father had made sounds about wanting me to go into business, hadn't he? I didn't recall his ever saying what kind.

"I am splendid, madam, and thank you for asking," I called up to her, and gave a tip of my hat. I believe I smiled. I may have even winked. "I should like a room, though, where I can await my uncle's return."

She didn't answer me. Instead, she looked down at Willie and, her tone reproachful, hissed, "Didn't you mail that damn letter?"

He slapped a hand over his heart and solemnly said, "First thing, Belle. Pinkie-finger swear."

"What letter?" I asked.

Apparently it had nothing to do with me, for Belle ignored my inquiry. She stood erect and smoothed her hair, for what little good it did on those wild russet gypsy curls. She pulled her flimsy negligee close about her, an action for which I was heartily sorry, and then pointed past me, to my dusty trunk. "That thing all you brung with you?"

"There are two more trunks and a valise at the Butterfield office," I allowed.

She said, "Willie?"

Grumbling, "Yeah, yeah," he tossed his bar towel to a table and exited the saloon, presumably to fetch my remaining luggage.

Belle fairly floated down the stairs, a vision in pink, dripping tiny feathers as she neared. As she stepped to the floor I doffed my hat and gave a slight bow. "Madam," I said.

"If you say so," she replied.

Now that she was closer, I saw that she was older than I by at least ten years, although still quite beautiful. And I also realized that she looked vaguely familiar. Just as this realization struck me, a door off the upstairs balcony — Belle's door — banged open, and a man wearing nothing but his long johns and his pistols marched out, waving an empty whiskey decanter.

"Goddamn it, Belle!" he roared. "How

long's it take to fetch a bottle?"

I recognized him at once. It was Cole, my rough and silent companion from the stage-coach, and Belle was the woman who had so eagerly greeted him on the boardwalk. I believe I flushed, for my face and neck felt suddenly twenty degrees hotter.

"Gonna be a minute, sugar," she called to him. "Got something to take care of." She jabbed a thumb in my direction.

Cole snorted and dangled the decanter over the railing.

"Don't you dare," she said firmly. "That's German crystal."

And without a second look at him, she took my arm and shepherded me back through the empty barroom, back through a curtained doorway at the side of the stage, and into a little hall. She opened the door to a room that bore a brass plate announcing OFFICE, and just as she ushered me through it, we both heard the distant crash of shattering crystal.

"I ain't cleanin' that up, you sonofabitch," she shouted up the hall before she pointed me toward a leather chair. With a tiny flurry of feathers, she perched on the edge of the desk, crossed one arm over her bosom, and heaved a sigh.

Carefully covering her knees, where my

vision was riveted at the moment, she said, "Gotta tell you something kinda rough, kid. You want a slug first?"

About ten minutes later, I took her up on that drink.

I do not recall the exact words she used to tell me about Uncle Hector. I only remember that I kept repeating, "Dead, everybody's dead!" over and over. I also remember that I must have wept a little, because she offered me a pressed linen handkerchief from the desk drawer.

The gist of it was that eleven days previous, while I was readying to leave New York, Uncle Hector had visited one of his mining concerns. He was alone for some reason, and had gone better than two hundred feet below the surface when the shaft collapsed.

And that, as Belle put it, was all she wrote. I hadn't known Uncle Hector was involved in mining, but by this juncture I was surprised by nothing.

Apparently, they were still trying to dig deep enough to retrieve the body.

Belle poured me two fingers of bourbon from Uncle Hector's private reserve, and at her urging, I downed it all at once.

I do not recommend this procedure.

While I sputtered and coughed, my eyes

still tearing from the liquor, she aided me from the office, across the main floor of the saloon and past a preoccupied Willie — who was sweeping up what I assumed to be the last of the crystal decanter and who mumbled, "McGinty's goddamn hogs are loose on the street again" — and up that long flight of stairs to the balcony.

By this time, I was once again capable of speech and asked her, "What's to become of me? Where will I go?"

While I'd like to believe otherwise, I imagine this came out as a sort of gravelly whine.

But Belle dragged me up the last few steps, patted me on the hand, and said, "Now don't you worry, sugar. Belle'll take care of you. And you're gonna stay right here."

I wouldn't take charity, couldn't. It wasn't in my nature. I was a Smith after all, and I had my standards. Gone, however, were my dreams of those actresses squealing and showing fleeting glimpses of their under-drawers. Gone were my hopes of learning the business under Uncle Hector's tutelage, and of having a place again, one I could at last call home.

Despite the whiskey burning my throat and belly, I took hold of the hand rail and forced myself erect.

"I . . . I thank you for your very great kindness, Miss Belle," I said, forcing the words out. "It is deeply appreciated. However, I have no wish to be a burden. I shall be on my way."

I turned myself around and started dejectedly down the stairs. I hadn't the slightest idea where I intended to go, only that I wished it to be someplace where no one knew me, where I could crawl into a hole and pull it closed over myself until I thought what to do.

But with a shake of her head that set all those fiery curls bobbling, Belle caught my arm. "This is your place now, honey," she said in a tone that was soft and convincing. All things about Belle were soft and convincing. "Ain't you figured that out yet? I reckon near everything Mr. P owned, he left to you, Lord love him. There's no need to be runnin' off."

In my addled state, this possibility had not occurred to me, and frankly, I was stunned. I simply stared at her, open-mouthed.

Now, during this conversation, Hanratty's had officially opened for the day's business. I turned my head at the sound of footsteps and saw the batwing doors creaking open and closed on their hinges and the customers slowly wandering in, their boots and spurs making clunks and clangs on the scarred planks. Willie was behind the bar, already pouring whiskey and drawing beer.

"This . . . all this belongs to *me?*" I asked, afraid to believe that my good fortune, so suddenly snatched away, had returned tenfold.

"This, and the Lucky Seven and the Aztec Princess," she said, smiling wide. "Oh, and I reckon half ownership in the Two Bit, down to Tombstone."

"And those would be . . . ?"

"Mines, sugar, mines. Two silver, one copper. 'Course, they ain't much. They was mostly a hobby with him. Mr. P didn't exactly have a nose for bright metal — leastwise bright metal that kept on comin'. But they're haulin' a fair amount of copper outta the Lucky Seven. Or they were, till it caved on poor Mr. P," she added, and placed a hand over her heart.

I was about to halfheartedly quip that perhaps the Lucky Seven had been misnamed, when someone brushed past me. And giggled.

Two steps down, the girl turned and looked up from under a mass of blond curls, and said, "Hiya, sweet pants." She winked a heavily painted eye.

"Get a move on, Pony Girl," said Belle.

I was shocked! The creature had on little more than her underthings, and more and more similarly attired women were following after her, parade-like, to the whistles and hoots of the men downstairs.

One by one they shouldered past us and down to the main floor. They wound their way through the barroom, draped themselves over the laps of customers, leaned provocatively against the bar. One of them called for a whiskey, then plopped down at the piano, spraddle-legged, and began to play Chopin's "Minute Waltz." It crossed my mind that at her present tempo, the piece would take a good three or four minutes.

A girl in powder blue leaned over, laughing while a man stuffed money down her cleavage with one hand and patted her behind with the other. Another girl had already snared a victim, and was leading him up toward us.

I had been sheltered, to be sure, but not so sheltered that I believed actresses — even common dancers — would do things like this!

I had been a complete dolt, and reality overtook me like a douse of ice water.

"We're all yours, honey," announced Belle, her smile broad.

As the girl and her grinning client climbed past us, I stammered, "It's a . . . it's a . . . it's a . . . it's a . . ."

"Best damn whorehouse in the whole damn county," Belle said proudly, and dragged me back up the stairs.

The rooms to which Belle showed me were in a corner of the building, just down from her door. There was a good-sized main room, in which Willie had deposited my trunks, with a small bedroom opening off it at far left to make an L-shaped apartment.

"Mr. P had it done up special," Belle confided as she threw wide the dark blue curtains and opened the windows. "Used to be, it was four rooms for the girls. See?" she said, pointing to a faint vertical imperfection that buckled the cobalt wallpaper. "They busted down a wall here, and another one over there. Only the best for Mr. P."

After she commented that I looked a bit green and determined that I hadn't eaten since breakfast, Belle promised to send somebody up with food, then left, confiding, "That Cole's gonna be madder'n a wet cat!"

Which left me alone to stare at Uncle

Hector's wallpaper. I tossed my hat to the horsehair sofa, stripped off my suit coat and vest, unbuttoned my collar, and fell into a leather wingback chair. I was sweated through, and the leather felt cool and comforting.

Poor Uncle Hector had gone to join Mother and Father, but unlike Father, he hadn't lost all his money on Wall Street. He'd left me a going concern and three mines. Well, one mine and two others that were little more than holes in the ground.

I wondered what might constitute a fair amount of copper. It sounded like Uncle Hector had a crew working the Lucky Seven, and one didn't hire a crew of men unless the mine was producing sufficient ore.

Or did one? More to the point, did Uncle Hector? It had sounded as if these mines of his were mere playthings, and only one was divulging anything of value. It might be better to divest myself of them as soon as possible, I reasoned, and hang on to the Lucky Seven until I could determine if its output was worth the payroll. After all, I thought with a sniff, penny wise, pound foolish.

There is nothing so haughty as a sixteen-year-old tycoon.

Someone rapped at the door. I opened it,

fully expecting to see Willie. Instead, I found a sour-faced, middle-aged woman — this one fully clad, thank God, down to her stained apron and stout shoes — bearing a covered tray.

She shoved it at me and growled, "Ain't much."

And with that, she clumped down the stairs while I stood looking after her, open-mouthed. The hoots and laughter from below soon snapped me back to reality, however, and I closed the door between us.

Her "ain't much" turned out to be a thick roast beef sandwich on fresh sourdough bread, still warm from the oven. This was accompanied by a small plate of sweet pickles and a large slice of apple pie smothered in cheese, along with a rather dusty bottle of sarsaparilla. I ate it up, every scrap and crumb, and carried the last of the soda pop back to the bedroom with me.

Whether it was the heavy meal, the abrupt intake of bourbon, or the revelation that I had been thrust into the role of teenage whoremaster — or perhaps all three — I was suddenly exhausted. I wanted nothing more than to lie down.

Like the outer room, the bedroom smelled faintly of good cigars and witch hazel, but there the similarity ended. The first room had been spacious and airy, with good quality furnishings, better than I had thought to find so far from civilization. But Uncle Hector's sleeping quarters were another matter.

The room was stuffy and papered in emerald — the latter being nice, I supposed — and the bed was almost elegant, if you happened to be a Spanish ambassador.

It was dark and heavy and elaborately carved with scenes of the Spanish court, circa fifteen hundred, and so large that it took up most of the floor. Shoved hard against the flocked wallpaper at the head and the far side, it left just enough room for a small chifforobe and a washstand at its foot, and a narrow walkway at its side.

The room's sole window was almost entirely covered by the massive headboard, and I saw immediately that there was no hope of getting to it, let alone getting it open. The bed itself proved quite comfortable, though, if you could ease past the idea that you were about to be carried off to the Inquisition. Or that possibly the bed itself was a device of Torquemada himself, and that at any moment spikes would jut down from the canopy and slowly lower to impale the sleeping victim.

I couldn't for the life of me imagine how

they had gotten it up the stairs, let alone shoehorned it into that tiny room.

But it was there, all right, so I took off my shoes and prepared for a nap. However, once I got settled on Uncle Hector's mattress, I couldn't stop my mind from whirling. I lay there, staring up into the dusty underside of a green damask canopy, thinking about Belle and that Cole person, and about Mr. Aloysius Dean and the fifty dollars he'd kindly stuffed into my hand back in New York.

I thought about poor Uncle Hector buried beneath all that copper ore, and about that strange, out-of-place woman who had brought my food. A vision of Mother and Father, their bodies caught in the tide and battered by rocks, entered my mind, and was quickly replaced — thank God — by one of Clive Barrow's shaggy head, bent over the letter that I still had to write to him.

Clive and I had roomed together at Tattinger's for the past three years, and were known collectively as "Salt and Pepper." Clive was dark, almost swarthy, with sharp black eyes and an athletic build. I, on the other hand, was blue-eyed and so fair that when I returned from one of my "educational trips" at summer's end, my blond hair

44

was nearly white from the sun. It wasn't until the last term that I had shot up to surpass Clive's height, if not his weight. When I left Tattinger's, the jovial cries of "Salt and Pepper" were being replaced with "Scarecrow and Squat."

Though he bore it with good humor, I daresay that Clive was not amused. I know I wasn't.

And so I determined to give Clive a good account of what had transpired so far, and was mentally composing my letter when I heard sounds on the other side of the wall.

Now I am not by nature an eavesdropper. At school, when I could have easily over-heard Mr. Dillard dressing down Skinny Whipple for allegedly cheating on his trigo-nometry final, I walked right on down the hall. And did I listen, ear to the door, when Franklin Hower and Fats Bentley had that fistfight over Franklin's sister? I should say not! I only stayed for half of it, and Clive filled me in on the rest later.

However, on this occasion, I didn't believe I could lift an arm, much less get up and walk into the next room. Out of sheer inertia, I lay there and tried not to listen.

But, boys being boys, I soon pressed an ear to the wall. The speakers were Cole and Belle, her room being next to mine, and they were arguing.

"Why not?" demanded Belle. She sounded quite angry. "Why won't you tell him? It's his goddamn mine, ain't it?"

"Knock it off, Belle," Cole snapped. "Ain't had the time to digest it."

"What's there to think over? He's here, and it's his. Why not tell him?"

"Because."

"Don't you 'because' me, Cole Jeffries! 'Specially after what we just done."

Cole laughed. "And will again, Belle. Now put down that doo-bob."

She snorted. I could almost see her crossing her arms over her chest. "It ain't a 'doo-bob.' It's a glass horse. And I'm about ready to crown you with it, you sonofabitch, if you don't come clean with that kid. Besides, you busted the last of my German crystal. I brung that set all the way from El Paso!"

It was at this point that I belatedly determined it was me they were arguing about — well, me and the crystal — and I suddenly wished for a drinking glass to amplify the sound. I pressed harder against the wall.

"Belle, baby," Cole said, a bit softer, "I'll order you new stuff, a whole set. And it ain't safe to tell him yet. It's for his own good. I can't prove nothin', but I still got a feelin' that Heck didn't exactly die accidental."

I gulped, for Heck had to be none other than Uncle Hector.

"But you can't prove nothin'," Belle insisted. "You said so yourself."

"I just got a feeling, okay?"

Belle made a hmphing sound.

"Trust me, baby," he said, so quietly that I barely heard it. "Just wait. From what you told me, he's had it pretty damn rough. Let him be a kid a while longer."

"Funny, you bein' so soft."

"Ain't soft. I just remember what it was like, that's all. Bein' a kid and havin' it yanked away."

There was a small sound, as if Belle had just put down whatever it was she was going to throw at him, and then she said, "You promise? About the crystal?"

"Promise," he said.

And then they lapsed into silence. Shortly thereafter, I lapsed into sleep.

3

When I woke, the raucous music and laughter vibrating the floor told me that Hanratty's was still in full swing.

I lit the lamps in my rooms, opened one trunk, and found fresh clothing. But none seemed right, somehow. I seemed to have grown at least a half inch since leaving New York City, and in more ways than one.

The last half day in Tonto's Wickiup, more than the last ten days in transit, had proven to me that I had been plunged into a vastly different world than I was used to inhabiting. My usual dark suits, no matter how immaculately tailored, had no more place here than a duck in a wolf's den. With a sigh, I laid the suit of clothes aside and opened Uncle Hector's wardrobe.

He'd had very good taste. I'll give him that. I was soon attired in a pair of tan striped britches, a light blue shirt, and a silk-fronted vest that were only a little too big for me. It was a welcome change to be able to move my arms.

I stood before the mirror and had a good look at myself. The clothes were more in keeping with my present situation, but the boy inside them seemed hopelessly out of place. No matter how I tried, I looked pasty-faced and startled, for all the world like a rabbit caught in a train lamp's glare.

Sleep had brought me back to reason, and despite my earlier — if brief — sense of confidence, I was totally out of my element. I could only hope for the kindness of Belle and her cohorts to see me through, to ease me into this strange new world.

And I intended to see if I couldn't find out why Cole was suspicious about my uncle's death — without letting on that I'd eavesdropped, of course.

I gave my vest a forceful tug, stood up to my full height — currently five feet and eleven and one half inches, with no end to it in sight — and stepped out to the balcony. Below, Belle caught my eye, and interrupted her conversation with one of the girls to lift a hand and beckon me down the stairs.

By the number of men crowding the bar rail and the tables, it was obvious that while the girls of Hanratty's were a draw, they were not the principal business of the place.

I passed a faro game with men crowded all around, and heard the rapid clicking of a roulette wheel's marble. All manner of men — brocade-vested dandies; gun-toting cowboys; weary shopkeepers and rough customers in fur hats; white and colored and Chinese and Mexican alike — played cards or threw the dice amid fan-churned clouds of yellow smoke.

Cole was nowhere to be seen. The girls were present, however, colorful dots floating on the crowd. A red speck atop the piano, an amber shimmer at the bar rail, a teal flutter in a cowboy's lap, and so on. They didn't overwhelm the place as they had seemed to earlier, but seemed more like a sprinkling of sugar candy, added for color.

Willie was still working the bar, but he had been joined by two more bartenders, and they were all busy pouring whiskey and beer and taking money. Despite my unease with nearly everything else, the money made me happy.

Once I'd made my way over to Belle, I half-expected her to instruct me to stand on a chair while she announced to one and all that I was the new proprietor. Perhaps all the men in the bar would raise a glass to Uncle Hector's memory while I stood there, beet-faced.

But instead, she slapped me on the shoulder, kissed me on the cheek, and shouted, "Well, ain't you a daisy! Helped yourself to Mr. P's clothes, did you?" Before I could reply, she added, "You hungry, puddin'? I know how boys are."

It struck me that if anybody would know about the appetites of men and boys, it would be the beauteous Belle, but I wisely kept my mouth shut and simply nodded a yes. After a word to Willie, she led me through the noisy crowd toward a small, unoccupied table beneath the stairs. Someone yelled a rather rude comment at her — something about robbing the cradle, although it was phrased far more indelicately — and she responded by shouting, "Aw, go suck an egg, Abner!"

I didn't get a chance to see who Abner was, because just then Belle shoved me between two tall gentlemen — one of whom I guessed to be an undertaker, because of his somber dress — and pushed me down into a chair. She plopped down opposite me, and with an arched brow, said, "Better?"

I assumed she meant better than shouldering our way through the throng, and nodded. This evening she was dressed more chastely than she had been earlier, if you could call anything ever worn by Belle chaste, and she appeared younger, closer to my age. I was beginning to fall for her, I suppose. Beginning? Part of me had already toppled.

I leaned toward her, looked into those big blue eyes, and said, "Why wasn't anyone sitting here?" The place was packed, but not a soul had so much as pulled out a chair at this table. I half expected that someone had sawn through the legs as a joke, and that any minute it would give way.

She cocked her head and pointed to her ear, and I asked again, this time shouting the question.

She grinned. "Mr. P's private table. Don't you fret about this mob. Willie'll push 'em out by two. Here comes Ma!"

I looked up in time to see the approach of a napkin-covered tray, held high overhead, and then the woman beneath it, the same one who'd brought me the roast beef sandwich. Cowhands, gamblers, miners, and field hands alike parted before her like the Red Sea. I could see why. Just as grumpy-looking as before, she slid the tray to my table with a scowl.

"Thanks, Ma," shouted Belle.

Ma grunted and disappeared into the sea of bodies again.

I gulped. "Your mother?" I asked. I suppose I had some lunatic idea that I'd marry Belle, and that this cow would be my mother-in-law.

But Belle replied, "You fooling?" without further explanation, then added, "Eat up, kid."

With that, she was gone, leaving me to my tray and my thoughts, and the fifty-some bodies laughing and carousing and jostling the back of my chair.

Mother had once told me to chew every bite of my food thirty times, and since she had said so little — that I can recall, at any rate — I remembered her instruction and adhered to it. Thus, it was a good twenty-five minutes before I finished my meal, which turned out to be half a cold roast hen, nicely seasoned, with parsleyed new potatoes swimming in butter, green beans, and another slice of that good apple pie. This was accompanied by a large glass of buttermilk in addition to a bottle of sarsaparilla, although this time someone had dusted the bottle.

By the time I enthusiastically scraped my pie plate of every last crumb, Willie and his fellow bartenders had nearly emptied the place out. The music had stopped, and push brooms were already at work on the floor.

There had been at least a hundred bodies crowding the bar when I came downstairs, but at the moment, only three nonemployees remained. Two were slumped over tables and snoring peacefully. Another lay in the middle of the floor, his head centering a small pool of greenish-brown vomit. One grimy thumb was tucked into his mouth, and his chest slowly rose and fell. As I recall, he was smiling.

"Finally!" said Belle as she emerged from the curtained hall, next to the stage. She strode toward me, shapely legs flashing beneath her short, frothy skirt. "Thought we'd never get rid of 'em tonight."

As she pulled out a chair and settled in — and I wrested my eyes from her pretty dimpled knees — I asked, "What about them?" and pointed to the men at the tables and the one on the floor.

"Well, we usually leave 'em be till mornin', but we can pile 'em up outside on the walk if they're botherin' you," she replied, and raised an arm to beckon Willie.

"No, no," I said quickly. "Don't change anything on my account."

She shrugged. "You're the boss, kid."

"That's a laugh," announced Cole's voice. Startled, I twisted in my chair in time to see him step down off the last riser of that long staircase. He had changed and washed and shaved since I'd last seen him, but he still wore those pearl-handled pistols on his hips. He walked with a slight swagger, too.

Well, I shouldn't say it was exactly a swagger. It was more a thing of total ease in his body, a sort of artless grace. Everything about his body and manner said, "Watch out, you. I am a man to be reckoned with."

Everything about mine said, "I am a clumsy dolt. Kick me."

I suddenly found myself as envious of him as I was intimidated.

I wanted to crawl under the table and stay there until I was twenty-five.

But I sat up straight despite my inadequacies, knowing full well that to Belle — and likely everyone in the territory — I was nothing to this man. I was nothing to anyone, really, except maybe a few fellows at Tattinger's. I was prepared to be put firmly in my place.

I'd make him work for it, though. I was a Smith!

I said, "I don't know why that should strike you as humorous, sir. I am the proprietor now."

"On paper, maybe," Cole said. "Ownin' it and runnin' it's two different things." He pulled out a chair, turned it around backward with one move of his wrist, and eased himself down, his arms crossed over the back. "You got a name?"

I glanced over at Belle, and she said, "It's Horace, um . . . Horace . . ." My heart sank. She obviously didn't remember the rest of it, which knocked me down more pegs than Cole could possibly have done.

To top it off, Cole rolled his eyes and said, "Jesus."

Still, I said, "It's Horace Tate Pemberton Smith, sir." I believe I was a trifle testy. I know I was flustered.

"Yeah, that's it," Belle said with a nod.

"Well, don't go spreadin' it around," Cole growled, and signaled to Willie, who somehow knew that he wanted a beer and began to draw him one. "It'll get you laughed at or shot. Don't think you want either."

I took some umbrage at this, and began, "I don't see why —"

"Trust me, kid," he said.

I didn't reply.

"Now Tate's good," he went on. "I don't recall ever meetin' a Tate. You, Belle?"

"Well, there was Lambert Tate," she said with a toss of her pretty head. "He got himself hanged for thievin' chickens over toward Plano, Texas. And then there was

Bob Tater, which is close, I mean the Tater part, but the last I heard he was down to Sonora, raisin' hell."

She was dressed in a sort of powder blue, and it did the most wonderful things for her eyes. I had already forgiven her for forgetting the whole of my name, and I was impressed — no, proud — that she could talk so calmly about a man who had been hanged for stealing chickens. She was so worldly!

"But I don't recall nobody with that for a first name, though," she finished up.

"Met a few Horaces," Cole said offhandedly. "Rubes and candy-ass greenhorns, the lot. The one that lived the longest was dead inside two weeks."

I had never heard the term "candy-ass greenhorn," but I feared it fit me to a tee.

"Tate," Belle said, and smiled. "I like that."

Suddenly, so did I. Then, I would have liked anything that Belle did. If she had liked short men, I would have run right out and had my feet chopped off. That's how smitten I was. I already had a change of location, I reasoned, so why not a change of name? It was still mine, or one of them, anyway. I was making a new start.

"Tate Smith," I said, rolling it around in my mouth, trying it out. It had a good feel to it, a nice bite. I believed I could get used to it.

"Your folks throw out the Donovan entirely?" Cole asked. "Would'a thought it'd be there somewhere in the middle."

I arched a brow. "I beg your pardon?"

Belle clucked her tongue and hissed, "Mayhap he don't know, Cole."

"Don't know what?" I asked, looking back and forth between the two of them.

"That your jackass daddy changed his name, boy," Cole said as his beer arrived. He took a long sip while I sat there, openmouthed, and then he added, "Didn't want anybody to know he was Irish. Can you beat that?"

"He certainly did not change it!" I said, leaning away. "My father was . . . was . . ." It occurred to me that I really had no idea who or what my father was, not really, and I stuttered to a stop. Lamely, I added, "He certainly wouldn't change his name."

Cole snorted. "Have it your own way, kid." He lifted his beer again.

Something about the accusation — and the demeanor in which it was delivered — made me more angry than the circumstances justified. But Cole was ignoring me now, and I returned the compliment. A change of subject was in order.

My face hot and my hands balled into fists beneath the table, I turned toward Belle. "I should like to see the books for this establishment. The mines, too. Perhaps tomorrow?"

"Sure thing, kid" had barely passed her lips when I could stand it no longer.

I twisted back toward Cole and nearly shouted, "Whyever would my father change his name?"

"Calm down, Horace," Belle soothed. "It's all right." She looked a tad alarmed.

"Told you," Cole said with a smirk. " 'Cause he didn't want anybody to know he was one a' them high-strung Irishmen."

I would have struck him if I hadn't been absolutely certain that he would gleefully pound me into pulp. So I unclenched my fists, gripped the edge of the table, and said, through gritted teeth, "I'll have you know, sir, that my father didn't have the slightest hint of the brogue on his tongue. His people were from London. They were all financiers. They were pillars of polite society!" I made those last three parts up, I admit. I had no real ammunition to throw.

Cole still had that smirk on his face, and Belle turned to him, whispering, "Why you gotta do this now, you sonofabitch?"

"Do what now?" I demanded. "Tell

me lies?"

Belle caught my right hand in both of hers, and said, "Now, Horace — I mean, Tate, honey — Mr. P used to go on and on about it, you know? About how his only sister married a shanty Irishman . . . that is, an Irish feller —"

"Who didn't have the balls to own up to it," Cole cut in. "Never did know what was so consarned bad about bein' Irish in the first place," he muttered into his beer.

"Your daddy come over when he was a baby," Belle said. She was still hanging on to my hand for dear life, probably to keep me from hitting Cole. I was exceedingly glad for the excuse not to. "And his folks died when he was just a kid. And he did right good by himself, right good by you and your mama, didn't he? Even if he took a new moniker, I mean. It never bothered your mama — hell, he was a Smith before they ever met up, the way I heard — but Mr. P? That was a whole different colored bangtail, I can tell you!"

I felt as if somebody had let all the air out of me, and slumped back in my chair. Each new affront — my parents' deaths, the train, Uncle Horace, this den of lewd women and drunkards and, for all I knew, white slavery — seemed the final blow, but this topped them all. I wasn't even a Smith! I was a Donovan, and a member of a race that my father had always despised, or at least appeared to.

I could recall a time before I went away to school, when some of the silver came up missing. Father had dismissed pretty Miss Moira O'Hara without a reference, even though she was an upstairs maid and probably never got within twenty feet of the silver service, saying, "The filthy Irish. Thieves, every last one."

But he should have known, shouldn't he? I thought dismally. Aloysius Dean, his attorney, had mentioned something about father being deep in debt. I wished I had paid more attention.

I supposed that my father, the great Theodore Smith (nee Donovan), master of Wall Street and captain of industry, had been a thief, too. His pedestal, which had been slowly sinking into the mire since that fateful conversation with Misters Dean and Cummings, and which I had been trying to shoulder up ever since, had now dipped well below ground level, and Father already was up to his hips in the muck.

I stared down at the table and whispered, "I'm a *Donovan?*"

I heard Belle whisper, "Now you done it,

you sonofabitch. He's gone all flummoxy. Doggone you anyhow, Cole!"

4

I couldn't stand much more of this, I thought the next afternoon as I stared blankly at the so-called ledgers. Uncle Hector's bookkeeping system was beyond appalling, past cryptic, and into the realm of the surreal.

That, along with the collection of rusty Spanish bridle bits I had found in one of the dresser drawers — and a collection of cut-glass doorknobs that had toppled from a cupboard shelf and onto my still-aching head earlier in the day — had convinced me that although Uncle Hector had possessed good taste in clothing, he'd been one step away from the loony house.

I'd had doubts before, but I was quickly learning that everybody west of the Hudson was, well, crazy. Even Belle — who, I had to keep reminding myself, was a prostitute, a profession that couldn't be redeemed by her beauty — seemed a tad addled in the head at least some of the time. Asking me to change my name, of all things!

In the end, I had informed her that I would be referred to as Horace Smith, period, and that I was having none of this Tate Donovan business. Cole could go to the devil, so far as I was concerned.

I had decided the latter that morning. I had popped awake at seven on the dot, as usual, but found Hanratty's as silent as a tomb. After thinking it over, I'd gone back to bed and alternately dozed and puzzled over my situation until nearly noon, when the heat — and Uncle Hector's toppling doorknobs — drove me downstairs.

There would be no Tate Donovan, I thought as I rubbed the bumps on my head. My parents had named me Horace Tate Pemberton Smith, by God, and I was going to stick with it. The way things looked, that name might be the only thing I had left of them.

And this business about Father changing his name? Why, I only had Cole's word for that, didn't I?

Belle's, too, but that was beside the point.

Father might well have done it. He may well have been a thief, too. But he was my father, the only one I'd had, and if he'd been a thief, he'd at least been of the high-class variety. There was some comfort in that.

I convinced myself that Uncle Hector had some sort of petty grudge against Father, perhaps no more than that he'd married Mother, and had spun the name-changing story out of all proportion.

And if someone was going to shoot me on account of such a piddling thing as a first name — a first name, I might add, that I had worn perfectly well up until last night — then let him pull the trigger.

So there.

And when you got right down to it, I had nowhere else to go. Uncle Hector's enterprises had landed squarely in my lap, and I intended to do as best as I could by them. I steeled myself to living in this insane asylum — although firmly in the role of keeper, not inmate — and see it through.

But now, as I sat in his office surrounded by all the paraphernalia I hadn't noticed the afternoon before — among them a collection of brass elephants and another of assorted rocks and minerals — I branded Uncle Hector with the immutable title of collector gone mad.

As I said, his books, to put in bluntly, were a catastrophe. More than half the time, in the place of numbers, he had entered arcane symbols or a little series of dots, or even tiny pictures of birds or reptiles or cacti. Sometimes they'd be all jumbled together, so that a line might read "7-duck-4-lizard-dot-dot-dot-snake." I could make neither heads nor tails of it. So desperate was I that I even tried turning the books to a mirror, a trick I'd gleaned from one of Clive's auxiliary accumulation of mystery books.

It didn't help.

The ledgers for the mines were in much the same shape as those for Hanratty's, although they were far slimmer. I couldn't make sense of them, either. Nobody could have, except perhaps Uncle Hector, and I had my doubts about that.

I had no idea where we stood on anything. I searched through the desk drawers and turned up nothing more interesting than a stack of receipts for whiskey, beer, and bar supplies, another stack for foodstuffs, and one that was a jumble of bills marked PAID for everything from lamp oil to French letters to quicksilver to silk stockings.

Uncle Hector might have been as mad as a hatter, but at least he was a prompt-paying madman. I'd give him that.

I called for Willie, who after some difficulty helped me locate the combination to the wall safe. Inside it, I found a few things of note. The deed to Hanratty's and the land upon which it stood, for one thing. It appeared to be free of encumbrances, and for this, I was grateful.

An envelope disclosed the deeds to the three mines Belle had mentioned: the sole proprietorship in the Aztec Princess and the Lucky Seven, and half ownership in the Two Bit, the other half being owned by someone named Lop Ear Tommy Cleveland.

The records for each girl were in there, too, plus those for Ma and the bartenders. These, thankfully, were much more straightforward than the books for the saloon, being written entirely with actual numbers, and in English instead of hieroglyphs. There was a page for each girl: how much she had taken in on a day-by-day basis, and what she had been paid.

There seemed to be a great deal of money in whoremongering.

But the most interesting thing I found inside the safe was contained in a very small but exceedingly heavy cardboard box. It was another stone, but not like the collection of rocks and minerals displayed on the desk and side tables.

I gasped, I think. At least, I sat down hard in Uncle Hector's chair.

It was an igneous rock, seemingly chiseled

fresh from the earth. I remembered that much — the igneous part, I mean — from Mr. Case's geology class. The thing was roughly square, and on two sharply cleaved sides, it showed pale milky quartz tinged with pink. That wasn't the thing that had me sitting on the edge of my chair though, for right in the middle of that quartz, there was a thick vein of gold.

At least, I was fairly certain it was gold. I could have kicked myself for not paying more attention in class! The whole of the stone — from the rough rock exterior covering most of it to the quartz with its astonishing contents — was smaller than a hen's egg, yet far heavier than it should have been.

Gold was heavy, wasn't it? But then, perhaps fool's gold was, too. Mr. Case had shown us some of that — pyrite, I think it was called — but that had been in shiny little metal crystals, and this certainly was neither shiny nor crystalized. It looked as if it had been poured into a channel in the rock millions of years ago, when the earth was new and the rock was molten.

Trembling, I slapped my pockets until I found my penknife. Afraid to set the stone down lest it should vanish into thin air, I managed to pry open the knife with my teeth and press the blade, hard, into the precious metal.

It left a small dent.

I dropped my knife to the desk and hugged that rock to my heart for a period of perhaps fifteen seconds, until reality took hold of me. It was gold, all right, but hardly a monumental sum.

But why had Uncle Hector locked it away instead of displaying it with his other rocks and minerals? After all, there was a chunk of milky quartz eight times the size of this sitting right in front of me. That one contained black streaks of raw silver, a large protrusion of which had been worked and polished to a sheen. Uncle Hector had been using it for a paperweight.

"Snoopin'? You been busy."

I looked up to see Cole standing in the doorway, and for moment I felt horribly guilty. But then I remembered who I was, sat up a little straighter, and said, "I'd hardly call it snooping, sir."

"Knock that 'sir' shit off, kid," he said, and slouched down in the chair I'd sat in while Belle told me about Uncle Hector's death. Cole glanced at the open safe, then the empty box, and then nodded toward my hands, which still clutched the ore to my vest. "Found it, huh?"

I tilted my head. "Found what? And I'd

appreciate it if you'd stop calling me 'kid.' Horace will do, thank you."

He ignored all but my first sentence, replying, "Heck's gold." When I didn't answer, he grunted and added, "Jesus. You can stop hidin' it. I seen it before."

"Seen what before?" said a voice from the hall. Belle stepped into the doorway. She grinned, and I believe I sighed. My thoughts of her, it seemed, were stern only when she wasn't in my presence.

But Cole kept his eyes leveled on me and said, "Go away, honey. Me and the kid got things to talk over."

He was really beginning to irritate me. I began, "I told you before, please don't call me —"

"Sure, sugar," interrupted Belle. "You eat, darlin'?" she asked me with a bat of her lashes.

"Thank you, yes," I replied. "Willie was kind enough to —"

"What you got there?" she interrupted, pointing to my clasped hands.

"Get, Belle," Cole snapped. "Now."

That pretty smile turned into a prettier scowl. "You're 'bout as fun as a singed wolverine this mornin', Cole," she grumbled as she pulled the door closed between us, then slammed it the last two inches. The etched glass in the door rattled.

Cole, who had not taken his eyes from mine during the entire conversation, parroted, "Sir and ma'am, please and thank you." He was not smiling. "You're just about too goddamn polite to live — you know that?"

"And you, sir, are becoming an annoyance," I said sternly.

I had never in my life spoken to a grown person in this manner, and the moment the words left my lips I was torn between apologizing and crowing.

Oddly enough, Cole didn't seem to notice the difference. "You tryin' to push that rock out the other side of you?"

I realized I was still clutching the ore to my chest, and reluctantly set it on the desk. I pointed at it. "You say you've seen this before?" I asked, arrogance fairly dripping from my voice. "Is it your habit to go through my uncle's safe?"

"You know where it came from, boy?"

"The safe, of course!" The man was an idiot.

He leaned back in his chair, rolled his eyes, and said, "Fine. Never mind. But I'd put it back in there if I was you. Won't pay none to flash it around."

As much as I would have liked to leave it

out, if for no other reason than to vex him, I snatched up the rock, put it back in its little cardboard box, and returned it to the safe.

"Happy?" I asked.

"Overjoyed," he said dryly, and yawned. "Can't you tell? See you been goin' through Heck's books. You make anything outta them pig squiggles?"

"No," I said, sitting down again. It did no good to get angry at a man who didn't seem to care. Or even notice. I made a conscious effort to tamp down my irritation. And also, to glean what information I could from him. "I haven't a clue."

"Same here. Ol' Heck was real secretive 'bout his books and things."

"So it would seem." I hadn't yet come across anything to tell me whether I was about to sink to the bottom of the financial sea or not. The filing cabinets might hold something, but there were four of them with four drawers each. Daunting, at best. I'd be looking until Christmas, and even then, I'd likely find nothing more than what Cole called Uncle Hector's pig squiggles.

But Cole had obviously seen the books, even looked in the safe. It occurred to me, somewhat belatedly, that Cole might know how Uncle Hector had been financially fixed.

A slight hitch in my voice, I began, "Would you know . . . is there a bank account?" I had come across nothing that even vaguely resembled a bankbook.

"Sure," he said, with no hesitation. "Two of 'em. Doubt if there's more than a hundred bucks betwixt 'em, though. Heck pumped near everything he had into the mines. Well, just the one, lately. Mines're awful pricey hobbies, kid, and they sucked every penny out of Hanratty's. More'n once he's had to ask your daddy for a stake."

"Pardon?"

"Money to get a new one up and runnin'."

"Oh, marvelous," I said with what I am afraid was a little wail, and dropped my head into my hands. Uncle Hector was broke and dead, Father was in the same condition, and I was halfway there. At least I was keeping with family tradition.

But then it occurred to me that by itself, without the drain of Uncle Hector's hobbies and eccentricities, Hanratty's might do quite splendidly. It didn't appear to be in debt. At least Uncle Hector had died solvent — technically speaking, at any rate. That was more than I could say for Father. And as to the moral dilemma of renting out scantily clad soiled doves by the hour, well,

73

I'd deal with that later.

"These mines of Uncle Hector's," I said, slowly raising my head until I met Cole's eyes once again. "Are these other two — the Aztec Princess and the Two Bit, I mean — worth anything? The land?"

Cole shrugged. He had lit a cigarette, and it dangled from one corner of his mouth.

"I should like to inspect them."

He stared at me with no change of expression.

Well, he likely wouldn't be pleasant company, but he was the best that was handy, and I was in a hurry. I swallowed my pride completely. "Would you . . . would you consider accompanying me?"

Slowly, he sat forward and took the cigarette from his lips. "All you had to do was ask, kid."

He rose, ground his smoke out on Uncle Hector's polished floor — my floor — and said, "Well, we'd best get you outfitted. It's a long ride. And you'd damn well better not be as tender as you look."

We made a stop at the bank, and I learned with some satisfaction that Cole had been wrong about the money. There was more than a paltry hundred dollars in Uncle Hector's accounts. There was a total of two hundred and twenty-four dollars and thirty-seven cents, to be exact.

However, since the Lucky Seven mine also had access to the business account — and since Cole told me that it had been producing barely enough copper to break even — I left those funds alone. I instructed Willie and Belle to deposit all profits from Hanratty's into that account, also. They were still digging Uncle Hector out of the Lucky Seven, after all, and I had a feeling that the exhumation would prove expensive.

I just hoped they were digging up a little copper while they were at it.

I took fifteen dollars from Uncle Hector's personal account. This, when added to the last of my travel money and a portion of the petty cash from the till at Hanratty's, was enough to outfit me for ten days' worth of roughing it on the open plain, and leave twelve dollars cash in my pocket.

When we left the mercantile, loaded with gear, I was wearing a brand-new Colt Peacemaker on my hip. Cole had insisted I'd need it, and despite the fact that it cost me dear, I didn't need much coaxing before it topped my pile of purchases.

Oh, it was a beautiful thing, a precision instrument! It wasn't so fancy as Cole's pearly eagle butts, but it was heavy and solid and shiny and quite deadly-looking, with ornate etchings on the barrel and ebony grips. Cole loaded it with five cartridges, firmly instructing me to keep the hammer on the empty chamber.

"Be just like a greenhorn to shoot off his own damn knee," he grumbled.

We dropped my purchases off at Hanratty's, which was by this time open for business. There was a fight going on in the back corner, near the stage. I started to move toward it — to do exactly what, I had no idea — but Cole caught my shoulder.

"It's just them Fisk brothers again," he said, as one cracked a bottle over the other's head. The bottle broke and the crackee staggered, but didn't go down. "Willie'll see it don't get too serious."

It looked pretty serious to me already. There was quite a bit of blood involved, at any rate, but nobody seemed terribly upset, save the two combatants. To the sound of the man with the bleeding head breaking a chair over his brother's back, Cole and I left Hanratty's and made our way to the livery stable.

This was more for Cole's benefit than mine, because he bought a horse. I soon learned, to my great delight, that I already had one — another hand-me-down from

Uncle Hector — and I fussed over him while Cole dickered with a couple of mustachioed horse traders.

Tellurium was my mount's name, and he was a sleek gray gelding, well conformed and roughly fifteen hands, with a silvery sheen to his dappled coat. He had a black mane and tail, making him very flashy, I thought, with clean, sound limbs, and large, well-spaced eyes, which gave every indication of a gentle nature.

When I asked Cole what the horse's name meant, thinking it might be the name of a local politician or a Western hero of some sort, he shrugged. "Some kinda rock, I think."

Leave it to Uncle Hector. I considered myself lucky that he hadn't trained the horse to commands in Aramaic or ancient Sumarian. Then it occurred to me that he might have done just that, so I took hold of Tellurium's halter and said, "Back, Tellurium, back."

He backed up a few steps, and I said, "Good fellow."

Tellurium proved a mouthful inside five minutes, however. I straightened his forelock, ran my hands over his neck and withers, and said, "I shall call you Tell, then. What do you say to that?"

He snorted softly. I took it for a yes.

I will admit something to you. When I saw that horse and learned he was mine, all mine to keep, my eyes flooded with tears until I had to turn away so Cole couldn't see.

My mount at Tattinger's, Cavalier, had been just a stable horse, true, but I had been terribly fond of him. I'd ridden him exclusively since I'd first enrolled, and out of all the things I missed about school, I think I missed him the most. When Tell rubbed his broad forehead against me, then lipped at my pockets, looking for carrots or sugar, it was the first true sense of "home" that I'd had.

"You and me, Tell," I whispered to him in that stall. "Us, forever." I meant it, too.

Cole argued with the traders for over an hour, and finally settled on a handsome dark bay gelding named Ranger, with two white socks behind, and a snip and a star. I thought this was strange. Not the horse, mind, but that Cole had to buy him at all.

When I asked why he was purchasing Ranger — I thought that every Westerner owned a mount, for goodness' sake! — he scowled at me and said, "Why you figure I come back to town on the damn stage, boy, with my saddle and gear tied up top? Some yellow bastard shot the sonofabitch out from under me."

"What?" I asked, shocked to my soul that anyone would shoot a horse for no reason, let alone while a man was riding him! "When?"

"When I was up seein' about Heck," he snapped and led Ranger out to the paddock, effectively halting the conversation.

5

We rode out of Tonto's Wickiup early the next morning, after a tearful farewell from Belle — which I admit was delivered entirely to Cole, not me — and after Ma wordlessly shoved a parcel at me, then stomped back inside.

"Give it here," Cole said gruffly as he snatched it away and tucked it into his bulging saddlebag.

"Who *is* that woman?" I asked as we jogged south, down the ragged main street and out of town. I was having some trouble with my stirrups.

"Shorten your leathers a notch" was all he said.

We were past the fringes of town before I got my stirrups even — a clumsy thing to attempt when you're trying to ride at the same time — and by that time I had forgotten all about Ma. I was full of youthful fervor about the journey. The thought of rattlesnakes and the like — not to mention the realities of camping in the wilderness — cast a bit of a pall over the proceedings, but were not enough to dampen my spirits.

I would see this country firsthand, and not just from the enclosure of a speeding stagecoach or train. I would inspect the mines, and then I would sell them to the highest bidder. I would have quite a tale to tell Clive Barrow, who I hadn't got around to writing yet.

Additionally, this would be my first true step toward taking charge, toward actually doing something that would affect my own future. Having been thrust into a grown-up world, I intended to make the most of it.

I wished I had slept better the night before, though. Between my anxiety over the trip and the noise from downstairs, I managed to get a total of two and a half hours before Cole came banging on my door at five. I was running on nerves and Ma's coffee, of which I had downed three strong cups.

However, I was not so enthusiastic about Cole's company as I was about my new gun, or my new hat, or my new leather chaps. He had done little but grouse and complain — or worse, kept irritatingly silent — for the whole of the time we were making our purchases. Frankly, I was torn between admiration for the man and wanting to throttle him.

He was certainly well-versed in the ways of the wild country, or at least seemed to be. I didn't really know that I was one to judge. But I watched him carefully, and as I rode along behind him, I gave wide berth to the same cacti he did, aped the low tilt of his hat, and watched the way that the top and bottom halves of his body seemed to move independently of each other. It was entirely graceful, and I tried to emulate it. His was a far different equestrian posture than I had been taught, and it took a while to get the hang of it, but it seemed, well, more comfortable.

I daresay my riding master at Tattinger's would have given me a stern dressing down if he had seen me, though.

We stopped every so often to rest and water the horses, and I soon saw why Cole had insisted we bring along so much water. Our horses were loaded with the stuff, both in canteens and large canvas bags, which sweated and dripped continuously and kept both my knees damp.

Most of the time, we kept to a walk or a very slow trot to which I didn't have to post — and which Cole, in a rather derisive tone, was quick to inform me was called a "jog" — mainly on account of the water's extra weight.

Cole said very little to me, either while we rode or when we stopped. I noticed that he glanced me over at each rest, as if he were looking for a weakness of some sort that he could exploit, but he rarely said more than "Loosen your girth, kid" or "Hand me that jerky."

I was too goggle-eyed at the scenery and too thirsty to instigate further conversation.

Now about the jerky. This was a food I'd never seen before, and once I tasted it, I hoped never to see it again. It was meat, or so they claimed — dry, tough, relentlessly chewy, and for the most part tasteless. I finally broke down and asked, "How the devil do they make this wretched foodstuff?"

He said, with a perfectly straight face, "They butcher a goat and nail it to a tin roof for a week." And then he studied for a moment on the chunk he was eating, said, "Maggot," and plucked off a little piece of something.

I felt the last swallow of water I'd taken rising up my throat, but managed to hold it back. I dropped the jerky I'd been gnawing into the low scrub behind my back, though. Maggots! I grabbed my canteen and downed half of it, just to get the imagined taste of filthy carrion bugs out of my mouth.

Cole smiled a little too smugly and said, "Cinch him up again, Tate. Daylight's wastin'."

"Don't call me Tate," I growled as I tightened Tell's girth. It was the second time that day he'd called me by that name.

He swung a leg over Ranger. "All right, Donovan," he said, and started out again.

Honestly, I wanted to punch him for calling me that. I would have if he hadn't been far ahead by the time I mounted Tell, and I might have gotten in one or two good swings before he flattened me. After all, I'd been on the boxing team at Tattinger's until I turned all knees and elbows. I wasn't sure exactly how much credence Cole would put into the Marquis of Queensbury rules, though.

Shadows were growing long, there was a pinkish cast to the horizon, and my backside felt like a well-pounded steak. The first all-day stint in the saddle is rough on the most seasoned rider, even when he has a fine, soft-gaited mount, such as my Tell.

I'd had my fill of endless vistas, soaring eagles and hawks, darting quail, and skulking coyotes for the day, and for the past half hour, I had been half-expecting — no, actually praying a little — that Cole would call a halt to the proceedings. So when he reined in Ranger and sat there for a moment, waiting for me to catch him up, I breathed a small sigh of relief. I wanted nothing more than to stand on solid ground again, and I wanted to stand on it for a good deal longer than fifteen or twenty minutes.

But once I rode up beside him, he turned to me and said, "You're pretty fair on the mosey, kid. I'll give you that. Let's see what you can really do."

And with that, he dug his heels into Ranger and sped away.

I was so surprised that it took me a second or two to realize that I was supposed to follow him, that this was some kind of idiot frontier test. My Tell was game and eager for the chase though. He half-reared, I gave him his head, and we thundered after.

We were gaining on Cole before I knew it! Out of habit, I crouched low on Tell's neck, moving my weight forward over his withers, balancing in stirrups that still felt too long. All my reservations vanished in a twinkling, though.

Tell's dark mane slapped at my face. The wind pushed at my hat and I held it on with one hand. It was like flying, and I was laughing, actually laughing!

I saw Cole briefly turn to see if I was still following. I think he was surprised that I'd gained at least four lengths on him, and was at that moment within two of him. He cut to the left, around a thick clump of cactus, and barreled straight toward what appeared to be a sharp drop-off.

I was enjoying myself too much to stop, let alone question his path. As nimble as a rabbit, Tell followed him around the cactus, across the flat, and then down the incline. It was a perilous slope, and I was on it and sliding down before I knew it. The instant that Tell started down, I clenched my teeth, tightened my reins so that I had contact with his mouth, and prayed that he'd make it to the bottom without killing us both.

But oh, he was nimble!

Skidding and hopping in a manner that would have been the end of any rangy prep school hunter, we reached the bottom after what felt like five minutes — but was probably only a few seconds — to find Cole waiting for us with a smirk on his face.

I rode up to him, anger having replaced my previous exhilaration, and shouted, "Are you crazy? You could have killed us!" I jumped off Tell to check his legs for cuts. That slope had been rocky.

I found no abrasions, thank God.

"You did good, kid," Cole said calmly. "Guess they taught you how to ride back east, after all."

I stuck my foot back in Tell's stirrup. "You thought I'd lie to you?" I huffed in irate disbelief. "If you were going to put me through some kind of moronic test, why didn't you do it earlier, when the horses were fresh?"

"Too much water weight," he said, without a change in expression. "They drunk almost half of it by now." He reined Ranger away and started down the draw I had just realized we were in.

I rode up beside him. "Cole, I don't think I like you very much at the moment." I scraped sweat off Tell's pale silver neck with the flat of my hand, then flicked it to the ground.

"You don't gotta like me, kid. I'm doin' this mine thing for Heck. And I done that" — he pointed over his shoulder, toward the path our free-for-all race had taken — "to find out just what kind of pluck you had."

"Pluck? *Pluck?* You nearly killed my horse — not to mention me — to find out if I had pluck? Are you mad, sir?"

"Been accused of worse," he said. "And I'da only killed you. That horse you're ridin' is one tough old brush popper." He rode on.

Once the horses had cooled out, the sunset had nearly passed, and the sky had gone to deep purple tinged with orange, Cole finally stopped and we made camp.

I had expected a roaring fire and a cozy tent, but instead I got a feeble blaze just big enough to heat coffee. That, and a blanket on the ground. We took care of the horses and I got my bedding laid out, all in silence, and then Cole tossed me my rope. I caught it and stood there, staring at him.

"Ring your pallet, Donovan," he said.

I had halfway calmed down from that impromptu race, but this stoked my fires again. "If you don't stop calling me that, I will have to take measures, sir!"

"I'll think about it, soon as you stop callin' me sir. Now ring your bed with that rope."

"Why?"

"Snakes."

I think I sucked in a good bit of air. "Snakes?" I asked weakly, and immediately looked down at my feet and the ground around me. Would snakes be brave enough to venture so near the fire?

Cole wasn't watching me, though. He was spreading a loop around his own sleeping place.

Quite conversationally, he said, "Now some fellers say the little hairs on the rope tickles their bellies, and they don't like that. Some'll tell you the rattlers think it's another snake, and that's why they don't cross. Me?" he said, straightening up again. "I just figure whatever works works."

I got busy with my rope.

For our dinner, we delved into Ma's mystery package. There was an entire chicken, cut up and fried, which was delicious, plus hard-boiled eggs — enough to last for several days — and a few small, wizened oranges. Shriveled or not, these last were a real delicacy after a day in the heat. I don't believe that I had ever sweated so much — or downed so much water — in one day.

While we ate, I pondered how in the world to broach the subject that I'd been trying, to no avail, to open with Cole. Namely, why he believed Uncle Hector might have met with foul play. This was more difficult than you might suspect, because I'd overheard the conversation, and a gentleman never admits to eavesdropping.

Well, to put a finer point on it, a gentleman never eavesdrops in the first place.

But in the end, I didn't ask, not that night.

It seemed so complicated, and I was so bleary-eyed and weary — and yes, sore — that the moment I swallowed the last of my second orange I fell asleep, still clutching the peel in my fingers.

"We're here," Cole announced.

It was roughly two o'clock in the afternoon, and as far as I could tell, we were in the middle of nowhere. Low, rocky, gravelly hills had replaced the flatland of yesterday, and the vegetation, while sparser, was no more interesting.

The only things to set this landscape off from what we'd been riding through for the past four or five hours were a couple of widely spaced pits, for lack of a better term, each only a few feet across.

I couldn't tell how deep they went, but I thought they were awfully big for animal dwellings. An army of badgers, all denned together? A vast family of coyotes?

"We're where, exactly?" I asked, craning my head back and forth, and hoped that a phalanx of mountain lions wouldn't suddenly emerge from one of those holes and come barreling toward us, fangs bared.

He stepped down from Ranger, then took off his hat and wiped his brow on the back of his sleeve. "Aztec Princess," he said as he led the horse away from me.

"Where?" I repeated. I stood up in my stirrups, but there was still no sign announcing that this was the Aztec Princess, not even a remnant of one. No miners' quarters, no stamping mill. No mine, period.

I gave Tell a little nudge with my knees, and rode up beside Cole, who had pulled down his last water bag but was still on foot, leading Ranger.

"Would you care to explain yourself, sir?" I asked, trying not to sound too huffy.

He stopped and looked up at me. "I'd get off that nag if I was you, Donovan."

I opened my mouth to say something utterly cutting, but before I could, he added, "They tunneled too close to the surface in more'n a few places. Best spread out your weight and the horse's lest you find another and fall through." He pointed toward a pit to my left, and repeated, "Get down. Now."

I still hadn't seen any mine shaft, but Cole sounded serious and I grudgingly dismounted. He snagged Tell's reins from my hands and nodded toward the pit. "Go and take a look if you don't believe me."

"Fine," I said. "I shall. And don't call me Donovan."

He grunted and led the horses off, toward the feeble shade.

I grunted right back at him, although I doubt that he heard me, and set out to have a look in this pit of his, thinking that if something fanged or clawed or hoofed boiled up out of it and attacked me, I would take my chances and try to thrash Cole.

Provided I survived the animal onslaught, of course.

But when I reached its edge, all my tenuous bravado fled. There, perhaps twenty feet below, was what remained of a wagon. And worse, the remains of a horse. Nothing but bones, harness fragments, rusted rims and broken wheels, and timbers all jumbled together like a jigsaw puzzle waiting to be worked.

I swallowed, hard.

The hapless creature had fallen through the roof of a tunnel, all right, wagon and all. The north end of the pit was blocked with debris, but I could just glimpse the opening that went south. Something alive scuttled beneath the skeleton's rib cage.

"Get back from the edge, you horse's butt!" Cole shouted.

I jumped back just as a little spray of gravel, right where my boot had been, sifted over the rim and spattered the bones below.

For once, I didn't correct Cole. I probably was a horse's butt.

Walking carefully, I joined him. He had already unsaddled Ranger, and was sitting in the shade at the base of yet another of those seemingly endless low hills, rolling himself a smoke.

"Is this safe?" I asked. My eyes were darting every which way, looking for shifting earth.

Cole snorted. "If you mean, are there any tunnels under us? No."

"There was a horse down there."

"Mule, actually. They got the other three out without a scratch." When I stared at him, he shrugged and added, "Heck liked to tell about it. Over and goddamn over again."

I shifted from foot to foot. "This is very interesting, I'm sure, but would you mind telling me where the mine is? The entrance, I mean."

He thumbed back his hat. "You're standin' thirty feet from it."

"Where?"

"There," he said, and pointed with the hand that held his tobacco pouch.

Even when my eye was directed to it, it took a second to see the thing: an opening in the hillside, low and camouflaged with planks the same dusty color as the clay and gravel of the ground. Also, a bush of some sort had grown up in front of it, so I think I can be excused.

"Ah," I said.

"Ah, indeed," said Cole, lighting his cigarette.

I scowled at him, although being busy with his smoke and match, he didn't see me. Was there ever a more maddening man?

"Well?" I asked.

He tossed his match to the ground. "Well, we're here. Do what you want. I ain't goin' nowhere." He drew deeply on his cigarette, and exhaled a yellowish plume. "If you're smart, you'll take yourself a little siesta." He leaned back, propping himself on an elbow, and proceeded to ignore me.

I should have hired somebody in town, I thought as I stripped Tell of his tack. I should have hired a complete stranger. At least he would have been civil, if only to get his pay.

That stranger would have called me Horace — no, Mr. Smith! He would have warned me about that jumping cholla I'd ridden too close to earlier in the morning. Oh, Cole had said something about it, but only when I was mumbling curses and picking spines out of Tell's legs.

By the time I'd given Tell a drink and put his hobbles on, Cole had finished his smoke and was flat on his back on the ground, his hat pulled low over his eyes.

So much for you, I thought. I pulled a candle and matches from my pack, stuffed the gloves Cole had made me buy in a back pocket, and set off toward the mine entrance.

But when I got there, I didn't immediately start ripping down boards. Something caught my eye, something about forty yards to the west.

The weather had muted their color and half-covered their forms in sand and grit, but I could see a few broken boards peeking from the brush. And beside them, jutting up behind a clump of brush and perhaps twenty feet away, there was a rusted pump handle.

Long ago, someone had dug a well, and there might even have been a building. Still, it didn't bode the best for me. I hardly thought there would be resale money in this property. No one in his right mind would want to live here, and I couldn't see that there had been decent grazing for even one lonely steer in the last five miles we'd traveled.

Oh, well. As long as we were here.

The place had been boarded up chockablock. Raw planks were nailed willy-nilly to other planks, so that the thing resembled something organic rather than man-made. It took me a moment to figure out where to start.

Glumly, I settled on a board, tugged on my gloves, and prepared to pry. The plank came away easily, the wood being brittle and the nails nearly rusted through. The second came just as readily, and the third, but I had trouble with the fourth. Upon closer inspection, I saw why.

New nails, still shiny once the dust was brushed away, secured it. The board was new, too. I frowned. Someone had entered the Aztec Princess, and quite recently. Several new pieces of lumber were tacked over the lower-right-hand part of the opening, in fact, and the bush that covered them appeared to have been transplanted there.

None too well, either, for it was dying. When I moved the lower branches away, the ground directly below it showed the marks where boots had stomped mud that had dried hard and brittle.

Curious.

I thought about calling for Cole, but a quick look showed him still stretched out and breathing deeply. I'd do this on my own.

I worked to the left, ripping down jury-rigged older planks, and soon opened a hole big enough to climb through.

I took the candle from my back pocket, lit it, and stepped inside.

6

The Aztec Princess wasn't exactly the best place to be alone.

Within five minutes of creeping along the disused main shaft — littered with fallen rock, webbed here and there by spiders spinning up fat roaches and crickets — I found myself wanting company, any company. Even Cole's. But pride can be strong in a young man, especially a foolish one, so I girded my loins and kept on.

To tell the truth, I really had no idea what I was looking for. Oh, silver, I suppose, but how would I be able to spot silver ore? Men far more seasoned than I had claimed to have mined it all and gone home. Within ten minutes, I had talked myself into believing I was on a fool's errand — which, in fact, I was. Cole, asleep up there in the purple shade, had known it all along.

I was angry at him for riding out here with me and thus fueling my hopes, angry at myself for thinking I might find something of value. The land was completely worthless. Any fool could see that.

I'd probably have to pay someone to take it off my hands.

But at this point, my fears — despite the spiders, the scurrying lizards, the squeaking rodents just beyond the range of my candle's light, and my intermittent "collywobbles," as Clive Barrow used to quip — my excursion had taken on something of a heady quality. There was something to be said for exploring, and a small thrill in discovery, even if you only found the occasional rusted chisel.

Within a half hour the whole business was beginning to pale, however, and I was wondering if I wasn't lost. I was about to turn and retrace my steps — or at least, I certainly hoped to — when I saw light up ahead, dusty and dim. Could I have come all the way back to the entrance and not noticed? I hardly thought so, even though I had lost all sense of direction and there had been several turns and twists and an abundance of side tunnels.

But I crept forward, closer to the light, holding my candle at an angle so the wax wouldn't drip on my hand. I had a wrist- and cuff-full already.

The light wasn't the entrance. It was another of those caved-in places. Not the one I'd peered into from above, for this one was far deeper than the first, being a good twenty-five feet from the top of the cave-in debris to the surface.

Also, it contained no mule's skeleton, only the remains of a freight wagon, half covered with detritus.

I was standing well back in the tunnel, puzzling over how in the world they ever got the mules out, when something stirred in the rubble. Something big.

Gooseflesh raced up my spine, and I took a step back. My candle shook.

"W-who's there?" I asked, like an idiot.

At the sound of my voice, amplified by the shaft, a dusty board exploded upward with a shower of dust motes. Something screamed.

I bolted.

I ran hard and fast back up the shaft, my heart pounding louder than my bootsteps, barely retaining the presence of mind to shield my candle's flame as I pounded onward. I wasn't sure that the screeching thing was still coming, but I didn't want to waste even a split second looking over my shoulder.

And in my rush to escape that which I was

convinced was a mountain lion, possibly several, I took a wrong turn. I tripped headlong over an old barrel and straight into a muddy wall, and knocked myself unconscious.

"Don't move, kid" was the next thing I heard. It was Cole's voice, couched in a whisper. "Don't twitch so much as a finger — you hear me?"

My head ached, there was something poking me in the back, and my arm was twisted beneath me at a most uncomfortable angle. I croaked out, "Whyever not?"

Immediately, there was a new sound, much too close. A sound like steam exiting a pipe under pressure.

"Don't talk, dammit," Cole hissed.

I opened my eyes. I could see Cole now, standing a few feet away. He held a flickering candle in one hand and his rifle in the other. "Don't even think about takin' a deep breath. You've got a rattler roostin' on your belly."

I gasped — I think anyone would have — and the hissing sound increased in volume. I cannot describe the fear that coursed through me, save to say that my bladder instantly emptied of its own accord, and the hand beneath my body tightened into a fist.

I held still, though.

I have said that I was lying in an awkward position, but when I got up the nerve to look down my nose, I could just see the top coil of the snake and his head above it. I could feel his weight then, too, shifting heavy and sinuous upon my shirt and trousers. Cole waved the tip of his rifle near the snake's face, and when it shifted position and struck at the barrel, I nearly screamed.

"Don't," Cole warned through clenched teeth.

He was lucky I wasn't vomiting.

Cole waved the rifle again. I saw the candle's flame glint off the end of it just before the snake actually found his target. The rattler's strike was like lightning, and it clung to the tip of the rifle's barrel for perhaps a second before it let go. The thing immediately recoiled on my belly, ready for the next onslaught.

Cole took a step back, muttered, "Shit," and turned the rifle's barrel toward him. He studied it in the light of his candle. *What are you doing?* I wanted to shout. *Checking the blasted metal for damage?*

"Lookin' for venom," he said quietly, as if he were reading my thoughts. Or at least, part of them. "Can't shoot him without bringin' the roof down on us or blastin' a hole through you. Mayhap I can milk the poison out of him. Got a few drops that last time."

On the edge of hysterics, I thought, *Oh, marvelous. Just champion.*

If the serpent bit me, perhaps I wouldn't completely die. Perhaps I'd just have convulsions, run a fever of a hundred ten, permanently lose my mental capacities, and spend the rest of my life drooling quietly in some asylum.

How comforting.

Cole set his feet and swung the rifle out once more, teasing until, with a sudden, nauseating flex of muscle, the beast struck again.

This time, he didn't wait for the snake to release. In a split second he jerked the rifle to the side and up, taking the snake partway with it until its fangs slid off the metal. Then, almost faster than I could see, nearly as fast as the snake had struck, he flipped the rifle about and brought the stock of it down on the snake, close to the beast's head, to pin it against the wall. Quickly, he set the candle on a barrel, trading it for a good-sized rock I hadn't known he'd had in his pocket, and brought it down savagely on the snake's head.

I lay there, too terrified to move, while he bent over and picked up the still-writhing body. He stood for a moment, holding it out, and then he said, "Big one. Been eatin' fat ol' mine rats for a good long time. You know, you didn't have to go to all this fuss just to rustle us up some grub, kid."

For all I had wanted to say before, I found myself wordless, with only a sour taste in my mouth.

He leaned his rifle carefully on the keg that held his candle, and held down his hand. The one without the snake in it, I mean. It had only just stopped rattling.

"Anything busted?" he asked as he helped me up. "Besides your bladder, that is."

Heat raced up my neck. "No, sir," I said in a cracked voice. I was careful to stand on the other side of him, away from that wretched snake. The horrid thing was still twitching. "How long have I been . . . I mean, how long . . . ?"

"Been lookin' for you for 'bout a half hour," he said without meeting my eyes. "It's nigh on five."

"Five?" I said. It couldn't have been three when I first entered the mine. I had spent some time walking, but I must have been unconscious for better than two hours. *You never do anything by halves, do you, Horace?*

I thought.

"Here," he said, and thrust that filthy snake at me. "Hold this. You're damn lucky he didn't set up shop inside your pants leg."

I held the snake for perhaps two seconds, and then it twitched in a great spasm, coiling over my wrist. I dropped it to the ground, bloody and squashed head first, as a wave of nausea swept through me.

Cole wasn't paying the slightest bit of attention, though. He had moved forward to stand where I'd been lying. I now saw that we were in a dead-ended tunnel, perhaps no more than eight feet in length. By the looks of the debris that had been cast into it — empty crates, a few rusted shovels, the empty powder keg I'd tripped over plus several more, and so on — it had been the storage closet of choice for the workers.

Cole was holding the candle high, staring at the wall. Water was seeping in from somewhere. It left a faint, damp sheen on the left side of the wall. I hadn't the slightest idea where it was coming from, but perhaps this was the reason the miners hadn't pursued this particular shaft any further.

The dead snake, still wriggling obscenely, bumped against my boot, and I jumped. Telling myself in no uncertain terms that it had gone to its Maker and couldn't bite me — and besides, I doubted that Cole's blow had left any fangs in its mouth, if it still had a mouth at all — I gingerly picked it up and tossed it a short distance behind me, then wiped trembling hands on my trousers.

"Can we go?" I asked. I wanted nothing more than to see the sun again. And change my pants. I also had some reservations about the advisability of standing about in a tunnel that had mountain lions prowling it.

"I think there's a wildcat or something down here," I added a tad urgently when Cole ignored me. "Maybe two or three."

But he was busy pawing at the wall. It was clay, which I thought was a bit odd, since the rest of the mine's walls had been for the most part rock. And indeed, the seeping water, in concert with Cole's glove, had sloughed away part of the mud to show the rock beneath.

More to himself than to me, Cole muttered, "What the hell?" Without turning around, he thrust his gloved and muddied hand back toward me. He said, "You see a pick anyplace?"

I scanned the ground and spied one under the old shovels. Using my foot to move the shovels aside — and to make sure there weren't any more snakes — I picked it up and handed it to him.

"Good. Now hold this and back up." He handed me his candle.

"All right, but —"

He swung the pick into the wall.

I hadn't been expecting it — the sound, I mean — and I jumped again, right onto the snake. I tripped, fell backward, and went down, all before the clang of it stopped ringing in my ears.

The light went out, too, just like that.

But I hadn't dropped the candle, thank God, and while I fumbled for my matches, Cole just kept swinging that pick.

"How can you do that with no light?" I shouted over the echoing racket. It was the darkest place I'd ever been in. I imagine it was the darkest place anyone had ever been in, outside of the grave.

He was making so much noise that he didn't hear me. I finally found my matches and gratefully lit the candle again. I chanced a quick look behind me, although I was fairly certain that any tunnel-dwelling mountain lions lurking in the shadows would have fled to Mexico by now, holding their ears.

And then the noise stopped. "Took you long enough," Cole said, but his voice had lost its usual growl. Instead, he almost sounded excited. "Gimme that candle."

Carefully, I craned myself to my feet and handed it over. Cole had cast his pick aside, and was kneeling down, looking through the rock he'd loosened. For all that banging, he hadn't loosened very much.

Then he stood up, tucked something into his pocket, and held the candle close to the wall. It looked as if he'd made a little hole, but I could see no more than that. He stood there for a good three minutes, peering and poking, while I rocked from foot to foot, my damp trousers chafing, and then he came out into the main shaft to join me.

"Grab that snake," he said.

It had finally stopped moving. I still held it far from my body, though. "What on earth do you want this filthy thing for?" I asked.

"Told you. Dinner."

I thought surely he must be teasing. Surely he only wanted its skin! He'd make a hatband of it — yes, that was it. Phillip Belvoir, back at Tattinger's, had brought one back to school with him the last term. A gift from his uncle, it had come all the way from New Mexico. It was a handsome thing — certainly handsomer off the snake than on — although Phillip had absolutely no use for it. Clive Barrow had tutored him in Latin for a whole term just so he could see it every now and then.

Perhaps I could convince Cole to give it to me or let me purchase it, and then I could send it to Clive so that he could have one of his own. Perhaps I'd even send him a hat to put it on!

"What?" I asked, alarmed when Cole nudged my arm and rocked me out of my thoughts.

"You gone deaf, boy? Let me take a look at that noggin." He felt the bump I already knew was the size of a hen's egg, shook his head, and asked, "It hurt much?"

"A little." Actually, it felt like there were a dozen angry dwarves in my skull, all trying to push their way out through the one spot.

"Well," he said, "you'll live, I reckon. Can't see as it's bleedin' much." Then he added, a bit angrily, "Christ! If you'da let that rattler get you, Belle woulda never let me hear the end of it."

I stared at him, mouth agape. If *I'd* let that rattler get me? And he just had to mention Belle, didn't he? An opportunity didn't pass but what he was reminding me that I was inferior: a kid, an Easterner, a person Belle would never be interested in.

Well, in that way.

Perhaps I was from New York, but that didn't make me inferior: things were the other way around, the way I saw it! And maybe I was only sixteen, and Belle might never see me as anything more than a boy, not even when I was all of twenty. But a man — even a boy — has a right to his dreams, doesn't he?

If any of these mental gymnastics showed on my features, Cole didn't appear to notice. He never did. He bent over, snatched my hat up from the floor, and after slapping it sharply across his thigh a few times, handed it over.

"You all right to walk?" he asked.

I nodded. I was a bit dizzy, but didn't mention it. I just wanted to get out of that mine and back into the sunshine again. And as far away from nature as possible.

"How the hell'd you knock yourself out, anyhow?" he asked as he moved ahead, leading the way up the tunnel.

"Something chased me," I replied, and took a quick look over my shoulder. Nothing but deep shadows, and the faint outlines of endless rock and intermittent timbers. At least our echoing conversation drowned out the tiny squeaks and rustles of the living things in the shadows.

When Cole didn't reply, I added, "I think it was a mountain lion."

He snorted. "No self-respectin' puma'd

get caught dead down here, kid. They like to prowl up high. Reckon you got spooked by a bat or somethin'."

Despite the embarrassment of my damp trousers and the throbbing ache in my skull, despite the reference to Belle, and the fact that I was having to consciously put one shaking foot in front of the other just to keep up, I managed to take umbrage at this. "It was not a bat, sir! It screeched at me!"

Cole paused a moment, for we had come to an intersection, then set off again, this time to the left. We were walking steadily uphill, and on top of everything else, my new boots were beginning to bring up blisters.

"Probably an owl, then, Donovan," he said at last, in a patronizing tone. "Never hearda no owls living underground, though."

He was impossible! It was plain that I was never going to win the point — or convince him to stop calling me that wretched name — so I changed the subject. At least he was talking to me. He had probably said more to me in the last ten minutes than in the whole of our acquaintance, not that this was necessarily a good thing.

Scratching my arm, I asked, "Why were you stabbing at that wall?"

He was ahead of me and I couldn't see

his face, but I believe his gait faltered, just slightly. "Thought it was funny, that's all," he said. "That rock bein' covered up with clay mud. Guess some fool was tryin' to hold back the water."

"Was that why they stopped that tunnel so short?" I had another scratch at my arm. Something must have bitten me, I thought dismally, because the itch was really beginning to become annoying. "Did they stop because of the water?"

Cole grunted as he trudged on, holding the candle before him. "Likely. If your mine floods, you're sunk. Literally. Pumps cost dear. Sometimes they cost more than the mine's worth. One of the shafts, down a couple levels deeper, is already flooded."

I realized that I was following Cole unquestioningly. I was impossibly turned around and I firmly believe, had I been left to my own devices, that I'd probably be down there to this day. But Cole — despite his many flaws, of which I could have made you a very long list — only faltered twice, and then only for the second it took him to make out our tracks on the floor of the tunnel intersections. We were back up at the surface and crawling out through the boards in less than ten minutes.

By this time, my arm was driving me mad.

Before I had walked twenty feet from the mouth of the mine, blinking into the sunlight, Cole grabbed my shoulder. "Let's see your arm, kid," he said with a look of concern.

"Wouldn't you rather go play with your snake?" I snapped, and was surprised at my own crankiness.

"Give it here," he said gruffly. He took the rattler from my grip, dropped it to the ground, and grabbed my elbow.

I gasped. Not because he'd grabbed it, but because I hadn't looked at my own arm until that second. On the inside of my forearm, where the flesh is tender, there was a huge, flattish red welt that itched and throbbed — more so, once I'd had a good look at it. Additionally, the arm felt heavy and achy now, more with each passing moment.

Cole reached toward my face, and I ducked backward.

"What?" he demanded. "I ain't gonna hit you, kid."

"Sorry," I mumbled, and stood still while he held the back of his hand to my pounding forehead.

With a shake of his head, he dropped his hand. "Hot, all right. You feelin' feverish?"

Actually, I was. I nodded.

"Well, you sure been through the wringer today, boy. That's a black widow bite you got, there. Looks like she's took hold, too."

He studied my arm again, poked at a little pit that had formed in the center of that angry welt and was oozing clear fluid. For my part, I never wanted to see the Aztec Princess again. I wanted to tuck my tail and go directly to my nice, quiet whorehouse and crawl into that nightmarish bed and pull the covers over my face until I was twenty-one. Possibly thirty.

Cole let go of my arm. "Ain't surprised," he said. "There was a whole lot of webbin' back where you knocked yourself out. Best change your britches and get settled in while you can."

"While I can?" I nearly shrieked, even as I scratched frantically at my arm. "What do you mean, while I can?"

Visions of Muskrat Hutchins's testicle-biting black widows raced through my mind. He'd said that I'd swell up like an eggplant or a melon or something, and then . . .

I swallowed. "Am I . . . am I going to die?"

Cole bent to retrieve the snake. It appeared quite a bit the worse for wear. At least, it was missing quite a few scales. I knew just how it felt.

As he rose up again, Cole said, "Oh, probably not."

"*Probably?*"

He looked at me. "You ain't dead yet, are you?"

Numbly, I shook my head.

"Them spiders hit different folks different ways," he said, as if he begrudged the time it took to get the words out. "Some, it don't bother a whit. Some folks swell up and go half-crazy. Every once in a coon's age, somebody dies. But you're still walkin', ain't you?"

In truth, I felt a trifle wobbly in the knees, but I nodded.

"Your head poundin'?"

I nodded again.

"Your arm gone all a-throb? It feel heavy-like?"

It felt like a sack of cement, as a matter of fact, and was thudding to the beat of my heart, stronger and more painfully with each passing moment. All the scratching in the world didn't seem to alleviate either the itch or the ache.

Worse, my thinking processes seemed muddled. For no reason at all, a picture of Clive Barrow popped into my head. He was shaking his fist at me, shouting, "You didn't get me my hatband, you moron! Look at that fine snake. You ruined it! What will the Master of Hounds say, Horace?"

"Sorry, Clive," I muttered.

Thank God Cole didn't hear me. "Well," he said, drawing out the word as he turned on his heel, "you'll probably just go a little crazy."

He headed back toward the horses, the battered snake dangling limply from one hand. His rifle, sending off dull glints in the dying sun, swung lazily in the other. Over his shoulder, he called, "And change them damn britches. I don't wanna smell your piss all night."

7

I suppose things could have been worse. About an hour later the delirium set in full force, but I don't think I was ever completely out of my head. I knew where I was, and that Cole was there through the night, changing the damp cloth on my forehead. And I knew that when my father appeared and lectured me on the proper way in which to eat a lobster, he was no more than a fever dream.

I finally settled into a fitful sleep, and woke midmorning, free of the worst of the fever and its delusions. However, my arm, while improved, was still itchy and swollen and red, and felt as heavy as a lead bar.

"Why didn't you wake me?" I asked Cole as I shakily stumbled to my feet. Besides the weight and itch, my arm still hurt like the devil, too — not a sharp pain, but a pounding ache — and I sat right back down again. I was weaker than I'd imagined.

"Thought I'd let you sleep," he replied. "You were shoutin' and tossin' half the night."

I found this small show of kindness touching until he added, "Hell, you kept me and half the critters in a two-mile radius wide-eyed. You really let somebody named Bartholomew teach you needlework?"

I colored hotly. "I was seven, all right?" Had I talked about every detail of my life?

"Found your cave monster," he said, ignoring me.

"You did? Where?" I sat forward, and was immediately sorry.

"Gone. Bobcat. Good-sized one, too."

A smile of satisfaction had not more than begun to bloom on my face, when he added, "Course, a bitty ol' bobcat's got nothin' on a puma."

I ground my teeth, then asked, "Did you shoot it?"

He scowled. "Why the hell would I do that? It wasn't hurtin' nobody. Came in, looked around, and hightailed it when I threw a rock." He rifled through his pack, pulled out the bag of hard-boiled eggs, and tossed it to me. "I was always kinda fond of bobcats. Better eat somethin'. I finished off the snake."

■ ■ ■ ■

Tombstone and the Two Bit — and my unmet and colorfully named partner, Mr. Lop Ear Tommy Cleveland — were next on our itinerary, although I would just as soon have given up the entire excursion and ridden north, to Tonto's Wickiup and Hanratty's. The Two Bit was bound to be just as disappointing as had been the Aztec Princess, if that were possible, and I wanted to return to some semblance of civilization.

But I was in no shape to argue with Cole, who insisted we ride southeast to a town called Poco Bueno, where I could see a doctor.

"What could a doctor do that you couldn't?" I asked while Cole helped me mount Tell. Much to my dismay, I was too weak to climb aboard by myself. "Let's just go home."

"What? And put a halt to all this goddamned fun you're havin'?"

And so, sickly swaying in the saddle, I rode to Poco Bueno on the end of Cole's tether line. We arrived just as the sun was setting, and after Cole checked us into the so-called hotel, he set out to look for a doctor.

Now I have said that it was nearly dark

when we came into the town, but even I, in my fevered condition, could see that it was little more than a wide spot in the road. And the "hotel" consisted of a one-room shed, roughly ten feet square, owned by a rough and unbathed woman called Mrs. Wiggins.

There were beds, all right, but they had not seen an occupant — or a change of linens — in months. Moonlight peeked between the raw boards of the walls, and when I turned down the lantern, I could actually pick out practically the entire constellation of Orion through one particularly large chink. An hour later, when Cole returned, I was still lying stiffly on top of the covers.

"Where's the doctor?" I asked, and turned up the lamp again.

"Ain't one," he replied. He set a bottle on the wobbly three-legged table. "Why ain't you under the covers?"

"The bugs had a previous reservation," I said snidely. When I'd pulled back the blanket, they'd been as thick as pepper on a pork chop.

"Well, la-dee-dah," he said, and uncorked the bottle. He proceeded to pour some of its contents into the single shot glass he produced from his pocket, then handed it to me. "Drink up."

I eyed it. "Is this some sort of backwoods remedy?"

"Nope," he said. He tilted the bottle to his lips, took a long swallow, then wiped his mouth on the back of his sleeve. "You're about over it, anyhow. The Who Hit John'll help you sleep. And it'll help me get good 'n' plastered."

Just what I needed on top of everything else, I thought as I took a sip. Cole, drunk.

"Don't drink like a sissy, kid. Toss it back."

I did, and immediately fell into a fit of coughing. "If I die," I said hoarsely, once I could speak again at all, "I'm telling Belle on you."

"Be about your speed," he snarled, and raised the bottle again.

I was exhausted and must have dropped off immediately, but I didn't stay asleep long. When I woke it was still dark, and there was no Cole in evidence. No bottle, either. When I dug out my pocket watch and checked it by the feeble light of the lantern, it said nine thirty.

I sat up on the edge of my cot. I was still feeling a bit woozy, but I had to admit that my arm seemed to be feeling a good bit better. Whether this was a side effect of the whiskey or the result of the passage of time,

121

pure and simple, was a moot point.

I sat there for perhaps ten minutes, bored out of my mind. While I didn't feel energized enough to run a footrace, I was no longer sleepy, and there was nothing to do. I supposed I could take a foot tour of the town. It would only take about five minutes, by my estimation, and would consist primarily of a turn around a hog pen and three or four shacks. How much trouble could befall me? So I splashed some water on my face from the cracked pitcher on the table, put on my hat, and opened the door.

The night was soft and clear and temperate, with a touch of a breeze. About thirty feet across the way, for I could hardly call it a street, was the aforementioned hog pen, with the dozing sows looking far more quaint in the moonlight than they had a right. I supposed the fact that the wind was behind my back had something to do with this.

I set out toward my left down the rutted path, then about a half block later turned left again, toward the light that I had just spied pouring from the open door of the largest structure in town. The building was only about twelve feet by twenty-four or -five, long and narrow and a single story, with a covered porch across its narrow front.

As I neared, I began to make out the crude sign depending from the overhang: JANEWAY'S, it said. WHISKEY AND DRY GOODS. And then I realized that Cole was sitting on the porch, his back against the wall, his arm looped over a nail keg, and the bottle in his hand.

"Hey, kid!" he slurred as I walked up, and lifted the bottle in a wide arc.

There appeared to be only a quarter inch or so of liquid remaining in it. He polished this off posthaste, and tossed the bottle out into the weeds, where I heard it break.

"You got any cash money on you?" he asked hopefully.

"I don't believe you're in need of any more to drink, sir," I said sternly.

"The hell I'm not," he replied, and thumped his head, hard, backward against the wall. I cringed at the sound, although he seemed not to feel it. He only straightened his hat and said, "I'm celebratin'."

I hardly knew what he had to celebrate, unless it was his joy at having seen me humiliated in every possible way, and all in less than seventy-two hours.

I said, "Get up," and held down my good hand. The other one was feeling better, but scarcely had the strength to lever a medium-sized dog up from the ground, let alone a grown man.

Happily, he took it.

Unhappily, he gave it a firm yank and pulled me down to the ground with him.

"Sir!" I sputtered. I crawled off him and tried to regain my feet. "That was completely uncalled for!"

But despite his drunkenness, he was strong, and he pulled me down beside him again. "Janeway!" he bellowed upward, toward the open window. "Another bottle!"

I heard boots on the floor inside, and then a bald head emerged from the window above. "No credit, Jeffries. Why don't you climb on your bangtail and get the hell outta town 'fore the law comes lookin' for you?"

Cole waved an arm. "We don't need your goddamn credit, Janeway. My pal here will pay."

I began to say something, most probably that I certainly wouldn't pay, but Cole threw his arm about my shoulders and took a vise-like grip on my spider-bit arm.

"Won't you, kid?" he asked.

"Yes," I said through clenched teeth. "Certainly."

A hand snaked down from the window and dangled in front of my face, fingers snapping. "Two bucks," said Mr. Janeway. "In advance."

Cole released my arm, and I reluctantly placed two silver cartwheels into Janeway's dirt-etched palm. It seemed a terrible waste of cash, but Cole was intent upon it.

"Ain't you gonna ask what I'm celebratin'?" Cole asked as Janeway thumped off.

"You're drunk," I said.

"That I am."

"You're disgusting."

"That, too, kid."

I started to get up again. "I'm going back to —"

He grabbed my shirt and yanked me back down. "Y'know, Donovan," he slurred, "for all them pleases and thank-yous, you're sure a rude little shit."

Mr. Janeway stepped out through the door at that moment, and handed down another bottle of rotgut. While Cole struggled with the cork, Janeway looked at me and said, "If you two are up to trouble, I don't want none of it. Neither does anybody else in Poco Bueno. You see that he gets out of town first thing tomorrow — you hear me, boy?"

I opened my mouth to protest, if nothing else, being tarred with the same brush as Cole, but Janeway disappeared inside before I could organize an argument.

"The nerve!" I said to the closed door.

Cole had the bottle open by then, and

proceeded to take a long swig.

"Will you come with me now?" I demanded. I stood up, and this time Cole didn't try to stop me. Through the window, I saw that Mr. Janeway should have been a good deal nicer about taking my two dollars. There was only one man in the establishment, and he appeared to be snoring peacefully, his head on the yard goods. Mr. Janeway, himself, was slouched at the far end of the room, his nose in a seed catalogue.

"Don't get your knickers in a twist, kid," Cole grouched, and slowly levered himself up. This time, I was wiser than to try to help him. I moved to stand well out of his reach. "Where we goin'?" he asked, once he was more or less upright and leaning heavily against the wall.

"To bed," I announced.

"Ain't the same without Belle," he mumbled, and started walking, using my shoulder for a prop.

Gad! He was lucky I helped him at all. Here I was, the next thing to dying, and he had gone out and gotten himself inebriated — and furthermore, brought up Belle again.

As we tripped and wove our way through the brush, I said, "I wish you wouldn't talk about her in that way."

He staggered, and suddenly dragged me a jolting two feet to the right. "She won't marry me, y'know," he said sadly, once he had his balance again. "Asked her twice."

"Good," I said.

"Ain't got no money," he added. "You got money, though, you little skunk. Piles 'n' piles."

"You are delirious, sir," I said. Our rented shack was less than fifty feet away, and I heaved him toward it. "I only have twelve dollars, of which you've spent thirty cents on what laughingly passes for our lodgings, and two dollars more for that rotgut whiskey."

"Oh, you're a rich little bastard, all right," he said, punctuating the comment with a swing of his sloshing bottle. "Gonna be, gonna be." He took another drink, then stopped stock-still and regarded me fiercely. "You keep away from Belle, understand?"

In the state he was in, it was best not to disagree with him. I nodded, and took the opportunity to scratch at my arm.

"Understand?" he demanded.

"Yes, I understand that you want me to stay away from Belle."

"Damn right."

We started walking again.

"Don't be buyin' her trinkets and doodads," he muttered.

It didn't appear that I'd be able to buy anything for anyone for a long time, considering the disappointment of the Aztec Princess, and that Cole seemed hell-bent on squandering my meager pocket money. "No trinkets," I repeated, and propped him against the side of the shed while I opened the door. "And no doodads."

He fell, rather than walked, in. Feeling that I'd carried him long enough, I simply stepped over him and sat on my bed. My arm was worse again, aching and itching all at the same time, and I had a long satisfying scratch while he crawled the rest of the way inside and sat on the floor, against the side of the other cot. He closed the door with one flick of his boot and tipped the bottle back again.

"Can you keep a secret, Donovan?"

"Why do you insist on calling me that?" I shouted. "It's not my name!"

"So you keep sayin'," he said, a smile curling over his lips. "You know what I got in my pocket, Donovan?"

I threw up my hands, an action I immediately regretted, and rubbed my sore arm, which only got it itching again. "I give up, Cole. Or should I say, Mr. Jeffries."

"Colton Hezekiah Jeffries is the whole of

it," he announced almost grandly. "Colton Hezekiah Jeffries, friend to rich men the world over, destined to never have more'n a three cent nickel in his pocket." He toasted me with his bottle.

A nasty smile took hold of my face, I'm afraid. "Colton Hezekiah? It would seem you have nowhere to stand when you make sport of my name, then, sir."

He sniffed. "Don't see me usin' it, do you? And it's gold."

He was off on a new tangent, delirious with drink.

"I would hardly call Colton Hezekiah a golden name," I said with a sigh. I wished I had something to read, and glanced around the little shack. Nothing, not a scrap of newspaper, not even a seed catalogue such as was currently fascinating Mr. Janeway.

"No, you jackass," Cole said as if I were dense. "In my pocket."

"There's gold in your pocket," I repeated flatly, humoring him.

Swearing beneath his breath, he set the bottle down and, with some difficulty, dug into his pants pocket. A moment later, he held his fist toward me. I leaned forward and reached out my hand. He deposited four rock chips in my palm with a soft rattle and clink.

"Told you," he said, grunting as he fell back. "You'd best keep your trap closed about it, too, young Mr. Horace Tate Pemberton Smith."

"You called me by my right name!" I said, surprised.

"Won't last," he said, and immediately passed out.

I didn't look at the rock chips, not until I had poured out the rest of Cole's whiskey (although I took a small drink of the foul stuff myself, thinking it would help me sleep) and gotten him up and onto his narrow bed.

But when all that was accomplished, I scooped the rocks off the table where I'd laid them, and held them in the lamplight.

I gasped.

Gold.

Thin, spidery veins of it ran through the quartz, and fine specks dotted the whole of each rock. I turned the chips over and over, squinting at them again and again, and all the time my insides were knotting with excitement.

They had to be from the Aztec Princess. They had to be the chips that Cole had freed from the wall of that tunnel, and stuck into his pocket, pretty as you please.

And not a word, not a word till now!

I regarded him in the lamplight, and over his snores, I whispered, "Would you have told me if you hadn't been drunk as a lord? Would you have breathed a word, you bastard?"

What could have been his reason for keeping this a secret, other than to cheat me? To think that Cole — a man who, I readily admit, I alternately admired and despised — was low enough to take advantage of a boy! It was almost too shabby a thing to contemplate.

But hadn't he said he was simply a friend to rich men? Hadn't he said he was destined to never have more than a few cents in his pocket?

Still . . .

He was drunk. Who could guess at his true motives?

I stuck the rock chips deep in my pocket and blew out the lamp. Alternately feeling very sorry for myself and rubbing my pocket with excitement, I pondered Cole's reasoning until sleep overtook me.

8

Contrary to my expectations, Cole seemed none the worse for wear when he jostled me awake at dawn. In fact, that morning, and for all the mornings I knew him afterward, he never once manifested the slightest hint of a hangover, no matter how much — or what — he had imbibed the night before.

At any rate, we were moving south before the sun was entirely clear of the horizon, and once again I found myself marveling at the wondrous heavens Mother Nature had hung over the vast desert. It didn't seem to me that they could be made of the same stuff as New York skies, and were probably too magnificent for white men's eyes to behold.

Nonetheless, we were far away from Poco Bueno by the time those intoxicating shades of purple and crimson and orange and pink had faded to the white-hot sky of day, and Cole was still slapping his pockets. It was all I could do to hold back my laughter.

Before we left Poco Bueno, he'd told me to wait outside with the horses, then had gone back into the shed and tossed the furnishings about for a good ten minutes. At one point, the sound of this cot and table slinging — and the tenor of his curses — reached a high enough volume that Ranger spooked a bit. Even my Tell, steady as he was, gave a few nervous hops.

I couldn't have been more pleased.

It served Cole right, I thought, served him right for not telling me about the ore samples the moment he'd found them, for teasing me about Belle and the bobcat and a dozen other things. It served him right for that breakneck race over the desert, too.

Let him sweat a little longer, I thought. If God wasn't inclined to make Cole suffer a hangover, then I could make him suffer this.

Besides, I had never before seen a grown man actually give in to his anger. All the grown-ups I had known back in New York had been of relatively high social standing and good breeding, and were therefore unwilling to show emotions of any extreme, good or bad. It just wasn't done.

Even my teachers had been composed. So to see an adult act mad when he was angry — or conversely, bubble over with laughter, as Belle was apt to do — fascinated me.

But as the day stretched on, I began to feel a tad guilty. Oh, Cole hadn't mentioned the rock chips. In fact, he'd barely spoken at all, although this, in itself, was nothing out of the ordinary. However, by the time we stopped for the noon meal — jerky and hardtack again — Cole unpacked all his belongings and began to search through them like a man possessed.

I could stand it no longer.

"What are you looking for?" I asked him. It had fallen to me to water the horses, and Tell was lipping at the bag I held for him.

"Nothin', damn it," he snapped. He didn't even look up from his empty saddlebag, which he was currently holding upside down and shaking fruitlessly.

This display of ill temper nearly put me off revealing the ore. As I have said, I rather liked it when people displayed their emotions instead of walling them off, but I didn't particularly care for it when that anger was aimed at me.

However, I reminded myself that no matter how vile Cole's manner was, he'd brought me out here in the first place, and at my request. I had never so much as thanked him for that, let alone for nursing me through my spider bite. If nothing else, my ingrained sense of common courtesy was off-balance.

I sighed, and said, "Cole?" When he didn't so much as acknowledge me, I said, a little louder, "Damn it, Cole!"

This time, he looked up and glared at me.

I dug into my pocket and produced the rock chips. "Are these what you're looking for?"

He was up in a twinkling and snatched the chips out of my hand before I could think to prevent him.

"You little turd," he growled, his nose three inches from mine. "You went through my pockets."

I was intimidated, but I stood my ground. "Most certainly not, sir! I have been accused of a few things in my life, but never of being a thief, let alone a pickpocket. You gave them to me last night."

He backed off a foot, and I was grateful since my insides were trembling. Cole was not what one would call overbuilt, but he was a smidgen taller than I and well-muscled, and most likely could have snapped my neck in a trice.

Especially when he was this angry.

But his face softened a little. He tucked the chips deep into his pocket, mumbled something incomprehensible, and turned away.

"I beg your pardon?" I asked.

He knelt down and began stuffing his possessions back inside his saddlebags. Without looking up, he replied, "Said, they're nothin'. Just some rocks, that's all."

"My rocks," I said. I was braver when he wasn't standing next to me. "You said there was gold," I went on, improvising. "You said I'd be rich."

He looked up and stared at me as if I'd just read his private journal. Not that someone like Cole would have kept one.

"I was just wondering when you intended to tell me about it. When you were sober, I mean. And by the way, I was remiss. I should have thanked you for watching over me the other night. I'm almost healed, see?"

I pushed back my sleeve a few inches and held out my arm. Although the arm still suffered somewhat from that odd, aching numbness, the swelling had almost completely receded. All that was left, aside from the occasional urge to scratch, was a flat reddish welt, little bigger than a silver dollar. The center of it, which had wept and itched so badly before, was crusted over and healing.

Cole didn't say a word. He continued to stare at me for a moment, then huffed a short, sharp, half-puzzled, half-annoyed sigh through parted lips. He proceeded to wordlessly refill his saddlebags, fasten them back on the rear of his saddle, snug Ranger's girth, step up, and gather his reins. From that lofty perch, he finally said, "Well? You comin'?"

I stood my ground. "When were you going to tell me?" I repeated. "Never?"

His mouth tightened in what I could only read as disgust, and he rode out.

It was five minutes before I got Tell ready to travel and caught him up, and even then he didn't speak for another ten. At last, he growled, "You think I'd do that, kid?"

I matched his tone. I said, "I don't know. I don't really know you, do I, Colton Hezekiah?"

Oddly, a tiny smile crooked the corner of his mouth. "Told you that, too, did I?"

Honestly, the man was a complete cipher. I didn't say a word.

"Musta been crocked, all right," he added with a shake of his head. "And I didn't say nothin' 'cause I didn't want you to get your hopes up. There's gold, all right, but there's no sayin' how far it goes. Ol' Heck, he was pullin' gold outta that hole along with the silver all along."

I twisted in my saddle. "He was?"

137

"Don't go settin' off skyrockets. Lots of times they're mixed together. But the silver assayed out at about seventeen hundred bucks a ton. That's raw ore. The gold only assayed out at maybe a hundred and a quarter, a hundred and fifty to the ton."

I tried to visualize how much rock it would take to make a ton. I couldn't imagine that it was very much.

He continued. "Now I don't know how far this pepperin' of gold goes. Could be there's a fortune for the takin' about two feet past where that shaft dead-ends. Could be I chipped out about all there was. Could be that once we start swingin' picks with a little more gusto and set into blastin', that water seepin' through the wall'll turn into a gusher that'll drown the whole damn mine."

"That sample," I said, my voice cracking with barely contained excitement. "That ore sample I found in Uncle Hector's safe. Do you suppose it came from there?"

"Calm down, kid," Cole said, although for once, he didn't say it unkindly. "I reckon it did. There was a hole already dug into that wall when I started in to pick at it. Looked to me like Heck mudded it up, too, to hide where he'd found it."

I recalled the bush, dead and recently planted, and told Cole about it.

He nodded. "Saw it. Ol' Heck was awful closemouthed. Didn't even tell me. A feller learns to be that way when he's been nosin' the ground for bright metal as long as Heck."

With some excitement, I said, "But if he knew it was there, if he had a strong suspicion there was gold for the taking — knew it! — why on earth didn't he —"

"Money," Cole said, cutting me off. "Costs a heap of cash to get an operation up and running. Likely he was puttin' a deal together. Heck was sure one for deals."

I slouched in my saddle. I had no money and no contacts. It didn't seem fair that I was inches away from ensuring my future and had no way to get at it. And then I brightened. "Why couldn't we go back there and mine it, just the two of us?" I asked, adding quickly, "I'd certainly pay you a fair share."

Cole snorted out a laugh. "Green as grass, kid, that's you. Sure, we could do it. Until the water comes gushin'. Or some claim jumper puts a coupla slugs in our skulls. Gold makes men loony — don't you think no other way about it. And the whole populace is gonna go plumb peach orchard crazy the second anybody gets a whiff of the first load of ore you bring in. Maybe before."

I sighed. Each way I turned, he cut me off. "What do you suggest I do, then? Simply ignore it?"

If he noticed the sarcastic edge to my words, he didn't react. He said, "Been thinkin' about that. I figure the best thing to do is ride on down to Tombstone and have these assayed there." He patted his pocket. "I figure they'll come in high grade. Maybe as high as twenty-five, twenty-six hundred to the ton. And then you'll take that assay paper, and you'll sell the mine, real quiet and real private. I know a couple fellers who deserve to get rooked," he added with a smile that verged on mean. "Let them monkey around with the floods. Let them blast ten feet back into that rock and find nothin' but more rock."

It was a two and a half day ride to Tombstone, and all the while I kept thinking about the Aztec Princess, and about Uncle Hector.

I wanted, in the worst way, to ask Cole why he'd had suspicions about Uncle Hector's death, and if he still held them. It had crossed my mind that if Uncle Hector had met with foul play, his discovery of gold in the Aztec Princess might possibly have had something to do with it.

It was a fairly wild supposition, but Cole had said that gold made men go mad, hadn't he? Of course, he'd also added that Uncle Hector was very tight-lipped when it came to things of that nature. It was a puzzle. And every time I came close to admitting that I'd eavesdropped and heard him and Belle in the first place, something happened to put me off it.

I thought over Cole's plan to take advantage of those investors. I wasn't much in favor of it, although I didn't voice my dissent. I figured that there would be plenty of time to do that, once we'd found out what the assay report said, and especially once we got back up to Tonto's Wickiup. There, Belle could intercede on my behalf and hopefully prevent Cole from causing me bodily harm.

I hated to think of myself hiding behind a woman's skirts, scanty though they might be, but not so much as I hated to think what Cole might do to me if he were angry enough.

Of course, if the assay report was disappointing — I still had a few nagging doubts that it wasn't gold at all, that Providence wouldn't possibly be that kind — then we could forget the whole matter. I had no intention of bilking total strangers, no matter what Cole thought.

But if the report was heartening, I had secretly determined to put together a crew of miners and set to the business of bringing out every scrap of ore I could. I was fairly certain I had a foolproof plan for putting together the cash to fund it, too.

As we rode down toward the boomtown of Tombstone, Cole informed me that once upon a time, the place had been known as Goose Flats — a meager collection of shanties and lean-tos on a windswept plain. There had been an itinerant miner there, a man named Ed Schieffelin, who had been told by scoffers that the only thing he'd find in Goose Flats would be his tombstone. He found silver instead, and the little collection of shanties was rechristened.

Tombstone had since boomed into a busy, if rather distasteful, metropolis.

The outskirts of town were an impossibly deep, mazelike hodgepodge of tents and shacks and open-air cooking sites, teeming with all manner and races of people. I saw Chinese, Mexicans, tame Indians, Negroes, and whites mixing and milling about, and more than one fistfight was taking place back in the spaces between the tents.

Squawking chickens fled from our path, as did a few squealing shoats and a plethora of cur dogs, and a man was butchering a steer's carcass right on the street.

The place was a whirlwind of stinks and smells. The odors of animal waste and unwashed humans mingled with those of roasting meats and cheap perfume and boiling laundry, and the vaguely sweet undertone that Cole told me was opium smoke. Taken as a whole, it hit you like a fist.

But as we rode deeper into the town, things began to get more organized. The stench faded. The narrow, livestock- and human-clotted lanes between tents became wider and turned into streets. Brand-spanking-new buildings, some looking as if the painters had vacated only moments before, gradually replaced the shanties and tents and open-air ramadas. By the time we ambled into the center of town, there were gaslights dotting the streets.

However, this was not to say that Tombstone, even the best part of it, was civilized. Quite the contrary, for it was a hive of questionable activity. Dangerous-looking men crowded the sidewalks and streets, disreputable cowboys and grubby miners and dandied-up gents alike. Half-naked women of all shapes and sizes, even a woman with one arm and another with a thick, dark mustache, hung out of windows and leaned against buildings, hawking their wares. Raucous music and laughter — along with stumbling drunks — spilled from door after door.

If you had taken Hanratty's on its worst night and multiplied it by fifty or sixty, then that would have been Tombstone. And it was only four in the afternoon.

After we settled the horses in a nearby livery and Cole dropped off the ore samples at the assayer's office, we found rooms at a tiny, one-story hotel called Fred's Deluxe. I do not know who Fred was, but I have to say he didn't have very high standards. The wallpaper was peeling, the curtains were in rags, and ancient mouse droppings crunched underfoot. However, there weren't many bugs — probably because of the mice — and the sign said they served lunch and dinner.

Immediately, I sank my weary bones onto one of the room's two beds. I adored my Tell, but several days on horseback would make anyone long for a perch that had no intention of moving.

Cole, however, tossed his saddlebags and pack on the other thin mattress and announced, "I'm gonna go have a look-see."

And then, as an afterthought, he said, "Gimme your gun, kid."

I handed it over straightaway, but gave him a curious look.

"Gonna turn 'em in at the marshal's office," he explained. "They got some kinda damn rule here about not carryin' sidearms inside the town limits."

Just then, we heard a gun's discharge. It couldn't have been more than a block away. I said, "I don't believe everyone knows about that particular rule."

Cole grunted, and tucked my Colt into his belt.

"What about Mr. Cleveland?" I inquired. "And when did the man say he'd have our report finished?"

"I'll ask around for ol' Lop Ear. Ought not to be awful hard to find." His hand was on the latch. "And the feller said tomorrow afternoon. You keep your mouth shut, hear?"

He had warned me against breathing a word of our strike roughly three thousand times while we were en route from Poco Bueno. I breathed a long-suffering sigh and said, "Yes, sir. Who is there for me to tell, for heaven's sake?"

He studied me for a moment, then said, "You'd best come along so's I can keep an eye on you. Tombstone ain't for kids, Donovan, not even for kids locked up in a hotel room."

I stood up and followed him through the door, saying, "Stop calling me kid. And stop calling me Donovan! My name is Horace."

"I wouldn't let that get around," he said with a smirk as he shut the door behind us. "Especially down here."

Amazingly, Tombstone had a bookstore, and this discovery helped greatly to temper my anger at Cole. While he hiked up the street and checked our pistols with the authorities, I picked out two dime novels. I recognized neither as being members of Clive's collection — and suffered a momentary guilt pang for not having written to him yet — and happily purchased them.

I thought I'd best read up on the West, now that I was living in it, and surprised myself by being excited at the prospect. Well, more the prospect of reading about it than the actuality. I had missed having something to read, and justified the expense by telling myself that I would send them to Clive when I was finished.

With my new books — *Panhandle Slim and the Two-Timers* and *Doc Holiday: Death Comes to Tombstone* (a very popular title, according to the clerk) — tucked firmly in my back pocket, we set out to look for Lop

Ear Tommy Cleveland.

Cole inquired at several drinking establishments, each one of which was more ragged and run-down and scofflaw-filled than the last. At the fifth one, whose staff consisted of a one-legged bartender and three elderly soiled doves leaning on a sawhorse-propped plank inside an open tent, Cole at last got the information he sought.

We hiked for what seemed a mile farther into the rapidly degrading outskirts of town, dodging goats and cockfights and drunkards and beckoning women.

The sun was slowly settling into the horizon and the sky had turned those wondrous colors again, but my stomach was growling and I was impossibly turned around. As I tried to politely dislodge myself from an opiated Chinaman who seemed intent, for some unknown reason, on wanting my boots, I said, "Cole, can't we look tomorrow? I'm tired and I'm hungry, and we're never going to find —"

"Aw, not again!" Cole said, cutting me short, then took off through the crowd at a dead run.

It turned out to be a very good thing that we had arrived when we had, for Cole was sprinting toward a little old ragtag man standing on a wobbly barrel, with his hands tied behind him and a rope knotted around his neck.

9

I knew this was going to be trouble. I shoved my way after Cole, through the mob and toward their intended victim.

The odd thing was, only a couple of them seemed angry. Some were laughing and more than a few were holding beer glasses. On the whole, they appeared more like a group of citizens — granted, the dregs of society, but citizens nonetheless — out to watch an impromptu horse race than to see a man die.

But the two men doing the stringing up were quite serious, and Cole reached the first before I was halfway there. Even over the hum of crowd noise, I heard a pop as his fist connected with flesh. The crowd roared. I couldn't see him very well, though, only glimpses through the shifting crowd, for he had taken the ruffian down to the ground. The poor fellow on the makeshift gallows wobbled precariously on his barrel when the second tough dived after the first.

Excited that their entertainment had been expanded by this new occurrence — a double bill, so to speak — the catcalling crowd moved back to give the battlers more room. I pushed forward through a thicket of elbows and body odor. I reached the small clearing they'd created in the nick of time, for the barrel suddenly spun out from beneath the little man's feet.

I lunged forward and caught him before the rope could pull tight, but the weight of another human, even when it is a small man, is quite a load to unexpectedly come into your arms. I stumbled and nearly went down. Somehow, though, I managed to keep my legs under me, and I quickly shifted my weight and hoisted him up so that his narrow backside was balanced precariously on my shoulder.

The crowd gave another roar — I don't know if it was because one of the combatants had delivered a particularly exciting blow, or that I had saved their intended victim from a premature demise — and the ongoing fistfight on the ground tumbled toward me.

Above, I heard my burden shout out, "Whee!" just before Cole — who was fighting off two big men with no help whatsoever from the throng of onlookers — landed at my feet with an *oof.*

I hopped back, directly into the telegraph pole, and heard the man on my shoulders shout, "Watch it, kid!" and then, "Thick 'em! Thick 'em!"

I had no time — nor inclination — to dwell on this curious remark, for Cole had already regained his feet. I watched, open-mouthed, as he landed a blow that broke the first man's nose. It sprayed bright blood over the crowd, and they cheered again.

No sooner had the first man dropped to his knees, wailing and holding his face, than the second man, a rough fellow with a scarred face, closed in and delivered Cole a crippling punch to the kidneys.

Cole grunted, and I squinted in sympathetic pain. He staggered forward and the second ruffian came after him. But Cole wheeled, low and bent over, and rammed him in the belly, headfirst.

Now it was the second man's turn to double over as all the air went out of him. Cole rose up, locked his fists together, and clubbed the thug over the head with them. He, too, went down.

Cole stood there, half-crouched, panting, and eyeing the crowd. "Anybody else?" he wheezed after a moment.

Apparently not a man of them was that big a fool. Also, they seemed to have little stake in the outcome of the execution, other than as an amusement. They slowly moved away and went on with their business, which, by the looks of them, was clubbing babies.

I realized I'd been holding my breath, and filled my lungs again in a rush just as Cole, blood running from a nasty gash above his eye, looked up at the man on my shoulder. He set his mouth in that disgusted expression with which I was rapidly becoming all too familiar, and said, "Jesus Christ! What was it this time?"

"Right good t' thee you, too, Cole," came the cackled, lisped reply.

Cole dusted himself off, raising a cloud in the process, and picked up his hat. He settled it on his head before he took out his pocketknife. I was awfully glad to see that knife. Even with the brace of the telegraph pole at my back, I didn't know how much longer I could bear up under the extra weight.

A moment later, the man on my shoulder was cut free and down on the ground. Well, not really on the ground, because Cole held him, dangling, by his collar. He was a good deal closer to the ground than he had been, though.

"I should've just let 'em croak you, you old buzzard," Cole growled.

"Theems to me like you coulda," the fellow said and inexplicably grinned. He had a wide gap where his front teeth should have been, and all his "s"s came out whistles.

During this, the tough with the broken nose had crawled off, but Scar-face was still there, and was slowly rising to his feet.

"Cole?" I said.

But his back was turned toward the thug, and he was intent on the man in his grasp. "If I'd had time to think about it, I woulda just kept on walkin'," he went on. He lowered the little man to the ground, adding, "You beat everything, Lop Ear — you know that? Why were they tryin' to stretch your neck this time? Poker? Thimble-riggin'?"

By this time, the thug had gained his feet and picked up a length of board. Staggering and weaving, he started forward with an unsteady menace.

"Cole!" I said more urgently.

But he paid no attention. "See this piece'a shit, Donovan?" he said, jabbing his forefinger into the little man's birdlike chest. "This here's your goddamn business partner!"

The thug was within striking distance. He

raised his makeshift weapon, and I did the only thing I could think of. I shoved Cole out of the way.

The board came down and missed Cole by inches, but landed squarely on the grizzled head of Lop Ear Tommy Cleveland. Looking faintly surprised, Lop Ear crumpled to the ground at just about the same time Cole swung around, realized what was happening, and changed his target from me to the ruffian.

Cole's punch flattened the bounder, and across the way, a man standing in a tent opening applauded. The whore on his arm stuck two fingers in her mouth and whistled her admiration. And it suddenly crossed my mind once more that I had absolutely no business being in a place like this.

I didn't have time to think too long, though, because Cole was already picking up Lop Ear. "Grab an arm, kid," he said, and together, we dragged an unconscious Lop Ear Tommy Cleveland out of that warren of miscreants and back toward the center of town.

My business partner in the Two Bit mine revived moments after we reached our rooms at Fred's Deluxe. Which didn't stop Cole from emptying a pitcher of water over his face.

Lop Ear sat up fast, and sputtered, "Why the hell'd you do that?" He shook his head like a dog fresh from the river, and a spray of droplets spattered my face and shirt.

"And why did you have to do it on my bed?" I wailed, wiping my face with my sleeve. My pillow, where Lop Ear's head had rested at the moment of dousing, was soaked.

Cole lit a lamp and turned it up. "Felt like it," he said, shaking out the match. Having dumped out all our water, he snatched my soggy pillow from the bed and, with it, proceeded to wipe the blood from his face.

"Sir!" I said. "That's mine!"

"It's Lop Ear's now," Cole replied with a grumble, and having cleaned the blood off, tossed the sodden, stained pillow to the floor. He peered into the badly silvered mirror above the bureau, touched his cut, and said, "He's bunkin' with us tonight."

I expected Lop Ear to protest, but instead, he broke out into a damp grin and said, "Beholden to you, Cole. Long time since I slept on a piller." Then he turned to me, water still dripping from his face and frayed collar, and said, "Cole's a good boy, even if he's a tad free with that damn water pitcher.

Why, he's thaved my bacon more times than —"

"Yeah, yeah," Cole said, cutting him off. Apparently satisfied that he'd stopped the bleeding, he settled his hat back on his head. "Let's go find some grub."

I had a million questions, but my stomach had been growling practically since the moment we'd arrived in town. Hopefully, I said, "The sign said they serve dinner here." At that moment, closest was best.

But Lop Ear shook his head, and a big droplet of water flew off his nose. "I wouldn't eat at Fred's, no, sir. Least, nothin' that you can't tell what it is right off."

Cole appeared to take this under brief consideration. "Aunt Deet's?" he said as he opened the door.

Lop Ear's face lit up, and he levered himself to his feet immediately. "Hell, I can taste that good fried chicken already!" Then he scowled. "You buyin', Cole?"

"Yeah," Cole grunted. "Blow out the lamp, kid." I did, and dumbly followed.

Aunt Deet's turned out to be a café on Allen Street, I believe, and the fried chicken was excellent indeed. Our dinners came complete with country fried potatoes and thick, peppery gravy, green beans with bacon, creamed corn, hot rolls, sweet pickles, and jalapeño peppers. I had never seen nor tasted the latter, and Cole and Lop Ear laughed and carried on when I downed a full glass of water after taking my first — and last — bite.

While we ate, Cole explained my presence to Lop Ear, who seemed genuinely distressed at the news of Uncle Hector's passing. "Goddamn," he repeated over and over, shaking his head. "Goddamn!"

Neither was there good news about the Two Bit. "Drowned," said Lop Ear around a mouthful of mashed potatoes. "She's clean underwater, and even a little baby pump to empty her out's gonna run about a hundred and sixty, seventy thousand. That's U.S. dollars, boy," he added, shooting me a rare glance.

And then he shrugged. "Well, she were about cleaned out when the floodin' commenced. That were thomewhere around five hundred feet or so. Reckon we can just let her drown and say amen." He placed a grubby hand over his heart. "She were a good 'un in her time."

He went back to his potatoes.

During dinner, I had a good opportunity to observe both men, since they were engaged in conversation and paying scant attention to me. Both were eating voraciously

— at Aunt Deet's, you could have all the second helpings you wanted at no extra charge — and in this, I joined them.

Both had red checkered napkins tucked into their collars, as had most of the patrons, and both had taken their hats off. This was out of the reverence everyone seemed to have for Aunt Deet, a short, stout, jovial, middle-aged woman who passed from table to table, greeting most everyone by name and asking if everything was to our satisfaction.

It was.

Lop Ear's gray and grizzled hair looked as if it had been cut by a threshing machine gone mad. A variety of lengths, it poked from his head every which way, as if his entire scalp were an unending series of cowlicks. I am tempted to say a good barber could have done wonders for him, but I will not. There was his face to consider, you see.

I don't believe he had been too handsome to begin with, but his nose appeared to have been broken so badly that it lay to, more than protruded from, one side of his face. One cheekbone looked to have been badly broken at some point, too, for his face dented inward on one side where it should have swelled.

The other cheek was striped by three old,

long scars, evenly spaced, which ran from just above his eye to nearly his jawline. One of these wounds had caught his eyelid, which, because of the scar tissue, had healed with a distinct droop.

He was not a pretty man.

I couldn't judge his age with any accuracy, but if he was less than sixty, I would have been quite surprised. And I could not for the life of me discern why he had been saddled with a name like Lop Ear. His ears seemed to be the only normal things about him.

After dinner, I wanted nothing more than to go to bed. I hadn't been party to most of the dinner conversation, which had consisted primarily of stories about people I didn't know and didn't care to, or local matters. Besides, Cole had introduced me to Lop Ear as Tate Donovan. Even though I quickly said, "Horace Smith, sir," and held out my hand, Lop Ear apparently thought Cole knew better, and addressed me as Donovan when he addressed me at all.

Loath though I am to admit it, I was becoming resigned to the name.

I yearned for my bed, though. The faster I went to sleep, the faster it would be tomorrow, and the faster we would receive the assayer's report. Also, the faster we would ride north, out of Tombstone.

But the moment we left Aunt Deet's, Cole said, "Let's go get a slug," and took off directly, Lop Ear on his heels. I had little choice but to follow.

Tombstone after dark was frightening, but exciting. Its daytime exuberance had metamorphosed into what I could only call a full-blown, nonstop, rough-edged glamour. The gaslamps on the street glowed bright. Light, both plain and colored by stained glass, poured from every window on the street.

The sounds of enthusiastic music and shouts and laughter had risen by a factor of ten, and the sidewalks were jam-packed with milling bodies. In fact, it was all I could do to keep Cole in sight.

In just a few minutes, however, he disappeared through an open doorway and into an adobe building. I glanced up at the sign as I elbowed my way after him. THE BIRD CAGE, it said.

This turned out to be a theater as well as a saloon. However, it had nothing on Hanratty's, which, in comparison to this and Janeway's, I was beginning to think of as quite refined. Narrow and oblong and ill-lit, the Bird Cage had more in common with a giant, tinseled coffin than an entertainment establishment.

There was no one on the stage at that moment, but soiled doves were everywhere, including balconies that overhung the area where we stood, and swings that depended from the ceiling. Cole pushed me into a chair just in time to narrowly avoid being kicked in the head by one of these giddy, gamboling damsels.

"Whee!" cried Lop Ear.

Cole signaled for drinks all around.

The noise was deafening and the room was cramped, and more than once I saw someone's coat pull back to expose a firearm. This aggravated me out of all proportion. Why had I been forced to turn in my lovely Colt pistol when everyone else was armed to the teeth?

I leaned toward Cole and shouted, "They all have guns! Someone should summon the marshal!"

He grinned slyly and pulled his vest away from his chest to momentarily expose a small pistol, one I hadn't known he'd owned, protruding from an inside pocket. "There's laws, kid, and then there's laws," he shouted cryptically, then pointed at my untouched glass. "Drink up!"

"And mind your own beeswax, Donovan!"

yelled Lop Ear. *Beeswax* came out *beeth-waxth.*

I do not know if there was no stage entertainment scheduled for that evening or if we left too early to see it, for by nine thirty both Cole and Lop Ear were almost too drunk to stand up. After some cajoling on my part, they were at last convinced to go back to our hotel.

All the way down the street and around the corner, Lop Ear would stop every fifteen feet or so and, at the top of his lungs, cry, *"Loretta!"*

This wasn't too embarrassing while we were on the main street, since every third man in the crowd was shouting something or other nonsensical. But once we turned onto Fourth Street, which was much quieter, I cringed at every yodel. I didn't know who Loretta was, but it didn't appear that she would be joining us tonight, if ever.

I finally said, "She's coming later, Lop Ear."

Amazingly, this seemed to satisfy him. Drunkenly, he slurred, "You know my Loretta, Donovan? Probably curled up with some goddamn rock breaker." He said something else, too, but just then he walked right into the side of a millinery shop, and I could make out nothing but the "Thumbitch!" that came after.

At last I herded the both of them inside Fred's Deluxe, down the hall, and into our little room. Cole plopped on his cot and made a brief show of elaborately taking off his spurs, but fell asleep — or passed out — before he had the second one all the way off.

Lop Ear simply walked in and fell down.

Unfortunately, he fell directly onto my bed, which left me the floor. I shouldn't have poured my drinks into Cole's glass while he wasn't looking, I thought belatedly. He'd had four or five extra shots that he didn't know about, and I'd had none. If I'd imbibed a whiskey or two, I probably wouldn't have minded so much sleeping on a mattress of mouse droppings.

But there was nothing else for it, and I was so weary that I could scarcely keep my eyes open. By lamplight, I worked a thin blanket out from under Lop Ear and another from under Cole and made a scanty mattress on the floor. Then I blew out the lamp and lay down, head toward the open window on my bloody and still-damp pillow, gave a last scratch to my arm, and fell into blessed sleep.

I was awakened most rudely in the middle of the night. At first, I thought that Lop Ear must have tumbled off his bed and directly onto my chest. Before I could begin to scramble out from beneath it, something big and furry dug its nails into my chest and launched itself onto Lop Ear's cot, squeezing all the air from my body in the process.

Terror gripped me. "Puma!" I tried to shout. "Wolf!" But no sound came out. There was no air to push it.

And then, just as the air whooshed back into my lungs, I heard Lop Ear joyously slur, "Loretta! You come back," between the sounds of happy little whimpers and a dog's tongue slurping a greeting.

"Lord," I grumbled and, with a grump and a grunt, turned on my side and went back to sleep.

10

The next morning, while Lop Ear lay suffering a hangover, I took Loretta out into the open lot next door and threw a stick for her over and over. She never tired of it. But then, I supposed that when you looked like Loretta you'd take any attention people paid you.

Lop Ear's dog was a match for him, for I had never seen any beast remotely like her. Knee-high at her shoulder and of medium build, she had a coat that couldn't quite decide if it wanted to be short like a Labrador's — which it was, on her face, back, and sides — or long and silky, like a spaniel's. Which it was — or would have been, if all the burrs and snarls and dirt had been brushed from it — on her legs, chest, and thighs, so that she appeared to be wearing a matted bib and pants.

When she was at attention, one ear winged out to the side and the other stood straight up. Both her lower canine teeth were broken off halfway down, and she had no tail at all, not even a vestige of one. There was no mistaking what she was feeling, though. When she was happy, the entire back half of her body wagged.

These features, taken one at a time, would not have been so awfully odd had it not been for her color. Colors, I should say. First off, there were her eyes: one was a dark brown, marbled through with a soft green-ish amber color, and the other was a clear but disconcerting blue. I wondered if she was blind in it.

Her coat was a curious shade of dark, steely blue-gray. Flecked and splashed all through this were patches of black, some quite large, some merely specks. It was as if she'd been black in the first place and some fool had splashed her with a bucket of laundry bleach. The only white on her was the grizzle on her muzzle, and that was not particularly attractive, either.

But she certainly had energy. After an hour and a half of steady toss and fetch, my throwing arm was aching but she was still leaping into the air, anxious for the next fling of the stick.

At last, I could throw no longer. Someone had dumped a battered wooden chair onto the lot, and after I checked it for spiders, I righted it, dusted it off, and sat down. "We will now take a break from our festivities, Loretta," I announced.

She seemed to understand. She lay down in the weeds and crossed her front paws. Quite the lady. I supposed she couldn't help that hideous color.

Actually, I had taken something of a liking to her, the poor thing, but I supposed I'd best not let myself get overfond. Soon we'd be in receipt of the assayer's report, good or bad, and then we'd be off. I teetered between salivating at the thought of all that gold (and all of it mine), and the idea that it would turn out to be pyrite or some such and I'd go back to Hanratty's to live the rest of my life among gamblers and whores.

They were very nice whores, I reminded myself, especially compared to those who populated Tombstone. And Belle . . . ah, Belle. But technically, they were gutter snipes or soiled doves or prostitutes, whatever term you wished to use, and I was unhappy — not to mention morally unsteady — with the thought of riding herd over them.

Not that I couldn't make a go of Hanratty's if I set my mind to it, but . . .

Well, there you were.

"Seen you hurlin' the stick for my Loretta, Donovan. Right nice a' you."

I turned to see Lop Ear walking out toward me. I didn't bother to correct him about my name. We'd be leaving him behind soon enough. Loretta shot to her feet and wagged her matted hindquarters enthusiastically.

One hand shading his eyes against a glaring sun that, in his current condition, must have seemed four times as bright, he said, "Where'd that Cole take off to?"

I shrugged.

"Like always. Him and Loretta, they got a lot in common."

I raised a brow. "Beg pardon?" At least Cole was reasonably handsome.

"Always runnin' off to somewhere," Lop Ear replied, and scratched the dog's head. She licked his hand in return. "Never tellin' nobody where they's off to. I oughta take that there throwin' stick and give you what for, Loretta."

I was about to protest this course of action when he abruptly squatted down and stuck his face directly in front of the dog, who proceeded to happily lick him from chin to hairline while he cackled.

"That's right, girl. Don't you go forgettin' my ol' ears," he said, turning his head from side to side. It was obvious that his scarred and lopsided face didn't bother her a whit. It was also obvious that she was mad about him.

I simply stared.

A moment later, he stood up again, his whole face shiny with dog spit. "Well, that was refreshin'. You got any cash money, boy?" he asked.

"A little. Why?" If he expected me to buy him a meal, I could afford it, but I had no wish to see this become a habit.

He walked off, beckoning me over his shoulder. "C'mon, then," he said. "We gotta go take care o' Debby."

"Debby?" I asked as I trotted to catch up with him, Loretta on my heels. For a little man with a powerful hangover, he walked at a clip, I can tell you.

"My mule," he explained. "Vin Tucker's squawkin' about the board. Told me yesterday as how he was gonna turn her into mucilage unless I paid her up-to-date. You got four bucks?"

I had it, although it was over half of my remaining cash. But I supposed that Lop Ear had been my uncle's partner — and was my partner now, albeit in what I now assumed to be a lake roughly ten feet to a side, but five hundred feet deep — and therefore I owed him something. I nodded in the affirmative.

"That's fine, just fine," he said as we turned the corner. "Y'know, you favor your uncle Heck a bit. He were a big gi-raffe of a critter, too, though he were fleshed out a mite better than you. And I do believe you got his jaw."

Rather than take umbrage at that giraffe remark, I changed the subject. "She has rather unusual eyes," I said, pointing at Loretta, and added, "One's blue."

Lop Ear looked at me as if I'd just said, "What ho, there's air to breathe today!"

My face heated slightly, and I quickly added, "I just wondered if she could see out of it properly, that's all."

He stopped and I stopped, too, and he craned his face up toward mine. "You got blue eyes, don't you?" he said.

"Well, yes," I replied.

"You can see out of 'em proper, can't you? Don't they got no blue-eyed dogs back where you come from?"

We had reached the falling down stable wherein Lop Ear's mule resided, and the moment the balding proprietor, Vin Tucker, laid eyes on Lop Ear, he raised his pitchfork and set loose a string of blistering invectives, which I will not repeat here.

However, after I nervously counted out four dollars and fifteen cents for Debby's back board, he softened a bit. At least, he put his pitchfork down long enough to shoot out a filthy hand and grab the money.

I stood by the open door, just in case Tucker changed his mind about the whole thing, but Lop Ear went back down a row of dim, dank stalls and spent some time with a shadowy beast, who I assumed to be Debby.

"That's just through today, Lop Ear," Vin Tucker called after us with a glower. "Tomorrow she starts addin' up again, and next time I ain't gonna be so dang kind about it!"

Lop Ear turned around, stuck his thumbs into his ears, and stuck out his tongue. Fortunately, Tucker had gone back inside and didn't see. He could have come out again at any second, though, so I grabbed Lop Ear's arm and pulled him around.

He shook himself free and frowned at me. "They manhandle their elders where you come from, too? Must be quite the place." And then he brushed off his grubby sleeve as if my touch had soiled it.

I didn't know whether to be more shocked at what he had done or his attitude about my having stopped him. I couldn't think of a word to say, although I believe I emitted a puzzled huff.

It seemed Lop Ear didn't hold a grudge, however, and soon we were walking back up the street while he commented on passersby. He tipped his hat to one diminutive lady, and after she passed, he said, in a hushed tone that bordered on reverent, "That there was Miss Nellie Cashman, bless her heart. Owns the Russ House over on Tough Nut, raisin' her poor dead sister's five kids single-handed, and the Lord never made no finer angel nor better cook."

And then he tipped his hat just as graciously to a second woman. "Pepper Alice from over at the Purple Garter. Different kind than Miss Nellie, but she'll sure as shit make a man behold his Creator." He followed this up with an exaggerated wink and an elbow in my ribs.

A block later I found myself sitting atop a small barrel in the mouth of an alley. Lop Ear was seated opposite me on a wooden crate so large that his feet dangled. There were quite a few crates and barrels stored there, for the building next door was a mercantile. And while we sat there, Lop Ear had pointed out the sheriff, the man who ran the newspaper, three ladies of the evening, and a luckless miner named Helmut Gehring, who had blown his own leg off with an ill-timed blast, and who hobbled past on a crutch. It seemed he knew every ne'er-do-well in town, either in person or by sight.

"How'd you meet Cole?" I asked. Frankly, I was becoming bored with all the names and faces. I'd be leaving soon, and would have no need to remember any of them, and I trusted I'd never have call to see Tombstone again.

"Cole?" he said, leaning down to give a scratch to the tangle of knots behind Loretta's ears. "Why I knowed him back when he was a pup, round your age. Couldn'ta been more'n fifteen, sixteen."

Strangely enough, the fact that Cole had ever been my age surprised me. I suppose it shouldn't have, but he seemed so completely grown-up and rough and tough that I couldn't begin to imagine him as a mere boy.

"See that ornery-lookin' feller across the way?" Lop Ear asked, changing the subject. He pointed toward a small knot of drunken cowboys who had stopped to harass a Chinaman.

"Which one?" I asked. They all looked reasonably nasty to me. "Shouldn't we do something about that?"

"That tall feller with the black hair and the blue shirt," he said, ignoring my question about the Chinaman entirely. "That there's Apache Tom, and he's a real bad 'un. A for-hire killer. And that feller in the checkered shirt — the one about to throw that rock? That's Johnny Ringo."

He said this as if I should be familiar with the name, but I wasn't. "Johnny Ringo?" I asked. Ringo had put the rock down, and the Chinaman scampered away, down an alley. I breathed a sigh of relief. Not so much for the Chinaman's safety, I admit, but because I wouldn't be called upon to do the right thing.

Lop Ear closed his eyes — not a long journey for that scarred and dropping lid — shook his head sadly, and said, "You don't know nothin', do you, boy? Just keep clear of Ringo, too."

The men moved on down the sidewalk, probably to look for someone else to torment, and I said, "You were telling me about Cole?"

"Oh. Well, your uncle Heck brung him down one time," Lop Ear replied. "That was when I —" Abruptly, he jumped down to his feet, narrowly missing poor Loretta, and waved an arm. "Well, hell and damnation, here comes Cole now!"

Things happened swiftly from then on, because the assayer's report had come in early: over four thousand to the ton! When Cole pulled me aside and whispered the news, I could scarcely contain my excitement. And when Cole then turned around and asked Lop Ear if he'd like to ride north with us for a while, why, I could have throttled him! I wanted nothing more than to be able to jabber at somebody about this great good fortune — even if it had to be Cole — and now it looked as if I wouldn't even be able to do that.

But while Lop Ear collected his mule and Cole went to get provisions and to reclaim our guns from the marshal, I made a stealthy side trip to the telegrapher's office. Cole had said it took a great deal of money to work a mine, and I knew of only one source for that. After all, Uncle Hector had always wired Father, or so Cole claimed. And Father never made a move without consulting Misters Dean and Cummings, his attorneys.

And so I sent a short wire to Mr. Aloysius Dean. I stated no specifics, so as not to inflame the clerk's curiosity more than absolutely necessary. I simply said:

A GREAT FIND! KINDLY EXTEND LOAN TO COMMENCE MINING A. P. SOONEST POSSIBLE. ARRIVING T. W. FOUR DAYS. RESPECTFULLY, HORACE SMITH.

It was a good deal longer than ten words and cost me dear to send, but my excitement was such — and the time so lean — that I couldn't think how to make it any briefer. At least I had the presence of mind to abbreviate both the Aztec Princess and Tonto's Wickiup, which I hoped would throw any Nosey Parkers off the trail. And it never once occurred to me that Mr. Dean might say no.

When I skidded back to the hotel, out of breath and barely able to contain myself now that I was going to be rich, Lop Ear, with Loretta and Debby — who turned out to be a colossal mule of nearly sixteen hands — and Cole and our horses were already waiting for me.

"Where the hell you been?" Cole demanded as he fastened the last pack into place.

"Prob'ly been visitin' one'a them fancy gals I was pointin' out," Lop Ear cackled.

"Sorry," I panted as Cole handed me my pistol. It felt good to have it back, and I paused a moment to run my fingers over the sleek and shiny metal before I tucked it into my holster. "It's almost noon. Couldn't we have lunch at Aunt Deet's before we —"

"You'll eat on the trail and like it," Cole said, and swung up on Ranger.

Cole had proven to me — and all those onlookers back on the outskirts of Tombstone — that he was a ready and able man with his fists. However, he certainly took his time about getting any answers from Lop Ear. We were camped for the night before I found out why those men had been so willing, not to mention eager, to hang him.

We were sitting around the campfire on a vast plain, having eaten a dinner of biscuits, rabbit, and gravy. Loretta was curled at my feet, and I was reading one of my books. It was the Panhandle Slim title, and I didn't believe I had ever seen such wretched prose in my life. Most every sentence in the book was followed by at least three exclamation points, even if it was, "Mary churned the butter!!!" and both the narrative and dialogue were terribly contrived.

I didn't know how Clive Barrow could read such trash. After all, it wasn't as if he'd never been exposed to finer things.

And so I was rather relieved when Cole

broached the subject of the impromptu hanging with Lop Ear.

"Aw, them fellers was just bad sports, that's all," Lop Ear lisped. "You'd think they'd appreciate a good-trained trick dog."

"Trick dog?" I put the book down and eyed Loretta suspiciously. She gave her backside a little wiggle.

"See, we goes into a store," he said. "Well, one'a them open tents out there that barters food 'n' such. Don't rightly know if you'd call one of 'em a store. . . ."

Cole shook his head and looked up from the fire, which he was stirring with a stick. Sparks flew up as he groaned, "Tell me you weren't doin' that again, Lop Ear."

Lop Ear just grinned wide, exposing that hole where his front teeth should have been.

I said, "Doing what?"

Cole sat back. "This old buzzard goes in a place and asks for somethin'. A pound of bacon or a short sack of cornmeal or such. And while he's pretendin' to dig into his pockets for his money — of which he never has none — that dog of his comes in, whippet-quick, snatches it off the counter, and runs like hell."

" 'Course," Lop Ear said, "I al'ays pretend to be riled, see? I tell 'em, 'I ain't gonna do no trade here if you can't keep wanderin'

178

curs from mouthin' the merchandise!' I tell 'em their whole inventory likely carries rabies or fleas or somesuch. Oh, I pitch a holy fit, and I pitches it real loud!"

While Lop Ear cackled, Cole said, "Then he catches up with Loretta out of eyeshot and takes the grub. If she hasn't eaten it yet. Goddamn, Lop Ear, it was the same crud in Tucson last fall, when I had to cut you down from the Presidio wall. Hell, you were half choked! You get caught nine times out of every ten. Don't you never learn? Don't you know half the territory knows that damn dog by now?"

Lop Ear grinned wide. "You cut me down, didn't you?" He looked over at me. "Cole here is practical my lord an' savior. He's delivered me from rope and blade that many times, and snatched my butt end from the gapin' mouth of perdition. You picked a good 'un to travel with, young Tate Donovan, you goddamn did. You want to keep your hide on, keep close to ol' Cole."

"Yes, sir," I said. I had no intention of doing anything but that. At least, not until we reached Tonto's Wickiup and Hanratty's, and I was in receipt of a loan from Dean and Cummings.

"You think it over?" Cole asked Lop Ear. " 'Bout the mine, I mean."

179

I stiffened.

"Reckon I could take a ride out there and have a look-see, maybe do a bit of blastin'," Lop Ear said. "I'd wanna pick up ol' Jingles Beldon, though. There's no better man with dynamite or a flick'a bang juice. You know Jingles, Cole."

Cole opened his mouth, but before he could get a word out, I blurted, "What mine? What mine is he going to blast, Cole?"

Cole's jaw muscles worked a couple of times before he said, "Yours, you little peckerwood. Whose did you think?"

"But you told me not to tell anybody!"

"Settle down, kid," he said sternly. "I told you not to open your mouth, but I never made no such promise. That sample assayed out so rich, I figured we'd best have a gander back into that rock 'fore we go sellin' the whole shebang off to the highest bidder."

While I simmered, he turned to Lop Ear and said, "Course I know him. You introduced us yourself, you ol' buzzard."

Lop Ear smiled. "Just checkin' to see how good you remembered. And you can get down off that high horse, young Tate Donovan. I been breakin' rocks a lot longer than you been alive, and I sure ain't gonna tell nobody about your gold."

Cole rolled his eyes. "Where's he at? And if you tell me he's back in Tombstone, I'm gonna wring your wattled neck."

But Lop Ear waved his hand, which Loretta took for a signal. She got up and went around the fire to sit beside him. He started to scratch her back as he said, "He's up somewhere around Poco Bueno, I heard. Reckon we could go up there and ask around." Loretta closed her eyes, groaned softly, and leaned into him.

"We just came from there," I said through gritted teeth. It seemed to me that people everywhere were rushing into the knowledge of my gold, people I didn't even know. By the time we actually got back to the Aztec Princess, we'd probably be leading a parade of every hard-luck miner and hanger-on in the territory, all of them set on stealing my fortune.

Well, I didn't want Lop Ear Tommy Cleveland and this Jingles person and Lord knew who else working my mine. I wanted things orderly, businesslike, and with a distinct chain of command. I wanted people with ordinary names like Bill and George and Harold to call me Mr. Smith, or at the very least Horace, if they couldn't bear to be so formal with someone so young as I. And I wanted them to dig so much gold out of the ground that I could eventually go back east, back to Tattinger's, back to New York and civilized people, and never have to think about anything west of the Hudson River, not ever again.

Except possibly Miss Olivia MacKember's Academy for Young Ladies of Good Breeding.

I was absolutely positive that anything in which Lop Ear was involved was bound to end with him dangling at the end of a rope, and me likely strung up beside him. I didn't want to go to Heaven that way, and I particularly didn't wish to meet Mother and Father on those gold-paved streets while wearing dungarees and a Stetson, with a rope around my neck or a big, messy bullet hole through my skull.

"Poco Bueno it is, then," said Cole, and stretched out on his blanket. "There anyplace to roost there besides that shack Mrs. Wiggins has got?"

"Hell," grumbled Lop Ear as he, too, lay down on his blankets. Sighing happily, Loretta burrowed her head into the crook of his arm. "I'd druther sleep under Janeway's saloon than in that bug hole."

11

It took us just as long to ride back up to Poco Bueno as it had to ride down from it, so I was forced to keep uncomfortable company with Cole and Lop Ear for another interminable day. This wasn't to say they were the worst traveling companions — at least, they didn't bludgeon me and leave me for dead at the side of the trail — and Cole's natural stillness was more than made up for by Lop Ear's conviviality.

He was so convivial, in fact, that by the middle of the first day I was ready to speak sternly to him. By the second, I was tempted to simply strangle him. And Cole? Oh, he was silent, silent as the tomb. But on those rare occasions when he did say something of import, it only served to remind me of his betrayal of my trust.

I do not mean to say that everything imparted by Lop Ear was mere babble, only ninety-nine percent of it. When he did have something important to say, it was very important.

I had taken to reading as we rode along through that dusty, cactus-speckled, godforsaken land. My wonderful Tell never spooked and seemed perfectly content to follow the other horses right along, and it made no difference to Lop Ear whether I actively listened or not.

I had given up on the Panhandle Slim book and was reading the Doc Holiday, which proved to be only slightly superior in the writing, but much more exciting. At least, there was no one named Mary in it, and therefore no long, boring, introspective scenes while she churned butter or milked the cow or stood out on the purple-prosed prairie watching interminable sunsets, waiting for Panhandle Slim's return.

I had just come to the part in which Doc Holiday is about to face off with three rough and deadly gentlemen, cattle rustlers by trade, when out of the blue Lop Ear said, "Well, now, I believe you was just a mite, Cole. 'Bout fifteen, wasn't you? That were right after Heck commenced to carry you. I mean, after them damned Apache and all."

Cole grunted, which was his preferred manner of keeping up his end of most any conversation, and I peered over the top of my book. Doc Holiday had experienced some dealings with Apache — fictionally, anyway — in *Death Comes to Tombstone,* and they sounded like very nasty fellows indeed.

"What about Apache?" I asked.

Lop Ear appeared surprised that someone was actually listening to him, and his scarred face fairly twitched with excitement. To let me catch up with him, he reined Debby down to a shamble, which nearly unseated the dog. Loretta rode behind his saddle, and although she braced with all four legs and dug in her nails to keep from sliding off Debby's slick and sloping croup, Debby didn't seem to mind. She was a rather nice mule, if one liked mules. I did.

"Oh, they was terrible," Lop Ear confided, once we were riding head to head. "Them devils, they killed Cole's folks when he was about your age, maybe younger. Course, it were hard to tell with Cole. He didn't get his full, towerin' size until he were practically twenty."

Cole shouted back, "Shut up, Lop Ear," but he didn't turn around.

I was anxious to hear! I dog-earred my page and tucked *Death Comes to Tombstone* in my back pocket. "Where?" I asked. "Why didn't they kill Cole, too? How did it happen?"

"They was headed to California, him and his folks," Lop Ear said, and gestured toward the west rather grandly. "There was several wagons, I'm thinkin'. They stopped 'bout two miles out of Monkey Springs and . . ." He scratched at his ear, then shouted ahead, "It were Monkey Springs, weren't it, Cole?"

Cole, who was riding about fifteen feet ahead, suddenly hauled Ranger to a halt and spun him around. "You talk too much, old man," he snarled, then wheeled Ranger back around and loped out ahead. He didn't slow down to a walk again until he'd put a good hundred yards between us.

As if nothing out of the ordinary had happened, Lop Ear continued. "Yup, I'm pretty sure it were Monkey Springs, 'cause Heck had digs around there back then."

I will admit that I felt a little guilty listening to Lop Ear. It was a bit as if I were going through Cole's bureau drawers, but I hung on every word.

Apparently there were several wagons in the party, and someone had broken a wagon wheel in such a manner that it necessitated a wheelwright. Since they had just passed the little town of Monkey Springs, and since Cole, being smallish, would be no help with blocking up the wagon and wrestling off the wheel, he was sent back to town on horseback. When he returned, leading the wheelwright, the wheelwright's wagon, and a new wheel, there was not one soul left alive.

In grisly detail, Lop Ear described the carnage the Apache had wrought, although — or perhaps because — I cringed. It was horrible for me to hear. I could only imagine what it must have been like for Cole, and by comparison, my experiences with snakes and spiders and bobcats — which I had previously thought horrendous — suddenly seemed trivial.

I shall spare you the specifics, which is a kinder thing than Lop Ear did for me. At any rate, the upshot was that Uncle Hector, hearing about the massacre, had taken young Cole under his wing.

"Right about the time Cole got his height," Lop Ear said, "he took it into his head that he was a fast hand with a gun. Well, he was. So fast it was downright scary, and damned if he couldn't hit what he was aimin' at, too." Lop Ear shook his head, and added, "That's right unusual, I'm here to tell you. But Heck weren't gonna admit it to him. I weren't either, not if I knew what was good for me."

He cackled brightly. "Ol' Heck had him

some ideas, he did, 'bout sending Cole back east to school, and he were madder'n a fried toad when Cole took off! Down to Mexico, it was. And damned if he didn't stay gone about four years." He pulled on his ear. "Well, mayhap it were five."

He paused. I was still a bit queasy after hearing — in more detail than anyone needs to know — about the mutilated bodies, and how Cole had thrown himself on his mother's corpse and tried in vain to close her wounds. So I said nothing. There are some pictures you cannot pry out of your head, no matter how hard or how long you try. It is still a scene that I picture with chilling clarity after all these years, and I was only told about it.

I remember being glad that if my parents had to die, that they had done it far away, in France, and that they had ended their lives quickly in warm, blue Mediterranean waters. Not at the end of an Apache knife.

Lop Ear paused his narrative long enough to take a drink from his canteen, and the moment he stoppered it again, he said, "Now whilst he were gone, we started hearin' rumors about some gringo gunslinger down in them parts. Didn't have no real name, they just called him El Diablo Dorado. Means "the Golden Devil." Or somethin' like that."

I tried to fix on the name. Anything to shake that bloody picture from my head. It seemed Loretta had heard enough, too, because just then, she jumped down to the ground and raced ahead, toward Cole. Lop Ear watched her go.

"Fickle ol' bitch," he muttered.

"What does this El Diablo Dorado have to do with anything?" I asked.

"Maybe nothin'," Lop Ear replied, switching his attention back to me again. " 'Cept me an' Heck, we thought as how it was kinda funny that after Cole came on back home, we never heard anymore about —" Suddenly scowling, he scanned the horizon. If he'd had ears like a dog's, they would have been pricked to attention.

I heard it, too. "What *is* that racket?" I asked. I noticed that Cole had reined in Ranger, and was staring toward the northeast.

"Whoa up so's I can hear better," said Lop Ear. I did and he did, and a second later a big grin spread over his face. He snatched the hat from his head, and with a sudden and piercing cry of "Whee!" fanned Debby's rump with it. She took off at a fast trot, then broke into a lope.

Tell tossed his head, eager to be after

189

them, but I took hold of him and said, "Easy, son, easy." Cole still hadn't moved from his vantage point, and I didn't think it wise that I did, either.

But a few moments later, a wagon slowly breasted the top of a shallow slope in the distance, and Lop Ear was headed straight for it. Cole eased Ranger into a slow jog, and I followed suit.

As I grew closer, I saw that it was a very curious rig indeed. It appeared to be an ancient short-bed Conestoga wagon, although it was missing its canvas cover. The supports for it were still there, though, and they were strung thickly with what sounded like thousands of small bells of all kinds, all ringing and tinkling and jangling.

But the team that pulled it was odd enough to make the wagon appear almost normal. First of all, there was a ratty-looking sorrel with far and away the worst swayback I had ever seen. You wondered how the poor beast could walk, let alone pull a wagon.

Harnessed next to him was a grumpy, shaggy black-and-white pony. She had a roached mane that stood a good three and a half inches, straight up, and her ears were pinned flat to her neck. I guessed her at barely ten hands high, and the little thing had to work double time to keep up with the sorrel's plod.

The moment the driver reined them to a halt and the bells stopped jangling, the sorrel appeared to lock his knees and doze off. Believe it or not, the pony actually sat down in her harness, sat down just like a dog!

All this happened when I was still a distance from them, and when I got closer, I saw that I had been overkind to call what they wore a harness. It was jury-rigged with more cotton rope and twine than leather, and was strung along every length with more of those bells.

Cole and Lop Ear and the driver were deep in conversation by the time I rode up. I hung back on purpose, stopping a good twenty feet out, staring at those impossible horses and hoping against sinking hope that the creature driving the wagon wasn't the Jingles that Lop Ear had been so keen on having help search for my gold.

He looked a bit taller than Lop Ear but was just as wiry, and had startlingly light blue eyes. They were piercing, even from where I was sitting. He could have been five or even ten years older than Lop Ear, and although his clothing was in better repair he was certainly every bit as much the lunatic.

"That's a right fine horse Heck has left

you, Donovan," he called without any preamble, then pointed to the drowsing swayback. "You watch him with my Comanche, you hear? He will savage most any beast what comes near him, and that is a fact. I would surely hate for him to tear up ol' Heck's nice horse."

He took off his floppy hat and held it briefly to his heart, exposing sandy hair shot through with gray, and an odd little bald spot, perfectly round and the size of a silver dollar, just off center on the top of his head.

Then, just as suddenly, he stood up in the driver's seat. Settling his hat back in place, he motioned for Lop Ear to rein Debby out of the way, then hopped down to the ground. "I hear you have got a lot of gold in the ground, Donovan," he said as he went to the back of the wagon and pulled out a long wooden plank. "Me, I have got me a good claim with no bats, but she's goin' to take a lot of blastin', yes, indeed."

As he carried the plank up toward his team for reasons unknown, I shot a puzzled look at Cole. He grinned, just a little, and said, "Kid, this old coot's Jingles Beldon. He's agreed to come have a look at your Aztec Princess."

Jingles had walked to the rear of the wagon again and unloaded a very large rock, and was presently engaged in laboriously carrying it from the back to the front.

"Crazy," I said softly. "They're all crazy." I was totally bewildered. Angry, too — angry that Cole seemed to be hell-bent on telling every madman we passed about my mine. And this Jingles gave every indication of being a madman times two.

As if to drive this point home, Jingles, who I was certain couldn't have heard me, suddenly piped up, "Ain't crazy, young Donovan. Could a crazy man have caved in practical the whole town of Hanged Dog, and neater'n a pin to boot? I should say not! Did a good job of it for Miss Gini and got paid in gold, but I woulda done it for free, yessir. Woulda done it if I had to pay!"

He dropped his rock a few feet behind the seated pony and made a few adjustments, then picked up his plank. She whipped her head back toward him and clacked her yellow teeth inches from his pants leg.

He ignored this, but plucked a gigantic wad of dirty cotton from her ear and shouted, "Will you take your feet, you midgety she-devil?"

As if all this were perfectly normal, Cole backed Ranger out of the way, and Lop Ear backed off a few more feet, too. Loretta, who had been standing several yards off to the side, ran behind a clump of brush and peeked out around it. As the sorrel, Comanche, commenced to snore rhythmically, the pony swung her head back and forth, ears still pinned flat.

"So much for you, then, Grace," said Jingles, and reinserted the cotton.

The pony yawned in reply.

I watched, gape-mouthed, as he picked up the board, worked one end of it between her rump and the ground, then turned it so that the middle of it was sitting on that rock, like a child's seesaw.

Without warning, he leapt straight up, onto the high end of the board, and just like that he levered that pony up onto her feet. Well, I don't know that he actually levered her, because it seemed to me that the pony stood up a fraction of a second before he landed. But still, it was an amazing piece of business. I had never seen anything quite like it.

"Whee!" cried Lop Ear, and smacked his thigh.

Cole just sat there.

Jingles lugged the rock back and settled it in his wagon bed, then tossed the plank in after it and climbed back up to the driver's seat. "Well, I'll be seein' you, then," he called, and picked up his reins.

I believe I gave an audible sigh of relief. It seemed that he had forgotten all about my gold, and was going home. But before he had time to snap the reins over the team's rumps, Lop Ear said, "What about the Aztec Princess?"

I could have murdered him.

Jingles paused. "Got to get my supplies back to camp first. Everything in its order. Got me some bang juice and bottles, lots of bottles, and a smidge of flour and grease and feed and the like. Had to order the bang juice special, clear from Tucson. Can't get it around here, no, sir. Bunch of dang dirt farmers and low women and robbers in Poco Bueno. That Janeway will steal a man blind."

Cole thumbed back his hat. "You tellin' me you're hauling a load of nitro around in that thing?" He pointed at the wagon.

"Not exactly, not exactly," allowed Jingles. "But if she sits around long enough, she'll commence to sweat like a Texican well digger. Course, I used to fling it at my bats, but . . ." He shrugged.

Cole nodded as though he knew what the devil Jingles was talking about. "How much you got?"

Jingles screwed his face up. "Ten cases," he said, then confided, "I like to be prepared for the worst."

Lop Ear locked his hands on Debby's saddle horn and leaned back. "Ten cases?" he cackled. "Hell, you just like the blastin' better than the findin', Jingles."

"Like you're one to talk, you old rake-faced coot!" Jingles snapped.

"Scalp head!" Lop Ear rejoined, and stood up in his stirrups.

But before the squabble could turn into a full-blown fight, Cole said, "Whoa, whoa, whoa, you two! How 'bout I buy those bang sticks off you, Jingles? Save us time and nosy clerks. I'm especially wantin' to avoid nosy clerks, if you take my meaning."

Jingles squinted and scratched the back of his neck for a moment. "That'd do, I reckon," he said at last, much to my disappointment. "Well, let's be off to the Aztec Princess, then. Still in the same place, ain't she?" He slapped his reins over the team and hollered, "Git up!"

The bells started jangling as Comanche started sleepily plodding again and the pony Grace trotted to keep up. Cole, riding beside the wagon, had to shout over the racket for about five minutes to convince Jingles that since it was almost four o'clock and Poco Bueno was a scant three miles away, we'd best spend the night there.

I think what finally convinced him was that Cole offered to buy the drinks.

Which, of course, meant that I would.

An hour later, we had entered Poco Bueno and settled the horses into Mrs. Wiggins's makeshift corral. While Tell and Ranger and Debby went straight to work on the hay we pitched them, little Gracie went directly to the far end of the enclosure and sat down. No one so much as commented on this, and in fact, Jingles carried some hay down to her.

He also insisted that Comanche be staked out, away from the other horses, since he feared the gelding would do them damage. Had anyone asked me I would have said a half-starved jackrabbit with enough incentive could have killed that horse, or at least crippled him for life. But as no one asked, I kept my own counsel.

At the insistence of Cole and Lop Ear, we walked over to Janeway's, kicking the tumbleweeds from our path as we went.

"Don't know how they got the nerve to call this a town," Lop Ear commented.

"Well, they have sure as shootin' got them a sheriff," Jingles said. He pointed down the street, which was vacant as far as the eye could see, save for four or five widely spaced buildings with multiple weedy lots between them. Someone had dreamed big dreams for Poco Bueno, but they hadn't come to fruition.

"That overgrown outhouse is where Biggs hangs his badge," Jingles continued, pointing to the smallest structure. "I don't believe you could get a full-grown cow in there, not horns and all. And for sure not a longhorn, like they have over in Texas. Why, some o' them got horns that spread eight, ten feet! Cole, I ever tell you about the time I rode me an elephant?"

Mercifully, we had arrived at Janeway's, and Jingles's story was cut short.

"You again?" Janeway growled when we walked in. I did not believe Mr. Janeway had much chance of success if he treated all his customers in such a fashion, but I kept my mouth closed. It was getting to be a habit.

"Not thrilled about it myself," Cole replied, then nodded at me.

I plunked two silver cartwheels on the splintery counter.

"Bottle of whiskey," he said.

Grumbling, Janeway fetched it and the glasses, and the four of us found places to perch amid the calico bolts and nail kegs and flour and sugar bins. Cole poured the whiskey.

There was one other customer in the place. A large man — not quite so tall as Cole, but certainly bigger in girth and vastly more repugnant in expression — stood at the small bar in the rear of the store, sipping a beer. I decided that he was passing through, also, as he had a good bit of desert dust on his clothing and boots. And also because his horse — anyway, I assumed it was his horse — was tied out in front of Janeway's. He nodded at Cole, who nodded back. It wasn't a nod of recognition, simply one of acknowledgment.

Cole and Jingles and Lop Ear started up what they must have thought was a cleverly deceptive conversation about the various catastrophes that could strike cattle. Mercifully, they didn't seem to expect me to participate. One could only take so much of hearing about blowflies and hollow tail and scours and such, and when Cole wasn't looking, I poured the last of my drink into his glass. I had tasted it, and found it as vile as the last time. Then I stood and carried my glass to the bar, in order to keep someone from filling it again.

Just as I set it down next to a gigantic jar of green and slimy-looking pickled eggs, Janeway wiped his beefy hands on a filthy bar towel and announced, "I'm goin' to the shitter. Anything's gone when I get back, Jeffries, I'm gonna know who took it." He sent Cole a nasty look.

Cole snorted and went back to his conversation.

Now, since we had come into Janeway's, the rough-looking man at the bar had been watching me. I don't mean to say he was blatant about it, but every time I looked around I got the feeling that he had just taken his eyes away from the back of my neck.

And as Janeway went out the door, the big man said, "Hey, kid. You from around here?"

I was torn between being a little afraid of the brute, and being pleased that he'd noticed my manner was vastly more civilized than my companions'. I took the middle road. I said, "You have guessed correctly, sir. I am a native of New York City."

The conversation behind me trailed off into nothing.

The big man smiled, although there was nothing friendly in it. "That right?" he said. "And what would you be called?"

Automatically, I replied, "Horace Tate Pemberton Smith, sir. And you?" Manners are a hard thing to let go when one has been drilled in them, and automatically, I stuck out my hand.

What happened next came so fast that it is difficult to put it all together, but I will try.

Instead of taking my hand and shaking it like a gentleman, the man let his unfriendly grin broaden into something wholly evil. Low, he said, "Well, ain't this my lucky day?"

Like lightning, he drew his gun.

Before I could think what to do, he fired. Except that I heard two shots, not one, and I wasn't dead. At least, I didn't think so. My knees turned to aspic and I grabbed the bar to keep from crumpling to the floor. I remember catching a glimpse of Jingles as he wrested my Colt from its holster and shoved Cole's still-smoking pistol into my numb hand, even as the brute collapsed face-first into the yard goods.

I remember Cole growling, "See? What'd I tell you about that Horace shit? And why'd you give him my goddamn gun, Jingles?"

A rolling bolt of calico came to a stop against my boot just as Janeway, trying to rebuckle his belt and run at the same time, came barreling back through the door, followed directly by a medium-sized man with a bent tin badge pinned to his chest. The man with the badge was shouting, "What! What!" And then he saw the body.

Janeway had taken it in, too. He bellowed, "Cole Jeffries! I knowed it! I just knowed it!" With both hands balled into hamlike fists, he went past me toward Cole, hopping bolts of cloth and crates of supplies the falling body had scattered.

I hadn't the presence of mind to turn around, but a second later I heard a loud thump and a wet crash, and Janeway stopped yelling. Dozens of pickled eggs rolled out across the floor, spraying brine and strong pickling smells over boards and boots.

The sheriff was kneeling beside the body by this time. "Goddamn," he said, ignoring Janeway's plight entirely. "Deader'n my wife's iron." And then he looked up at the gun held limply in my hand, and at me.

I have no idea what was on my face at that time. I was incapable of speech or rational thought, and my boots were rooted to the floor. In my defense, I had never had a man drop dead in front of me before, and with absolutely no warning. I probably would have soiled my trousers again if I'd had time to think about it.

Lop Ear stepped forward into my range of vision, carefully avoiding the eggs. "I theen the whole thing," he lisped, pounding his chest. "It were thelf-defense."

"That's the truth, Sheriff Biggs," Jingles chimed in from behind me, as serious as a bishop on Sunday. "This big wad of nothin' drew on the boy, and for no reason a churchgoin' man like yours truly could figure. Now one time when I was up Colorado way —"

"Shut up, Jingles." Cole, looking well past annoyed, stepped forward, kicking eggs and brine-spattered yard goods out of his way. "Just close your pieholes, both o' you. What happened was —"

But the sheriff, who had rolled the body over on its back, cut him off. He let out a long whistle and said, "Well, paddle my ass and call me Dorey! You yahoos know who this sombitch is?"

My companions shook their heads in unison. I was still too stunned to do anything.

Smiling ear to ear, Biggs picked up an egg, wiped it on his shirt, and took a thoughtful bite. Chewing, he said, "This here's none other than John Henry Strider hisself!"

12

The name meant nothing to me, but some-one — I think it was Jingles — suddenly hissed in air. I heard Cole murmur, "Aw, shit!" He sank down on a pile of crates and wiped his face with the flats of both hands.

"You done the shootin', did you, boy?" the sheriff asked me.

I moved my mouth, but nothing came out. Images flashed through my mind, images of being marched to the gallows, of being hanged, of my body left to rot as a warning to others, and of my entire class from Tattinger's being shipped across country to view it.

Sheriff Biggs's eyes flicked to Jingles. "What's his name?" he asked, still chewing.

"Donovan," Jingles piped up far too glee-fully.

"Tate Donovan," added Lop Ear.

"More often called Kid Donovan," Jingles corrected, and stepped on Lop Ear's foot by way of punctuation. "Oh, he's a good hand with a gun, 'specially for a fella so short in years. Why, the mind boggles, thinkin' how fast he'll be once he hits his majority." He elbowed Lop Ear in the ribs. "Killed himself John Henry Strider! My, my. Chalk up another one for you, Kid."

Softly, Lop Ear growled, "Stop pokin' at me, you consarned scalp head." He took a step away.

"Claw-faced old coot," Jingles happily muttered back. "Oh, young Donovan is fast with a gun, Sheriff Biggs. He has got the population of Tombstone what is dastardly — that's more'n three quarters, by my reckonin' — fearin' to go out in the daytime lest they incur the might of his saintly wrath. Why, he is a terrifyin' messenger of good, and a defender of kids, and —"

"Shut up, goddamn it!" shouted Cole — a little too late, by my book — and he was so angry that veins stood out in his forehead. Behind us, Janeway twitched and moaned, and a new shower of those smelly pickled eggs came bouncing out across the floor, spraying juice and picking up dirt.

Hands clenched into tight fists, Cole rose from his perch. Visibly struggling to keep himself under control, he said, "It wasn't like that, Biggs, and these two old desert rats damn well know it. I was the one that did the shootin'. And then this mule's pizzle," he said, jabbing a finger toward Jingles, "he grabbed my gun and switched it with the kid's."

Biggs got up from the floor and dusted his knees. "Just like you to try an' swipe the credit, Jeffries," he grumbled with a disgusted shake of his head. "Well, I'm here to tell you that I ain't buyin' it for a slap second, no, sir. Why, I practically seen Kid Donovan shoot him my own self. Ain't he still holdin' the gun?"

"That's right, Biggs," Jingles chimed in. "Amen and pass the gravy!"

Cole thundered, "But it's my gun!"

Biggs closed his eyes and wagged his head. "No buts about it, Jeffries. There's a gun already stuck in your holster, so shut your face and save your lies for those that'll believe 'em."

Biggs turned back toward me. "Sorry to say there ain't no bounty on John Henry here," he confided apologetically. "He al'ays managed to pull off his killin's legal-like, rat bastard that he was. He was up to thirty-seven, the last I heared."

Jingles scratched his head. "Forty-one, I was told. Course, I heard he was in New Mexico, too. Hired himself out to Mammoth Mines, they said. It's a big operation, Mammoth," he added. "Lots of silver, lots of skulduggery."

Lop Ear snorted derisively.

A hatchet-faced man, painfully thin and dressed in patched overalls and a sagging hat, peeked around the doorway and surveyed the scene. "E-everythin' all right, Biggs?" he asked nervously. "Me and Electa heard a couple shots."

"Will you listen to me, Biggs?" Cole tried again. "This idiot kid didn't —"

"I told you to shut the hell up, Jeffries," Biggs half shouted. "You think I'd take the word of some lyin', thievin', no-'count, go-to-Mexico, gunslingin' sonofabitch over Jingles? He might be half cracked, but he don't lie."

Jingles rocked back on his heels and slid Cole a smirk. Cole angrily raised a threatening hand, but Lop Ear, who was standing between them, put a stop to it.

"And would you mind holsterin' that pistol, Kid?" Biggs continued. "You're makin' me nervous." He turned around to face the door. "It's all right, Carl. Kid Donovan just shot hisself John Henry Strider!"

"John Henry Strider?" Hatchet-faced Carl gasped and took off down the street as if the devil himself were on his tail, shouting,

"Kid Donovan shot John Henry Strider at Janeway's!"

"Now you listen to me," Cole began, and took a step forward.

"How many times I gotta tell you to shut the hell up!" shouted Biggs.

Somehow, I managed to slide Cole's Colt into my holster, and at last I found my voice, or the beginnings of it. I put one hand on Cole's chest in an attempt to hold him back, and said, "Sh-Sheriff Biggs, sir, this gentleman drew his pistol with no warning. Cole was only attempting to . . . Sheriff?"

Biggs wasn't listening, for he had dropped to his knees again. My first thought was that he was diving for another of those putrid eggs, but he put his hand on my boot. "Holy shit," he muttered. "Will ya take a look at that?"

I had not moved my feet a fraction of an inch since I first offered my hand to the dead man, but now I looked down to where Biggs was pointing. The late John Henry Strider's bullet had entered the floor right next to my foot, leaving a round and splintered hole. It had also taken a small, crescent-shaped bite out of the edge of my boot's sole.

"I'll be damned," said Biggs, and levered himself up again. "I'll just be dinky-double damned. Kid, I'd like to shake your hand."

Not knowing what else to do, I numbly stuck my hand out and he grasped it firmly. "Steel," he said, pumping it over and over, "that's what you are, Kid, pure steel. I'm right sorry I ain't never heard of you before, but we're kinda the armpit of the prairie out here in Poco Bueno. Don't get much news. Kid Donovan in my town, by God! Faced off with John Henry Strider point-blank and didn't flinch!"

We vacated Poco Bueno immediately, at the suggestion of Sheriff Biggs. He was worried that I'd take down Mr. Janeway, too, once he woke up. He confided to us that Mr. Janeway was a bullheaded bastard, but he was the bullheaded bastard who owned Poco Bueno's only store, and therefore he'd rather not bury him.

"I trust you see my meanin', Kid," he'd said. "No offense."

He was most solicitous. I'll give him that. He didn't even object when Lop Ear, whose shirt bulged as if he had gained ten pounds since we had entered Janeway's, started calling, "Loretta! Loretta! Where you got to, dagnab it!" at the top of his lungs.

"No offense taken, Sheriff," I replied. I'd gotten over the worst of my paralysis and confusion while Biggs — along with a fawning Carl and most of the citizenry of Poco Bueno, which amounted to about two dozen people — trailed after as we marched down to the corral. However, I hadn't had a single second out of Biggs's earshot to confer with any of my companions.

Although I was heartily tempted to try, once again, to press the truth upon Biggs, I was also leery of it. This John Henry Strider person had died, after all, and had died by violence. Even though he might have been a bad man — and I had every indication that he was — someone needed to shoulder the blame. Preferably the perpetrator.

But Sheriff Biggs seemed to already know Cole far too well, and bore a dislike for him so strong that he wouldn't listen to a word Cole tried to say. The basis for this enmity was unknown to me, and I thought that I'd best ferret out the reason before I started pointing any fingers in Cole's direction.

At least Biggs — and in fact, all of Poco Bueno — seemed delighted over John Henry Strider's untimely and violent demise. It seemed an odd position for an officer of the law to take, but all things considered, I was not about to argue.

Besides, with a depth of gratitude I could not fathom, Mrs. Wiggins tearily refunded the money we had paid for the use of her corral and one night's rental of her shack. Men took off their hats to us, and a couple of them shyly shook my hand. A little boy pointed at me and asked, in a rather loud voice, "Is he the one, Daddy?"

And all the while we were tacking up the horses in preparation to vacate the town, and children perched on the fence and grown-ups whispered and doffed their hats, Lop Ear and Jingles chortled softly and Cole grumbled under his breath.

The sun was still hovering above the horizon as we rode north to the clatter of Jingles's bells, out of Poco Bueno. The tardy Loretta caught us up and leapt behind Lop Ear's saddle just as we passed the final shack and noisily headed out into open desert again, dodging stray tumbleweeds.

Two hours later it was dark, and we were camped well away from that paltry excuse for a town. I had kept to myself since we left town, distanced at first by the awful racket of those bells, and later by purposely offering to see to the horses, single-handed. I couldn't help but overhear Cole and those two old goats, though, and I was getting awfully sick of it.

The smells of good cooking rose to meet

me as I finally and reluctantly joined the others at the fire, and as I sat down, Cole was saying, for at least the thousandth time, "I shoulda just shot you, Jingles."

I was almost hoping he would make good his threat. There would be one less crackpot fiddling with my gold, and one less person carping around the campfire tonight. All I wanted was some silence in which to sort it out.

At the end of my figurative rope, I asked, "Why don't you do it, then, Cole? Go ahead. Just shoot him. If you get it out of your system, will you be quiet?"

Cole set his mouth and glared at me over the fire. Lop Ear, having suddenly lost his extra weight, had the coffee going and a skillet of biscuits baking. Another sizzled with the fragrant ham that I had smelled all the way down at the picket line, and that I was reasonably certain he'd stolen from Janeway's store. Compared to everything else that had happened in the past few hours, the theft didn't seem worthy of comment.

"After all," I added stubbornly, "one man has already died at your hands today. What's another?"

Lop Ear chortled and reached around Loretta to crack stolen eggs in with the ham.

Jingles made a sour face. "Now what kind

of an attitude is that to be takin'?" he asked, and theatrically slapped a liver-spotted hand over his heart. "I have saved your bacon today, young Donovan, not to mention Cole's. I have taken a sorry situation and turned it around into a tale of masterful glory and gunslingin' to tell round the fire. And now you're incitin' him to massacre me." Jingles shook his head sadly. "Why, I have not been subjected to such unfair treatment since Dewey Hoofman tried to throttle me in my sleep for being a hog thief. Never thieved so much as a shoat in my life! I have took a few chickens and a cow or two, mind, but never a hog, and Dewey never kept no chickens."

Fiercely, Cole jabbed at the fire with a stick. There was a light wind, and Lop Ear had to scurry to the side to avoid the sudden shower of sparks that billowed his way. Loretta didn't move as fast, however, being preoccupied with an eggshell. Over the faint stench of singed dog hair, Cole demanded, "And just how do you figure that, old man?"

Jingles's brows shot up. "Why, Dewey never had so much as a feather on his place! Couldn't abide a bird, not after the vultures polished off his poor daddy's molderin' corpse down in —"

"Hold it," Cole said with a wave of his

stick. "I mean, how you figure you saved anybody's bacon?"

Jingles pursed his lips. "I suppose you have forgot how you crossed Janeway's brother-in-law up in Flag that time, or —"

"He deserved crossin'," Cole cut in.

"And he was still a man's brother-in-law," Jingles said, lifting his nose into the air. "Mayhem and rowdy-dow don't count diddly when it's a man's kin that's accused of them, even kin by marriage. And the ones with the god-awfullest, scum-suckingest kin is the most defensive." He shook his head. "As for Sheriff Biggs, I don't know why he has it in for you. But he surely does, and by doubles."

He brightened a little, and added, "Now this reminds me of the time I was down around El Camino, and these two brothers . . . I believe Nate and Dave Blanchard was their names . . . Well, old Dave had a purple birthmark over near half his face, and they had an old red cowdog named Susie with 'em. Anyhow, they showed up in my camp madder'n a couple of boxed bobcats on account of they thought I'd made off with their camel. . . ."

"Mayhap it were in them years when you was down to Mexico, Cole," Lop Ear cut in happily. "When you was down there, did you shoot Biggs's brother, too?"

Cole glared at him.

"Why," said Jingles, miraculously back on the subject again, "if I hadn't switched that pistol of yours, you'd be danglin' by your neck from Janeway's porch right this minute. A man can die a lot of places, Cole, but Janeway's front stoop is not one I'd pick."

Cole grumbled something I couldn't make out, and then he tossed his stick into the fire. He looked at me, ignoring Jingles completely. "I should have stopped it, kid. I'm sorry. Shoulda put the kibosh on the whole damned thing."

I softened a little. Hearing Cole actually say he was sorry about something — about anything — was what did it, I suppose. I said, "Well, everything was so confusing. I should have said something myself, except that I was —"

"Pure dumbfounded, boy!" cackled Lop Ear, and he slapped his thigh. "Never seen another white man so thunderstruck in all my borned days!"

"I suppose I was," I admitted, and smiled a bit sheepishly.

"You're takin' this way too light, kid," Cole said. He leaned forward. "Don't you know about John Henry Strider?"

"He was someone who killed a lot of people?" I ventured. It was the sum and total of my knowledge of the man.

"Damn right," replied Cole. "He was a hired gun. Worked for the mining interests, or anybody who'd hire him. And he had a reputation."

Serious for once, Jingles nodded.

Lop Ear, turning the ham, muttered, "That he did, that he did."

"A reputation for what?" I asked.

Cole let out a quick little huff of air. "For bein' fast, you idiot. For bein' deadly. I'm tellin' you, I should have stopped it — somebody should have — because once word gets out that you killed that shootist, you're gonna have every quick-draw Johnny in the territory on your tail."

I'm ashamed to admit it, but I honestly did not understand him. "Whatever for?"

"Tryin' to kill you, that's what!" Cole roared, and swept his arms wide. "This ain't New York! This ain't even Missouri, goddamn it! Out here, bein' fast with a gun's the only claim to fame some men have got. And if gunnin' you down is a way to make that claim bigger, they're gonna come after you. Make no mistake."

Belatedly, the gravity of the situation settled over me. Men, coming after me? I had yet to fire my pistol, and I couldn't imagine aiming it at another human, not even to save my life. I hunched over my knees, hugging them. "Dear," I muttered. "Oh, dear!"

"Oh, dear," parroted Lop Ear. "Goodneth grathious!"

Jingles rubbed at his nose. "Well now, I reckon I didn't think about that, Cole. A feller can't be perspicacious every dadgum second of the day, you know. Young Donovan, I hereby humbly apologize for any grief that may come to you."

"Please!" I said, wearily closing my eyes and fervently wishing that my parents had never gone to France, that they'd never been killed, and that I was back at school, innocently studying Latin and mathematics and feeling sad for myself because my allowance was late in coming. "My name isn't Donovan. For the millionth time, it's Smith!"

"First time I heard of it," remarked Jingles, and stared out into the darkness. "You tether my Comanche far enough from those other horses?"

"Whatever your name is, what's done is done," pronounced Lop Ear. "And so's these biscuits."

13

It took us nearly a full day to ride from our camp outside Poco Bueno to the Aztec Princess, mostly because the wagon slowed our progress over the increasingly rugged terrain. While Jingles's wagon rattled and banged and bumped over dusty ruts — or worse, virgin desert — the noise of those damnable bells kept our conversation to a minimum. This was fine with me, as I had a great deal to mull over.

John Henry Strider, for one. Why on earth had he asked my name? This had only flickered back into my memory somewhat after the fact, and it struck me as very curious. And what had he said when I'd told him? "Ain't this lucky," or some such. Why, it was as if he were looking for me!

I tried to banish this impossible notion from my mind. Perhaps Cole had been right after all. Perhaps hearing the name Horace simply brought out the worst in Westerners.

And, all things considered, I supposed I could forgive Jingles for snatching the pistol from my holster and filling my hand with Cole's gun. After all, now that I'd heard about the bad blood between Janeway and Cole — and, more mysteriously, between Biggs and Cole — switching pistols must have seemed, to Jingles's twisted logic, his only recourse.

I wished it had occurred to him to stick the firearm into Lop Ear's hand instead of mine, though.

Additionally, I had a case of nerves about the telegram. I thought that perhaps I should have given Mr. Aloysius Dean a firm figure for commencing operations on the mine, but then, I hadn't the slightest idea what that might be. Not without consulting Cole, anyway.

But then, I reasoned, hadn't attorneys Dean and Cummings — on father's behalf — done this sort of thing for Uncle Hector many times before? They, above all others, should be able to ascertain the proper funding. With any luck, the money should be waiting for me when we got back to Tonto's Wickiup. If we ever did. Our progress was so slow, what with having to clear brush every few minutes so the wagon could get through — and Jingles having to "lever up" his pony every other time she stopped — I was beginning to wonder.

Each time we paused to rest the horses and that damnable din of bells stopped, Jingles babbled without cease. By late afternoon, I was fully informed on subjects as diverse and dubious as the native savages being the Lost Tribe of Israel; the care and feeding of pachyderms, canaries, and camels; the proper weaving of Navajo blankets and the nurture of Apache boys; the Mexican War, in which I gathered he had played some role; and the life and times of a lawman named Wyatt Earp, including those of his many brothers and associates.

This last part I had some interest in, because one of Earp's closest companions was Doc Holliday. The stories Jingles told were quite different from the one in my book, however, and I didn't know which to believe.

There may have been other topics, but frankly, I can't remember them. Jingles was inexhaustible. Cole didn't even attempt to get a word in edgewise, and I was limited to an occasional "Really?" or "My goodness." Lop Ear's comments filled in the lulls, although they were far too few.

It was nearly nightfall when we traversed the last brushy valley and came upon the

Aztec Princess. Jingles, without being warned, halted his jangling wagon and team a good distance away.

"I'm not goin' to take a chance on winding up in one of those sinkholes, no, sir," he said as he climbed down from his wagon. "We have had them in Tombstone, too, right smack in town. Miracle they got the horses out. Roan and a nice buckskin, as I remember. You sure you got no bats?"

"No bats." I had already reassured him countless times there was not one single bat in the Aztec Princess to the best of my knowledge.

"Can't be too careful about bats," he said.

My head was still ringing, and I rubbed at my ear as he began to unharness the team. The others had ridden ahead, but I lingered.

"I've been meaning to ask you, Jingles," I said, probably a bit louder than necessary. "Why on earth do you want such a noisy wagon?"

"Apache," he replied, and slid me a conspiratorial glance, as if this should say it all.

But it didn't, and I asked, "What about Apache?"

He had just pulled the cotton from Gracie's ears. As she made an abortive attempt to take a bite out of his leg, he said, "Why, they're afraid of the noise! They think it's ghosts coming. I am not bothered by Apache anymore, I can tell you that much. Keep your choppers to yourself, pusscat."

Grace groaned and sat down, and I leaned on my saddle horn. "But Cole told me the Apache have all been rounded up. I don't see why —"

"You never can tell when one of those devils is goin' to jump the reservation, young Tate Horace Smith Donovan, or whatever your name is," he said, leading Comanche from the traces. That poor sorrel looked more swaybacked every time I looked at him. If you had balanced a straight board from his withers to his croup, I honestly believe the drop from the plank to his sagging topline would have been a good two feet.

"I figure to be prepared, that's all," he continued. "I have had my run-ins with Apache — yessirree, Bob — and I do not care to repeat the experience. Now, when I know you better, I will tell you the story about how I came to get my gold bar."

And then, although the swayback gave no visible sign whatsoever of a change in attitude — his eyes were, in fact, half lidded — Jingles suddenly took a firm hold on his bridle.

"Easy, boy! Down, I say!" He turned to

me and hissed, "You'd best ride on down after the others. My Comanche is getting worked up, and you do not want to be around when a foul mood strikes him."

Although I was mildly intrigued by that gold bar, I had already learned not to press Jingles. Any questions were liable to lead into a dislocated tangle of how to trim a burro's hooves or mule skinning on the Santa Fe Trail or somesuch, and never get back to the point. So I touched the brim of my hat and clucked to Tell.

Later that evening, Jingles and Lop Ear and Cole lit candles and went down the shaft to have a look. I stayed up top with the horses and Loretta. I'd had enough of mine shafts already, and didn't see any point on trudging down into that claustrophobic — and snake-infested — darkness when I didn't absolutely have to.

They were down there quite some time, during which I called Loretta to me and started making her over to pass the time. She really was quite a nice dog, once you got past her looks, and she seemed more than appreciative of the attention. I even went to my packs, dug out the body brush I used on Tell, and gave her a good going-over.

Oh, she loved that! The hair and burrs and nettles fairly flew, and with them a good bit of dirt that had me sneezing. She closed her eyes and stretched out her neck, and made all sorts of contented moans and whines and what I can only describe as gurgles, and leaned into the brush so hard that had I not physically held her up, she would have toppled over.

I was just looking her over, amazed at the transformation a little elbow grease had achieved, when she suddenly ceased licking me and stared off into the distance. A low growl, which I felt through her body more than heard, rose up in her, and she stiffened. I threw my arm over her shoulders and across her chest to hold her back — from what, I didn't know — and looked in the direction that seemed to disturb her.

The moon was fairly bright that night, but all I could see, other than the night-silvered shapes of the fallen building, the old pump, and the surrounding vegetation were the shadows of two of those gaping holes, where the mine had caved in on itself.

Loretta's growl rose audibly. She lunged forward, but I caught her before she had gone an inch and hugged her tighter. Whatever was out there, I didn't wish Loretta, brave thing, to fall victim to it.

And just then, I saw it. A shadow at the edge of one of the holes in the ground, the one farthest from me. Well, it wasn't a separate shadow at first. It was more like the hole was suddenly growing, had come alive, like something out of an Edgar Allan Poe tale. All the hairs on the back of my neck stood up, and I swallowed hard. But then the swell of black suddenly separated from the main of the hole, and moonlight eerily struck a bobcat's silhouette.

Abruptly, Loretta burst into a frenzy of furious barks that nearly deafened me. I must have loosened my grip on her, because she gave a tremendous push and vaulted through the ring made by my neck and my restraining arm and shoulder. The bobcat sprinted away with Loretta hard on its heels.

They were out of site in a nonce, and I didn't realize until they disappeared that Loretta had very nearly broken my jaw.

We rose with the sun the next morning and bid a hasty goodbye to Jingles and Lop Ear, who were happily unloading explosives from the wagon when I lost sight of them. Loretta, back from her late-night cat chase and, full of new burrs and grit, stood atop the wagon seat, overseeing.

"Are you certain they're entirely trustworthy?" I asked Cole. The question had plagued me for days, but it was the first chance I'd had to be alone with Cole. Frankly, I was certain that Jingles, although well intentioned, was half mad. I wasn't too sure about Lop Ear's sanity, either.

But Cole only scowled at me. I was becoming adept at reading those scowls and grimaces, though. This one said, "Don't be an idiot." Well, it was probably phrased a bit rougher than that, but I got the gist of it, and didn't ask him again. If he trusted those two old coots, I supposed I had no other choice but to go along with him.

We rode on in blessed silence, free from ringing and jangling and wagon thuds, punctuated only by the gentle scrapes of horse legs against brush, the soft creaking of saddle leather, and the occasional clatter of a bit against teeth. In fact, neither of us spoke another word until Cole called a halt at noon.

We watered the horses, and around a mouthful of jerky, Cole, completely out of the blue, asked, "You wantin' to learn to use that pistol?"

The question startled me, but not enough to keep me from nodding eagerly. "Yes! Certainly!"

He motioned me to follow, and walked

about twenty feet away from the horses. We were well out of those hills now and on the flat, where the growth was all thigh-high scrub and tall cactus with wide, twisty, gravelly bare spaces in between. He pointed to a large prickly pear about fifty feet away.

Still chewing his jerky, he pushed back his hat. "See if you can manage to hit that, Donovan."

I tucked my jerky into my pocket, drew my revolver, and rotated the chambers so that the hammer rested on a full one. Then I raised my gun with both hands, closed one eye, and sighted down on the cactus.

"Hold it," he snapped before I had a chance to pull the trigger.

The gun sagged in my hands.

"One hand," he said.

"It's heavy!"

"You'll get used to it. Jesus."

One-handed, I raised the pistol once more. Again, I closed one eye and sighted on the cactus.

But just as I was about to pull the trigger, he said, "Wait!"

Exasperated, I said, "*Now* what!"

"Keep both your eyes open, boy."

"Why?"

He growled, "Because I said so."

I arched my brows, hoping he would

notice what pains he was putting me to. But he didn't, so I sighed and raised the gun again.

This time, I pulled the trigger.

The gun jumped in my hand with such explosive force that I nearly dropped it. And worse, the cactus seemed to have suffered no damage whatsoever.

I was fully prepared to endure Cole's laughter, but all he said was, "Squeeze that trigger real easy, kid. Don't yank it."

I sighted and tried again.

This time I did better. I was prepared for the kick of the gun, and this time I gently squeezed the trigger. A pad on the left-hand side flew into the air! Of course, I had been aiming for the center, and this particular clump of prickly pear was perhaps eight feet wide, but I felt a thrill of accomplishment in having hit it at all.

Grinning, I turned to Cole. His face was void of expression, which took some of the wind out of my sails. He said, "Again."

He never asked me what part I was aiming at, which was just as well because I never hit my selected target dead on. But by the time I'd fired the fifth bullet from my trusty Colt, I was within a foot of my mark.

"Fair," he said, turning back toward the

horses. "We'll try again tonight."

We did. In fact, from then on, he let me practice every chance we got. I got better, if I do say so myself, and by the last time we practiced, just before we rode back into Tonto's Wickiup, I was drawing from the holster and firing in a reasonably smooth manner, and managed to puncture a hole less than a half foot from where I was aiming. Give or take an inch or two.

I was proud of myself. I was also aware that Cole wasn't doing this just to be nice, although he didn't offer his reasons. Oh, I knew that he felt bad about what had happened in Poco Bueno with John Henry Strider. I thought that Cole, in some sort of lopsided fashion, was trying to make it up to me.

But it dawned on me, when I was dozing off that first night, that Cole was readying me to face that which he was certain was coming — every quick-draw Johnny, as he had put it, in the territory.

I didn't really believe this would happen, if truth be told. After all, once I was back in Tonto's Wickiup, I would wrench my own name back into place and take care of this Donovan business. No one, I was certain, would think to look for me at Hanratty's.

We had Tonto's Wickiup in sight, on the

distant, flat horizon, when I finally asked Cole the question. I had thought how to work up to it over the last day, but it still took a great deal of throat clearing to muster the courage to start.

"Somethin' wrong with your lungs, kid?" Cole asked me.

"N-nothing," I said as I got hold of myself. "I was just wondering . . . that is . . ."

"Spit it out," he grumbled.

"Why did someone shoot your horse out from under you?" There. It was finally out, at least the first part of it. "When you were up north, seeing about Uncle Hector, I mean."

"I know what you mean," he snapped. "It ain't like somebody drops my pony every other Tuesday." He took a moment to pat Ranger's neck, and then he looked over at me again for a long time before he said, "I don't know. But I'm thinkin' it was on account of the mine. Your mine."

"My copper mine?" Frankly, I was puzzled. Why on earth would anybody shoot Cole's horse over a copper mine that was barely breaking even?

"No, the Aztec Princess. Now Heck didn't say a word to nobody. He could keep a secret, all right, so I can't figure how anybody would have known about it." He reined in Ranger and sat there, his palms pressed into the saddle's horn. "But somehow somebody found out. And they killed him for it. Tried to kill me, too. Missed and hit Brownie instead."

"But why on earth would someone . . . ?"

"Kid, I don't know." He shook his head. "It's just . . . well, I can't figure any other reason anybody'd have to give old Heck a shove down that shaft, that's all. Everybody liked Heck."

I didn't argue with him, but it seemed to me that he was just guessing, both about Uncle Hector's "murder" and the reasoning for it. There was no need for me to embarrass myself any further. I simply nodded, said, "Thank you, Cole," and rode on.

Riding in silence once again, we came into town and were most of the way to the livery stable when my life changed. That was when I first saw her, you see, there on the walk in front of the milliner's shop, and instantly knew she would be the one. She was small and blond, with the face of an angel: bee-stung lips, a pert little nose, and big blue eyes, bright with intelligence and twinkling with humor.

I nearly fell from the saddle, and in fact, Cole reached out and grasped my arm. "You all right, boy?" he asked. "Your color's off."

I shook off his hand and pointed to the sidewalk, asking, "Who is that girl? The one with the older woman." I had guessed the latter to be her mother and had already wondered whether she would approve of her daughter marrying the local whoremaster.

"Those gals in front of the hat shop?" Cole said. "That's Mrs. O'Brien and one of her daughters. They've got about ten of 'em, I reckon. I think that one's Annie. Third from the oldest. Their oldest girl, Jane, she's teachin' in the school now. Why?"

By this time, we had ridden past the milliner's shop, and I was turned halfway round in my saddle, staring. Annie glanced up, and without knowing it, I raised a hand in greeting. She smiled and daintily waved a delicate hand to me before her mother spoke to her, distracting her attention.

I righted myself in the saddle. Cole was staring at me, expecting an answer to his inquiry.

"Because I'm going to marry her," I said. And that was that. Some things, you just know.

14

After settling the horses at the livery, we started up the street toward Hanratty's, carrying our saddlebags and pack rolls. Cole finally spoke. "Marry her?" he said, with a twinkle in his eye.

I felt heat creeping up my neck, and snapped, "I don't appreciate being the brunt of your private jest, sir." I already regretted blurting out my intentions, but it was too late to take the words back. The intentions, however, I wished to stand by. Just not to Cole.

Cole laughed softly, but didn't press the point.

We were about a foot from Hanratty's swinging doors when I heard a shot, and at the same time felt my ear sting. I must say that I didn't put the two together. I simply slapped a hand to my bloody ear, insulted that in addition to venomous snakes and spiders, Arizona had boy-biting bees!

Cole put a hand to my shoulder and shoved me through the batwing doors before I had a chance to remark on it, though. I landed on the floor in a heap, and watched as, beneath the doors, Cole's belongings dropped to the sidewalk and his booted feet took off, toward the sound of the shot.

And then Belle was at my side, wailing, "What happened? You're hurt! Where's Cole!"

I do not remember if I answered, for I had just then realized that someone had shot at me — at me! — and scrambled backward, across the floor, until the stairway's first step pressed into the small of my back.

Belle pressed a damp bar towel to the side of my head, and repeated, "Where's Cole?"

Just then, two more shots split the air, fired in rapid succession. Then a third!

Belle rose to her feet, crying, "My God, Cole! What is it?"

It was then I knew that Belle would not keep me from my Anne. It was Cole and Cole alone she loved. There was a tinge of sadness upon my heart, but also joy. Now nothing stood between me and Anne — other than the fact that she had never met me, of course.

And I must admit, with a great deal of

shame, that it was only then that I came to my senses and realized that Cole had more than likely gone to apprehend whoever it was who had fired at me. He was out there, protecting me with his own life! I tried to spring to my feet without much success, but on the third try, I made it. With Belle screaming for me to come back, I rushed to the doors and pushed through, to the sidewalk.

Cole was nowhere in sight. I started up the street in the direction he'd taken — trembling hand on the butt of my gun, fear so thick in my veins that it was a wonder I could walk at all, and clinging close to the storefronts. There was no one else around, but a hint of movement behind the window of a store across the way told me that everyone had gone inside.

To hide, no doubt. It seemed as if the entire town had suddenly been lifted into Glory.

Which was exactly what was going to happen to me, if I wasn't careful. But by the time I managed to drag my trembling form one block, I saw a man's shadow, up ahead, emerging from the mouth of an alley.

Cole had trained me well. I "skinned leather" and smoothly drew — and just stopped myself from firing in time. The man was Cole, and he was holstering his gun.

I stood there, frozen into place, while he walked the two blocks between us. Up and down the street, doors slowly creaked open. Shouts of "Everything all right, Jeffries?" and "What the hell's goin' on out there?" rang through the streets.

Cole, still walking, called to one man, "Get the sheriff, Red. Undertaker, too, I reckon." His face was deadly serious.

Red, whoever he was, ran up the street and out of sight at about the time Cole reached me. He gave me a long stare and said, "Thought I shoved you outta harm's way, kid."

I squared my shoulders. "Only for so long. And I'm not a kid."

"Remains to be seen," he muttered, and pushed past me.

I followed him into Hanratty's, and slouched beside him when he pulled out a chair at Uncle Hector's special table. "Beer," he shouted to Willie, just as Belle joined us.

"I was so worried!" she murmured, and started to fawn over him. "Who was it this time, Cole? The Blakely brothers? Seth Thompson? I heard he was headed down this way."

"Wasn't me they were shootin' at." He

pulled his watch from its pocket. "Walt Eli must be out to lunch." He glanced at me, and added, "Eli's the law around Tonto's Wickiup, such as it is," before he turned to Belle again and shook his head. "Ol' Walt probably dived under the table the second he heard them shots."

At that moment, the sheriff — dark, short-ish, and husky — pushed his way through the doors and approached us. "Miss Belle," he said, touching the brim of his hat, then immediately focused his attention on Cole. "What did you ever to do Big Johnny Hill to make him mad enough to take a shot at you? More to the point, what'd you do to whoever hired him?"

Cole's beer appeared at about that time, and he took a long drink before he said, "Damned if I know, Walt. I 'specially don't know what this boy, here, did to get him riled."

The sheriff suddenly took a good look at me and said, "You're bleedin', boy!"

"Willie, I forgot," the negligent Belle piped up. "Go get Doc Hastings."

Cole briefly capsulized what had hap-pened — while I marveled that Belle could have forgotten I was injured — and then he came to the part I didn't know. It seemed that this Big John Hill character was a wanted gunman, one who hired himself out, usually to someone who wished somebody else dead. Cole remarked that Hill had thirty-three notches on his gun. Sheriff Eli remarked that it was a "pure-D miracle" that it wasn't thirty-four, to which Cole replied that he knew what he was doing, thank you very much.

I had no reason to doubt him, although the sheriff just shrugged. My anger with Cole over the mines and Lop Ear and Jingles had transformed back into the admiration I had once held for him. He had saved my life, and I was grateful.

The doctor came and patched my ear, remarking that it was "goddamn miraculous" I hadn't been killed. As it was, a small piece had been nicked from the upper cartilage, so my ear, if you looked at it closely, would forever have a notched appearance. All in all, however, it was a very small thing.

After the wound was cauterized — a much more painful procedure than the original injury, I assure you — I went back downstairs. Hanratty's had opened for the day during my absence, and the customers were already two and three deep at the bar. Cole was still slouched at Uncle Hector's private table — sans the sheriff — and the lovely Belle was nowhere in sight.

I strolled over to Cole, dodging two miners and a cowhand along the way, and sat down.

Cole looked up from his beer. "Why ain't you in bed?" he asked.

"I wasn't hurt that badly. Cole, I want to go up to the Lucky Seven."

"What the hell for? You aimin' to get yourself killed for real this time?"

I sighed. "Cole, two men have come after me in the past four days. I don't know why, because you keep killing them before they can be questioned. I want to find out why."

He glowered at me, but said nothing, for just then, Belle joined us.

She flounced down onto his lap, said, "Hiya, Horace!" to me, and planted a kiss on Cole's lips. It lasted a considerable time.

Again, I felt a pull toward Belle, but this time, it was with nostalgia, of all things. The beautiful Anne awaited me, after all. I filed Belle in the past with the other silly, overreaching, and ludicrous dreams of my childhood, and decided to concentrate on my future. I would be serious. I would be steadfast. And I wanted to get this thing cleared up before I brought my sweet Annie O'Brien into it.

Already, she was "my sweet Annie."

"You're liable to get yourself dead, kid," Cole said.

I thought quickly. "Not if you come along!"

"Whoa!" said Belle. "Just what are you boys up to now?"

Before Cole had a chance to answer, I said, "I'm attempting to learn who is trying to kill me, Belle, and why."

Her brow furrowed. "Kill you? I thought it was Cole that Big John Hill was after!"

Grudgingly, Cole said, "No, Belle. I'm afraid he was after Donovan, here. And we ran into John Henry Strider a coupla days ago. He was ready to gun down the kid, too."

I said, "Then you're just as puzzled as I, Cole?"

He stared at his half-empty beer mug for a second, then said, "All right, yeah, I am."

"John Henry Strider?" Belle cried, loud enough that a few men turned their heads our way. "John Henry Strider's out after Horace, too?"

"Was," I said. "Cole killed him, although I got the blame."

"Cole . . ." she began, but he hushed her.

"Let's talk about this upstairs, honey," he urged as he stood up.

She stood up, too, saying, "Horace, don't

you set one blasted foot outside! You hear me?"

"Yes, Belle," I said. I had no intention of going through Hanratty's doors again. At least, not until we set out for the Lucky Seven.

Once Belle and Cole had gone upstairs and closed the door behind them, it occurred to me that it might be a smart, although not honorable, idea to go upstairs, too, and listen to their conversation.

I had a brief tussle with myself over this, but in the end, intelligence won out over ideals, and I climbed the stairs. I quickly made my way to the bedroom, wrestled off my boots, and lay on the bed, my good ear to the wall.

"Well, how did Strider know who he was?" Belle was demanding.

"Because the little idiot told him," Cole replied curtly, and I flushed with shame. It is one thing to hear someone call you an idiot to your face, but another entirely to overhear it said to another person. Especially to one you like.

Belle muttered something I couldn't make out, and then Cole answered, "I don't know, honey. I don't know why the hell Strider was lookin' for him, and I can't figure Hill, either. Unless it has somethin' to do with the mine."

"What mine?"

"Never mind. C'mere."

"Don't try to pretty talk me, Cole Jeffries! What's going on?"

"Belle." He sighed. "I can't tell you. I promised the kid, okay?"

Of all the times to keep his word, after he'd told nearly everyone else in the territory!

And Belle didn't press him, drat her! She said, "All right, Cole Jeffries. I'm letting you off the hook, just this once."

Afterward, there was no more conversation, just the sounds of grown-up things taking place, so I went back out to my parlor, sank down in the leather chair, and slept.

I awakened to the thuds of a fist pounding on my door, and realized that I had slept through the afternoon and the night in Uncle Hector's chair. Morning was just breaking outside my windows when I groggily called, "Just a minute!"

Cole, fully dressed, was at my door. "Well?" he demanded.

I ground fists into my eyes. "Well, what?"

"Thought you wanted to take a ride up to the Lucky Seven."

"Now?"

"Good a time as any," he said as he turned toward the landing. "C'mon, kid. Get a move on."

We traveled to the northwest, and by dusk, we found ourselves just outside the beehive of activity that was the Lucky Seven mine. It was, as Cole said, a full-tilt operation, with a smelter, barracks for the miners, a cookhouse, and other assorted buildings, even a small church. Men were everywhere, whistles blew, dogs and burros and goats meandered through the crowd of grubby miners coming off shift and the slightly cleaner ones starting to work.

The landscape had grown quite hilly for the last few miles, and the main shaft of the Lucky Seven started in the top of the highest hill I'd seen thus far, and went straight down. I say this, because there was a cage of sorts, rigged to go up and down in the mine on a series of chains. It was powered by a trio of mules who walked round and round, turning a giant spindle, which lowered the cage. When they wanted to bring someone up, an employee would go fuss with the rigging, and the mules would start walking again. I was fascinated to see how it worked!

Cole and I rode directly up to a door at the end of a long building, and dismounted.

There was a small sign that said, LUCKY SEVEN ENTERPRISES, HECTOR PEMBERTON, PROPRIETOR.

Cole tossed his reins over the rail. I did, too, and followed him through the door and into what proved to be the office.

A harried-looking man sat at the desk, hunched over a ledger. He looked up quickly, frowned, and thumbed his visor back a hair. "You again?" he growled at Cole. "What now?"

"Brought the new owner up to inspect the place, Trimble, and nice to see you, too. You find Heck's body, yet?"

The clerk's frown deepened, but he stood up and reached a limp hand over the desk. I took it, saying, "Horace Tate Pemberton Smith, at your service, sir," and gave it a firm shake.

"You think you got enough names, kid?" he said, pulling away. He stuck his hand under his armpit and added, "That's quite the handshake you got there."

"Just call him Donovan," Cole said. His eyes narrowed, and he looked straight at Mr. Trimble. "Now about Heck . . ."

Cole had a way with people. Pretty soon, Mr. Trimble was disgorging more information than anyone needed to know. They had found Uncle Hector's body — much the worse for wear, I imagined — and they had also come across a fresh vein of copper ore. The crew was mining this now. Trimble had, indeed, also seen a man of Big John Hill's description around the site at the time of Uncle Hector's death, and after, when Cole had come up to see about him. And had his poor horse shot from beneath him.

"It's a puzzlement, kid," Cole said to me, once we'd walked a distance from the camp and the sun was going down. "I'll be hanged for a chicken thief if Hill wasn't the rat bastard what gave ol' Heck a shove down the shaft, and killed my Brownie horse, too. But . . ." He threw up his hands, then pulled out his tobacco pouch and proceeded to roll himself a cigarette.

He pulled a match from his tin and flicked it to life. "This whole thing is way beyond me," he said around the smoke he was lighting. "C'mon, kid. You're the one with all that fancy education. You got any ideas?"

I shrugged. I honestly didn't have a clue.

That night, Cole and I slept apart from the others — which meant on the ground, ringed by our ropes. I had barely nodded off when I thought I heard a familiar voice.

Willie? Willie from Hanratty's?

I opened my eyes and sat up.

"Cole?" the voice came again, in an exaggerated stage whisper. "Cole! Horace! Shit, I mean, Tate! You out here?"

I stood up and whispered, "Willie?" into the darkness.

I heard stumbling feet approaching, then made out Willie's bulky form emerging from the darkness. I waved a hand, and whispered, "Willie, over here!"

"Thank God," he muttered. "Bad enough I gotta ride up here, half in the dark." He neared and stopped, facing me. "Worse still that you two lunatics had to sleep on the ground instead of in a nice building. With lamps 'n' candles." He paused to dig through his pockets, during which time, Cole came awake.

"What!" he said, jumping to his feet and drawing his gun all at the same time.

"No need for theatrics," I said, with a touch of superiority. "It's Willie. From Hanratty's."

"I know where he's from," Cole snarled before he turned to our visitor. "What is it, Willie? Somethin' wrong with Belle?"

"Naw," Willie grumbled. "Got a wire for the . . . Got a wire for Horace — I mean Tate." He produced a crumpled wad of paper and held it out. "Belle thought it might be important."

246

I took it and smoothed it, a feat that took no small amount of time.

"You rode up here in the middle of the night?" Cole was asking.

"It was light when I started out," Willie said defensively. "Ain't my fault. You know how Belle is, Cole, when she gets an idea in her head 'bout something."

I looked up from the telegram, which I was squinting at in the moonlight. It was nothing, after all. "It's all right," I said, folded the mangled paper, and tucked it in my pocket. "Just a wire from Mr. Aloysius Dean, Father's attorney." I believe I said it a bit grandly, as if Mr. Dean were my attorney, as well. Which I suppose he was.

As one, Willie and Cole said, "Well?"

I blinked. "What?"

They looked at each other, and then Cole said, "A man rode near thirty miles, some of it in the dark, to bring you that paper. Least you can do is to read it to him! Ain't you got no manners?"

I snapped, "Of course I do!" although I didn't add that I failed to see the sharing of private information as socially relevant. Additionally, I had no wish to share it, for Mr. Dean had wired to ask me how much money I needed.

I continued. "Mr. Dean asks after my

health and wonders if Uncle Hector is doing right by me, that's all."

Willie scowled. "Well, why the hell couldn't he put that in a regular letter, 'stead of gettin' everybody all riled up?"

Cole put his hand on Willie's shoulder. "I reckon everything's a big emergency to New York City folks, Willie. You want to bed down with us? You had any chuck yet?"

While they talked, I wandered across the camp to a torch left blazing before one of the buildings. In its unsteady light, I once again read the wire, then again. I supposed I would have to share it with Cole, after all. Not that I really had a reason to keep it to myself, but one likes to think one has some bits of discretion left, even if they're nonsensical.

And besides, perhaps Cole would know how much cash would be required. Or at least, he would be able to communicate with Lop Ear and Jingles, something I feared myself inadequate to do.

Understand anything that came out of their mouths, I mean.

I tucked the telegram away and picked my way back to my bedroll. Apparently Cole had rustled up something from the cookhouse, because Willie was fully occupied with a plate heaped with something roughly resembling food. I sat down on my blankets, after giving them a quick kick in case of snakes.

"You're learnin', kid," Cole muttered.

I made no response, either to the "you're learning" or the "kid." I simply eased my head down upon my saddle and closed my eyes, and let my thoughts ramble pleasantly from Annie to my impending riches and back to Annie, until I nodded off.

I learned very little at the Lucky Seven, aside from the fact that Uncle Hector's body had been swiftly buried again once it was rescued, and that I could count on a small income from the mine itself. For an undisclosed period, at any rate.

However, I did not think the copper income would be nearly sufficient to cover the costs of reopening the Aztec Princess. That was the preeminent matter weighing upon my mind. After we paid our respects at Uncle Hector's grave, we bade Mr. Trimble goodbye and rode out of the camp, and Cole said, "How's it feel?"

"How's what feel? Uncle Hector, you mean?"

"Realizin' all those boys back there depend on you for a paycheck," he said.

I hadn't honestly thought about it, not like

that. To tell the truth, I hadn't really given much thought to all those buildings, all that livestock, and all those men, well, being my responsibility. After a pause, I said, "It is quite a commitment."

I glanced back, to where Willie was riding, and deemed him far enough away to be out of hearing range. "Cole, Mr. Dean wishes to know how much money will be needed to put the Aztec Princess in operation once more."

"Dean? The telegram Dean?"

I nodded and he snapped, "How the hell does he know anything about it?"

I was taken a bit aback, but replied, "Well, *you* told everyone that would hold still! I sent one wire — that was all."

"From where?" he demanded. "Where were we that had a telegraph office, Horace?"

His use of my correct name sent chills through my limbs, and I meekly replied, "Tombstone?"

He made a sound I cannot describe, but one I took to be intended to denote his total disgust, and he lashed Ranger with his reins. They sprinted out ahead a good fifty yards before Cole reined the horse back down to a walk.

I held Tell back, although he was game. If

a little thing like this could put Cole into such a foul mood, I had no intentions of keeping pace with him. Let him sulk on his own, I thought. Let me play the part of adult.

I could almost hear Cole's voice adding, in my head, *For a change.*

15

We were roughly ten miles from Phoenix when Willie, who at that time was riding off my left, exclaimed, "Where the hell's he goin'?"

"Why?" I asked. I had noticed that Cole, far up ahead, had veered off to the right, but I imagined that he knew where he was headed. This land all looked the same to me.

"Because he ain't goin' back to Tonto's Wickiup, that's why," Willie said and kicked his horse ahead, apparently intending to catch up with Cole, which he did in a moment.

Once again, I held my Tell back. I wasn't sure that I wanted to talk to Cole yet. I had been rolling his actions around in my mind, and frankly, I was irritated with his attitude! It was my mine, wasn't it? I surely had more business telling Mr. Dean — who might be of some financial use — about the strike than Cole had telling Jingles Beldon, the dynamiting, bell-ringing, camel-grooming king of the territory!

I watched while Cole and Willie appeared to hold a discussion. Then Willie came back onto the trail that we had been following — which would take us back to Tonto's Wickiup — and pushed his horse into a soft lope. I decided I had best find out what was going on, and despite my misgivings, I determined to check with Cole first.

After all, I reasoned, he had brought me.

So I urged Tell forward, and caught Cole in an instant. When I reached him and slowed down to ride alongside, though, he didn't acknowledge my presence.

"Cole?"

He still stared straight ahead, through his horse's ears.

I reached over and grabbed his shoulder. *"Cole!"* I repeated, half shouting.

At last, he acknowledged that I was breathing, if only with a curt nod. Still, it was something.

"Where are you going? Why is Willie going back to town alone?"

His jaw muscles worked for a long moment before he said, "Gotta talk to you, Donovan." He suddenly twisted toward me and snapped, "And don't tell me not to call you Donovan!"

After that outburst, I was almost afraid to prod him for more information — let alone correct him — and waited a good minute before I spoke again. "Well, I'm here, Cole. Go ahead and talk."

"Not now, kid. Not until I get a couple drinks in me, anyhow."

"What?"

He pointed up ahead. I saw a small cluster of shacks huddled on the horizon. "What is it?"

He said, "Whiskey," and pushed Ranger into a gallop.

Leave it to Cole to find a saloon in the middle of nowhere, I thought.

I had no choice but to follow.

Fifteen minutes later, we were seated in the shade of a rough saguaro-rib ramada, and Cole was tossing back his third shot of red-eye whiskey. The man in charge, one Lucius J. Crooke, seemed impressed with my being the owner of Hanratty's, and kept prodding me with nonsensical or plainly stupid questions, always followed by "You know, businessman to businessman?"

While I tried to keep Mr. Crooke entertained until Cole was well oiled enough to speak his mind to me, I noted the other

254

patrons. Both were seated deeper inside the ramada, in purple shade, but I made out two men, I thought, in opposite corners. One seemed a rough sort, the other a bit more cultured. I discerned this by looking at their boots, mind you. The toes of them were the only parts I could truly make out with any clarity.

Cole ordered himself a beer, this time, and added, "Give him one, too, Lucius."

When I declined it, he pressed the point, and I actually had to drink half of the warm brew before he was satisfied. I was not, however. There was a dead fly floating in it.

Cole waved Mr. Crooke off and leaned across the three-legged table, toward me. "All right, kid. I hope I got enough whiskey in me to hold me from swattin' you clean to Mexico." He stopped a moment to clear his throat. "You sent a telegram back east, the day we left Tombstone, right?"

I was still back on the part where I went to Mexico, powered by the force of one of his fists, and it took me a second to say, "Y-yes. Yes, I did."

"And you been tellin' everybody your real name's Horace Tate Whatever, even though I told you a dozen times to stick with Tate Donovan?"

"But I don't see what that has to do with —"

Something bumped my chair, and I looked up to see a rather large man standing at my shoulder. A quick glance down at his boots told me he was one of the fellows who had been seated in the shadows. The rough one. "You Horace Smith?" he asked, although it emerged as more of a growl.

I nodded, unsure of what to make of him.

He turned his attention to Cole, who was sliding out of his chair to stand. "You Cole Jeffries?" he grumbled again.

"What about it?" Cole replied, and I heard a dare in his voice. Frankly, at that moment, I was terrified of both of them.

"I'm Duffer Atbrun," the man said with a scowl as he stared at Cole. "Old John Hill was a friend o' mine, and you're the one what dropped him."

"Only after he nearly dropped me!" I heard myself saying, and slapped a hand over my own mouth, too late.

For at that second, one of Duff Atbrun's hamlike hands shoved me out of my chair, to the ground, and with his other, he drew his gun.

Thank God that Cole was faster! I heard two shots, so close in succession that one might have been the echo of the other, and

Duff Atbrun fell to his knees.

He wasn't dead quite yet, though, and he twisted to point his gun at me. More from training and instinct than any sense of bravery, I drew and fired, only realizing afterward that it was a living man I was shooting at, not a cactus.

But Atbrun tumbled, nonetheless. He went over backward and lay still.

I was still, too — frozen into place by the fact of what I had just done. *Oh, dear Mother and Father,* I remember thinking, *thank the Lord you're dead so I won't have to tell you about this!*

"Couldn'ta done that if he hadn't been drinkin' all afternoon," said Lucius Crooke, breaking the silence. "Hell, I didn't even know he could wobble up!"

Cole holstered his gun and came round the table. He kicked Atbrun's gun clear of his hand before he said, "Lucius, did you know he was gunnin' for me?"

Mr. Crooke shrank back somewhat under the blistering heat of Cole's accusatory tone, but he said, "Can't say as I did, Cole. He were madder than a bagful o' badgers when he rode in, but he didn't share no names with me."

Cole snorted. "Christ, Lucius, you coulda warned me. When's his lordship get back, anyway?"

Lucius shrugged. "Don't know. He's passed out." He indicated the second man in the shadows, the one with nicer boots.

I shook off the last of my paralysis, holstered my weapon, and said, "His lordship?"

"Forgot you were down there, kid," Cole said, and gave me a hand up. "His lordship's the proprietor of this ramshackle excuse for a saloon. Lord Daryl Duppa, that is."

"A real lord?" I had never heard anything so fantastic in my life as a real lord living practically on the open prairie!

"That's up for discussion," Cole said, and righted his chair. Atbrun's right leg had knocked it over when he toppled.

"No, son, he's a real one," Lucius said quickly. "English. His family, they pays him to stay over here, 'cross the pond."

"Oh," I said, staring at the corpse. I vaguely recalled hearing of such bounders as Duppa, ne'er-do-well shirttail royals whose families doled them out an allowance, so long as they didn't go back to England and embarrass the old coat of arms. But right at the moment, I was more concerned with the body, and the fact that I'd changed it from a living man into a deceased one.

Lucius was pouring Cole another beer. I

said, "Shouldn't someone . . . do something about him?" Neither Cole nor Lucius nor the man passed out in the shadows seemed the least bit concerned about him. In fact, Lucius stepped casually over the body to bring Cole his beer.

"Oh, too hot to do any diggin' now," Lucius said. "He'll keep till the sun goes down."

Cole said nothing, just tipped back his beer and took a long drink.

"You'll read the Bible over him?" I asked.

"Why?" Cole interjected before Lucius had a chance to answer. "You think that'll iron the wrinkles out of you killin' him? Or get him in good with God?"

Actually, I think I did. I shrank down in my seat and stared at my hands.

"From now on, kid, you listen to me, and you pay attention," he continued. His tone indicated that if I had ever listened to anyone, I should now be doubly heedful. And I was. "You will not tell anybody else about this Horace shit. That's ended right this minute. Got that?"

I nodded, vaguely offended. "Yessir."

"You won't send anymore goddamn telegrams or letters, not even to the Queen of England!"

"I don't see why I'd have any call to —"

"Shut up! Dad blast you, Donovan! You have a real goddamn knack for stirrin' up trouble," he shouted, "and by trouble, I mean gettin' people killed!" He kicked the late Mr. Atbrun's rib cage for emphasis, and a small cloud of dust rose from the corpse's vest.

"Yessir," I said, cowed. He'd made his point.

"I don't know how much trouble you dragged up, but I got a feelin' this is only the start of it, kid. From now on, you do what I say and *only* what I say — you got that?"

I nodded.

Cole seemed reasonably satisfied, and turned his attention to his beer and away from me.

I was glad.

We left the cluster of ramadas and lean-tos behind before dark — and therefore before anyone started digging a last resting place for the late Mr. Atbrun — and headed back toward Tonto's Wickiup. I cannot say that Cole was in an improved temper, but at least he had enough liquor in him that he didn't hit me. Nor did he preach at me anymore. He just rode on in silence, and I followed suit.

We came into Tonto's Wickiup just past sunset, and we were back at Hanratty's, which, at only seven thirty, was filled almost to the rafters. After I placed a dinner order with the mysterious Ma — I had yet to discern whose mother she really was — and tipped my hat to Belle, I went on up to my rooms.

I was exhausted. In the space of less than forty-eight hours, I had been shot in the ear, killed a man who pointed a gun at me, been offered a great deal of cash by Mr. Dean, discovered what had become of Uncle Hector, and learned that my copper mine would support me for a little while longer. And my ear still hurt.

Well, Mr. Dean hadn't exactly offered me cash. At least, it was not a firm deal as yet. And I hadn't had a chance to ask Cole about it. Not that I would have asked, even if I'd had a chance. I didn't dare make him angry again.

As I sat in Uncle Hector's leather chair, waiting for my dinner, I couldn't cleanse my mind of one image: the face of Mr. Atbrun, as he fell that last time. He had looked surprised, I recalled. He had looked as if he couldn't believe he had been killed by a child, and as if he was offended by the fact!

As awful as I felt about having pulled the

trigger, and as appalled as I was about what I perceived to be his reaction to my doing so, I found his attitude somewhat . . . off-putting. I cannot explain it better than that, other than to say it made my stomach queasy and my sense of right and wrong seem somehow tilted. It just didn't fit together — at least, not in any sense to which I was accustomed.

Willie was the one who delivered my supper, and I ate it alone, and deep in thought. I managed, somewhere during the entrée, to turn my thoughts to the charming and beautiful Annie O'Brien. I imagined meeting her by accident on the street, or perhaps in one of the stores of Tonto's Wickiup. I imagined how sweet and funny and kind and loving she'd be, and then imagined that she'd be simply wretched and not at all the girl I'd guessed when I'd glimpsed her shining face.

That was a little unsettling. I blamed it on Cole, naturally. His actions today had predisposed me to look on the ugly side, the unexpected side.

And I suddenly realized that he hadn't finished whatever it was he had started out to tell me. All he had done was lecture me on the merits of being his puppet, but he'd given me no concrete reasons for playing the part.

Well, tomorrow I'd ask him, straight out, just why he thought that the whole world had seemed to descend upon my head because I had sent a simple wire! It made not a lick of sense to me.

Of course, neither did John Henry Strider, nor Misters Hill or Atbrun. I was totally at a loss.

I tugged off my boots, climbed out of my clothes, and eased into that leviathan of a bed. And despite the muffled giggles and groans coming through the wall, I resisted the temptation to listen by falling directly to sleep.

I rose early the next morning, full of good intentions about writing that long overdue letter to Clive Barrow, and about arranging a meeting with Annie O'Brien. However, I had barely set pen to paper when there came a knock on my door.

It was Willie. My first thought was that he had come for last night's dirty dishes, but when I moved to get the tray, he said, "There's a feller, Horace. Tate. Boss."

I stopped and turned. "What 'feller?' "

"The one in the street. He's standin' out on the walk, and he keeps hollerin', 'Kid Donovan!' I reckoned that was you. . . ."

"Well, ask him to come in, for heaven's sake," I said, annoyed but curious. "I'll come downstairs in a moment."

But Willie didn't leave. "Already asked him. He said he's callin' you out."

"He's what?"

Willie rolled his eyes. "Callin' you out. Don't you know nothin'?"

"Apparently not," I replied, then tapped my lips. "Is Cole still in the next room?"

"Far's I know."

"All right. Thank you, Willie." I handed him the tray, then marched myself out into the hall and to Belle's door. I had to rap several times, but Belle herself finally straggled to the door and cracked it open an inch.

"Pardon my early intrusion," I said, "but I need to speak with Cole."

"Cole!" she yelled groggily, but at me, not at him. "Horace is here for you!"

I heard a groan in the dark, from behind her.

"I don't know. He didn't say," she replied. It seemed that while his grunts were indecipherable to me, she made them out with no trouble.

He grumbled again.

"What's it about?" she asked. By this time, her eyes were drifting closed again, and I was afraid she'd fall asleep while standing at the doorjamb.

"It's about the gentleman who's calling me out into the street," I said.

This time, I heard a quick rustle of bedclothes, the thud of boots and the jingle of spurs, and the soft curses of a man trying to dress hurriedly. It was as I feared, then. Whoever was out there had come to kill me.

Yet again.

I was growing weary of the gesture.

Belle moved aside, and Cole stepped past her and out into the hall, still buckling his gun belt.

"Who is it?" was all he said.

"I don't know. Willie told me," I replied, then added, "You said I should do nothing without consulting you."

He looked up, and the expression on his face was, well, amused. I didn't quite know how to take it. "That's right, kid. I did. And just what did I stop you from doin' this time?"

"Going out to see what he wanted."

"Good thing you stopped, then." He moved past me and started down the stairs. I followed on his heels. "Probably some quick-draw Johnny lookin' to make his reputation," he said as our boot steps echoed hollow in the empty bar. "Either that, or another one of Johnny Hill's ilk."

He started out across the floor toward the doors, asking, "Willie? You ever seen this yahoo before?"

"New to me, Cole, and about all of twelve years old," Willie replied, polishing a glass.

Cole breathed, "Damn!" under his breath, and pushed through the swinging doors.

I watched him, from inside them. He walked out into the center of the street and shouted, "What you want, son?"

"I want Kid Donovan!" came the answer, and I had to stand to the side to see the young man, braced and ready to draw, a block up the street. He was most certainly not twelve, but he didn't appear to be much older than I.

"What for?" Cole called.

The question appeared to confuse the young man, who hesitated a long moment before he replied, "I wanna kill him! He killed John Henry Strider, didn't he?"

I saw Cole's chest heave with a sigh. His prophecy had come true, after all. He said, "As a matter of fact, son, he didn't. I did. Cole Jeffries is the name. You wanna draw on me?"

The boy's posture changed. He seemed to pull into himself, somehow, and he said, "Huh?"

"I asked if you wanted to call me out, instead," Cole said. Once again, I read amusement on his face, although I could see nothing remotely amusing in his situation.

Belle had followed us down the stairs, and she stood at my shoulder, watching the street. I whispered, "What on earth is he doing?"

She put a gentle hand on my arm. "Just playin'," she answered, with a little smile. "Honest. That Cole!"

The boy down the street appeared to be thinking it over, and not too happily. Finally, he said, "D-did you say Cole Jeffries?"

Cole nodded.

"If y'don't mind, sir, I'd a whole lot druther you sent the Kid out."

Cole said, "Well, you're gonna be disappointed, then, ain't you?"

The boy's face screwed up and he looked as if he were about to throw a tantrum when the sheriff moved into view. He leaned against a post across the way, and folded his arms. "Got trouble, Cole?" he asked. Down the street, the boy watched with keen — if nervous — interest.

"Nothin' I can't handle, Walt," Cole said, all confidence and bravado.

"Well, I don't want no fresh bodies in my

cemetery today," Sheriff Eli said, and swung his gaze down the way. "You're not from around here. What's your name, boy?"

The lad hesitated, then called, "Joe Turner."

"Well, be off with you, Joe Turner," the sheriff said. "Go on, now. Scat!"

Young Turner threw a glance toward the saloon — and right toward where I was standing, although I don't think he could have seen me in the shadows — then turned and slouched back down the street, toward a horse tied at the rail. He was on his way out of town before Cole relaxed.

"Thanks, Walt," he said with a wave.

"No trouble, Cole," replied the sheriff. "But I'd appreciate if you'd get Heck's boy outta town for a while." He walked off, and Cole came back inside, leaving me to wonder why the sheriff seemed to think it was *my* fault!

Cole walked right past me with no further explanation and muttered, "Beer," at Willie. Then he sat down next to Belle, who waited at Uncle Hector's private table.

"You're alive, darlin'," she said, and kissed his cheek.

"That I am, Belle," he replied, and took her into his arms.

She giggled.

16

If Cole planned on getting me out of town, I was going to make certain he didn't do it before I got to meet Miss Annie O'Brien. While he sat alongside Belle, nursing his beer, I sauntered casually over to the bar and whispered a question to Willie.

"Two blocks south and over one west," he said as he polished a glass. "Can't miss it. It's the white one with the big front porch and the double swings. Why?"

I didn't bother to answer him. I simply thanked him and set off, down the street, letting Cole's "Hey, kid!" ring unheeded, behind me on the air.

I was glad I had taken care when dressing that morning. Uncle Hector's pants and sleeves were a bit long, but a much better fit than my own clothes. And I fancied the blue of the brocade vest looked nice with my eyes. As I neared the O'Brien home, I pushed my hat — one of Uncle Hector's best beaver Stetsons, actually — down a little lower to disguise my bandaged ear.

The house was as Willie had described it — unmistakable. It was the only wooden house on the block and the largest; it had a long front veranda with a wide porch swing on either side of the front door. I supposed they needed two swings, if they had all those daughters; then I felt heat flood my face when I imagined myself sitting and swinging with Annie. And kissing those bee-stung lips.

I stopped across the street and waited for my face to cool.

I had given much thought to the correct way to approach Annie, and had finally settled on that which I considered most proper. I girded my loins, cleared my throat, and strode across the street, trying to appear full of confidence. I opened the gate of her white picket fence and stepped onto the porch. I knocked.

Almost at the same instant, the door opened, and I believe I jumped a little. There stood Mrs. O'Brien, Annie's mother. I gulped.

"Mornin', son," she said. Her eyes had the same hint of veiled amusement that Cole's had shown earlier, and for a moment

I wondered why everyone was laughing at me.

But I collected myself, nodded my head, and said, "Good morning, Mrs. O'Brien. My name is Horace Smith, and I wondered if I might speak to your daughter, Anne."

"You're the new owner of Hanratty's?" she asked, her amused look deepening.

"It seems that word travels quickly in a small town such as this," I said, forcing a smile of my own.

"Yes, it does, Mr. Smith," she replied. She showed no intention of going to fetch Anne, though.

"I hope it's not offensive to you, Mrs. O'Brien. I mean, my having inherited a . . . drinking house. I have every intention of divesting myself of —"

She turned, and called down the hall, "Annie! It's that boy from yesterday!" She turned back to me. And smiled openly. "You can't help the business your uncle was in." She gestured to the porch swing on the right. "Have a seat, Mr. Smith. She'll only be a moment."

"Mr. Smith?" asked the vision before me. I stood, instinctively, although I daresay my knees were knocking.

"C-call me Horace, Miss O'Brien."

271

Her face screwed up a tad, and she repeated, "Horace?"

"Or you could call me Tate," I quickly added. Perhaps Cole had been correct when he said not to mention my real name to anyone.

"Tate, then. I like that. Won't you please have a seat?"

I did without looking, and was most grateful when my backside met swing instead of porch. She sat beside me, although on the far side of the bench. "And you must call me Annie," she said, folding her delicate hands in her lap. When I sat there, mute and unable to think of a word to offer, she said, "And what brings you here this morning, Tate?"

"I . . . I wanted to meet you, Miss — I mean, Annie," I muttered. "That's all." Actually, I wanted to ask her to be my wife, bear my children, and allow me to spend the rest of my life worshipping her, but that seemed a bit much. At least, for our first meeting. I added, "I wanted to ask your permission to . . . keep company with you."

There. At least I had that part out. And suddenly, I wanted to drop right through the floorboards, lest she say no.

She tipped her head, and the light danced on her corn silk locks and twinkled in her clear blue eyes. "Keep company? But I don't know you, do I? Except that you're polite to ladies on the street, and wave rather than shouting catcalls or whistling."

"What better way is there to get to know each other than to keep company?" I parried.

"True," she said with a nod, and relaxed back into the arm of the swing. "Well, let's get started, shall we? Tell me about yourself, Tate."

I was growing increasingly relaxed with her — and was nearly up to the point where I spent my thirteenth summer in Ontario, with a paid companion — when Pony Girl, of all people, came traipsing up the street. She was dressed in her work clothing, and wore a generous display of face paint. Horrified, I watched as she opened the gate, leaned provocatively on its post, and said, "Hiya, sweetie. Cole wants you back up at the place. Hey, Annie."

I wanted to die.

But Annie smiled and said, "Morning, 'Randa. I was just about to offer Tate a glass of lemonade. Would you care for some?"

While I was still puzzling over the 'Randa part, Pony Girl said, "Thanks, but I gotta get Horace back. Cole's in a toot." Then she frowned at me and said, "C'mon, boss!

Daylight's burnin'!"

I rose, although I'll be damned if I remember how. But I do recall asking, as I walked out the gate, "May I call again, Annie?"

And I most assuredly remember her reply, which was "Surely, Tate," delivered with a wondrous smile.

The next thing I knew, I was being pulled back toward Hanratty's by Pony Girl. "Oh, Cole's pitchin' a fit, sugar," she said, attempting to hold her little robe closed with one hand and drag me with the other. "He wants you in there yesterday! What'd you do to piss him off, anyhow?"

"I — I —"

"Stop jawin' and start goin', honey!"

"I am!" I was stumbling over Uncle Hector's boots to keep up with her, as a matter of fact. "Who's 'Randa?"

Pony Girl looked at me as if I had seven eyes and eight ears. "Miranda's me, you fool!" she said, and pushed me through the doors of the bar. "I'm 'Randa!"

"Well, how was I supposed to know?" I asked, even as a hand — connected to Cole — descended upon my shoulder.

"Get movin', kid," he said, and gave me a shove back outside — and down into the dirt. He set out at a brisk clip toward the livery. "Don't worry," he said after I caught up with him. "Belle packed for you." He disentangled my bedroll and saddlebags from his and tossed them to me.

"Why?" I demanded, out of breath and struggling with my gear. "Where are we going?"

"Anywhere but here."

"But —"

"And I thought I told you not to write any letters, goddamn it! Belle found one in your room, half wrote!"

"But it was only to —"

We had reached the livery. Cole stopped and broke in, quite firmly, "When I tell you something, boy, I mean it. No letters. No telegrams. No communicatin' in any way, shape, or form!"

I gulped and blinked. "All right, Cole," I said. "I simply didn't think —"

"That's just the trouble, Donovan," he growled as he grabbed his saddle off the rack. "You don't think."

And I hated him again, because he was right.

We headed south, and were several miles from town before he deigned to speak to me again. "How you feel about Yuma, kid, or maybe Mexico?"

"One is as dismally bleak as the other, I

suppose," I said.

Part of me was still back on the O'Briens' porch with Miss Annie, and I couldn't begin to compare the warmth of her back-east-styled home — not a speck of adobe in sight! — with the sorts of shabby dives I imagined Cole would lead me to.

They would probably all be like that place yesterday, made of dried cactus and mud, and reeking of bad whiskey.

"Well, I don't reckon anybody's heard of you in Yuma, yet," he said, more to himself than me. "And they speak English there."

I actually perked up at this tidbit. "Yuma it is," I said, almost eagerly. With all the reasons I had to stay in Tonto's Wickiup — Annie being first on that list — it never crossed my mind to tell Cole I'd rather not go at all. I suppose he had cowed me that much. And also, I suppose that I saw in him something of a father figure, although he was far too young. He certainly acted the part, though.

Cole nodded curtly. "Fine. Yuma."

And then he lapsed back into silence again. After a few minutes had passed, with no sound other than the plod and crunch of Tell's and Ranger's hooves, the swish of brush underfoot, and the gentle creaking of leather, I dared to ask, "Cole? Yesterday, when that Mr. Atbrun tried to . . . I mean, before that, you were telling me something. And you didn't finish. What was it?"

Cole stared at me for a second and I feared I had stirred up a good bit of trouble, but then he said, "Been thinkin' it over, kid. Don't trouble yourself, yet. I'm thinkin' that I need to see a good paper."

"A good paper?"

"A good newspaper. You know, like one from back east, with the whole news in it. Not just the local crud, like back in town."

I said, "Oh." And then, "Why?"

Cole sniffed. "Just gotta check on a couple things, that's all. Don't want to go off half cocked."

I was only more puzzled. I asked, "Do you care to explain that?"

He grinned at me. "Nope," he said, then fanned Ranger's backside and took off at a dead gallop.

I had no choice but to follow.

Three evenings later, after camping out each night and not being snake- or spider-bitten, attacked by wandering camels or bobcats, or swarmed by disgruntled scorpions, we arrived in Yuma. I cannot say the town had much to recommend it, but then, I wasn't expecting much, and it was dark when we rode in.

After sleeping on the hard ground for nights on end, I was looking forward to a hotel bed, even if it did prove a tad buggy.

Cole, however, had other things on his mind.

We didn't even take the time to settle our horses at the livery. At his insistence, we tied them to the rail outside a little place called Cantina de Maria, and went inside, where Cole ordered dinner for both of us, along with a round of cervezas, which he translated for me. Beer.

At least this beer had no flies in it, and I choked down half a warm glass before they brought our supper. This was some foreign concoction that I hadn't understood when Cole ordered it, and still didn't comprehend after he explained it to me.

"That there's your enchiladas, kid," he said, pointing to my plate with his knife. "Beef, or so they say, with lots of goat cheese. Good sauce, too." The knife moved. "Those are *refritos* — that's refried beans to you — and that there's guacamole. Made from avocados. You can spread it on the tortillas," he added, pointing to a curious side dish that looked something like bread, but wasn't.

I stared at him, probably as blank as a

sheet of paper just pulled from the note-book.

"Oh, hell," he muttered, disgusted again. "Just eat up." He dug into the mess on his plate.

I watched him for a few seconds. He didn't seem to be seizing up, so I tried a bite of my beans. Surprisingly, they were quite good. I hadn't realized how hungry I was after having shared just one meager jackrabbit with Cole for lunch, and began to eat like a stevedore.

"This is Mexican food?" I said around a mouthful of enchilada. "It's wonderful!"

Cole just nodded and kept on eating. I avoided the little plate of jalapeño peppers that they brought with the meal, however — once burned, twice shy, as they say. Cole ate them all and washed them down with that horrible warm beer, and I kept expecting flames to shoot out of his mouth each time he opened it.

They didn't, though. And for dessert, he ordered us some kind of wonderful custard in caramel sauce, called flan. I must say, I hadn't enjoyed a meal so much in quite some time! Our table was cleared and I was ready to find a hotel, but Cole was not. We sat there, listening to a rather dreadful musical group — which he called a mariachi band — while he downed tequila after tequila and I began to feel rather . . . bloated.

Actually, I was in distress. I tried to ask Cole if there were any outhouses, since he seemed to know the town and the place, but the band was so loud that he couldn't hear me. When I could wait no longer, I stood up to head for the rear door.

I elbowed my way through the crowd standing on the open part of the floor — which, I suppose, was meant for dancing — and was nearly to the far edge of the mob when I heard someone say, "Donovan?"

I turned to find the source of the voice, which was thickly accented, gruff, and low, and I suddenly realized that the crowd through which I had been working my way was heavily armed, in addition to being rowdy and loud. I couldn't pick out the speaker, though. A cold chill gripped my spine, and I turned toward the rear door once again.

I twisted, only to face a rather broad, muscular Mexican man, thick of mustache and armed to the teeth. He stood there, blocking my way. And he smiled. I cannot say it was the most wholesome smile with which I have been greeted. I backed off a step, fully expecting to bump into some other patron, but there was none there. The floor had cleared, just like that, and I stood alone in the center of the room.

A hush had fallen over the gathering, as well, and for a moment there was no one in the world but myself and that horrid man, who still smiled coldly at me through yellow teeth.

"Donovan!" someone called behind me.

I wheeled once more. Three men stood behind me, spaced an arm's length apart, and any one of them might have called my name. All were staring at me, all were armed, and two were smiling, although none of them appeared particularly friendly. The last of the rest of the mob was quickly funneling out the front door.

I felt the chill in my spine turn to ice.

"Don-o-van," someone said in singsong. And then it was repeated by a new voice, and another, and another.

A quick glance toward my table told me that Cole had fled me, too. How could he? How could he desert me now?

And then I heard his voice, shouting, "Drop!"

I did! I hit that floor faster than gravity could account for, and landed on my face just as the place exploded with gunfire. It was as if ten cannons went off at once in a confined space, and abruptly my ears were of more concern than my burning bowels.

But I hadn't been shot, I quickly realized and, hands still over my ears, chanced a glance upward.

Another single shot turned my face downward again, and my eyes seemed to seal closed. From that dark, terrifying place, I heard the ring of spurs as boots neared. And then I felt a boot's toe nudge my side. I opened one eye.

"It's all right, kid" came Cole's familiar baritone, which, at that moment, I greeted as the voice of God Himself.

I climbed slowly to my feet, while taking in the six dead men that ringed me. One of them still twitched rhythmically.

"W-what happened?" I asked. I don't imagine it came out very forcefully. "W-was I supposed to ask permission for the outhouse?"

Amazingly, Cole chuckled, which nearly knocked me back to my knees again. However, I managed to hold my ground while he said, "Go on ahead, kid. It's out back."

I took a stiff step before he added, "Just be ready. I'd draw my gun, if I was you."

I complied and slowly made my way to the back door, stepping over two bodies of my would-be murderers along the way.

There was no trouble in the alley, and the outhouse was easy to spot — and to smell. As I sat there in the dark, one hand holding my testicles above seat level, I realized what had happened. Or at least, what I thought must have happened. Those miscreants had surrounded me. If they all fired at once, they would've naturally hit each other, I reasoned. And Cole had been there to take out the one that wasn't felled in the initial blast.

Thank God for Cole!

I decided, right then and there in that dark, dank, wretched outhouse, to cut him in for exactly one half of my profits from the Aztec Princess. As exasperating as he could be, he was my savior many times over and, I realized, the best friend I could possibly have. Even if he did call me by the wrong name.

Needless to say, we didn't stop the night in Yuma. We only stayed long enough for Cole to have some heated words with the sheriff, to most of which I was not privy. We rode a few miles out of town, then camped. By then, I must have imbibed a good half gallon of water — on top of the beer I'd had in town — and had to call a temporary halt to the journey twice. It seemed that Mexican food didn't agree with me, which was a shame, because I very much liked it.

When I explained this to Cole, he just said, "Don't worry, Donovan. You'll get used to it."

I wanted to know just what he meant by that. And I wanted him to offer an explanation of what had gone on while I was facedown on the floor — and later, when he spoke with the sheriff — but Cole was not forthcoming with any information.

This did not surprise me.

I ringed my pallet with my rope, snuggled down into the thin comfort of my blanket, and fell into a fitful slumber.

17

For the next few days, we simply wandered aimlessly. We rode to the edge of a vast and endless sea of drifting white sand, which Cole told me was the Yuma Desert. I have never seen anything so beautiful or so forbidding.

We journeyed across the Colorado River and into California without incident, and I was beginning to relax somewhat. I think Cole was, too. At least, he managed a few words to me.

"John Henry Strider's killin' brought those idiots in Yuma down on you," he said. "Same for that yahoo kid back in Tonto's Wickiup. Well, maybe he wasn't such a yahoo after all. He had the sense to leave, anyway."

"Joe Turner," I reminded him.

"Yeah, whatever. So I figure Yuma and Tonto's Wickiup are Lop Ear and Jingles's fault." He lit the smoke he'd rolled a few minutes before and, as he shook out the match, added, "But Strider himself, and Big John Hill, and Duffer Atbrun, those were different."

"How so?"

"Cause they're hired guns, kid. Their kind don't go round killin' folks unless there's money in it. Or revenge. The first two, I figure for the money part."

"And Atbrun for revenge? Because of Mr. Hill?" I offered. Actually, I was completely lost.

Cole nodded. "Now who in the hell would have call to dislike you so much that they'd hire a killer? It don't seem to me you're old enough to have made any enemies that bad."

I shook my head. "I can't imagine . . ."

"There are more out there you should be worried about. Red Nose Dakota — he's part Crow — Ralph Biggs, Elias Jenkins, and Apache Tom, just off the top o' my head. Guns for hire, every one. Tell me, Donovan. How'd your folks die, anyways?"

I told him the whole story from the beginning, and how Mr. Dean had pressed cash upon me and put me on the train.

He was silent for a few moments before he said, "Well, you've had it hard, Donovan. Mighty hard. Tell me more about this Mr. Dean. I recall old Heck mentionin' him a few times."

I told him everything I knew, which, granted, wasn't much, and then we drifted into silence again.

We decided, however, that perhaps it was safe to go up to the Aztec Princess again to check on the "diggin's," as Cole called them. We turned back east to cross the muddy Colorado again.

Privately, I wondered how long I could actually survive. I had been in the territory less than two weeks, and already had every killer — both amateur and professional — in the West following me around, or so it seemed. As long as Cole was around, I had a good chance, I surmised, but I would have to be alone sometime, wouldn't I?

And there was Annie. My sweet little Annie. Oh, she looked so much more beautiful seen from close up, without a street between us! Those eyes of hers weren't just blue, but sparkling, cornflower blue, and her hair wasn't just blond, it had the color and sheen of corn silk pulled fresh from the field.

And her face! Oh, I could have written sonnets about her face. Except that just then, Cole thumped me in the side.

"Wake up, kid," he said. "We're pullin' in."

The Colorado ferry we had been riding

had indeed pulled into its dock across the river, and we led our mounts off. While Cole settled with the ferryman, I stroked Tell's soft neck. He was a beauty, too, and hadn't spooked at the ferry either time we'd ridden it. That is an important thing for a horse, and shows its trusting nature.

I swung a leg up, smoothed his ebony mane into place over those silvery withers, and waited for Cole's return. It was quicker than I'd thought. He fairly leapt to Ranger's back and said, "Ride!"

"Where?" I shouted back, alarmed.

"Just go!" he yelled, and slapped Tell's backside.

Tell almost left me behind, his exit was so hasty! I can't even tell you which direction we took off in, but I can say that it was fast. I clung to the saddle, trying to figure out from whom we were fleeing, while Cole, bent low over Ranger's neck shouted, "This way! Come this way!"

I did.

Soon the terrain changed from gravel and rocks to sand, white sand. I gave Tell his head and prayed that there would be an end, and soon. Both horses were lathered by this time, and Cole showed no indication that he wished to stop, or even slow down.

Over dune after pale, featureless dune we galloped, our horses laboring, sinking deep into the sand, then clattered rapidly over the places where the wind had swept it from the hard substrate. We were climbing yet another of those endless dunes when the first shot came.

It was from behind us, and Cole gestured at me to hurry, hurry. But I couldn't go any faster. Tell was at his limits, and heaved with every breath. I followed Colt to the crest of the dune and was nearly over when, abruptly, another shot sang out, and Tell dropped to his knees.

At first I thought that he had simply given out. In my mind, he was impermeable to bullets. I was the one they were after.

But it was not to be. He lay there, just over the crest, his breathing labored and a damp red stain blossoming across his belly. I threw myself across his neck, crying, "Tell! Tell, no!" and felt Cole wrench me back by my collar. I tumbled down the dune, white sand sticking to my tear tracks, my heart broken.

"But he's in pain," I shouted at Cole, who had crawled back to his spot, and was peering out, over the top of the hill of sand. "Who did this?" I demanded. "How dare they?"

Cole's head whipped toward me. "Get your ass and your gun up here," he snarled. *"Now!"*

From the top of the dune, the only sounds were the wind's whistle and my poor Tell's labored breaths. I had stopped myself from crying, and tried not to hear them. I looked out across the expanse, and saw nothing.

"Cole . . ." I began.

"Shut up," he said.

I closed my eyes for a moment, wishing for all the world that I had gone over that cliff with Mother and Father, and that none of this had happened, none of it at all. But when I opened my eyes, Tell's sides were still heaving, and the desert was still there.

And a speck of movement.

"There," I said, and pointed. "Something moved at the top of that dune."

"Seen it," said Cole.

"This is my fault again, isn't it?" I was feeling sorry for myself, sorry for Tell, sorry for the world.

"Not this time, kid," he said, his attention on the dunes.

My eyebrows flew up. Not my fault? Not my fault that my horse was dying, not my fault that I was horseless in this desert, not my fault that we were being shot at? I couldn't believe it, couldn't believe Cole.

"Slide down and get my rifle," he said curtly.

Still in a daze, I did as he said. The trip down was much easier than the trip back up, but I made it. And when I at last got back and handed him his rifle, Tell had stopped his labored breathing.

A glance told me he was dead. His sightless eyes stared out over the desert. The air no longer teased his nostrils. Flies had begun to find and settle on his flank injury, and his muscles didn't twitch to shoo them away.

I broke down.

"Knock it off!" came Cole's voice. I didn't look up. All I could think of was my poor Tell, his life stolen by some ne'er-do-well with a grudge.

"I said, knock it off!" This time, Cole hit me in my bad ear, and it started bleeding again, through the bandages. The pain also snapped me to reality, which, I suppose, was what he intended.

"Better," he said, the moment I stopped wailing. "I'm sorry about your horse, kid, but right now, we've got other snakes to —" He cut himself off and fired three rapid rounds at the dune where I had spied movement, then sat there, silently staring, his eyes intent.

My head snapped toward the dune when I heard the scream — thin and distant and very high. Cole waited another moment, then said, "Go get your gear off Tell."

Slowly, I finally moved. I reached Tell's body and, unable to hold my tears back, silently pulled free my saddlebags and pack. He was so beautiful, even in death. I stroked his neck for the last time, then went back to Cole, who was still staring across the sand.

"You got hold of yourself?" he asked without looking up.

My "Yessir" came out in a choked whisper.

"Get down the hill, then."

"But —"

He turned and glared at me.

I slid down the dune's far side once more, and went to where Ranger was standing. When Cole came down, he found me with my arms locked around Ranger's neck and my face buried in his mane.

"It's all right," he said, almost kindly. I heard his rifle slide back into its boot. "Gimme those," he added, and took the gear from my arms. I heard the complaint of leather as he secured my things on his saddle.

And then I felt his hand on my shoulder, which surprised me out of crying further. He said, "It's all right to cry, Horace. I had a first horse, too." And then he swung into the saddle. He held a hand down to me.

"But aren't we going to . . . b-bury him?"

He shook his head. "We have to git. He don't mind, kid. I promise. Now step up."

Grudgingly, I did, but my eyes were on Tell the whole time.

"Who were they?" I asked as we rode away. Ranger was a strong horse, but he could travel no faster than a walk carrying both Cole and me. "Are you sure they're dead? You didn't go check."

"They're the Barlow brothers," he said, keeping his eyes on the trail. We were out of the sand dunes by then, and back in the desert. Brush was beginning to show, low on the ground, although the distance ahead promised more growth. "I saw 'em back there, headed down the river toward us."

"They were in a boat?" I think I asked.

"No, ridin' down alongside the river," Cole said, and I heard him snort. I supposed I deserved it, that time.

"So who are these Barlow brothers?"

"Fellers I knew from . . . from a long time ago. Like I said, sorry, kid."

"You mean that your long-lost past caught up with you?"

I took Cole's silence for assent.

"From when you were down in Mexico?" I added.

He reined in Ranger and said, "Get off."

I did, against my better instincts. I wouldn't have put it past him to just ride off and leave me.

But then he dismounted, too. "Let's let Ranger take a little breather," he said, and began walking and leading the gelding. I kept up with him.

"Why were they trying to kill you?"

Cole looked down at his boots for a moment, then straight ahead again. "Because I killed their daddy."

"And that's why you ran from them? Instead of . . ."

He turned toward me, and he had that amused expression on his face again. He said, "Instead of holdin' my ground and facin' them like a man?"

"I wouldn't have put it exactly that way," I said, trailing off.

"No, I s'pose you wouldn't. But yeah, that's why I took off. Their papa, old Jake — he was one tough customer and meaner than a sack full o' rattlers, but I never had nothin' against those boys of his. They been comin' for me, off and on, for about ten years now. Some people just won't let the past rest."

This time, I was the silent one. I was trying to imagine Cole as a very young man — as El Diablo Dorado — hot-blooded and in a strange land. Was it then that these brothers started coming after him? I wondered. How many more were there? How did he sleep at night, knowing so many people wanted him dead?

"Forgot to ask you," he said, breaking into my thoughts. "What'd you think of Annie, once you saw her up close?"

"She's beautiful," I replied. Somehow, I didn't want to talk about her so soon after such ugliness. "Were they dead? The Barlow brothers, I mean. How many were there?"

"I don't know, and two. Arlo and Carlo."

I stopped stock-still. "You're joking."

He stopped, too, and his face screwed up. "About what?"

"Arlo and Carlo Barlow?"

His mouth crooked up into a grin and he scratched his head. "Never thought about it that way," he admitted, then laughed. "Well, the third one wasn't so funny. That was Juan. He's not around anymore."

By the way he said it, I thought I'd best not ask what had happened to Juan. I said, "I don't have enough money to buy another horse. Not one as good as Tell, anyway."

We started walking again, and Cole replied, "There won't ever be another one like him for you, Donovan. But we'll try and find you somethin' close."

Later that day, we walked into Yuma and went directly to the livery, where I found a nice chestnut gelding in a horse trader's string. Cole looked him over, but found him lacking. "He's fourteen if he's a day," he said. "Try again."

I picked out a bright buckskin. He had a black mane and tail, like Tell's, and I suppose I thought that would be lucky. But Cole said, "Nope. Fistulous withers. Sorry."

At last, we agreed on a five-year-old gelding, strawberry roan in color, with the rather feminine name of Cherry. He wasn't any too pretty, but he had kind eyes and small, tipped-in, wide-set ears, and he nuzzled me when I spoke to him. The trader assured me he was sound and well trained in all the basics — although he'd not been schooled in any "ropin' or cuttin' stuff" of which the trader was aware.

I didn't need a horse trained to cut cattle, although I said nothing. Cole was doing my negotiating for me, and for once I had the presence of mind not to open my mouth. He ended up buying the gelding for only thirty dollars, and only because "the damn thing ain't even trained to cut cows!"

Once again, we didn't tarry in Yuma. Cole wanted to keep moving, and I can't say I had any desire to argue with him. For all I knew, one or both of the Barlow brothers were closing in on us, and would shoot yet another unfortunate horse from beneath me.

We camped well to the northeast of Yuma, in the shelter of a little copse of palo verde trees, which are a most curious creation. They have no leaves and a sickly green bark, which is, for the most part, smooth. I found them strange and alien. However, Cherry was proving a very good horse, although he couldn't be compared with Tell. His gaits were soft, he was tender of mouth, and even though he had a tendency to be a bit eager, I was most satisfied with him.

This didn't help me from thinking about Tell nearly nonstop, however. I missed him terribly.

Two days later, we came upon the Aztec Princess, and Jingles and Lop Ear greeted us enthusiastically. They had been blasting and the mine had failed to flood, for one thing. And for another, they were finding gold!

"Oh, she's a rich one, all right, young Tate Donovan," Jingles said, cackling. He dug into his pocket and pulled out three chunks of rock, one almost solid gold, and I gasped. "You're goin' to be the richest dang-blasted kid in the territory," he cried. "Mayhap the whole danged country!"

"He'th got him a point," Lop Ear added. He was cooking dinner and Loretta was under his arm, her tail a-wag and her colorful eyes dancing. I wondered how she was hitting it off with the resident bobcat.

"After you strike it rich, young Tate," Jingles went on, "I'd appreciate one of those gold bars like you rich people al'ays have around. Like to add it to my collection!"

"Collection?" I asked, but Cole cut me off.

He said, "You pair o' miscreants got any idea how much it'll take to get this thing up an' runnin'?"

It was a question I had very much wanted to ask, too, and would have thought of it if I hadn't had so much else on my mind.

Jingles rubbed his neck. "Well, I think that's more in Lop Ear's line. I been on my own for a good many years, now." And then he turned his head and shouted into the darkness, "Comanche! Blast you, you rapscallious villain!" He got up directly and disappeared into the murky night, muttering, "I told those boys not to tether their horses so close . . ."

Cole said, "Well?" and stared at Lop Ear.

He simply shrugged and smiled, showing the gap where his two front teeth used to be. Lisping, he said, "Don't figure we need nobody, Cole. Why, Jingles and me been haulin' it out just fine. After we blasted a few feet down that little side spur, we hit the mother lode. Been buryin' our metal bearin' ore down a secret place in case of bandits, so don't you worry none."

He gave a turn to the rabbit frying in his skillet. Loretta licked her chops. "And don't you trouble your mind about floodin'," he went on. "That little trickle that she was is all she's ever goin' to be. Hey, Jingles!" he added, addressing the deep shadows to my far left. "Check Debby for me!"

All sudden impatience, I said, "I wish someone would come to a finite amount. Mr. Dean wishes to know how much to advance me for the costs."

Cole twisted toward me. "He does? And when did this happen?"

His face had gone dark, and suddenly I was afraid to tell him. But I said, "In his t-telegram. The other day."

"I thought he was just askin' after you!"

"He w-was. In a way. He only —"

"Well, I guess I don't need the damn

newspaper, do I?" he snapped, and I cringed.

"What's everybody so riled up about?" Jingles called as he entered the campfire's circle of light. "I could hear you all the way over to the horses!"

Cole jabbed a thumb in my direction. "This little fool managed to set the whole of a hired militia on us, that's all."

I blinked. "What?"

"You still got that wire on you?"

"Yes," I said, patting my pockets. "Some-where . . ."

I produced it at last and handed it to him. Frankly, it went against my most basic beliefs, letting someone else read my mail like that, but at the moment, I was too shocked to do anything else.

He unfolded it unceremoniously, and stared. His teeth clenched and his jaw muscles worked while he read it over and over, and then fairly threw the paper back at me. "You idiot," he snarled. "You blamed fool!"

I scooted away from him, to keep safely out of arm's reach. He was a little too close and a little too angry for my taste. I asked, "What did I do, Cole?"

"That!" he shouted, pointing at the tele-gram, which had fallen from my hands and was burning to ashes in the fire. And then he jumped to his feet and began pacing. The ensuing spray of dirt barely missed Lop Ear's frying pan.

"I know about this Mr. Dean of yours," he said as he marched back and forth. "Heck was mighty closemouthed, but he told me a lot more than he did most people. I remember him sayin' as how this Dean had sold shares in the Aztec Princess."

"So the gold isn't all mine?" I asked, crestfallen. "How much stock did he sell? I mean, what percentage is left for me?"

Cole waved the question off. He said, "Don't you read? Don't you know nothin'?"

He stopped and threw his arms wide. "Y'know, it struck me funny at the time, why anybody'd want to buy shares in a dried-up ol' silver mine. But I figured Heck knew best. It was his mine, after all." He dropped his arms and resumed pacing — head down, arms folded. "I think Heck managed to get himself — and your folks, too — killed. And all because of this goddamned hole in the ground!"

Lop Ear looked up, cocked his good eyebrow, and said, "Damn hole in the ground? Well, now, Cole, she's a lot better than —"

Jingles, now returned and standing across

the fire, hissed, "Shut up, you ol' rake face."

Lop Ear started to respond, but after one look at Jingles, he closed his mouth.

Cole simply stalked off, into the night. I heard him out there, kicking rocks and muttering.

"Rabbit's done!" Lop Ear cried joyfully.

18

Cole recounted his suspicions the next day, while we were riding aimlessly north. He thought that Mr. Dean was most probably a stock swindler. Now this was a very strong charge, but I'll admit he had the circumstantial evidence to back it up.

He told me that Misters Dean and Cummings had suggested taking the mine public three years after it had completely stopped producing. That struck me as odd — I mean, in that Uncle Hector had agreed to it at all — but Cole said Uncle Hector had told him it was a common practice, and he'd need the money to put new machinery in the Lucky Seven.

Cole said he hadn't thought any more about it, until I mentioned having sent the telegram scant days before John Henry Strider faced off with me at Janeway's, only to be shot and killed. Strider was famous nationwide, Cole said, as a hired gun for the mine interests. It wouldn't have been at all difficult for Mr. Dean to locate and wire him, and send him after me.

But still, I was stuck on the first question I had asked — why?

"Let's backtrack, kid," Cole said. "Your uncle Heck sent his wire, askin' for a stake, about a month or six weeks before your folks died, right?"

"Yes," I replied carefully. "They were just leaving for the Continent when his telegram arrived."

"And they got killed about three days after their ship docked, right?"

"Yes. But —"

"And your uncle Heck, he was killed about a month or so after they were," he broke in. "Then somebody took a shot at me."

"And killed your horse." My mind was on dead horses at the moment. "They killed your Brownie."

"Well," Cole went on, "it seems to me like a lot of people get killed after sendin' off a telegram to Mr. Dean about that mine."

"But Father didn't send . . ." I began, then added, "Oh." He had shown it to Misters Dean and Cummings. He had always shared what he called Uncle Hector's "begging wires" with Aloysius Dean.

Cole had been right last night. I was an idiot.

"Misters Dean and Cummings have over-sold the mine, haven't they?" I asked dully, feeling as if I had just been punched in the stomach.

"Bingo!" Cole said and rolled himself a smoke.

I also knew that if another strike of any kind were made in the Aztec Princess, it would ruin Dean and Cummings. I had read about such things — selling many more shares than there actually were in a property — and although I had no idea just how much of the Aztec Princess had been sold, I knew that it was likely more than she was worth, or could ever produce. I suddenly felt violently sick to my stomach, and leaned over Cherry's side — and my knee — to vomit on the desert floor.

"You got that right, kid," Cole commented, while he lit his cigarette and I scrubbed at my lips with my neck scarf.

The more I thought about this business, the worse it got. By the time we had eaten lunch and moved on again, my mind had embroiled Misters Dean and Cummings in the most malevolent of schemes, in which my entire family were merely pawns.

I had also decided they had more than

likely stolen Father's money, and that he had been innocent all along.

I will admit it did not take much self-convincing for me to believe my father blameless. Father may have had his humbugs — Irish maids among them — but a born thief, he was not. Not Theodore Smith!

When we made camp for the night, I asked Cole how many shares he thought Dean and Cummings might have sold.

"You got me," he replied. He loosened his girth and pulled the saddle from Ranger's back. "Maybe six, seven times what there really was to sell."

My jaw dropped. "Six or seven times?"

He shrugged, and put the saddle down. "Happens," he said. "I knew a fella once, sold one hundred percent of his mine shares nine times over."

At long last, we sat down on our blankets and Cole fixed a supper of biscuits and beans. At least we were in no immediate danger. The Barlow brothers seemed to have vanished from our trail, and no one knew where we were, even me.

And if Cole knew, he wasn't telling.

A few days of travel later, we were both sick of campfire cooking and sleeping beneath the stars. We had gone quite a distance north, and Cole said we were near the town of Diablo.

This name gave me some qualms, I will admit. I had seen more men die in the last few weeks than anyone should expect to observe, and wasn't looking forward to another fiasco such as we had experienced in Yuma.

"It's a pretty damned rough place," said Cole, when I voiced my reservations. "But we have to pick us up some chuck. I don't believe I can squeeze another feed out of the beans, and we're gettin' short on grain for the horses, too."

"Very well, then," I said, resigned to the situation. "We can't hide forever."

Actually, what I was thinking was that I had been victimized — not by God, or the Fates, or whatever one wished to call it, but by a man: Mr. Aloysius Dean. I couldn't fight God, but I could bloody well fight a person! I could fight for my father's good name, and mine.

Let their minions come, I decided. Misters Dean and Cummings would not win.

We rode into Diablo a little before dusk. It was a ramshackle place. Poorly built buildings rose from the ground like ill-spaced teeth, and on either side were canyon walls. One rode down into Diablo, rather than found it on the flat, and the main road ran the length of the canyon.

Most of the people I saw — of which there were few — appeared disreputable and dangerous, not to put too fine a point on it. There was not a female in sight.

It crossed my mind that the future husband of Miss Annie O'Brien should not be caught dead in such a place. And then I shuddered when I realized it was possible I would be.

Eyes followed us as we rode down that dusty excuse for a street. Heads turned slightly with our passage, as if no one wished to officially recognize us, but all knew who we were. I had a very bad feeling again, and was happy I had nothing left in my stomach to throw up.

While I fought the uneasiness in the pit of my belly, we stopped before a livery and arranged for our horses. Then I followed Cole across the street, to what passed as a mercantile.

While he ordered beans and flour and canned peaches and ammunition, I stared out through the windows, at the street. The few men we had passed on our way into town were gathering now, in little knots along the street, and an ominous sense of foreboding filled me.

"Hey, kid!" Cole called from the counter, breaking into my thoughts. I turned to face him. He said, "Grab a couple of those blankets from the shelf there. No tellin' how long we'll be out here, and the nights are gettin' bone cold now that we're up in altitude."

I went to the back of the store and pulled down two new blankets, both brown and nondescript, and took them to the counter, where I placed them on the mounting pile of Cole's purchases.

"Thanks," he muttered. He rummaged in his purse and paid the storekeeper, asking if we could leave the items and pick them up later. The storekeeper nodded in the affirmative, and Cole said, "Let's go see about grain, and then . . . I'm thirsty, kid. How about you?"

I shrugged. I supposed that it didn't much matter one way or the other. When Cole was thirsty, we drank.

Rather, he drank and I gagged.

He led me up the street to the feed and grain, and then next door, to the saloon. This turned out to be a very poor excuse for a bar, in which we found three rickety tables with two scarred chairs apiece, and a bartop consisting of a raw plank balanced on two barrels. It was little better than those makeshift "places of business" in Tombstone, which I was beginning to think of as the Prince of Cities.

Cole pushed a squawking hen from the closest table and indicated that I should sit down, then crossed the room and leaned over the plank. "Two beers," he said to the bartender, who made our rough and muscular Willie, at Hanratty's, look like a scholar and a gentleman. He had exactly four teeth that I could see — one upper front tooth, an eyetooth, and two lower incisors — and they were all four mossy and gray-green.

Cole didn't seem to think this odd, though, and joined me without comment. Our beers arrived — unfortunately — and while I played with my mug and Cole drank, I let my thoughts drift to happier things. Miss Annie, for instance.

How I wished that I was safe in Tonto's Wickiup and ensconced on her lovely porch swing, and that she was there beside me, laughing at my stories, batting those big blue eyes, and asking me if I wanted lemonade.

What a life I would have, if only I lived long enough to see it! I pined for her.

That was, until Cole tugged my sleeve to get my attention, and then nodded toward the window. Outside, on the walk, one of those little knots of men had moved close and swelled in number. Six or eight men conversed among themselves, but glanced up and in through the window on occasion, then turned quickly back to the group.

We were being sized up, I thought.

Apparently, Cole thought so, too, and quickly grabbed my untouched beer. "Hate to waste it," he said in a mumble, and tipped the glass to his lips, all the time keeping his attention on the street.

He put the mug back on the table, and said, "C'mon."

I did. I followed him out the back door and into an alley, of sorts, then to the edge of the building.

"Who is it?" I whispered.

He checked his gun. "Red Nose Dakota, Elias Jenkins, and the Hastings boys," he said, keeping his voice low. "Among others."

"And who are they after?" I pressed him. "Me or you?"

"Good question," he replied. "But it's probably you. You go that way," he said, pointing back to the other side of the saloon. "I'm goin' out here." He slipped away, against the side of the building. I followed his instructions and went the opposite way.

Pistol in hand, I crept forward along the opposite side of the building, nervous sweat coursing from my brow and dripping from the end of my nose. I hoped the men in the street had come for me, I admit. It may sound crass, but if I was to die today, I didn't want it to be for something Cole had done in Mexico, while I was still in diapers!

Just then, Red Nose — or so I guessed from the strawberry birthmark that covered his olfactory prominence — turned round the corner and faced me. He appeared as surprised as I and immediately raised his gun. But mine was already raised, and I fired.

I hit him in the shoulder, and the shot spun him around and back. He didn't go all the way down, though, and fired, crying, "Horace Smith, you little shit!"

I felt the bullet sting my forearm, but I still fired again. This time, he fell straight backward, the slug having hit him in the throat. I saw the blood bubble, then stop, and I immediately retraced my steps.

I was nearly back to the alley again and feeling the bitter sensation of bile collecting in my throat, when two more shots split the silence. "Cole!" I shouted, and ran to the street again.

I rounded the corner just in time to see

one man dead in the street — besides Red Nose, that was — and Cole diving down behind the horse trough across the road. He didn't appear to be hurt, though, and I immediately fired on the man who appeared to be shooting at him, and who had just that moment glanced over at me. He was a mere ten feet away and hadn't heard me come around the corner, so it wasn't really fair. Still, I admit that I shot him dead without a second thought.

More shots. I dodged behind the building's corner and watched Cole's head come up as he fired down the street, then ducked again.

"Where?" I shouted.

"This side of the livery!" came his cry.

I didn't think. I only reacted. I sped off, holding my arm and running alongside the saloon and back to the alley, then down it until I reached the last building before the livery. The hostler had turned all the horses out before fleeing the hail of bullets, and they stood between my position and the gunman's. Between Ranger's legs, I could plainly see him — or at least bits of him — crouched in the open side door of the stable, firing at Cole.

I did the only thing I could think of. I lay down on my belly and tried to find a clear shot between the horse's legs. But every time Ranger moved out of the way, Cherry or another innocent horse took his place.

At last, I gave up and moved forward, I suppose with some idea of skirting the rear of the corral and getting behind the gunman. I had almost accomplished it and was nearly to my goal when the gunman abruptly twisted toward me and opened fire. It was nearly in one motion, so I had no time to dive out of the way, although I tried, too late.

His slug bit deep into my thigh, and the wound sprayed blood through the air as I landed behind the stable, tears stinging my eyes. The blood was flowing freely, but at least I had the presence of mind to pull the bandanna from my neck and tie a hasty tourniquet.

I pulled myself to my feet once more. Stumbling one-legged to the back door of the barn, I finally paused at its edge and peeked around the door. The gunman, having apparently given me up for dead, was firing up the street again.

I managed to creep inside, and actually aimed my gun at his back.

I had a clear shot.

I could have fired.

Something held me back, though. At least,

until another man slid into the stable's front doors and took a shot at me. He hit me in the leg — again, although this time in my calf — and when I fired, he went over backward. My second shot was for the alerted first gunman, though, who was wheeling to take aim even as I pulled the trigger. And in doing this in such rapid succession, I lost my balance and fell to the floor, knocking over a bucket of water on my way down.

His shot went wild and he hit nothing but the rafters. But my returned fire pushed him backward in the mucky straw and out into the corral amid the milling horses' hooves. I shot him in the chest.

I toppled to the ground, holding my hurt leg, the blood thick and sticky on my fingers and palm. I remember thinking that a man wasn't supposed to lose this much blood and live. When I looked up, I realized that I had disturbed more than a bucket.

In the stall behind me, a broken lantern had set fire to the straw on the floor. Flames were already climbing the wall. I tried to get to my feet, failed, and ended up crawling out the front door, past the dead man who lay there, and dragging a bucket. I suppose I had some foolish idea that I'd get to the water and put the fire out.

I was halfway between the doors and the blacksmith's water trough, just outside, when I heard a burst of fresh shots, and did my best to hurriedly crawl back inside the burning building.

I couldn't see the men involved. I couldn't even see Cole. He'd moved from behind the trough up the street to God knows where.

Men were up there somewhere, though, freely exchanging shots across the wide-open street.

But I realized they hadn't seen me yet.

Smoke roiled wildly in the freshening breeze of evening. Flames devoured old straw, fueled by dry manure and the detritus of years. I heard a window explode.

It was at this point that I realized I couldn't save the livery. I crawled in to rescue the only creature still trapped inside, a rabbit locked in its hutch, and set it free. On both hands and a knee, dragging one leg behind me, I followed it out the front doors, albeit somewhat more slowly.

By the time I had crawled halfway across the street, keeping my head low and pulling my leg as stiffly as possible, the whole place was engulfed. One of the horses broke down the corral's gate, and Cherry and Ranger raced off into the distance — after narrowly missing me — along with three or four other mounts.

I looked up the street again, toward the gunfire. In the fading light, the small traces of gunshots — powder flares — were vaguely visible on the side of the street I had come from. I wondered if I should cross back over the street and attempt to sneak up from behind them, or whether I would do better to continue on my original path.

I admit that I also tested my leg, seeing if I could move it — I could, although with immense pain — and making certain that neither bullet had hit bone. I had forgotten completely about my arm.

In the end, I followed my original course, and made it the rest of the way across the street, opposite the fiery livery.

Intermittent shots continued to slice the evening stillness. The livery, cobbled together from what I was sure were very old, dry boards, was blazing away, and sparks had caught the buildings on either side afire. I feared the whole town would go that way, as no one, including the stableman, had come running to fight it. It seemed everyone in town was either in the gunfight or hiding from it.

I tried to crawl up the street, but I was growing weaker by the moment. Additionally, I was losing a great deal of blood —

my tourniquet had little effect, no matter how tightly I twisted it — and a terrible cold seemed to grip my bones. I made it a few feet before I could go no further.

Consciousness began to slip from me, and the last thing I thought to do — the *only* thing I could think to do — was to fire my gun several times and draw their fire down the street. I remember thinking that I did not have much time left, and that it didn't really matter if I were shot again.

I emptied my gun straight up middle of the road.

The gun slipped from my fingers.

I saw no more.

I was shocked to open my eyes and see daylight, and not the daylight surrounding Diablo, either. We were back down at the Aztec Princess — although how we'd gotten there I had no idea — and Jingles was bending over me. His mouth popped open in surprise and he yelled, "Hot diggity and pass the biscuits! He's awake! And alive!"

Then he clasped me by the shoulders and kissed me with a loud smack, right in the middle of my forehead. "You're alive, young Donovan! Alive and breathin'!"

I hardly knew what to do. And I had no time to do it in, for Lop Ear, Cole, and Loretta all crowded in right then, and an enthusiastic Loretta began to lick me from collar to hairline.

"Well," said Cole with a grin. He pushed his hat back. "I'll be damned. Thought you were a goner for sure. Welcome back, boy!"

I was in a weakened state, but I attempted bravado. "You didn't think I'd die and leave this mine in your laps, now, did you?" I asked, and tried to lever myself up. I failed miserably, and fell back upon the blankets, weak as the proverbial kitten.

Jingles chuckled and Lop Ear lisped, "There you go, boy! Want me to hit you up alongthide the head while you're at it?"

I looked toward Cole. "What happened? What day is it?"

"You've been out for three days, Donovan," he said. "I was pretty damn sure we were goin' to lose you for a while there."

"But how'd we get here?"

"After those last eight or nine got through shootin' at me — and by the way, thanks for that last salvo you made — I wandered down and found you. Right careless of you, kid, losing that much blood. Don't do that again."

I smiled, I think. "I'll try not to." And then I belatedly added, "There were eight or *nine* of them up there?"

Cole settled back on his heels, and Jingles and Lop Ear walked to the mine's entrance, arguing — once more — over the Lost Tribe of Israel. Cole nodded as if his entire life had been nine-to-one and the matter was worthy of no exposition, and said, "I walked down the street and whistled up Ranger, and he brought Cherry and a couple others in with him. After I cauterized your leg and arm, I packed you down here."

I remember the cauterizing of my ear, and was most thankful I had been unconscious for this occasion. I gulped. "Over Cherry's back?"

"Just like a sack of feed," he said with a smile. "I pulled us some new saddles off the horses on the rail," he added. "You're riding Red Nose Dakota's rig, I think. I've got Elias Jenkins's."

When I began to protest, he cut me off, saying, "Ours were in the livery. What started that fire, anyway?"

"Me," I admitted.

"Well, you done a damn good job of it. Took out near the whole town before it burned itself out."

I closed my eyes, wishing that it would all go away. Now I was doomed to be jailed for arson, if I wasn't first killed by some fool with a gun and a grudge.

But Cole, seeming to read my mind, said, "I wouldn't worry about anybody comin' after you for that. The whole damn town was put together with spit instead of nails. Blows down or falls down every few years, anyhow. I don't reckon a good fire could be much tougher to repair."

I heaved an internal sigh of relief, opened my eyes, and said, "Thank you, Cole. For saving me yet again, I mean."

He sat back, grunting. "You know, ol' Red Nose Dakota had a grudge against me from a long time ago. Least I could do for the feller who killed him, now, wasn't it?" And he smiled at me.

I grinned back.

POSTSCRIPT

Dear Trey,

Well, as I said, it's been years since those events, and the world has changed a great deal in that time. No longer is this a country where men make their own laws and freely murder one another, just to see who's the fastest hand with a gun. Except in Chicago, where, until recently, gangsters shot one another over pin money and liquor.

I never did ascertain just how Cole managed his escape from those villains that day in Diablo. He was never one to talk at any length, and frankly, I wasn't in the mood to press him. I was in the process of learning to just let some things be, or, as Cole would say, learning not to prod every beehive I came across with a short stick. Most bees, I had discovered, did just fine on their own.

But we had survived, and that was the important part. It is even more important to note that our gun battle in Diablo put a quick end to most of the unpleasantness.

Upon our return to Tonto's Wickiup, Cole sent telegrams to the territorial governor as well as to some old friends in New York — although how he managed to have friends so far away, I can't imagine — and the next thing we heard, Misters Dean and Cummings had been arrested. Both of them served a long time in jail, too, and the scandal was horrendous.

You perhaps recall reading about the Great Stock Swindle of 1882 when you were at Yale, wherein a couple of thimble-rigging brokers had sold up to twelve thousand percent of a number of worthless Western mines? I was at the heart of uncovering it, my boy. Cole and I both.

Cole helped me get things straightened out on my end, and I retained a new attorney, back east, to see to the final details.

In the end, we waited a good year before bringing in any of the gold from the Aztec Princess. Cole said it would just complicate things if we announced a strike while all the paperwork was being sorted out. As it was, we never really announced a strike at all. Jingles and Lop Ear, who were having the time of their lives between the gold and the blasting, rigged up a shack where the old miner's quarters had been, got the pump working again, and even hitched Debby and Comanche to an *arrastra,* to grind the ore.

They smelted it fresh from the ground — although I still have no idea how they ever constructed a kiln hot enough to do it — poured and stamped their own bars, and sold them in California. That is, with the exception of one rough bar, which Jingles carried beneath his wagon seat until his death.

To this day — well, up until 1933, anyway, and the Gold Recall Act — I wondered where the gold in my coins and your grandmother's jewelry came from, and if it was mined at the Aztec Princess. I suppose that most of it now resides at Fort Knox, guarded behind steel doors. A shame. Whenever I touched a gold coin, I felt that a little of me, and Clay, and Jingles and Lop Ear, as well as all the girls was back there, in Tonto's Wickiup: young and carefree and alive.

The mind can play tricks, can't it?

But I was telling you what happened afterward.

I married Annie, of course. We spent the rest of that year swinging on her front porch and sipping lemonade and laughing together and getting to know each other, and were wed on the following Christmas Day. We were very young, of course, but it was the fashion in the West to marry young and we truly loved each other. Still do. Your grandmother is my world.

Hanratty's was a little more difficult to deal with, and I stayed in the whoring game for another few years, albeit only publicly. I had to have a place of business in order to explain the income from the Aztec Princess, you see. Belle ran the place, although I went to the saloon each afternoon and came home again each night. I unofficially gave Hanratty's to her on my wedding day, and officially turned it over three years later, on Christmas, by which time I had reached my full and preposterous height of six feet, five inches, and added another fifty-five pounds to my skeletal frame.

By that time, Annie — who never measured in at more than five feet, two inches — and I had quite a substantial nest egg saved up and had built the biggest house in town. We also had your dear father. And by then, no one would have mistaken the prosperous family man Mr. Smith for gangly Kid Donovan.

The legends grew, though. Kid Donovan was credited — or damned — with more kills than smallpox, and was rumored to be in Mexico, waiting for the heat to die down.

We simply let him stay there.

Cole stayed around town, more or less. And on more than one occasion, he saved my life by stepping from the shadows at just the right moment, guns blazing. For the most part, though, the threat to my life had gone away, simply vanished in the billowing smoke of Diablo. I suppose that leaving that many dead and an entire town in ruin tends to put off the weaker sisters.

Cole married Belle at long last, some seven years after Annie and I wed. Annie and I held their wedding in our home, in the parlor. Jingles and Lop Ear came up for it, along with Loretta and the rest of the creatures. We had to ground-tie Comanche out in the vacant lot next door, for by that time he had tried to savage Debby, Lop Ear's mule, and even I had to admit that the silly old swayback posed a threat.

Lop Ear passed from this earthly plane in 1905. He died in his sleep, long after he and Jingles had cleaned out the Aztec Princess, and went to his rest a happy man. I was awfully glad for that. Annie and I took in Loretta's replacement, a bubbly, shaggy herding dog of the same type — what they're calling, these days, an Australian Shepherd — and she had four more years with us. She was your father's dog and his constant companion.

Jingles died somewhere down around Tombstone at the turn of the century, and not of old age. He was blasting in his new mine, and didn't make it outside before the charge went off. Cole went down to see about him. He said it appeared Jingles had suffered a heart attack during his escape run, and never knew what had hit him.

Cole buried him with his gold bar from the Aztec Princess, and one more that he carried alongside it for all those years. Jingles never did divulge where that one came from, so I think it was likely better off entombed with him.

When your father was fifteen, your grandmother and I moved to Phoenix. There wasn't much left of Tonto's Wickiup by that time, and I was in the state legislature by then. We thought Phoenix made more sense. We bought the big green house that you remember from your childhood, when you came to visit us with your mother.

Your father went off to Yale, and we waited patiently for statehood. It came in 1912, the year your uncle Cole left to follow in your father's footsteps at college. We, in Arizona, were the last state to join the Union, and justifiably so. We were the wildest of the wild places.

Cole left his gunfighting, ruffian ways behind, and he and Belle tried ostrich farming outside of Phoenix. Sometimes he would compete in a local rodeo, or one of the quick-draw contests. He usually won when riding broncs, and always did when the contest was any with a gun.

When ostrich plumes went out of fashion, he went into turquoise mining. He and Belle had three fine children, who grew up to become pillars of Phoenix society, and a testament to good stock coming from bad beginnings.

He tried to enlist when the Great War came, but they turned him down. Too old. If they had taken him, I daresay the war would have been over in a week.

Belle passed peacefully in 1920, and just two years later, Cole was out working in the garden when he was shot dead. We never learned who did it, although their youngest daughter, Rose, was home. She said she ran outside at the sound of the blast, only to see the dust of a rider galloping away.

I never said as much to Rose, but I like to believe it was a surviving Barlow brother who had done the evil deed. Then, at least, Cole's own past would have sealed his fate.

I could make better sense of it that way, I suppose.

I was known as Tate Smith from the time we rode back into Tonto's Wickiup, and thereafter. It seemed easier to handle than all the trouble that both "Horace" and "Donovan" had brought me. And we carried it on. Your father was Horace Tate Pemberton Smith Jr., but we called him H.T. And you were the third Horace, called Trey.

There seemed to be some degree of symmetry in this.

So you see, there is more myth than truth in the story of Kid Donovan. I never did most of the things that they said I did. Some of "my" efforts were never done by anyone, and a few of the rest by someone else, mainly Cole. I supposed that the press was hungry for someone new to deify or laud and the carnage at Diablo — and that which led up to it — gave them their wish — that was all. It was an accident of time and place, and a case of the fourth estate taking unfair advantage.

I don't know how many died that day in Diablo. I myself can only account for three — and the fire — and I have asked my Lord and Savior for forgiveness. Cole's body count, on the other hand, will forever remain a mystery. As will most everything about him.

I never had a better friend than Cole Jeffries, and I very much doubt anyone else has, either.

Oh, and I never did write to Clive Barrow, although a year later, I anonymously sent him a snakeskin hatband along with a hat to go under it. The whole affair was just too complicated to explain.

You understand, don't you?

I hope that Clive did.

Love,
Grandfather

The employees of Thorndike Press hope you have enjoyed this Large Print book. All our Thorndike and Wheeler Large Print titles are designed for easy reading, and all our books are made to last. Other Thorndike Press Large Print books are available at your library, through selected bookstores, or directly from us.

For information about titles, please call:
(800) 223-1244

or visit our Web site at:
www.gale.com/thorndike
www.gale.com/wheeler

To share your comments, please write:
Publisher
Thorndike Press
295 Kennedy Memorial Drive
Waterville, ME 04901